FIRST NIGHTS

FIRST
NIGHTS

SUSAN FROMBERG SCHAEFFER

ALFRED A. KNOPF NEW YORK 1993

This Is a Borzoi Book Published by Alfred A. Knopf, Inc.

Copyright © 1993 by Troglydyte, Inc.

All rights reserved under International and Pan-American Copyright Conventions. Published in the United States by Alfred A. Knopf, Inc., New York, and simultaneously in Canada by Random House of Canada Limited, Toronto. Distributed by Random House, Inc., New York.

Library of Congress Cataloging-in-Publication Data
Schaeffer, Susan Fromberg.
First nights / Susan Fromberg Schaeffer. — 1st ed.
p.   cm.
ISBN 0-394-58820-7
I. Title.
PS3569.C35F57   1993
813'.54—dc20   92-10181   CIP

Manufactured in the United States of America
First Edition

FOR EVADNE LAFAYETTE

Time is longer than rope.
WEST INDIAN SAYING

CONTENTS

PROLOGUE

BEAUTIFUL LADIES IN SNOW

BY ANDERS ESTERSEN

SHE WAS SO BEAUTIFUL. You have no idea. So beautiful. Not in her daily clothes, without her make-up, going about her business. Then she could be plain. I remember when I first saw her, an awkward sixteen-year-old whose hand fluttered to her mouth when she smiled. She was ashamed of her crooked teeth. Later of course she had them straightened. But on the screen! Then I would forget I knew her, in ordinary life tripping over her own two feet, and sit in the dark, enchanted, like everyone else, watching Anna Asta with unbelieving eyes.

She always used to say, Oh, Anders is not impressed by beautiful women. Often I think that is why she trusted me.

In the beginning, at premieres of her films, people would come up to her and try to touch her. She's so beautiful, she's unearthly, they'd say, and they looked at her in disbelief. And later she would say, *How stupid they are! The whole world burns with beauty! In summer, the flowers, the snow blossoms in the winter, the sun coming through the leaves in the spring! Beauty is the rule! It is earthly! It is only not human!* And she would go on, indignant, about how beautiful the world was, and how, when you were miserable or upset, the beauty of the world was so stunning it could stop the suicide leaping from his bridge, but when you were too miserable, too upset, you looked around and nothing beautiful any longer meant anything and then you knew you were already dead. That was when beauty tormented you, sealed up in itself, indifferent to you and your troubles. She said beauty belonged to the nonhuman world. Humans with their pale skins, their furless bodies, their beady eyes and large ears, their bad teeth, they were not beautiful, so naturally they worshipped beauty when they thought they saw it in something human. *Of course* they were puzzled by a beautiful man or woman.

She had plenty to say, believe me, when she was angry. When she lost her temper—and she did that frequently—she was no sphinx.

She never thought it strange that people tried to pull her hair to see if it was real. She never thought it odd that people wanted to touch her skin to reassure themselves she was, like them, made of skin and bone. Instead, she felt pity for them, pity and disdain. You see? she would say. They cannot believe anything human is beautiful. What contempt for themselves they must have! If someone is born beautiful, everyone else must carry on about it. They must set us apart. They must make *things* of us. They must hang us on the wall and worship us. Well, that is how it is. We are all lizards. I am just a more beautiful lizard, but believe me, Anders, when I look in the mirror, a lizard is what I see.

But in public she was shy and for years she spoke English badly and so people said she was stupid. Let them think what they like, she said. They will anyway.

Once I was known as the most famous director in the world, and probably I was. Every time I stuck my nose out of doors, someone in one country or another handed me an award. There are even awards named for me. But after a few minutes of conversation, a couple of minutes spent praising this or that in one of my films, the conversation always turned to Anna Asta. "You directed Anna Asta in two films. You knew Anna Asta from the time she was sixteen. Tell us what she was like." Of course I could not answer such questions. If anyone she knew spoke of her in public, she never acknowledged them again. They simply ceased to exist. They became what the Russians later called *former people.* I know some former people who adored Anna Asta but made the mistake of opening their mouths and then they longed to be people again. She would not allow it.

Well, once Anna Asta was the most famous woman in the world, an actress who came from my country. It is hard, now, to imagine how famous she was or how important she was to the people who came to see her films, and without knowing that, it is also impossible to understand the effect fame had on her. In those days, after all, films were still new. Daily, arguments raged over how films should be made. There was endless theorizing about what effects this or that technique would have on the audiences. Walter Drake, one of Anna's favorite co-stars, used to sit in his canvas chair on the set, holding forth on the danger, the inadvisability, the positive immorality, of close-ups.

Close-ups! Who today can imagine a film without them? Who can imagine an Anna Asta film without them? Her later films are virtually a series of close-ups, interrupted every now and then by sequences that further the action. But in Anna's films the real action took place on the planes of her face.

Yet Anna would sit there and agree with Walter Drake. Yes, yes, it was true. Close-ups were terrible. Let's get rid of them! And Drake would go on—he was a boring man, very sweet, but a terrible bore of a gentleman—about these huge floating faces on the screen, nine feet tall, sixteen feet tall, huge disembodied heads floating up there, frightening women and children, causing them to scream and duck for cover. These close-ups are a terrible thing, he would say. They will ruin the movies for everyone. And Anna would smile and say, Yes, yes, no more close-ups. And Max Lilly, the man who brought her to America, the man who is famous now—if he is famous for anything— because he discovered that face of hers, would listen in astonishment and in Swedish demand of her, "How can you listen to such nonsense! Tell him off! Tell him the truth! That big face floating up there like a planet, it's the recovery of awe! It's the face the little child sees in his cradle. It's the second time in a person's life when a face is a planet and that planet is heaven! Tell him, Anna! Don't listen to such nonsense!"

And she would smile at Drake and say, "Oh, terrible, those close-ups are terrible! Heads without bodies! What can people make of it? Of course they are terrifying!" Perhaps she was teasing Max. Who knew what went on in her mind? But one day Max looked at her and said in a cold, low voice, "You are a blasphemer. You are the shadow that falls over the shrine." After that they didn't speak for weeks. They called her the Ice Princess, but she had a temper. A *cold* temper, Max would say: if he were here.

This is what you must try to imagine. In movie theaters all over the world, people would come in from the bright light in the street, hand over their five cents, and sit down in seats to watch Anna Asta's films. They were silent then, of course, and in the darkness, an organist would begin playing. And onto the screen would float this beautiful, beautiful face, larger than the full moon ever appears in the night sky. And one eyebrow would rise slightly and that small movement was like an earthquake. And that beautiful mouth, that elongated cupid's bow of a mouth with its glistening lips, the lips would part over those shiny white teeth, so slowly, so very slowly. And people would watch every movement of this face, the effect of every thought on every facial muscle, watch so closely that the slightest movement of the eyes, the mouth, the least wrinkling of the forehead was as violent as an earthquake in the real world. Anna used to insist that any face would fascinate, if it were blown up so big, if it were photographed as if it were the most important thing in the world. After all, while it was on the screen, it was the only thing in the world. Who would not be interested in the single thing in the world? But of course many faces were photographed exactly as hers was and people showed no desire to see those faces again.

Whereas their appetite for Anna was bottomless. They all but devoured her. People waited for days in the rain outside her house, hoping for a glimpse of her. A lovesick man with more courage than sense rented a hot-air balloon and landed in her back garden and for his efforts was rewarded by sirens, arrest and five days in jail. Terrified grocers gave interviews to national newspapers, telling reporters what Anna Asta bought when she stepped into their stores. Her shoe size was better known than the name of the country's president. And for one reason or another, she did not like this attention. She would say, Oh, yes, I know how many become movie stars so that the world will look at them. Believe me, I am not one of them.

I think, really, she was not. We worked together often. I never saw an actress less inclined to work under public scrutiny. What she did—her acting—the most public of the arts, she did in private. Before she came onto the set, she knew how she would do each scene. She had rehearsed every gesture of hand or foot, every movement of eye or mouth. When she came on, she was finished. I cannot rehearse, she would say. When I come onto the set, it is already hardened, like concrete. So of course she hated filming, because then, what she had done in secret was made public and to her this was always a desecration. And yet it is also true that she loved the camera, that when the camera's eye was on her she was most truly herself, felt herself most beautiful, most loved. She was a complicated woman, very difficult.

Long after we had both left Hollywood and had grown quite old, I began to visit her in Manhattan. By then, she had a housekeeper, a woman from Green Island named Ivy Cook. Together the two of them hypnotized me.

It seems to me that I started them talking into microphones, writing in notebooks, talking, during the summers when I spent the day with them. I, with my constant talk of getting to the bottom of things. Oh, he knows everything there is to know, Anna used to say, and I let her say it because it made the two of them happy, to talk and think they were understood. As for me, I understood nothing, and I understand nothing, but when I listened to them speak, I hoped: out of their stories would come some truth that fit me, some poor coat I could put my thin arms into, with one button right over the belt. I could fasten that button and in the coat climb up the long ladder into the sky. That poor coat was just what I needed, all I needed. Always, everywhere, we are seeking meaning. This is one of the things I learned from listening to them, although they claimed I knew this all along, that my films were evidence of what I understood, and it was because I understood everything that they spoke to me.

When Anna left the movies, at forty years of age, she was an extremely wealthy woman. If she had needed to earn a living, she might have been better off, but who knows? What could she do but act? The world agreed she had genius, was a genius. If she had had nothing, if she had ended up in a store basement selling hats, would that have improved her character? She would have said yes. She didn't hold a very high opinion of herself.

Ivy Cook, who came to work for her when she was forty years old and Anna was sixty, was raised on Green Island by her father and stepmother. Her family lived in Catherine County where there was no such thing as electricity and all water had to be carried up from the spring or the standpipe in buckets. They raised what food they needed: oranges, grapefruits, pineapple, breadfruit, pigs, goats and cows. To listen to Ivy recite a list of what grew naturally on Green Island was to listen to someone take inventory of the Garden of Eden. Of course, to her it was no such place.

They were both very intelligent, although neither of them knew it, and they would mock you if you said such a thing to them. Both of them were finished with school by the sixth grade, but I never met anyone who had a higher regard for education than Anna Asta or Ivy Cook. People like that often turn against books, saying things like, "It's all common sense. It's experience that counts," when in fact they have no sense and a mongrel hunting food in the cans on the street has more experience. But not these two.

When I came to America, no one was ever sure of my nationality. They weren't certain if I was from Sweden or Germany, but they knew I was foreign. The mistakes I made when I first came! The mistakes I still make! And Anna! She said when the gossip columnists had nothing to write about, they wrote about the feet she put in her mouth. But Ivy was another kettle of fish. If she was not angry, she talked, as Anna always said, like a book. She had almost no accent at all. Once I asked her about this. You speak the language so well, I said. You never make mistakes. How do you do it? And she said, Well, it is the British, isn't it? They taught Miss Blue and Miss Blue taught me. Miss Blue's right hand was covered with scars from a metal-edged ruler, one hit for every mistake she made when speaking the King's English. Miss Blue spent so much time carrying me up and down the island I naturally learned from her. But you know, she told me, when I go home to Green Island and I do my higglering and I want a bit of saltfish, I speak like every other crow in the tree. And it was true: when she spoke on the telephone and lost her temper, I thought she was speaking a language I'd never heard before. *And she say, I told she off. And I say, what? And he say: yes.* And when I asked her what language that was, she laughed at me and said, You don't know English when you hear it? Then she was sorry, afraid she'd embarrassed me. Oh, she said, if I spoke slowly, then you would know it.

Anna Asta began poor and Ivy Cook began poor. Here the resemblance ended. When Anna died, her assets were chronicled in the national newspapers. When we read Ivy's will, Anna and I sat there and cried; we might have been reading a document from the eighteen hundreds. *To my sister, Monica, my good black dress. To my daughter, Priscilla, my black cape. To my son, Junior, my color television. To my brother Jack, my black Bible and my good red pen. To my brother Herbert, my gingerbread clock.*

Anna had little use for family. She used to sit on the couch and ask Ivy how many brothers and sisters she had brought to this country, and as Ivy talked, Anna would enter figures on a little calculator. "You know," she said one day, "if you'd left all of them there, you'd be a millionaire now. Well, maybe not a millionaire, but a very wealthy woman." Then she would begin listing the relatives she still had, or thought she had, in Sweden and how much it would have cost to bring them over. Always she came to the same conclusion: "If I had brought them here, I could be living in poverty today."

Ivy Cook never had the least interest in money. Her aunt, Tita Lu, left her a small house on Green Island, in Mare River, where she grew up, and she always intended to go back there when Anna died. She used to say, I have a place to live and people who love me. Is there something more I must want?

This made me curious. I would say to her, This woman you work for, she has so much money. You don't become envious? No, she felt no envy. The world had given her some things, Anna others. Who could question the order of the world? It would have been like saying she thought stones ought to fall up. She might think so, but what good would it do? As it was, it seemed to her better, on the whole, that stones fell down. This way when you looked up at the sky you saw something clear and blue and you were not forever walking with your arms protecting your head in case the stones changed their minds and once more began falling down. I grew accustomed to sitting in the parlor, listening to the two of them talk, and after a while, they grew used to me, sitting there. This, people always said, was a gift I had, making myself invisible, although what kind of gift it is, I don't know. A stone has such a gift. After a few days, who notices the stone sitting in the front yard?

One day Anna looked up from her book and said, "Ivy was married for fifteen years, you for fifty, and I was never married at all, and here we all are, digging in a stony field looking for company just as if we all followed the same road."

"They are different stony fields and different things we are digging for," Ivy said. "Mr. Anders, what do you think?"

"Oh," I said, "I don't know how different any of us are."

"Please," said Anna. "That is sentiment. Some of us are better than others. Some of us are not even human."

"What nonsense!" I said.

"I wish it were," Anna said.

They were alike, too, in their love of privacy. "She chats too much," Ivy said when someone asked too many questions. "Let the woman go about her business." She called her youngest sister "Miss Carry Go Bring Come" because when she was a child her sister told their father that Ivy was hiding her shoes in a hollow tree so that when she was ready to run away she would have something to put on her feet, but meanwhile no one would suspect her of having such plans, because who would think she would run away from home bare-footed? *Miss Carry Go Bring Come,* the very name of gossip. Her sister would flush with shame when Ivy said it.

I liked to think that Ivy would live forever, she enjoyed living so much, whereas Anna was another story. She was always looking for a reason to live. I don't know if she ever found one. But she lived to be ninety. Perhaps that kept her going: looking for a reason to be alive.

Well, we always had something to talk about, Anna and I. In the old days when I was pronounced the most famous director in the world, I was brought to this country to teach others to make films. Now who remembers? I directed Anna two times. So when I visited, I would remind her of those times, and one afternoon, she said, You know, someone was talking to me about the way those silver nitrate films decay. And I said, Oh, let's not talk about that, Anna! It's a sad business. Fifteen, twenty of my films gone! Someone said, You wait, Anders! They will show up somewhere in an archive in Kiev. So I've been waiting sixty years and still they don't show up.

You know why they're destroyed? she asked me. Remember how the dialogue was spliced in at the last minute? The titles were not washed so well as the rest of the film because everything was quick, quick, quick, get the film released. Then fifteen, twenty years later, someone would smell that awful smell, they would open up a can and the smell would get worse, and they'd say, Oh, this one is going. It's decomposing. Let's get rid of it. But really, only the words were going. Isn't that something? Only the words! And you could watch those films without the words and still you would understand everything! All those beautiful pictures destroyed because of a few words! Oh yes, people should keep quiet. People should keep their mouths shut. Such beautiful pictures, all gone! Those beautiful faces of yours, those wonderful landscapes, people travel all over Sweden looking for them, all of them gone because of a few words!

Words have their use, I said.

You! she said. *Artist, don't speak. Do your work.* So you always said.

I said, That's not what I meant. We cannot live without words.

Well, I'm not so sure, she said. Look at those paintings. I love paintings. They say a lot but they don't say one single word.

I said, There are some people who paint with words.

Good for them, Anna said.

She and Ivy were looking at Ivy's photograph album. I stood behind them, looking at the album. Photograph after photograph of Green Island, photograph after photograph of the two of them standing in front of wood shacks. One shack was striped, its boards painted alternately aqua and pink.

What a place to make a film! I said. You remember, Anna? You made one there. She ignored me. Sometimes you could talk to her about her films, other times, not.

I sat down in the brocade chair on the far side of the room and watched them. They were absorbed in the pictures and I thought, What if that album were a book that recorded every scene in their lives? What if you looked at the pictures long enough? Would you see a pattern? Was there some kind of code, a scene that repeated itself over and over again? The critics say so of my films. Always, they say, beneath the surface, it is the same story: a lonely person suffers from guilt—sometimes senselessly—and must find a way to expiate it. Why would I make film after film about guilt when I never remember suffering from any such emotion? Still, the critics find it in every film I made.

Was it the quiet, the way they turned pages, *slap, slap,* so that the sound of the pages turning reminded me of waves breaking on the shore of the lake where my family spent its summers, was it the orange glow in that room, as if we were sitting inside a segment of an orange? Whatever it was, I began thinking aloud. I said, "You know, I've always believed everyone has a favorite story they follow like a map throughout their lives, and if you know that story, you can know the person's life."

Anna looked up and said, "I knew someone who had a story he read again and again. He never read it to me. This is what it was about. An island was in danger, and to save it, someone had to be thrown into a volcano. Or maybe not a volcano, but a pool full of sharks. Anyway, they had to be thrown into something. Do you know that story? Always when he finished reading it, he would look up and sigh, and say, 'Why me?'"

I said there were a great many stories like that and could she be more specific? She said if she could be more specific she would be a retired professor living in a small town in the Swedish countryside.

Ivy said that when she was a child, Miss Blue used to tell them stories and riddles. Anna asked her if she remembered any of them and if she had a favorite.

"I had a favorite," said Ivy. She was not one to waste words. If you didn't put the question exactly right, you didn't get the answer you wanted.

"What was your favorite?" I asked.

"'Mr. Johncrow's Wedding,'" she said.

"Tell it," Anna said.

"Mr. Johncrow is a vulture," said Ivy. "You know vultures?" she asked Anna. Anna nodded. "This is the story," Ivy said. "Once there was a beautiful girl, the most beautiful girl on Green Island. Her mother and father decided it was time for her to be married and the news went around, and suitors began to come to the house. But with everyone who came, the girl found fault. This one was too tall, this one was too short. This one was too thin, this one was too fat. This one was too poor, this one was too rich.

"Finally, the girl's mother beat her. 'Everyone on Green Island has chopped a path through the bush to our door,' the mother said, 'and you have turned them all back. You will grow up to be a poor spinster and eat dust in the courtyard of a house that is not your own.' But the girl was not worried and only said, 'Mother, when the man who shall be my husband comes, I shall know him.'

"Now Mr. Johncrow was flying high above Green Island and he could not help but notice how every man on the island seemed to be traveling back and forth to this same house, and he flew down low and asked Mr. Dog, 'Why is everyone going to that house on top of the mountain?' and Mr. Dog told him that the most beautiful girl on the island lived there and was looking for a husband, but no one who came pleased her. 'I will marry her,' said Mr. Johncrow. Mr. Dog laughed at him.

"But Mr. Johncrow dressed himself up in a fancy black coat, and he bought a fancy black carriage and two fancy black horses and he stopped outside the girl's house. 'A man is here to see you,' called the girl's mother, and the girl came down, drew aside the curtain and looked out the window. 'That is the man I will marry,' she said to her mother. 'I will marry him and no other.' And so the mother announced the wedding and began to prepare meats for the wedding feast.

" 'Sister, sister,' said the girl's small brother, 'I see him clearly, as clearly as can be and he is not a man at all, but a johncrow.'

"The girl was enraged and thumped her brother down.

" 'Take off his jacket and you will see his wings, his bony wings,' said her little brother, but his sister only laughed at him. The wedding feast was prepared and Mr. Johncrow took his bride away in a carriage to a house on top of a high cliff, so high that the grass ran out and there was nothing but naked rock. The little boy followed behind. He hid in the bushes down beneath his sister's house and ate berries and fruits he picked there, and when it grew dark, he sneaked up the hill and spied upon his sister. He looked in the window and at night he saw Mr. Johncrow, his black bird's body on top of hers.

"During the day when he saw Mr. Johncrow soar off into the skies, he would crouch down beneath his sister's window. 'Sister, sister!' he cried. 'You have married a johncrow and must run away!' but his sister only laughed at him and threw stones to chase him down the hill. Then one day he sneaked up the hill and saw Mr. Johncrow swooping down from the sky and he watched him dive into a ravine. The little boy crept along the rocky ground until he came to the edge and looked down. There was Mr. Johncrow tearing at a stinking carcass!

"The little boy ran back to his sister's house. 'Sister, sister, come with me!' he said. 'Your husband is in the ravine tearing at stinking meat!' Finally the sister was sorry for her little brother and she said, 'Oh, all right, I will come with you.' She followed him to the ravine and when she looked down, there was her husband, tearing at the carcass with his huge beak and claws.

" 'What must I do now?' asked his sister. 'I see I am married to a johncrow,' and she began to cry. Her brother said they must wait for her husband to fall asleep, as he would soon, since he had eaten so heavily, and then they would sneak back to their parents' house, and this is what they did. The townspeople went up the hill and found Mr. Johncrow's nest and burned it and Mr. Johncrow flew off to save himself. Now the girl lives safe at home and listens to her little brother when he speaks, for she knows that even the least one can have something worthwhile to say.

"Yes," said Ivy. "That is my favorite story."

"Mine," said Anna, "is 'The Many Dancing Princesses.' Every night they went out somewhere to dance, but no one knew where they went. They went down through a trap door and they had a jolly time. But a prince fell in love with one of them, and one of the princesses dropped a slipper, so he followed them. Do you have to like all of the story? I don't like the story after someone finds out where they're going. But the first part, that's my favorite story."

" 'The Twelve Dancing Princesses,' " I said. "Not 'The Many Dancing Princesses.' "

"Does it matter how many?" Anna asked me.

"Well, if you wanted to look it up," I said, "you wouldn't find it under 'The Many Dancing Princesses.' "

"Why should I want to look it up?" Anna said. "But if you only like part of a story, can it tell very much about you? Probably not."

"Probably it tells more."

"There's another one I used to like best, many long years ago, in Finland," she said. "A woman marries a beautiful prince but she has to promise never to look at him at night, and of course she can't keep her word. One night, she lights a candle—these fairy tales," she said to me, "they wrote them in the time before electricity—and she bends over her husband and a drop of hot wax falls on him and wakes him up and he turns into a beast, I don't know, a man with a hog's head or something like that, not the kind of hog they kill for ham, but a wild boar with tusks, that kind of a hog, and she spends the rest of her life trying to break the spell and turn him back into a beautiful prince. She does it, I think, in the end. That was my favorite story, once, long ago. Not anymore. Now it's all those dancing princesses."

"Which one is your absolute favorite?" I asked.

"Now, the princesses. Then, the princess who turned her husband into a beast."

"One story per life," I said.

"Perhaps I've had two lives," Anna said, "not one. And perhaps it is not your favorite story, either, but the story that most frightens you, the one you see only in bad dreams. And if you only see it when you're dreaming, how can you remember it when you wake up? So, think about that, Anders!"

I didn't have to think about it. I knew she was right. What story did I dream about, again and again? Was it a story full of guilt and expiation? As far as I knew, no such story had ever made much of an impression on me.

"Now that you know our favorite stories, Mr. Anders," Ivy said, "come! Explain our lives."

Anna laughed and stood up. "He has the key but no doors," she said. "Or he is at the right door but he has the wrong keys!" Anna Asta could be a very infuriating woman. Believe me. I know.

I see that to the last I am to be a kind of impresario, the director. Now I sit here with their notebooks, their taped conversations and confessions, and my own memories. If memories could fill boxes, I would need several warehouses. And I tell myself, Anders, this will be a big job. You are almost one hundred years old. What makes you think you will live long enough to finish? And then I said, Stop this self-pitying. Who asked you to do it? But who ever asked me to do anything?

This, really, is my last film, and it is the right one for me. I will pick up all the images I have of their lives, and put them together into a photograph album, the supreme photograph album that tells the truth about them, an album such as the recording angel might have! Oh, it cannot be done, of course, but at my age one can forget impossibilities. And of course the truth of this album will be my truth, and now that I am the only one left, I will be the omniscient one. Finally, a purpose to this silence in which I live, absolute as God. There will be no one to contradict me, no one to ask, Why does Ivy first tell the story of her life as if she were telling the story of someone she does not even know, and then speak in her own voice? But Ivy would have known why. Anna would have known why. When your life begins, in those first years when everything is most important, the individual memory fails, and so you rely on what you are told. You are only a character in someone else's story. You are the main character, every event concerns you, but the story is not yours. You cannot tell it. It is only later, when you come to count the cost, when you have grown old and have time to look back, when it is too late to change anything: then you become the story teller. Perhaps that is the moment you are truly born.

I will have them tell their stories as I want them to tell them and this will not be so bad. I will let one talk until I am tired and then the other one will interrupt. When I am finished, I will go back and smooth it all out: like God. But of course I am not God and so I shall hurry myself a little. I never believed in tempting fate and at my age I worry about fate more than I once did. It is the only thing left on earth still tempted by me.

And I am the one to do it, the only one who can. Everyone always said I adored women and it is true. And because these two were both beautiful, very beautiful, and because, at the end, the three of us so often walked up and down the street in snowstorms, I will call it "Beautiful Ladies in Snow." I leave myself out, you see: out of the picture. But I am there. I am the one telling you everything. I am the story teller. How important I make myself! But in fact it is they, those two, who tyrannize over me. Somewhere I hear Anna laughing. Let the men think they're free, she says. Or is it Ivy who says so? Wherever they are, they look at each other and nod. They smile like cats. They have me in the palm of their hand. Their fingers close over me like bars in a bird cage. Well, I could do worse than sing for them.

If I can live long enough to finish the song! Well, I am still here for some reason. I think I can do it.

FIRST NIGHTS

BY ANNA ASTA AND IVY COOK

PART ONE

WILD ORANGES

ANNA ASTA

THE PAST, WHAT IS IT? A series of pictures that grow fainter and fainter with time. After a while, you don't want to see them anymore. They are only pictures. You talk to them but they don't talk back to you. Pretty soon the photograph album is like a history lesson and all the time you are failing it. *Who is that? I don't know that one. And this one? Oh, that was my mother. How do I know? I studied that face hardest. And this one? That was my father. How do I know? It's the same face: my face.* Someday I'll look in the mirror and let out a scream. I won't know the face I see there. That's how you'll know my mind is gone. No one ever studied a face as I studied mine. Strictly speaking? I suppose that's not true. Everyone who makes a living by his face studies it in the mirror.

They say my face was the most famous face in the world, and I'll tell you something: it's true. All of you would know me if you saw me on the street: *if* I had make-up on. No, *know me* is the wrong way to say it. This terrible language! I still can't manage it! You wouldn't know me; there's one person left in the world who knows me. Long ago, of all the people I knew, there were only two who knew me, and sometimes, even then, I wondered.

One of them wanted to make something out of me. The other one wanted to marry me. They both succeeded, in their way. He made something out of me, Max did. Today I can't walk down the street without photographers swooping out of the sky like sea gulls. Everything dies but photographers. They don't die. One of them spends his days following me. I came out of the hospital, and there he was with his camera. I'm eighty now. I look like a bag lady. You'd think they'd give me some peace. No peace. I came out of my house last week and he was there and he wore something around his neck and I saw it, and I thought, That's a shrunken head. Whose head is it? And right away, I knew it was my head.

I pointed at it and started to laugh and I said to him, I'm dead and I don't know it! So they gave you my head! Who said you could have it? And I picked up my walking stick and ran after him and he ran away! He ran away from me! I should have thought of this before, being crazy. In New York, people walk along with guns but no one is afraid of guns anymore. They're used to guns. A crazy person, that's another story. I'm not afraid of dying. Why should I be when I died such a long time ago? This won't make sense to you, because you'll ask, if you died a long time ago, who is this walking and talking now? Don't ask.

But one thing I am afraid of. They'll have me stretched out on my slab and some kind of stiff sheet thrown over me, and my head pointing up at the ceiling and my eyes will open, they'll snap open one last time, and what will they see? A bright light, a very bright light, like a klieg light. It won't be God. I don't believe in Him. It won't be heaven. I don't believe in it, either. It will be the flash bulb of a camera. I believe in cameras and I believe in photographers and I believe in the devil. I wouldn't believe in the devil, really, but I have to, because I believe in photographers.

I remember the first time I came to New York, and I wanted to walk, I always wanted to walk, and I took a taxi and I said, Take me to Central Park, and the taxi stopped at Ninety-sixth Street and Central Park West and I went into the park and started to walk, and it was wonderful, there I was in New York, and it was warm, and the sky floated in the ponds just the way it does in Sweden when the weather is fine, and I walked toward the tall buildings I had seen downtown and a photographer, well, he grew right up from the ground, to this day I think he was a crocus that grew arms and legs at the sight of me, and he began following me, and I walked faster, and he walked faster, and someone else joined him, and they began saying my name, Anna Asta, Anna Asta, and I started to run, and they ran after me, and when I got to the statue of the general on his horse, there was a pack of them after me, and I saw it was no use, so I turned around, and I said to the photographer, I feel sorry for you. What a life you have.

Who knows if he even heard me? Who knows what language he spoke? Who knows what language I spoke? When I get upset, I don't know what language I'm speaking; especially then, I didn't. I used to say, Soon I will be like my famous cousin who went from country to country, learning a little bit of German and a little bit of Spanish and Swedish and Russian and French and finally no one could understand a word he said. He was a walking Tower of Babel.

Well, he wasn't the only one. What it was like on the sets in those days! Everyone speaking their own language, and I said to the leading man, "I love you," and then I looked at the director to see his expression: Did I say it right? You know, some directors cared that you said the words properly even though the movies were silent, because if you didn't, if the titles said one thing and your lips said another, then in came complaining letters from the deaf mutes. And some of the directors, like Anders, cared very much about the deaf mutes who could read lips. So I had to say it properly. And then the actor took me in his arms and whispered something, I didn't know what it was, maybe it was insulting? And I pushed him away from me and glared at him and the director was yelling "Cut! Cut!" Or at least that's what he was yelling if he knew the language. "Go! Go!" Max would yell when he meant "Stop! Stop!" And everyone would get confused. Sometimes I thought they understood him but only pretended to be confused, Max was such a hard man to work for. All they had to do was follow his directions and they made him look bad. Bad? Terrible! And the tantrums he would get into when they told him they were just doing what he ordered them to do! So if they wanted to get rid of him, they found the way. I saw that and I took it in. But he was the one who was great. He was the one. When they finished with him and he got back on the boat and returned to Sweden, and went from there to Germany, I thought, He is doing the right thing. He is the one the world will remember.

And Charlie got what he wanted, I suppose he did. I didn't marry him but for almost six years we lived together in his house on Cliffside Road. Charles, Chuck, Chuckie. I used to call him Chuckie. He taught me. He ordered books from Finland and Sweden for me. He saw how much trouble I had making myself understood and he said, Someday you will not even understand yourself. He gave me a journal bound in leather with a little lock, but what are locks? They are flimsy things. You cannot trust them. Then he said, You really want to lock it up? Write in Finnish. Who knows Finnish but you? Well, Max knew Finnish.

But now I had an idea. I began to write in this tiny handwriting, so small no one but me could read it. And to make sure, I would leave out certain letters, so it was really a kind of code. But still I wasn't safe. He would look over my shoulder, Chuckie, and he'd say, Oh, the letters are going straight up and down. So what are you mad about now? Everything's slanting to the right. Put on your coat. We're going for a walk.

He's dead, of course. He died young, and no one remembers him, although then everyone knew: he was the greatest actor there was. Half the women in Hollywood blamed themselves for his death. His funeral looked like a fashion show, all those women who blamed themselves coming to say goodbye. I don't know how long they had him on their consciences, but I still have him on mine. I didn't kill him. I don't believe that. I'm not a sentimentalist, you see. No one killed me. I'm still here. It's in the genes; it's what you're born with. My genes are strong. I think of them, each one of them, like a sturdy hiking boot. Charlie wasn't so lucky, genes like soft leather shoes, and always tripping over his laces. I didn't kill him, but I didn't help, either.

And maybe, who knows, if I'd been different, he'd have lasted longer. In Sweden, before I came to this country, before I had any money, I had a pair of soft leather boots and I patched them and patched them until there was nothing left of the pair I bought at the store. But maybe he didn't want to be patched. Maybe he saw it all coming and thought, Well, enough of this. I try to think of him sometimes, eighty, like me, living where there are telephones and televisions and calling him, and he gets up from his chair and answers the telephone, and I can't imagine it. Charlie old!

But just this instant I *can* imagine it. He gets up, he holds on to the table, he leans over and picks up the phone. "Anskie!" he says. "You ugly thing! Don't let them tell you you're beautiful! A person who can't read isn't beautiful! A person who can't speak isn't beautiful!" Well, of course, now I am crying. So I say, "You haven't been sitting there waiting for the phone to ring? Not all this time?" And he says, "Yes, I've been waiting all this time." And over the phone I hear the clink, clink, clink of ice in a glass. "What's that noise?" I ask and he doesn't answer. He sighs only. So I know. He's drinking. "I don't appreciate your drinking," I say. "Anskie," he says, "I last as long as this drink," and I hear the ice clink, and his voice says, "I'm almost finished," and now I can't see him anymore, now I'm not in the room with him, watching him, but at the end of the telephone wire, listening, and he says, "One more sip, Anskie. Call me again, Anskie," and the ice clinks, he is gone.

There are nights when I dream of him. Nothing special happens: he is back, the old times are back, we're waiting behind the flats of the set, waiting to go on, and he starts to talk about something, about tennis, something, it doesn't matter, and the dream goes on and he decides to sail a boat out to a little island and a storm comes up and

I can't sail out to meet him, or he and I are talking and I say, Yes, I'll marry you, and we sit there, my hand on his knee, on the smooth gray flannel of his knee, my arm around his shoulders, around the white wool of his sweater, and I think, All right, this is what you want. You've knocked around enough, now you must marry him, and I look down the beach and a woman is walking toward us and I turn and look at Charlie, and I see his eyes flick toward me and then he looks out to sea and I know. When the woman is almost in front of us, she stops and he smiles sadly, I never saw such pity in anyone's eyes, perhaps once before, once only, and he gets up and says, "Well, Anskie, I'll see you," and the woman reaches out her hand to him. He takes it. They walk away. They walk away together.

When I wake up, it is as if he is still in the room. I smile at whatever my eyes fall on. I love the coverlet my hand rests on. I see his face, not as it was in life, but as in the dream, as if all this time he lived, unknown to all of us, aging as I've aged, and I love every vertical crease in his face, every wrinkle around his eyes, the wobbling turkey-skin of his throat, I love every proof of the years he has gathered to him. And then, as if I am watching a film, the dream advances, and we are sitting on the beach, and the woman walks toward us and before she stops I begin to cry, not tears, but sheets of water that wash over my face, splash onto my clothes, and I lie there and cry until I am exhausted. I can't get up that day. The rest of that day is death. My bones turn to water. The sun goes out. I expect to hear wailing in the streets. If Ivy comes to the door, I wave my hand at her: Go out.

2

IVY COOK

THESE THINGS I REMEMBER, or they are remembered about me, and were told to me, so that now I may think someone else's memories are my own. This is the way it happens. I can say this shoe is mine or it is not. I can say, This is the red felt hat I wore to church the day I sat in the balcony and looked down and saw all the ladies of the town wearing their round straw hats so that the church seemed to be filled with beautiful floating plates that nodded and bobbed on the hot currents of air, stirring as Preacher Beckwith spoke, Brother Beck, leaning forward and back, the hats bobbing up and down. The shoes are mine, and the red felt hat, but was I there in the balcony, or was it Tita Lu who told me about looking down on the hats as they floated on the air like so many lily pads on the rippling sky of her father's heart-shaped pond in Mare River?

In a court of law, the magistrate asks, "Do you remember? Do you remember flinging that stone?" and people feel no guilt when they answer, because they have thought it over and think they know they are either telling the truth or hiding it. They know if they picked up the stone and threw it. Yet they turn pale and shake with fear if they go up the eleven steps to the courthouse and before they have time to think, the same man asks them, "Is that your red felt hat?" This is how fragile memory is, how little we trust our own memories, how much we fear our memories are untrue. And yet, what do we have but our memories? Our past lives in our memory. We are the sum of our memories. And still, we are asked, "Is that your red felt hat?" and we tremble with fear. Then we pause and think. We remember the day someone gave us the hat. We breathe a sigh of relief. Yes, I remember. It is my hat.

Of course the day comes when the sky goes dark, and the teacher, Mistress Banford, closes the shutters against the storm, and inside the school it is dark, and everyone gropes for his shoes, and when he gets home, he has on two left shoes, or one of his own shoes and someone else's, and it is always that way on Green Island. When you close your hand on something, how do you know it is yours, and even if it is, how do you know you will be able to keep it? It is all a storm, and after the storm, no one cares who has whose shoes. Everyone is happy to stand on his own two feet.

"Her memory is good, you know," says my father. "Her memory is real good."

What use is it?

I used to say, When I grow up, there are four things I will never do. I will never wear stockings, I will never wear dentures, I will never wear glasses, and I will never get married.

Why not?

Because I don't see the use of them.

When my teeth hurt me, I had them pulled. Nothing will ever hurt me twice, I said. When I put on glasses, the bridge of my nose complained, but I was on one side of a river, and my books were on the other, and I had other bridges to cross. When I met a man who took me to a dance, I pulled the thin woven web over my legs and admired their sheen in the moonlight. When the parson came and said to me, "Do you want his soul to burn in hell because you refuse to live as man and wife?" I gave in and married. Better to tie a wild horse with a vine than to guide your life down a path by the frail, dusty spider-reins of memory.

We were sitting on the veranda steps. The day was very hot. A fat fly buzzed through the air. Everyone was too tired to swat him. The fly hovered over each of us as if deciding where to settle. He hovered over my stepmother. She sighed deeply. Shadows were dark black and sharp. The black shadow of a coconut tree cut across the yard and painted itself upon the glaring white wall of our house. The chickens slowly emerged from the coffee walk, felt the sun on their feathers, and went back in. The pigs lay in their wallow like alligators waiting for prey. A mule cart passed in front of our house raising enough dust to blot out the mountains behind the meadows. We could hear the river running. *Sweet, sweet, sweet,* it sang. *Cool, cool, cool.* A man with a megaphone stood up in the cart, and as he passed our house, he shouted, "Storm warning! Storm warning! Nail everything down! Storm warning!"

Miss Blue came to our gate and called out, Hold the dog! She was smiling. We smiled when we saw her. The very water in the stream could boil in the sun, but Miss Blue was always cool and dry. Her skin was cool and dry to the touch. A fine powder seemed to cover it. In the last life, I was an alligator. She used to say that, and we used to believe her. Her clothes did not dampen and stain and stick to her, exposing the outline of her body, as ours did. We thought she had powers.

She came into the yard and sat down on the bottom step.

"Riddle me this riddle," she said. "Guess me this riddle and perhaps not."

"I have a riddle for *you*," said Mr. Cook, my father. "Not even the king could guess it, and so that man went free." But what was my father doing there, in the middle of the day? Why wasn't he at the plantation, spraying bananas?

"Guess me this riddle and perhaps not," said Miss Blue. She ignored my father, perhaps because he wasn't there. I couldn't pronounce my name. What is your name? they asked me. *Icy*, I said. I was actually named after my Aunt Lucille, but everyone called me Ivy. Few people on Green Island are called by their proper names. "I have a hard shell," said Miss Blue.

"A turtle," I said.

The first one to guess a riddle didn't have to carry water from the spring to the house for the next meal.

"A cockroach," said my brother Jack.

"I have a hard shell and many heads and many feet. In the morning, I have two heads. In the afternoon, I have three or four or ten. In the evening, I have two again. By midnight, I have one. At the last dawn, I have none."

"Birds in a nest," I said, and it seemed to me that Miss Blue gave me an evil look.

"I have a hard shell," said Miss Blue. "In the morning, I have two legs. In the afternoon, I have six or eight or twenty. In the evening, I have four again. By midnight, I have two. At the last dawn, I have one or none."

"Cockroaches in the hen house," I said. "The chickens eat the cockroaches one at a time."

"No," said Miss Blue.

"Will you tell us?" said Mrs. Cook, Bea, my stepmother. Her youngest child, my half sister, was fanning her with a palm leaf.

"No," said Miss Blue.

"Bring some lemonade, come," said Mrs. Cook to Jack, my half brother Jack.

Was there a storm? Did it break hard over the ridge of our roof? Did Miss Blue tell us the answer to the riddle? Now, when I ask, no one remembers the riddle, much less the answer. *Oh, those riddles are old-time things.* Was my father there, or had he gone to work? Who was in the donkey cart, shouting into the megaphone? Once I used to know. He worked, I think, for the post office. The post office owned the megaphone. Why didn't the police own a megaphone? Did anyone listen? Did they nail their windows shut? It was very hot. It was like moving through butter. I remember how hot it was.

These are my earliest memories. I am going to school with Kathleen, whom I love and who lives in my yard. The school is down the road and then up a steep grade. As I walk up, I put my hands on my hips. I say, "Queen of Tiverly, coming up."

I am still living with my mother, my grandmother, whom I call Auntie Tina, and my great-grandmother. I call my great-grandmother Nanny and Nanny is completely blind. I believe that one day she will open her eyes and see me. I believe that Nanny chooses to be blind as she chooses to keep her eyes shut, although when my great-grandmother is frightened, she opens her eyes and the pupils of her eyes swim wildly about.

Someone has died up the hill. His name is Poppy Zeke. All the children fear him. His house is just above the riverbank where the river runs wide and flat and clear and the stones beneath the water are tear-shaped and flat and perfect for throwing. All the children wade there. The older ones bring their younger brothers and sisters because the water is not so deep as to be unsafe. On their way to the fields up in the mountains, children, taking the goats up to the mountain pastures where they will feed, stop here and let the goats drink, and while they do, the children call back and forth to one another. Up behind them, the blue mountains rise, layer upon jagged layer, until the last of the mountains resembles a thin skin of cloud about to burn off in the sun. Men too stop here on their way to work, and women, on their way back from town, stop to wet their feet and splash their faces. They call to the children they find there: *Didn't I hear the school bell? Your mother knows you are eating that store cake? Good morning, Mr. Johnson. Why does my donkey cry out when he sees you?*

This is a great trial to Poppy Zeke, who complained all his life that he was born with bat's ears and could not bear any noise. Whenever the children ran through his yard, he picked up a stout stick and chased them. Once Kathleen took me into his yard to fill my tin cup with water from his standpipe, and he rushed out of the doormouth, his face twisted up. "Beast face! Beast face!" called Kathleen, and then ran for her life. I stumbled and fell and when I looked up I saw Poppy Zeke bearing down upon me. I was so frightened I lost consciousness. I awakened on my great-grandmother's bed, the old woman's hand stroking my forehead. "To annoy the man on such a hot day!" said my great-grandmother.

Up the hill, there was a great sound of hammering. "Can we beg some cedar boards from you?" asked Poppy Zeke's daughter, and my grandmother went behind the house and produced one pine log, saying it was all she had. "Bring the child to the funeral," said Poppy Zeke's daughter. "You know it is right."

It was still cool. Everything was still covered by a thin sheet of cool water. The roosters crowed and the dogs barked and the women began dragging their tin wash basins out into their yards but nothing disturbed the early morning quiet, which existed behind these sounds, independent of them, and which made every noise—the rooster crowing, the clatter of a wash basin against a stone—different and more remarkable than it would be at any other time of day. Each of these noises was made new by the early morning silence, which was itself, every day, something remarkable and cool and new.

My grandmother brought me up the hill and sat me down with the other children in Poppy Zeke's yard. Poppy Zeke himself, because he is dead, is lying in his own bed in his own room. One of the bolder children has already been to see him and says he looks the same as ever, his face twisted up with rage. Someone says, "What do you think dead people do? They are just the same in death as they were in life."

The children are plucking chickens and I am on my knees, plucking feathers, my back to Poppy Zeke's house. I stop to admire the rooster who struts in front of me, his bronze and gold and red feathers and the red comb on his head, all so suddenly lit up by the sun. Without warning, someone stuffs a handful of feathers down the back of my shirt, and the children start to shout, "It's Poppy Zeke! It's Poppy Zeke!" I think Poppy Zeke has come for me and I try to shake the feathers from my blouse but they stick there like nails puncturing my skin. I begin to scream and dance up and down and then I remember nothing. "To scare the child into fits!" I hear someone saying. "I'll come for you with my machete!" I see my grandmother's face looking down at me. I hear a chicken clucking and I shudder. In my imagination, the flesh of the chicken and the flesh of the dead man have become one.

At the funeral, my grandmother passes me across the coffin to my

Uncle Kenneth, who passes me back to my grandmother. All in all, I
am passed back and forth three times. I remember sobbing. I remember my fear that they will drop me and no one will dare pick me up
and take me from the coffin and I will be buried alive with Poppy
Zeke, who is also alive, alive and glaring. At night, I look up at my
ceiling and see Poppy Zeke's face staring down. His expression is always the same: terrible, terrible fury. Sometimes, when I look up into
the sky, his face appears in the clouds.

"Now," says my great-grandmother with satisfaction, "he will look
after you. The loving dead must protect the living."

So, I think, Poppy Zeke is still alive. I do not want to be protected
by him and I do not want to see his face in my ceiling. He will protect
me? Protect me from what? There is nothing to fear on Green Island.
Months go by and I see no sign of Poppy Zeke. I begin to forget him,
unless, of course, he appears in my ceiling.

I see *her* standing in the doorway, the sun at her back. The house is
darkened against the heat. Outside, the sun is so hot it is not yellow,
but white, so when I look at her, the woman is only an outline, an
outline of a person, black against the sun, in the house, an aura of
white light around her. On one shoulder sits an enormous parrot. I
cannot see her face. Perhaps the woman is standing with her back to
me after all. She has a lovely shape, a shape like a Coca-Cola bottle.
This, I know, is my mother. It is the most distinct memory I have of
her. Her hair is tall, tall, tall, and she wears it in a long braid down
her back. The woman has taught the parrot to talk, but I don't remember what it says.

Someone has taken me down to the cliffs. We have walked all day
and now we are at the edge of the island. This is where Green Island
ends, says the woman, but I think, No, this is where the water begins.
There is no end to Green Island.

The cliffs are green and steep, layers and layers of them, plunging
toward the sea, arching their backs like the dolphins that fly out of
the water. Here and there small houses, houses made tiny by the
distance we have come, dot the hills. One house seems cut out of an
impenetrable forest wall. The path leading up to it is a thin red thread
wound around the mountain. A small twist of smoke rises from the
chimney of the house, grayish brown against the painful blue of the
brilliant sky. As we watch, the whale swims slowly by. His back is
shiny and enormous. He is larger than any house I have ever seen. He
turns his head and his shiny black stone of an eye finds us on the cliff.

He swims slowly, utterly indifferent to us. On his back, he bears two huge sea turtles who have gone along for the ride. They are gray-green and the day is so clear we can see the pattern of their shells, their wrinkly heads, their gray-black feet.

The gray whale swims slowly by, attended by dolphins. They leap in and out of the water. Suddenly the whale blows a great column of water, a waterspout, and the sun catches the drops as they begin to fall back. "All of those," says the woman who is with me, "are jewels. Men go down to the sea and bring those jewels home for their women." The sky is blue, the sea is green. Everything on land is vivid and solid and beautiful.

The sun shifts. The water is green where it laps at the edge of Green Island, but farther out it is blue, the same color as the sky. We are up so high we can see clouds reflected in the water. The sun moves again. Now the water looks like the endless pastures and meadows of Green Island. Some day, I think, I will walk on the water. "Lovely turtles," says the woman. "Flying fish. Did you see the flying fish?" All the way home, I look up, looking for the flying fish. I see a large black bird. I point at it. "A johncrow," says the woman. I don't know what that is. "A johncrow is a vulture," says my blind great-grandmother. "Don't look at it. If you see one look at you, you must bathe in the river and you must wash the clothes you wore." I forget about the black bird. There is no end to Green Island. Some day I will walk upon its waters.

My great-grandmother is sitting on the bed, cross-legged, and I am sitting in the space between her knees. She is combing my hair. "You have tall hair," says my great-grandmother. "And fine." She combs it gently. Her fingers have eyes. Soon my hair will be free of knots and then my great-grandmother will begin plaiting it, expertly, quickly. "What the eyes can't see, the fingers remember," she says. Snap, snap, snap goes the rubber band, holding the braid in place. Snap, snap and snap, snap again. She had made three plaits of my hair. Just then the dogs begin barking and the chickens begin squawking and the rooster crows. "Who is here?" says my great-grandmother. Her eyes are open and her dark pupils are swimming. Her pupils are black with fear. "Who is here?"

Outside, there is a black car, my uncle's car. I run over to it. Someone picks me up and puts me down in the back seat.

"Who is here? Who is here?" I hear my great-grandmother calling again and again. "That's my child, you hear! Bring her back!"

The car drives off. In the back seat of the car, I see a strange woman. I sit quietly. I see the woman staring at her feet. I am wearing socks. My great-grandmother was about to put on my shoes when the black car came. The woman says nothing to me.

When the car stops, I get out. I see a man standing near a gate in front of a strange house. "You are going to like it here," he says to me. I recognize him. He is my father. I say—I think I say—I want to go home, but he says, No, your mother is sick and she wants me to keep you. You will like it here, he says again.

He takes me inside and gives me a glass of lemonade. A large woman—is it Miss Blue?—looks after me. She starts to tell me a story. "At the edge of Green Island, if you look very carefully, you can see the Sunken City. Many, many years ago, there was an earthquake and the whole city slid into the sea. We can take a rowboat and go out and look for the city. Wouldn't you like to see it? There it all is, just like Mare River, the whole town, the city hall, the police station, all the houses, and the church and the church steeple. When the tide is low, the steeple rises out of the water and you can tie your boat to it. Do you want to see the Sunken City?"

I do. I nod my head.

"Don't tell the child nonsense," says the woman from the car.

"It is not nonsense," says the man I recognize as my father. "That woman in the car, now?" he says to me. "She is your new mother."

"Stepmother," says the woman in the car.

"New mother!" says my father impatiently. He has great authority. I feel it, as does the woman in the car. She turns her attention to Miss Blue.

"And have you no sense, Miss Blue?" she asks. "Your own daughter nearly drowned looking for the Sunken City! You have no sense at all?"

"You're going to like it here," says my father. "And you, Mrs. Cook!" he says to his wife. "How can you talk to Mistress Blue that way? Regain your senses, madam!"

This is the story of my kidnapping, as they told it to me later.

My father and Mer, my mother, do not marry. Instead, my father marries Miss Bea and he and his wife leave Cinnamon Bay and go to live in Mare River. They name their first child Jack, their second, Cynthia, and their third, Cherry. I stay with Mer, my mother, in Cinnamon Bay.

My father has a friend named Lazarus who still lives in Cinnamon Bay near my mother's house. They are playing dominoes. Lazarus tells my father everything that happens there, so that my father knows what man my mother lives with and when she has children. My father never asks Lazarus about her, but at times a silence falls, and Lazarus says something about the drought or how bad the expected storm is likely to be, and my father does not answer. "Your daughter," Lazarus says, "she is a pretty one," and my father listens to him as if he had been in a deep sleep and had just awakened.

"She still looks like her mother?" asks my father.

"She is the picture of Mer."

"But from the side she resembles me?" he asks.

"I didn't notice," Lazarus says. "Next time I'll look." He has little interest in children who, to him, all look more or less the same. My father's questions about Mer and his daughter in Cinnamon Bay make Lazarus uneasy. He likes lives that run smoothly. He doesn't like storms or explosions or people waiting for one another behind bushes with sharpened machetes. He doesn't like women going to the magic men and then going home to brew up dangerous teas or softening candles out of which they make wax dolls. "Your mind runs on that Clifton woman too much," Lazarus says. "You chat too much about her. Your wife will think something about it, you'll see. You're in Mare River, the others in Cinnamon Bay. Let it stay."

"If I stop by to see her? She is my daughter. So she knows her father's alive?"

Lazarus looks up from the dominoes set up on the table in my father's yard. "You want to own her, don't it?" he says.

"Who?"

"The girl. Ivy," Lazarus says.

"She is mine," my father says. "I could think about it and say, I want to have her in my possession. No one would disagree. Look at the mother, with one man after another, and the child not with her all week, but with the grandmother and a blind great-grandmother."

"She is a happy child right where she is. You want to play or you want to talk?"

"Their cousin, Kenneth, he is a great pal of mine," my father says.

"Leave it alone, sir!" Lazarus says, striking the table and almost upsetting it.

On his way back from Gray's Mansions, where he works as foreman of the banana sprayers, it is my father's habit to stop at a roadside rum shop, an establishment that is nothing more than an octagonal bench built around the trunk of a huge persimmon tree. Behind the tree is a large cart on wheels painted shocking pink, the back of which is lined with shelves holding bottles of liquor. One particularly hot Friday evening, my father stops there and sees Kenneth Clifton, my mother's cousin. They talk about the state of the drought in Cinnamon Bay, the fungus that has been attacking both the banana trees and the palms, and finally my father brings the conversation around to my mother, her family, and to me.

"The child is living quite nicely," says Kenneth. "The women love her, and Lucille, she dotes on her, and the two sisters, well, that is an old story. They are living and loving as always."

He tells my father that when I was still living with my mother, before I went to live with my grandmother, my Aunt Lucille came in and found me crying. "Why is she crying?" my Aunt Lucille asked my mother, and my mother said I was crying because she had beaten me. "Why did you beat her?" my Aunt Lucille asked, and my mother said, "You see that china wagon there? She broke one of my cups."

My Aunt Lucille left without saying a word and came back with a huge box and unpacked everything in it and put the things on the floor. Then she packed up everything my mother had on her own china wagon. "Now she can break my things and not be beaten," my Aunt Lucille said. That was how devoted my aunt and my mother were to me. And Lucille particularly, since she had no child of her own and people were starting to say Brother Beckwith had married a mule.

"She cannot have children?" asks my father.

"She hasn't any yet," Kenneth says.

"Let me talk plainly to you," my father says. "That child is my child and I want her in my possession. Why shouldn't she live with her brothers and sisters? She lives now with an old woman and an even older blind woman. Her mother has too many men. Perhaps she is happy, perhaps not. If I had her here, then she would be happy."

"And how would you come by the child?" asks Kenneth.

"You visit them?"

"It's my family," Kenneth says. "More than it is yours."

"And during the day, the grandmother is working in town, dressmaking, and there's only the blind old lady?" my father asks. Kenneth nods. "So if you came into the house, the old lady wouldn't think anything of it?" Kenneth nods his head. "You could go into the house and take the child and hand her out the window to me," my father says.

Kenneth says nothing. "A woman with three or four men, a child with a blind old lady," my father says, watching him. Kenneth works for the airport in Greenstown. Every year he is promoted higher up. He wants everything to be right, Lazarus says of him. Everything has to be right. Kenneth would not think it right for a woman to have four children by four fathers. "What do you say?" my father asks him.

Kenneth drinks and says nothing. "It is my family, you know," Kenneth says at last. "If the child wasn't happy, you would bring her back?" My father nods and orders two more glasses of rum. "The child doesn't like me, you know," Kenneth says. "My voice is deep and it frightens her. Sometimes when I come in, she runs and hides."

"She is used to seeing me," my father says. "I have made sure of that."

"The grandmother works in town on weekdays. On weekends she sometimes goes to the market to see her crops and when she goes she takes the child with her. During the week she takes her to the shop in town. I came in there one day and Ivy was picking up all the little threads from the floor, pulling them where they catch in the rough boards. Friday she works late. Everyone comes in wanting their dresses for church or for parties. She doesn't take her on Fridays. I could help you," Kenneth says.

"In two weeks," my father says. "We could drive to Cinnamon Bay, get the child, and come back here. I can talk to Bea. She will sit in the car to soothe the child if she starts to cry. It will work out quite nicely. I can see it."

"But if she's unhappy, you will bring her back?" asks Kenneth.

"Oh, yes, oh, yes," says my father. "I can promise you that."

Two weeks later, early Friday morning, a black car draws up outside the Clifton gate. No one is in our yard.

"She must be inside with Nanny," Kenneth says. Just then, I come to the window, look out, see the car and run over to it. Uncle Kenneth gets out and calls to me but at the sound of his voice, I run back into the house. "Go around by the window, there where the standpipe is," Kenneth tells my father. "I'll go inside and say hello to Nanny. She won't think anything of it."

He goes inside. The house is still and silent, as if no one has ever lived in it.

"Granny!" he calls. "It's me! Kenneth!"

He goes into the bedroom that opens off the hall, and in the middle of the bed sits my great-grandmother, his great-aunt, her long braid trailing down over her cotton nightdress. "Good morning, Granny," he says.

"You're not at work?" my great-grandmother asks him. "Why aren't you at work?"

"I wanted to see you, Granny," he says. His eyes were elsewhere, looking for a sign of me.

"Here I am," my great-grandmother says.

"Anything you need?" he asks her. "You have gas in the cylinder?"

"I don't know," my great-grandmother says.

"I'll shake it and see," he says, walking back into the kitchen. "You're low," he says, coming back. "I'll throw it in the back of the car and fill it up in Enfield and bring it back."

"So you're going?" Nanny says.

"I had a cinnamon stick and some coconut drops for Ivy, but she must have gone with Auntie Tina," Kenneth says.

"Ivy!" Nanny says. "Come out from behind my back there!"

I slide out from behind her but I do not get down from the bed.

"Come, girl, show some manners," Uncle Kenneth says. "Manners take you through the world. Come and take these candies from my hand and thank me properly."

"You must do as he says," says my great-grandmother. I get down from the bed and walk toward my uncle, my eyes on the ground.

"Come now, look up," says Uncle Kenneth. "Am I so ugly?"

I look up at him, and as I do, he grabs me beneath my arms and hugs me tight to his body and carries me to the open window. My great-grandmother turns this way and that, searching for me. "Did you thank your uncle?" she asks me, but all she heard was my screams, scream after scream.

"Kenneth!" shouts my great-grandmother. "Why is Ivy screaming? Bring her back to me! Put her back on the bed! Ivy! What happened? Ivy!"

But Uncle Kenneth has already passed me through the window into my father's arms and my father runs with me, through the gate and into the car. "I'll see you later, Granny!" Uncle Kenneth calls out, running through the front door and getting into the front seat next to my father. "I'll bring back the cylinder!"

"Where is she?" my great-grandmother calls again and again. "Where is Ivy?" We hear her voice, high and shrill, frantic and desperate, curling out of the window like thin clutching fingers with long, long nails.

"I'd steer clear of Cinnamon Bay, if I were you," Lazarus tells my father. They are sitting on the shocking pink bench of the rum shop. The owner has painted the base of the tree aqua. "There's some hard feelings there."

"Some hard feelings," my father says.

"The blind old lady ran out in the road, crying like a wounded thing, and she ran up and down, crashing into trees and a donkey cart, and she was so frantic no one could lay a hand on her. Anyone who caught her, she tore away from them. You ask anyone about it who saw it and they start in weeping. When they caught her and brought her back to her house and set her down on her bed she started clawing out her eyes, that's what she wanted to do. They had to tie her hands behind her back.

"And then Auntie Tina came back from Albion Bay and a heap of wailing like you never heard in your life, and when Lucille heard of it, you don't want to know about it, sir. And Mer, she sits and cries all day. No one knows what to tell them. The old lady and Auntie Tina and Lucille, they went to church Sunday, and the congregation sang hymns for them and prayed for them and they testified to the assembly. You want to talk about something in Cinnamon Bay, first you talk about the old blind lady and Ivy and how her father came and snatched her like a chicken hawk over a chicken coop."

"They say that?" my father asks.

"They say worse. And Kenneth, he was walking down the street, going through the market, and a rock hit him on the side of his head and he carries a lump like a goose egg. It was no child threw that stone, sir. Don't try to tell me so."

"Lucille, she'll come up here," my father says.

"They say she is saved," Lazarus tells him. "You better hope so. She's mean with a stone and good with a machete."

"The child is happy where she is," my father says. "She has her brothers and sisters and she runs and plays all day. She does like the Mare River School."

"Don't tell me she doesn't miss the women who cared for her every day of her life," Lazarus says. "Even a dog stops eating when its master's gone."

"She eats," my father says.

"She does not cry?"

"Oh, yes, she did cry, but now she is happy. That's the children's way," my father says.

"I am glad I had no hand in it."

My father said nothing. What was done was done. The villagers would think it over and say, The child is with her father. She's well cared for and she's happy. He was well liked in the town, by the men, certainly, but especially by the women. In a few months, the women would say his car is not a catch-a-man car, waiting near the school to steal unsuspecting children. He came for his own daughter. Someone would say it was no life for a child, sitting in a darkened room with a blind old lady. Someone else would say that if my mother gave me up to her mother and grandmother, then she must have had a reason. Many women were raising their children alone because the children's father had deserted them, disappeared one day and never returned. They would look at my father and see a husband and a father who loved his child. They would compare my father to the men who had vanished and wish they had chosen a man like him instead of the shiftless beast they cursed every morning. Because they liked him, they would find excuses for him.

My father knows all this well. He took it into consideration before he enlisted Uncle Kenneth's help. Still, my father does not like to think of the blind old lady running wild in the street, in her nightdress, and when he thinks of my mother, Mer, sitting in her room weeping, he wants to rip his own clothes. But I am his and he wants me in his possession. My father is sure he has done the right thing.

Two grown men, my father and my uncle, sat down together and plotted all this out. Two grown men, my father and my uncle, decided this would be best for me. They believed they were right.

The story of my life begins with that kidnapping.

Later, I will remember nothing before it (though I will want to remember), only a few flares and flashes, disconnected lights in a long darkness, as a firefly winking on and off in the night marks his path as he passes. But there is *something* I remember, a place, a feeling that is not a person but is also a person, a landscape that is warm and safe and alive and that speaks with several voices. It is the place I come from and the place I will return to. At night, when I am frightened and fall asleep, and, falling, feel the day's fears floating from me one by one, I know I am returning to that place. In the morning, when I awaken and turn onto my back and stare up at the ceiling, I catch a glimpse of that place, I feel it touching me like fingers drawn gently and lightly across the back of my hand, I hear the faint murmur of voices and so I am protected against the rest of the day.

3

TIME PASSES AND PASSES and stays the same, stays as strong as ever. It is only we who wear out. Why is that? I used to ask, Why is that? No more.

In the corner of this little room I call my study is a tall, thin grandfather clock. I brought it all the way from Sweden. They say my great-grandfather made the cabinet with his own hands. Every Sunday, my father used to wind the clock and as he did, he told me that my grandfather went into the forest and picked out a tree, a big oak tree, and he marked it. He tied his red scarf around a branch and he went back for it with his brothers and they cut the tree down. Two red oxen pulled it through the forest over the snow, back to the house. Then he cut the tree into planks and for two years he cured them in the shed.

While the wood was curing, he drew pictures of the clock he saw as if it were standing in front of him. Tall and thin it has to be, like a church tower. On Sundays when the roads were passable he would travel the countryside, looking at belfries. Then, one Sunday, he stayed home and began to draw. After that the clock grew from the wood.

I heard this story so many times I thought I could smell the wood shavings as they curled up from the plane. I could smell the stain and the varnish. I watched the grain as the stain took it and brought it out. I loved the clock as if it were a person. Well, to me it was a person, even better than a person, simple, predictable, its workings intelligible. It stood there in the corner speaking its language, Bump, bump, Bump, bump, and out of the clock poured blessings, poured time itself.

Then one day a few years ago, I looked at the clock, looked at it suddenly, you know, not as I usually look at it, staring at it happily the way you stare at an old dog asleep on the floor, not even aware you are looking; no, in that instant it was as if the clock were not there. For a second only, but that was enough. There was a sudden great hole in the world. My eyes, because they showed me such a thing, were intolerable to me. And suddenly, it was a bad clock. Its side panels were bulging, or so it seemed to me then, and I saw that the clock was swollen with time, gorged with it, like a wild animal that brings down its prey and eats too much and can't move and lies on the plain and prays that no other animal will come upon it while it lies there, eyes glazed, stomach swollen, and I got up and went over to the clock, threw myself upon it, really, and began beating on its door, screaming, Give me some of it! Give me some of it! Give me some of it! Then I fell down at its base, sobbing. Give me some of it, give me some of it, I said over and over, but now I knew it was not time I was asking for, but something for which I didn't have the words. Well, that's how it's always been for me. I never have the words when I need them. Probably that's why I've been so careless with language, never learning any one properly, because what difference does it make, if one has nothing to say?

But this time, this time, I would have given anything to know the words. *Give me some of it.* Finally, there was something I wanted and it had no name. There was no word for it.

The tall brown clock, darkened now almost to black, the incessant blanket of snow on the infinite fields around our house, so many fields, so much snow, only something flying almost as high as the sun could take it all in, the sharp smell of pine trees in the cold, the crackling of the snow like popcorn beneath our boots, the way our boots struck the frozen earth and the earth rang out like struck metal. The grayish-blue corkscrews of smoke rising from the chimneys into the gray sky, the sound of water running beneath the gray and white ice over the gray and black stones in the river, sleigh bells growing louder and then fading, a small gray and brown bird that sees the bread crumbs on the windowsill and, excited, flies into the window and lies stunned on the sill, then recovers and eats the crumbs, and far away, the faint whistle of a train.

Well, I was glad no one was there to see me attacking the poor clock or lying at its feet like a mad penitent. This is what happens when you live and brood alone. When I got up, slowly, my joints snapping and crackling, holding on to the clock, steadying myself, I thought, Good for you, Anna. That could have been a scene from one of your silent movies, flinging your arms, beating them against your body, against the poor wooden body of the clock, falling to the floor, not as if you'd fallen of your own accord, but as if you'd been struck on the head by a giant fist from the sky (did Max teach me that or did he praise me for knowing how to do it without being told? I don't remember)—but in that movie, the one I'm thinking of, I put on my coat and rushed out over the ice and was drowned in black water, only my white scarf floating up to the surface: I ask you, what kind of world is this, when you make films and become other people and live out their stories in their worlds and even then you can't have a happy ending?

But I've complained about this before. I'll complain about this again. Still, this time when I got up from the floor, I was a happy woman. The room was full of a white light, as if outside it had snowed heavily and now the sun had come out and I weighed nothing. I forgot my creaking bones and floated to my chair and looked at the clock and tried to think: what was different?

And then I saw what it was. Before I flew over to the clock, before I attacked it I didn't think. Always, always, before I do something, before I say something, there is that instant, an instant, no more, but it is enough, when I hear myself saying what I am going to say, when I imagine myself feeling what I am going to feel. And that split second throws everything in doubt. Do I really feel what I think I am feeling, or did I, in that split second, rehearse becoming the way I now am? Is there nothing that comes from so deep inside me, that comes without asking, comes suddenly, so that I know it is really mine?

I used to sit before the mirror in Charlie's house on Cliffside Road and lean in, deep in, until my face slid out of focus, became hazy, and I would grip my head with my hands, and ask the face I saw there, Is there nothing at all genuine about you? And there were days I saw Charlie staring into the mirror with that same desperate look and I knew what he was doing. All right, when I flew at the clock, I was melodramatic, I was extravagant, above all I was silly (and, you know, I *am* all of those things), but this time I didn't think. I didn't see myself flying against the clock like a crazy little bird after some crumbs. So now I know: there's something I want that I don't have, something I don't have the word for. But I can make a good guess all the same. Is it youth? I don't think so. Do I want back the people who died? Am I cruel enough to summon them up again? No. Is it death I want? No one who eats red carrots and yogurt day after day wants to die. As always, I give up. I can't think in a straight line. I start out for one house and end up at another, everyone at the window, looking surprised. What, she's here again? Someone tell her there's a main road out there somewhere!

Why does it have to be complicated? Max says. Why give yourself a headache? What is life, an astrology course? Anna, listen to me. You ask a question, you already have the answer. You want some of it? What just made you happy? Look around you, Anna, before you start thinking. You use thinking as a way of hiding from the truth! Look first and then think!

Well, I don't know, I say to Max. Why would I lie? Why should I say I don't know if I do?

Onion! Radish! Max shouts at me. Brains of a potato without its eyes! Soon he will grab me by the shoulders and shake me until my head jerks back and forth on my neck, and then he will be sorry and cry and call me his little radish.

Why a radish? Because it tastes sweet when you bite into it and then it is bitter? Because it is onion-shaped and reminds him of his beloved domes in Russia? But then why not call me his little onion?

The straight road, Anna! he cries. You are at the wrong house again! Stop thinking, Anna! Oh, when she thinks, Methuselah himself grows old! Anna, look at the clock!

I look at the clock, black and tall and thin, and Max is right. It is simple. I know what I want. I want to think what I think, feel what I feel. I don't want to come between myself and the world. Perhaps it is not too late? But it is too late. So much of life wasted! An entire existence lived as if I were in a film in thrall to the demands of a director I'd never met. But, you know, I must meet that director. I *must* meet him. Who is that director, that stranger with the strong hands? He must be me. *Ah,* Max sighs.

Now I curl up in my chair, happy as a cat in the sun. One is never too old to be praised.

Or to get started! Max shouts. What are you waiting for? When did you last see someone look back and turn into a pillar of salt? Look back, Anna! It won't kill you.

But does Max know what will kill me? I look back often, not over my own life, which is what Max would like me to do, but at Ivy's. Why must it be my own life I look back on? I already know that story. Yet there are times I think I didn't live my own life at all, but walked through it with someone's hands over my eyes, someone, a person like a film director, and that person said, Go left, Go right, Cry, Laugh, Go home, and I did all those things and I was richly rewarded. I was the most beautiful, the most clever, the most obedient, the most soul-less puppet of them all.

THESE ARE THE FEW THINGS out of many I remember after leaving Cinnamon Bay and going to live with my father in Mare River. I remember that my new grandmother would never let me taste from the pot in which I was cooking. I could not even put the spoon into the pot and taste its contents as I stood next to the stove. Instead I had to take the spoon, go into another room and taste the food there. To this day I do not taste food when I'm cooking. If it is not salty enough, salt can be added at the table. If it's too salty, the damage is already done.

I remember the spring at the bottom of the yard and how the water that came from it was always ice-cold, and I remember the little cup we left there, tied by a string, nailed into an old cedar log.

I remember how many layers of clothing my new grandmother wore and wondering how she stood it in the heat. She wore several chemises, several slips, several petticoats, and, on special occasions, a corset. She always wore two skirts. She had a very sweet smell because when she cooked she used a great deal of cinnamon and she had three cinnamon trees in her yard and several pieces of cinnamon bark in each pocket. She had never cut her hair and so it was very tall. She wore it in three braids and sometimes she coiled the braids along the back of her head and secured the bun with long metal pins. She didn't want to be called Miss Lize, but because she was so old, she wanted to be called Mother Lize and that was what I called her.

I remember our dog, Gelert, who convinced me that the time of signs and wonders was at hand, Gelert, our brindled dog, who would walk into a bedroom, and if anyone's hand was hanging from the edge of the bed, he would walk beneath that hand, and with his head lift the hand and slide it back onto the bed. At the time this seemed so strange I thought it was one of the signs and wonders the preacher talked about, something that meant the strange times before the end of the world were about to begin.

I remember the plague of butterflies, and later, the plague of parakeets. I remember that the plague of butterflies looked like a yellow haze moving in from the sea, and while we watched, the butterflies began settling everywhere. They covered the roof of our house so that the roof seemed to flutter as if it were alive. They covered the trees near our house where they fluttered like yellow leaves. They blanketed the roof of our chicken coop. They covered Gelert, who was sleeping outside the house. Until two landed on his nose he didn't notice them and then he woke up and shook himself and the yellow butterflies rose in a thick cloud around him and he barked in confusion. The goats standing in the field turned bright yellow and when they ran, the butterflies flew up and danced around their heads. The butterflies didn't want anything; they didn't appear to eat anything.

My brother Jack went outside and stood still and was covered with butterflies. When he came back to the veranda and brushed the butterflies away, he was covered with a fine yellow dust, like pollen. There was a shift in the wind, or a slight, fine rain, and the butterflies rose up in a cloud and flew off in the direction of Cinnamon Bay. They never got there. Only people in Mare River saw the plague of butterflies. For months afterwards, when the breeze blew, a yellow wing would spiral down out of a tree like a falling leaf. We would open a book and out of its pages would fall a yellow butterfly wing.

I remember my father announcing that he intended to go to England to earn more money so that he could buy more land because he had so many children, and as it stood now he could not leave enough to any of us. I don't remember his going, but I know he did go. It was during that time that I began to visit my Aunt Lucille in Cinnamon Bay. I remember the plague of parakeets in Cinnamon Bay, when the trees were filled with chartreuse parakeets eating up the green leaves and whatever seeds they could find on the ground. I remember falling asleep one night listening to their singing. There were so many of them their tiny voices drowned out the sound of the waves crashing against the sea wall in the bay. I remember deciding to catch a pair of them and keep them in a cage and when I got up early in the morning the red sun was rising up behind the hills and I was too late. I saw the parakeets rising up as if by a signal and they flew off in the direction of the bay. The people of Mare River did not see the plague of parakeets, only the people of Cinnamon Bay.

I remember sitting on the steps of the veranda at night while the men who had finished playing dominoes told ghost stories and how frightened we were by them. Some of the men would not tell stories, saying that was women's business, but when a woman told a story, the men would interrupt and say, "No, no, that was not how it was," and they would tell the story in their own way. I remember how late we sat there on the steps, listening, because we were too frightened to go to bed.

I remember Christmases before my stepmother became too moody to enjoy them, and how we washed down everything in the house and repainted all the rooms, and on Christmas Eve, in the middle of the night, we hung new curtains because we didn't want any of the neighbors to know what kind of curtains we would have, and how, earlier in the evening, my stepmother would take her pans full of batter into the bakery in the village, and the baker would put them into his huge oven, sliding them in on long wooden paddles, and he would give us a receipt for them, and as he wrote it, he would chant aloud, "Three fruitcakes, seven sponge cakes, five layer cakes," and how we would smile, because we always had more cakes than anyone else, and it was important that everyone in the village know how many we had. I remember my father waking me up at four in the morning to take me back to the bakery to get our cakes. I remember children in school saying, "You must be rich because you wear shoes and your father has a radio." I remember eating so many mangoes on the way home from school that I forgot to eat dinner and when I woke up in the middle of the night, I thought, Oh, I forgot dinner, and went back to sleep.

I remember how I knew Cynthia was my stepmother's favorite. Cynthia did the cooking and she divided the dinner into ten portions. The first was my father's, and when that was in the hot dish, and placed on the dining room table, she served the other nine portions: one for my stepmother and one for each of the eight children. Cynthia served herself, too, but she always left another serving in the pot, and she ate that, too, and no matter how we complained, my stepmother never scolded her.

I remember hiding under the bed, pretending to be a ghost, and poking whoever was on the mattress above me. I remember when we all pretended to be ghosts, and since ghosts are not known to walk with their feet touching the ground, we raised each foot high in the air before we put it down.

I remember taking the goats up into the field in the morning and bringing them back in the evening, and persuading my father not to butcher Gretchen the Goat, because she would follow me when I called her and all the other goats would come after her. I remember the palm tree at the end of the world. I remember fighting with my cousins when my father told me that if anyone took their goats or cattle up through the fields of guavas, I was to tell them they must not go that way because the animals were snipping all the buds off the plants, and when my cousin still went through, how I fought him and beat him and my Uncle Gusta came and cursed me and said to me, "You believe this is your mother's place?"

I remember my father sending me to look for Uncle Gusta up at the crossroads, a place we called Mile 68, and telling me to ask who-ever was there if they had seen him, and if they had, to tell him to wait there until Vidal Cook came for him. I saw some men standing at the crossroads and I didn't know if they knew my uncle, so I asked them if they had seen a coolie man with his shoes over his shoulder, because Uncle Gusta never wore shoes in the country. He tied their laces together and threw them over a shoulder, and then when he approached the city, he put them on. "Who is that man with the shoes on his shoulder?" one of the men asked me, and I said he was my Uncle Gusta, and they told my uncle what I had said, and he told my father. I remember my father asking me why I had said that, and I answered that I didn't know if the men knew who Uncle Gusta was, but they knew what a coolie man was, and Uncle Gusta never wore his shoes on his feet, but on his shoulder, and my father laughed, and after that Uncle Gusta never liked me.

I remember an uncle who stopped at Mother Lize's every Friday on his way from Mare River to the Greenstown Market, and how one Friday he came and left her some grapefruit and said he would see her next week, and when I went to work at the grocery store, a news flash came on, and the announcer said that a man driving a truck full of grapefruits from Mare River to Greenstown had met with an accident and three men had been killed. I remember saying, "That's my uncle," because when you are that age, you are sure that everyone and every-thing is concerned with you and I could not believe there was another man who would be driving a grapefruit truck between Mare River and Greenstown, and I left work and went with a friend to look at the accident, and when we got there, there were grapefruits all over, some of them split open, their insides blood red, and three men covered with gray blankets, and I picked up the blankets and looked at the dead men, but none of them was my uncle.

I remember waiting at the crossroads for my father to come home for the night. I remember hiding from my father when he came home because I knew he would beat me. I remember wanting to run from my father when I knew he would beat me, but I knew better because he would then fling something at me, and when he hit me, that would be worse. Whenever I think of my early days, I think of my father, how he came to school and told Teacher Williams, "They are not your children. Don't hit them," how people were afraid of him because he would tell everyone, "I have a thirty-eight. I'll fill your mouth full of lead."

I remember the clay pots standing in the middle of the dining room table, beading with water, the water inside them ice-cold and growing colder. I remember washing dishes in the stream. We didn't use soap, but susumber leaves, and to scour pans, we used the husks of coconuts, and I remember how clean everything was, and how Mother Lize would come and say, "You think this pot is clean?" and pick it up and wipe out its inside with her white apron, and if there was a mark on the apron we had to take it back to the river, but after a while she never found anything to complain of.

I remember so many childhood things and they seem so bright to me, as if the sun had never shone on them or faded them, and how each of those memories seems to take up more space and time than years of my adult life, so that now, when I look back, my adult years seem dull, almost colorless, as if what color and high spirits belonged to me had been used up years before, how any sense of uniqueness was already bled from me by the time I married, how everything seems, compared to the time in Mare River, black and white and flat, like a diagram all of us followed, how everything was already settled, how we knew the ending of every story almost as soon as we knew the beginning, but probably that is a deception caused by passing time. Time passes so much faster when we're older and so everything seems closer together, like buildings with no space between them that cannot let in the light. There was so much more space between things when I was a child.

I remember cooking with my brothers and sisters in the outdoor kitchen when we tried to make our own breakfasts. I remember so many things and over each falls the long shadow of my father. I don't believe he will die before me. I will be surprised if I outlive him.

I remember when my brother Jack went to technical college in Greenstown and my father forgot to send him his weekly pocket money and I took the bus to the college and gave him the money myself. I remember when my youngest brother, Herbert, went to the same college some years later and wrote to my father asking him for money for books and clothes and my father sent him a watch, and when he opened the package and saw what was in it, he dropped the watch into the office wastepaper basket and walked out.

I remember when my father went to England and wrote me and asked me to come and go to school there, but I refused because I was newly married and said I wasn't ready to leave my husband, and suggested that my father bring Iris over instead, and after that, he wrote to me weekly, asking me to come, and Jack said, "You want Daddy to stop writing to you? Write and ask him for something." And I wrote him and said I'd seen someone wearing a lovely sweater and she said it came from England, and I'd love to have one like that, and after that, he didn't write me again. I didn't know he was back on Green Island until I met a friend in the Greenstown street and he asked me, Aren't you going to visit your father, and I said, Are you crazy? He's in England! I will go that far to visit him? And he said, No, he wasn't. He was back in Mare River. He had taken sick in England and come back. A few weeks later, Jack and I drove to Mare River and there he was, but his wife, my stepmother, wasn't with him. She stayed behind in England saying she wasn't ready to come out yet. Later we found out that we had many brothers and sisters growing up in that country.

I remember sitting in Tita Lu's parlor when a man knocked at the gate and asked if Ivy Cook was there, and I said, I am Ivy Cook, and he said, I am your brother, and I said, Oh, no, not again. But he was my brother and we had gone to Cinnamon Bay All Age School together and had never known we were related. I remember when the cricket team from Vulture's Beak came to play the Mare River cricket team, and the teachers asked who could take one of the students to their house until the bus came for them the next day, and I asked my father, and he said I could. The boy could sleep with my brothers in their room. I remember bringing home a boy named Robert Cook, who was my age, and when I introduced him to my father, my father looked at him carefully, and asked him about his people. The boy said he didn't know who his father was, really, because his mother had left Goose Landing before his father knew she was pregnant. My father asked him, What is your mother's name? and he said her name was Joy. I guess I am your father, said *my* father, because I did live with a woman named Joy in Goose Landing, and she left in 1930, the year you were born.

When my father came back from England without his wife, I went to see him in Mare River and he was living with a woman named Hilda, who had begun by taking care of him but now they lived as man and wife. Do you know my age, Daddy? I asked him, and he said, Yes, I know your age, and I said, No, you don't, because if you knew my age, you wouldn't be living with that girl. She is younger than I am. And he laughed at me and said, Oh, so that's it. But when you're with someone young, you feel young.

There are so many things I remember about him: how he always wore a hat, how, no matter how hot and damp, his trousers always kept their sharp crease. How he cried when he came into my room after I was burned and felt how hot my breath was when I breathed out. How he told the father of my first child not to marry me out of pity or duty because later he would resent me. And I remember how he kidnapped me. Oh yes, I remember that. And for years, I thought I was bitter over it, and once I asked him why he did it, and once I said, You should have died instead of my mother, and he cried when I said that, and told me not to say such things, and then I cried all night because I was sorry for what I had said. But still I knew: not everyone is kidnapped. Not everyone is wanted so badly that someone comes for him secretly in a car. When my father beat me and I protested, he said, The teacher always beats the best pupil first.

Yes, it is his shadow that falls over everything, but inside his shadow is her shadow, concealed by his, my mother's shadow, the shadow of the woman who did not want me enough to find a way to snatch me back. She stands there watching him take me from my uncle who hands me out through the window and her hands are at her sides and then she walks back down the road to her house and she ties a cloth around her hair and she begins her daily chores and I don't think she cries. I have been looking for her all my life. What I remember best is her absence, or, at times, a sound, like a snatch of song that means she is coming, but she never comes. Her absence is what I remember best.

NOW I AM IN Miss Anna's room, sitting on the edge of her bed, my back stiff, reading her what I have written down, and she says, No, no, Ivy, that won't do. A story isn't a broken mirror, pieces of glass all over the place. A story is a whole thing, it has a beginning and an end, like a bolt of cloth. You must say, One day I was born, and then this happened and this. Otherwise how to make sense out of it?

And I say, Lady Clare (because that is what I sometimes call her), Lady Clare, you know you won't be able to tell your own story that way so why must I? Anyhow, I cannot do it.

She says, You can do it. You must. We want to make sense of ourselves. We told Anders we would try.

Who is going to make sense of us? I ask her, getting up. I have a kitchen to clean.

You won't try? she asks me. Her lower lip is trembling. I sit back down on the bed. The teacher always expects the pupil to do what he himself cannot accomplish.

Everyone on Green Island is a story teller, I say. I know the story of my father's life and how he came to Green Island, and what the years were like when I lived with him because Miss Blue told me, but I myself do not remember those days. I only remember her story.

Then you must tell her story! Anna insisted.

And you? I ask her. I suppose you have been up all night trying? Where are all the pages?

I spoke into a recorder, she says sullenly.

And you have done much better than I have done? I ask her.

Well, I am trying, she says. I don't think in straight lines.

Who does? I ask her.

My lines are more crooked than most, she says.

Oh, Lady Clare, I say, you are only finding excuses.

Her room, her whole apartment, except for my room, which I have painted blue, is the color of apricots although she claims it is the color of peaches and Anders says the walls are the color of salmon. When the sun comes in, the rooms glow like the inside of a conch shell. Next time, I say, we should paint the ceilings and the trim pure white, it is so dusty here. In a few months the cream color is too dark.

This paint job will last long enough for my lifetime, she says. Don't go getting any ideas.

5

ON GREEN ISLAND, when you see a starving dog with his ribs sticking out, you point at him and say, Oh, you live with your aunt! I didn't live with my aunt, but my stepmother. Still, when I saw a mangy dog who was all bones, I knew how he felt. I don't know what she had against me, but she had something. When we were in the third form, we had sewing class, and in that class we made a brush-and-comb holder; it was square and had two pockets. After mine was inspected, I took it home, ripped out the stitches in the bottom, folded over the top, ran some thread through the seam and made myself a pair of panties. This is how things were when I was growing up. Perhaps this is why I'm so grateful for whatever I have now. Now there is no one to say, Yes, she can have this, or No, she can't have that. There are times when I think back to my childhood days and I wonder why I am not bitter, but really, I am not. I am not even bitter against my stepmother.

I used to tell Anna about her and Anna said, "Why you bring that woman anything is beyond me. Well, of course, it makes you feel superior to bring her things from this country, but even so, I would let her starve. Is it because you're so religious? I wish I were religious. When you pray, do you really believe someone listens?" And I said, I don't know why, but I do believe it, and she sighed and said she wished she did.

Of course I cannot say why I have any faith at all. When I was quite young, we used to go to Brother Isaac's church in Mare River, a little church that started out in a small wooden building with a hard dirt floor. But Brother Isaac soon became famous as a preacher and then the church moved to a bigger building made of cinder blocks plastered over and painted a bright pink. Shortly after that, Brother Isaac began to hear the voice of God and he was the talk of the island. God had told him that he must give away all his possessions, and his followers must do the same, and on the seventh of June, they were all to go to the highest cliff on the eastern side of the island, and when they jumped, God would lend them wings and they would fly straight to heaven.

Many of his parishioners believed every word he said and some of them even claimed to have heard God speaking to Brother Isaac, and many of them gave up everything. One morning, we were sitting on the veranda when a man and his wife came to our gate and called out for my father, and when my father came from the house, the man handed him the reins to his two donkeys, each of which was loaded down with crates full of chickens and pigeons. After that, he went to the cliff where he intended to fly off with Brother Isaac.

When Brother Isaac jumped off the cliff, he broke both legs and one arm and his back was black and blue. After that, the villagers sang this song:

> "Brother Isaac called the tune,
> But he jumped a little soon.
> He'll jump again, this time in March,
> Give me rum, I'm dreadful parched."

My father gave back the donkeys, the pigeons and the chickens, and we began going to Brother Beckwith's church. "Any man who jumps from a cliff has nothing to teach me," my father said. "Oh, it is quite all right to go to church, quite all right, but as for me, I prefer to talk to God in my own church where the sky is my roof and the floor is the earth beneath my feet. Still," he said, "you children, you must go."

So I don't know why I wasn't more unhappy when I was a young child, but I think it had something to do with the porches and the front steps. Every night, we would sit, either on our own steps or someone else's, and people would tell stories. They told stories about the little unbaptized children who died and came back as mischievous spirits, their feet on backwards. That was how you recognized them. But you couldn't follow them, because if you followed their footprints, you were walking the wrong way. They never harmed anyone but they pulled clothes from clotheslines, they pulled people's hair, they upset buckets of water. And then there was the woman who waited for unfaithful husbands at the crossroads and smiled at them and friended them up and lured them to their destruction and afterwards they were found at the bottom of a cliff. So when you meet a woman at the crossroads, Miss Blue used to say, you must always look at her foot. If she is the bad woman, one of her feet is not right. It is a cloven hoof.

There were stories about ghosts, there were stories about earthquakes, there were stories about families, and of course there was gossip. After my father kidnapped me and I began to sit on his porch at night, swatting at mosquitoes drawn in by the kerosene lantern, my toes wriggling against the cool earth, the moon looking down, I began to hear stories about him and his mother and father before him. These stories were repeated over and over. In his house there were eight children and every one of us could tell the story of his life and this is how I know it so well. Who knows if it is true? It is what I heard again and again, so I do believe it.

My father, Vidal Cook, was born in Cinnamon Bay, on Green Island. His father, Asad Cook, was born in India where he earned his living driving a donkey cart. When the owners of the sugar plantations from Green Island sent a group of overseers to India to hire men to work their plantations, they found a willing volunteer in Asad Cook, who had no property of his own and had lost three children to cholera. The men who made the long journey to India by ship were reluctant to hire Asad Cook, whom they correctly judged to be sickly, but a donkey cart loaded down with mangoes stopped in the middle of the road, and its owner could not persuade the animal to move, nor could he beat him into submission. Asad Cook left the group of men who were standing on the side of the dusty road, went over to the donkey, and asked the beast's owner if he would like some help.

"What you can do, please do it," said the donkey's owner. "He is forever stopping. Night will fall and still he will be standing here."

Asad Cook put his head next to the donkey's ear, began stroking the donkey's head, rhythmically, stroking him between the ears to just above the top of the nose, speaking to the beast as if it were a man whom he knew well.

"It is a hot day, donkey, isn't it?" he asked the beast. "You don't want to take another step. Who can blame you? The road is rocky and there is no shade anywhere. But what will you accomplish, standing where you are? The sun will beat down upon you and soon you will be even more thirsty and the load of mangoes will be even heavier. Whereas if you move, there is a spring down the road and a cluster of trees and a nice patch of thick green grass. The water in that spring, donkey, is cool and clean and it is not so far away."

Asad Cook did not attempt to pull the donkey or to push him. He continued stroking the beast's head. "I would go with you, donkey," he said, "but I have to stay here and work the fields. But if you would go with your owner there—the man is your friend, you know, he only beats you because he must get his mangoes to market and he knows if you stand in the sun, you will die here—if you would go with him, you will be a happy donkey tonight and you will make your owner happy. If you think it over, you will see that going forward is the sensible thing to do."

He stopped stroking the donkey's head and took a step away from the beast. The donkey, perhaps anxious to hear more of the man's voice, took a step toward him. "Oh, no, donkey," said Asad Cook, "You must not come with me. I must work the fields. See how I have tied up my pants? Today my job is to work the fields. Tomorrow my job is to take my donkey into town. Perhaps my donkey is your cousin." He took another step and the donkey moved after him.

"He is a good donkey, a frightened beast," Asad said to its owner. "He saw something along the road and it frightened him. He needs reassurance. You must speak to the donkey so he does not feel so alone."

"Speaking to a donkey, what nonsense!" said the owner.

"You shout at him and there he stands," said Asad. "You have a cart of mangoes going nowhere. Will you not try it?"

"Will you help me drag him?" asked the beast's owner.

"If you will first speak to him, and then if he does not move, I will help you drag him," said Asad.

"Come along, you stupid donkey!" said the owner.

"That is not speaking," Asad said. "That is shouting. Naturally the donkey will not move. Should I say to you, 'Speak to the animal, you stupid ass!' would you listen to me?"

"You are calling me an ass?"

"If you don't want help, the fields are calling," said Asad.

"Talking to a donkey!"

"You hate your animal?" asked Asad.

"I raised him!" said the owner. "Why should I hate him?"

"Then you are too proud to speak to him?"

"I am not too proud to speak to him!"

"Speak to him, you fool!" called a man watching from the side of the road. "No one can pass! Your cart blocks the way!"

"Don't speak to him because a man on the side of the road tells you to speak," said Asad. "If you speak now, all will think you speak because you are afraid of that shouting man on the side of the road."

"I'll speak if I want to speak!" said the agitated owner of the donkey. "Donkey," he said, turning to his animal, "have mercy upon me. The heat is killing. It beats down upon my head and I can feel it through my turban. If you don't come with me, the mangoes will rot and I will have no rupees to take home to my wife and she will cook nothing for tomorrow's supper. Have I treated you badly? On days when my own stomach was empty, did I not find fodder for you? Truly, it is a sad state of affairs when my own beast shows this ingratitude. You were a scruffy beast when I got you, a walking mange, and now your hide is fine and strong. Last week the cart overturned and we got to the market late and everyone had his mangoes and we sold ours for almost nothing."

"Must you tell the beast the story of your life?" shouted the man from the edge of the road. "Must you begin with yourself in your mother's belly?"

"I will talk to my donkey as much as I see fit!" shouted the animal's owner. "Donkey," he said, turning back to the animal, "see how they mock us? Because I stand here in the middle of a dusty road speaking into your ear and not beating you with a stick, which is what they all expect? I will sit down in the road next to you and look up at those violet mountains and the men from the side of the road will come and beat me. Then you will be satisfied, you miserable lump of lard!"

"Don't lose your temper now," said Asad. "When you are doing so well."

"Donkey," said the man, weeping out of frustration and embarrassment, "will you not move?" He tugged gently on the donkey's bridle. The donkey moved obediently forward.

"And if I get into the cart?" the owner asked Asad. "Will he go forward?"

"He is quite ready to go. He is quite nice, your donkey."

The man climbed into the cart, jiggled the reins and the donkey moved forward, proceeding at a steady pace down the road.

The men from Green Island came over to Asad Cook. "You can handle all kinds of animals?" they asked him.

"Anything that is not a snake, that beast I can handle," said Asad.

"Should we take him?" the men asked one another, and fell to discussing him as if he himself were not present. His chest was sunken and his arms and legs were sickly, and the whites of his eyes were yellowish. "He'll die of jaundice before we reach Green Island," one of them said, but another said a rest, the sea air, a diet of fresh fruit, and not even his own mother would recognize him. "And we need a donkey driver," he said. "We need a donkey foreman."

"Here my wife has her family and I have my mother and sisters," Asad said. "Our life here is not bad."

"Green Island is a fruitful place," one of the men told him. "There is never a time when there is no fruit on the trees. As soon as the breadfruit is over, the star apples come in. There are bananas ever-lasting. You walk through the fields on your way to the grazing goats, and you pick and eat from this tree and that tree, and when you come home, you are too satisfied to eat your dinner. No one starves to death on Green Island and the people there say they live forever. 'You will live so long we'll sun you,' that's what they say, and the old people live so long they put them in chairs and set them out in the sun and take them in again for their dinners. And it is a beautiful island, moun-tainous and green, and whales are seen spouting off the coast. There is a saying the people have: No one ever leaves Green Island."

And so Asad Cook, his wife, daughter and mother came to live on Green Island. Asad went to work for Mr. Gray on Gray's Mansions, a sugar plantation between Cinnamon Bay and Mare River, and was soon put in charge of the field animals. After four years, he earned enough money to buy five acres with a small house outside of Cin-namon Bay. He planned to add more rooms himself. The first thing he built was a chicken coop right behind the kitchen. He planted two ackee trees in the front yard. The land was already heavy with fruit trees. Bananas and coconut trees grew behind the house. Pineapples grew on one side. Oranges grew in the front yard, grapefruits in the back. There were plum trees, cinnamon trees and persimmons, almond trees and pecan trees. Asad Cook looked forward to living on his own property.

His son Vidal, my father, was born six months after he arrived on Green Island. He grew up on Gray's Mansions, following after his father, observing him with the animals, and tagged along after the owner of the plantation, Mr. Gray, a man who was known for his ability to engraft one plant to another. His star-apple trees bore grape-fruits and his orange trees bore apples. Vidal would stand in back of him, observing. He watched the men when they built houses, and was given a few bricks, mortar and cement.

When Vidal was five years old, his father, who was taming a wild horse, heard someone call to him, turned his back on the animal, and was kicked in the kidneys. His urine turned bright red and his body was racked first with chills, then with fever. In three weeks he was dead.

"So," I said to Anna, "now are you happy? This story has a beginning and eventually it has an end. Now are you satisfied?" But she was staring at me as if I were a pickle.

"Oh," she said, "it's very good."

"What is wrong with it?" I asked her.

"Oh, it is hopeless, hopeless!" she cried. "I cannot tell a story like that! What I know I know in bits and pieces!"

"Then you must tell the bits and pieces," I said. "If I told you only what I remember, if I described what happened the way I remembered it happening, it would all be bits and pieces too. This is only a story I heard again and again, one story among many."

"But you believe it? You believe it is true?"

"I suppose it is true," I said, "or why would they tell it? Of course they embroidered here and there, they always do, that's the way on Green Island. There were no televisions, few radios, just people sitting on steps, telling stories."

"If you believe a story, then it is true," Anna said. "And if there is no story, then you are empty."

"Lady Clare," I said, "maybe we should tell our stories to the tape recorder and not tell them to each other until we are finished."

"Oh, well, I will do the best I can," she said grumpily. "But you must finish telling me the story about your father! You cannot tell a person a piece of a story!"

"And you are working on yours?" I asked her.

"Oh, very hard," she said. "Very very hard."

"Good," I said. "Then you are ready for bed and will get a good night's sleep."

"You know I never sleep," Anna said.

6

WELL, TO BEGIN. I suppose I should tell my earliest memories. Everyone always wants to know that, although they are completely arbitrary, so of what consequence are they? At a certain point, the miserable, helpless little organism begins to register impressions and one of them sticks. Why should this matter? Does the flypaper care whether it catches a bottle fly or an ordinary house fly?

I know: I have to argue about everything. When I tell myself something, then I argue with myself. In my own defense, I must tell you that usually I argue silently, but those who know me, they know what's going on. I stand there with a mulish look. Max had no patience with it. *The donkey is braying to herself.*

Well, frankly, this bores me, you see. I'll explain why later, how stupid it is to try and find something interesting in the life of an individual.

This is what comes to mind now, naturally not a scene from my own life, because a scene from my own life is what I am trying to summon up.

A man and his wife have run away and now they are living in the snow-covered hills. He has committed some kind of crime and someone is looking for him always, but for a long time no one finds them, and so they live happily. He hunts for food and she cooks it and they bathe in a beautiful lake at the foot of the high cliff they live on. They have a child, a beautiful blond child, not human at all, like a Botticelli angel.

But then they are discovered. If they don't flee the man will be taken and he and the woman will be separated. It is snowing through all this. It is always snowing and it is very cold. The woman is afraid they will take the child from her or she is afraid they cannot flee fast enough with a child. The child is about three or four. She takes him to the cliff where she used to stand looking out, waiting for her husband to return from his hunting. Often he would return with a wild goose which he held by its long neck, its body swaying, bumping into his leg as he walked. This time, she picks up the child and holds him over her head. Across the frozen plains, she can see her pursuers coming closer.

What does she think about? We don't know because she's so far away and the light is behind her so that she and the child are only a black silhouette. She holds the child over her head and then she holds him out over the cliff, his feet dangling in air, as if to frighten him. Perhaps this is what he thinks, that he did something wrong, and now his mother is punishing him. We don't know. They are very far away. Then she drops him. The cliff is so high that when she looks down the body is barely visible. And now she and her husband flee.

They sleep in a tent even higher up in the mountains and when they come in from gathering water, the snow has melted and frozen again on their faces. His beard is matted with ice, and his eyebrows. They are made out of snow and ice. They argue all the time now. Finally, she goes out and lies down in the snow, and when he comes out, he sees she is dead, and lies down beside her. Now they are both asleep.

The child, what happened to him? Well, who cares, really? We are all flying through the air. Something is always pushing us off a cliff. Sooner or later we all lie down against the ground.

What was the man's original crime? Whatever it was, it was a small thing. But it grew.

This was a dream of a friend of mine, long dead. There was much more to it, of course. He said, We must preserve our best dreams, and I asked him, Is that what you do? And he said, Yes, but my dreams are not very good. Still, his dreams were his own.

Can someone tell me why I think of his dream when I am trying to recall my first childhood memory? Snow is in both of them. I suppose that's it.

Snow is the first thing I remember, no surprise when you are born in the Finnish countryside. Snow is falling outside a window and someone is holding me up to the windowpane. How old could I have been? One? Two? I grew so fast, no one picked me up and carried me for very long. *Oh, she's such a big girl.* Everyone said it as if that meant I had decided to grow big, big and gangly and falling over my own feet. She can trip standing still! my mother said, and it was true. One day I was standing outside the classroom door and the teacher was coming in with books, a tall pile, the top book wedged under her chin, and I moved to the left to get away from her, and then to the right, then left, then right, and the next thing I knew I had a terrible sprained ankle. Three weeks at home, my foot in plaster, hopping through the apartment like a crazy stork.

So here I am at the window, and it's settled: I'm not very old. Who's holding me up? It must be my father. My mother didn't have time and she didn't like windows. When I think of her in those days, she is always saying one of two things: Let me see your hands, or Get away from that window. So it wasn't my mother.

I am held up to the window, the blue-black window, and snow-flakes have hit it and melted and there are crazy paths running down the pane. Outside the snow is thick and edible and I put my two hands on the pane of glass and lift them off and when I look, there are my hands, still on the glass! I look down at my own hands and back at the glass and the hands on the window are gone. I wiggle my fingers. There they are. I press my mouth to the window. The window is cold and wet and salty and I start to howl. I want the snow. This cold, hard thing is between me and the snow. The snow comes in waves, now it weaves from right to left and suddenly it comes flying straight at me, into my mouth and my eyes, but again the cold glass stops it.

Behind me, my mother lights a kerosene lantern. Now I look out in surprise. The whole room is suspended in the night air, my mother, my father holding a bundle whose hands keep pressing on the glass, a floating table, floating chairs, oh, I like it better out there! And now I really start wailing and won't stop. I want to go out there, into that room painted on the darkness.

I did, you know. I went into those rooms. Everything that can happen takes place there. Every disaster under the sun takes place there. These are the rooms and people built of shadows, but real calamities occur in them. You sit in a dark room and look at the faces on the screen, and you say to yourself, These are rooms without ceilings or walls. Nothing is real here. Very good. You are sane and intelligent.

But the eye is insane. What it sees it believes in. The woman held the child over her head and dropped it. So you tell yourself, That wasn't real, that wasn't a real child, but what you feel is real. And now the falling child and how you felt when you saw it fall, all this is part of you. You can't get rid of it. You can't cut it out. You can fall very far in these rooms.

Who likes to admit to the contagion of dreams? If, when you went to sleep at night, your dreams suddenly became visible to millions of people, and in the morning you heard people had jumped out of windows, thrown their children off cliffs—well, of course most of the time they don't begin so dramatically, not at first. At first they change the style of their hair, have their teeth filed down—all because of your dreams. If this happened, wouldn't you be afraid to go to sleep? Well, as Charlie used to say, Why me?

Everyone dreams but not everyone's dreams are put on display for the whole world to see. And among the few whose dreams travel around the world, only one or two come along who make the others dream along with them. I was such a one and believe me, it ruined me.

I hear a key turning in the lock. Thank God! Ivy is coming back. Now I can think about important things, like how much a pound of salami costs today, and I can look at the date on the sour cream carton and see if Tuesday is still the day the store gets it in fresh. Well, this is what my life is made up of now. These things are important. I can see Max, wherever he is (and he is nowhere, none of us are anywhere), watching this, bent over with laughter. Oh, he is roaring. *You face-maker! Stupid cow! Washerwoman! Peasant! Don't call yourself an actress! You expect me*, and now he gestures to someone in the wings, perhaps it is Anders, *to make something out of that?* Well, if he'd been interested in the price of onions, he might be here today. They wouldn't have sent him back to Sweden. Anders stayed here. He made great movies. Once he said of Max, "He has two tones of voice, The Bellow and The Shout. If he could lower his voice, what a happy man he would be." This was true. But when Max lowered his voice, it meant that for him the world had gone black and who knew what might happen next?

While Max was still here, we had a circus scene in a movie and he had to have an elephant. And a white elephant, to match the white horse I rode on. Where do you find an elephant, much less a white one? He should have known better. There's an expression in this country: white elephant. The production people looked from the elephant to Max, and they thought, They're the same, two of a kind. So the cameras came to a halt, nothing happened on the set, and outside, in an empty lot, they began whitewashing the gray elephant, and then someone led the elephant onto the set where there was this crazy circus going on, people screaming and dancing and streamers flying down from balconies, and naturally the elephant panicked. Naturally he did. *I* panicked and I understood what was going on.

Then the zoo doctor came—what do you call an animal doctor? Never mind. I'll think of it. And he gave the poor elephant a shot. I think he was a very old elephant. His eyes were tired and full of little people throwing things at him, taunting him, making loud noises, trying to see if he would move. Oh, I had sympathy for that elephant. Anyone who wants to be a movie star should go to the zoo and look at that elephant and see how happy he is to be famous, because that's what he is, famous, at least while the zoo has visitors, all throwing things at him, hoping he'll get up and trumpet for them.

And then the elephant was painted and Max yelled *Stop!*, meaning Start the cameras, and for once the cameramen began cranking, because, really, the crew always knew what he meant, but they were so tired of his tantrums they pretended they thought he meant what he said, and the zookeeper began leading the elephant around and on went those hot, hot lights.

The whitewash dried out and caked under the heat of the lights and I was riding my white horse in circles, minding my own business, and what did I hear? *The elephant is crumbling! The elephant is crumbling!* In Finnish naturally, because Max was hysterical, and when he was hysterical, and no one could understand him, he became violent.

Now Max is grabbing the zookeeper and trying to turn his head toward the crumbling elephant, the patchwork elephant. The zookeeper, understandably, knows only that a maniac has hold of his head and is trying to twist it from his neck, and he is no weakling either, so he begins to fight back. Now he has his hands on Max's throat and Max is still trying to twist off his head as if it were an apple on a tough stem, and the elephant, the flaking elephant, the drugged elephant, folds his front legs and lowers his head to the ground, and then he folds his back legs, and now he is sitting on the set, in the middle of this crazy circus, like a giant paperweight.

Somewhere, Mr. Pinsky, who has come from the main office—probably they sent someone for him when Max began painting the elephant—is shouting, "You know what this is going to cost? How many shots do we have of the elephant? How many shots do we need of an elephant? Get rid of the animal! Separate those men! We don't need this kind of attention in the papers!"

Naturally he doesn't. The Queen of the Lot, a thirty-five-year-old woman whose husband has just died, you know, a widow, the papers are full of sympathy for her, has been caught by a studio detective having an affair with a sixteen-year-old boy, her co-star. So far, no one outside the studio knows, but all day, from Mr. Pinsky's window, you can hear him shouting, "We don't want to draw attention! We don't want to draw attention!"

The cameramen stop cranking. The extras stop dancing. "Separate those men!" Mr. Pinsky shouts again. The stagehands come alive and pull Max and the zookeeper apart. "Get Flat Foot down from her high

horse!" Mr. Pinsky shouts. That's what they called me in those days
before I could speak English: Flat Foot, Square Head, the dumb Finn,
the dumb Dane, they couldn't tell one country from another. If it
wasn't in America, it didn't exist. But by then, I understood the language when I heard it spoken. You know, you don't forget things like
that. If you're like me, you'll wait years to get even.

I got even. I am the one who is remembered, not them. But what
a cost! Green fields so slick with blood the soldiers lose their footing
and the horses slip and fall and not an extra bullet left to put anyone,
man or animal, out of his misery. That's what it was like, there in the
middle of all that sun and glamour, slick green grass, red with blood.
Well, whenever one person wants something and another doesn't,
there's going to be blood shed. Of course I knew this before I left
Sweden. Some things I was born knowing.

How do I know it is Ivy I hear and not one of the muggers' apprentices
who practice in the park outside my window? Because the person who
just came in is humming "Sheep May Safely Graze." It is a bad sign
when Ivy hums, like the distant rumble of thunder when the sun is
still shining through the green leaves, splashing them all over gold. If
she hums, okay, but if she hums and puts up the ironing board in the
middle of the parlor, then we are in trouble. Other people complain
that their housekeepers won't iron, everything goes to the Chinamen
for 150 kronor a shirt, but Ivy irons when she is worried.

When I say, I like the brass tarnished, look at the interesting colors
it turns, all she sees is visitors coming in and looking at the tarnished
fender and going home saying, That woman who works for Anna
Asta, she's worth nothing! Nothing! She can't even polish brass! And
the picture frames are tarnished, too! Of course the picture frames are
tarnished! I like watching them turn from silver to gold. For a while
you think, well, maybe they are *really* changing. Maybe they know
the secret. Like me, in front of the camera, turning from lead to
gold. When they start turning from gold to black, then I let Ivy polish
them.

What did I start out to say? All these years of not working have
worn down what discipline I once had. Ironing. That's it. Ivy irons.
She irons everything, especially when she's humming. She irons no-
iron clothes I pay a fortune for so when I travel all I have to do is
wash them out and hang them up. She is deaf to my recriminations.
"The iron will wear them out! Don't iron them!" Some day I'm going
to walk in and she'll be up on a ladder ironing the walls.

I am bored to death, says Max. Bored to death. Candles, picture frames, shirts, ironing. This is what I pulled you out of the earth for? So you could tell the world about the price of salami? A sphinx should talk about salami and sour cream? I am going for a swim. Oh, if he were only here. He goes out saying, as usual, *A straight line for once, Anna! A straight line!*

7

AFTER HIS FATHER DIED, Vidal Cook, my father, cried for days but probably believed the stories people told him about how his father had gone to a better place where he watched over his family. His mother moved her three sons, one daughter and her mother-in-law to the little house her husband had bought before his death. The three children slept in one room on one bed, and she and her mother slept on a mat in the main room they called the hall. The three acres produced bountiful crops, and his mother, who during the week worked as a cook for Gray's Mansions, took the bus into Jasmine Bay to peddle her crops on weekends. Occasionally a neighbor who was driving his truck to market in Jasmine Bay would stop at their gate, shout for her, and she would climb in on top of the crops in the back of the truck, taking Vidal with her. The other children stayed with her mother-in-law.

When Vidal was old enough, he was sent to the Cinnamon Bay All Age School where he learned to read and write and although he learned quickly and distinguished himself as a student, it soon became clear that his great gift was his appeal for females of all ages. His teacher made much of him. The girls in his class lingered after school and walked him to his gate. When his mother was working at Gray's Mansions, Mrs. Gray bought him books, asked him to read to her, praised him for his progress, and took him for rides around the plantation in her horse and buggy.

At first he thought nothing of it. Since his father's death he had lived in a house of women. There was his mother, who occasionally spent the night, and his grandmother, who every night washed and ironed the clothes he wore to school the next day. When his mother was away, he slept on the pallet with his grandmother. Margaret, his sister (the whole family had taken English names), was appointed his protector and took her job seriously. She walked him to school every day and was soon expert at flinging stones when other children taunted him for his small stature and thin legs, once going so far as to climb a tall boy as if he were a tree in order to claw at his eyes. The tall boy had chased Vidal, caught up with him, and bore down upon him, so that in order to escape him, Vidal began backing up and, not able to see where he was going, had fallen into the muddy ditch at the side of the road.

A sudden spurt in growth when Vidal was ten, accompanied by a gain in weight, changed the boy's appearance. It was no longer necessary for his sister to protect him. He played soccer with the boys from the All Age School and was soon captain of the team. Now girls from his school walked him home, frequently appearing out of nowhere along the road, offering to share their spice cakes with him. His mother and grandmother took note of this new state of affairs and were quick to take advantage of it. They sent the boy to market on Saturdays with instructions to buy from stalls kept by women. Frequently, after he left with his purchase, the woman at the stall would look at the change in her hand and say, "That boy is thief! Look for what he made me give him my saltfish!" But the next week when he came back, she would make the same mistake.

In school, the boy did well, but his ambition was to go out to Gray's Mansions and watch Mr. Gray at his grafting, or the men at their mortaring and bricklaying, so that one day, in exasperation, Mr. Gray asked him, "What are you studying up on? How to be a jack-of-all-trades?" The boy answered that as far as he could see, it took a lot of skills to get through this world. "What about a doctor or a lawyer?" asked Mr. Gray. "You don't want to be one of those?"

"What do they do?" the boy asked.

"Doctors carry black bags, drive a horse and buggy, and cure sick people. Lawyers wear long black robes and take cases to court where they appear before judges. They study for a long time to get their black bags and black robes and they live in cities and make a whole packet of money."

"I like it where I am," said the boy.

And he was happy on Green Island, in his house with his mother and grandmother and sister, and his two brothers who looked up to him and were told to listen to him ("Obey him! He's your older brother!"), learning to graft and to build, and when he was tired from cycling up and down the hills between Gray's Mansions and Cinnamon

Bay, he would walk slowly through the fields behind his house, beating down a trail in the tall grass, which eventually became a thin red clay path, until he reached the highest point behind his house, and there, where the fields became an impenetrable wall of jungle, he would sit on a large gray stone beneath a pecan tree and look out over the town of Cinnamon Bay to the bay itself, where on stormy days great waves hit the sea wall and exploded like gigantic white flowers, and beyond, where the light turned the sea water to silver. From his perch, he could see the patchwork of fields, the network of hard-packed dirt roads connecting village and field, the people riding in their carts or walking beside them, the hang-upon-nail vendors going from house to house, carrying their valises packed with ready-made dresses and panties, the pack of yellow dogs running into the field of sugar cane, the school with its little bell tower, the church and its steeple, and on Friday nights, the choir making its way to the church for choir practice. Green Island, he said to himself, was a good spot and it was only a matter of time before he took his place among the people who walked so purposefully along the roads on their way to their own homes.

"You don't have any ambition, you know that?" said Mr. Gray, surprising Vidal, who thought himself driven by ambition: the ambition to grow up entirely, to become a man, to learn what it was to love a woman, to have children of his own, and beyond that, to own enough property so that it was impossible to walk from one end to another between dawn and noon. If he could satisfy that ambition, what more could he ask for?

"How these girls come round here, banging on the gate!" his grandmother complained. "They are rude and out of order!"

"Very rude," said his mother. "Vidal, you must not encourage them, you know."

"They say sweet words to him and flatter him and turn his head," his grandmother said.

"He doesn't know they are there," his sister said. "One and all, they are the same to him."

"Is that true?" his mother asked him.

"I have no time for girls," he said. "They feed me spice cakes and criss cakes until I cannot bear the sight of sweets and they come and watch me play cricket and they don't even know the game!"

He accepted women's affection for him as part of the natural order of things. He expected it as well as accepted it, just as a beautiful woman accepts the fact of her beauty and expects heads to turn, and when they do not, is insulted, not because she cares for the particular head that has not turned, but because the right and proper thing, the inevitable thing, has not happened. He had come, without realizing it, to rely on his charm, which affected both men and women and even animals. In his family it was said that he could talk a starving dog out of its bone or a vulture out of its dead meat. He heard all these things but made little of them, convinced that anyone could do the same if he cared to or if he tried.

And meanwhile, he was becoming a competent young man who could do carpentry, build a foundation for a house, spray the plantation's banana trees, resolve arguments among the crew who worked on the plantation, boil soursap leaves into a tea that soothed the irritable workers, tell riddles and stories to the men when they sat in the shade of lemon trees eating their luncheon. He was Teacher Williams' best pupil, and won the fourth-form reading contest, although his handwriting was deplorable ("An illiterate chicken writes better than you!" his teacher said. "What kind of job will you get with this writing?" And then, changing tack, "When you find a girl, how will you write her love letters? She will open an envelope and look for someone else!") and no amount of scolding could make him work.

When he was thirteen and still in short pants, the Clifton family moved to Cinnamon Bay. This was a family of women, two young daughters, Lucille and Mer, their mother, whom everyone called Auntie Tina, and a great-grandmother known only as Nanny.

Auntie Tina soon became known as an exceptionally skilled dressmaker who could make up dresses in the latest style simply by looking at pictures of what was wanted, and who could, moreover, take an old dress apart, cut it, sew it again and make it into something not even its previous owner would recognize, while Nanny, her blind mother, did elaborate beadwork entirely by feel. Her specialty was beading fabric with roses. Soon bridal dresses from all over the parish were brought to her.

Lucille and Mer appeared at the Cinnamon Bay All Age School, and within days they had been quizzed (Where was their father? Dead. Where did Auntie Tina go on weekends? She peddled crops from her fields or sold her embroidery in the larger town of Albion Bay) and taken in. The other girls began to copy their dresses and, before weddings or celebrations of any sort, Auntie Tina was much in demand.

The Clifton sisters, Lucille and Mer, were inseparable, and regardless of how happy the other children were to accept them, always seemed to stand apart. The other children noticed, for instance, that they would never eat food anyone offered to them. When Teacher Williams told the class not to bring lunch because they were having a party for a teacher who was retiring, the Clifton girls obeyed instructions and did not bring lunch, but neither did they eat. "We ate too much for breakfast this morning," they said. On the way home from school, the girls, who were starving, stopped to pick guavas and ate the fruit all the way home. If they visited the house of another child, they had always just eaten or were about to eat, or, when pressed, complained of stomachache. The boys swarmed thick about them. They laughed and joked with everyone, but when people thought of them in their absence, the two girls always seemed turned to one another, as if listening for the end of a sentence of which no one else had heard the beginning.

Vidal Cook fell in love with Lucille Clifton, whom the other children called Lu. He drove her to school on the handlebars of his bicycle. He emerged from behind trees when she walked along the road. There was no shadow in her path that did not seem to contain him. She, for her part, appeared to favor him. She went to parties and dances with him. Her younger sister, Mer, showed little interest in him or in anyone else but her sister.

At the end of the day, in their bedroom, as they undressed and got ready for bed, and put out the candle, the sisters would sit and talk over the day's events. "He says someday he is going to graft a parrot onto a vulture, so when something is dying in a field, the last thing it sees circling above it and coming closer and closer will be beautiful and not ugly," Lucille said.

"A parrot onto a vulture!" said Mer, with a sharp intake of breath.

"It is ridiculous. It cannot be done," said Lucille.

"Oh, he is a dreamer," said Mer.

"Like you."

"I am not a dreamer," Mer said, but she did dream, and lately she dreamed about Vidal.

"Look at this," Lucille said, coming into the bedroom abruptly and throwing something round into her sister's lap. "Tell me what it is."

"It looks like an orange," Mer said. "It smells like an orange. But it is green."

"It is an orange," Lucille said with a sigh. "It is an orange he grafted onto a lime tree."

"Does it taste like an orange?"

"It *is* an orange," Lucille said impatiently, "but it is a green orange."

"A bowl of green oranges," said Mer dreamily.

"Mother said you bought a hat," Lucille said. "Show it to me, now." When it was handed to her, she inspected the red felt hat with its broad red brim that dipped to cover one eye. "Put it on," she told her sister, who sat down in front of the vanity and settled the hat on her head. "It doesn't suit you," Lucille announced. "It makes your head look pointed and your other eye look blackened. Your forehead isn't high enough for a hat like this. My black straw hat, that's the hat you should have for church."

"Can I wear it then?" Mer asked.

"What will I wear?" asked Lucille.

"You can wear my red hat," Mer said.

"Let me try it on, then." Lucille put on her sister's hat. It was a beautiful hat, shading one eye, a glamorous hat. Even an ugly woman would look beautiful in such a hat. "It doesn't flatter me," Lucille said, "but it makes you downright ugly. I'll wear it for you."

That afternoon, Vidal, who was on his way back from Gray's Mansions, saw the two girls walking back from church and got down from his bicycle and walked along with them. So fascinated was he by Lucille and her romantic hat that he almost tripped twice, once stepping into a hole, and once stepping on his own shoelace. He walked the girls to their gate and then rode his bicycle back toward his own house, then changed his mind and drove back to the Clifton house. He got down from his bike and propped his bicycle against a tree near their house.

The girls were unaware of his presence, absorbed in some conversation of their own. He watched Lucille take off the red felt hat and hand it to her sister, who settled the hat on her own head. Lucille inspected Mer, and with a disgusted look, shook her head. In that instant, Vidal saw how it was. The hat was Mer's. Lucille had taken her sister's hat, and now that she had worn it to church, and had impressed the neighbors, she was handing the hat back to Mer. Now if Mer wore that hat, everyone would think she was wearing a hand-me-down of her sister's. In that instant, he lost all interest in Lucille. Mer was the one who intrigued him, Mer, the gentle one, the one who let herself be taken in, the one who always smiled, who laughed at the least thing, a small golden puppy worrying a pumpkin vine, Mer who cried when the teacher called her sister to the front of the room and took out his ruler, and who went up to take Lucille's punishment instead, Mer was the one he thought about now. He thought about her after he decided to leave school and work for Mr. Gray at Gray's Mansions.

ANNA IS ASLEEP. I am sitting in my little blue room waiting for the storm to break. Outside my window there is a single flash of lightning and inside everything is lit by it, the same kind of light a television gives off. I count to ten before I hear the sound of thunder, so the storm is still far off. On Green Island, storms could be far off but move so fast whole villages were flooded without warning. One morning in Cinnamon Bay, Daddy held me up to the window and a donkey swept by on his back, his feet in the air, his big brown eyes staring, and Daddy said, He won't stop before he reaches the sea wall.

A few minutes later we were up on the roof of Tita Lu's house and the most amazing procession of armchairs and tables, birdcages and china wagons, dressmaker forms, cats, dogs, chickens and calves went sweeping by. Every house in Cinnamon Bay had a thick long rope tied to the main beam and now I saw why this was so. If anyone was caught up in the flood, someone safe on a roof would throw the rope.

Well, we will have a different kind of storm inside, I thought, when Mr. Anders tells Lady Clare he is going back to Sweden.

"Do you think she will be upset?" he asked me when I let him in. "You know how she stays," I told him. He sighed and said that at his age he didn't really have the strength for friends.

What is wrong with these people from her country? Other people wear them out more than a hard day's work in the fields. Any minute I will hear the bell ring and I will have to go in and watch her crying and Mr. Anders glaring. I pay close attention to the news. A disaster, that would come in handy, that would distract them, but no, for once no dreadful thing has happened. The worst is the crash of a small plane in Paraguay.

My phone rings and it is my daughter, Priscilla. She wants me to know that if I am missing my white handbag and shoes, she has them. No matter how old they are, this goes on.

Anna's phone rarely rings because she gives almost no one her phone number. Instead she collects other people's numbers and when the spirit moves her, she calls them. As a result, when I am dusting, or standing still in the middle of the room, and her phone rings, I jump as if a ghost had touched me. I pick up the phone and speak hesitantly into it. Most of the time it is a wrong number.

Well, now Lady Clare is ringing for me. "Mr. Anders would like some more tea," she says.

When I come back with the tea, he says to me, "Ivy, you are a good girl, to put up with this one here," and I say, "Mr. Anders, all my life I like helping people."

He looks me over, he studies me, he says, "The golden rule, eh?"

I say I believe in the golden rule and he says, "What is the golden rule but another kind of selfishness? The way you behave teaches the way you want others to behave toward you. If only other people were smarter, they'd catch on sooner, and then you could misbehave a little more, eh, Ivy?"

"Lady Clare," I say, "I don't know what he's talking about," and Anders laughs and says, "She doesn't want to know what I'm talking about."

"I don't know what you're talking about either," says Anna.

"You are the best illustration of what I've just said," Anders replies with a sigh.

"Ivy, sit down," Anna says. "Anders is threatening to go back to Sweden."

"At my age you can't afford to stay too long in one place," he says. "You stand still too long, they begin throwing dirt over you."

Outside the lightning flashes, flashes again. The lights overhead flicker, dim, regain their strength. *The Cat and the Canary*, remember that, Anna?" he asks. "In the old days," he says, looking at me, "if there was thunder and lightning there was also a murder."

"Or a seduction," Anna says, her voice bored.

"Anyway, some kind of calamity," says Anders.

The lightning snaps through the air, snaps again, and the lights flicker and go off. "Now I must light the candles," Anna says, and when I say I will do it, she says, "No, no, I like to light candles. You take the candelabra and put it on the mantel."

In the candlelight I study Anders' face and his snow white hair, so pretty, I would love such white hair, but I have Indian hair and it will be black when I die, only a few gray strands here and there.

"Yes, what a face he has," says Anna. "Even today they want him for films. Well, look at him, the picture of wise and dignified old age, it's enviable."

He says that while he is gone, until he comes back, we must keep up telling our stories.

"Yes?" says Anna. "Why must we?"

From her tone, I know she is flirting. When I next look at her, she will be transformed, the years will have fallen from her.

"You know, Ivy," she says, "not many years ago someone wrote Anders' biography, very long, very detailed. Not one word about his likes and dislikes, did he eat fish, did he like his mother or his father. Not one word about his wife or his children, only that he had them. He worked, he tired himself out, he took vacations. So he must have cooperated very much with his biographer! The biographer should have come to me!"

"Who can I talk to about Esther?" Anders asked. "If someone knew her, that's something else."

"I knew her," Anna says.

"Well, you outlive yourself, it's not such a pleasant thing," he says.

"They say the worst thing is outliving your children. Of course I don't know," Anna says.

"Another form of outliving yourself," says Anders. "Ladies, tell your stories! Think of it this way. In two cinemas, side by side, divided only by a wall, two films are playing. If you could run fast enough, between one cinema and the next, so that you could see both films at the same time, then you would have one complete story."

"Who knows what he is ever talking about?" says Anna. "Right now he will say anything so we will not ask him why he must go back to Sweden."

"My daughters are there," Anders says. "Two women, almost old."

"Old!" says Anna. "I remember them when they were four and three and had bright gold curls."

"Now they dye their hair and complain about arthritis," said Anders. "But Bibi, she says, Poppa, when you come I feel like a little girl again."

"Would you do it over?" Anna asks.

"Would you?" he asks her.

"Ivy, would you?" she asks me.

None of us answers. The lightning flashes, I count to three, the thunder explodes and shakes the ornaments on the mantel, the candles flicker, we watch each other like people in a movie theater where the film has broken and now the only thing left is the faces of the other spectators.

8

MY MOTHER, Hedvig Martenson, was born in Finland in the little town of Ekeborn, the daughter of farmers. She was the youngest child, ten years younger than the one before her, a change-of-life child, and often said that she grew up thinking she had seven parents, two very old, whom she called mother and father, and five more, whom she called sister and brother. As a result, she was completely spoiled and understood nothing of the meaning of life. While her brothers and sisters got up well before dawn to feed the animals, light the wood stoves in the house and barn, and shovel out the barns and sheds, she had nothing to do but follow them. Often they would carry her so that it wasn't even necessary for her to walk from the house to the barn. Her sister Tora wrapped her in a carriage blanket, and her brother Tomas picked her up, threw her over his shoulder and walked off with her as if she were a feather.

Her job was to nurse the newborn animals whose mothers had died, a task she welcomed since it was no more taxing and far more pleasurable than playing with dolls. While her brothers and sisters worked in the stalls, she sat on the floor with a bottle of milk and a baby lamb in her lap. She knew how to test the milk on the inside of her wrist to see if it was warm enough, but not too warm. Usually, as the animal grew, it became very fond of Hedvig, my mother, and then it would follow her everywhere. Occasionally her parents would pro-test, especially if someone wanted to buy the sheep or the cow or the pig, but her brothers and sisters always overruled them, and so she grew up with her own odd children.

Because my mother, whom everyone called Vigi, thought of the animals as her children, she expected a great deal of them. She expected, really, that they would walk and talk and so she trained them. None of them learned to walk or talk but truly her animals were remarkable. She had a dog and a cat which she raised as litter-mates and eventually the dog would lie on the bed, purring, and the cat would lie on the floor, on its side, feet stretched out, as if it were a dog. Someone had told her that a neighboring farmer had raised his bull as if it were a horse and he rode it when he went out hunting. She wanted to do the same. She raised her bull calf so that it came when she called it, and when it grew large enough, she began to ride its back. People used to stop at the farm and knock on the door and ask to see Vigi riding her bull.

Her pig was her greatest success, and when I was a child, people still talked about my mother's pig, Mona. Pigs are intelligent, but this one was unusual, even for a pig. First my mother taught it to fetch a ball. That took no time, so my mother began holding things up to the pig, and saying their names: book, boot, pot, whatever came to hand. Then she would hide the object and tell the pig to fetch it. When she said, Mona, fetch the pot, the pig would trot into the kitchen and come back with the pot. When she said, Mona fetch the book, Mona would come back with a book in her snout. One day she said, Mona, fetch my dress and pointed to her hem, and the pig began squealing. Mona, she said, fetch my dress. The pig rolled over on its back, its legs in the air, and squealed louder. So my mother said it again. This time the pig got up, walked sideways to her, and gently took the fabric of her skirt in its mouth. My mother threw her arms around the pig and kissed it.

She also taught the pig to jump through the snow after her, and to follow her around the room when she danced so it seemed as if the two of them were waltzing together. When she told the pig to stand, it would throw itself up on its hind legs, my mother would grab its front legs, and the two of them would dance about for three or four steps. Eventually, the pig grew too heavy for this. My mother was, she said, a child in a fairy tale. As a result, she wanted nothing more than to marry and have children of her own.

Later, she had cause to regret the extreme happiness of her childhood. The family had difficulties, of course, some of them terrible. Two children before her had died of diphtheria and one of tuberculosis, a disease then almost unknown in Ekeborn. She lived through years of drought when the crops withered in the fields and her brothers and sisters took mules to a neighboring farm and carried water back from their spring. All of this was hidden from her. She remembered the drought years as bright times and warm, when she and her animals could play outside every day.

She clearly remembered coming into the house from the sunshine and, because the house was dark and her eyes were still stunned by the light, she could see nothing, and as she rubbed her eyes she heard the sound of someone sobbing. She followed the noise, and in the corner of her parents' darkened bedroom, her mother was sitting on a straight-backed wooden chair, its seat caned, leaning forward, her back straight, her elbows propped on the whitewashed windowsill, her body shrouded by the thin white curtains that fell over her shoulders and back like long spider-webbing, sobbing and sobbing. Gradually, she could see that her mother's body was not really motionless but that her shoulders and back moved up and down in rhythm with her sobs. The walls of that room were whitewashed, and the furniture was hand-hewn and stained almost black. The ceiling was whitewashed and its beams were also stained black. The feather bed was white, and the bed cover and the pillows were white. White sheepskin rugs lay on the floor. It was a room built of snow, and in the corner, her mother, dressed in black, was sobbing against the white windowsill. It struck my mother as wonderful and mysterious to be sobbing that way, dressed in black, in a darkened white room. It did not occur to her that her mother was sad, nor that she was suffering. "I was a very stupid child," she said to me. "I had no one to think of but myself. It's a wonder they didn't beat me."

I used to love to listen to my mother talk. In an instant, she could summon up the farm of her childhood, its gray painted buildings with their black roofs rising up out of the snow-covered fields, the trees black like dancing women the witch froze and left to stand on the horizon, their arms out to the sun, the warmth of the barn, the smell of the wood smoke rising gray up into the gray sky, her sisters and brothers, her mother and father, coming and going like great shadows who had one purpose, to take care of the little princess who in the mornings sat on the barn floor in her bare feet, wrapped in a carriage rug, feeding a goat or a lamb out of a glass bottle.

My mother met my father one winter when he was sent from Stockholm to live with relatives in the country who thought the pure, cold air would do his weak chest good. He was, according to her, the most handsome man she had ever seen, and apparently her family agreed with her. Well, that is no wonder: he *was* handsome. To this day I believe I have never seen a more handsome man. They say I am the image of him. Probably I am. He was not so much handsome as beautiful, his features too delicate for a man, at least for a man who would work most of his life delivering packages for stores and at night earn extra money driving hearses from the funeral home to the church around the corner.

I loved my mother, but he was the one who understood me.

When we lived in Ekeborn, my sister Marianne told me a story about a man who murdered his wives. "He waits until they come to him in their shifts," she whispered as she sat on the edge of my bed. "A white shift, with embroidery at the neck, gathered just beneath the breasts, a white shift with long sleeves, pleated at the wrists, a white shift *just like the one you have on!*" she said, and she threw herself at me and caught up my shift in her fist. "And then," she said, "and then— Anna!" she asked, "are you listening?" I nodded. I was afraid to blink, afraid to let the world go dark even for one instant. "You're not listening!" she said. I said I was. "And *then* he grabs them up, he holds them in *one hand* as if they were nothing but a sheet of paper, and he takes them to the attic and you know what he does with them there?" She watched me. "You won't guess," she said. "He doesn't boil them in large pots. He doesn't saw them in pieces. He doesn't shoot them or thrust knives into their hearts. He picks them up and hangs them from hooks, like meat in the butcher's market. But you know what, Anna? They are still alive!"

I asked her how they got down. "Oh, they don't," she said. "They stay there until they die. And you know where all the bodies are right now? They are in *Pastor Lundquist's attic!* Lars and I are going to look tonight. Do you want to come? No, you can't come. You're such a baby. You'll tell mother where we went." Of course I swore I wouldn't.

Later that night, we were in front of the deserted parsonage on the outskirts of Ekeborn. I don't know how we got out of the house, what excuse Marianne and Lars gave my parents, but there we were, standing in the snow, the house empty, the moon full in the sky, the moonlight reflected in the perfectly black windows, and my sister Marianne prying open a window and climbing in. Lars handed me up to her and climbed in himself. And then we were going up the stairs and our feet stirred up the dust. No one had lived in the parsonage for a long time, I don't know why. Had Parson Lundquist died or had he gone away? I don't remember. Marianne pushed me up the steps in front of her, whispering every inch of the way. "Anna was always afraid of him and his black and white beard, like an animal," she said, "and his smell, from the green cigars, when he hugged her, she said she couldn't breathe, she said she was going to be sick, but he liked Anna, he wanted Anna for one of his hooks. Now, Anna, you're going to see what he wanted you for and where you'd be now if it wasn't for me and Lars, always watching you."

I don't remember going up the steps, but we were in front of the attic door. "Now, Anna," Marianne said, "go in and see what we saved you from," and she reached over my shoulder, I could smell the damp wool of her dark green coat, and she pushed the door open, and I could see the bodies, hanging on hooks from all the walls, all in white shifts, just like the one I wore under my wool coat, and she pushed me through the doorway, and the bodies I saw there, all these I had already seen. I was sure of it. That was the most terrible, thinking to myself, I know this! From somewhere I know this already! I opened my mouth to scream but I couldn't make a sound.

When I next opened my eyes I was flat on my back in the snow outside Parson Lundquist's house, the parsonage looming up in front of me like a huge train bearing down, and Marianne was rubbing ice on my forehead and Lars was pounding on her upper arm with his fist, shouting, "Idiot! Idiot! I knew it would come out like this!" He was crying and Marianne was staring and crying.

"We have to get the bodies down," I said.

"There weren't any bodies," Lars said.

"No bodies?"

"Only in your imagination," Lars said. "Marianne, you idiot! I'm telling Mother!"

"The story's in all the papers," Marianne said sullenly. "I didn't tell her anything she couldn't find out anyway."

"She can't read, Marianne! I can read and I didn't see anything about bodies hanging from hooks!"

"You tell Mother," Marianne said, "and I'll tell her about you and Krista," so I knew he would not tell Mother. When I stood up, the parsonage leaned over me like the skull of an unimaginably huge animal and the ground was like water beneath my feet. "You have to carry her," Marianne said carelessly. "She's such a baby!"

I began to have terrible dreams but I kept to myself what had happened. At times, I thought I had dreamed all of it, the story Marianne told me, the walk to the parsonage, climbing through the window and walking through the house, raising little clouds of dust on the steep, narrow stairs. Lars told me the bodies I saw were only chairs covered in sheets and that I must not listen to Marianne's nonsense but be quiet and forget about it. Still, it all came out when my grandmother read aloud from the Bible. "And God created man and woman," she said, and I spoke up from beneath the table and said that was a very bad idea. Everyone laughed and asked me why God's idea was such a bad one, and I said it was bad because men liked to hang women on hooks and leave them there until they died.

"Where did the child hear such nonsense?" my grandmother asked, slapping shut the huge cover of the Bible. "Marianne? Do you know?" Marianne shook her head. A cabbage in the field couldn't look more innocent.

"Never mind," my father said. "I'll talk to her." And so I told him the whole story. "I saw the bodies," I insisted. He asked me what they looked like and I told him. They were green with dark black lines through their skin, and their hair had fallen out, and the tops of their heads were shiny, and when you looked at them, they made terrible faces. "No," he said. "A dead person is a nice-looking person. He is only sleeping. He looks just the same as he did in life, only sometimes better. Now nothing hurts him and he dreams a happy dream forever."

"But the faces!" I said.

"A dead person never makes faces," he said. "A dead person is very kind and polite and *even if* someone had killed him, even if, Anna, he would not mention it because the dead are always happy. They are so happy they sleep and not even the loudest noises can wake them out of their wonderful dreams. You are afraid of the dead, aren't you?" he asked. I said I was. He said I should envy them. "Just before a person dies, there's a funny sound in the air, the sound of a hummingbird's wings, and gold dust comes down and settles on that person's face, and as soon as he dies, the gold dust turns to perfect happiness. Perfect happiness, Anna! Everyone dies happy."

You know, I believed this for a long time, a long, long time. But it's not true. Of course it's not true. Max died in a hospital, in Anders' arms, sobbing so that Anders could not understand the very important thing Max wanted to tell him. They told me later that after he died, they pried open his fingers and he had a picture of me in his hand. I don't believe it. By that time everything that happened was embroidered by the vultures, as if my life—and Max's life—weren't bad enough.

They say that before I went to the pastor's house, I was like the rest of the family and slept like one of the dead, but afterwards, I was a bad sleeper. Who can believe now that I ever slept like a stone, so deeply that no one could rouse me? Lars remembers Mother throwing a glass of water at me one morning, she was so infuriated at my sleeping through her shouts and shakings and she wanted to get to church. And what happened? I mumbled, brushed at my cheeks, turned over and went back to sleep on my wet pillow. But by the time I met Charlie, I couldn't sleep, and neither could he. I suppose he had his own bodies on hooks. We used to walk around at night, me with my glass of warm milk, Charlie with his glass of pure gin. "I don't like to bruise gin with an olive," he used to say. "Or insult it with water." For a while, when I first met Charlie, I slept well. We both did. But not for long.

Why are they sharpening long knives at Hogeborn?

When my mother met my father, he lived with his aunt and uncle, the Rasmussens, the wealthiest farmers in the district, and so it was assumed that my father too had money. By the time my mother's parents learned that he came from an extremely poor family, and had left school at ten to help support himself and his brother, it was too late. My mother was hopelessly in love with him. Her parents tried to argue with her, but all she said was, "I want to marry and raise children. One man is as good as another." They finally consented to the marriage which was, in any case, inevitable. Their one condition was that my parents remain in Ekeborn. And for many years they did live there. I was carried into the barns by my uncles and played with the animals, although I don't remember any of it. My father was called home to Stockholm when I was six, and by then he was already coughing.

I suppose I understood, even at a very young age, even while I was listening to her stories, that my mother knew she had made a mistake and now looked back on her childhood through narrowed eyes, accusing it as she would a kidnapper: It was you who brought me here. When she had one of her headaches, she would sit on the bench in front of the wooden table and rest her head in her hands, and, when she thought no one was there to hear her, would say again and again, Oh, what a mess I have made of my life. Now, when she thought of the pig who leaped through the snow after her, she would twist the knife, telling herself she was more foolish than that pig, that the pig knew the world was full of danger, how could anyone have been so deceived, how could they have permitted her to be so deceived, to think that everything would always be as it was, that she would always be carried across the snow? Why had no one explained that when you had children you must have food to give them? Why had no one told her how difficult it was to feed children, how expensive they were, how much they ate? If she had known, surely she would have done things differently! For one thing, she would never have left the countryside. On a farm there is always something to eat, but in the cement city, nothing grows. I was very young when I came to understand that too much happiness can be poisonous. But too much misery, that was no good either! What did one strive for?

I used to ask myself these questions when I walked with my father through the streets of Stockholm. What should one want? Too much happiness and one became miserable. Did it follow that if one was miserable, misery turned to happiness? I believed my father, who said that the dead were always happy, but I didn't want to wait that long. I couldn't have been more than eight when I concluded that the purpose of life was to please oneself. And I had very strong opinions. Oh, yes. People who are afraid are often like that. So everyone in the family came to me to ask advice. Why should I know what I was talking about? A child doesn't know anything. But they used to listen to me, and so the youngest became the oldest, or so they thought.

"Is there someone on earth more selfish than you?" Charlie asked me one day. We were filming a great love story and that day we were doing most of the love scenes. Mr. Pinsky came down from the head office, he came out from behind his crescent desk, and he watched. Charlie was lying on a couch and I was draped over him. "You are the most selfish woman on earth," he whispered to me as I bent over him. He knew my head shadowed his lips. Oh, he knew all the terrible curses, just like Max, and when he was angry, he liked to use them, and the lip readers who came to his movies made his life miserable. Some of them used to type up what he was actually saying and circulate "the real dialogue" among themselves, and sometimes, of course, "the real dialogue" got in the papers, and then he would be summoned into Mr. Pinsky's office for one of Pinsky's famous lectures. "This is an honorable profession, a serious profession, there are millions of people who learn about life in movie theaters! I won't have you swearing like a drunken sailor!" And Charlie would lose his temper, he never had any control over it, and shout, "These are *silent* pictures. No one's supposed to know what I'm saying. Can I help it if the world's full of deaf mutes?" God knows what he would say. He couldn't stop.

"This is going to burn up the screen," Mr. Pinsky said. "Today we make film history."

"Doing what?" I wanted to know. All we'd done was spend the day kissing each other. Charlie and I were fighting and now my lips were chapped. My lips were all I thought about, how rough they were and how any minute they were going to split and bleed and I had no camphor to put on them, and tomorrow they wouldn't be able to do close-ups.

Mr. Pinsky looked at me—Flat Foot, Square Head, dumb Finn—and said if I didn't know what we were doing he couldn't tell me. I grabbed Charlie's arm. He was always ready for a fight if he thought someone had insulted me, and I said, "Look, Mr. Pinsky, we are tired and my lips are chapped and we are going home."

"Each to your own home, of course," Mr. Pinsky said. He had antennae. Probably he felt the rough soul of a gossip columnist.

"Of course," said Charlie.

"Of course," I said.

"The most selfish woman in the world," Charlie said, the instant we were off the lot. I didn't argue. How could I? It was true. All frightened people are selfish. They do what makes them feel less afraid. When nothing is worse than the fear (and for a long time that was how it was with me), then you are completely selfish. Of course, then I didn't understand my own nature. I tried to change it. It would have been better for everyone if I hadn't.

"Oh, wonderful," said the funeral director when my mother died. "She died with all her teeth. You have no idea how much easier that is for us." He was speaking, of course, as one professional to another. He assumed that's what I'd be worried about: what my mother looked like, lying on her back in the coffin. It's true I had my teeth capped after I came to the United States, my teeth capped and my nose narrowed, all in the same week. For two weeks, I walked around thinking my life was over. Every nerve in my head throbbed, my nose was badly swollen, misshapen really, it spread all over my face like a mushroom, and I had two black eyes that turned, as the days passed, purple and then greenish-purple and finally greenish-yellow. My lids were so swollen I could barely see and I would push up on the lids when I tried to read the newspaper. "Don't look at me," I said to Charlie. "Give me an aspirin, please."

I awakened in the middle of the night and Charlie was leaning over my bed, studying me. His cheeks were wet. He touched my nose, then each of my eyelids. "Anskie," he said, "it isn't worth it, is it?" I think, if I had known then what I knew later, if I had understood what he meant, I would have sat up in bed and said, "No, it isn't worth it. What should we do now?" But instead, I saw this beautiful man looking down at me, a man who was more beautiful than I was, and everyone said I was a beautiful woman, his curly black hair, his high coloring, his perfect white teeth, his long straight nose, and I thought, He doesn't know what he's talking about! His teeth are perfect! His nose is perfect!

"Oh, Charlie," I said. "The cow is already out of the barn. Let me sleep." Yes, he said. Go to sleep. I believe he sat there and watched me all the rest of the night. Whenever I opened my eyes, he was there, swaying sometimes, so sleepy he was, but watching. If my eyes opened, he gently traced the shape of my eyebrows with his index finger. He had large hands, so large he tried to hide them, but to be touched by them that night was to be touched by the wing of a moth.

Well, my mother's face. She had the face of a doll, a cookie-dough doll, but I have her eyebrows, high and arched and wide and mobile.

When she raised her eyebrows they seemed to fly up and disappear into her hair. What things we would say to her to get her to raise her eyebrows!

"Tape her eyebrows!" Max told the make-up man. "I can't do anything with her! Does anyone know what you're saying?" he asked me. "Does anyone know what you're thinking with those eyebrows going up and down like guillotines, waving around like two flags? She says, 'I'm happy to see you,' and up go the eyebrows! Now we're waiting for them to come down again! It's a roller coaster, not a face! She's taped? Good. Anna, say something. 'I'm happy to see you.' Say that. Ah, now she looks like a normal person. Keep the tape on. Comb the hair down over the tape. Put on a droopy hat. Women don't wear hats indoors? *This* woman wears hats indoors! Think of a reason for it! You want people all over the world coming out thinking I made a movie about eyebrows? I *never*," he said to me, "*never* had to tape Lena Martin's eyebrows!"

Of course I was crying. I cried a lot in those days. I shouted, too. Go to hell and take Lena Martin's eyebrows with you! I picked up my handbag and blindly threw it. I heard a shriek of pain. Evidently I had hit a cameraman.

"Hah!" Max said. "Now *she's* insulted! Look what I have to work with! Look at that human blot in the middle of my movie, spoiling everything, and *she's* throwing things. Well, that's how it is. You try and try and you take a piece of clay and turn it into marble and the clay sits up on its wheel and insults you. What can you say to that? There's nothing I can say to that!"

He walked over to the long table on which sat scale miniatures of the sets, and when he got to the mansion, in which I was to be trapped at the film's end, he took a match and held it to the little door of the tiny great house. The flame from the match leaped halfway up the wall of the scaled-down house and suddenly it was on fire. Flames ran along its base, and then, like a mad kind of ivy, began climbing the walls. When the whole house was ablaze, a crewman ran over and doused it with a can of beer.

I looked at the grand house on the table, blackened and sodden, dripping and still steaming, and of course I began to cry.

Anders, who had watched all this, didn't say anything. He was always very calm. He grabbed Max by the back of his jacket collar and propelled him toward the studio door. After a few minutes, I walked off the set and looked out of the studio window. Anders had a firm grip on Max and was walking him up and down, up and down, talking constantly. Every so often, he would stop walking and talk even faster. When Max opened his mouth to say something, Anders gestured angrily with his free arm. Max was a huge man, perhaps six foot three, but Anders, I saw now, was taller. Eventually, he finished what he had to say and released Max. The two of them walked back toward the studio.

"So, you're still here," Max said, avoiding my eyes. "Go home and get some rest." I started to put on my coat. Max fumbled in his pocket. "Take a taxi," he said and pressed some bills into my hand. Anders watched him.

For all I knew, Max had another miniature model of the great house and tomorrow morning it would be sitting there on the table. Or nothing would proceed until another scale model was produced, and while we waited, Max would glare at me, and soon everyone would do the same. And this was one of the more peaceful days on the set.

From the time I met Max, people began to tell me stories about him, about his extravagance, his legendary temper, his complete absorption in the world of movie making. All of it was true. When Max was on a movie set, he was always shouting. If he had something to say to the script girl standing next to him, he shouted.

"His trouble," Anders used to say, "is that he thinks he's Napoleon and he must have read somewhere that Napoleon never lowered his voice."

When Max, Anders and I were on the train crossing the country from New York to California, Anders found me alone, crying in my compartment, and he began to talk about Max. "You know," he said, "Max is really something of a monster. People don't tell these stories for nothing. Once we were driving out to the mountains to scout out some locations for *Winter Reindeer* and there was a car accident at the side of the road. Naturally we had to stop and look. And a beautiful woman was standing there, her face twisted up in grief. Max went up to her. You know what he said? He said, You have a wonderful face, just the face I need for my movie. So I was horrified and pulled on his arm. I said, Max! Someone the woman cares about was just hurt in this accident! And he said, Is that a good reason to turn down a chance to be in a great movie?

"Another time, we went to a friend's funeral and another group of people were coming out of the cemetery, and Max said to me, Look at the old man! He's just what I need for *The Bridge Builder.* So: the man's face was swollen and puffy with crying and two women were holding him up. He was dangling from these relatives. And I said, Max, if you go anywhere near him, I'm not talking to you again. Of course he was astonished. He said, If God didn't want me to see this man, why did he cause both funerals to take place at the same time?

"Once the head of the Lagerloff came to see us and he brought the great financier Billquist and Max looked him over and said, You're the financier? Someone else could play your part better. Everyone laughed because they thought he was joking but believe me, he was not. What are you going to do with someone like that? When he's obsessed, his blinkers go on and he sees what he wants to see, nothing else. The rest of the world doesn't exist. It's terrible. When he gets this way, my wife walks out of the room. And then other times he'll pick you up and carry you for miles because he thinks you look a little pale. He's not easy. He's not sensible. He's not predictable. But then who wants those things all the time? And he's a genius, he's proved that again and again, so you forgive him everything, and what's worse, he *knows* you'll forgive him everything. Naturally, no one can do anything with him. But probably you know this already," Anders said.

"Yes, but sometimes," I said.

"Oh, sometimes," Anders said, smiling. "Sometimes he's the most wonderful man in the world.

"But obviously he is also the spoiled son of a doting mother, don't you think so? Can you imagine him, a little boy, one or two, in a little lace dress? And then a bit older, but still his mother carries him across the floor? He told me she did that, you know. How old do you think he was before his feet touched the ground?" And as the train rocked us back and forth, we dreamed up scenes from Max's pampered and indulged upbringing so that, when he finally came back into the car carrying magazines and hot chocolate, he found us shrieking with laughter, tears of hilarity streaming down our faces.

"So, if it's such a good joke, tell me what it is," he said. When we didn't answer him, he set down the magazines and the hot chocolate, his gestures elaborately polite, and then he stalked from the compartment, banging the glass door shut behind him.

Once, before we began filming *The Mansion of Father Bertil*, Max called me where I worked at the confectionery shop, and when I picked up the phone, I heard someone's voice shouting, "Will you shut up? Do as I tell you and shut up about it!" Then the voice said, "Hello? Hello?" and I said, "Hello. Who is this?" And the voice at the other end, Max's voice, said, "Would you mind telling me who I called?" I said, "This is Anna Asta," and he said, "Oh, Anna! I forgot what I called you for. I'll call back later," and he hung up. And when he called back, he was cross because I ought to have known what he was calling for in the first place and I ought to have reminded him.

In the old pictures, my father and I have one face. His was almost a perfect oval, but long. He had finely arched eyebrows, huge blue eyes, and his nose was long and aquiline. We have the same mouth, a full, almost pouting lower lip, and an upper lip that seems carved out of stone, thinner but beautifully shaped. The make-up men painted my upper lip to exaggerate its shape: a capital M. But my father's ears were small and delicate while mine are like my mother's, two door-knobs, one on each side of my head. "Can't those ears be glued?" Max asked, and the make-up man looked dubious, but they got some airplane-model glue, or something like it, it smelled foul, and dabbed it behind my ears and then pressed them against my skull. For a while the glue would hold, but then, under the hot klieg lights, it would begin to soften, and then melt, and then run down my neck and drip onto my costume. "Her hair should be a cloud around her head, so those ears can't keep coming out like crazy planets—do I have to see to every single thing?" Max said, and then the hairdressers took hold of me. But when he was ready for close-ups, he glued my ears. Once when I did something that annoyed him, he grabbed me by the side of the head and accidentally pulled me by the ear and a piece of skin ripped. All day long, whenever the camera wasn't cranking, I dabbed at the spot with cotton and glycerine water. Every time Max looked at me, he flushed, turned, and shouted at someone else.

My mother always said my father was handsome, but to me he was not. He was beautiful. My mother should have had his looks, and he hers. His face belonged to an aristocrat, a ruler of countries, a famous artist, but he was none of those things. Instead, he delivered packages, drove hearses, and finally cleaned out privies.

Could he have been something other than he was? Could my mother? They were good people. When they were young they were happy, but later their life was terrible, so poor and so hard, there was no room for happiness in it, or unhappiness either, only exhaustion. If they had not married? If they had remained single? If someone had come along and grabbed them up, as Max grabbed me up, and said, Look, here is another road you can go down?

On our long walks through the city, my father had a sharp eye out for pieces of wood, gray and jagged and water-softened, and we would come home laden down with them. Then after we finished eating, he would sit in the middle of the bench, at the kitchen table, whittling little wooden animals with his jackknife. Later he would sand them down, and before every birthday or Christmas, he would paint them. These were my toys, these wooden animals, these, and one doll my sister was given by my grandparents. I inherited it when she tired of it. The doll did great things and told the animals of her adventures. One year, my father built me an ark for them, but I was unhappy. My animals should live in a house! So he began to build me a house for them. I remember my mother complaining about that dollhouse, saying it was the only kind he could build for his family, and he kept on working, not looking at her, and I thought, Good, nothing she says to him bothers him, but when I went around the table to get a better look at the fretwork he was carving to go over the doorway of the little house, I saw the tears running down his face.

You cannot forgive your mother those things, even though, later, you grow to understand them.

I always knew when my father was coming because his cough came in before him and in no time he was gone. Well, if you don't mind, I'll talk about my father later.

In Ekeborn, we lived in a large barn my grandparents converted into a house. When we moved to Stockholm, we moved into an apartment house on the south side of the city. I was ashamed of it. We had a small kitchen almost entirely taken up by a large, rough wooden table my mother covered with oilcloth, and long wooden benches ran the length of two sides of the table. When we sat down to eat, we had to bend forward if my mother walked behind us to get a pot from the stove.

We had only one bedroom and one bed. I remember waking up at night and seeing my arm and trying to move it and, although I felt it move, it lay still on the covers. The mystery was solved when I realized I was looking at Marianne's arm, not mine. The bed was a sea of arms and legs and heads, and someone was always twisting this way and that so that the blankets were soon in a hopeless tangle and of the seven of us on that bed, only one, or perhaps two, were warmly covered at night. So we lay close to one another to keep warm. On nights when I could not sleep, I would go into the kitchen and stretch out on one of the benches, but usually someone had gotten to the bench in front of the stove before me, so I would crawl under one end of the table and come up like a diver in front of the other bench. The bench was hard and narrow, so I never slept for very long. In the morning, I would pretend to sleep while the others got up. Then I would burrow beneath the covers, waiting for my mother to start a fire in the wood stove, and I could do this because I was the youngest. In some ways I was as spoiled as my mother had been.

I would never let anyone I knew come to the house. If they did not already live in the building, I would not invite them. They would see the one bedroom and want to know where we all slept. When my mother asked me why my friends never knocked at the door, I would say, my business is my own. Later, people found out where I came from, and they looked at where I had gotten to, and suddenly everyone took credit for what I became. I don't know how many people walked around telling the newspapers, "Actually, I was the one who first suggested that she attract attention by *not* giving interviews." It is all nonsense. I made myself. This sounds like a great thing? We all make ourselves. If we're lucky, someone comes along and says, Well, you can also do this, and if you have it in you, you can. So I made myself, like the child makes cookie dough into a doll. And I didn't do such a wonderful job, believe me. I had moods. You don't want to know about the moods I had. I still have them.

Someone invites me to a party and I don't want to say I'm coming. If I know I have to go somewhere, my stomach starts to hurt, or my head, or my hand is too heavy to move, or I can't wash my hair. No one knows what agonies it is to wash my hair. But must the whole world know what's going on? So if someone invites me to dinner on Thursday night next week, I say, How do I know I'll be hungry next week? And they think, What a pest!

I made myself, but also I didn't. I came into this world with moods, one minute happy, the next minute death itself couldn't be blacker. I learned to protect myself. You can be as crazy as you want behind closed doors. Who calls in the neighbors when their face swells up from a bug bite? So if I didn't want to be seen more often than other people, what of it?

And I got so fed up with people and their questions, always the same ones. What are you doing now? Did you have a good night's sleep? Is it their business how I slept? And in the evening, So what did you do today? From morning until night, Did you sleep, what did you do all day? You know, you can be sitting still in a chair looking like you're doing nothing, and still, you're accomplishing a lot. But who understands that unless they're the same? So I became very good at answering questions but not answering them. I said if someone offered me the role of a clown, a male clown who was really a woman, I couldn't refuse it. And all the women would write to the male clown and they wouldn't get an answer, because the clown was really a woman and she wasn't interested. I meant something by that, you know. I meant there was one role I wanted to play. Whoever figures that out can have whatever I own. Well, they can have something, at least.

Charlie came in one day and said, "I know!" And he did. He thought it was so funny, how I was telling everyone what they wanted to know and no one had the slightest idea of what I meant.

"If I could do that," he said. "Teach me how to do it!" But I couldn't. "You're devious," he said, looking me over. Right then and there I should have dropped what I was doing, that life I was leading, and said, Let's try to be happy. If I could have backed into it, slid into it, then maybe it would have been possible, but always he wanted an answer right away. And I was never in a hurry. Once you make a mistake, you live with it forever. Better to wait. I always thought there was more time. I was right, about myself anyway. But not about Charlie. He died very young and I am still here.

Maybe our bodies talk to us and tell us what to expect. I always knew I'd live to be old, not that I saw any particular point to it. So after a while, even if something disappointed me, I didn't care. Next year I'd do something better. But for him, disappointment was the end of the world. "I work hard and I'm going to die young and I won't accomplish what I want to accomplish!" How did he know? How did either of us know?

He was such an intelligent man. No one believed it, of course. He was too handsome. What a curse that is, really. As if you were nothing but a face and a body, a figment of someone's imagination, a thicker version of a beautiful shadow someone saw on a screen in front of a great, dark room.

The day after the burning of the great house on the studio table, we heard the sound of pebbles hitting our windows. When I looked out, a little boy was standing in the snow, and Max was handing him something, probably a coin. During the night, fresh snow had fallen, and Max, tall and thin, standing there in his black wool coat, looked like an enormous raven. I drew back from the window, hoping he had not seen me, but again pebbles hit the windowpane, and when I glanced at it, I saw it had begun snowing again. When I looked down, Max was still standing there, his fur hat in his hand, the snow turning his thick hair gray. So I put my coat on over my shift and put on my boots, and as I was going down the steps, I put on my gloves.

"Well," I said, pulling my hood up over my hair, "why are you here? So early in the morning?"

"I want to talk to you," he said.

Why are they sharpening knives at Hogeborn? Why are they sharpening long knives at Hogeborn?

"You like coffee?" he asked me. "I know a nice coffee shop. Very good pastries," he said, not looking at me. A few days ago, he said I would sell my soul for a pastry. "My car is parked around the corner."

"You shouldn't bring your car here," I said. "The neighborhood isn't good."

"How far would they get with it? A peach-colored sports car. There's only one like it in Sweden."

"In the world," I said.

"In the world," he agreed.

We sat in the little pastry shop and he ordered two small coffees with cinnamon sticks stuck through their little dome of whipped cream flaked with dark chocolate and he called over the waiter with the pastry cart. "I'll select for you," he said and I stiffened. Surely what I ate was my own business! But he chose an enormous white plate and pointed at each heap of pastries, and the plate was set before me with one of each. I threw my hands up. How could I eat so many? But he said, "Don't worry. What you don't finish you can take home. We're not wasting money." I started to laugh. Max worrying about wasting money! If he wanted a shot of ice breaking up at the seashore, the whole company was packed up and put on a train. Not for him a miniature beach built in a sand box, a miniature ocean whose water could be whipped into waves or stilled and then frozen.

Of course, money meant something to me then. It still does. We didn't have any. A pair of shoes was one hundred kronor, but mending a pair, that was twenty, so I mended my shoes and when Max had expensive shoes made for me even though my long dress would cover my feet, I scolded him. What difference did it make what I wore on my feet? "You will feel like a queen when you are wearing scuffed shoes with holes in them?" he asked me. "A queen must be a queen from head to toe. And is it only you I'm thinking about? When I look at you, *I* want to see a queen. What do I see when I look at you and know you have on shoes with holes in the soles, probably lined with newspaper? I see those shoes and wonder why I'm not making something called 'Tragedy of the Streets.'" It was easier to wear the shoes than to argue. In those days, I was very cooperative.

"If you will eat your pastries and listen, then I will let you go. I know how stingy you are with words," Max said. The pastry stuck to the roof of my mouth. Was Max discouraged, disappointed in me? Was he going to let me go? How often had he told me that even when the picture was finished, he could reshoot scenes with someone else as the beautiful young girl and no one would know I had ever been in it?

"Most of this you won't understand," he said. "Not because you're stupid but because you're too young. I know I call you stupid, but really, I am angry because you're too young to understand. So," he said. "To begin. I know how easily things go from this earth. Some men with astrakhan hats ride into the village and your family is gone. No one's left. There's no one to bury them but the villagers or a few people from the synagogue, and they don't have much money, and they're afraid the men on horses will come back, so they bury your family in the middle of the night, they say prayers in the middle of the night, and they put up wooden markers and no one has time or money, so they write the names and the dates on pieces of paper and nail them to the pieces of wood, and in a few months no one knows who's lying where. Well, what difference does it make? Dead is dead.

"So I came to Germany, and to Sweden. I won't have children. I'm not the sort. Still, I'm human enough to want something to last that has my name on it. Not just something with my name on it, but something that keeps me alive. It's not a child but it is a child. Such my films are to me. I dream them and then I film them. They're dream children. This is how I think of films. They're dreams you see when you're awake. You know how hard it is to dream when you're awake? There are two ways to do it. Either you go crazy—I don't have any use for craziness, it's such a waste of life—or you have a lot of money, *a lot* of money. One way or another, dreaming when you're awake is a very expensive proposition. But if you can do it, if you can dream when you're awake, and make the whole world see your dreams! Do you understand? Then you never die!"

"Oh, I don't know," I said. "It is so important not to die? The doings of humans are so important? One day, I was sitting in art class, and I looked around me, and I thought, The human being is an ugly thing. Look at it. A long tube with arms and legs dangling from it. They're like lizards, lizards with a few alterations. And their heads! Swellings on top of their necks with a face-plate nailed to the front, and behind the face-plate, all the senses jammed together, the nerves for the eyes and the nose and the mouth. So some of these lizards are more beautiful than other lizards, but none of them are beautiful, not compared to a cat or a dog or even a cow." I traced a path on the shining glass of the table top. I observed the white latticework that turned the coffee shop into a café in a garden. It looked like a stage set.

"Lizards," said Max.

"Lizards," I said.

"Of course you are joking," he said. I didn't answer him. "It was art class," he said. "So you were looking and looking, probably at the model you were sketching, and suddenly everything lost its meaning and made no sense. It's the same when you repeat a word over and over again. Say a word again and again and soon it won't mean anything at all. When you're a child, you repeat the word again and again until it attaches itself to the thing, but when you're older and you repeat it over and over, it comes loose. Strange! So," he said, thumping the table, "lizards!"

"No," I said. "It isn't like that. I look around and often I see lizards."

"I see," he said, but of course he didn't. He didn't want to see. "I interrupted you," I said.

"Yes, well," he said, looking at me. For the first time, he seemed unsure. "So, yes, I want to save my dreams. They're the best part of me. But that's not enough. Film is film, after all. It's not alive. I want to take a human being and make it wonderful. Everyone who looks at that person will envy it. It will be special, a miracle I made happen. Well," he said, laughing nervously, "a very miraculous lizard. You're the one I want. When I'm finished, everyone will know you. People in Lapland will have your picture on the wall. People walking along the Great Wall in China will want you. You will have everything you want. You say, *I want this,* and you'll have it. Everything I put you in will shine forever. We'll shine together, like the moon up there when it comes out. Can you want what I want? Can you do what needs to be done?"

"It is important?" I asked him.

"It is important."

"Why?"

"Is this life," and he waved his hand, "is this life good enough? For you? For anyone?"

"No," I said. But perhaps I hadn't seen enough of it. Two years before, when I was fifteen, my father had died before my eyes. I split into two pieces. This must happen to many people, but I hope not everyone knows it. I knew it. There were days when nothing was good enough, when I thought, What a silly business it all is. We're born, we live in houses, we go about our business, and we die. Why this interest in what we do before the last thing happens? And then on other days, it was a wonderful thing, this life, full of surprises. I looked up at Max, and the day turned. Life was again wonderful.

"So," he said, "do you want to be part of it? Can you want what I want?"

"Yes," I said. "I can."

"You will let me teach you?"

I nodded. He placed his hand over mine, that huge, hairy paw. It was warm and beautiful, long thick fingers like the roots of a tree. The features of his face were exaggerated, as if a caricaturist had drawn him. His face was long, his forehead high, his eyes deep-set in dark sockets, so dark it was hard to look into them, like deep ponds in the wood. A deep, vertical crease bisected each cheek. At that instant, I foresaw how those creases would deepen, become crevices, how his forehead would wrinkle, how the vertical creases between his eyebrows would also deepen, how his face would every year more closely resemble a face carved out of a cliff. Even then, I thought everyone resembled a particular animal, and as I looked at Max, I thought, Which animal does he resemble? And I thought, a baboon. A very intelligent baboon. I looked at him and thought, If it is true we have come from animals, and of course we have, then to look at Max is to see how far we have come from the apes. And then I felt fright. There were times when Max read my mind. If he could do so now, what would he think? He was so vain, far more vain than I was—even then. The best of clothes, his own tailor, nothing that was not absolutely elegant. A baboon! He would think I had betrayed him. But to me a baboon is a very beautiful animal.

His skin was leathery and tanned, but in the light it had a yellowish tint. Perhaps he was not healthy and already suspected he would not live long. So, at seventeen, in the coffee shop, I felt pity for him and took my right hand and put it over his hand, and we sat there hand on hand on hand. I noticed how wrinkled his hand was; he was almost twenty years older than I was. I said, I want you to teach me to dream in the daytime, and still we sat there. In an enormous quiet. The waiters moved back and forth in silence in their black suits, their starched white shirts, their black ties, through the whitewashed rooms, through the white-latticed arches, everything black and white, like a photograph. I felt as if I had chosen a husband, taken vows, given over my life. What would happen to me now?

"And you," he said, looking over at me, "you don't even understand this movie we're making. That's the funny part."

"Certainly I understand," I said. "A drunken priest is cast out by his congregation—" but Max waved his hand and I stopped speaking.

"The priest doesn't matter, the sixty-eight sets I built don't matter, the chase across the ice doesn't matter. What matters is the fire. The whole movie is about fire. It burns everyone up! Not just the great house. It is about passions, fire, how they burn everyone up, the woman who took a lover, the lover who died and left her his house, the husband the woman takes later who throws her out into the snow, the old mother whom that woman throws out who stays alive all those years out of her passion to see her daughter, the door locked against the disrespectful daughter, that's the father's passion for his daughter, how it flares up in him when passion flares up in her! The passions flare up, little sparks, then great flames, then embers, then ashes. But always, always, somewhere, the fire is raging. That's what it's about. That's why the faces are so important. Those faces! Old ones, young ones, ones in the middle, they all have to be there! Oh, well, the pretty ones like you, they have to be there for everyone to sigh over, but once you get people inside sitting in the dark, then they see the plague is everywhere, scarring all the faces, making them what they are in middle age.

"In middle age, people have faces. The face of the countess, so old and haggard! What a face! Destiny is written on it! The history of the species is written on it. She's not beautiful, no, but wonderful, she is wonderful, something you can contemplate forever, and you can learn more than the philosophers who sit there studying a skull. The skull has only one lesson to teach. It teaches fright. The face of the countess, that teaches awe, and after awe, humility. But your face, it's still blank. It can't teach anything. What can it reveal? How everyone loves to watch you? How even a washerwoman with red, swollen knees loves beauty? But in thirty years, or forty, oh, then you will have a face. You understand?"

Did I or didn't I? I was to be the bait who lured people into movie houses to see what was really important? Was that it? Was that what he meant? "You're not satisfied with my face?" I said.

"I came to you for your face," he said.

I had disappointed him. I knew it. So I said, "In the sleigh scene, when the wolves chase us across the ice, what is it the priest throws to them to make them stop pursuing us?"

"Great God!" he said. "That's what you want to know? You're like the fisherman's wife! She gets three wishes and each time it's for the wrong thing!" He picked up a piece of apricot cake from my plate and chewed on it slowly, looking at me, as if to say, She is stupid now, but later she will learn, or perhaps he was thinking, For now, she must be stupid. She doesn't want to understand what I tell her. My face was burning. For an instant, I thought I had a fever. And then he nodded at me and smiled. *You will do*, said his eyes.

"Eat your cakes," Max said at last. I took my hands from his and began to eat. Suddenly, I was starving. As I remember, I ate every pastry on the plate. There was not a crumb left. I should have asked Max for a box of pastries to take home, the boxes were so pretty, closed with an embossed gold seal, and tied with pink and green ribbons twisted together. I still feel guilty about that. But let's forget about it. If I were to list all the things I feel guilty about, I would fill up every notebook I own.

9

AFTER VIDAL COOK fell in love with Mer Clifton, several years passed. Perhaps he forgot he had fallen in love with her. Perhaps he mistook what happened for something that occurred in a dream. These things happen. Something takes place quickly, a storm blows up, and whatever it was is forgotten except every now and then, when it seeps through into the light, like an undercoat of paint that never properly dried.

The village went its way, which is to say that some of the old people died and their places were taken by the newly born. Vidal Cook became Mr. Gray's foreman, responsible for overseeing the men who sprayed the bananas on the plantation. Vidal's sister, Margaret, moved in with a man she liked, and after having several of his children, went to Albion Bay and married him. That was the way on Green Island. The villagers had a saying: Befriend in the country, marry in the town. Mer moved in with a young man who did masonry work and her sister Lucille moved in with a farmer who had a talent for giving speeches and who sometimes conducted services at the Pentecostal Church. Mer and the mason moved back to Cinnamon Bay and lived in the house with Lucille. Lucille began conducting rehearsals of the church choir, although as everyone pointed out, she could not sing a note, and it was like watching a duck conducting a tree full of nightingales.

One day on his way home from work, Vidal saw two women fighting in the street. One woman had the other down, and as he drew closer a friend called out to him. "Vidal! It is two women fighting over a man. Stay out of it!"

"I will, sir!" said Vidal, and the two of them joined the thickening crowd gathered to see the fight. The woman on top was hitting the other on the head with a closed fist. Vidal looked around and saw he was standing in front of the Clifton house. One of the women who had been watching the fight suddenly bent forward, looked more closely, turned around, and banged at the Clifton gate.

"Lucille! Lucille!" she shouted. "It is that woman come from Albion Bay beating upon your sister!" A window in the hall flew open and Lucille thrust out her head.

"Is that my sister lying there in the road?" she shouted.

"It is Mer!" the other woman called to her.

"Tell Mer I am coming!" Lucille said. By the time she reached the road, Mer had turned the other woman over, taken off her own flat-heeled slipper and was hitting the other woman over the head with it.

"Here, take this!" Lucille said, taking off her leather-heeled shoe. "Beat her with this!" Mer took the leather-heeled shoe and began to beat the woman on the head. "Stop!" the woman beneath her cried. "Stop!"

"Say you're sorry!" demanded Lucille.

"I'm sorry," said the woman.

"Say you'll go back to Albion Bay and stay there!"

"I will," said the woman.

"Let her up, Mer," said Lucille.

The woman got up, looked around her, and ran down the road. She stood there, staring back at the crowd, wiping away her tears. Without taking her eyes from Mer, she began brushing the dust of the road from her skirt.

"We don't need a dirty person like you in Cinnamon Bay!" said Lucille, who bent down, gathered up a handful of rocks and began flinging them in the woman's direction. The woman ran off down the road like a frightened, starving dog, but then she stopped and called out, "I throw out my dirt but your sister takes it in."

"Not even garbage will stay with you in your nastiness," Lucille shouted at her.

"What is this all about?" she asked, turning to her sister. "Why was that woman after you?"

"She said she was friends with my man years ago and I had no business with him," Mer said.

"Is that a reason?" Lucille asked, appealing to the crowd. "Something she threw out years ago, and now no one else can have it? And not even a chair or a curtain? A man! Her name is on him some-where?"

"Good for you, Miss Two Shoes," someone said to Mer, and for years afterwards, that was what everyone called her: Miss Two Shoes.

"You told her you were leaving that man you're living with?" Lucille asked her sister.

"Why should I tell her what is not her business?" Mer asked.

Vidal walked up to them. "Mer?" he said. "You want a ride on my bicycle?"

"Come in and have a cup of bush tea," said Lucille.

"I'll take a ride," Mer said.

He took Mer back to his house. "Come in and meet my grand-mother," he said, but she said, No, she was still hot all over from fighting. "I didn't think you were the fighter," he said. "Everyone says Lucille is the teg reg who fights for you."

"I'm too old for that now," she said.

"Up above there," he said, "at the end of that little red path behind the house where the chickens go, there's a beautiful place where you can see to the other side of the sea. You want to come up?"

They went up and looked out over the town, to the far horizon, the seamless place, where it was no longer possible to tell where the sea ended and the sky began.

"From here," said Vidal, "the town looks like a pretty, very well made machine."

"Or an anthill with many two-legged ants," Mer said. She looked at him and said shyly, "I won the fight. Didn't I win the fight?"

"You did win it," he said.

"My sister and my mother, they say if I don't learn to fight for myself I will never survive in this world."

"You did fight and you did win," he said.

"If you want something and that is the right thing, then why should you have to fight for it?" Mer asked as if thinking out loud. "If it is right for you, it should come to you."

"The world is not that kind of place," Vidal said. "When fruit falls from the trees, it is full of rat-bite or it is rotten. When it is ripe and good to eat, you must go up in the tree and pick it."

"You reach out and pick it?" Mer asked, smiling.

"Oh, yes, oh, yes," said Vidal.

"And if I reach out for you and pick you, then I will have you?" she asked.

"Oh, yes, that's how it will be," he said.

And that night, Vidal helped Mer move out of her sister's house,

and moved her into his room, where they lived with his mother, grandmother and sister.

"They are young and foolish, and like all young foolish things,
they are happy," said Vidal's mother to his grandmother.

"Oh, yes, young and foolish and happy is one thing," said the
grandmother, "as long as it is their story alone. But if the girl becomes
pregnant?"

"He will love his children. He loves all children."

"Your story is not your story long," said the grandmother. "My
story was not my story long. It was my story and your father's story,
and then you came along, and our story was your story. How soon
one person's story becomes someone else's! How long can you call
your life your own? You go up on a hill and never have you been
more yourself, but you are like everything else, pushed about by the
sun. And then your children come after you and they are unhappy
with their lives and they ask, 'Why did you do things this way?' and
what can you tell them?"

"We never reproached you with anything," said her daughter-in-
law.

"The young are so careless. If a child should turn around and ask
you why he had to be born?"

"You tell him the truth," said Vidal's mother. "You say you don't
have the slightest idea. Does a banana ask the banana tree why it was
born? Does a coconut? If everything that was born wanted to know
why, the noise would be deafening, everyone would be asking the one
question that cannot be answered, and soon the gourd would be dead
upon the vine and the world would come to an end. You cannot ask
why you were born. You are born and you look around the world
and ask, 'Where is my place in it?' "

The grandmother sighed. "That girl," she said. "She has wide hips
and the look of a woman who will have many children."

"They say she has a sweet temper and loves to laugh," said Vidal's
mother. "The family is good. The mother we know. The sister is a
teg reg and no one dares cross her. The Cliftons stick together like
glue and they say the girls are closer than flies on flypaper."

"She is a restless girl," the grandmother said. "Don't you feel it?"

"Everyone that age is restless," said Vidal's mother. "I was restless."

"Not after you married," said the grandmother.

"I persuaded Asad to come to Green Island," said Vidal's mother.

"One move in a lifetime is not restless," said the grandmother.
"And besides, Asad thought he persuaded you to come."

After Vidal and Mer had been living together for six months, the weather turned stormy and the banana trees were invaded by pests. Mr. Gray asked him to stay on the plantation during the week. Mer took a job working with a dressmaker in Albion Bay. Every morning she got up early to take the bus and every night she was back at eight o'clock. Vidal's grandmother kept dinner warm for her on the table. After Mer ate, she and the grandmother would play cards. Two years passed, and during that time, Lucille, her mother and grandmother moved back to Albion Bay although they kept their house in Cinnamon Bay, renting it to Miss Blue, a widowed woman who was famous for telling stories, many of them about herself. After she moved in, she nailed a sign to the door: STORY TAILOR.

Teacher Williams passed the house, saw the sign, and snorted. "No one in this village can spell his own name," he said. "Story Tailor indeed!"

But Miss Blue had not misspelled anything. A story tailor was what she considered herself to be. She let it be known that if people were having trouble or were unusually happy, they could come to her and tell her their stories, and she would change the story for them, a nip here, a tuck there, until, like a dress that made you uncomfortable because it caught you around the ankles, it was made to fit. If, for example, a story was about a wolf who ate a child, you could change the story so that a bear ate the child. Or a wolf might eat a goat and not eat the child at all. A nip here, a tuck there, what a difference it made, how much happier you were with it, just as you were not happy in a dress that once was too long for you, but couldn't tear yourself from the mirror once it had been properly shortened.

"That's the way," Miss Blue told Mer, who had come to visit to see how she liked the house and to be sure the roof wasn't leaking, "you get power over your story. You know," she said, lowering her voice to a whisper, "your story is clever and doesn't want to be changed. It hides inside you and when it knows you're coming for it, when it feels you coming closer, it jumps behind the wall of the heart! It hides under the roof of a toenail. To remain hidden it must do everything it can. It doesn't want to be changed. Nothing in this world wants to be changed."

Mer was fascinated. "You change people's lives!" she said.

"Oh, yes," said Miss Blue. "Tell me your story and I'll show you how it's done." Mer said she was too young to have a story. She lived in a friendship with a nice young man and his mother and grandmother.

"You'll have a story if you live long enough," Miss Blue said.

"You know," Mer said, "I never can think of myself as old. My

sister, Lu, she is always saying, 'When I am old and am sitting on my
porch with my black dog,' or 'When I am old and can only eat strained
carrots,' but when I try to picture myself old and wrinkled, I can't see
anything at all."

"Nothing?"

"Nothing."

"I never heard of that before," said Miss Blue. "You should have
your hand read."

"What do you think of it, Grandma?" Mer asked that night.

"Think of what?"

"Can you tell her a story and she changes your life?"

"If she could do that, why should she be living in Cinnamon Bay
and not in a mansion in Greenstown? I win," the grandmother said,
laying her cards down. "You don't pay attention."

"How do you keep your hair so straight? Or is it just Indian hair?"

"Indian hair," said the grandmother.

"In Albion Bay, they pay a fortune to get it straightened," Mer
said. "This morning I was on the bus and a fat woman got on with her
head like a pin cushion in those hair-straightening curlers and wearing
a satiny black dress with a big red rose pinned on the lapel and she
saw an old Indian woman sitting there and she said, 'Coolie, get up. I
want to sit down.' But the people on the bus came against her and said
to her, 'Who gets on the bus first sits down first,' and when she went
on telling the old lady to get up, a big woman said to her, 'Shut up,
girl, or we will put you off the bus.' "

"They did put her off?"

"They didn't have to. The old Indian lady looked up and she said,
'You may be coolie up there on your head'—she meant the fat lady
was going to have straight hair when she took the rollers out—'but I
am coolie up here,' and she pointed at her head, 'and coolie down
here,' and she pointed between her legs and the people on the bus
laughed the fat lady to scorn."

"When they told my husband Asad about Green Island," said the
grandmother, "they forgot to mention the ill treatment we would find
here. You know, I think you are pregnant."

"Oh, no. I can't be pregnant. Lucille and I agreed we would both
be pregnant at the same time."

"Whose idea was that?" asked the grandmother. She was smiling.

"Lucille's. She said that way, if anything happened to either of us,
the other one could take both children."

The grandmother yawned. "There's a lot of stealing from the fields
at night," she said. "They haven't caught anyone?"

"No, but when I was walking home from the bus I saw Lazarus and he was sharpening his machete."

"It's time for bed," said the grandmother.

"Grandma," said Mer, "I did tell Miss Blue that when I think about myself as an old lady, I can't think of anything. I can't imagine myself with wrinkles or aches and pains or swollen joints or black speckles on my skin. I don't see myself at all."

"Why should you see yourself as an old lady when I can't believe I'm old myself and all I have to do is look in a mirror? If Miss Blue upsets you, stay home."

"I'm only curious," Mer said.

"You're not curious, you're pregnant," said the grandmother. "Go to bed."

In August, Mer gave birth at home to a baby girl. The birth was quick and without complication, and afterwards the grandmother gave her a drink of rum and told her to sleep. Vidal's mother sat next to her bed fanning her with a palm frond. After a few minutes, Vidal's mother laughed and said she felt like Mr. God, the man who spent his days fanning the judge in the courthouse, who was so impressed with the importance of his position because, if he did not fan the judge, the judge could not dispense justice, and if the judge did not dispense justice, the country would go to rack and ruin and be run by alligators. All of Green Island, dependent on his fan! After work, you could see him, nodding to the left and right as if he were a visiting eminence. But the girl didn't answer, so she thought Mer had fallen asleep.

In the corridor she heard her mother quarreling with Vidal.

"What's this I hear about a Miss Bea? Who is this Miss Bea? You have this woman here and now you have a child! Who is this Miss Bea and why must I hear stories about her living in your hut out at Gray Mansions?"

"There's no truth in it, Grandma," Vidal said.

"You are lying like crazy!" said his grandmother.

"There is no Miss Bea!"

"She doesn't exist?" asked his grandmother.

"She doesn't exist for me. There's a Miss Bea on the plantation. She comes from St. Mary's. What has she to do with me?"

"Now she exists," said his grandmother. "A minute ago she was not yet created."

"I talked to her one night."

"If you are lying!" said his grandmother.

Vidal's mother came into the corridor. "Every word you say out here you can hear in there!" she said. "Go into the yard and argue!"

"I am going to bed," said the grandmother.

Just then the baby began crying. "What a sound," said the grandmother, smiling.

For nine days, Mer stayed in the house, waited on by Vidal, his mother, his grandmother, and Mer's sister, Lucille. She was not allowed to walk on the floor without shoes. In spite of the heat, she was not permitted to sit in the doorway without a sweater. At the end of nine days, she got up, got dressed, and said she was taking the baby, whom they had named Ivy, to St. Mary's to see her mother and grandmother and to register her there.

"How long are you going to stay?" asked Vidal.

"A week, maybe two," Mer said. "You will come for me?"

"I will send and tell you when I'm coming," he said.

Ten days later, Vidal took the bus to Albion Bay. It stopped on the corner of Princess Street. Vidal had no trouble finding the house.

"She is a beautiful baby, isn't she?" he said, picking up the infant. "She has my eyes. Look, I brought a blanket, everything we need to take her back."

"I'm not coming back," said Mer.

"You're not coming back?"

"Not yet."

"Why not?" He looked at Mer's mother, who turned away. Mer's blind grandmother shook her head and turned in his direction, her eyes closed. "Someone has said something against me?"

"Is there something to say against you?" Mer's mother asked sharply.

"I am not a saint, ma'am," Vidal said.

"From the time we were children," Mer said, "women followed after you."

"You are the one I love."

"I am not ready to come back," Mer said.

"You go back and get her!" his grandmother shouted at him. "Someone told her about Bea! That woman sleeps on your mat at Gray's Mansions! I know all about it! She knows all about it!"

Vidal didn't answer her.

"Stubborn mule!" she shouted, striking him with her coconut broom. "You will go back! Don't tell me that if a tooth hurts you, you pluck it out! Don't tell me nothing will hurt you twice! You go back and get her! You bring her back here!"

"You want your card-playing companion back again, eh, Grandma?"

"Don't joke with me! The bus leaves in a half hour. Come! Go run and catch it! You have a daughter in Albion Bay! The Cliftons will let you see her if you don't bring back the mother?"

He came back late that night, alone. "She says she doesn't want to come back," he said.

"Because she knows about Bea!" said the grandmother, who sat down at the table, placed her head on it, and began to weep.

"She is young and ambitious," Vidal said. "Maybe she thinks she can do better. I'm Indian, I like the countryside, I'm happy spraying bananas. All I want is some property."

His grandmother picked up her head and glared at him. "She likes Indians!" she said.

"There's no hope?" his mother asked him.

"No," he said.

"And the baby will stay with her?" asked his mother.

"Do I know who the baby will stay with?" he shouted, slamming his fist against the wall. "She will not come back. That's all they told me."

"This living like a ram goat, this is what comes of it," said his grandmother. "I did love that girl."

A wave of sadness overcame him, so powerful it heated his body and threatened to knock him down. Immediately the sadness turned, as it will, to anger. "I cannot marry for you, Grandma!" he shouted, and, leaving the room, banged the door behind him. Then he went out behind the house, climbed the narrow path of the uppermost field, and sat still in the darkness listening to the sound of owls, the ugly croak of swamp frogs, the rustle of the breeze in the palm fronds and the distant but distinct sounds of the sobs of the women of his family.

"If she will not come back, what can I do?" Vidal asked Lazarus. The two men had tired of waiting for the bus to Gray's Mansions and gone back for their bicycles. They were now at the foot of the long, steep hill leading to the plantation. They dismounted, and walked their bikes up. It was early morning still.

"Look at that boy there," Lazarus said, pausing to get his breath. "What is that big silver thing he is waving? It looks like a soup ladle. Where would he get a thing like that?" He turned his attention again to Vidal. "If she is making you wait," he said. "If she heard stories about Bea."

"I told her!" Vidal said. "I told her I would marry her!"

The men resumed walking. "That Clifton family, they are fancy people," Lazarus said. "The sister Lucille and her choir and her church and the two of them with their fancy hats and their Albion Bay manners, marriage is not enough for them. She will expect cleaving, too."

"Cleaving? Speak plainly," said Vidal.

"*Cleaving,*" Lazarus said impatiently. "The Bible says you must leave your parents and cleave to your wife and you must not go sniffing after other women. You did no cleaving while you were at Gray's Mansions, sir."

"Cleaving," said Vidal. "Well, that is a hard job, but I could do it."

"Not if she doesn't want you," said Lazarus. "You could go ask again."

"I will not go again," he said. "I went twice. Now she must come to me but she will not come. Lucille herself told me. Mer will not come. She will stay there with her family in Albion Bay."

"I don't see any cloud of dust on the road resembling the Clifton family wagon," said Lazarus.

Lazarus, who had gone to the All Age School with Vidal, was tall, thin, pale and had a shock of blond hair that bleached white in the sun. When the plantations were not hiring and when work was scarce, he would go down to Cinnamon Bay and wait for the tourist boats to come in. He was a well-advertised attraction. "Laugh for the tourists, Lazarus," one of the fishermen would say, and he would laugh his high, piercing, unearthly laugh, a sound like nothing else heard on earth. The sound called forth nervous laughter in the tourists, admiration tinged with fright, and they threw coins overboard in a golden shower. Lazarus would dive for the coins, staying submerged so long that the tourists, and even the fishermen, who were accustomed to this performance, would become agitated, and just as someone was about to cry out, Lazarus's head would burst through the thin skin of the water, and in his fist would be a handful of coins. "Your laugh would wake the dead," someone said when he was a boy, and the name Lazarus had stuck. Who remembered his given name now?

"You will take this woman Bea?" Lazarus asked him.

"Her family is good and she does love me. I do love Mer more but she will not come."

They walked along, pushing the bikes uphill. On the morning breeze came the smell of charcoal. The mists in the valleys below them had almost cleared and here and there they could see small ribbons of smoke, women up early in the morning, cooking breakfasts and dinners for men working in the fields. Below them, a child drove a small herd of goats along a red clay path.

Vidal had already been to talk to Bea's father, Mr. Bell. "No man will fool her again," Mr. Bell said. "This time any man who fools around her, he has to marry her." Bea, a tall, slender woman with enormous round eyes, sat on an overstuffed chair in the corner of the room, her eyes fastened on her shoe buckles.

The two men and the girl sat there in silence. Vidal was aware of the sun nibbling at the edges of the windows, but inside it was cool. There was a real carpet on the floor and the furniture in the hall was not homemade. It came from Greenstown, a city to which he had never been. Mr. Bell wore a suit no tailor in Cinnamon Bay had made, the waist band eclipsed by the globe of his belly, and red-patterned suspenders held up his pants. His white shirt was starched and ironed and his black leather shoes shone. The sunlight coming through the window was reflected in them. Vidal watched the flicker of light on the shoes, fascinated.

Afterwards, he would say that he was perhaps more taken with Mr. Bell than with the daughter. There was a father sitting in that room, a man, a person of authority. Vidal was angry and rebellious and made to feel small, and at the same time he was overcome by his desire to submit to this man's authority, somehow embodied in the man's thick neck, so thick that the collar of his shirt barely fastened, and a fold of flushed skin was pushed up by it. He was conscious of his own thin neck, still the neck of a boy, as his thighs and arms were those of a boy. He was undone by Mr. Bell's thick thighs straining against the fabric of his trousers, the thick arms pushing against the fabric of his shirt. There was the smell of green cigars about him, the odor of his own father, long ago sunken in memory, now evoked only by that odor. He was helpless before his enormous and unsuspected desire to submit to Mr. Bell, to relax his fists and let his hands lie open and empty on his own thin thighs, palms up to heaven, to cry like a child and ask the man, What should I do? Tell me what to do and I will do it.

"I will marry your daughter," he said.

"And you will forget the other woman?"

"I will forget her."

"And the child?"

"I make no promises about the child," said Vidal, his face flushing. "She is my flesh and blood."

"That is right and proper," said Mr. Bell. He nodded and called to his wife. She poured a glass of rice wine for each of them and he and Vidal shook hands. Vidal observed the expression on the father's face, the satisfaction of it, a good piece of business concluded.

Bea was now standing and looking from one man to the other, smiling. "She does not come with an empty trunk, you know," said

Mr. Bell. "She has a bit of her own. You might buy some property, perhaps not so close to Cinnamon Bay."

"I think I will never marry," said Lazarus, breaking into Vidal's thoughts, "never marry and never take a woman into my house."

"That life will be simpler," Vidal said. "As for me, I like the company of women." Vidal thought of the child, Ivy, with her mother in Albion Bay, and of his grandmother, who had asked whom the child resembled, and of Mrs. Clifton, who said the baby looked just like Mer from the front, but when you looked at her from the side, there was Vidal's profile. "I would like to have the baby," he said.

"Vidal, stop," said Lazarus. "That way lies trouble."

"She is mine," Vidal said.

"She is yours but she would be an outside child. You know what they say. The black vulture always thinks his own children are white. The preacher always baptizes his own children first. I am a yard child. I know."

"All the same," said Vidal.

And so he married Bea at the Pentecostal Church in Cinnamon Bay where Lucille Clifton directed the choir and cast poisonous looks at the happy couple. His mother and grandmother wept through the ceremony, a state of affairs Mrs. Bell attributed to the happiness that seized them when they saw their son standing with Bea before the altar.

"What an odd choice of hymns," someone said afterwards. " 'Nearer My God to Thee.' The choir generally sings that at funerals. Miss Lucille! Why 'Nearer My God to Thee'?" Lucille gave back a murderous look.

Several days after the wedding, an odd story began to circulate. It was said that early in the morning, on the day of the wedding, the stationmaster looked out from his little booth at the end of the platform and saw Vidal standing there, peering into the distance as if looking for a train, a small suitcase resting on the ground before him. "Isn't this the day he is to marry?" the stationmaster asked himself, and decided that something was not right. He walked over to Vidal. The early morning air was cool and the sky was gray but there were blue rips in the gray canopy above them. The day would be clear and bright.

"Vidal," said the stationmaster. "What are you doing here?"

"I am waiting for a train," Vidal said.

"What train, sir?"

"Any train that stops, wherever it goes, that is where I am going," said Vidal.

The stationmaster ran down the road to the Cook house, fetched Mrs. Cook and Vidal's grandmother, and the two women came to the station, talked to Vidal, and brought him home.

It is said that when Lucille heard the story, she said nothing. She smiled.

10

I GET UP from my little bench in front of my desk, and my knees are creaking. In another room, Ivy is humming one of her hymns. She knows more hymns than I know words in English. She is so cheerful, really. Even when she is sad and humming, she is more cheerful than I am. It is a question of expectations, isn't it? She expects something will make her smile and then the sadness will pass. But I, when I am miserable, expect something will make me more miserable and so I am paralyzed and made more unhappy by an event that has not come and may never come.

I can smell freshly ironed cotton, me with my nose like a wolf's. The poor journal, it is time for me to close it. Look at how long I have had it, Max, how it outlasted you. But who wins? Gone fifty years and who am I writing about? You.

Outside I am surprised to see it is snowing furiously. Little black-and-white people are scurrying about on the street fifteen stories below, their heads bent into the wind. Great, fat flakes falling, lining the inside curves of the few trees that manage to cling on in New York City, covering the cars that line the streets until they look like large animals, covering the drooping necks of the streetlights, almost blotting out the pods of light hanging at the ends of their stalks. A man goes by, his head bent down, his shoulders covered by inches of snow. Oh, this happens so seldom now. Every year there is less and less snow in the city. They say the whole world is getting warmer. I don't believe it. There's no nature in the city. The whole place is dead.

You look around you and what do you see? Concrete and brick

and tar. All stone, none of it natural, everything man-made, everything covered up. One day, I was out walking. I came up to a mountain of garbage bags near a big building and suddenly a rat ran out. He heard me and he ran across the cement walkway and through a chain-link fence protecting an empty lot. From what was the lot protected? From what are they protecting this empty, rubble-filled space? He was wild, that rat, and the fear on his skin, you could almost smell it.

I stood there and looked into the lot to see where he went, but wherever he lived, he had his house well hidden. He was gray and black like the rubble. I shouldn't have expected to see him. I would have liked to, though. We were two of a kind, wild and frightened and stunned, probably, wondering what we were doing in the middle of all this concrete. That's why there's no snow. Who knows what nature is anyhow? Maybe one morning it got up and looked around and said to itself, I don't live here anymore. I'm going to live some-where else. And it took the snow with it. Every so often, this thing called nature flies over the city, on its way somewhere else, some-where luckier, and to remind us, so we'll stop and think what's hap-pened, it opens its hands and lets some snow fall down on us. How do you even know the seasons here? If you stayed inside and never came out, you wouldn't know. Only if you go out and find it's cold, well, then you know it's not summer. Or you can do what I do, and go for a walk, and look for the last tree in the city and see if its leaves are green, or yellow, or if they've fallen off. These are the clues.

Who can walk around this city and not feel sorry for these trees? Someone breaks a hole in the cement for them the way fishermen at the North Pole break a hole for their fishing line, and then they pound stakes of wood into four corners of a little square, and they put a rubber teething ring around the tree, and they fasten wires to the teething ring, and to the wooden pieces they fasten the wires. In Fin-land where I was born, winds howl like the end of the world and still the trees stand up without the help of human beings. There it is dark most of the time, but still the trees grow. Here, the tree gets a little sun, an hour or two. These buildings go up so high that you can't see the tops of them when your neck grows arthritic. They block out the sun. You can't have respect for a tree in New York.

But the weeds, they give you hope. No matter how hard the con-crete bears down on them, they push their way up. They say, what's this hard thing on top of my head? I will break it to pieces. So they do it and the city spends a billion dollars getting rid of them. Am I a flower or a weed? Of course a weed. All that time spent trying to make me into a flower, what a waste!

"Ivy," I say, "it's snowing. I'm going for a walk."

"What nonsense is the woman talking now?" she says, without bothering to look at me.

"A walk," I say, going to the front closet and taking out my boots.

"There's a snowstorm out there," she says. "You were looking out the window?"

"That's why I'm going out." I take down my wool coat with the mink lining. Eleanor gave it to me, the year she moved to California and that fancy rest home they call a hotel. "I don't need it anymore," she said. "You take it. It's a good coat. I know how you hate to spend money."

It's too short on me, of course. Eleanor was tiny, but such a good actress. And what a big head! They all had big heads, those silent film actresses, great big heads on top of little tiny bodies. Except for me, who was like a stork, gangly and big all over. Next winter, the tailor can sew a border onto this coat so I don't walk around like a gawky teenager who overnight grew out of her clothes. "So, I will see you later," I say, waving at Ivy, but just as I am out the door, she says, "Oh, no. You crazy? I'm coming." Ever since I broke my hip I can't get out of the house without an escort.

In the elevator, she taps my pocket and taps it again until I take out my hand and show it to her: gloves. My hat, of course, is firmly settled around my ears. I never go out without a hat. We start to walk.

"Oh, it is wonderful!" I say as we cross the street. "It is just like home!" I stick out my tongue and let the flakes settle on them. Ivy clicks her tongue. The snow is falling through the city sky and the city is polluted. But for tonight the snow is falling straight from the stars and is absolutely pure. What do I know about pollution or health or bodies? In the snow, I do not have a body. I am no age at all. I am as I began.

A piece of paper blew across the road and frightened the horse. The horse panicked and began to gallop and smashed the carriage into a tree. The bride was thrown from the carriage. When her new husband climbed down and ran over to her, she lay on her back, smiling. But she was dead. And then he bought a ship and sailed to the South. He docked near a beautiful antebellum mansion and went ashore because he needed water. There he met a beautiful girl. But ever since the Civil War, her father was frightened of strangers.

He tries to take her away but an escaped murderer prevents her from going. He sails away but comes back for her. Does someone knock over a kerosene lamp? The house is on fire. Everything is in flames. But they are safe on the water. He and the girl are safe on the water. For the time being, everyone is safe.

What am I thinking about now, can someone tell me that? A piece of paper, everything on fire. Something Max told me, one of his stories, probably one of his stories, and a man who sails away with a girl, probably into a storm and ends up on the bottom of the sea. What a patchwork of stories I am!

"You know," I say to Ivy, "it is a little bit cold."

"A little bit!" she says.

"Well, for you," I say.

"And I am a little bit tired, I suppose?" she says.

"Yes," I say. "You are."

"We can stop in the nice shop around the next corner where they have the fried plantain and cornmeal cakes. You like cornmeal cakes," she says.

"Not too oily," I remind her. "You know my stomach."

"As well as you do, ma'am," she says. So we walk on. "In here," she says.

We sit down in one of the booths. Ivy orders a large plate of fried plantain, salt fish and cornmeal cakes. I order three cornmeal cakes, and we share a pot of tea. "Don't drink it so hot," I tell her. "Hot is not good for the lining of your stomach."

"Whose stomach has the trouble?" Ivy asks me, pouring a steaming cup. We eat in silence. Then I look up and see a man's face pressed to the window. He is wearing a fedora, an old-fashioned hat, with a lady's ribbon, pink, tied around it.

"That man is following us," I tell Ivy. "This is the second time I've seen him." Ivy looks up and says, "I can't make him out. He is black or he is white? Where his face should be, there is the kitchen counter. But I know that hat."

"Even in a snowstorm, they follow me," I said.

"Why you?" she asks me. "Yesterday, I went down street for some fish heads when I saw that hat. You were out yesterday?"

All day yesterday I stayed in my room, in my bed, the covers pulled up to the top of my head. Once or twice I sat up, looked at the wall and lay down again. With moods like mine, how will death surprise me?

"Oh," I said. "So maybe he is following you. So it is not for me to worry about." Then I think how that sounds. Nothing must happen to Ivy! What would I do without Ivy? "If he is following you, then we must call the police," I say.

"You crazy?" she asks me. "The police!"

"I tell you, the police here are not the same as on Green Island, mixed up in everyone's business. You call them, whatever it is, they take care of it."

"When I need the police, then I will call them," Ivy says. We both look up at the window. "It is an old-time thing, that hat. You won't get those old-time things again," she says.

The cakes are good and filling and not too oily and the tea is warming. "You have been writing in your journal?" I ask her.

"You can tell me why we are scribbling in these books all day?" Ivy asks me. "Who is there who wants to know the story of my life? I am a big old woman."

"Anders and his crazy ideas," I say. "Once a director, always a director. He sees us milling around the apartment like extras, so he puts us to work."

Ivy has many sisters. At night I can hear her in her room, talking to one, then another. And her brothers and her children and her grandchildren. On her vanity table is a forest of silver frames, each one enclosing a face like hers. I give her one of those frames every time I go on a trip. "I cannot go home without a silver frame," I moaned in Warsaw. "I want a silver frame." And so someone got it for me, beautiful, worked silver, with a huge amber stone, pear-shaped over the arched top. "Oh, Ivy will love it," I said, and my friend's face sagged and went gray. Never, never can I learn to keep my mouth shut. People say I don't speak, but they don't know. I speak all the time, and always the wrong thing.

At night, when I can't sleep, I translate what I've written in my journal into English and read it to Ivy. If I still can't sleep, she reads me what she's written in hers. Her journal is a notebook, no lock on it, not like mine, a lock, a zipper, everything but a land mine, covered with flowered red cotton, really very pretty. She is not always coming to the end of a page and telling herself, Look, I'm at the end of the page, now I can stop. Every page in her notebook is equal to six of mine. "So what were you writing about?" I ask her.

"Shrimp," she said. Shrimp! I am disappointed. She promised me to begin at the beginning, to tell me how her father got from India to Green Island, all those things. I think, sometimes, that I would sell my soul for a story.

Outside, it is still snowing, harder than ever. "I don't think it is stopping so soon," I say, and we get up. Ivy picks up her handbag, ready to pay for her part of the check, but I tell her I dragged her out in the storm and today I will pay. Always we used to split the check because I thought that was how it should be. I paid her a salary and all the rest was extra. Better not to complicate what is good with questions of money.

But Ivy insists and starts dividing up the check—mine is sixty-five

cents and hers is one dollar and fifteen cents—and the waiter begins
to mumble. "She comes in here with her fur coat and she makes the
poor lady pay the few cents there!" I turn red like a cabbage. "Go
about your business, sir!" Ivy says. "The lady should give away her
money? This is my life I'm living here! You hear me complaining?"
The waiter tears up the check and rewrites it so only my sixty-five
cents shows up. "You want to cut off your head to spite your neck,
go on," Ivy said. "I am not proud before a fool. I know where to buy
a pair of slippers for one dollar fifteen." He goes off muttering something about how people like her are why people of color are impossible to liberate. He slams the cash register shut.

"He is too fool," Ivy whispers to me. When we leave, she says to
him, "Tomorrow the prices, they will be the same?" and when he
opens his mouth to speak, she laughs at him. "Go on with you, man!"
she says. "Interfering with your customers!"

It is a real blizzard now, the snow so thick we can't see in front
of us. We hook our arms together and bend forward into the snow.
In snow like this, there is no time. We are walking now down an
avenue of huge lindens, centuries old. In a minute, the drunken priest
will drive up in his carriage and offer us a ride. The wild wolves will
chase us but they will not get us. Oh, after all, life is wonderful.

Ivy is pulling me into a doorway for a rest. I know she is glaring
at me, so I don't look at her. She bends forward and peers up and
down the street. Nothing but snow. "That man with the hat," she asks
me. "You think he was following you?"

"So if he was?" I say. "I know who he is. It is always the same
ghost following after, always the same one." Now I am all laughter and
silliness, from one swing of the pendulum to the other.

"His face was white or black, this ghost?" Ivy asks. So she is
worried.

"We will warn the doorman," I say. "If you are worried."

"I am not worried," she says. "I sleep with a machete under my
bed."

"By now," I say with a sigh, "it must be a pile of rust."

"It is as sharp as death!" Ivy says. "Let's go."

I have no idea how far from home we are, one block, two, three,
it could be miles. And then we are in through the big plate-glass doors
and I turn to look once more at the thick snow, that swirling white
wall, anything can come walking out of that whiteness, but she has
me by the arm and is steering me to the elevator, clucking, saying our
boots are filled with snow and wet snow is down our collars and we
are wet to our brassieres, our coats are wet and now we must dry

them on sheets stretched over the radiators, and the whole apartment will smell of wet wool, wet dogs everywhere, that smell, and in the morning, I will have pneumonia and again and again I will say, How did this happen? Just yesterday I was a healthy young woman!

Then, when everything is off, the boots upended in front of the radiators, the coats spread out, our dresses swaying from hangers like hung people over the bathtub, I get it into my head that I am going out again. "Fine," says Ivy. "Go." She will not come? "I eat no salt, I eat no fat, no cholesterol, I live on fish heads, all to live a long time," Ivy says. "If whooping cough is to cut me down, it will have to look for me. Such foolishness!" And she starts to say something about Miss Blue, who also didn't know when to stop, and I forget about the snow and sit there listening.

Now I am in my old flannel robe and under it is my long underwear, gray bottom, pink top, and on my feet are fuzzy pink slippers she bought me last Christmas. I am sitting in the big French armchair as I always sit, my back against one side of the chair, my legs up over the other arm. I am wide awake. Ivy is not happy about that but I am warm enough, and so she is satisfied.

"Sometimes you speak of ghosts," Ivy says, "but to you they are a joke. To me they are not. I've seen ghosts many times. Everyone on Green Island sees them. Now they don't see them as frequently as before because of the refrigeration. It used to be that the bodies lay in the houses waiting for the coffin to be built and the relatives to come from all over the island, and then there was the funeral, but before the funeral, the ghost walked. Now the bodies are refrigerated and the ghosts are cold and stiff, so they don't walk as often. Everyone says it. I believe it. Maybe I am stupid, but stupid or not, I've seen them. Who hasn't? The children walk around like ghosts, lifting one leg straight in the air, then putting it down again. They say that's how new ghosts walk, stiff-legged, because they are not people anymore and yet they are not practiced as ghosts. The old-time people say a ghost walks just like you or me but his feet don't touch the ground. When you look, you see a little line of light right under his feet. Well, so they say. The ghosts I saw walked with their flat feet right on the ground. Did you ever see a ghost?" she asks me.

Once in Stockholm, when my father was delivering packages, he took me with him. It had been snowing all night. There was not a sound in the city. As we came to a corner, we began to hear shouts and wild singing, and when we turned the corner, there were kings and queens standing in the snow. Their crowns sparkled in the light and they bowed low to one another. They raised gold goblets encrusted with jewels to their lips and then clinked their goblets together.

"Oh, ghosts!" I said, but my father said, "No, they are real. Look at their feet. They are wearing boots just like yours. And see where they come from." He pointed to a three-story building painted brown. On the walls were all sorts of posters. The kings and queens saw us and waved, then turned, and, with their arms around one another's waists, walked back into the building. Every now and then someone turned to look back at us.

I tugged at my father's hand. I wanted to follow them. I pulled him after me, toward the brown building. He looked down at me and laughed. He said, No, no, it would be better if we went on. I would remember what I saw here, kings and queens playing in the snow. Then I pulled my hand from his—I pulled my hand out of its gray mitten—and ran into the building and the guard at the door was too surprised to stop me. I could hear some of the kings and queens inside and I ran down the hall until I came to a room where their voices were clear. Two of the queens were out of their velvet and fur robes, although they still wore their crowns. "Oh, look at the little girl!" someone said, and then one of the queens pulled on her skirt. She stepped into it and pulled it up from her ankles, a plain gray wool skirt, and while I watched her, she zippered it. Then she took off her crown and put it down on a wooden table. The wood was gray and stained, but the crown gleamed there. She picked up a black sweater and pulled it over her head and straightened it over her hips. She sat down at the table and looked into a triple mirror. With a dirty rag she wiped off the black outline around her eyes and her eyes grew smaller, like the eyes of rats. She wiped the redness from her lips and cheeks. She became pale. Suddenly, she looked up at me and said, very slowly, Little girl, I can become a queen anytime I want to. Then she laughed, jumped up, and put the crown on my head. Here, she said. How do you like it? Oh, she should have a scepter. Berthe, who has the scepter? Someone thrust a scepter into my hand, and automatically my hand closed over it, but I was lost in what I saw in the mirror. There I was, in my gray wool coat which was once Marianne's, far too long for me—the sleeves came almost to my fingertips—but on my head was a crown! She's a little fat, said the queen, but what a face! When she loses that baby fat, she'll be something! What do you think, Carl? And Carl the king said, She's not so bad now. She could be our princess. Do we need a princess?

"Anna, come," said my father, who was standing in the doorway. For a minute, I had forgotten why we came out. I wanted to ask them,

Can I come back, or do you disappear? My father says you are not ghosts, but what are you? "What are you?" I said aloud.

"We are actors," Carl said dramatically. He was enormous and his face was thick with whiskers. He looked like a great bear who had, for that one day, put on a human suit. "One day we are kings and queens and the next day beggars and murderers. We live on stages in theaters and when we finish our performance, we are just like you. We are silly people, really."

"Silly people!" said one of the queens. "We are magic people! Like a book that changes its stories every night while you sleep!"

"Are you the people who come and take little children away in the middle of the night and chop them up with axes?" I asked him. Now I was hiding behind my father, holding on to his thigh.

"We are the people who come and take children away at night when the moon is full and the snow is falling," roared the big man and he put his arms up before him and made claws of his hands and bent from the waist as if he were about to pounce on me.

I shrieked and my father reached down and patted my head. He could not pick me up because he was carrying a large package. "Stop frightening the child!" the queen said, her voice deep and angry, but already I was no longer frightened. Already I wanted to come back and see what they would become when they stopped being kings and queens. And my father began to cough.

All dead now, those kings and queens, the man who coughed, the girl who saw the kings and queens in the snow. She breathes in and out, but really, she is dead. Oh, I can see ghosts whenever I look at my old films. There they are, ghosts, legions of them, their lips moving but no sound coming out, as lost as words in a dead language. Who watches silent films now? Only a few crazy people who come to this building, sneak past the doorman, ring my doorbell, and try to give me roses. But if the dead could come back! If they could really come back and if they could speak! If they could hold out their arms and say my name! Then I wouldn't mind if they did come after me with an axe. No, I wouldn't mind. If the dead would come back! But they don't come back.

"No," I say to Ivy. "I've never seen a ghost."

"I've seen them, many times," Ivy says. "Once, when I was a small child, after my father kidnapped me and I went to live with him and my stepmother, I was visiting my grandmother, not the grandmother who had me before I was kidnapped, but my father's mother, Mother Eliza. They called her Mother Lize. She was a full Indian, you see, with her hair in a braid she wore down her back, all the way to her knees, but when she went out, she was a midwife, she wore it up on top of her head and then she looked taller. She was tiny, not five feet. She was cooking some curry and I was sitting on the veranda, looking down the lawn to the ackee tree at the edge of the garden where it ended and the road began. The sun was beginning to go down, but it was still light and it was still very hot.

"I had on a cotton dress and no shoes and I was fanning myself with a palm leaf when I looked up and saw a woman pulling dresses out of a basket and hanging them on a line between two big trees. I watched her hang the clothes, first the dresses, and then men's shirts and men's trousers, until the line was almost full. Every so often she would stop and mop her forehead—it was so hot even though the sun was going down. I thought, Why is she hanging clothes out now when the dew will catch them, and in the morning they will still be wet? And just then Mother Lize walked out, 'Look there, Granny,' I said. 'Down there,' and I pointed. 'Why is that woman hanging out clothes and the sun is going?'

" 'No one is hanging out clothes,' she said, and she slapped down my hand. 'You must not point,' she said.

" 'But Granny, look! The line is almost full. See where she's taking up her basket and walking across the road!'

" 'Nothing at all do I see there,' said my grandmother.

"The next day I was sitting out on the veranda and again the woman came. 'Look, Granny!' I said. 'She's back!' and my grandmother again slapped down my hand and said, 'No one is there, and it is not polite to point at ghosts.' Just then a woman from Cinnamon Bay came walking up with a basket of mangoes for Granny, and when Granny went inside to get her a glass of water, I said, 'Miss Ames, do you see that woman hanging up clothes on the line down there at the bottom of the yard?' and Miss Ames said, 'Oh, yes, she hangs out clothes there all the time. She's been dead for long years now. That is a ghost, you know.'

"I asked her why she hung out clothes.

" 'When you are a ghost, you do just what you did when you were alive,' Miss Ames said. 'The Bible tells us that when we die we are changed in body but not in spirit. Every day she hung out clothes on that line when she lived, and every day she does it now.'

" 'What, the same thing all over again?' I said.

" 'All your desires are the same,' said Miss Ames.

" 'It is a pretty poor thing, being a ghost, if you still go down to the river and scrub the clothes on stones, spread them to bleach on the rocks, wash them again and walk all this way to hang them on a line,' I said. Miss Ames said I was too young to understand.

" 'Who is she, hanging out her things?'

" 'That is Miss Blue's mother, who almost lost her life looking for the head of the river,' she said. 'See,' she said, looking toward the foot of the garden. 'Now she is gone, and the clothesline and the clothing with her.'

" 'Miss Ames,' I said, 'you must please tell me about Miss Blue's mother.'

" 'When you run your father's goats up into the pasture, come knock at my gate,' Miss Ames said, getting up. She drank the glass of water Granny gave her and walked through our gate, down the path, and back to the road."

"SO, MISS ANNA," Ivy asked me, "you are not asleep yet?"

"Who can sleep with such exciting stories?" I said. "A ghost comes back and hangs out laundry."

"But that is what she did in life!" Ivy said.

"She did more in life than hang out laundry," I said. "If you ask me, that is. It is a wonderful thing, on Green Island hanging out laundry?"

"Of course it is not a wonderful thing," Ivy said impatiently. "Washing clothes at the river, that was not wonderful, but it was very nice. Every woman with her head tied up in a kerchief, trying to keep her secrets, but they come out as she suds up her clothes with blue soap or brown soap, that was nice, and spreading them all soapy on the stones and seeing them start to bleach in the sun, that was very nice, but hanging the laundry up if the clothes were still wet, that was hard work."

"So she was being punished, that ghost," I said.

"Janga Mumah, that's what her daughter, Miss Blue, called her when we were children," Ivy said dreamily. She was growing sleepy. "Janga Mumah because she so loved shrimp. She almost drowned herself because she so loved shrimp. Janga, shrimp."

"I loved shrimp, back in the old days, before my stomach developed thoughts of its own," I said. "But no one cared. They didn't care what I ate. They didn't care what I thought. If I was tired, what was that to them? On the screen, I looked so sad, so beautiful. If they could make me move so the shadows fell the way they wanted them on the screen, well, that's what they cared about. Did they know I had a body? I didn't have a body. Back then, I was a ghost. Oh, it is exhausting, thinking about those times."

"No one ever starved to death on Green Island," Ivy said, speaking as if she didn't hear me. "Wherever you went, there was food.

"But janga, they didn't grow on trees. You had to get them from Snake River, out where it widened in back of Cinnamon Bay, going toward Mare River. And some nights in the summer, it was so hot, hot, hot the people would make up a party to catch janga, you know, after the work was done, and then they'd come back and cook up the janga on a charcoal fire and eat them until they could eat no more.

"They'd make torches out of bottles with a few inches of kerosene in the bottom and their wicks made of newspaper twisted tight, tight, tight, and they'd set off, along the banks of Snake River. And they would go along, hitting the rocks and turning over the rocks, until they had their pails full, keeping to the bank, going upriver where the janga were bigger and sweeter, or so the old-time people said, sweeter and bigger the further you went, sweetest and biggest at the head of the river, but no one ever got to the head of the river, not that anyone knew.

"I wasn't born yet, but still I can see it, the inky sky, the stars like rock salt, the people going along the black bank, their gold torches bobbing in the darkness, the black palms stirring, the birds calling, the big moon on the water, the waves breaking the moon up, like glass, then putting it back together again. How can I see it so clear if I wasn't born yet? I see it clearer than I see nights of my own life."

"Probably it was a movie," I said. "Probably you saw it in a movie. Once, we made a movie on a tropical island. I think it was Green Island." Ivy didn't hear me.

"So one night, when they had their pails full, they began to start back. Someone called out to Miss Blue's mother. 'Ida! Time to go back! You are too greedy! We are going back.'

" 'Just a little farther,' Miss Ida said. 'Wilfred! You will come with me?' And Wilfred said he would. But sooner or later, Wilfred had a big pail full of big, big janga and he turned back, and he called out, 'Ida! I'm going back! Let's go!' He thought she was behind him and so he turned around.

"But Miss Ida saw the river was getting wider, and her pail was not full because she held up each shrimp and looked at it, and if it was not fat enough, she threw it back, and now the shrimp she grabbed up were bigger and bigger, big, big, big.

"Wilfred didn't look behind him because he thought Miss Ida was following him out, and every now and then, he'd say something to her. 'These will be good to eat, don't it?' 'We should do this tomorrow and the next night until we faint from janga,' and when she didn't answer, he thought she was watching her footing. When you get tired, then it seems that the stones of the river are treacherous and the water is deep. So when he came to the bank and saw the torches of the other people, he turned around to give Miss Ida a hand and she was not there!

" 'Oh, she will be here in a minute,' everyone said. 'Don't fuss so.' They were eager to eat their shrimp. So they sat on the riverbank and shelled their shrimp and started to put them on sticks and hold them over the charcoal fires. Every now and then someone would say, 'That Ida, she is so fool for janga,' and when they had all eaten themselves full, someone looked up and said, 'Wilfred! She is not here yet?' and Wilfred, he said, 'What?' and someone, he said, 'No. She is not here.' So then at last they realized she was lost and they must look for her.

"They filled up their torch-bottles with kerosene and made more wicks and went up the river looking for her, and they came to the place far, far, far, where the river branches, and they looked at each other. She went which way? No one knew. So half went up one branch and half went up the other.

"And they didn't find her, so they went on. And someone said there were tigers at the head of the river and everyone stopped and held their torches and looked, but then they started again. 'She is so fool for shrimp, we should have tied she with a rope,' one of them said. And then they heard the sound of someone crying, and there was Miss Ida, sitting on a rock at the side of the river, sobbing and sobbing. And they brought her back down, and when she got back, oh she was cold, cold, cold, she said, 'I saw the head of the river,' and everyone's mouth was nailed shut with coffin nails. 'The water is broad and white and there is a waterfall,' she said, and someone pried open his mouth to ask what else she saw there: were there tigers? But she wouldn't say anything else. And after that, they called her Janga Mu-mah. If she got in an argument, she didn't have to take off her shoe to beat you. All she did do was say, 'I saw the head of the river.' Once when she was so sick everyone thought she was dying, Wilfred leaned over her, and he said, 'What you saw there at the head of the river?' But all she did was smile and not answer him.

"Other people went up the river, looking for the head of the river, but they would go to the right or the left, down this branch or that, and they never found it. She did find it, I believe she found it."

"At the head of the river, she found kings and queens," I said, "and so she was punished. Something she found there she shouldn't have found, or something she lost there she shouldn't have lost. Otherwise, isn't it so, when she was a ghost, she would have gone back to the head of the river? But what did she do? She came every night and hung out clothes on a clothesline."

"She was married to Wilfred and had many fine children," Ivy said. "Two fine boys and three fine girls. Her granddaughter, Elaine, she drowned looking for the Sunken City, but that was Miss Blue's fault, always filling our heads with the people who walked there under the waves, ladies and gentleman in fine clothes, and when your boat sailed over and they looked up and saw you, their words floated up to the surface in bubbles and burst and when they did, you could hear what the deep-water people were saying. And you, Miss Asta, you are ready for your bed now? I think you are ready."

She seemed so tired as she came over to me, as if she herself had been upriver, and when she came to my chair, she clasped her hands together and held them out, and I grabbed on to them and she pulled me up. "Settle yourself," she said and nodded while my joints adjusted themselves. "Why must you sit like that!" she said, and I said, "Ivy, don't fuss."

"You will sleep tonight," she said.

"Oh, I am still awake," I said. "You must tell me how you came to this country."

"Lady Clare," she said, "I am going to sleep." *Lady Clare.* What she called her daughter when she would have the last word.

"Lady Clare is going to sleep," I said. And I knew I would.

The woman stands in a doorway looking into a room. There is no light in the room, but the moon is full. In there, everything looks like an undeveloped negative. The big, square bed is crudely made, a huge sheet of plywood on top of cinder blocks, a mattress on top of the plywood. The whole family—mother, father, sisters, brothers—sleep in that bed. In that bed it is like a great soup.

The woman watches the figures in the bed. They stir, they float. A girl raises her arm. It floats away from her, it becomes someone else's arm. Above the bed, on the bed, arms and legs are floating, heads are floating, attaching themselves to one body, then another. There is no such thing as male or female on that bed. Who is who?

On the bed, someone rises up, looks blindly around. Oh, the woman says, standing and watching, he is drunk. He doesn't know what he's doing. Probably he thinks he is dreaming. He sees a floating breast and grasps it. He sees another and grasps that too. He turns over and lies on the body next to him. His grunts and groans fill the room. Everyone else in the bed sleeps or seems to sleep. Thank you, Mother, he whispers and rolls away and into his own place on the bed. Next to him his daughter lies still, for an instant staring at the ceiling, then rolls on her side. Her father is lying on his bed, naked. She inspects his body, his moon-colored sex. Then she turns on her side, turns toward him. Around her float bluish arms and legs, breasts and profiles, bellies and buttocks. Sometimes she has her body to herself, sometimes she does not; sometimes she is a female, sometimes she is not. She looks at the window. She imagines she is wearing a crown on her head. She reaches up to touch it. It is sore between her legs, but in the morning, it will feel better.

The woman in the doorway watches them on the big, square bed and says aloud, That is not how it was. *Nevertheless she covers her eyes with the back of her hand.*

11

THIS IS HOW I met Max. This is how it all started.

My father died when I was fifteen. We knew he would. He had the white plague and the doctors could do nothing for him and we had no money, so if there were doctors who could do something for him, as some of the people to whom he brought packages said there were, we could not afford to find them. I would take him to the clinic and the doctor would say, He must have rest and fresh air, and I would become angry and say, All day long he walks the street, delivering packages! How much more air can he get? And they would say, Well, then, rest. But how could he rest? If he did not work, we had no money. In the end, he was too weak to work and he sat in the kitchen whittling wooden animals while my mother scrubbed the floor, cooked or ironed. Sometimes she did embroidery for a large department store and then she would stay up into the small hours until she grew so tired she began to prick her fingers and stain the thread and cloth she worked on.

My sister Marianne went to work in a bakery. My brother Lars shovelled coal onto a cart and developed a cough of his own.

Long ago, I had understood that the kings and queens I saw in the snow were actors and actresses and at night I would go to the stage door of the Lagerloff Theater with Marianne or one of my friends from the building and wait for them to come out. I loved to listen to them talk, I loved to see them as they left, sometimes still wearing their make-up, and often, when we were lucky, actors from other shows would rush up to the stage door, still in costume and make-up from their own dramas, eager to see the last act of the play at the Lagerloff. Once I saw Erik Grissom, his face painted dead white, his eyes outlined in black, his lips red with lipstick. He smiled at me. Marianne pushed me forward, but I could not speak. I wanted to be one of them, to forget that at night we all slept in one bed, a bed that shook with coughing, to become, at least in the evenings, a princess, a queen, a woman to whom things happened. I obtained the application forms to the Dramatic Academy and filled them out. Now I shamelessly pestered the actors and actresses when they came through the stage door: who was the best acting coach for someone like me, someone who would give anything to be accepted into the Academy, and finally, I had narrowed my list down to two names. I went to see both of them, both women, both retired actresses and as I was sitting on the bench at the kitchen table daydreaming about which one I would choose, my father walked in the door. It was the middle of the day. I knew he would not work again; I knew there was no money in the house, not even for the poor medications my father needed. I began looking for a job. I tried to forget the names of the acting coaches: Erastoff, Hulson. I was the youngest child. My mother had had special hopes for me.

The night before I was to go with Marianne to look for a job as a shop girl, my mother began to cry and nothing could console her. I picked up the carved wooden giraffes my father made for me and made them dance but this time she didn't laugh. She threw them across the room. "Go ahead, earn your money!" she shouted at me. "But don't bring it home! I don't want it!"

"She doesn't know what she's saying," Marianne whispered to me.

"Don't bring it home," she said, over and over again, all night.

My father, who was sitting on the bench, resting his arms on the table, and his head on his arms, looked at me trying to comfort my mother. "Go to bed," he said. "This is how dreams die. A person dies easier."

"I had to marry a handsome man!" she screamed in rage. She was gripping the edge of the table, as if, were she to let go, she would spring on him and kill him. My father closed his eyes, his head still on his arms, and appeared to have fallen asleep.

I thought then that my mother had begun to hate my father. She would be stirring something on the stove, look up and see him whittling, and say, "Can't you do something else? I'm sick of these splinters all over the floor. Always I'm using the needle to get splinters out of my fingers. We eat food with wood in it. No one can walk on a floor with bare feet." He would ignore her and continue his whittling, and then she would turn on him. "You stupid man! Look at Anna! She is too old for wooden toys! You want to make something, make a coffin! How are we going to afford to bury you? Maybe I won't bury you, you know! Maybe I'll put you out with the trash!" Then she would burst into tears and my father would put down his knife, sweep aside his woodwork, get up and put his arms around my mother's waist, and they would stand there. She would have her back to him, stirring the stew pot, and he would embrace her from behind, his head against her broad shoulder. "Sit down and rest," she would say at last. Her voice was rough.

Of course she was afraid. I know that now. But then she was filled with pity and anger, and because she could not express the first, because there was nothing she could do, she expressed the second. And probably her anger was easier for him to bear than the sorrow he saw in our eyes, and the fear that dilated our pupils and made us stare, so that, whenever he looked up from his carving, our eyes were on him.

A man and a woman lived on an island. It is always good to live on an island if you are happy, and they were very happy. They had a child. Then a woman from the city came between them. The man agreed to murder his wife. He would overturn the boat and she would drown and he would come back to the island and marry the other woman, but when it came time to kill his wife, he could not do it. As he stood over her, he saw her face as if he had never seen it before, and suddenly he was in love with her all over again. Because she had almost died, his love for her was revealed to him, yet he was the one who had tried to kill her!

Later, they went to the city together, and she ran away from him, but then she saw he loved her once more, and they took wedding pictures, as if they had just that moment been married. In an amusement hall, they danced a peasant dance while people watched and clapped. The husband caught a runaway pig. On the way back to their island, a storm came up and their boat was overturned. The husband thought his wife had drowned, and in his grief, he tried to kill the woman from the city. They found the wife, half drowned, and she lay in their bed like one who was dead, but she rose up. She rose up because he had tried to kill her.

When I saw that movie I thought, I must not marry. I thought, hollow reeds float. I must remember hollow reeds float. Someday I will be out in a boat and it will overturn and it will be important to know that. The man's wife was saved because he tied a bundle of hollow reeds to her. I didn't understand that love can turn to anger and then back into love. There was so much I didn't understand. There is so much, even now, I don't understand. People have said I was bad, selfish, and I was both those things, but in my defense, I hold up my hand and say, Look at me, how old I am. How old I am and I am still trying to find out.

Marianne worked at a very fancy bakery near the biggest department store in Stockholm, and one day she came home and said that the confectioner's next door wanted a salesgirl who could run a cash register and clean the shop when there were no customers and tomorrow I must dress my best, brush my hair away from my face, wash my hands and file my nails, and come with her to see Mrs. Berger.

Mrs. Berger hired me the same day and that same day she taught me how to powder the glazed fruits, and not my clothes, with confectioners' sugar. She would stop my hand from going to my hair when it was covered with sugar. She taught me how to fill the fancy, velvet-covered boxes with colored tissue so that the boxes seemed stuffed with their few pieces of fruit, and she said I must smile at the men who came in for a quarter of a pound of glazed figs as if I were in love with them. That way, she said, when I gave them their change, they might tell me to keep it. "I started out as a shop girl," she said, "and my smile bought me this shop."

One day a tall, very distinguished-looking gentleman came in and asked for four pounds of glazed dates. "I will take care of the gentleman," said Mrs. Berger, who was grinning from ear to ear, and she began heaping the dates onto the big brass scale. While she fussed with the dates, I studied the gentleman. He wore a black coat of a sleek fur I had never seen before and an astrakhan hat. He wore soft, fine beige leather gloves, the backs stitched with dark brown thread, tiny, tiny stitches that formed a many-pointed star. In his hand he carried a riding crop. His mouth was very wide, and his lips narrow. He held his head so that his chin was elevated, as if he were trying to see something in the far distance, as if whatever was in front of him was not worth noticing. He was, I guessed, almost as old as my father.

"Why not let the girl pack them?" he said. "She has such long, white hands."

The smile fell from Mrs. Berger's face like a dish from a shelf. She handed me a huge white box, its rim banded in gold and told me to pack the dates for the gentleman and to take care not to drop them.

I had arranged the first two dates in the center when I realized I had not yet put in the tissue paper, so I removed the dates and one of them dropped to the floor. "Never mind," the gentleman said. "Wrap that one specially. I'll eat it later." Mrs. Berger passed in back of me. "Smile at him," she whispered to me, but I could not. My face was frozen.

I began again: two dates in the center, then a circle of dates around the two in the center, radiating out toward the rim of the box, then another layer, then another, until eventually, the box was full. "Very good," he said. Two other customers had come in and were waiting behind him. "You don't mind if I confer a bit with the girl?" he said to Mrs. Berger. "I need so many things." Now she smiled a real smile. This was a good customer.

"Tell me," he said, "if you were picking something for your father, what would you select? Here there are so many things. I am helpless," he said. He threw up his hands.

"I have no father," I said idiotically. I was horrified to hear myself say it. In back of me, I heard Mrs. Berger snorting. Now his eyes were on me. I knew now what people meant when they spoke of men with burning eyes.

"Well," he said. "No father. Nor do I have a father." He seemed to stop and consider. "But I have an actor who must be pacified. Perhaps you have heard of him? Erik Grissom? He is starting a whole new vogue in European cinema. He will not learn his lines. And why? Because he does not like to learn them. But he does not say so. Instead he says that learning the lines first is a sterile exercise, a monkey's trick, and he will only learn them as he understands their meaning. Really, he is very funny, but he is very lazy, and the whole company is catching his laziness. So, as expected, I shouted at him, all kinds of ridicule, and today he is home with a cold and cannot come in."

"He is ill?" I said. My voice quavered, my hands shook, and my eye began to twitch.

"He is fine! This is how actors punish directors who shout! This is a game we all understand! No, two pounds of glazed fruit and he will be cured and he will know his lines in the morning. What kind of fruit do you suggest for him? Picture him at home, reclining on his green chaise longue, sighing and sneezing into a perfectly clean handkerchief. He is a good actor, you know. The doctor would take him for a dying man, but I see the gleam in his eye. What kind of fruit do you suggest and I will take it."

My lips were glued shut. My tongue was stuck to the roof of my mouth.

"If you cannot choose, I will have to bring you to his house with a little tray, like a waitress in a nightclub, and he will select himself. Your employer won't mind?"

"Her employer will mind very much," said Mrs. Berger, and suddenly, I was smiling. This gentleman had come in for some glazed fruits and from this he had created a drama. Everyone in the shop was listening and smiling.

"So," he said, and leaned toward me as if he were studying my face. "So. Well, go on."

"Pineapple," I said, "is the most expensive, but if he is really so badly behaved, give him pineapple rings with glazed cherries in the center." He was nodding, smiling at me. Emboldened, I went on. "Children like them best, you see. When aunts and uncles come in to buy something for children, I always show them pineapple rings with cherries in the centers."

"Three pounds of pineapple rings with cherries in the center," he said. "Is there a special box for children?" Mrs. Berger picked up a box with a great gold clown embossed on the lid. "In *that* box," he said. "The girl will wrap it," he said to Mrs. Berger.

"Tell me, madam," he said to her, "this girl is your daughter? Oh, she is not? Do you know," he continued, as if I were not there, "has she any ambition to act? I have been looking all over for a certain face and she has it. I would like to borrow it for a little while."

Mrs. Berger said that if she had a krona for every man who came into her shop and saw the face he wanted stuck to her salesgirl, she would be a rich woman. The gentleman laughed and said, "But you *are* a rich woman, to work every day with someone who has a face like that. Here," he said, and took a small silver case from his vest pocket, and from it he took a cream-colored card. He gave it to Mrs. Berger, and then he took another and put it on the counter for me. I was still arranging pineapple rings. *Max Lilly, Director,* said the card. *Lagerloff Studios.*

"You are Max Lilly?" Mrs. Berger asked. He bowed slightly. "And you are really taking that fruit to Erik Grissom?" He bowed again. "Who can forget him as the murderer fleeing across the ice!" she said. "And such eyes! Who can forget his eyes?"

"They pop," Max said. "Like a frog's. A metabolic disorder, but very handy for the camera. How it affects his disposition, that's another thing. And as you probably overheard, he has no discipline whatever."

"When the women carried the girl's body back over the ice, I cried until my sides hurt," Mrs. Berger said.

"Yes, well," said Max, "that was what we wanted." He sounded, now, bored.

"This girl," Mrs. Berger said. "What do you want with her?"

"I want to borrow her for a few shots. She must get up from a sofa and go crazy, implore the gods in heaven, throw herself on the floor, a few things like that. But she is so busy here, and she likes her work so—"

"You will borrow her," said Mrs. Berger. "And when she comes back, she will bring back a picture of Erik Grissom? Signed, of course."

"Signed, pop eyes and all," said Max.

"When do you want to borrow her?" asked Mrs. Berger.

"Tomorrow morning at six and for the rest of the week," Max said. "But no one has asked her. Do you want to be borrowed, Miss . . . ?"

"Asta," I said.

"And your last name?" he asked.

"That *is* my last name," I said.

"And your first?" he inquired patiently. Mrs. Berger looked at me as if I were an idiot.

"Anna," I said.

"Anna Asta," he said. "It might be all right."

When he left, I threw my arms around Mrs. Berger and she threw her arms around me. But we had not been careful about the confectioners' sugar and on the backs of both our dresses were the white, dusty prints of two palms, and all day, we swatted at one another as we went from counter to cash register, and then I thought, What if he didn't pay me? What if I had no money to bring home at the end of the week?

"Go the first day," Mrs. Berger said, "and then see. Besides, he gave you the change. How much was it?"

I fished in my pocket and pulled out four bills. Two hundred kronor. "It will be all right," Mrs. Berger said.

And it was. Just like that. As in a fairy tale. My mother said, "If you want to do it, you must try."

Of course there were problems. When I came into Lagerloff Studios no one paid any attention to me. When Max finally saw me in my costume, an Empire dress, my hair piled in curls on top of my head, he said, "Good. Now go crazy. Implore the gods, pull down the heavens, then throw yourself on the floor." But go crazy just like that? I was so happy and excited, what was I supposed to implore the gods about? I started to laugh and couldn't stop. Here I was, just a day from the confectioner's shop, and I was supposed to go crazy all at once, for no reason. Max was furious and stalked off the set.

Erik Grissom came over to me and said, "Look, little girl, this is how you go crazy," and he threw both arms into the air. His face contorted with pain, his whole body writhed, he shouted, I could have sworn he was shouting, "Pineapple with cherries! Pineapple with cherries!" and then he threw himself to the floor as if he had no bones he cared about. "So," he said, getting up and dusting himself off, "do that."

But now I was hysterical with laughter, and watching me, Erik began to laugh too. And then Max was back. "Both of you, go home!" he thundered. "You can't act. Go home. Tomorrow I have two new faces. Today we'll do the scene in the farmhouse. Go home!" I began to cry and beg, No, No, don't send me home, but Max turned his back and began calling, "The scene in the farmhouse, the flats are in place? Bring the furniture. Go home," he said, turning to me. And I began pleading. "Aha," Max said. "*Now* implore the heavens!" So I did what he wanted and he was very well pleased.

Later, when I went to the Dramatic Academy, Max still "borrowed" me for his films, and although he always said all he wanted was my face, somehow my part was always large. And yet I could not act! I heard him one day saying to Anders, who wanted to borrow me, "Of course she is beautiful and when you see her through a lens, you don't recognize her, she isn't even human. But you tell her, Look sad, and her face sags and she stares. She can't act." Anders objected. "That scene," Anders said, "where she looks at Erik with such longing!"

"You know how I did that?" Max asked him. "You know how she loves sweets? I saw it was hopeless. I got in my car and I went to a store and bought a fishing rod. I don't have one, I hate fishing. For three weeks, I had her on a diet, vegetables, a little piece of chicken. I hung chocolate truffles on the fish hook and I dangled them in front of her, right in front of her nose, just out of range of the camera. You never saw such longing! That's how I did it! She can't act. You want to spend your life with fishing rods and melting candy?"

"She's better than she was," Anders said.

"They say the same about the dead," Max said.

I remember those chocolate truffles. I don't remember why I was supposed to look at Erik with longing. And Erik was no help. He always knew where the camera was, and if he knew Max wanted a close-up of me and the camera wasn't on him, he made the funniest faces. So I would laugh and Max would explode. But eventually I must have learned something.

Last night, I dreamed about Max. Usually my dreams are like me, suspicious. They take care to put on sunglasses and big hats, so I never know what they are about, but in this dream we were having an ordinary conversation, just as if we were in my parlor. "This morning," I told him, "I got a letter from some crazy person wanting to know about Walter Drake. Walter Drake! Is there a person on earth other than me who remembers Walter Drake? He was famous on the stage before I was born, but when I came to this country, no one knew who he was. But now you see what happens? People watch my movies, and they are so tired of me, they start to look around at the rest of the scenery. Just like the Statue of Liberty! Who lives in New York and pays attention to the Statue of Liberty? You have to come from a faraway place to look at it, Paris or Chicago, then you pay attention to it. Otherwise, what do you know about it? It's standing there in the water. You've seen it, enough. So it is with me. They've seen me, enough. They look around. And who do they see? Walter Drake. How can they not see him? He was in all my movies, an old man, always with an unfaithful wife, yours truly.

"Last week someone writes. He wants to know about Dorothy Abbot! And I had to stop and think: Dorothy Abbot, who was she? Oh, the one who was always so tired. If she had to sit in a chair and sleep and the camera was going, she was tired. Finally, someone worse than me. But Dorothy Abbot! Imagine wanting to know about Dorothy Abbot! So when I get a letter like that, I know: now I am the Statue of Liberty. Everyone knows my face and that's enough for them. No one's really interested. Dorothy Abbot, Walter Drake!"

"But always," Max said, "you had to have Walter Drake. Why was that? He wasn't an actor. A nice man, yes, but stiff as cardboard in a shirt from the laundry. The only man to collect a pension from the studio."

Before my eyes, Max turned into Walter Drake. They had the same face. "If you don't mind, Mr. Drake," I said, "I was talking to Max."

"You are complaining?" Walter Drake asked in Max's voice. And that was the end of that.

So that is how it all started, a fairy tale absolutely. When I was not working with Max, I was at the Academy, but gradually the Academy began to seem less useful to me. Whatever I learned there during the day, Max would undo.

Because we were students, we were given cheap tickets to all the plays, and sometimes the tickets were free, and in the evenings, when we finished work, we would sit together in a café and talk about this and that, mostly gossip that floated around the Academy halls, but it had begun to seem to me that people looked to me for rumors, for tips about directors who were going into production. After all, I was in Max's film and there was so much talk about it, how expensive it was, how it once again would make his name, this time as an international figure, and I didn't like it. I wanted to belong. I wanted to sit back and laugh and listen. That was my nature. "Oh," someone said one day, "when the camera is not turning, it is not worth her while to live!" How often I was to hear that from then on. And you know, when a thing is true, you are not so happy to hear it.

A tall, dark-haired girl, Helga, and I became good friends. Like me, she was poor, and when we had no classes, she would come to my house and throw stones at the window and I would come down and we would go to the basement apartments of women who sold expensive clothing that had been worn before, but nothing was damaged, there was no sign of wear, and so you did not know.

Max would see me coming onto the set in the morning, in my brown wool coat with the worn elbows, and a scarf tied under my chin, and he would say, "All right, here you can come in flat on your feet as if you were delivering groceries, but an actress must walk in as if she owns the world. And of course there are days when you feel like you don't own it. I know. So then you must have something to wear that says, 'The person inside this thing, she owns the world.' If I walked in like you, what would they give me to make a picture? Ten kronor and a cup of coffee!" I said I had no money, and also, how did I know where to find such a thing to wear, but Max said all women knew such things, and an *actress*, of course *she* would know.

So there we were, that morning, walking twenty-five blocks to save trolley fare, under the gray skies promising snow, everything drained of its color, like a hand-tinted photograph, the colors so mild you had to look twice—was it black and white, or was there color in it? And we came into the basement apartment laughing, and we took off our coats, and for once it was warm in one of those places, the woman must have had a good sale that week, and we got silly and the woman fell in with us and she began to bring out her most dramatic things, gowns with sequins, with bodices that barely existed, little strips of crepe de chine, held together by a rhinestone chain, or backless gowns with rhinestone wings rising from their shoulders, and we posed in front of her triple mirror flecked with little black tarnish scratches, laughing until we had to hold our sides and lean against the wall. And then I put on a gray gown, plain but cut low, a long-sleeved gown that swept the floor and I moved this way and that, one hand on my hip, tilting my head to one side, and suddenly I noticed it was quiet and Helga was staring at me, the woman was staring at me. "So," said Helga. "Now we know why Mr. Lilly picked you."

"That's it," said the woman, one hand raised, covering half of her mouth. "A changeling. Every so often, they come along."

I was embarrassed, but I was also staring. Who was that, looking back at me from the mirror?

"Ah," said the woman, "this is the beginning of the seduction. When they fall for themselves. When the way their hair looks is more important than if the country goes to war."

"I need something to wear," I said, "something that can cover up my bad clothes when I go to the theater."

"Take that," said the woman.

"No," I said, "this is no good. I have nothing to wear over it."

"So," said the woman, as if to herself, "she has not gone completely crazy. She holds on to her money. Learn from that, Helga," she said.

She went into another room and came back with a black velvet cape, long and lined in aqua silk. Its collar was wired and stood up high, framing the face with its black wings. The collar was studded with rhinestones, but the cape itself was absolutely simple and plain. "Put this on," she said. Now there was something brutal in her face and her voice. I put on the cape. In the same hard voice, she said, "There is also a hood." I put the hood up and looked in the mirror.

"How much?" I said.

"How much?" said the woman. "How much do you have?"

"Fifty kronor," I said.

"Fifty kronor!" said the woman. She shook her head and smiled to herself, as if I had insulted her dreadfully. "Then fifty kronor is what it costs." Still wearing the cape, I took the fifty kronor from my purse and handed it to her. I felt I was moving slowly, as if drugged. "Someday you will come back here and buy something expensive," she said and she laughed strangely.

I looked at Helga, who was staring at me like a sleeper having a bad dream and trying to wake up. As if to clear it, she shook her head slightly. "Whose cape was it?" she asked the woman.

"What does that matter now?" the woman asked her.

"Well, you know I like to ask," Helga said. She sounded piteous, as if she were pleading.

"She is dead, the woman who wore this," the woman answered her. "Dead and gone and she won't come back for it." Then her mood changed. "Wear it well," she said. "The dying are funny, are they not? When my daughter was dying, she called me to her house. We hadn't talked in ten years. She said, 'Take my new red dress. Give it a good time.' I took it and wore it and I gave it a good time.

"So," she said to Helga, "what can we do for you?"

"Oh," Helga said, "I don't want anything."

"Though the eagle flies, still the mouse must live," said the woman. "Try something on."

After that, it was not the same between Helga and me. She would say, in a bitter voice, that I had been to her apartment, I had seen how her family lived, but I would not let her in my house. Or: Where are you going now? To the studio? This was hatred and I knew it. It made me bitter. So I began to turn away from people my age and although it seemed I was one of them, I was not.

I am the oldest daughter of a very poor man. All night I wait on line at the butcher's. Finally, I lose my job and a terrible woman takes me into a house of pleasure where I can earn money to feed my family. The first time I go there, I am dressed up in a white evening dress that exposes my breasts. Someone I love sees me there and shouts insults at me. Even though I have done nothing, I am ashamed and try covering myself with my hands. Soon, all is explained and I leave the house of pleasure and live virtuously ever after. Not happily, but virtuously, which the film gives me to understand is better.

Max and I are again sitting in a pastry shop. There are times I dread these expeditions, these conversations. Always I must be wonderfully dressed because people will notice me. They are already on the lookout because they know I am featured in Max's new film. All this attention, the knowing stares of waiters, the murmur that greets us when we walk in and people begin to recognize Max, and at this moment I like it. I like it there in front of the camera, taking the first step out of myself, out of my body, into someone else, for an instant, in danger, suspended in air, a long drop down, while everyone watches over me as if I were very ill. The director watches, the cameraman watches, the man who does the lighting watches, the make-up woman, the costumer, everyone's eyes are on me. There is such drama in this! As if everyone were watching to see the instant my breath left my body.

But these conversations with Max, I am coming to dread them. Now he is saying, "Every role you play casts a shadow. Well, it follows, doesn't it? You become the role, the role becomes part of you. So you must choose your parts carefully. In America, they talk of the dangers of typecasting, but there it is always about money. The danger is playing a role so long it grows bigger and bigger and what you were in the beginning is not big enough to fight it down. Come, *Dr. Jekyll and Mr. Hyde* is playing around the corner. We'll go see it. All these stories that seem the most fantastical, they are the most true. When a story is told again and again, then it is more than true. Then it is universal."

He says all this leaning forward, talking to me as if his words were nails he would hammer into my skin. I want to say, Stop, Stop, what is the hurry? You have years to tell me these things! And then I know: he doesn't think he has very long. He is always planning ahead, but he doesn't think he will have time and so he is trying to teach me everything and *I am not worthy. I am not strong enough.* I want to get up from the table and run away. I want to be back in Mrs. Berger's confectionery, selling candied fruits and trying to smile at the customers. I ask if we can see the movie tomorrow. This afternoon I have something to do. He looks at me. Something to do? With a young man, someone my own age? And yet he is not interested in touching me in that way. Oh, all right, he says. Tomorrow. If you have something to do.

He offers to drop me where I am going, but as he knows I will, I say, No, I want to walk. I walk and walk in my black cape, in the middle of the day, the heavy clouds threatening snow. People on the sidewalk stop and stare as I pass. They are dressed for work, in plain, warm coats and sensible hats and gloves. They wear thick, clumsy boots and carry packages or leather portfolios. What an apparition I must be, walking in this thin black cape, in this gray wind, under gray skies, in my thin black shoes.

I come to the confectioner's shop. "Mrs. Berger!" I call out.

"Yes, madame," she says, coming toward me. Oh, this is not the smile she turns on the well-dressed gentleman. She has an obsequious grin reserved for wealthy ladies. I stand still, waiting for her to recognize me. "Oh, it is you!" she says, clasping her hands over her breast. "It is you?" she asks uncertainly.

"Oh, yes, it is me," I say. She smiles at me, a large, happy smile. I know what she thinks: I told her to smile at the wealthy men who came in here, and look where she has gotten, listening to me! But I could not smile at Max when he came in. Already she is rewriting my story. "Mrs. Berger, I forgot your signed picture of Erik Grissom, but tomorrow he is going to play a trick on Mr. Lilly. If you can come to the studio, tell them you are my friend. They will bring you to the set."

"When can I come?" she asks. She is breathless. She looks at me as if I were a saint who had appeared out of a cloud of flour.

"Come at seven-thirty and you will see the trick," I say. She cannot stop thanking me. "Is it true, what they say about Mr. Lilly's terrible temper?" she asks me. Already I have become protective, some say secretive, but to me these are the same things. "He is a great director," I tell her, and I am out the door, walking toward home. At this time, I still want to bring the strands of my life together into one rope.

"Anna!" says my mother when I come in. "Are you out of your mind? You want to cough like your father?" And she takes my cape from my shoulders, oh, with such reverence it breaks my heart even now, and she hangs it up, and then she sits me down in front of the wood stove. She lifts up my legs and places them on the ledge of the stove. She hands me a hot cup of tea. She rubs my cold hands in her warm ones. More than ever she looks like a person formed from cookie dough. She takes her woolen shawl from her shoulders and puts it around mine. "So," she says, as she continues chopping vegetables for the night's stew, "tell me what you did today," and I tell her we went to the café, I went to Mrs. Berger's and asked her to come to the set, and everything I say pleases her. Everything I say fascinates her. I bring word from a world she never knew existed, one she still doesn't believe exists. I notice I am watching her as if she were in a film, as if I were far away in time and distance, as if, now, this was the only way I could see her, on a screen, a shadow flickering on a wall. I start to cry, and she says, "Oh, Anna, you are exhausted," and she puts me to bed.

12

IN THE MORNING, she hears them arguing, her father and the woman they say she is to call Mother. But she does not call her Mother. When she lived with her own mother, everyone called her Mer, although her given name was Marie. "Call her Mamma Bea, now?" says her father, but she cannot do it.

"You should hit that child, you know," says Bea, her stepmother. Bea is hugging Jack to her, Ivy's stepbrother, who, although he is younger than she is, took possession of their house first. Still, she is the oldest child, her father's first child, because he was with her mother, Mer, before he was with this woman. Young as she is she knows this and knows it is important.

She says, *Yes, ma'am* and *Thank you, ma'am* when Bea gives her something or does something for her. *You must always answer Yes, ma'am, or Yes, sir, or Yes, Daddy*, says her father. *Never just yes or no. Manners will take you through the world.*

One thing her stepmother does is comb her hair, which is very long, very straight, and very very thick. When her stepmother combs her hair, it is early in the morning and cool. The chill, lightly moist air feels like the color of the sky, blue, cold and remote, as if the day had not yet settled down on the earth, so that everything around them seems to be floating still. The roosters are clucking and crowing. They can hear the invisible ducks trying their wings down by the river. In the morning, the trees are not green but golden in the rising sun. Across the river, a thin gauzy mist is slowly rising, thinning out as it goes. For a while, the sun is behind it and it is blinding. Soon it will be gone and from the valleys will come thick puffs of fog, breathed out, says Miss Blue, the giants who sleep there at night. During the day, says Miss Blue, the giants take the shape of trees. "You must always be careful when you climb a tree," she tells Ivy, "whether a coconut or a rose apple. You must apologize to the tree and say, 'I am sorry, tree, if my feet are hurting you.' Out of pity for the tree, you must never wear shoes when you climb. If you feel a branch giving way beneath you, you must say, 'Tree, bear up. Many a time has my father cut down a green tree and left an old tree standing,' and if you say so, the tree will not let you fall."

In back of Miss Blue's yard is an orchard of rose apple trees whose branches weave together, so that Ivy can climb into one tree, and from that tree to another, from one white blossoming tree to another, escorted by bees that do not sting. Miss Blue has told her they will not sting. They hum to her as she climbs.

She pays attention to whatever Miss Blue says. She treasures whatever she tells her. Miss Blue knows her mother, Mer, and sees her when she goes to Cinnamon Bay. Ivy imagines that Miss Blue's voice is really her mother's voice, that Miss Blue says to her what her mother would say if her mother were nearby. When she visits Miss Blue, Miss Blue gazes at her, shakes her head and says, Ivy, you are the picture of your mother. Ivy imagines that Miss Blue visits her mother and tells her that Ivy looks exactly like her. Sooner or later, her mother will become so curious she will have to come and see her. She imagines

Miss Blue and her mother, sitting on the veranda on hot Sunday afternoons, and her mother tells Miss Blue the things she would tell Ivy
if she and Ivy were together. These are the things Miss Blue tells her.
These are the things her mother wants her to know. "Tell her the
story about how to climb trees," Mer says, and when Miss Blue comes
back to Mare River, she speaks with her mother's voice.

She wishes she knew more about Miss Blue. She thinks about Jack
and her stepsister, Cynthia, and she cannot see them without seeing
her stepmother in back of them. She looks at her stepbrother and
-sister and thinks that it is as if they are painted onto their mother.
But she is not painted onto anyone. If someone were to stand in back
of her, they would see a hollow black shape, its outline the same as
her own. She likes to pretend that Miss Blue is her mother (until Mer
can come for her) and that she is painted onto her. But days can pass
and she does not see Miss Blue and on those days she realizes how
little about Miss Blue she knows. And Miss Blue herself seems to come
from nowhere. Miss Blue is not painted onto anyone either. In back
of Miss Blue is the same hollow black shape.

Young as she is, she is aware of how children flicker, warm but
insubstantial, like flames against the solid walls of the world. So little
of their minds belongs to them. So much of what they say is not their
own but repetitions of what they have heard their parents say. They
are shadows their parents cast. Fathers cast their sons' shadows upon
the ground; mothers cast their daughters' shadows, but she has no
mother, and so she wavers and flickers more than most. She is like a
candle, always afraid of burning out. Whatever Miss Blue says she
gathers up like something precious because it is precious. Miss Blue
fills her in and fills her out. Miss Blue helps her cast a shadow upon
the ground. Miss Blue stands behind her and she pretends Miss Blue
is her mother. When Miss Blue tells her stories, she pretends those
are stories of her mother's life. Miss Blue notices how Ivy watches her
and calls the child, with some pride, her apprentice.

"Hold still," says her stepmother, who stands in back of her brushing out her hair. She separates Ivy's hair, strand by strand, trying to
undo the knots, and then she loses patience. She yanks the brush
through her hair and jerks Ivy backwards. Ivy tries not to shout out.
This process is repeated uncountable times. By the time Bea is finished
and Ivy's hair is combed and plaited, they have travelled from one end
of the veranda to the other. The veranda runs the length of the house
and then goes around the corner. Ivy's neck is sore and her voice is
hoarse from calling out to everyone who passes her yard. "Good morn-

ing, Miss Iron Front! Good morning, Teacher Masters! Good morning, Teacher Williams!" Long ago her brother Jack left for school, leaving her there.

When she comes home from school, her stepmother gives her a short broom made of twigs and tells her to sweep the porch, which, from one end to the other, is littered with strands of her hair. Her head throbs while she sweeps. Miss Blue says her head will be bald as a johncrow's, but every day there is as much hair to comb as there was the day before.

Her father and stepmother are still arguing about shoes. "I don't have money for a lampshade or drawers and she needs a pair of shoes?" says her stepmother. "Is this how it will be?"

What is she talking about? Ivy knows what a lampshade is, but drawers? Why does she need drawers? Her chests have all the drawers she needs.

Later, she hears the sound of sawing in back of the house and sees her father through the window. He has cut two shoe-shaped pieces of board and is drilling holes in them. Then he pulls rope through the holes. She understands that those will be her shoes.

She doesn't know when she began thinking of herself as a motherless child.

She lived in her father's yard for three years, and during that time, she rarely thought of her mother, Mer, her grandmother and her great-grandmother, sitting blind in the sun or on her bed, knowing where she was only by the feel of the heat on her skin or the sounds around her. Now she had her stepbrother Jack, and her stepsister Cynthia, and her stepmother Bea, who was always pregnant, and who had two more girls, so that when Ivy was not at school, she was kept busy by the babies.

A new grandmother, Mother Lize, appeared at the house, coming and going from Cinnamon Bay, and when Mother Lize was there, she combed Ivy's hair and placed herself between the child and her stepmother.

Then one night Ivy dreamed of her great-grandmother. Someone had put a goat in her house and its cry confused the blind old woman, who thought if a goat was crying and then butting her side, she must be outdoors. So she began to walk as if she were indeed in the yard, and when she came to the wall of her bedroom, she walked right through the wall as if it weren't there, and walked down the path in front of her house, that path that led so close to the sea anyone walking there was drenched by the spray of the waves crashing against the

sea wall, until she came to Vidal's yard. She knocked at the gate and
then held to it, turning her blind head from side to side.

A heat filled Ivy's chest. She got up from her bed and went to the
window. The brilliant moonlight filled the yard where earlier the men
had been playing dominoes by its light and where she and Jack had
used the bits of crockery they collected from every house they visited
to make a moonshine baby. She had lain on the ground and Jack took
the pieces of broken crockery and outlined her body and then she got
up carefully, trying not to disturb the outline.

"Take that up," said her stepmother, "or a ghost will come along
and lie down in that shape on the ground there."

She looked into the yard and there was her great-grandmother
leaning on the gate. Her great-grandmother walked through the gate
and lay down inside the moonshine baby. Then she sat up and beck-
oned to Ivy.

Ivy was sure her great-grandmother had died. But when? She
wanted to ask the ghost sitting inside the outline of the moonshine
baby who she was, really, and what had happened to make her a ghost,
but how did she know she was seeing a ghost of the loving dead?
Perhaps it was someone else, someone evil, who had taken the shape
of her great-grandmother. She went into father's room and lay down
on the floor on his side of the bed. Her stepmother rose up on her
arm. "What does your woman want now?" she asked, but her father
was asleep and did not hear her. "Let the child stay," said the voice of
the great-grandmother. She fell asleep listening to the wind rising,
stirring the fronds of the palm trees in the yard. She could tell from
the feel of the air on her skin that it was going to rain.

"Where are you going now?" calls her stepmother. Her father does
not answer, but gets on his bicycle and begins to pedal off. He changes
his mind and turns back and asks Ivy to come with him. Bea hears the
front door to the house bang shut. Where are they going? They are
going to Mr. Darlington's where Vidal intends to build a coffin.

They ride downhill, going fast, and for a while their dogs follow
them. Then the dogs tire, and when Ivy looks back, she sees them
pushing their way through the underbrush on the side of the road,
down to the river to get something to drink. At the bottom of the
road, almost at the bottom of the mountain, is Mr. Darlington's house.
His wife has just died. The trouble is, says her father, that Mr. Darlington is an awful man and his wife was an awful woman. She used
to do tailoring work, and if a young man came to pick up his first
suit, a thick wool suit, because that's what you needed to make an

impression on a girl's family, and if he was even tuppence short, she'd bawl it out so everyone could hear it: "Go, take the suit you don't have money to pay for if that's how you stay!" And this young man would ride off with his suit, his eyes wet and his cheeks hot, and the suit would be worn thin and food for moths before he'd forget his humiliation at the hands of Mrs. Darlington.

"You need someone to build a coffin for you, sir?" Vidal called out as he came into Mr. Darlington's yard.

An enormously fat man came out of his whitewashed house. He didn't have a hair on his head and he leaned on a cane. "If you can do it for me, do it," he said. "Don't joke with me."

"I'm not joking," said her father. "I have three small ones. See this one here? I am going down but they are coming up. I'm doing it for them. Good deeds go before you in the next world and store up credit for those you leave behind in this one."

"The boards are on the other side of the house," said Mr. Darlington.

"Go send your son to Rudy and tell him I beg his carpentry tools," said her father. "I don't have the things I need for the job."

Mr. Darlington dispatched his son, who cycled off up the hill. Ivy watched him go, standing up on his pedals. The hill was steep. She watched Mr. Darlington watch her father. "Don't coax his dogs over," Vidal said to her. "He has bad dogs."

"My dogs are not bad," said Mr. Darlington. "You're here to make a joke of me, isn't it? You stole my land and now you want to make a joke of me in the hour of my misfortune."

"Don't say that in front of my child," said Vidal. "Tell the truth in front of her or I'll fill your mouth with lead, dead woman or no dead woman on the board to cool in there."

"I had all intentions of buying that land," said Mr. Darlington. "You stole my intention from me."

"That land was in the paper month in and month out," said my father. "I bought it and then everyone wanted it."

"You stole my crops right off it," said Mr. Darlington.

"Your lease was up," said my father. "You tried to pull the law over you like the skin of a sheep but we knew you for a wolf. Two shoots of banana and two bushes of cocoa!"

"If I had a crop on the land," said Mr. Darlington, "it was mine to rent. As long as I had a crop."

"It was my land," said Vidal.

"And a pig came and rooted it up?" shouted Mr. Darlington. "A pig came with pick and shovel?"

"The whole of Mare River came against you," said her father.

"The whole of Mare River! A lot I care for Mare River! Where a pig comes with pick and shovel and roots up a man's crop!"

"Will you shut up?" said Miss Coffin Cover, coming out of the house. "Will you wake the dead? Your wife's not stiff yet, and her teeth aren't out, and I hear this heap of shouting going on!"

The two men fell silent. Ivy looked at her father and tapped her teeth. "When a person dies, they take out his teeth," he said.

"Why do they do that?" Mr. Darlington asked, half to himself. "She doesn't need her teeth in the next world?"

So the dead had no teeth? Dead men's teeth came out.

At night, her father took out his teeth and put them in a glass. At night when her father slept, he was dead, and in the morning he came alive again. "Get me my teeth, now," he would say to her in the mornings and she would bring him the glass where they swam.

Mr. Darlington's son had returned. "Rudy says he doesn't want his tools used on dead boards," said the son.

"Go to Lazarus's house and get his tools," my father said.

"Way down there in Cinnamon Bay?" asked the boy.

"Go!" roared Mr. Darlington.

All morning, she watched her father measuring the cedar boards and sawing them to size, and when he had the bottom cut out, and then the sides, a crowd began to gather in the yard. "Mister Vidal," someone cried out, "I didn't know you knew carpentering."

"I don't know carpentering," said her father. "You have no shame? The woman's *dead* for two days. Dead and cold in there on the ice. She's going to come back as a duppie, you know, and when she comes back, she won't be coming for me. You can tell the whole island I killed your wife," he said to Mr. Darlington, "but the whole island knows better. Would I be here making a coffin for a woman I killed? Did I kill her because I took back the land that belonged to me?"

"Chaw!" said Mr. Darlington and walked away.

Ivy looked up and saw a johncrow flying in circles over the house. They were enormous birds, black and baldheaded, their beaks like razors. They floated high above on the warm currents of air and they came down when they saw something to feed on. If they made a mistake and found nothing to eat, they died on the ground. They did not have the strength to climb back up the steep stairway of air.

"What's this child doing?" cried Miss Coffin Cover, rushing out of the house's doormouth and grabbing Ivy up. "None of you see what this child is doing? You want to mark her?" She pointed skyward at the johncrow. "Look how she's winding these cedar shavings around her wedding finger! Bride of death! Bride of death!"

"It is all superstitious nonsense and I don't want to hear any more of it," said her father, but he stopped work and came over to Ivy. "Never tempt fate," he said. "Fate is stronger than any person. Never tempt it. Wait for it to tempt you and even then you must run for your life."

"He's pondering on the day he got married," said one of the jocular men in the crowd. "He should have run for his life that day."

"And what's he doing here now?" asked Kenneth. Was he the same man who came for her in the black car and took her from her mother's house in Cinnamon Bay? "What's he doing here now where the man and his wife hate him?"

"Are you speaking to me?" asked Vidal.

"I am speaking to the moon," said Kenneth. "A man may speak to the moon."

"I am going down and they are coming up," said Vidal. "I am doing it for this girl and the others at home."

"That is very smart," said one of the men. "Good deeds must recommend you."

As soon as the men saw Vidal attaching the first side of the coffin to its bottom, they began to feel ashamed, and they moved to help him. They hunkered down and picked up pieces of sandpaper and began working the cedar. "It is smooth as satin," one of them said. "It is a coffin fit for a queen."

Queen of Tiverly, coming up.

"Hurry with the coffin cover," said one of the men. "See how the sun is going down there?"

"What's this child doing here all this time?" called Miss Blue from the road. She sat on an old white donkey whose eyes were narrowed to slits and whose ears were at right angles to his head. The animal looked as if he had seen the end of the world. Miss Blue's long, heavy legs almost reached the white, pebbled ground. "She has no home to go to?"

"Take her then, Miss Blue," said her father, and he lifted Ivy up and sat her down in front of Miss Blue.

"That man does love a funeral," said Miss Blue. "He gives Coffin Cover a run for her money."

Ivy sat down on a mat in the corner of Miss Blue's thatched hut while Miss Blue made tea. The usual double column of red ants was climbing from the floor to the thatched ceiling.

Since leaving her mother's house in Cinnamon Bay, this was the place she loved best. It was to Miss Blue that she was brought when her ears hurt and no medicine would stop her crying, when she would spend sleepless nights with one ear, then the other, pressed to the clay water jug that sat in the middle of the dining room table and kept the water ice-cold all day long. The water in that jug was always colder than the water they drew from the spring to put in it. When Miss Blue came to the house and began to tell her stories, and when Ivy complained of the throbbing in her ears, Miss Blue said what she heard was the sound of the sea, lapping and lapping at Green Island, sucking and sucking at the cliff stone, chewing with its white frothy teeth, until one day Green Island would begin to shrink, first to the size of a large rock, then to the size of a pebble, until it vanished completely. On the day that Green Island vanished beneath the sea, said Miss Blue, the people of the island would grow pale green wings, fly once round the island like dragonflies, flying until they came to a great branch on which they would all settle and that branch would be the great arm of God. The sound of blood in her ears turned to the sound of wings and soon Ivy was asleep on the mat of her floor.

"Tell me a story," she asked Miss Blue.

"Once I had a daughter who used to say all proper stories were about the sea."

"A story about the sea is fine," said Ivy.

"Oh, no," said Miss Blue, "it's not that simple. You must be very careful about the stories you tell a child because each child has her own story, and nothing can change it, any more than you can change the lines on someone's hand, but sometimes, when you tell a story, either because it's the perfect day to tell it, or because you tell it so well, or because in the child is an empty place through which the wind whistles, then the story fills that place up and after that the child can't hear her own story. The child is deaf to her own fate."

Fate, thought Ivy. First her father mentioned it, and now Miss Blue.

"I knew a young woman once," said Miss Blue, whose mind had wandered, "and she went to a palm reader just to make a fool of the woman. I don't know what she had against her, but it was something, the usual quarrel probably, that the palm reader had put a spell on her, something like that, and she knew the palm reader was almost blind, and what did she do?

"She drew lines on her palm with blue ink, and the palm reader read her palm, or what she thought were the lines of her palm, and the woman went home and laughed at the palm reader and told everyone what a trick she'd put over on her, and how the old lady couldn't read anyone's hand but was really a blind old fraud, and you know what happened? Everything the palm reader said would come to pass did come to pass. Every little thing she said came true. Finally the young woman died just the way the old lady said she would, going to look for the Sunken City. One night she went out in a boat and she rowed out until she found the steeple that pierces the ocean water, and she looked down and saw the people, men and women, walking along through the streets below the water, and the people saw the shadow of her boat going over and looked up at her and said things to her, and bubbles rose up from their lips, and when they reached the surface of the water, she heard them speak quite plainly.

"And she anchored her boat to what she thought was a bit of land, a little island far from shore, but it was only a patch of floating vegetation, and when she woke up in the morning, she had drifted far far from land and all that she could see was the vast curve of the sea stretching into the distance, and the great red sun sliding up from under the waves and floating up into the sky, and that was how they found her, in her boat, asleep on her back, staring up at the sky.

"It happened just as the palm reader said it would. When I heard that," Miss Blue said, "I thought, We all know our own stories. We know the lines in our hand. And you, you might know yours already, if you weren't too frightened to see it. You're born with it and it's your job to listen to it and change it when you can and gain power over it."

"What was her name?" Ivy asked.

"Oh, her name, I don't remember," said Miss Blue. "Someone young and foolish. She's dead now, of course." She sat on her mat, her arms wrapped around her knees, her head on an arm.

"Once," said Miss Blue, "there was a girl who wanted to marry, but she was not satisfied with any man who came to court her. 'I will not have him,' she said; 'his feet are too big.' Or again: 'His ears are too flat against his head.' Or 'His teeth are like fangs.' Finally all the men in the country had come to see her and been sent away."

Ivy knew this story well. It was her favorite story, about the very choosy girl who ends by marrying a johncrow. Somewhere in the middle of Miss Blue's telling it, she fell sound asleep, deep into a confused dream in which her mother, Mer, walked into the fields and saw her father, who had the body of a bird, but his own face, diving and diving again into a deep gully. She turned away and when she turned back, four johncrows with the faces of men were diving and diving into a deep gully as her mother watched, her hand to her mouth, two fingers across her lips as if to seal them.

13

IVY SAYS SHE MUST go back to Green Island. Ivy's Aunt Lucille, whom she calls Tita Lu, has died, and so Ivy must go home and do the right thing. At least she has stopped crying. I am always angry when people cry. I never know what is expected of me. Should I burst into tears with them? Will that show the proper degree of sympathy? How will that make things better? Then there are two people crying, not one. And if I start weeping, aren't I implying that whatever happened is as bad for me as for the other person? And if I start in crying, how do I know the other person won't think, Oh, she is an actress. Those are actress's tears. Should I say, The worst has happened, this is the worst thing in the world? Then the person may collapse altogether and what will I do with him? And maybe he doesn't think it is the worst thing in the world, but now I have said it, he feels obliged to act as if it is, and then we have a great drama on our hands. Or should I say, Well, of course it's terrible now, but in a few weeks you will feel better? How do I know he'll feel better? He may be like me. He may not want to look on the bright side.

  Face it, Anna, said Max. *There is no bright side.* And when I tried to comfort him, he turned into a maniac. And Charlie, was he any better? One day I was at my wits' end, and I said, This is terrible. This cannot go on. This is like death, and he looked up at me, he lifted his head from the pillow and said, It is not *like* death! It *is* death! *You* understand! And Charlie was so happy to think himself understood he got right out of bed, started to pack a picnic lunch, remembered he hadn't shaved in a week, and went off to the bathroom, while I made sandwiches and packed a basket. Of course, he took care of the wine. We couldn't go anywhere without wine, which is how the highway police got to know us quite well. They would stop us and call Mr. Pinsky and he would say, But they are working! Tell me what the fine is and

I'll pay it, and such was the studio's power, they would let us go. I imagine Mr. Pinsky paid more than a fine, the police were always so happy when they realized whom they had pulled over.

So I don't know what to say. I pat Ivy awkwardly on the shoulder, and say, of course you knew it was coming. *If we can get the fluid out of his lungs, then he can breathe,* the doctor told me. I knew it was coming, but it didn't make it any better. Now, because I don't know what to say, I am getting angry. This is always my way.

She will not rest now until she tells me all the details.

"Brother Beck was talking to her. He said, So what do you want for breakfast? A cup of tea? and she didn't answer him. A cup of tea? A piece of toast? She didn't answer him. He walked over and stood in front of her and she tapped her mouth with her hand. She couldn't speak. He ran next door and got Mr. Louis and they carried her right down to the hospital in Cinnamon Bay in his donkey cart and they put her on the ward right away. He talked to her and talked to her, but all she did was touch her mouth. She couldn't speak, you know.

"Well, to tell the truth," Ivy says, wiping her eyes, "the first time was worse. He woke up and reached over to her and she was cold to the touch and lying there stiff as a board, her eyes open, and he thought she was a dead woman, and they carried the doctor to the house, and he said, 'Mr. Beckwith, your wife here had a stroke. Come, we will carry her to the hospital.' And her blood pressure, it was one hundred over two hundred or something higher, and when they got her there, *he* looked so bad they put the band around his arm, and guess what? His pressure was worse than hers! So he had to stay there, too. That was the first time I flew out, last Christmas, you remember?"

I remember. I know all this.

"It's a nice hospital out there, but it's on the sea. It's a hot country, but when the wind comes in from the ocean, you can chill yourself, so last time when I went, I went out by Alexander's and I bought her a few warm nightgowns, white flannel ones with flowers, like mine," Ivy says. "When I was leaving to come home here, you know what she asked me? 'You thought I was going to die, don't it?' she said. I said, 'No.' 'Yes,' she said. 'Isn't that why you carried shrouds out here and dressed me in one?'

" 'What craziness you talking now?' I asked her. 'What shroud?'

" 'Didn't you bring the white gown with the little flowers?' she asked me.

" 'Yes, I did bring it,' I said. 'What does that have to do with shrouds?'

" 'It is shroud,' Tita Lu said. So I went to her dresser and opened her top drawer and I took it out.

" 'This is a shroud?' I asked her.

" 'Yes, what you dressed me in,' she said, clamping her lips together so she looked like her false teeth were out.

" 'Tita Lu,' I said, 'this is not a shroud. This is a *nightgown*. I have one in my own carry case,' and I went and got it and held it up in front of her. She started to cry. 'Why you crying for?' I asked her. 'Everyone in America sleeps in these nightgowns.'

" 'That is not shroud?' she asked me.

" 'Tita Lu, this is a *nightgown*,' I said again. 'I brought it because it is cold in the hospital when the wind blows in and I thought, Tita Lu, she gives away whatever she has, all someone has to do is look at it and say, Isn't it pretty? And she says, You like it? Take it then. I know how you stay, Tita Lu. So I thought you might not have a nightgown clean and nice to take to the hospital and why should you be ashamed in front of the nurses?'

" 'I told her, didn't I, Brother Beck, that Ivy would not come and put me in shroud while I still drew breath, didn't I tell her?' Tita Lu said, and I said, 'Who? Who did you tell?'

" 'Jasmine is the one I told,' she said. Jasmine, that ungrateful dog! Tita Lu took in her children for six years while she came up here to work, and she never sent a dollar down for them, and they weren't children like mine who would be satisfied with one finger of banana and a piece of toast. From the time the sun came up until it went down, they ate and starved her out and she never said a word. So I went and got my sister Jasmine and I said, 'Look here, I may not live here anymore but some day I may come back and I don't want anyone saying I put my aunt in a shroud while she still breathed. I may live up there, but I lived here all my young days and I knew how to use a machete then and I know how to use it now,' and Jasmine, she began babbling, saying, 'Miss Pinky' (you know that's how they call me), 'Miss Pinky, I saw the gown and it was so nice and white and she was lying so still, I thought it was a shroud and I told her how lucky she was you brought it all the way out here,' and I grabbed her up and shook her and she is a big woman, and I said, 'Jasmine, my life is my life and your life is yours and if you want to keep it, you stay out of mine. You tell me one more lie on me and you won't tell another, you hear? You hear me, Jasmine?' And that creature is my half sister!

"When I left Tita Lu's house, she was sitting in the doormouth, wearing the nightgown, she was so proud of it. 'Come, Pinky,' she said. 'I am not dead yet, but one day I will be, so you come and bury me, give me a good burial, hear, and watch over Brother Beckwith, all these years together, not even our own child to come between us, you watch over him, hear?' I promised her, but I did not like it, to hear her going on about her own dying.

"Well, now I have to go out on the street and get something to bury her in. And something for her head. They say after she was dead a day, all her hair fell out."

"Her hair?" I say. "It fell out?"

"Every little string of it, and it was so black and tall and nice when I saw her last Christmas."

"Well," I say, "you must go." This, I know, is where I should stop, but I cannot help myself. "I am fine on my own," I say. "I will go for long walks, and as for food, that store on the corner, you tell them what you want and they pack it in a paper bag for you. You can even call them and they'll bring it straight here but then they charge you a dollar extra and a dollar for the delivery boy, it adds up."

"She is the woman who raised me and I promised I would give her a good burial," Ivy says stiffly.

"What about her husband?" I ask.

"I knew her before her husband. They are keeping the body for me. I will be the one to wash it."

It is Wednesday now. "When will you be back?" I ask her, and she says she will be back on Monday. "Will you call Lee for me and get me tickets?" she asks me. "When I go out on the street, I'll stop at the bank."

She comes back with a white flannel nightgown and a cheap white lace mantilla. When she gets there, will she really wash the body? What a terrible thing to do! Can she love someone that much?

You will have plenty of time later to learn to be a human being, Max says.

When she leaves for the airport, I am so angry I can barely bring myself to speak to her. I try to pretend I am overcome with grief, but Ivy knows better.

After she is gone, I go out for a walk, all the time telling myself, You will slip on the ice and break your hip and it will serve her right when she comes back, fetching and carrying, not a minute to herself. It is what she deserves. I stop and look in the window of a jewelry store. Necklaces of colored crystal beads are strung across the window. Oh, I remember necklaces like that, and then in the window, I see the reflection of an old-fashioned fedora, a pink satin ribbon tied around its brim. I turn suddenly and point my umbrella at the man who is on the other side of the sidewalk staring at me.

"What do you want?" I demand loudly. Is he black or white? His face is powdered. He might be a black man. He looks like a black man who has powdered his face, but I am not sure. "What do you want from me?" I shout. Now people are stopping. The man turns and runs into the street. Why he is not hit by a passing car I don't know. They never hit the right people.

I don't break my leg. I stop in the little store, buy a sandwich and an olive salad, and go up to my house and eat sitting in the middle of my bed. I turn on the television and watch someone cooking a four-course meal. These are heroes, these people who do such everyday things and enjoy them. Once I had a cook, but she quit, complaining, as all my help did in those days, and then there was nothing in the house but jars of apple butter. For a week, that was all I ate. It was easier than going to the store.

Who is this man following me? He seemed surprised when I turned around. Perhaps he thought I was someone else? That would be something, people following me all these years, and I am murdered by a stranger who thinks he knows me.

The emptiness of the apartment jumps on me. The television is not enough, so I turn on the radio, too. Still not enough noise. I turn on the record player. This is good. This is noisy, like our old place in Stockholm. I will sleep for a while and then take another walk. It will be Monday before I know it.

When *The Mansion of Father Bertil* was almost finished, something was on Max's mind. Whatever it was, it must have been serious. Although he was known for his shouting, his ranting and raving, now his sarcasm had an unusually sharp edge and people did not forgive him as quickly as they often did. So Erik had resolved to play a trick on him, a silly trick, but afterwards Erik would feel better, because he would no longer be the only person who was laughed at. Some of the things Max said were so outrageous and so funny at the same time, it was impossible not to laugh, even if your sympathies were not with him. Believe me, people laughed at Max's imitations of me lying ill in bed or walking across a room. There were weeks when I was afraid to move lest Max imitate whatever it was I had done. I was never so inhibited as I was when I worked on that film.

Erik had had enough. Whatever he did, however he did it, Max would shriek and call upon God. What had he done to deserve this, and on and on. So that Monday morning, we all knew the trick was coming. There had been hurried, secretive conferences with the prop men and the camera crew. Someone was seen carrying a black bundle up the ladder and walking the rafters with it.

On Monday, no scenes were scheduled to be shot with Erik, but he let it be known that he was coming in to rehearse with Marta, a friend of mine from the Academy. Mrs. Berger, whom I had invited onto the set, stood in the shadows. When he arrived at the studio, he nodded politely but frigidly to Max, and he was gone.

"Good riddance," muttered Max, who promptly forgot about him. Instead, he turned his attention to the great classical actress Tora Tellson. Now it seemed she knew nothing, not even how to powder a wig. The shouting began. But nothing Max said ruffled Tora, who only smiled and nodded and said she would try again. This infuriated Max even further. In the scene we were to film, she had come upon her horse and sleigh plunged through the ice and was to run in circles, hysterical with grief and shock. His idea, as we could plainly see, was to reduce Tora to the desired state so that when the cameras turned, she would simply continue what she was already doing. Instead she smiled on and Max roared even louder.

"God is not good to you," said one of the grips, goading him, raising his eyes to heaven as he spoke. I knew, we all knew, that this was what Erik was waiting for, the instant when Max lost control of himself and began calling on God in His heaven to witness the hell on earth he presided over. We held our breath, but for some reason Max calmed down. I was in a corner of the set, looking up at the ceiling, and from where I sat, I could see a black bundle swaying back and forth just under the rafters. I looked again, squinting, and I saw a pair of shoes sticking out of one end of the bundle and I knew that this black bundle was a body and that the body was suspended by wires from a trolley that ran the length of the set. As soon as Max called on God, Erik would throw off the black cloth that covered him, the prop man would send him sailing across the ceiling, and Erik would answer in God's voice.

I wish I could remember what Tora did, because, naturally, she was in on it. I think she told Max she would like to sit down because she always needed to be calm before a dramatic scene, and Max looked at her, saw she was cooler than ice, and began to shout. "My God!" he thundered. "Where does this woman come from? Why is this happening to me? Answer me!" He was about to begin enumerating the tortures he hoped the next life would inflict upon poor Tora, when a deep voice from the ceiling answered him. "She comes from heaven, you hound of hell! How dare you address me! You ask why this is happening to you!"

Max stood still, flabbergasted. He paled. Then he came to himself. "Come out, Erik!" he thundered. At that moment, I saw Erik do something to the wire that suspended him from the trolley and, almost directly over Max's head, he plummeted through the air in the white robe he had put on for the occasion, shouting, "Hound of hell, here I come!"

Max saw him falling and instinctively reached out to catch him. Erik was extremely thin, but nevertheless he was a fully grown man, and he was falling almost fifteen feet. When Max caught him, he landed on both of Max's outstretched arms and Max made an odd noise, as if all the air had been forced out of his body. In the blink of an eye, Erik was standing in front of Max, grinning. Max was massaging his left wrist and smiling sheepishly. Everyone on the set was roaring with laughter. The prop man up in the rafters was wisely staying where he was because sooner or later he was going to have to explain how he let a man who was the star of the film risk falling fifteen feet through the air to the hard floor of the set. Max seemed to be laughing and crying at once, and when he walked around the set, he walked clownishly, one shoulder higher than the other. This seemed like the funniest thing of all, and we all shrieked with laughter. As soon as one calmed down, another would begin and we would start one another off.

"Well, that was very funny," Max said at last, "but someone better call a doctor." He had dislocated his left shoulder and sprained his right wrist. His left wrist was only bruised. The doctor who came to the set scolded him. How could a man who was almost forty, who had been in the business as long as he had, take part in such stupidity? Leave stunts to the stuntmen and the young men, he said, and the entire time he was bandaging Max's wrist and lecturing, Max said, Ja, ja, ja. If you were not strong as a horse, you would be in pieces, the doctor said. Ja, ja, ja, said Max. But he was not angry at Erik, not at all. Whenever he saw him, whether or not he wanted to, he smiled. After that, no one could separate them. When we came to America, Erik came too. He had a whole career in America, thanks to Max. "How can I be angry?" Max asked. "*He* was so mad he fell out of the sky on top of me. He's foolish but brave. He has passions. I am not mad at him."

"And if he does it again?" I asked.

"If he does it again, I break his neck," Max said.

The key is turning in the lock. Ivy is back. I want to tell her about the man watching me in the store window, the same one who watched us in the coffee shop, but I know I must ask her about the funeral on Green Island. I have *learned* I must do these things. I have learned there is something missing in me and I must watch other people and imitate what they do. Oh, I am not inhuman. Sooner or later I would work it out, I would understand I must ask, "How was the funeral?" and by then I would want to listen. Of course, by then everyone would be so fed up with me they would not care what I did. This too I have learned by experience.

"She looked so beautiful," Ivy is saying, "so peaceful, and her hair did not fall out after all. It was black and tall and all the gray was gone. I combed it, so I know. And Jasmine? She said she would wash the body, and my other half sister, Marie, she said she would wash the body, but they got in the cold room, and there were five bodies laid out in there, and they couldn't take it, so I did it alone. And there was one body who was burned to death, you couldn't tell if it was man or woman. The undertaker showed it to me. It was stiff and flaky, like toast."

"How did they wash it?" I asked.

"I don't know if they did wash it," Ivy said. "But she was beautiful! She looked like the young woman who took me in. And her skin went white, she was clear, clear, clear, well, it's as they say, in death we are changed in the twinkling of an eye. And the service, it was beautiful, beautiful, beautiful. Brother Beck said some things and Pastor Goldsmith repeated his remarks, because you know since his stroke his voice is not strong, and then everyone came up and made remarks about Tita Lu and how good she was and how she gave them food to eat when she had nothing for her own mouth and how when they passed her gate, she always had a good word for them, and all the children she took in over the years, they spoke for her, and Walter, he spoke for her, and Lisa, and people came to the house and told stories about how she played the organ in the church and how she taught herself and how she led the choir, Tita Lu with a voice like a johncrow! They went on praising her until the next morning.

"And Jasmine, my sister Jasmine's husband, he is a mason, he built her a fine tomb, a nice white concrete tomb, there isn't another like it anywhere in the Cinnamon Bay Cemetery, and I bought two black silk roses and we got a stone vase and we cemented the vase into the base of the tomb, and then we cemented the roses in so no one could take them out and we put our money together and bought a little wrought iron fence to go around the tomb, with a little gate in it. She will be happy in there, no goats and dogs walking on top of her, and it is a big stone, big enough for Brother Beck when he goes, so big and so fine no one will dig her up by mistake as sometimes happens. Yes, it was a fine funeral and a fine burial."

Her eyes filled. "Well, Tita Lu," she said, "go on your way now. You are on your way now, Tita Lu." She gestured with her right hand, as if brushing away a fly. "So, you went for walks?" she asked me. "You ate something?"

The thief's wife lay down in the snow and went to sleep and froze to death and the thief came out and lay down next to her and soon he too froze. The story ends there. Who found them? Did anyone find them? Did they slowly become bones and then powder or was it so cold in the mountains that whoever came upon them found them preserved just as they were the day they died, and if he did, what did he think happened to them? What story did he tell himself to explain it? The last I saw of them, they were beautiful snow statues, all their troubles over. That was how terrible life was for them. There was no rest for them in life. In death they found cold, everlasting cold, and rest. No one buried them. There was no one to bury them.

"You washed the body?" I asked her. "How was it, to do that?"

"Oh, it was nice, doing for her what she did for me. It was the last thing I could do for her. What else could I do for her except bury her? Well, go on your way, Tita Lu." She stood up and went into the kitchen. "I don't see any pots in the sink," she said. "You ate? What did you eat?"

"All the things that came out of those little brown bags you see there in the trash," I said.

"Tonight I will make a nice chicken and potatoes," she said, tying her kerchief around her head. "And get rid of all this dust. Where does it come from, all this dust?" She got to work and I sat in the middle of my bed.

After a while, she came in and gave me an envelope of pictures her son had taken at the funeral. There were many of Tita Lu lying in her coffin. She did not look peaceful. She looked stiff and ugly. Stiff and ugly, surrounded by white lilies already browning at the edges. *She washed her. With her own hands.* I stretched out on the bed and the bed began to drift and float, as it always does before I fall asleep. In the kitchen, Ivy was humming a hymn. You are on your way now, Tita Lu, I heard her say. You are on your way.

He has finally succeeded; he is standing on the stage and in front of him rows and rows of people, in stalls all the way up the ceiling, are clapping and clapping, slapping the flesh of their hands together, jarring the bones underneath, their eyes filled with tears, and some of them are holding back sobs until their throats hurt, their mouths tightening until the muscles in their face hurt, and is it because his play is good? It is good. But the people in their stalls, they are crying, some of them are crying, because he has succeeded. Oh, it is necessary for someone to succeed.

A long time ago, I went back to Europe and I gave a little talk, I drank coffee with some ladies, I signed some books. I must have been crazy. I never did things like that. A woman came up to me, tears streaming down her face. It was Helga's mother, Helga, who went with me to buy my cape. And I said, "Your daughter, how is she?" and she said, "It came to nothing for Helga. She was in a few plays, she met a man she liked, a nice man, and she has two children. Oh, she is very fat now, is Helga. But you," she said again and again, "you. It makes me so happy."

I couldn't understand it. Why did it make her happy? I was not her daughter. Why wasn't she jealous? I thought, she should hate me. But she didn't hate me. She was so happy to see me. So then I knew. So few succeed but everyone must believe someone does succeed. Maybe we are all one thing after all. Maybe when one bird flies from the nest and does not fall, that one flies for all the rest. Of course about people I don't know anything, but I think it must be true. Otherwise what did they see in me? Why was I so important to them?

But while he stands there, he sees her face. Her face floats in front of him like a moon, a huge planet. He cannot see through her to the people pounding the bones of their hands. What is success to him now? At the moment it comes to him, he sees the face of the one for whom it would have meant the most. Now he realizes why he wanted it. He wanted to give it to her, as his gift. But she is dead or she is gone and he stands with success in his hands, his lip trembling, his eyes skittering. To whom can he make his offering? He is like a madman who stands at the stage door, a bouquet in his hands, but there has been no performance. No one will ever open the door. No one will ever come out. This, he says to himself, is what success is. It comes when there is no one to see it, no one to take it from you. It is heavy in your hands. Nothing could be heavier. This is heavy enough to press him into the earth. This is a kind of death; this is death.

He says her name, and there where she lies on her sickbed in the poor quarter, she hears him call; she remembers her promise. If you call me, I will come. The doctor has already said she will not live through the night, but now she gets up. Her beauty is gone. Her bones come through her skin. Her eyes drown in the deep dark pools beneath them. The night is cold and she has no coat. Long ago she sold it. She goes out into the night and holds on to the street walls. She pulls herself along. Oh, what agony it is to move! She is pulled along by the force of his need for her; she is hooked on this need as a fish is hooked on the brutal, brutal line.

She is really dead. We know she is really dead. Yet she goes on. A truck passes and she lets it drag her. A carriage passes and she crawls onto its rear step and lets it carry her. In his room, the party goes on. He is not part of it. He stands by the window, calling her name. Because he does so, he forces her heart to beat, and because her heart beats, she goes on. Now she is at the door to her old room. She goes in. Now someone comes from the party and finds her.

She tries to straighten her hair. She tries to smile. They are going to bring him to her. He comes in. He rubs her hands; there is the sound of skin on skin, a kind of sighing, a rustling, as the wind rustles dry leaves. She is a dry leaf now. Oh, what a struggle this is, to breathe in and out until he is finished with her! But he has something to give her. He summons it up: the applause, the people in their stalls, you did this for me, this is what you wanted, take it from me. Oh, she does, she does, she smiles, she doesn't blink, she is afraid to blink, if she closes her eyes, how will she open them again? It will take too much strength to open them. If she closes them she will never see again. She smiles and with her eyes wide open, she dies. Now she is dead and he sinks to the floor next to her bed. In the next room the party goes on.

Here it all stops. Here the story stops. They do not tell you: how does he go on now?

What we do, we do for others, for the memory of their faces, their smiling faces. When they see this they will shine like the sun. We must please them! It is never enough to please ourselves. Never. No one tells us that.

Walter Drake said, "By the time I was a success, there was no one left alive to see it." Always I wanted him on the set with me. It was always his face I looked to: was it good? When he was pleased, it was good. He had Max's face.

Come back to me, come back to me, he says as he stands on the stage and the applause breaks over his head. He calls her name: come back to me. If I am the last person left on earth, why should I live? Come back to me. And then he knows—then we know—there are only two or three people on the earth, and when they are gone, you are the last one. There are no streets, the buildings are gone, one lone splintered tree and a howling wind, dust flying. Come back to me, he says, and the dead woman struggles, brought to life. It is cruel to bring her to life, but he does it. How can he not? How can he stand there in an empty world, the dead in their stalls clapping the bones of their hands together. How can he not call her up?

Come back to me, I say, burying my head in the pillow. Come back to me. Oh, it is terrible that she washed the body. Will she say, Tita Lu, come back to me? No, she has let her go. She will not call her up. That poor woman will not struggle to sit upright, lift her cement roof, begin her long journey here. She will rest peacefully because that is what Ivy wants for her.

There are lunatics who cannot let go. Even after they strangle their victims, they keep their grip on the dead man's throat. That's how the police find them, their hands clenched.

Now I stretch out my hands. Now I run my fingers over the wrinkles at the edge of my pillow. The wrinkles become the wrinkles in the faces I dream of. I stroke the wrinkles. I turn the pillow so the cold side is against my cheek. I turn it again and again. I begin to wonder why part of the pillow is always cold, even when the room is hot. I must remember to ask someone that.

Once I met a very famous scientist. The whole world knows his name. Before I met him, I objected. I said, Why does he want to meet me? Because he admires my mind?

But at the last minute, I showed up. He stared at me all night. Well, he was comparing me, the flesh and bone of me, to the woman he saw on the screen. He was telling himself he wasn't disappointed, that I was a different woman from that one who shimmered up there in front of dark rooms, but just as beautiful. Of course it isn't true but soon he will convince himself it is. I am such a convincing hypnotist? He wants to believe.

We begin to talk. So many disappointments in his life, how his knees hurt, and his wife, he misses her. She really loved you? I ask him. All those years, she really loved you? How is it possible?

I don't know if it was possible, he says. I wanted to believe it was possible. But someone has loved *you*, he says. I laugh and say, Oh, yes, my mother, my father, my sister. Dead, all of them. Some brothers live on but what are they to me now?

Life, he says, is terrible. So many disappointments. Well, my son—But you don't want to hear about my son.

Why not? I say.

Because I cannot bear to talk about it, he answers me.

Oh, I say, we are all the same. We grow up, we do our jobs in life as best we can, we make a mess of things. I start to laugh. Yes, that is what is interesting, how we make a mess of things. He is starting to smile. So what did you do? he asks me in German. What things did you make a mess of?

Well, where should I start? I ask him, and I begin with my arrival in this country, and how from the first day I knew this was a crazy place, a completely crazy country, and yet I didn't flee, I didn't jump in the river and swim back to the boat, so here I am, and he started telling me stories, and until he died, we were such good friends, everyone shook their heads at it. We knew what we had in common: what a mess we made of things.

I saw that film again last week: the playwright stood on the stage and called to her. The quality of the print was terrible. Sometimes you could see their faces, sometimes time had erased them. She groped her way down a ghost street. It was the world of the living calling to the world of the dead and the dead answering. I am glad I saw it but I am afraid to see it again.

I think, Look, Max, how time erases even dreams. And then I think, the negative may be okay. The film could be restored. Somewhere there is a good print. But what am I saying, really? *Come back to me.* I am always saying that, even when I am on line in the delicatessen, asking for a loaf of bread. Come back to me. But they won't come back, so I turn my back on all of them. This is the face I show to the world: a woman who has forgotten her own life. You know, when you forget what went before, then there is only one thing that can be important: what is happening this minute. So my stomach becomes very important. Why is it upset? Why doesn't it like olives? Should I go to a party tonight or will it be too cold? Will I get home early? These are the things that loom. I will tell you something. This living in the present, it is very boring. Sometimes I even bore myself.

Why is this part of the pillow cold even though it's the part pressing against the sheet? This question fascinates me. You don't know how I consider it, night after night. Sometimes I bore myself silly. But to be bored is to be calm, so calm you fall asleep. I am always sleeping. Sophisticated people say to be so tired means one is depressed, but what is wrong with being depressed if you are also well rested? If I were not depressed, I would be up all the time, hopping around the house, waiting for a late party so in the morning I could have circles under my eyes and a heart skipping beats. Let me tell you, if I were a little more cheerful, I would have been dead years ago.

The big struggle now is to stay awake during the day because otherwise at night you cannot sleep.

Who is going to burn this journal after I am gone? Who is going to stand over me and say, Come back to me?

14

SHORTLY AFTER VIDAL MARRIED BEA, he and his wife removed from Cinnamon Bay and took up residence in Mare River where they had recently bought property. Lazarus, who was their first visitor, reported that they had a beautiful piece of land and a lovely river that ran in front of the house, a river with steep banks, so that the family could bathe in privacy. A few months later, the Clifton family moved back to Cinnamon Bay. Lucille Clifton continued to live with the young farmer, Septimus Beckwith, who was likely to become ordained as a minister of the Pentecostal Church. Mer came home and lived with a young carpenter, but something about him displeased her, and she left him. He left Cinnamon Bay to look for work elsewhere, and after he was gone, Mer discovered she was pregnant. She had another girl, whom she named Catherine. After Catherine's birth, Mer lived with a policeman and had a third daughter.

"But what is wrong with the policeman?" Lucille asked her sister.

"He is not for me and I'm leaving him," Mer said. She moved in with Lucille, the policeman left Cinnamon Bay, and Mer discovered she was pregnant. After the baby, another girl, was born, Mer moved in with a house painter. She now had three daughters, Ivy, Catherine and Jasmine. When she moved in with the house painter, she seemed to settle down. She had a fourth child, a fourth daughter, Marie.

"Nothing satisfies you," Lucille said one day, sitting on her sister's bed. "What is wrong with these men? They beat you?"

"They don't beat me," her sister said.

"They drink?"

"This is a drinking country," said Mer. "They don't drink more than anyone else."

"Then what is the trouble?" asked the exasperated Lucille.

"They tire of me or I tire of them, and when they leave, I find out I'm pregnant," said Mer.

"You have no luck with men," Lucille said sadly.

"I went to Miss Blue's, and I told her the story of my life and she changed it for me. She said that the man I'm with now will soon bore me, but if I stay, the boredom will change into something else, something better."

"This story-tailoring business is nonsense," said Lucille.

"Belief kills and belief cures," said Mer. "I think I may be happy with this man."

"Mother and Nanny can't live forever," Lucille said. "If something happens to them? They're old people. Anything could happen. They already have Ivy."

"I stop in and see her every weekend! I give them money for her."

"And Vidal, you know he asks Lazarus about you and he wants to know everything about Ivy. He has three children of his own and if he decides he wants Ivy as well? He's her father and she does not live with you. He stops by and visits with the child. He wants her to know him."

"She will stay with Mother and Nanny," Mer said. "That's the end of it." Lucille sighed and looked at her. "He's not a patient man," she said. "He has a temper. He flings things at the children when they don't behave. He flung a machete after the oldest one when he wouldn't stop crying, and then he drove the child to the hospital in Cinnamon Bay and they said when Vidal got there, he was bawling worse than the child."

"He has his children, I have mine," Mer said.

Bea was cooking in the outside kitchen, and now, waiting for the cornmeal and grated coconut to boil down, she looked out the window. The chickens were eating the leftover coconut she had thrown out for them and a flock of yellow butterflies was settling on the chocolate bushes at the far edge of the yard. Men drove by on children's bikes, their knees akimbo. The sun leaned over the edge of the horizon. Outside, she could hear Jack and Ivy shouting together and then Cynthia's high-pitched crying. "Stop that noise!" she shouted and the sound of crying immediately ceased.

From experience she knew what had happened. Ivy had heard her shout and had picked up the baby to quiet her. She was still a baby herself but she was good with infants and animals. In that she was like her father. Vidal had put her in charge of a suckling pig that refused to nurse, and the child had soaked a rag in sweetened coconut water, sat the piglet in her lap, and soon had the animal sucking on her fingers, gazing up adoringly. The piglet was an enormous beast now, almost as big as the old sow, but it still followed Ivy wherever she went, and at night when it saw Ivy go into the house and realized it was once again separated from her, its high, agonized squeal was the last sound the family heard.

"Slaughter it, now," she said to her husband. He, however, ignored her. They had, he said, plenty of other pigs, and this one never had to be chased down and brought back to the pen. It came when Ivy called it.

Bea was not happy with her stepdaughter. Her stepdaughter was good to her children, she could see that. And her eldest son was especially close to Ivy. When Ivy took the goats up above the house into the fields, Jack went too, and when Jack was sent for the goats in the evening, he had Ivy for company. When they had nothing to do, they disappeared into the woods and time and time again, Bea had come upon them sitting under a tree, talking quietly and seriously. She did not wish Ivy real harm—certainly she did not wish her dead—although she often had dreams in which the child was falling from a pine tree, or caught inside a burning room—but she did wish her elsewhere.

Most of the time, she thought, the girl was happy. She ran about in the yard with the other children. They played games together. They bathed in the river and swam there when they came home for lunch before the school bell rang. She was hard on the child, but no harder, she told herself, than she was on any of her children. She didn't want the girl to think that she could get away with murder because she wasn't one of her own. She knew the neighbors had things to say because Ivy never had proper clothes, but then the child didn't show her proper respect. When she said that to her husband, he said, Yes, Bea, but what does the child do wrong? She couldn't think of any one thing in particular, and so she always ended by saying the same thing. She doesn't have manners toward me, not like the others. I don't like her ways. She has haughty ways.

The truth was she was afraid of the girl. Ivy was born knowing how to handle her father. She insinuated herself into his affections. She knew how to ask him for something so that it would break his heart if he didn't say yes to her. She didn't talk to him as a young girl talks to her father. No, she talked to him as a young girl talks to her young man. She cast down her eyes and spoke almost too softly to hear, so that he had to incline his head toward her, and she became the meekest of the meek.

When Bea watched Ivy with Vidal, she thought she saw duplicitousness in her, a precocious cunning. When Ivy wanted something— a spinning top carved from a piece of mahogany, a book borrowed from the owner of Gray's Mansions—she would cast her eyes down and her voice would change, and when she finished speaking, she would look up at her father with silent adoration, and she had a habit of drawing her left hand across her left eye as if to wipe away the tears that had formed there. Bea would watch these interchanges and whisper to herself, "Flirt! Little flirt! She is just like her mother!" Didn't the child remind him daily of Mer, who was now living with her fourth or fifth man? Of course, the townspeople, egged on by the Clifton family, had seen to it that she heard the story of how Vidal was found waiting for any train that came along the morning of her wedding.

The child followed after her father, stood up watching him when he repaired the house, was taken by him whenever he was not at Gray's Mansions. She appeared out of nowhere when he picked up his bicycle and held out her arms so that he could lift her up and seat her on the handlebars in front of him.

It seemed to Bea that Vidal showed less of an interest in their own children, for she did not think of Ivy as one of their own. She thought of her as Mer's daughter. Yet she was dutiful to the child. She fed her, and if she was not well, she had Vidal take her to the doctor. When the child first came to live with them, she had tried to show affection to her, but mistook her natural shyness and reticence for coldness, even malevolence, and no longer attempted to pretend that Ivy was her own. The child seemed intent on making a fool of her. When Miss Blue knocked at the gate, Ivy would run to greet her and throw her arms around the old woman's legs, and soon the two of them would be off together. It did not occur to Bea that Ivy had known Miss Blue from her time in Cinnamon Bay and so thought of her as part of the home in which she had been so happy. She saw Ivy's affection for Miss Blue as a mocking of her own efforts, deliberate ridicule, a deliberate pushing away. And just two days ago, it was crepes, a pair of crepe-soled shoes, and now thanks to Ivy, she and her husband were barely speaking.

Bea was there on the veranda when Ivy limped up to her father and said, "Daddy? You are going into town today for store groceries?" And when he said yes, she said, "I want to beg you a pair of crepes, sir." He asked Ivy what she needed them for, and she said that Miss Blue's niece said she would give her sewing lessons in town after school and she needed a pair of crepes to walk back home from the bay.

"What size do you need?" he asked her. She said she needed a seven. He came home late that night and in the morning, he left the shoes in their box at the foot of Ivy's bed, but as soon as Bea saw Ivy wearing them, she could not keep quiet.

"He buys you a pair of shoes and I don't have money for the children's criss cakes?" she said. "And you have a good pair of brown leather shoes!"

"Those shoes are school shoes," the girl said, "and Tita Lu bought them or I wouldn't have any, and if I have these crepe-soled things, I won't have to wear the leather ones out."

"So you'll only wear out what *we* buy you, not what your mother's family buys you?" she demanded. "That's it, isn't it?"

"You want the shoes, ma'am, take the shoes," Ivy said. "We wear the same size. You take them." And Ivy put on her brown leather shoes and went off to school with Jack. Sooner or later the girl would turn her own boys against her.

In the evening, Vidal came home and asked Ivy, "How are the shoes?" and the child said, "The shoes were fine, sir."

"What do you mean, the shoes *were* fine?" Vidal asked. "What happened to them?"

"Your wife, there, she said she didn't have the money to buy the children criss cakes and yet you brought me shoes and she said I had a pair of shoes I wouldn't wear out because my mother's family spent the money on them, so I gave the shoes to her."

"Where are the shoes?"

"Your wife has them," she said.

"Where are the shoes?" Vidal roared at Bea. "Go, bring the shoes!" She went and brought the crepes in their box. "You don't want them," Vidal said to Ivy, "and she doesn't need them, so nobody will have them." He went outside, came back in with his machete and chopped up the crepes. "Now everyone can have them," he said. "You, miss, you can have them, and you, Bea, you can have them, and the rest of the children, wherever they are, they can have a piece too. Is everyone happy?" He turned and walked out the door.

"Where are you going?" his wife called after him.

"To play dominoes," he said.

"When will you be back?"

"When you see me."

He jumped on his bicycle and pedalled off.

"You," Bea said to Ivy. "You go to the spring for water and then sweep the yard."

"I have to get the goats!"

"Get the goats and then go to the spring and sweep the yard!"

"But it will be dark!"

"Your father thinks you are a baby and only his children can do anything around the house, but we'll see about that," said Bea. "Go, get the goats."

Ivy started up the path and Jack caught up with her. "She didn't stop you from coming after me?" she asked him.

"Oh, I came thiefing out," he said, "through the bedroom window. She has more eyes than a potato but still she can't be everywhere at once."

"He will come back drunk," said Ivy. "He will come back drunk and I will have to undress him."

"Why is it he doesn't get drunk like other fathers?" Jack asked. "When he comes home drunk, he's quiet. He doesn't have a word to say."

"You know he's drunk because he doesn't lean his bike up against the house," Ivy said. "He lets it drop when he gets off it and he walks straight into the house." And then, she thought, he calls me and says, "Ivy, draw off my boots." And if he's not asleep yet, he says, "Ivy, draw off my pants now." How she hated that, taking off his boots and his pants, watching him turn to the wall and fall into a thick, sudden sleep from which nothing could wake him.

I will not see the light of his bicycle waver up the path until late tonight, thought Bea. He and that child are too close. The people in the village said Ivy was the picture of her mother but Bea had seen the mother once and did not think she was so much to look at, short and wide and smiling, like any other girl in the village. But she and her sister had airs. And when the mother was pregnant with Ivy, that was when Vidal began calling on her, and after a while her father took him aside. After that, Vidal said to her, "We are friends, Bea. We are just friends, isn't it?" But then Mer had the child and took her to Albion Bay to see her mother and she didn't want to return to Cinnamon Bay.

She knew Vidal had gone up twice to see Mer, and twice had asked her to come back. Whether she said no, she would not come back now, or no, she would not come back at all, Bea didn't know. But Vidal could not be told no twice, and certainly not three times, and the next time her father spoke to him, Vidal said, "All right, I will marry your daughter."

"She is not pregnant?" asked her father.

"I am not the one to ask that," said Vidal. But Bea was pregnant although she herself didn't know it yet.

"She will grow up one day and be on her own," she said aloud to the empty yard, and when she turned back to the kitchen, she saw a woman standing just inside the doormouth, a very slender, tall, elegant woman wearing a red felt hat that came down over one eye and cast one half of her face in shadow, a woman wearing a beautifully cut dress of thin cotton material, a red and purple print, and on her narrow, long feet were red sandals that matched her hat.

Bea, who was the oldest of eight children, had little schooling, finishing only the third standard, and even for Green Island, her family was unusually superstitious. She had been taught that spirits could appear whenever they wished and that they moved without sound, and although they usually walked so that their feet did not touch the floor, this was not always the case. A spirit you met outside was far less dangerous than a spirit who entered your house. Once it was in, it looked around, and if it liked what it saw, it might decide to stay. A spirit who took up residence in such a manner might, when your attention was wandering, take possession of you, and from that point forward, you would be forced to do whatever it asked. You would become its slave. There was no doubt in Bea's mind that the woman in the red hat, red sandals and flowered dress was such a spirit.

It had come through her gate, which was hung with chains of brass bells, yet not one of them had tinkled. This was the way of spirits, who could move without causing anything to stir, like a breeze that moved through trees without causing the slightest motion of the foliage. It had entered her kitchen without alerting her to its presence, although every floorboard in the room creaked like a swamp toad. She forced herself to look the spirit in the eye. The woman's languid posture did not change. She regarded Bea from beneath half-lowered lids, her expression one of amused condescension.

Bea picked up a handful of salt and threw it at her. Salt was well known to be inimical to spirits, who could not eat salted food, nor could they cross a threshold in front of which salt had been sprinkled. The woman shook her head slightly and stared at Bea.

"Is the spirit on you?" Bea asked.

If the woman in the red hat was a spirit, she would be forced to answer yes. The woman in the hat said nothing. Bea made the sign of the cross. The woman did not move. There was only one thing left to do. She began to curse, every bad word she could think of, shouted at the top of her lungs. This, her grandmother had taught her, was a last-ditch remedy. When you met a devil, you cursed him worse than he could curse you, and so, convinced he had come upon a bigger and more powerful devil than he was, he would disappear.

The woman did not disappear, but lounged against the door frame, staring at her.

"Well, well," the woman said. "I was told you wouldn't be happy to see me but no one told me to take the precaution of first stopping my ears with wax." She stared at Bea as if she were a new and particularly repulsive kind of insect. "You don't know me?" she asked. When Bea still did not answer, but continued to watch her as if she might at any instant rise from the floor and fly at her, the woman in the red hat said, "My name is Lucille Clifton. We've met many times on the street in Cinammon Bay. Not to say hello to, but we've seen one another many, many times. I suppose there's some reason you're cursing at me?"

"Lucille Clifton?" said Bea. "Who heads up the choir?"

"Ivy's aunt," Lucille said.

"Oh, Ivy's aunt," Bea said. She flushed deeply. The Cliftons, she thought, existed to make her ridiculous. Now this woman would go to Vidal and tell him what kind of greeting she met with when she visited her niece's house.

"Where is Ivy?" asked Lucille. "You can imagine, can't you? Her mother is concerned about her, and her grandmother, too. Her great-grandmother cries constantly and blames herself. They are all concerned about the child."

"She's quite fine," Bea said. "You can go out in the yard and wait for her and see for yourself."

"But she has no clothes," Lucille said flatly.

"She has clothes," Bea said defensively. "She has what she needs."

"Two little shifts and no shoes, and two pairs of panties with holes," Lucille said.

"Who is telling you stories?" Bea asked. "Miss Blue?"

"Every Friday the bus comes from Mare River to Cinnamon Bay and those who practice in the choir come down on that bus," Lucille said. "What goes on here is spoken of down there."

"I dress her as well as my own," Bea said sullenly.

"Where is Vidal?" Lucille asked.

"It's Saturday, he's up at the rum shop," Bea said.

"Up at the rum shop with his big-time friends. Straight up the road?" Bea nodded. "Lovely to visit with you," Lucille said. She stood up straight, walked through the kitchen door, through the yard, out through the gate, and down the road. Bea watched her. The breeze did not disarrange her hair. The dust of the dry road did not appear to touch her. In spite of the heat, which had turned the green leaves livid and caused the ripe oranges and lemons on the trees to glow like evil presences, she seemed perfectly comfortable. Bea mopped her dripping forehead and decided to immerse herself in the stream that ran below the house. She imagined that Lucille would have plenty to say to Vidal and if she stood still and thought about it, she would grow even hotter. "Jack! Ivy!" she called. "Bring Cynthia down to Blue Hole!"

Lucille walked along the dirt road until she came to the shocking pink and aqua rum shop. It was exactly the same as the ones outside of Cinnamon Bay, except that the Cinnamon Bay shops were painted in alternating stripes of pink and orange. A cluster of men were standing beneath an almond tree, each holding a bottle of beer in his hand. Lucille recognized Vidal immediately. He was taller than the others and even from where she was, she could hear him telling the others that he would fill someone or other's mouth with lead. She sighed. People did not change.

"He is telling people I killed his wife?" Vidal asked. "Again? I am going to put a stop to it. I know how to do it. That Darlington will not keep on saying it. Everyone says it is that lady in Ocher Bay who killed his wife. The woman went up there and laughed everyone's dresses to scorn and laughed at the people there for wearing socks with their shoes and the bride's mother said to her, 'She'll never laugh at anyone again,' and she didn't. So if it's magic that killed Mrs. Darlington, what do I have to do with it? Oh, I'll fix him good now!"

"Vidal!" Lucille called out. "I want a word with you!"

The men caught sight of her and fell silent. "Good afternoon, gentlemen," Lucille said, looking around. "Some of you know me, I believe, from choir practice."

"Good afternoon, Miss Lucille," someone said, and the others took up the greeting.

"Vidal," Lucille said, turning to him, "my business is with you. I hear my niece has no clothes. You know when you took her, you left all her things behind, so if you will give me a list of what I must sew for the child, I will bring it to you next weekend."

"She is my child and I will clothe her," Vidal said, reddening. "Go to Stanny's store and take whatever you need."

"And you will pay for it?"

"I will pay for it. I am her father."

"I'm going to Stanny's," Lucille said.

"Stanny's, his prices are high," said one of his cronies.

"I am the child's father," said Vidal.

"She didn't reproach you," one of the men said.

"No," Vidal said uneasily.

"Good afternoon, sir," Lucille said to Stanny, stepping through the doormouth. Over the door was nailed a sign that read STANNY'S FASH-IONABLE EMPORIUM. Lucille read the sign and shook her head. Green Island was full of such stores, a tiny shack bearing the sign MARE RIVER FASHION INSTITUTE, as if naming the thing would make it so. We are, thought Lucille, a hopeful, silly people. "I need clothing for a seven-year-old girl," she said.

Stanny's store was built of unpainted wood that had grayed in the weather, and the boards closest to the ground were lichenous. The boards were roughly cut, and inside, brilliant shards of light gleamed like molten glass. Long coils of amber flypaper hung from the rafters, all thickly clotted with large black flies, some still buzzing.

"What does she need?" asked Stanny.

"Everything," said Lucille. "Three of everything."

"Dresses?"

"Yard dresses and Sunday best, and of course a fancy straw hat and one plain, ten pairs of socks, mostly white, although some must match the dresses, and panties, at least ten pairs, fifteen if you have them, one pair of patent leather shoes, size four, two little sweaters, one parasol to keep off the sun—what have I forgotten?" Lucille asked, breaking off. "I have a list in my purse," she said, fishing it out, "but it seems incomplete."

"Some chemises?"

"Chemises, yes."

"I can't think of anything more," Stanny said. "You will pay for it?"

"Vidal Cook will pay for it. He's out by the rum shop. Ask him."

"Oh, no, miss," he said. "I don't need to ask him."

Lucille was inspecting a white lace dress whose waist tied with a light blue satin ribbon. "This is the best you have?" she asked. "Nothing with layers of lace?"

"Only a baptism dress," said Stanny. "That's the only one fancier."

"Let me see it," Lucille said. The dress was produced and Lucille said she would take it. And a red and green rubber ball and a small alaglaster doll. She looked around the shop and when she could find nothing more, she picked up a kerchief and added it to the pile that now covered the counter. "All these are to be charged to Mr. Vidal," she said.

"The child will do her father proud," Stanny said.

"Oh, yes. She will," Lucille said.

She walked back down the road to the rum shop. Vidal was still standing there. "You found everything you wanted?" he called to her.

"Everything," Lucille said. "Stanny's boy is taking it to your house right now." Vidal smiled and looked at his friends as if to say that he could afford whatever was asked of him. He is puffed up like a frog now, thought Lucille. If I could be there when the boxes are delivered to his door!

She was hot and tired and well pleased with herself, and so she walked down the road until she came to Miss Blue's. Since moving to Mare River, Miss Blue no longer lived in a house with four walls and a floor. Instead she lived in a shack whose walls were made of mats of woven straw wattled over with mud. The roof of her shack was thatched and the floor was hard-packed dirt on which her sleeping mat rested. On the door of the shack Miss Blue had nailed her familiar sign: STORY TAILOR.

"Good afternoon, Lu," Miss Blue called to her. "Come in and have a glass of lemonade."

Lucille came in, sat down on a mat, and leaned back against the wall of the shack.

"Wait, wait," said Miss Blue. "Let me put this mat behind you. We have red ants here till it hurts." She pointed to a corner of the shack where a column of red ants were marching across the wall and disappearing into the thatch. The shack must have been built over an ants' nest.

"How is the story-tailoring business here, Blue?" Lucille asked.

"Oh, it is quite good," Miss Blue said. "Last week a man came in and what is his trouble? He fell in love with a woman without even seeing her face. What did he fall in love with? He fell in love with the contents of her purse. She opened up her purse in church and he looked in and saw in there little bottles filled with aromatic oils, and an orange, and strange coins, and all manner of things, he couldn't remember them all, and now he can think only of her and he wants to marry her."

"How will he know her? If he hasn't seen her face?"

"Oh, he has seen it. He looked up from the purse and looked into her face and there he saw quite an ugly woman but all the same he wants her."

"And she does not want him?"

"No. She says a handsome man makes a bad husband. Can you imagine it? And she as ugly as a pork belly."

"You will help him," Lucille said, yawning. The heat was making her sleepy.

"And you know I work up at the great house? After a ball, I go up there with Miss Coffin Cover and we clean up. What the wealthy people leave behind them! And Miss Coffin Cover, she always brings something of her own with her, and when she thinks I'm not looking, she hides it in a corner, and then she pretends to find it and takes it home with her. And she sits up nights and pretends she went to the ball."

"I don't know Miss Coffin Cover," Lucille said.

"She was Myra Wilcox," Miss Blue said. "But here she is Miss Coffin Cover because she is flat and square and always wears black and cannot be kept from a funeral. Wherever there is a dead body on the board, there is Miss Coffin Cover. And you ask her, 'Miss Coffin Cover, what is the relation?' and she says, 'Oh, the deceased, she is my neighbor's cook's friend's aunt, so you see there is a relation between us.' "

"My God," Lucille said.

"You are here for a reason? You went to see Ivy? You saw Bea?"

"The woman is a raving lunatic," Lucille said. "Instead of saying 'Good afternoon,' she threw salt at me, asked me if a spirit was on me, and then cursed at me for five minutes. She is mad absolutely."

"And you did what?" asked Miss Blue.

"I did nothing. I went to the rum shop where Vidal was standing up with his big-shot friends and told him Ivy had no clothes and he told me to go to Stanny's and order whatever she needed and he himself would pay for it and when I could find nothing more to buy, I took a kerchief and put it on top of the pile. Don't be surprised if Miss Bea comes knocking at your front gate asking to have her story tailored so that it ends up with my body found under a calabash tree."

"For that she has to go to the magic man," said Miss Blue.

"You will let us know how Ivy gets on?"

"Carrying tales is a bad business."

"The child can't call for help."

"No harm will come to her if I can help it," said Miss Blue. "How does your grandmother get on?"

"A pitiful business," Lucille said, standing up. "Women from the church go up there morning and night and read from the Bible to her. It soothes her."

"And Mer?"

"Mer lives in a cloud." Lucille didn't know what to say about Mer.

"The hunted bird lives in a cloud," said Miss Blue.

Lucille only shook her head. She wanted to marry Septimus Beckwith, it was time to marry him, but how could she marry when Mer was always crying? She would bring Mer a flower, show it to her and say, "Look how beautiful it is," and her sister would sniff its perfume and for no reason begin to cry and when she cried, she would wave her hand at Lucille as if to say, Don't pay any attention. It doesn't mean anything. It was hot in the shack and she began to doze but awoke with a start. "Bea does not care for Ivy," Lucille said. She spoke suddenly and loudly.

"But the father does love the child hard," Miss Blue said. "He loves her more than the others. One day he was beating her and I asked him why he was at her and he said, 'The teacher always beats the best pupil.'"

"That will only make things worse," Lucille said.

"He may fear that what he did, you will do also, come and take the child back."

"I can't come for her. Only Mer can come and she won't do it. I won't be back, you know. It will make it worse for Ivy if I come. Bea won't like it and why should she like it?"

Miss Blue offered her another glass of lemonade, but Lucille said if she started on her way now, she could catch the last bus to Cinnamon Bay.

"You will let me know, Blue?" she asked. "If anything happens?"

"Nothing will happen," said Miss Blue. "If you want Ivy, you will get her yet. Time is longer than rope."

"Don't tell me that story, Blue," said Lucille. "What's done is done."

15

WHEN YOU BEGIN SOMETHING, you never know where it will end. This is a simple truth but it escapes even the most complex people. Certainly it escaped me. From the time I was quite small, I wanted to be an actress, and not any actress: a great actress. At that time, there was nothing I would not have done, nothing. There would be my face, up on the screen, and the world turned to me, as the faces of people on earth turn upward every night to look at the moon.

When I met Max, I studied him the way scholars study a text. There was nothing I would not have done to please him. Nothing. Erik Grissom knew that and eventually he had reason to fear and hate me. And then the day came and there I was, the star I intended to be. Now I was afraid when people watched me on the sets. At night, when I thought I had to go back in the morning, I would become sick to my stomach, so sleepy I would go to bed in my clothes and wake up in them the next morning. *I cannot do it. I cannot do it.* I said it again and again.

"This is neurosis," Max said. "Go, do your work, and before you know it, the day is over." They closed my sets. They chose scripts for me, roles that did not upset me. Nothing helped. Every day it was darker because every day added more bars to my cage. Eventually the day came when I could not go and so it all came to an end.

How could it be that I was so unwise? Why did I not know how unsuited I was to what I wanted? *Whom the gods would destroy, they first make mad.* This is what it means. I went my way. I did everything I could to become Anna Asta, the woman the world watches. And when I became her, I could not tolerate it. *This is guilt. That's all it is,* Max said. *Overcome it.* But I could not do it. Perhaps he could not do it either. With what genius he set about destroying himself when we reached Hollywood!

How does it happen? Is it true we are all collections of people, small selves loosely bound together, and for a time, one of us gets our attention? I think it is true. And then another self, a smaller one, grows stronger, secretly grows stronger while we are still ignorant of its presence. And then one day it declares itself and we are unprepared. We are like a small country, proud, independent, suddenly overthrown from within. Yes, I think that is what happens. Lucky is the person who knows what selves he has hiding in his closets and what they may do to him when they emerge. Then he can take care. He can take measures. He will not be surprised, as I was: surprised and defeated.

I look back and try to remember. Did we know what we were doing when we came daily to the set to film *The Mansion of Father Bertil?* Of course now it is easy to think we did know. We had hopes, yes. Max built sixty-eight separate sets. No one had ever built so many for one film before. And every day, someone was giving him more money, for the wolves chasing us over the ice, for the train transporting us to the frozen lake, for a real three-story house we could burn to the ground. You can still go and see it, the ruined house, standing outside Stockholm in the snow. One day Erik came up to

Max and said he was wasting money, spending so much on this film. Instead he should take all of it, hire an army, and invade a country. *A couple of thousand kronor more, Max. That's all you need.*

But day by day, what did we think? We were distracted by Max, his insults and his complaints. I was, he said, more wooden than a tree. He was going to chop me up for firewood. Erik was a wooden puppet. He flung his arms like a windmill. If Tora grew any calmer, he'd hold up a mirror to her mouth. Who knew if she still breathed?

Max wanted *The Mansion of Father Bertil* to turn out well, better than his famous film *The Sharp Knives of Hogeborn.* He wanted this so badly he was crazy with desire. Of course he was exhausted as well. At times he would rant and rave and scream and finally burst into tears and then he would have to stand behind one of the flats until the storm was over. So he pushed us and pushed us, and always we thought we were failing, and if we were failing, so was the picture. When all this was at its worst, Erik decided to fall upon Max from the rafters, and then we had a week of something like peace, if you can mention such a word in the same neighborhood as Max.

Then it was back to the same thing, even Tora in tears. All through filming, Max complained. She could not cry real tears. And now he had her weeping like a waterfall and what did he say? "This afternoon we are filming a comic scene, you damn cow, and you will have red eyes!" So that afternoon we didn't film at all. Tora stalked off the set and went home.

By this time I knew Anders Estersen. He was working on another set and I went to find him. "Max is making himself sick," I said.

"Over there!" he shouted. "Move that tree over there!"

Then he looked at me surprised, as if I'd jumped out of the ground. "He likes it that way," he said to me. "Just one tree!" he shouted. "Just move one tree!" He watched the tree move to the left, and then looked down at me and said, "All right, I have two minutes. Let's get a cup of coffee.

"So," he said, "first, you don't understand. He is a very superstitious man. If things are going too well, he expects the ground to fall away beneath his feet, so it is always the worst acting, the worst weather, the worst story, the worst everything. That way he suffers like a martyr so God will see him and reach down His hand. We take all this for granted."

"But," I said, "he says the picture is bad."

"Will he say it is good and tempt the critics to contradict him?" Anders asked. "When he releases the picture, *then* he will say it is good. More than good, the best, so good the angels are weeping and lining up for the best tickets. And if you look at him and raise your eye-brows, he will say, 'It's done, it's finished, it's hopeless anyway, so now we convince the weak-minded people who do not know what they think.' Then he will go on praising himself until it is truly outrageous. This is where the artist leaves off and the showman begins."

"I think," I said, "that this is worse than usual. He cries. He stands behind the flats and cries."

"You think the picture is bad?" Anders asked me. He frowned and pushed the hair out of his eyes: Anders of the massive forehead, the lantern jaw, the black, burning eyes, the neatly trimmed black mous-tache, the incredible sweetness that made everyone who knew him feel calm, feel happy.

"How can I know?" I wailed. "I am the worst thing in it. Tora cries her eyes out all the time and asks anyone who will listen, 'Is this a nervous breakdown?' "

"Even Tora is falling apart?"

"Even Tora."

"Tell Max I want to see the rushes," Anders said. "Not everything he's got, just an hour or so. I'll come tonight."

So he came. I was off in a corner of the set, quiet like a rat, making faces into my mirror. But wherever I was, I felt Max's eyes on me. I knew where he was even when my back was to him.

"I came to see the great disaster," Anders said. He had a booming voice. He could have been a great stage actor. Instead he starred in his own films. For this Max envied him. At the Academy everyone said that Max was a failed actor, that the archives had footage of Max in a filmed play, and when he was in front of the camera, everyone gawked, he was so large and brown and odd and his mouth moved so strangely when he spoke. "You know, over in Studio Seven I am making *Ghost Train*," Anders said, "and it is pretty good. So I want to see something so bad I will feel even better."

"I want you to tell me the truth," Max said. He seized both of Anders' hands and grasped them so tightly Anders grimaced. "Disguise absolutely nothing. Hide nothing. Don't think of my feelings. They are already broken, frozen, dead! Any detail that strikes you, if the pacing is off, if the acting is wooden, anything. If I can't do it anymore, you must tell me. If *The Sharp Knives of Hogeborn* must be my epitaph, you must say so. Will you say so? I can trust you?"

"If you will let go of me and run the projector, I'll tell you what I think," Anders said.

"It's not edited, of course," Max said. "Maybe when it's finished it won't be quite as bad as this."

"Who knows?" Anders said.

"Well," Max said, stiffening, "these opening scenes, they have a *few* good things in them."

"A few," said Anders. "I see."

"Well, see for yourself," Max said. His voice was gruff. He threaded the film and switched on the projector and the screen came alive. A minister was lecturing his congregation and reducing them to tears of repentance, and then someone came up to the minister and said, We must forgive you your trespasses if you can speak to us like that, and the minister turned on the congregation and denounced them. *Hypocrites! Drunks! You do not even deserve a drunkard!* And so they threw him out in the snow. He wandered in a storm, he was lost.

After that, all was out of sequence.

A middle-aged woman is thrown out into the snow by her husband. In the next scene, the same woman is young and disowns her elderly mother and orders her into the snow. Next an irate father drives off into a snowstorm and leaves his daughter stumbling through the drifts after him. A young girl who was beautiful before is now scarred by smallpox and refuses the minister's protestations of love.

Not breathing, I sat there. This is what we had done! We had done this! Then the screen went white and the film began to lash as it spun about, *snap, snap, snap!*

"So?" said Max. "What do you think?"

"You don't need to retire yet," Anders said.

"No?" asked Max.

"No," Anders said. "But as for me, I should think about it."

"What are you talking about?"

"Next month or the month after I'm going to America," Anders said. "Nothing wonderful gets done there so probably I'm the right man for them. But you, you stay here." He sounded utterly bereft. "You finish the movie the way you began it, no one is ever going to forget it. They will write about you in the history books."

"Oh, but it is nothing!" Max said, flinging out his arms. "The next one I do, *that* will be the one."

"So can I go home now?" Anders asked. "Anna," he said, "you are not so bad. Don't let him bully you. You can always come work for me. It's not so exciting on a set with me. Actors don't fall out of the sky on my sets." He turned back to Max. "Finish the picture and keep your mouth shut. You know the old saying. 'Artist, do your work. Don't speak.' Just do the work, Max."

Anders walked off the set and Max began crying with relief. "He was impressed," he said at last. "He was jealous. Did you see how he stooped over when he walked off? He was jealous. I know."

Then came a week of peace and we were finished. I was out of work and back at the Academy and the long wait began: for the editing of the film, for its release, held up while Max haggled with foreign theaters for the best time, when nothing else would compete with him, and it was still winter, and the long, dark days dragged on and the snow fell like a curtain and out of our window we could see the blurred, wet, gray slate roofs of the houses across the street, shiny with moisture, whitish smoke curling into the gray skies from the chimneys, the snow gathering in thick drifts on the roofs, then falling with a great thud, creating impassable drifts on the sidewalk. Or the day would turn foggy and we would look out the window and see nothing, and inside, the arguments went on: who would sit nearest the stove while my mother cooked and we did our homework, who would sleep next to the wall, who would sleep on the edge of the bed and from it fall to the floor six or seven times a night whenever someone else turned over. Already *The Mansion of Father Bertil* was an extravagance, a dream, but now I was awake at home and fighting to sleep next to the wall. What could be more important than sleeping next to the wall?

Then one day Max came to the Academy and called me out of class. "The preview is next Saturday night," he said. "You will be there, also Erik and Tora. And this time you must have something decent to wear. There will be photographers." He took a roll of bills from his pocket and pressed it into my hand.

"I can't take this," I said, flushing.

"Don't act like the daughter of a washerwoman," he said. "This money comes from the publicity budget. It's no use sending you to the store alone so I will take you. You'll buy a good dress and decide to scrimp on the stockings and shoes and all night you'll be pulling your stockings up or trying to hide your feet. Let's go."

So I was fitted out with a beautiful, very plain green silk dress, a silver metallic dress that had no back at all, four or five pairs of stockings ("What will you do if you get a run?"), and two or three pairs of high-heeled shoes.

"Oh, I do not like these! They hurt my feet!" I complained, and Max said if Cinderella had been like me she would still be home cleaning ashes out of the stove. Then he decided I needed something to wear over the dresses and my black cape was not warm enough for standing outside theaters in Berlin greeting opening-night crowds, and he took me to a furrier. I tried on many coats but the one I wanted was a silver fox. "Silver fox sheds," Max said, and the coat was taken back. "Persian lamb is not bad on a young girl," he said, "not if she is blond," and he nodded to the salesgirl, told her to shorten the coat an inch and a half, asked her when the alterations would be finished, and paid her for it.

"So," he said, "if you can do something with your wild hair, you will not disgrace me."

The preview was held in a small screening theater at the Lagerloff Studios. I sat between Erik and Anders Estersen. Max sat in front, turning around constantly. "He's counting the house," Anders said.

Max had turned around again and was looking in our direction. I waved. "Don't wave!" Max thundered from the front row and the people sitting on either side of him bent toward him. Who had he shouted at? Why was he shouting? "Just sit still," Anders said. He was clenching and unclenching his fists.

The lights dimmed and went out. There on the screen was Max's name and then the title: *The Mansion of Father Bertil.* So it was done. So it was real. Then came Erik's name, then Tora's, then mine. My hands grew cold. My lips were numb and the tip of my nose froze. How lifelike it was! Who would guess now that most of it had been filmed in a studio? Real snow swirled around real trees and houses. A young woman fell ill with a dreaded disease and was really disfigured. All the little things that had gone wrong—the way Erik turned to us before the cameras stopped rolling, the way Tora mockingly raised her eyebrows after a particularly dramatic scene—all of that, gone. This was life, compressed and purified. In the dark, I began to cry with joy. He had done it. There was his dream for everyone to see, immortal. And there was I, a small part of it.

Finally, the lights went back on. In the room there was a profound silence, as if a heavy invisible snow had just fallen inside.

Max stood and rushed up the aisle to us. "Let's get out of here," he whispered violently. "No one has a word to say! They're speechless with horror! I don't want to sit around and wait for all that malevolence and condescension they call sympathy!"

"Are you out of your mind?" Anders asked. "They are sitting there stunned. Go back to your seat! Keep quiet!"

And they *were* stunned. The next day the theater pages of the newspapers were dedicated to *The Mansion of Father Bertil.* Most of the papers had double-page spreads. Stills from the films were prominently featured and there, there, I was! When I got home that night, my mother stroked my hair and wept. "If only your father could have lived to see this," she said again and again. "If only he were here!"

Max threw a party for the cast and everyone came and laughed and drank and danced. Every time I passed Tora, she was saying, "Do you *really* think so?" We could not get enough praise. "Very beautiful from some angles!" Erik shouted, quoting from a review, throwing his arms around me.

And after that, we didn't see Max for days. He was giving interviews. When did he know that *The Mansion of Father Bertil* would be his masterpiece? Oh, he had known from the first. From the beginning he had insisted no expense be spared. Why else build sixty-eight sets? Was it true he was difficult on the set? Was it true Erik Grissom had broken Max's shoulder getting even with him?

Of course, he said, he was difficult on the set. He was creating a *world*, not a film. *The Mansion of Father Bertil* would explain Scandinavia to every other country on earth. He wanted no less than that. Perhaps if he undertook something less ambitious, he would be less trouble. Of course Erik had fallen from the sky onto his shoulder, fallen without the slightest fear. "We knew every minute we were in God's hands," Max said.

"What did I tell you?" Anders asked me. "Don't read any more of this stuff or you won't be able to look at him."

The picture opened in a heavy snowstorm and the lines stretched for blocks. We drove to the theater in our limousine, past the people standing in the snow, whitening as they stood, their breaths white clouds in front of them, and I asked Max, "Why don't they go home? They can see they won't get in."

"Everyone wants to be a part of success. People starve to death for it and they don't even know they're hungry. Well, tonight they know!"

When we got out, women pushed themselves forward and thrust flowers at me. One woman pushed a rose into my face as if she intended to take out my eye, but Max's giant hand stopped her. "Just push forward, don't look," he said. "Keep going, keep going," and then we were inside. "So how does it feel?" Max asked. "Good enough?"

"Good enough," I said. I was so excited I was shaking from head to foot. But the woman who tried to scratch out my eye with the rose, what did she want from me?

This, I thought, this is what I want.

"You don't feel it yet. It takes a while to sink in," Max said. "But let it sink in. My first two films, I was so busy working on what came next, I didn't stop to enjoy it. Eat now for the lean times. Don't do what I did. This should give you confidence. You can't do anything without confidence," he said, and then the crowd swept in behind us. Even in the middle of this commotion, Max watched me, instructed me.

And again the name of the film came on the screen, and Max's name, and mine. And it entered my head that Max was hungrier for the approval of the world than I was, that I was more solitary. I was after something narrower and harder and more selfish. What were crowds to me? Who were these people? I wanted to please myself. I was like the kings and queens I'd seen so long ago playing in the snow. I didn't need an audience.

Max leaned over. He whispered to me, "You think crazy things at times like this. Don't worry. In the morning, you'll take off that silver gown, you'll still be yourself." I was comforted. I sat in the dark and thought, In the morning I will be who I was. That person on the screen has nothing to do with me. But I was wrong.

The Mansion of Father Bertil was opening in Germany. The next thing I knew, I was shopping, packing, kissing my mother and sister and brother goodbye, getting on a train, waving at my family, all at the wrong speed, everything moving too fast, moving jerkily. When I sat down on the green velvet seat of the express, when Max bought cups of hot chocolate, when I felt the train jerk and start and stop and start again, when I saw the station flying by, I knew everything was changing.

I liked it when things went slowly, when I could think about them, decide what they meant, think about where they would lead, but now life rushed past, faster than the train, and I understood one thing only: the people waiting for us in Berlin were not interested in the girl who at night fought for her place on the bed near the wall. They were interested in the girl on the screen, the girl who on the screen looked like a woman.

I drank my chocolate. I was splitting in two. When I was a child, my father brought home decals from a fancy store. At first, the decals were lovely pictures on shiny sheets of paper but when I soaked the sheets in water, the decal began sliding from its paper backing. Then I fished it out—it was thin to transparency, and delicate, like a shed layer of very thin skin—and I would carefully spread it on a little square of glass. This was how I felt now. I was sliding from the paper, the backing that had held me all my life. My self was sliding from myself.

"*Now* you see what I meant?" Max exulted. Oh, he was triumphant.

"*Now* you see what I meant? Wasn't it worth it? Isn't it wonderful? Is there anything more wonderful?"

I said there was nothing more wonderful. I sipped my hot chocolate. I looked into the little cup. It was black, as I was, with terror.

From that instant I ought to have known.

On the train Max spoke as if this were his last chance to make himself understood. He spoke, in these moods, as one who was half hysterical. "What will I do next? What will I do next? Anna, it is like climbing a mountain! You stop and you freeze to death! Always you must have your eye on the next thing. But I don't know what the next thing is! Now is when I have to have faith. Now is when I have to remember that I never know the next thing until I see it. Once I see it, once I can't see anything else, when there is nothing else, when I profoundly believe only this thing will interest me for the rest of my life, then I know what it is I will do. It can be anything, you know. It can be that one cow under that one apple tree out there. That's all it has to be. The cow, whom it belongs to, what it's seen, what life looks like to the eye of that animal, one thing leads to another, that's how it is. But right now there's nothing. Terrible! That Anders, he is a lucky man. What he works on now is the whole world to him."

And so he would go on.

In Berlin we were met at the station.

In my hotel room, I lay on my bed, and when I couldn't sleep I tried to write letters. When I found I had nothing to say I got up and went out for a walk. What was Berlin but another city? Here too people fed children, bought clothes, combed their hair. As people passed me, I caught snatches of conversation. Here, too, I said to myself, they put on shoes, they answer the doorbell, they sweep the steps, they live in buildings you would never see in Sweden, they eat sausages, they drink beer, and they speak a different language. All this I knew before I came. Then why did I come? So I walked on, wondering.

The hotel was in an elegant section of the city. There the gray stone buildings were beautiful, their balconies curved, with wrought iron railings. There the streets were wide and statuary of men and women held up the little porches over the entrances. After I had been walking for some time I saw that the streets were narrower, the buildings meaner. Maids in full gray skirts and white blouses were hanging out laundry on lines strung from one side of an alley to the other. I was tired and leaned against a lamppost.

I walked. The houses thinned out. I saw train tracks and wondered which way they went. If I followed them, would I be walking toward home or away from it? Suddenly I knew I was lost and daylight was going. I would have to find a taxi. But there were no cars. Just then, a milk wagon pulled by horses shot out of a warehouse and when the driver saw me, he stopped.

"What are you doing down here, little lady in a fur coat? This is not a safe place. Where do you live? The Hotel Imperial and you've gotten yourself out here? Get up on the seat with me. I'll take you back. Just now a young washerwoman was killed out here, ja, by a postman. He strangled her. Oh, news flies fast. He was bringing her letters from her lover who went away and when she went to thank him, she found out. He was writing the letters himself! So she got mad and he got mad and he strangled her. They say he's gone. No one can find him. You know what he'll do, don't you? He'll drown himself. You watch the papers tomorrow, young lady. A postman will drown himself. A woman will throw herself from a high place. So, young lady, here you are. The Hotel Imperial."

"You have five minutes to get dressed!" said Max. "Five minutes. One of the greatest cities in the world and all you can think of is to walk, walk, walk like a dray horse. Get dressed. I'm not looking. Don't pull the dress like that! You'll tear it! You're ready? Thank God!"

Through its back entrance we were smuggled into the theater. We climbed a dark, narrow flight of steps to our stalls. I remember the steps creaked. The pale yellow plaster peeled from the walls. But the stalls! They were gilded (*This is real gold, Anna, gold leaf!*); the floor, the walls, the chairs were upholstered in burgundy velvet. This was beautiful. (*This is German opulence! The back steps are filthy, the cupboards are filthy, but everything that meets the eye, that shines.*) Our stall protruded out into space. It floated over the rows of seats below.

"Come, practice standing at the railing," Max said. "Place your hands on it *so*. Now lean forward slightly. Bend from the waist. Nod your head."

"Heights make me dizzy," I said. "I cannot."

"She cannot!" he said scornfully. "Heights make her dizzy! You want to go back to the ground and arrange pineapple slices? Bend from the waist. Don't sway like a lily in the field. Nod to the left, now to the people below, now to the right. What is so hard? Oh, sit down!" he said.

Only the aisle lamps set into the chairs were lit. People were admitted into the darkness. And then suddenly huge spotlights were trained on us. We were blinded. Max took my hand. "Get up," he said. "Smile and nod, smile and nod. Do it right or I'll throw you off!"

The people below were on their feet, smiling and clapping, and the lights below grew brighter and I saw many people holding round bouquets.

"Those are for you," Max whispered as he smiled and bowed, left, straight ahead, right. "After the showing, when we leave, take as many as you can carry."

He took my hand and raised his arm and mine over our heads. The applause grew thunderous and suddenly I was completely happy. My cheeks flushed, my body grew hot, and there it was, all of it, the Berlin streets I had walked that morning, the cobblestones slick and dark with rain, little fogs rising from the stones so that the people across the street seemed to float, to have no shoes and no feet, the squares filled with bronze statues, so that, in that moment, I knew I would remember the city as a city of statues, and the rooms of the Hotel Imperial opened before me, the lobby with its acres of mirrors, its shiny crystal vases and its dead white lilies, the tasseled peach chairs in my room, the chandeliers with their embossed glass globes dripping dagger-shaped crystals, the deep carmine carpets, the feel of the quilted red bedspread, my finger tracing the gold threads that ran through it, the shine of it, the coolness of it.

"You see!" Max said. "You see!"

They go into the department store, the two sisters. Oh, it is a beautiful store. The salesgirls ignore them. From the state of their shoes and their stockings, from the way they gaze, stunned, at the glass counters, it is evident they have no money.

"When I am famous," says one of the sisters, "I will buy this and this. I will buy this and this, and that, too. I will buy dresses and hats and I will have pairs and pairs of shoes, so many I will have to store them under the bed. Whatever I want, I will buy. I will buy couches and chandeliers and candelabra. I will buy curtains and silver and picture frames made of onyx. I will buy carpets too pretty to walk on. And you, I will buy you whatever you ask for. It will be wonderful."

Her sister looks at her sadly. "Even if it happens," she says, "you are happier now dreaming about buying these things than you will be when you can pay for them. And would I ask you for anything? Would Mother? We have our pride."

"Pride, what is that?" says the other sister. "Oh, I cannot wait to buy all these things!"

But when she could buy them, she could not bring herself to spend her money, and she asked herself, Why is it never as you dream it will be?

•   •   •

Ivy comes into my room and opens the blinds. From the way the heat settled on my chest, I knew the day was sunny. She waited for me to move, but I kept my eyes closed and so she went out. Later, she will come back in with a cup of tea.

She sets the teacup down on the table with a little clatter.

"It is already eleven?"

"Eleven-fifteen."

I feel a great contentment. Occasionally time passes as you want it to. Then there are so many fewer minutes in the day to get through. I run my fingers along the edge of the pillow until I find the cool spot and turn the pillow so that the cool patch rests against my cheek. "I have been thinking," I say. "Why is that part of the pillow always cool?" Ivy makes a clucking noise. "Is part of the pillow always cool? Even on Green Island where it is so hot?"

"Green Island is part of the earth," Ivy says.

"Well, of course Green Island is part of the earth," I say. "No one said it wasn't."

"Green Island this, Green Island that!" Ivy says.

"Something happened that I should know about?" I ask her. "Sit down on the edge of the bed here, not always roaming around like a caged cat."

"The man who was following us?" Ivy says. "This morning he spoke to me in the fish shop. He says Neville, my husband, is missing. For two weeks no one has seen him. His mail is piling up. No one at work sees him and his last two checks lie in the office. So I grabbed this man up by the collar and said, Look! I may be his wife in the eyes of the law but it is years since I laid eyes on him. Why do you want to bother me? Go talk to his women, them! And you know what he says? He says, 'Neville's unemployment, his social security, you can get it, you know. You're his wife. It belongs to you. Your name is on all the papers.'

"So I said, Whatever he has, let the man keep it. I don't want anything from his pocket. And meanwhile, the poor fishmonger, he's standing there holding a trout by its tail, so I said, Come, get out of the man's way. He has customers. And this man, the man in the hat, he says to me, What you throw away your children might not growl at. But you have to sign a paper. Sign a paper! For what! I signed a piece of paper when I married the man! I don't want to sign any more papers.

"And anyway, I said I wanted to know how he knew me. He had a piece of paper with my name on it and right away I recognized my sister-in-law Flora's handwriting. You remember I told you about Flora,

Neville's sister? So why must Flora have her fingers in my life? And why must he follow me up and down and why does he not leave me a note in your mailbox? He says Flora told him he must tell me the story in person, and he must ask me, Did I hear from Neville? How do I hear from Neville? I asked him. He doesn't know where I work. I don't tell him. No one but Flora and my children have this address and I told them, You give it to Neville and you never hear from me again. So now," Ivy said with a sigh, "that is the end of Flora. Let the man go about his business!"

I sit up and stretch.

"Signs of life," mutters Ivy.

"But that is off our minds," I say. "Now we know who he was, the man in the hat. Now we will sleep a little better." Then I had to remind myself: it was a relief for *me* to know who the man in the hat was but for Ivy it was another matter. Always my mind is drifting in a country of my own. Always I have to remind myself there are other people alive whose flesh and blood is also warm.

"Where do you think he is, this Neville of yours?" I ask her.

"I do not think, I know," she says, "and where he is we will not find him."

"You think he is dead?"

"He doesn't pick up his mail, he leaves his checks lying, and he never took up with a woman who had even two dollars, so he is not lying sick somewhere while someone supports him, so, yes, I think he is dead."

"But if he is dead, someone will find the body."

"If he was drinking—and when is he not drinking—and he sat down with his bottle, and it was cold out there, and he drank some more, another drop of rum from his bottle, and he fell asleep, and someone came by and said, Let's lift this man's wallet and all his papers, and he woke up later and saw a garbage scow, and thought, That looks like a comfortable place for an hour, and he climbed in and fell asleep, and he didn't wake up, and they came and took the scow off, and they dumped the scow out, then maybe they won't find him.

"Well, you take out of this world what you put into it and he put nothing into it, so out he goes and no one knows if he's in this life or out of it, and does someone worry over him? The last woman he lived with, she threw him out. Flora and her cousin came to help him move, and the man was standing up there cooking his rice and peas, and the woman, she picked up the pot from the stove and threw the rice and peas into the trash and said, 'This is my pot,' and she put the pot under her arm and walked out, and the man's lunch was steaming there in the trash. So let him go on! Fifteen years I was married to him and I have two good children I wouldn't have otherwise and when I last saw him, I wouldn't swear that was the man I married. You could see through him, that's how meager he was. So that is the end of Neville."

What lives we lead! Everywhere I go, tables covered with pictures, men smiling out of the frames, women smiling, children. You know, it is a rule: the more pictures on the tables, the closer that person is to the end of his life. And when that one is gone, to whom will the pictures mean anything? Oh, it is frightening even to think about it. And to everyone else, what are those pictures? Boring! Another person. Just another person. Oh, it is terrible.

"We come into this life with nothing and we go out of it with nothing," Ivy says.

"You don't regret him? You feel no guilt?"

"What must I feel guilty about? The man came to this country and found another woman and so had no money to send me. I came here, I took him back, he drank, he took up with other women, he brought one to my house, my son threw him out in the snow. I was in the hospital and he was so busy with his other woman and when he came and swayed there drunk on his chair the nurse threw him out into the hall and his sister Flora cursed him. For fifteen years we were man and wife and we were happy and I said, This is how life should be. Then he bought a car and stayed out all night with his new friends. The man who is gone, leaving his checks lying on a desk, that man is not my husband. So, Lady Clare, I have work to do. You cannot walk out in wrinkled shirts. People will say I am good for nothing."

People will say. People will say.

A short balding man came to visit us in the Hotel Imperial. He was American. Max paid him every possible attention. At first I did not understand why. He looked like the man who collected night waste where we lived in Helsinki. He is, Max said, the most important man in American films.

Why, I asked Max, is it important to make films in America? First, he said, there is the money. In a few years we can make so much money we can come back and do important things. We can do exactly as we please and not ask anyone for anything. And almost as an afterthought, he added, Nothing we do here calls as much attention to itself as the worst thing they do in America. He said that as if it were a small thing, something we will add in when we think the matter over, but really, that was the most important thing. That is why he wanted to leave. Attention and more attention, Max could never have enough of it.

Your passions kill you, I thought to myself and I shuddered. Then I thought, No. The wrong passions in the wrong body, those are what kill you.

When Max and the short, fat American finished their drinks, the American stood next to my chair and bowed to me. I looked up at him and saw his eyebrows were raised and the side of his mouth was twisted up. He was looking at me as if I were something he did not like but must put up with. I nodded and smiled but I was sure he knew I did not like him, wished he had never come.

"So," Max said after he'd gone, "it's all settled. We're going to America! You'll see the greatest city in the world! You'll meet all those movie stars you've been sitting and watching in the dark. In a year, maybe less than a year, the shopgirls are going to brush off their white aprons, go into the back of the shop and comb their hair, and come out of their shops into the dark streets, and you know what they're going to do? They're going to go into movie theaters and pay good money to see you! As for me, I'm going to make great European movies. In America. People will talk about them forever! They will last forever! This," Max said solemnly, "is what I want."

"Is it important?

"It is important."

"But Anders," I said.

"Anders is already in America," Max said. "He's making a film about dust. Dust! I have a telegram from him. He's bought up every fan in California and he has airplanes sitting in the desert blowing dust with their propellers. He says he's happy but his wife misses the snow. So if we go to America, where will we be going? Anders will meet us in New York. We'll be working at the same studio. We won't know we've left the Lagerloff!"

He said we would be in New York by the beginning of August.

I see I have not given a very good picture of Max. For one thing, I have forgotten to mention his dog, Gussie. How can that be? Max was never without that dog.

This is how you must picture him. He is a tall, elegant man, sitting very straight in a carved wooden chair, his right elbow resting on the arm of the chair, his arm straight up, his long fingers holding a cigarette, his palm, tilted back at the wrist, facing the viewer, almost as if he had been waving and had frozen in that position. A long white cigarette rests between his second and third fingers. He is wearing a black wool suit and a perfectly ironed white shirt with the high white collar of the time and his tie is dark red and of an intricate design. In his pocket is a perfectly ironed silk handkerchief. Gussie sits at his feet.

Gussie is a small bulldog, white, patched with black and tan. One black patch covers her left eye and gives her the look of a desperado. She is never far from Max. Often she sits on his lap and nuzzles him until her head is under the flap of his jacket. Right now, excited by someone coming into the room, probably the photographer who will take this picture, she is leaping and leaping into the air. And yelping, and of course, barking. Max remains immobile but smiles slightly. It is a very mischievous smile.

Once a famous ventriloquist performed with his dummy. Even when he ate or drank, he could make the dummy speak. Soon the dummy came to seem more alive than his master. At times Max and Gussie remind me of the ventriloquist and his wooden doll. Max is always sitting, elegant, perfectly composed, his eyebrows raised, his smile amused and ironic, and the little dog is leaping about like a maniac, exploding with energy, existing to please, and I think, The dog, that is *really* Max, not that elegant man sitting there.

And of course everyone must put up with the dog's antics, must brush the dog's hairs from their clothes, while no hair ever dares settle on Max's suit. Great fusses are made over the dog's walks, while Max sits elegantly in his chair and moves his right hand slightly to the side, holding its cigarette.

"How does Max stay calm through these negotiations?" Anders asked me once. "He is swimming with sharks. Doesn't he know he swims with sharks?"

Max was calm, yes, but the dog was uncontrollable.

The afternoon that dreadful American, that Mr. Pinsky, spoke to Max about us, Gussie tugged at the American's shoelaces and untied them. Gussie stood up, her front paws on the man's trousers and looked into the man's eyes and began to bark. She lay down at the man's feet and every few minutes she growled.

Even a stone could see that Mr. Pinsky was afraid of dogs, but Max was oblivious, or so he seemed. When the interview was over, we had first-class passage guaranteed, for me, for Max, and for Gussie. Max swore our salaries were higher than Mr. Pinsky intended. "He paid us about ten thousand dollars to get away from Gussie," Max said. "And she is such a sweet dog! Aren't you a sweet dog, Gussie?"

And he put a biscuit in his mouth, he bent down, and Gussie took the biscuit from his lips. Then he set Gussie on the floor and resumed his pose in the chair.

At first you must be taught these things, how to sit, how to walk, but after a short while, they become second nature.

I remember when Eleanor first came to Hollywood. She walked like a stevedore. Max would look out the window and see her walking and call me over. "Look at that," he said. "No one here knows how to walk. You walk like a flamingo with arms and legs, and look at that one down there! Day and night she walks up and down the studio streets practicing her walk."

Then one day I looked out and Eleanor was floating from one end of the street to the other. "You see what practice means?" Max asked me. And the training doesn't leave you. When Eleanor left New York for the rest home, giving me her fur-lined coat, she floated onto the train, off the train, and if she's still alive, she floats from her bed to the door. Every reviewer in the world mentioned Eleanor's extraordinary grace. It is funny, really.

To Max, appearances were everything, or if not everything, almost enough. "Never apologize," he said to me. "Never. Consider what people say. If you give in, give in graciously. Don't apologize." But once I saw him do it.

He was sitting in his chair reading a script. Gussie was sitting at his feet. Max was smoking a small cigar, held, naturally, in a specially made cigar-holder. "Good dog, good dog, Gussie," he said, and the dog, transported, jumped straight up and into his cigar. The cigar burned the dog's eye and Gussie let out a scream of pain. Max jumped up, he overturned the chair, the script settled like a leaf storm all over the floor, and he grabbed up the dog. "Oh, Gussie, I'm sorry, I'm sorry," he said over and over again. "I'm sorry, Gussie. Anna, call the car. We're taking Gussie to the hospital. Oh, Gussie, I'm sorry. It will be all right, Gussie, I didn't mean it, Gussie," and all the time he was crying.

Gussie died six months before Max and it was a good thing. Max died in a hospital. He would never have gone in unless the doctors had agreed to let him bring Gussie with him and of course they wouldn't have done it. Anders told me he thought Max would have gone into the hospital earlier, but Gussie was still alive and he didn't trust the dog with anyone else. But I don't think that was it. I don't think Max could bear to be separated from the dog. Who knows what that little dog stood for?

I would come in—I always moved quietly—and Max would be deep in discussion with her, what changes he would make in a script, who should be cast in a part, how to persuade the studio to commission an opera especially for his new movie, and he would pause and listen and say, "So *that's* what you think, Gussie!" Well, life is peculiar. I had very long conversations with my cat, and when she died, I said, No more cats. That's it. Now I am free to come and go. But these days I don't come and go so much. Maybe it is time to get another cat.

To understand Max, you must know he persuaded his backers to commission a new opera for his film. And it was a silent film! They say the opera is still performed. I don't know. I never heard it.

And Anders, I haven't given much of a picture of him either. They said he was more serious than Max, but who knows what serious is? Often he starred in his films himself, because, as he said, "You get tired of telling other people what to do. If I take the part, that's one less worry." When he played the role of an older man or a villain, he always grew a beard. "Now I look serious," he would say, tugging at the beard with satisfaction. "With a beard you can be any age. You remember that, Anna!" He was devoted to Max and devoted to me. Once he loved something he never put it down. I think his heart was simple but his mind was not. Once the vision was there, he could not abandon it. He would not rest until he had it on the screen. He wrote his own screenplays. He could do anything. I think Max and I envied him. I still do.

Once when Anders came here, he said, "One thing I am proud of. I never did anything just for the money. Never." Then for a while we said nothing because we were both thinking of Max and his last years when money was all that kept him going.

"He thought he could transform whatever he laid his hands on," Anders said at last. "But he was not God. He could not do it. Well, that's a sad story. Let the dead rest in peace."

We drank tea and ate our biscuits and he went home to Sweden and at eighty became the star of a wonderful film and for a while he was famous all over again. He would not appreciate my speaking of him. "Artist, do your work and keep quiet." That was what he always said. "What is best about me is up there on the screen," he said. "The rest is tying my shoes and how my wife bakes her bread." I think he was heartbroken when his wife died. The old charmer. Even in his seventies, women trailed him home. Today he lives quietly. What else can he do?

• • •

Ivy came back in wearing her coat, her scarf tied around her head, her head tie, as she calls it. "That man is downstairs again," she said. "I will run him off."

"Be careful," I said.

"I have a knife in my pocket and if he makes a sound, Flora's cousin or no Flora's cousin, I'll juke him."

"Talk to him in front of the doorman," I told her and she nodded at me and went out.

Three men are in a graveyard, sitting on a tombstone. One of them says, "Here no one can tell us what to do." In back of them, the church steeple rises up, its clock face like a full moon. There is always a full moon in that cemetery. Someone calls to one of the men, asking him to come along, but he refuses to go. The other two men begin to fight with him and they knock him down. He doesn't move. One of them picks up his wrist and holds it and then they run away.

The dead man pulls loose from his body. He looks just as he looked before only now the church and the gravestones show through him. The death cart drives up to him and the driver gets out. He asks to be taken to the hospital but the driver says he can do nothing for the living. The man begins to sob. Is it New Year's Eve? he asks. It is New Year's Eve.

Now he is reunited with his wife. For a few days they are happy. Then he begins to drink. He torments the children. When he goes into another room, she locks the door behind him. She dresses the children quickly, trying to run away. He begins to kick at the door and then slashes at it with an axe. Cracks begin to appear, then a small hole, then a large one. Then his hand comes through, turns the key, and opens the door. He stands over his wife with the axe. "It is not so easy to escape, is it?" he asks.

It is not so easy. I am tired of driving that carriage.

16

WHEN IVY CAME HOME from school, everything was quiet. Nothing had disturbed the routine of the household. She put her book bag down on the veranda and her stepmother handed her the coconut broom. Ivy went up to the top of the yard and began sweeping, working her way toward the house. She swept around the fallen chocolate leaves. When they fell, they grew slimy, and fat silvery gray snails clung to them. Inside the house, her stepmother was already cooking dinner. The smell of curried goat floated to her where she stood, stooped over.

"You're too lazy!" shouted her stepmother from the veranda. She flung a star apple at the girl, and without thinking, Ivy caught it and took a bite out of it. "He will beat you when he comes homes, you'll see," said Bea, and she flung another star apple at her. Ivy caught that one too, looked at Bea, and said, "Slip, you fool!"

Her stepmother came down from the veranda carrying a broom and hit her in the back. "You say 'Slip, you fool' to me?" she demanded, outraged. "Am I a child you're playing Last Lick with on your way home from school?" Again she hit Ivy with the broom. Ivy grabbed it and was about to hit her back when her father drove up on his bicycle and saw them fighting in the yard.

"What is going on here?" he demanded.

"She is too lazy," said her stepmother. "She stands around in the yard when she should be sweeping."

"She alone is sweeping the yard?" asked her father. Her stepmother's face fell. "And Jack? And the boy I pay from up the hill?"

"She hit me with the broom!" I said.

"Tell her why!" Bea said.

"You hit a girl child in the back with a broom?" he asked. "She is a girl, like you. She could be pregnant, like you."

I could be pregnant? thought Ivy.

"I hit your woman!" shouted her stepmother. "I flung an apple at her and she said, 'Slip, you fool.'"

"Vidal! Vidal!" someone called from the gate. "Come here, sir!"

"You two wait here," said her father, but Bea turned and went into the house. "I will wait where I please," she said. "You," she said, pointing at Ivy. "You stand there."

"Why you didn't go to Mer's funeral?" the man asked her father.

"What are you talking about?" her father asked.

"Mer Clifton, that woman in Cinnamon Bay. Isn't she the mother of that child standing over there? They buried her yesterday. You didn't know?"

"She's buried?" her father asked. "In Cinnamon Bay?"

"Yes, yes," the man said impatiently. "Your mother, she is walking up here to tell you. I passed her on the way."

Just then Mother Lize came into view. "Is it true?" he called out to her.

"It's true," Mother Lize said. "Two of her girls went to see her in the hospital and she was fine, but when they got home, there was everyone sitting on the veranda crying and when they said Mer was dead the girls began to laugh and said no, they had just come from seeing her, but the telegram from the hospital, it reached home before them. They came up the road and everyone was on the veranda crying and crying."

"It's a mistake," said Vidal.

"It's true. I saw her myself," Mother Lize said.

Vidal jumped on his bicycle and cycled off. Ivy stood and watched him go.

"Now what?" her stepmother called from the veranda. "You have nothing better to do than stand there? You believe this is your mother's house? That no-good woman with four children and four fathers for them? You believe you are home with her?"

Ivy continued to sweep, ignoring her. When she was finished, she laid down the broom.

In the kitchen, she could hear Mother Lize quarrelling with Bea. "Will you shut up?" Mother Lize was shouting. "The woman is just dead. It is the child's *mother!* Have you no sense?"

Ivy stood still, listening, and then went to Miss Blue's.

"A man came and said my mother died," Ivy told her.

"True?" said Miss Blue.

"I don't know. This is a bad story." She began to cry. She thought, When my stepmother told me to sweep the yard, steep and large though it is, when she told me to fetch water from the spring, a half mile away, and then refused to let me drink any of the water, but sent me back to the spring with a tin cup, I told myself that one day I would run away to Cinnamon Bay. Now I have nowhere to go. And my stepmother calls me my father's woman.

"You cannot change this story," she told Miss Blue.

"No, but I can put it in a different light," she said. "Once there was a motherless child who lived with her stepmother— Come, lean your head against me, that's it. The stepmother hardened her heart against her stepdaughter and never lost a chance to abuse her and dishearten her. Neighbors came to the house and told the stepmother that her stepdaughter was the picture of her dead mother. This incensed the stepmother even more. Whenever she looked at her stepdaughter, she saw her husband's first wife standing before her.

"The father loved his wife, but he also loved his daughter, and he did not know what to do. His mother came to him and complained of his wife's treatment of the daughter, but he could only say, 'Mother, what can I do? I work all day. I'm not at home,' and his mother would scold him and curse him.

"Time passed. The father tried to forget his first woman, but his wife would not let him. One day the father came home with a young man and asked him to paint his daughter's picture. He told his wife that if any harm came to that picture, he would leave her and not return. The young man painted the picture and it was hung in the hall. When his wife objected, the father threatened to leave.

"Eventually the wife could not bear the gaze of the woman in the painting, for her eyes always seemed to follow her wherever she went, and one day she sickened. But she did not die. Whenever she left the house, she again felt strong and healthy. One day she left and never returned and the stepdaughter lived with the family until she married."

"What happened to the woman who went away?"

"Oh, she found another man. And the husband found another woman. They always do."

"How long did it take him to find another one?"

"Probably years. But in the end the child was victorious over the stepmother and she did not have to blame herself for anything."

"I like the story," Ivy said. "Miss Blue? My stepmother says if she dies it will be my fault and then she will come back and tear out my eyes."

"You believe her?"

"When she takes sick, I wait on her hand and foot, I am so coward!" the child said.

"The dead do not come back," Miss Blue said. "The dead stay dead. You must ask your father." She stroked Ivy's hair. "Is there anything you would like to add to my story? A long illness for the stepmother? Anything?"

"Perhaps a storm," she said.

"A storm," said Miss Blue. "Come back in a few days and I'll add a storm."

"What good will it do to add a storm?" Ivy asked.

"It never hurts to embroider a good story," Miss Blue said.

The girl walked slowly home, past Stanny's son, Lemuel, who at first seemed to be sitting on a large brown boulder, but was sitting on the body of a slaughtered cow, waiting for his father to come with the truck for him and the dead animal. She thought about Miss Blue's story, which had turned black to white. The more her stepmother mistreated her, the more quickly she would pull doom down upon her own head. Of course, Ivy thought, Miss Blue might be wrong.

When she got home, her father had not yet returned. She walked back down the road, waiting for him. It began to grow dark before she saw his bicycle light wavering toward her, striping the trunks of the coconut trees. When Vidal saw her, he jumped off his bicycle and grabbed her up in his arms. "It's true," he said and held her to him. "She is dead and buried." They sat under a nisberry tree. Her father cried and held her to him. "Ask him now," whispered a voice. "Ask him about your mother."

The sky rippled with silver and the earth shook. A storm was coming and it occurred to Ivy that Miss Blue had already added the storm to her story even though she herself had not heard the new version yet.

"I don't know anything about my mother," she said. "I can't even remember what she looks like. When I try to picture her, I see her standing with her back to me."

"If you could see your face, you would know what she looked like," said her father impatiently.

"I don't know how you met her or why you left her and married Miss Bea," she said.

"Can't you think of anything better to talk about?" Lightning and thunder shook the earth. Her father sighed.

"When I courted your mother, I was still in short pants. Can you imagine that? In short pants. I had my first bicycle back then but I didn't do very well with it. I was forever falling off it. But we were sweethearts a long time. It wasn't your mother I went after to start with, you know, it was your aunt, the teg reg. She'd walk down the street and everyone would say, 'Here comes Lu Clifton, the teg reg.' She was a fighter, that one, not afraid of anybody.

"Your aunt, she always came to church in the most beautiful hats and one day I walked her home from church. I was loitering there near the gate and her sister—your mother—came out on the veranda and your Aunt Lu handed her the hat—it was a red felt hat—and said, 'Here, take it. Everyone said how ugly it was.' So I saw Lu was fooling Mer and cheating her. I couldn't see Mer's face from the gate, but she took the hat and went into the house and from inside came this great burst of laughter. I never heard such a laugh, you had to laugh yourself when you heard it. So I waited outside until she came and I asked her to come to the river for a walk and she did come with me. She was always laughing, your mother, and anything you wanted, she would give it to you. And she was pretty, too. A little bit, like you are. She never said a word to me about my short pants.

"And then some years passed and we became friends and we had you. I wanted to marry her, you know, but she said she never wanted to get married. And after you were born, she took you up to her mother's house in St. Catherine's, because she wanted her mother and grandmother to see you, and she didn't come back. And your great-grandmother, my grandmother, you know, she was in love with your mother, and she kept telling me, 'Go to St. Catherine's and bring her back.' But when I went to get her, she said she didn't want to come back. So I went home and my grandmother sent me back for her and when she said no again, I came home and I found Miss Bea."

"Why didn't she come back?" Ivy asked.

"Oh, she was young and giggly and she wanted her freedom and she had her mother and grandmother there caring for you and maybe she wanted to stay with her sister. You couldn't get a breeze between them, they were that close. I don't know why she didn't come back. Someone told me her family told lies against me. They said I had another woman at the house when she was in St. Catherine's but I didn't. If they tell you that, you'll know it isn't true. I wanted to marry your mother more than I wanted Miss Bea. I loved her more. But what could I do? In the end, your mother moved back to Cinnamon Bay and now the whole family lives there, but by then I was already married. Miss Bea is not a bad woman."

"She is," the child said.

"After the storm I will take you down there," Vidal said, "back to Cinnamon Bay, and you can visit with your great-grandmother and your grandmother and your Aunt Lu. They want to see you."

"Great-grandmother died," Ivy said.

"Where did you hear that?" her father asked sharply. "I saw her this afternoon with my own eyes. She's fine as can be. And your grandmother, and your aunt, the teg reg. She sleeps with a machete under her bed. She showed it to me. Once the storm is over, I'll take you down."

"It will storm?" Ivy asked.

"Is that a question? Is that what I feed you for? Lightning is gashing the sky and thunder is shaking the ground and you ask if it will storm. Of course it will storm."

"And what is her grave like?"

"Oh, a mound in the earth and a small wooden marker," he said. "Vin and I will tomb it in a few months' time."

They walked back to the house, bending into the wind. She helped her father push his bicycle up the hill. "You mustn't think I didn't love her, you know," he said. "I wanted you because you were her child."

The thunder crashed. The palm fronds lashed about and the wind flung coconuts and nisberries from the trees. "Tonight even the star apples will come down," Vidal said. "The rain will be a welcome thing. The drought's been long and hard."

Last week, her father had gone to Black River and come back to tell them that everything that grew there was blackening and dying. The women were emaciated, their babies were skeletons. "It is the land of the living dead," he said.

He put his palm against the small of her back and pushed her up the hill. The wind grabbed their breath and left them gasping.

Her stepmother stood on the veranda. "Your dinner is waiting on the table," she said to Vidal.

"Let it wait," he said. "I'm not hungry."

"Is the woman dead?" asked Bea.

"She is dead and buried," said Vidal, "and those in this house who fear spirits would do well to fear hers."

Her stepmother said nothing, but later, when Ivy looked out the window, she saw Bea had taken a bag of sea salt and was scattering grains of salt in a circle around the house. Miss Blue came later in the evening, saw the salt, found Ivy, and said, "You see that ring of salt around the house? She's afraid of your mother's spirit. The salt will keep her out. Spirits cannot stand salt. And when they try to cross a ring of salt, they cannot do it. They must stop and count the grains of salt, and of course it cannot be done, so they cannot come in." Then Miss Blue, who had come to their house to wait out the storm, lay down on the floor of Ivy's bedroom and fell asleep.

It was late when Ivy awakened and everyone was sleeping. Outside were the stars and the noise of the wind. She stepped over the sleeping bodies and looked out the window. A woman was crouched down just beyond it, just outside the circle of salt. She picked up a handful of salt and sand and let it fall slowly through her fingers. As Ivy watched, she began counting the grains of salt, but she would lose count and begin again. Ivy could hear her whispers over the voice of the wind.

Oh, I shall never do it. I shall never get in.

The woman was bent over, absorbed in her task. Ivy knew she could not get her attention.

The woman was a figure of such sorrow and hopelessness she made the child's bones ache. Ivy wanted to wake someone and say, *See, she has come for me,* but the child knew she wouldn't stay if anyone else came. She wanted to see her face, but the woman would not look up, or perhaps she could not, so absorbed in counting the grains was she.

Lightning flashed, she lifted her head slightly, and Ivy saw she was wearing a red felt hat. She was still there, sitting on the ground counting the grains of salt when Ivy fell asleep standing up at the window.

In the morning, Miss Blue told Ivy she had fallen down and landed on her during the night. At first, Miss Blue said, she thought the storm had come upon them and Ivy was a rafter falling from the ceiling. She did not ask what the girl was doing at the window and Ivy did not tell her.

The palm fronds lashed. In the yard, oranges and coconuts were raining down. Mr. Speckles, the man from the post office, went by in his donkey cart with his megaphone, saying the storm would soon hit and they must nail everything down. Vidal followed him down the road and Ivy followed her father.

"What of Cinnamon Bay?" asked Vidal.

"It's raining in Cinnamon Bay," said Mr. Speckles. "The gully will soon come down there."

"I want to see that," said Vidal. "I never have seen it."

"You and Cinnamon Bay are in romance once too often," said Mr. Speckles.

"The gully came down in Cinnamon Bay!" cried Miss Coffin Cover, running up. "It came down one solid wall of water! It took up a strong colt, two donkeys, five pigs, many chickens, and goats still bleating out! And the boats, they went after the animals, but the sharks, they got there first. They are shark food now."

"This child's house, it is still standing?" Vidal asked.

"Her people's house is still standing," said Miss Coffin Cover. "Think on your own place. Dry River is Roaring River today."

And indeed the river that ran through their property, the river in which they bathed every morning and evening, and in which they washed their dishes and clothing, was brown and muddy and roaring and foaming as it made its way downhill. Something white flickered along the length of the riverbed, the froth on the water.

At first it was a small rain.

"See, it is not bad," said Miss Bea, who went about her business while Vidal nailed up boards across the windows. "Every pigeon is not a flock," said Miss Bea, making up her bed. "Go sweep the yard," she told Ivy, handing her the broom. But as Ivy was sweeping, the wind began to rise. She bent double, trying to make her way back to the house. Her father's hand grabbed her wrist and he dragged her in after him.

"Anyone who comes in now stays in," said Vidal.

Then they saw a woman coming round the bend leading her donkey. It was Mamma Jane, who worked the land at the bottom of our meadows. Vidal got up, went out, grabbed the donkey's bridle and Mamma Jane's wrist. They watched the three of them, Vidal, Mamma Jane, and the donkey, struggle against the wind as they made their way to the house.

The rain now fell black and thick and solid, obscuring the windowpanes so that at times they could see them and at other times the sheets of glass seemed to dissolve into the rapidly falling water. The wind roared like an animal kept from its prey. Ivy began to cry. "What's wrong with you now?" asked her stepmother. "You're inside, warm and dry." She peered intently through the window. "That man is not bringing that donkey in here!" she said. "Don't bring that donkey in here!" she shouted.

Vidal led the donkey into the house and shut him up in Jack's bedroom.

"Donkeys can fly too," he said. "Everything that flies through the sky in a storm does not have wings."

"He will eat the sheets!" shouted Bea.

"Any dead in Cinnamon Bay?" Vidal asked Mamma Jane.

"Her family is all right," Mamma Jane said, looking at Ivy. "The living and the dead are all right. They tombed the blind lady last week, you know."

Now the wind had grown stronger but the rain had stopped and through the windows they could see clearly. The light was an evil greenish-yellow and while they watched, a white pigeon tried to regain its nest. Ivy knew the nest. Many times she had climbed high into the pimento tree to see if the pigeon's eggs had hatched, and after they hatched, she watched the nestlings lift their beaks and cry while they waited for the mother pigeon to come and feed them.

Now the pigeon struggled against the wind, beating and beating her wings, but she was tiring and growing weak. Just as she made a great, last effort, and they thought she would reach her nest in the tree, the wind picked up, and the pigeon was carried away by the wind and swept utterly from their sight.

"Now it is after us," said Vidal. The wind began shaking the house. From the dining room came the sound of dishes crashing. The sky had turned black and the water fell. When the wind swelled the rain would stop and each new burst of wind was more violent than the one before. Ivy felt her father's hand on hers and above her she heard a popping sound, as if many small stones were hitting the roof, then a whining, metallic noise, and when she looked up, she saw the roof beginning to lift from the house. As she watched, the wind howled once more and the roof was torn away.

For an instant, the sheets of zinc hovered above the house, suspended in the air like a fan, and then the wind carried them out of sight. They crouched in the corner, her father, her stepmother, Jack, Mamma Jane, Miss Blue, the babies, while the rain fell directly upon them and while they watched, sheets of zinc from other houses sailed overhead, *whew, whew, whew*, driven by the force of the wind. The headless body of a goat sailed by followed by the whirling goat's head.

"That zinc is sharp and deadly," said Mamma Jane.

First the rain died down and stopped. Then the wind grew weaker and the trees became still. When they went outside, most of their animals were still in their pens. "We did not get the worst of it, you know," said Vidal. "Come with me to look for our roof, now," he said to Ivy.

As they walked under the cinnamon tree, they heard a terrible squealing from the sky and when they looked up, the tree was full of piglets. "Miss Blue," called Vidal, "come look at this! See how the wind has wedged these five piglets into the forks of the cinnamon tree branches!"

"Mistress Cook!" Vidal called to his wife. "Get me a crocus bag, bring it, come!"

He climbed the tree and stuffed a terrified piglet into the bag and brought the bag down. The sow beneath the tree inspected her piglet and continued her pig screams. She did not stop until all five piglets were back on the ground and then she lay down beneath the tree and they began to nurse at her. Branches from the cinnamon tree were scattered on the ground around her. The air was fragrant with their smell.

"Where in the valleys am I to look for my roof?" Vidal asked Miss Blue.

"Up behind Mr. Darlington's house," said Miss Blue. "The wind does blow everything in his direction."

That was where they found the sheets of zinc, still attached to the rafters that had torn loose with them. Vidal had his hammer and pliers and pulled the nails from the sheets of zinc. He stacked the sheets neatly and neatly laid the rafters in rows. But by the time he went home, got his donkey cart, and returned to pick up the zinc and the rafters, the field above Mr. Darlington's was completely empty. Everything was gone.

"Where is the johncrow who eats wood and tin?" asked Vidal, "and what is his name?"

As they walked back, he said, "I know it is Darlington. He holds it against me because I built him the coffin when no one else would do it. He wanted the coffin but he didn't want to look ashamed."

"But where is Mr. Darlington's house?" Ivy asked as they passed it.

"You see this rock here?" her father asked, kicking it. "This is what's left of Mr. Darlington's house."

"Then will he go away?"

"No, he will build another. Where can he go? His family is in the ground here."

After the storm, I did not think about my family in Cinnamon Bay again. I had seen the bird blown back from its nest and the bird never returned. I had seen the five piglets wedged in the joints of the cinnamon tree. I was one of those piglets and if I was fortunate enough to be stuck in a tree, then no matter what tree I was in, I should not complain.

But there was something else: it was as if one of those sheets of zinc, flying over the house in Mare River, had cut me off from my previous life in Cinnamon Bay. I now forgot my mother, my grandmother and my great-grandmother. I no longer wondered why my stepmother complained endlessly about me. I didn't sweep the yard well enough. I was too lazy. This was my lot.

My stepmother's relatives would come to the house and tell her what a good woman she was, how good she was to take me in and put up with me when I was so ungrateful and so unmannerly. She would say, You don't know how I suffer. She has no manners, she talks back, she sets a bad example for my children. And she, only an orphan! Only a yard child!

And then their eyes would narrow, and they would say, children who run away from home come to terrible ends. Their parents get down on their knees and curse them, and God hears them, and the child is disowned and can never come back. From that time forward, everyone shuns the child and the child never again has a home. I believed them, but I also listened and thought, This is only the story she tells herself. It has nothing to do with me. Soon I will be grown and I will leave this house and that will be the end of Miss Bea.

PART TWO

THE WIND

THEY SAY IF YOU COME to America and you cannot see the New York skyline, that is bad luck. The day our ship approached land, a dense fog concealed everything, yet the people returning home seemed to know the land was close. I suppose you sense it, when you are returning to your own country.

We got off the ship in the thick fog. We were checked by immigration. There was some commotion over Gussie, who had to be examined and then came ashore in a box, but of course when Max was about, there was always commotion. Then we waited for the man The Studio sent to meet us.

We stood in the thick gray mist, waiting. We were the last ones on the pier. Everyone else was gone, taken off by people who knew them. Then a car pulled free of the mist and slowly drove up.

"I'm supposed to get some pictures," the driver said. He spoke German. "Just pose over there, would you?"

"Together or separately?" Max asked.

"One of each, it's safer," he said.

"One?" Max asked. "One?" So I knew: we were going to have a scene.

"Max," I said, "I am tired. I don't look my best. One is enough."

"One?" Max roared. In her box Gussie began to yelp.

"I have only three plates," said the poor photographer. "Two for you and one for the funeral."

"Whose funeral?" Max demanded. "Yours?"

The photographer tried to say something, *funeral, crowds, hysteria,* but Max was still storming. "Max," I said, "in a few minutes, it's going to be dark." So our pictures were taken. A few days later they were printed. There we stood, beaming, like two happy human beings. My stockings were wrinkled. I didn't have time to notice it myself. Max noticed it for me.

The photographer drove us to the hotel. "The streets are always so crowded?" I asked him.

"The funeral," he said, but Max cut him off.

"This is the funeral you're wasting your last plate on? I don't want to hear about this funeral."

We crept through the foggy streets toward the hotel. Outside the car it looked like winter in Stockholm, but it was terribly hot. I began to crank down a window. "Don't do that, Miss Aspen," he said. "The mob's unruly."

"Aspen!" Max said, thumping the back of the driver's seat. "Her name is Asta!"

We sat in the hotel room, deliberately not looking at each other. Two hours passed, then three. I was tired, bored and angry. The heat was nauseating and probably I was hungry. I was exhausted by the effort of keeping silent and the longer I sat still, my lips clamped together, the angrier I became. Can anything make you angrier than keeping quiet, not because you want to, but because you know, if you say one word, trouble will start?

Beyond the window rain was falling through the fog. Across the street the buildings were barely visible. The noise of traffic was constant. What could I say that would not start Max off? So I sat still, silent. Max's shirt was wrinkled. Soon he would complain about that. Gussie lay at his feet like a dead dog.

"This is not the Hotel Imperial," Max said. I pretended I hadn't heard. "Nobody here speaks Swedish! They said they would get us a translator!"

"Max," I said, "I am going for a walk."

"Are you crazy?" he said. "It's pouring out there."

Still, I put on my coat. I looked at my watch. Five o'clock. People would be leaving work, stopping at stores for loaves of bread, meeting one another for coffee. Outside there would be people laughing, walking arm in arm. "Nevertheless I am going," I said as soon as I shut the door behind me. "I am going out whether or not it is thundering and lightning. I am walking until my knees turn to rubber." So I talked to myself until the elevator stopped for me and took me down.

The doorman stopped me from going through the revolving door. He put his hand on my arm and said something to me but I didn't understand a word. He raised his eyebrows and spoke to the woman behind me. The doorman had also stopped her. She sat down in an overstuffed chair, and unbuttoned her coat. "How long will this go on?" she asked the doorman in German.

"For the rest of the day," he said to her. "But really, to go out now is not safe."

I went up to the woman's chair. "Excuse me," I said, "but what is happening?"

"Oh, it is the funeral of that famous actor," she said. "A terrible thing. Who ever saw anything like it? The crowds are so wild the police cannot control them. Three people were trampled this morning. This afternoon, four policeman were beaten up with umbrellas. The Red Cross set up tables along the route and they have their hands full."

"Route?" I asked.

"The route to the funeral home. Anyone who can walk is going to have a last look at him. And you know what they say? They say it isn't even his body in there. They say it's a department store dummy with a wax head. They're afraid the people will pull the body to pieces, everyone wants a little souvenir. Well, it is horrible, horrible. You can't walk out there. The doorman was right to stop you. You get swept up by the crowd, you can't get away again. They carry you along. This morning they pushed a policeman through a plate glass window when he tried to stop the line going into the funeral home, and everywhere, ambulances taking women and children with cuts and bruises, and women going into labor outside the funeral home! This is American craziness! What is he, really? Only an actor! No, don't go out there!" she said. "When you didn't listen to the doorman, I thought you were one of the crazy ones."

"I don't speak English," I said. "Not yet."

"I don't speak it so well myself," said the woman.

"Well, I will take a look at this crowd through the lobby window, and then I will go back up," I said.

"A sensible European girl," the woman said, smiling at me. "What country are you from?"

"Sweden," I said.

"Oh, I am from Germany," she said. "The German people are sensible. They don't get into such hysterics."

From the hotel lobby, I watched the crowd outside, impenetrable, moving like a thick serpent. Then I went back to my room.

"Anna!" Max called. "Come in here! What a surprise I have for you!" And there, sitting in the other armchair with Gussie on his lap, was Anders.

"What happened?" Anders asked. "Oh, I know," he said. "You saw the crowd out there. This funeral! Sit down! Drink something!"

I sat down and listened to them talk.

"What funeral?" asked Max. "Since we got off that ship, everyone talks about a funeral. The king of this country died?"

"A movie star, you know him, Rodolfo, the one you laugh at so much. 'I will teach you what all women must know.' *Him*," Anders said. "The streets are mobbed, the police are out, no one's ever seen anything like it. They don't know how to bury him without killing more people."

"Three today, dead, two yesterday, dead, heat exhaustion, trampling, eighteen children lost and looking for their mothers, a room full of lost shoes at the police station, the hospital emergency room full, tents set up on the street, it's terrible. It's a crazy country."

"They treat him like a god," Max said. "A movie star!"

"These are the two gods they know here, movie stars and money," Anders said.

"What a story this would make!" said Max. "A procession, a false god, a mob, the dead king, the whole city shining like silver. If I had seen it!"

"There was talk of a wax head," Anders said. "The papers said the police didn't know what the crowd would do if they saw the dead man and someone suggested an effigy. Why not? A wax mold of a man's head on top of a department store dummy? We would know how to do it, you and I."

"We missed something there," Max said. "Now we can only imagine it."

"Still," said Max. "I can buy the papers and keep them by me until the translator comes. I can go to the funeral."

"That woman, that Gemma Rambova, coming all the way across country, weeping and fainting every step of the way," Anders said. "Who needs movies here?"

I fell asleep in my chair. Then I heard Anders saying, "You know, they put the body in a wicker hamper. They had to do it to get him from the hospital to the funeral parlor."

"A hamper? Wonderful!" Max said. "This should happen to us!"

"And the studios, they're afraid that woman will spoil everything. He's dead but all the publicity's going to her. These peasants who become movie stars, there's nothing like them. I'd rather fight the Russian army! She faints, she has fits, she hints she'll throw herself on the coffin, so they have two trained nurses and a doctor with her. And everywhere the train stops, she gets off and announces that she can say nothing and she sways and faints and it's in all the papers again.

"You know I heard talk that The Studio wanted to have her assassinated. Why? When this man died, he owed The Studio a million dollars, so if they don't make the money back showing his old pictures, they don't get anything. If that woman keeps grabbing the publicity, they're afraid everyone will wait for her in the rain and no one will be in the movie theaters. So the rumor was they would kill her.

"Anyway, The Studio isn't worrying. They insured his life for one million dollars and I heard today from someone who works in Pinsky's office that he already took the check to the bank. But now the dead hero has a wife somewhere trying to come out of the woodwork, saying the money should go to her. But no one likes her. She used to be a set designer, the strangest sets you ever saw, let me tell you, even a German expressionist couldn't find a use for them. They're not going to let her get a penny. And there may be another wife somewhere. They're young, these people, they run off to Mexico, they get married there, they come back across the border, they have regrets, they cross over again and get a Mexican divorce, but sometimes it's not legal, don't ask me why. So all this they're trying to keep out of the papers. Believe me, it's easier to run a small European country."

"From the pictures it looks so quiet," Max said.

"It's a crazy place. Be careful," Anders said. "And *that* one, she's such a *Finnish* Finn, I don't think she'll like it."

"She likes money," Max said. "I never saw anyone hold on to a krona like she does."

"If she wants money, maybe she'll be happy."

"Who knows what she wants?" Max said.

My eyes are still closed. Ivy is humming. Outside it is raining. All over the city people will be putting on galoshes and getting out their umbrellas, huddling in doorways trying to keep out of the rain, standing back from the curb so cars don't splash them, all of them on their way to work, and I, as usual, lying here, deciding what to do. For forty years now I get up every morning and decide what to do.

Really, it is a great burden. It is easier to get up and go off to a job, even if you don't like it, than to ask yourself, What do I want to do now? Because, really, most of the time who wants to do anything? And then you get older, you've done everything so many times, it's not so easy to convince yourself you want to do it again.

It could be my nature. I was seventeen and making my first American film and I walked around my room with my monkey sitting on my shoulder and I asked him why I had to go to work. Already I was tired of it, tired of trying on costumes, of the make-up men working on my face, painting me like the side of a building. When they were finished, I didn't have blond eyebrows anymore but black ones, and the lipstick changed the shape of my mouth, and then they stuck a black wig over my hair and called Mr. Pinsky. "She looks too Spanish," he said. "But Mr. Pinsky," the make-up man said, "the movie takes place in Spain!"

"So?" he said. "She'll be a blond Spaniard. Americans like blondes. She's a blonde, why shouldn't she look like one? She'll wear a lot of mantillas, who'll know what color hair she has anyway? That's what you want her to wear? She looks like a washerwoman."

"But Mr. Pinsky, she's supposed to be poor so later when she comes home rich, everyone sees the difference."

"So let her be poor in a rich way," said Mr. Pinsky.

And then it began, the fussing over costumes. How to make me poor in a rich way? It couldn't be done. Eventually I wore the same clothes but they hid me behind flowers. All the time I was carrying orange blossoms or lilies and when Mr. Pinsky saw that, then he was pleased. "Good, good," he said. "Flowers cost a lot. Now she looks poor in a rich way. She couldn't carry maybe roses?"

I had hay fever. I sneezed through the whole picture. When they showed the rushes, I had huge black circles under my eyes. Later on in the film, when I became rich and wore fancy clothes, they let me put the flowers down, but then it was no picnic either. Half the costumes were so tight I couldn't sit down. Between takes I propped myself against a wall.

At first, I couldn't understand a word anyone said. My interpreter worked overtime. He had to translate every single word people said anywhere near me, and, since it was impolite or unwise to do this while the others were nearby, he had to memorize what they said and translate it for me the second they were out of sight. But how did I know he was telling me everything? I was a nervous wreck. And when he had nothing to do for me, he made himself useful to Mr. Pinsky. He was like everyone else there: he wanted to be in movies.

And Max gave me an argument. He said, What's wrong with you? Half the world wants to be in your shoes. And I said, Now I am only an apprentice! When I am a great star, then I will be happy! I believed what I said. Happiness was always around the next corner.

So outside it rains and I don't know what to do. If I turn on the radio, the news will be the same as always. Cars are running into one another, the traffic doesn't move, the trains are stopped in their tunnels. Nothing is ticking. Every year it comes as a big surprise. Rain! Snow! No one is prepared. What they call a big storm here, at home no one would notice it. And if a snowflake falls! Then no one dares go out: is it too icy to walk, or will I slip? Then everyone is just like me, crazy indecisive, sitting at the window, shaking their heads.

Any second Ivy will walk in and say, "What do you want for breakfast, Lady Clare?"

What do I want to eat and how am I supposed to know?

Well, bagels, once I used to love them, but how long can you love a bagel? It is like everything else. After a while the love affair is over.

I ate pickled herring and black bread every morning for ten years of my life and then one morning I saw pickled herring lying on my plate and I couldn't look at it anymore.

Now it is salami and cheese and brown bread, and Ivy objects. Salami is full of nitrates. For a while I tried to live on carrots, it seemed so simple, so simple that my hair started falling out. And the doctor said I must eat protein and asked what exactly *was* I eating and I said carrots, red and orange, and he said, What are you, a goat? Eat some meat. Eat some meat! And every day the papers are full of people falling over from clogged arteries. You are not falling over so fast, he said. You have no cholesterol at all. If you were an adolescent you would not be growing. Go home and eat what you want and don't drive your housekeeper crazy.

You get older, you have nothing to do, you get cranky. You begin to look at everything with a crazy eye: this might kill you, that might kill you. Once when we were in New York, Max ate a piece of cheesecake and he came home with a terrible stomachache and no matter what, he would never eat cheesecake again, and he was only thirty-seven.

You don't even want to hear the list of what I won't eat: artichokes, chicken liver, blueberry blintzes, red caviar, blue cheese dressing, red cabbage, candied ginger, Twinkies.

On my walks, I used to sneak out and get them. They were just like little cakes my mother used to make for Christmas except that hers were soaked in rum, so when I got home, I'd get out some rum and pour them over the Twinkies, wait a few hours and eat them. I did this on weekends, when Ivy went home to her family. Really, they were very good, but then one day I ate them and got sick and now I won't touch them. Instead I send Ivy to this fancy bakery on Madison Avenue where she pays a fortune and comes home with what? Twinkies soaked in rum but in a different shape.

"So," I ask Ivy. "You gave the salami to the doorman?"

"No."

"This saving!" I say. "We are both crazy on the subject. Sometimes when I tell you, throw something out!"

Now she puffs herself up. "All right," I say. "Why didn't you give it to him? Such a nice little spotted dog, what can the doorman feed him on his salary?"

"There was no doorman to give it to," she said. "Louie is gone. There's a new one in a red uniform standing there. I asked him, 'Where is Louie? He is on vacation?' and he said Louie is taking a little rest."

"He is dead," I said.

"No, he is not dead. Next week he'll be sitting in the basement sorting the mail and answering the phone. At least there he can dress as he wants. No more brown uniforms with gold braid."

"Oh, but you don't know what he thought of that uniform," I said. "Once, in Sweden, a doorman was fired and they took back his uniform. It was a ridiculous uniform, really, black and gold braid and medals all over it, and a few days later they arrested him. He had tried to steal it back! He was too old for the job, you know. It was a terrible thing, taking it away from him, just like peeling away his skin. He crept around, he couldn't look people in the eye, they found him floating in the river. A terrible thing.

"Eleanor, you remember her? She gave me the coat? Every week she calls and says she doesn't like Arizona. So I ask her, Why not, Eleanor? Is it the heat? No, there are no trees. I tell her there are no trees here either. Well, where I am, she says, you see a sign saying 'Forest,' and you get your hopes up and what is it? A cactus forest. To her that is not a forest.

" 'So what is it, really?' I ask her. No one is unhappy because of trees. 'Here no one knows who you are,' she says. 'Everyone spends all his time saying, *Once I was something. This is what I was.* It's so depressing, everyone sitting round reciting their credentials: *You didn't know me then, but once I was important.* A few hours sitting around the pool and you think you're a ghost. Once you had a life story but out here you live in the margin of the page.' No, she doesn't like it there. So now, wherever he is resting, Louie is sitting around the same pool. Really, life is too hard."

"So what can we do?" Ivy asks. "We must lie down and die?"

I get up and sit on the edge of the bed. "You want to watch that movie I made on Green Island where they shoot me in the end?" I ask her. "Have they found your Neville?"

"They won't find Neville; he is in a Dumpster," Ivy said. "If we are going to see the movie, let's see it."

"You can work the VCR?" I ask her. "I'm afraid of it. A big square bomb is what it looks like to me."

"Miss Anna, anyone with fingers can work it," Ivy says, exasperated.

"Maybe we should have someone come in to look at the wiring."

"For what, Miss Anna? Every night I watch it. What I tape in the afternoons I watch at night. Come, tell me the truth now. Why are you afraid of that VCR? Every time we set off to watch the movie, you have some excuse."

"Oh, you don't know what it's like. You can't imagine, it's—I don't know what it is. Those movies, I have books filled with stills from them. I like to look at them, you know. Such nice, locked doors! But the movie starts, everyone starts to move, the doors are not locked anymore, the ghosts come back, I can almost touch them! You don't know! Forever they will do the same thing!"

"Then why must you say you want to watch them? We can go for a walk. You want to return those red shoes? They pinch your toes? We will return them and have a cup of coffee and a pastry, I will buy some salted codfish, that will take up the afternoon. Come. Get dressed. We will see *Bitter Almonds* some other time."

"There are people who stay up all night and watch them," I say as I pull on my slacks. "And, you know, I don't think it's right. I think they should ask my permission to see them, each and every person. In my opinion those films belong to me. But of course no one agrees with me. Always I have such queer ideas!"

"It's stopped raining," Ivy says.

2

THE STORM DIED DOWN and disappeared and with it went visions of my mother, stooping beside the house beneath the window, counting grains of salt, and in its place came a kind of peace I had no right to expect, a time in which I was happy as any child and after school went with my half brother Jack and we climbed the trail up toward the fields where the men planted corn and peas and potatoes, up to an old, giant plum tree, which we climbed, and we sat in its lowest branches, looking down on our house, talking to each other.

From where we sat in the plum tree, the house was small and far away, and Bea, when she came into the yard, was only a featureless doll. Above us puffy clouds moved along in a stately way as if drawn by horses, and on windy days, frothy clouds scudded along like driven sea foam.

Oftentimes I went up into the fields alone, climbed up into the plum tree, and thought, *Nothing happens here and nothing is going to happen.* It seemed to me as I sat in the plum tree, feeling the bough move up and down beneath me, a subtle movement suggesting that everything on this earth wanted to move and would find a way to do so no matter how deep its roots, that I could hear the sound of growing things. I could hear the *creak, creak, creak* of the bark of the plum tree and the nisberry. I could hear the slow, viscous sigh of the banana as it pushed its way higher into the sky. Each blade of grass, when it felt the dew evaporate, made a tiny hissing sound, so that a grassy field sounded like an army of tiny, almost invisible green snakes. And I listened, too, to my own body: when I put my hand to the long bone of my arm, I thought I could hear a grating, a staticky crackling, up and down my arm as it grew along with the rest of my bones, every day making me taller, taller and closer to leaving Mare River.

In the mornings, four of us got up to go to school. I slept in one bed with Cynthia and Cherry and Eileen. Before he went to bed, my father set down one alarm clock in the hall, outside all the bedrooms, and whoever heard it first got up, turned it off, and woke the others. Then we put on our wooden sandals, took our towels, and went down to the river to bathe.

We bathed in Blue Hole, a little distance from the house, where the riverbanks were high and no one passing could see us unless he troubled to come to the edge and peer over. We bathed naked, splashing and sudsing one another with the leaves of the susumba plant.

If we reached the river early, we sat in the water, kicking the water to froth, talking about what the day would bring, what exams there were, mocking the songs we sang at school. We were accustomed to bathing naked, accustomed also to watching one another's bodies, to noticing our breasts when they began to swell, changing from small, hard buttons to soft swellings of flesh, to noticing when our stomachs rounded, our thighs fattened, and our hips began to curve, and at night, the girls, all in one room, all in one bed, tried to guess when each of us would begin our monthly bleeding and we went on to speculate about the other girls in our standard and the standards ahead of us.

Our brothers, if they paid attention, did not let on, any more than we admitted noticing the strange behavior of the organs that dangled from their groins. And meanwhile, the sound of our laughter could be heard back at the house where it mixed with the sound of the last crickets, the early morning birds and the snapping of fat in the clay cooking pans.

Then one morning a girl in my class came up to me and said, "You know your brother Jack?" and I answered, "Of course I know my brother Jack," and the girl said, "No, you don't know him. He is telling the other boys that when you bathe, he can see hair."

"Hair?" I said.

"Not on your head," said the girl.

"Oh," I said, and felt a hot flush rising from the pit of my stomach, spreading out like a wave to the top of my head, to the bottom of my feet.

"Daddy," I said that night, "is it wrong for Jack to tell the other boys that when we bathe he can see I have hair?"

"Hair?" said my father.

"Not on my head," I said, my eyes cast down.

"Jack, come here!" my father shouted.

By the time Jack came into the room, my father was waiting for him, his hand behind his back. Jack, who did not know what he had done, nevertheless began to back up. If our father's hand was behind his back, then he had a fan belt in it. A beating was coming. "Stand still!" thundered my father. "What's this I hear about you telling the other boys how your sisters look when they bathe naked in Blue Hole? You did do it?"

"Yes, sir," Jack whispered and looked around for a means of escape. "Don't try to run," my father said. "I will get you when you come into your room to sleep and then it will be worse."

Outside the window, we heard the sound of the fan belt on Jack's bottom. "Now you will have to go further upstream to bathe," said my father. "All the way to Banana Hole. If I cannot trust you with the girls, it is disgusting, isn't it?"

"Yes, sir," said Jack.

Now Jack bathed alone in Banana Hole. He came back every morning with a pailful of river shrimp which he handed to his mother and asked to have cooked up for his lunch. It was weeks before he offered to share his catch with us.

The school bell rang at eight o'clock, a half hour before we had to be in our classrooms, but the school was just up the road, and so we never left home before the bell rang. When Teacher Banford came in, we stood up and sang:

"Every morning the red sun rises,
Rises red and bright,
Rises from the dark, dark ocean,
Driving back the night."

Then we sat down and began to work. "Help me with this, now?" the others would say to me when we were assigned compositions or stories. "Help me with this, now?" they would say to Jack when we were given problems in arithmetic.

If we got to school early, Jack and some of the boys would sneak into Teacher Williams' room, find the cane with which he hit them when they were impudent, and begin to score it just at the joint, so that when he picked it up to hit one of the boys, it fell apart. They did this so often and so successfully and in the process produced such hilarity that Teacher Williams, who was a very young man, not long out of school himself, and resentful of challenges to his authority, produced a stout leather belt, which he wore along with the thin belt that held up his pants. He was soon known as Two-Belt Williams, and one day, exasperated by Jack's doings, he yanked off his belt, intending to beat him, but that day he was wearing only his thin leather belt, the thick one having been, for one reason or another, placed in his briefcase, and as he advanced upon Jack, a thin, enraged skeleton of a man, shouting about peashooters and spiders' nests, his pants fell down, humiliating him utterly and leading him to blame Jack for all his difficulties in this world.

When, the next week, Jack once again took up his peashooter and tried to shoot down a wasps' nest in the corner of the room, Teacher Williams ordered Jack to come to the front of the room and stretch out his arm. He picked up the belt to hit him, intending only to raise a welt on his skin, but he was so infuriated, he hit him with the belt buckle, breaking the skin and causing an enormous, swollen bruise.

The next morning as we were eating breakfast, Jack reached for his cup of hot chocolate, and my father, who was passing through the kitchen, saw his arm.

"How did you come by that, sir?" he asked.

"Oh," said Jack, "I was using my peashooter at a wasps' nest and Teacher Williams caught me."

"He did break up the skin like that?"

"He didn't mean to, Daddy," Jack said. He looked to me for help. The last thing he wanted was our father at the school, offering to fill Teacher Williams' mouth with lead. "He meant to hit me with the belt, not the buckle, sir. I deserved it, sir. If I had hit the wasps' nest, all of us here would be right now swollen up like balloons."

"Bea!" called Vidal. "Tell Lazarus to go on his way when he blares his horn. I'm going to the school." And he was out the door.

The children looked at one another. "We could," I said, "say we are too dizzy to walk and our ears hurt."

"I cannot think of one thing worse than Daddy up at the school threatening to fill the teacher's mouth full of lead," said Cynthia. "Not one worse thing can I think of."

"It is too embarrassing to stand," said Cherry.

"Your father is going to school to fight for you," said Miss Bea, appearing in the room, "and you are going to school where you will look proud of him. You hear?"

We crept off down the road and as we went we heard the other students singing:

> "Every morning the red sun rises,
> Rises red and bright,
> Rises from the dark, dark ocean,
> Driving back the night."

We heard this song, as invariable and predictable as the rising of the sun and we hoped that all might still be well. Our father might have heard Lazarus blare his horn and, persuaded by his shouts, might have jumped in and driven off to Gray's Mansions. Instead we heard my father shouting from the schoolyard: "Your piss don't burn grass yet and you hit my child and break his skin? What did he do that you should break the skin on his arm?"

The other children ran to the window and saw, as we saw, a terrified Teacher Williams cowering in front of my father, who had one hand bent behind his back, the fan belt clutched in his fist. "They are *my* children," my father said, "and as long as I live no one else touches them. They do something wrong, you send to me and tell me and I will take care of it. Not one Cook child is to come home bleeding or I will fill your mouth with lead!"

"My God!" said Cherry.

"I can never hold my head up again," Cynthia said.

"You know their names?" my father continued. "Ivy and Jack, Robert and Cherry and Cynthia and Iris. Those are mine. You understand me, sir?"

"Get back to your seats!" shouted Teacher Banford, the principal, and so we had no time to hear Teacher Williams' answer. "Is this a carnival, that you should be gaping out the window there?" Teacher Banford picked up a pointer and said, "Sing!"

"But, teacher," said Eugenie, "we already sang the song!"

"Sing it again!" said Teacher Banford.

And so, on that day, the sun rose twice in the Mare River School.

And from then on, we could have gotten away with murder, but after our father's appearance at the school, the last thing we wanted was to remind other children that he had come there. After school we could hear them reenacting the by now famous scene. "Your piss don't burn grass yet," we would hear from behind a bush and we would run. And two years later, when Eileen came to school and nothing could stop her chattering, Teacher Williams lost his temper and slapped her. She began to cry. One of the older children came up to him and said, "Teacher Williams! You know that child's last name? She is a Cook, you know."

And Teacher Williams picked up Eileen, hushed her up, wiped the tears from her cheeks, sat her on the edge of his desk, and made animal silhouettes with his fingers, trying to quiet her, while the rest of us watched from the window, choking with swallowed laughter and then we ran out of the schoolyard where we could laugh until we were completely exhausted.

From the day my father came to school, it seemed as if attention moved, like a spot of sunlight, away from me and settled on Jack.

On Saturdays we cleaned the house while Bea went to the market in Cinnamon Bay. One such Saturday, Jack took down the mantel clock and sat in the middle of the hall floor with it. Soon he had the clock pulled to pieces.

"He will kill us!" Cherry said. "If one of us does something, he beats all of us."

"I can fix it," Jack said, but of course he could not.

We pooled what few pennies we had and ran down to Mare River with the clock. An old Indian clock maker fixed it for us, and when our father came home, we had it back on the mantel, ticking trustily.

But the next week Jack decided to take apart the old Warren radio. He spread a sheet out on the floor and had the tubes strewn here and the wires there, but when he tried to reassemble it, it would not work. "Now what will we do?" I asked. "We don't have the money to fix a radio, and no one in the village can do it. This will have to go to Greenstown or Albion Bay."

Jack packed the insides of the radio back inside its case and set the silent object back on the mantel. "Sometimes he's tired and doesn't turn it on," he said.

"When? When doesn't he turn it on?" Cynthia asked.

That night, my father came home drunk, I drew off his shoes and his pants, and we all gathered in the yard and discussed how long our good fortune could last.

The next morning, my father got up, took a piece of bread from the dining room table, and went into the hall to turn on the radio. The radio remained silent. "Eh?" said my father. He tapped the radio's wooden case. No sound. He looked at the dial. No light. He turned the radio over and looked at its back, took out his pocket knife and undid the screws holding on its backplate. "Who was inside cleaning?" he called out.

"Ivy and Jack," Cynthia said.

"Jack, come in here. You had something to do with this?"

"Yes, sir," he said. We waited for the sound of the belt, the wails of our brother.

"All right," my father said. "Go bring me a brown paper bag and some string." Jack brought the bag and my father wrapped the radio in the paper and tied it up tightly. He motioned Jack to follow him and went into his bedroom, where he placed the package high up on the topmost shelf of his wardrobe, in the back, in the corner. "When you turn a man," he said to Jack, "that radio is the first thing you will fix."

Outside the truck blared its horn and my father turned to go. "But until then," he said to Jack, "until then you will not touch it. Whenever you pass that wardrobe you will remember it is in there and when you turn a man, you will make it good."

"He didn't hit you?" Robert asked.

"No," Jack said. "Worse."

One evening I came in after having brought back the goats. "What's this I hear about you running from fights?" my father asked me. "Is that what I feed you for? If you get in a fight, you fight. If you lose, you lose. If you do damage, don't worry. I will back you up. No child of mine runs from a fight like a dog with its ears down."

"I don't run from fights, Daddy," I said.

In Teacher Williams' class was a girl named Eugenie. The other children called her a eunuch and insisted that she was neither boy nor girl. I, who liked Teacher Williams, and would think all day about a word of praise he bestowed upon me in the morning, was unwilling to fight with her in his class. Now, however, the girl had taken to calling me Coolie.

"I am not a coolie," I said to Eugenie. "A coolie is someone who works in the fields for nothing, only for food."

"A coolie is an Indian and you are part Indian," Eugenie said.

"You better not call me Coolie again," I said, but every time no one was watching, her mouth would form the shape of the word. I will have to fight her, I thought, even if she is in Teacher Williams' class.

The next time Eugenie called me Coolie, I grabbed her by the hair and hit her in the head. Eugenie kicked me in the leg. Soon the two of us were on the ground rolling over one another. Teacher Banford saw us and ordered the older boys to separate us. That was on Tuesday. On Wednesday, Thursday and Friday, and then again on Monday, we fought on our way to school, on our way back from lunch, and on our way home.

On Monday, I followed Eugenie into the school toilet, intent on finding out for myself if Eugenie was a eunuch. I backed her up against a wall. The girl began to scream *Murder!* and *Help!* and I was pulling up her skirt just as the girls from the next form discovered us and pulled us apart. When the principal heard this tale he immediately sent for my father and Eugenie's mother.

"What is this fighting about now?" my father asked.

"She calls me Coolie!" I said. "I can only hear it so often!"

"And the toilet?" he asked. "Why were you in there?"

"They say she's a eunuch and I was going to find out," I said defiantly.

"And did you find out?"

"No. The girls from the next form stopped me."

The next morning we stood in the yard while the principal talked to our parents. We listened while our doings were rehearsed. This one called the other one coolie. That one called the other one eunuch. It had to stop. Our parents were in their Sunday best, nodding solemnly. I looked over at Eugenie and the girl whispered *coolie* and the fight began again. I thumped Eugenie on the head and knocked her down and within seconds we were rolling about in the dust. Then I felt myself yanked through the air by the scruff of my neck and knew that my father had me. Eugenie's mother had ahold of her.

"Any more fighting," shouted the principal, "and you will both be expelled and you will end up walking behind a donkey in the fields with a big packet on your head and nothing will become of you!"

Within a week, we were the best of friends. Eugenie was not a eunuch. I helped her straighten her hair. Once she had coolie hair, she was happy.

The days grew busier. One morning my sister and I were cooking lunch, grating cornmeal and coconut. We set the pot on the fire to boil down, and then added red peas and cooked it until it had the consistency of a pudding. This was our favorite dish, and it was our job to prepare lunch for our father, so we put a large serving on a plate and put it in his warming dish on the dining room table.

When my father came home, he picked up the cover, saw the cornmeal pudding and shouted, "Who is this for?" and I called out, "You, sir."

"Am I a dog, that you should feed me cornmeal?" my father shouted and hurled the dish out into the yard where the dogs fought over the food and ate it up. We looked at one another and shrugged and began cooking some mutton for our father, who had stalked out of the house and walked up the path into the fields.

"It is very good, you know," said Cynthia.

"I know," said Cherry.

"When I get married," I said, "if a man throws his dinner through the door, he will not get anything more to eat from me."

"I thought you weren't getting married," Cynthia said.

"If I'm even living with someone and they throw their food, they'll be hungry a long time."

We went into the yard and retrieved the tin dish. We were not upset. We were fascinated by the doings of those around us, the older ones, who acted, so it seemed to us, according to no law, but who were, like the weather, uncontrollable.

Now, when I came into a room, the older women did not stop speaking until I had passed by. My grandmother, Mother Lize, let me remain when she talked about delivering babies. Miss Blue let me stay while she told Miss Iron Front about a woman who died the day after one of her children had thrown lye mixed with water on the ground next to the woman's natal tree. The child and his mother watched in horror as the tree's leaves wilted and shrivelled and during the night everyone in their house heard a loud crash. The wind had brought the tree down.

In the morning, the woman whose tree it was did not wake. "Where is Mother?" said the woman's son, coming into the yard.

"Still asleep," said his sister.

"Mother doesn't sleep this long," said the son, and when he went into the bedroom, he found his little daughter sound asleep next to his mother. He woke the child and sent her out of the room. His mother was dead.

"That's how it is if you have a natal tree," said Miss Coffin Cover. "You have to take care of it. It's best not to have one at all."

"You are all too superstitious and full of nonsense," said Miss Iron Front. "If you are going to die, you will die, tree or no tree. With a birth tree in your yard, you know you belong. My son's birth tree still grows in the yard and he has been dead how many years but still he belongs in that yard."

I was coming to know the secrets of the town.

Why was I happy now? It was as if someone had waved a wand and taken away my stepmother's power. Suddenly I was in a world into which she could not enter.

After I began helping Daddy butchering goats, and after I began going up into the hills with Frankie, my father's helper, who carried the wooden-board box filled with goat meat, into the hills where I went from house to house, collecting money people owed me for the goat meat, taking orders for the next week, my father began to look at me in a new way. I was growing up. One Sunday I came down leading a goat he had never before seen.

"Don't tell me you bought that goat," he said to me.

"How much would you pay for it, Daddy?"

"Did you buy it?"

"First tell me what you would pay for it."

He came over and picked up the goat. "The live weight is good," he said. "Twenty-eight shillings."

"I paid twenty-three."

"We'll see how it works out when we kill it," he said. The next Sunday when we slaughtered the goat and weighed up the five quarters, we saw we would make a nice profit on the goat. "Don't go getting too confident, now," he told me. But I rarely made a mistake, and when I was up in the hills, bringing people the meat they ordered, and someone needed to raise cash quickly and wanted to sell a goat, I drove a hard bargain. "You're a bigger thief than your father, you know," people said of me.

I liked going up with the goat meat, wrapped for each person in brown paper marked with his name. I liked the climb up through the fields to the houses. I liked stopping in the different kitchens for a glass of lemonade and listening to the different people talking about their lives. If I heard anything interesting, I saved the information for Miss Blue.

Eventually I had a customer who wanted only the fifth quarter of the goats: the heads, the feet and the livers. Now when I climbed into the hills I carried a bag full of goat heads, five or six at a time. The children, and some of the adults, began to regard me with fear. They would stare at the bag I carried and hurry inside their houses.

"You think these goat heads can talk?" I demanded angrily when a woman ran from me. The next week, it was the same thing. "You think these goat heads can talk?" I asked again. "They can talk and they will curse you out if you run from them." The woman hesitated and stayed where she was.

The next week Frankie twisted his ankle and I had to go into the hills alone. "I don't like it," my father said. "There's a man loose up there who hurts girls."

"I will be fine," I said.

When I got tired, I stopped in a field to rest. I listened to the wind rustling the leaves in the trees. I thought I heard a twig snap beneath an animal's weight, but I was tired and wanted to sleep. I looked at the bag full of goat heads and took them out. I had eight goat heads and I set them in a large circle around me. Then I fell asleep. When I awakened, I shooed the flies away and put the heads back in my crocus bag and finished my rounds, selling the goat meat I had with me, and taking orders for next week.

Before I got back to my house, I met my father on the road. "You're not hurt!" he said, grabbing me up.

"Why should I be hurt?"

"A man came running down from the fields like the devil was after him! In shirt tails and no pants at all! Screaming and wild and quite mad! Right from the direction you went! Oh my God! I was frightened!"

"Here I am."

"He said something about goats."

"He meant ghosts?"

"He meant goats," my father said. "Everything he looked at, he screamed 'Goats, goats, goats!' "

"Maybe he saw my goat heads," I said, and I told him what I had done with them.

"You are terrible, you know," said my father. "You are your mother all over again. Let's go to Cinnamon Bay and visit them, your aunt and all of them. Let's go."

In Cinnamon Bay, Vidal knocked at Lucille's gate. "Come see your niece, Miss Clifton," he called to her. My Aunt Lucille, Tita Lu, came out and the three of us proceeded to my grandmother's house where I once more sat on the big bed while my grandmother wept and played with my hair.

After that, on Sundays, when I was finished with the goats, I took to walking from Mare River to Cinnamon Bay. On some Sunday mornings, my father would tell me to go on to my aunt's and he would take care of the goats. Then I would wrap my head in a bandanna and begin the long walk down. As I descended the steep, narrow clay path that wound in and out through the green wall of leaves, invisible to anyone who didn't know where it was, I had a good view down the mountain and could see all its terraced pastures and clearings.

In the meadows below, seven brown cows were grazing, white guarlings riding their backs or walking about in the grass. By the time I reached Cinnamon Bay and walked back, the white guarlings would have flown up into the trees. There were several trees they preferred, and just before dusk, I would see them, hundreds upon hundreds of them shining in a brilliant green tree, the golden light behind them, the most beautiful thing I ever saw.

I kept walking until I came to the bottom of the mountain and then began walking along the seawall on my way to Cinnamon Bay. I stopped in front of a yard and watched a small dun-colored puppy worrying and chasing a pumpkin vine. I went on, making note of a patch of fever grass growing next to the road where the sea wall cut off the view of the bay and the road ran straight into the horizon where a lone palm tree seemed to stand at the very edge of the world. Someday I would make up a story about that: the palm tree at the edge of the world.

I walked slowly past the grove of almond trees. Mr. Graves was hacking at his hedge with a machete. "Good morning, Mr. Graves," I called out, and he waved the machete in my direction. I went past the houses whose stripling fences were painted in diagonal stripes, pink and turquoise. Miss Curtis was no better, I could see that: her dwelling was still propped up by a crooked gray-white tree limb. Goats, horses, donkeys and dogs were tied on the side of the road, grazing. I said hello to each of them as she passed. One goat seemed to listen, and then, as if in frustration, stamped its feet.

I stopped near a mango tree next to a pink and orange fence. Under that tree they had buried Mr. Walterson. Two boys ran out of a lane, shouting, waving clumsily, their shoes weighted down with thick river mud.

When I got to the town, I walked slowly. I was tired and thirsty and the sun was up. Mrs. Bennett saw me and said, "Come in and have a glass of water," and I said I would like the water but I was on an errand.

"Here comes Mr. Granison," said Mrs. Bennett, and when I, who saw no one, asked her how she knew, she said you always knew when he was coming because all the dogs of Cinnamon Bay started barking. He had teased them as puppies, pulled their tails and their ears, thrown sticks at them, and now that they were grown, they barked and howled, and if you had any business with Mr. Granison, you listened for the dogs. They never disappointed you. Just then Mr. Granison passed her window.

He stopped to talk to a man who told him that Uncle Wood had died the night before. "It wasn't sickness that took him," said the man. "It was death."

We listened to them through the open window. "I saw him last night and he looked better than me," said Mr. Granison. The other man said that everyone looked better than him. A man with sheets of tin on his head passed the window, saying good morning to both men. A man with a donkey came by and the donkey began balking and screaming as it approached Mrs. Bennett's house.

"That is the country telegraph," said Mrs. Bennett. "That man, there, he beat the other man's donkey, and the donkey did mark him and now the donkey does scream whenever he sees them. So you hear the donkey screaming, you know the whereabouts of the donkey, and you know who is making the donkey scream. There are no mysteries in Cinnamon Bay."

Outside, Mr. Granison was saying, "God saw the road was getting rough and the mountains high, and so, he bent down and closed his weary eyes."

"Yes, indeed," said the other man. "He closed his weary eyes."

I went on until I came to my aunt's house where my Aunt Lu poured me a glass of lemonade. "Sometimes," she said to me, "I think I killed her. She died two weeks after I was married."

"Everyone thinks they killed my mother," I said. "My father thinks so and you think so, too."

"It was her life that killed her," said my aunt. "To be so unlucky!"

I stored each piece of information as if it were a grain to be eaten during some unspecified but expected famine.

My Aunt Lucille and I went up to my grandmother's house. It was high up on the mountain. A red clay trail reached it and from her little veranda you could look down over the town below, out past Cinnamon Bay, out to the ocean beyond. The boats in the bay were clear to the eye, but on the horizon they were specks, and, if their sails were unfurled, small splashes of white against a deepening blue. I picked a bushel of star apples and was about to go inside and begin juicing a soursop, which my grandmother said was very good for the nerves. In back of us, parrots were calling from tree to tree. My grandmother complained that a flock of parakeets had eaten all of her corn seed. They came down suddenly, like a cloud, and then they were gone, little greenish-gold parakeets, the pests! And she hadn't even gotten a pair for her empty cage.

I began the long walk back to Mare River. Someone had painted the trunks of their coconut trees with lime. A rusted drum was filled with water and a tin cup rested on the ground beside it. A drying goatskin was nailed to a tree. "Don't look," I said to a goat as I passed. It is a city of goats. Green Island is a country of goats.

Chickens drank from the trench of a train pipe. I looked up where the hill rose above the road. A woman was standing on a stone, the wind blowing her thin cotton dress. "Where are your teeth, man?" the woman called, turning and shouting to someone inside the house.

A man drove by on a bike, his child sitting before him. He pedalled hard in the heat. He wore a white shirt, a black suit and a black vest.

A perfect flight of cement steps climbed gracefully up to a tumbledown plank house. Well-dressed girls in high heels were coming back home, each of them carrying a plastic shopping bag, while at home their mothers washed dishes in the yard, their heads tied tight with scarves. A black guarling walked through a flooded ditch, carefully, slowly, stepping high, like a man who doesn't want to wet the cuffs of his trousers and so rolls up his cuffs, hunting for something. A dog skulked by, its ribs showing, pale-eyed, as if it had lost the outline around its eyes.

I passed a roadside stand cut out of a wall of vegetation built into the ocher clay of the mountain walls. The women I passed carried loads on their heads. There was the smell of burning charcoal. Ahead of me women turned off the main road onto the pumpkin-colored roads that led into what looked like jungle. Here the buildings were constructed of abandoned doors and stray pieces of zinc and the women used much-mended umbrellas for their parasols. They were orange and shocking pink. Vans and trucks whizzed by. In the yard across the road, a child was slapping at her head with both hands. The sun leaned over the top of the mountain, going down, and the road began its slow climb up to Mare River.

As I walked, I looked up into the hills and it seemed to me I could see myself there, walking with Frankie, carrying my wooden box filled with brown paper packages of goat meat. I saw myself coming down the narrow trails at night, followed by my father's fifteen goats. When I was as old as the women now returning home in their high heels, I would not remember walking up into the fields as I did now. That girl who walked through the fields would be gone, a ghost. There was no one left who had a picture of my mother, not even a piece of paper to show what she looked like.

In Paradise, said Brother Beckwith, everything was always the same. From day to day, year to year, nothing changed. The weather was the same, the trees eternal.

Then Green Island was a paradise. A storm could blow down groves of bananas, level acres of coconuts, and within months, everything was once again green. All had been replaced. Only the people came and went and did not return, thinking themselves solid and permanent, but as transient as the banana trees, soon to be replaced, to be blown about like pollen. Things happened, no one remembered them. The landscape erased all clues.

As I came to the curve in the path that would bring me to my father's house, I thought about the ghosts I had seen: my mother, my great-grandmother, the woman who hung out her clothes at the foot of my grandmother's garden. I believed that ghosts wanted what the living wanted and that the earth was crowded with the living and the dead, who were not so different and jostled together. They both wandered the earth asking, Why did this happen to me? I thought of my mother, who had died so early. Unfinished! My mother's life was unfinished. Everything on earth howled to be completed. Who ever saw a fish pulled from the sea only half created? Or half a plant growing from the earth? God finished His creation before He rested. But people died unfinished and so they walked the earth.

"What about your sweeping and your chores, miss?" Bea called to me from the veranda. "Every Sunday in Cinnamon Bay? We'll see about that!"

3

IT IS POSSIBLE to cross this country on a train and still see nothing. This is what you do: you sleep during the day and lean against the window at night. Thus you can go from one end of the country to the other under the impression that you are going through a very long tunnel. You can even forget what country it is you are travelling through. At night, when I lean against the window, waiting for Max to speak, the world outside is nothing but a reflection of this little one, an ice cube of light, the two of us frozen in it. I think it would be nice to paint. Then I would paint a head or a skull and pouring out of one side of it, all this darkness. I put my hand on the window: cold.

"You are going to keep this up?" Max asks me. "All the way to California, pretending we're not going anywhere?"

I tell him that I am not used to the time changes. At home it is night. He looks at me and goes back to his book. Somewhere on the train, in another car, Anders is also reading.

I am back home in the apartment in Sweden. My mother is hanging up my new dresses. We don't have a cupboard or a closet. A wooden plank is nailed across the wall, and large nails are driven partway into the wood. From these nails, hangers full of clothes are suspended. A metal rod runs the length of this piece of wood and two worn sheets have been made into curtains and hang from it. These curtains can be drawn aside when the clothes are hung up and then closed to cover them. My mother draws the sheets closed. I notice how puffy and red are her hands, how swollen her two thumbs. She sees me looking at her.

Once I had nice hands, she says. Small, small hands. You have your father's hands, big, long fingers. But mine were small. When I was a girl, I took good care of my nails. My mother bought me a silver vanity set and every morning I used the nail buffer. I never had a ridge in my nails. Now I have crevices. Of course it is from all this scrubbing, all this washing, so many of us in two rooms, nothing stays clean. At least you will escape.

She sits down on the edge of the bed. Tell me about Berlin, she says. I tell her again about the opening of Max's film, the car that came for us, the bouquets pressed upon us, my picture in the paper. I tell her about going for a walk in the poor section and how I lost my way and was brought back to the hotel in a milk cart.

"It is wonderful," she says, clasping my hands to her bosom. "Like a dream." But it was not all wonderful, not all of it. Some of the time I was frightened. She doesn't want to hear this.

"It was my dream," I say. She drops my hands and stares at her lap.

"You know, Anna," she says, "you are very selfish. Don't jump up. You are. Very selfish. Who do you love besides yourself? Oh, you love me because you don't have anyone else. You don't love Marianne. Your brothers, you hardly bother with them. Of course you are much younger than they are, but still, it's true. If we all died tomorrow, you wouldn't cry."

I stare at her. What is she talking about? Why is she saying this now? "And this Max, what do you see in him? Don't tell me he's only a teacher. No teacher comes to his student's house and throws stones at her windows! He doesn't take her to stores and buy her clothes! He gets you your clothes, I wash and iron them, that's what we're good for. You don't care about us. Berlin, that wasn't far enough? And now America! You're ashamed of us, you want to get away, you want to forget where you came from, I can understand it. But for once say the truth!"

Is it the truth? I don't know and so I don't answer.

"So," she says, "you don't even bother to explain. You let me think what I want to think, no matter how terrible. You are a cold and hard person and sooner or later this Max will find you out. You'll find a man you want, and everything will be fine, but Anna, watch out for his mother! She'll find you out!"

"What is it you want from me?" I ask in a cold voice. "You want me to tell you I love you? You want me to say how much I'll miss you?"

"I don't want anything I have to ask for," says my mother. The red spots in her cheeks are burning. I would like to reach up and touch them but my hands are leaden. Now I stubbornly stare straight ahead. I will not be bribed into saying I love her. I will not be shamed into saying it. And if it is true that I am ashamed of my house? Why does she scold me? She is ashamed and bitter. I have only learned the lessons she taught me.

"Still you have nothing to say to me?" my mother asks. Every word she says makes it more impossible for me to speak. "So," she says, getting up. Just then Marianne walks into the bedroom from the kitchen. "So, Marianne," she says, "try on some of Anna's fine things."

I never let anyone touch the clothes from the stores Max takes me to. I don't think of them as my clothes. They are his, paid for by his money: costumes I am allowed to wear as long as I play my role well. My mother knows this. Marianne looks at me, smiles questioningly. "Go on, Marianne," my mother says. "Try on the dress with no back."

"But she is heavier than I am!" I say. "She will tear it."

"Try it on, Marianne, just this once," says my mother. "After all, in a few weeks Anna is going to America and then you won't have a chance. Anna doesn't mind, do you, Anna?"

I say nothing. Marianne is overcome with curiosity and excitement and so she draws back the faded sheet, takes out the gray dress, and lays it next to me on the bed. I move my hand so the fabric of the dress will not touch it. I have nothing to do with this. "Hold this," Marianne says to me, giving me her blouse and skirt. She stands in front of me in her ivory slip. She picks up the dress and raises it over her head and raises her arms and begins putting it on. My mother gets up and helps her. Of course it looks ridiculous. It is a backless dress, cut low in the front. It is not meant to be worn over a slip. And now it will not slide down over her hips. "Just give it a good pull," says my mother. Marianne starts to object but my mother gets up and gives the dress a smart tug. We hear the sound of fabric ripping. "Oh, what have you done?" Marianne cries. She begins sobbing, struggling out of the dress. "Oh, Anna, I am sorry!"

"Don't apologize," says my mother. "She should have let you try it on long ago. You've seen her standing in front of the mirror holding the dress up to her," my mother says to me. "You never said, She's my sister, why shouldn't she try the dress on?"

"They don't fit me!" Marianne cried. "I don't need to try them on!"

"She is selfish and thinks only of herself," my mother says.

My brother Lars walks in and asks, "What's going on in here?"

"Your sister Marianne tried on Anna's dress and accidentally she tore it," my mother says.

My voice comes back to me, cold with fury. "*You* tore it," I say to my mother.

"I was too big for it," Marianne says, sobbing.

Lars is puzzled. Rarely have I fought with my mother. "What is this all about?" he asks me.

"Oh," I say, "I am selfish and cold, and I am going to America, and if you all die here, I won't cry about it."

"Marianne said so?" he asks.

"No," I say. "Your mother said so."

"My mother?" he says. "She is not your mother?"

"She has just found me out," I tell him. "How cold and selfish I am and how little I care for her and how all I want her to do is wash and iron my clothes."

"Mother?" he says. "How did this start?" As he stands there I think, he is the image of my father. My mother holds out her hands.

"Look at how red my hands are! Red, scalded flesh! Boiled flesh! And these swollen fingers, I have to soak them in hot water for a half hour, sometimes more, before I can fit them into gloves! Look at these hands!"

"What does she want?" I ask Lars. "Does she want money? Is that what she's blaming me for? I don't bring home enough?"

"Money is all you think about!" my mother shouts.

"You can have every penny I earn," I say coldly. "Every penny."

"I don't want your money!" shouts my mother.

I get up and take my purse down from its hook, empty it into my hand, and fling the bills and coins on the bed. "There! Now are you satisfied?"

"Anna, stop!" Lars pleads.

"Mother, stop!" Marianne says.

My mother picks up a handful of coins and hurls them at me. "Treat me like a landlady, will you? Like a scrubwoman? You are a monster! Selfish! Cold!"

Lars takes my arm. "You come with me," he says.

"That's right," my mother shouts. "Get her out of my sight!"

"Marianne," Lars says. "Talk to her."

"Out of my sight," my mother shouts again.

Lars and I go downstairs and begin walking. I am shaking with rage. "How did it start?" he asks me.

"I don't know!" I say, yanking my arm free.

"How?" he asks again.

"She was hanging up my dresses and I was sitting on the bed, and she said I didn't love her, I didn't love anybody, I was ashamed of all of you."

"Why?" he asks. "Why?"

"She looked at her hands and said once they were beautiful, small hands, not like mine, and the next thing I knew, she said I was hard and cold, Max would find me out, sooner or later everyone would find me out."

"Find out what?"

"That I'm hard and cold and no one can love me!" I shouted. "I told you!"

"I don't understand it," he said. "You must make it up with her."

"I must make it up! When I didn't do anything!"

"But you can't go on this way," he said. "I don't understand it. You get along so well."

"I understand it! Oh, I understand it! All these years she's worked to give us a chance, to give *me* a chance, the youngest, her little one, her favorite, and now I've taken it! I've taken it and she can't forgive me! She thought, Oh, Anna must have a chance but what she really meant was, Oh, I must have another chance! And now she sees *I'm* to get the dresses, *I'm* to be in the papers, not her! Well, that's too much! She made a mistake! And on top of that, I'm going to America where she won't see me and how will she brag about me every day to the neighbors? *That's* why I'm selfish! *That's* why I'm cold! And when she's tired now, what can she tell herself? That I need her? I don't need her! I have Max! Oh, yes, I understand it! She hates me!"

"She doesn't hate you," Lars said.

"Don't lie to me! Don't humor me!" I say, walking faster, in front of him. He catches up with me and grabs my arm. "Stop talking like a child!" he says. "So she had dreams for you! She didn't think they'd come true! Whose dreams come true? Did she stop and think you'd go to America if you succeeded? She can't think further than Stockholm. She can't imagine America! You might as well tell her you're going to the moon! *I'm packing my clothes and going to America.* What does that mean to her? *I'm going to the land from which no traveller returns.* If you stabbed yourself in front of her it would be the same thing! You don't see it?"

"She called me cold! She called me selfish! I cannot love anyone! She deliberately tore my dress!"

"Forget the dress!" Lars said.

"*She* tore it! Deliberately!"

"Forget the dress!" Lars said again.

"I am not going home," I said.

"You are," Lars said. "You are if I have to knock you down."

"I will not sleep in the same bed with her," I said.

"Then sleep on the kitchen bench like in the old days," Lars said, "but sleep in the house."

I nodded but would not look at him.

"Anna is sleeping in the kitchen," Lars said when we came in. Marianne was whimpering in the bedroom. My mother was in bed and said nothing. The clock in the church steeple across the road struck twelve. I put on my hat and coat and curled up on the kitchen bench and fell asleep. Much later, I felt someone's hand on my hair. "I am sorry," my mother said. "Your dress, in the morning, I'll mend it."

"I don't care about my dress," I said.

"You know I love you," my mother said.

"No, I don't know it," I said in a new, bitter tone. "Not anymore."

"What do you mean?" she asked me. "How can a mother stop loving her child?"

"Anyone can stop loving anyone else," I said. I was not ready to give in.

"I don't want you to go so far," my mother said. "That's all it is."

"I don't have to go," I said.

"Yes, you have to go," she said. "Everyone has a destiny."

"I'm too young for a destiny!" I said bitterly.

"It's too late for that now," she said. "Come to bed."

"I'll come later," I said. I waited until I heard her settle on the bed, waited until I heard the familiar sound of deep breathing, and lay down on the narrow strip next to the edge.

But now I knew: she didn't want me to go. If I did go, ambition would take me from her. Ambition would take my clothes down from behind the sheeting on the wall. I could stay in Sweden and make films, but I would not. I would go because I was ambitious and my mother was right: ambition is cold and hard.

"Oh, for heaven's sake, get up," Anders said, shaking me awake. "Look out the window." He flung up the shade. "Look at that landscape! Max, look outside! If we could film that. Wild horses, Max! Almost as good as your swimming reindeer!"

"I'm not interested in wild horses," Max said.

Outside the windows were cliffs, rugged cliffs scored deep as if by long, long nails. When the sun came out, the cliffs glowed rose-red. When the sun went back, the cliffs were brown and beige. The meadows stretching to the foot of the cliffs were brown. Everything looked dry. A herd of reddish cattle grazed and occasionally some sheep.

"Someone knows why, when it is going to rain, the cattle all fold their feet under and lie down?"

It was the first thing I'd said all day. Max didn't answer me. Gussie, who was sitting on his lap, got down and put her paws up on my knees. I patted my skirt and she jumped into my lap. "It is a long trip," I said, stroking the dog, but still, no answer. Nothing. Max stared at the cliffs like a cliff.

"All right," I said. "Enough is enough. I have said three things and not one has come back with a crumb in its beak. Let him talk to himself." I was not my mother, forever making conversation with a man who would not talk. I got up and left the compartment.

Who could keep track of where we had come from, everything changed so fast? First we went through the back streets of cities, gray wooden porches, women hanging out laundry, just like home, all the poor places to see first, men sitting on stone steps in front of red brick buildings drinking from their bottles in paper bags, again like home, but less snow, and then the city would lose its grip on us and we were out in green fields, little mountains, everything so neat and clean, the white houses in the green fields, all sharp angles, just like a children's picture book, and now this great flatness, all this sand, this big white light falling down from the sky like blocks of stone. In some lights, if I am careful, if I block part of the landscape with my hand, I can tell myself it is snow, but of course it is not snow, it is sand, it is so hot. When I get home, I will have a lot to tell. *When I get home.*

Anders was sitting in his compartment, his feet up, his back against the window, reading. I knocked at the glass door. He nodded. *Come in.*

"What is that you are reading?"

"A script," he said.

"Any good?"

"No."

I sat down across from him. "Max is sleeping?" he asked.

"Max is staring."

"Well, you know Max," Anders said.

"I am only seventeen and I am on a hot, fast train going across America to the country of San Bernardino, where someone from The Studio is going to interview us. Probably I will make a great fool of myself because I don't know the language."

"You must learn the language," Anders said. "You must not always cling to the Scandinavians you find there. Then you will speak only Finnish or Swedish or German and you will never learn."

"Max is not learning. He says, 'If they are intelligent, they will speak my language. A shout, a gesture is understood in any language.' "

"Learn the language," Anders said again. His eyes were returning to the page before him.

"If it is not good, why must you read it?" I asked him.

"How do I know it is not good until I finish? Lightning may flash at any time."

"What a great optimist you are," I said, sighing.

"You think so?" said Anders, putting down his book. "My wife says I am an optimist like Noah. I expect the flood but still I build an ark. Is that an optimist?"

The motion of the car, swaying, swaying, made my blood pound. I heard it thudding in my ears.

"So what is it like to be seventeen and cross the country on a fast train?" he said. "You feel success speeding toward you?"

"All the time I think it is like being in a war. When is the siren going to sound? When is something to happen?"

"Now you are talking about being seventeen," Anders said. "Everyone feels it."

"So nervous, so full of fear? I don't think so."

"Seventeen and high-strung," said Anders. "Seventeen and high-strung and intelligent."

"No, no, no. In the Academy, the other girls played their parts, they went for interviews, but really, you looked into their eyes, you could see it, the little rooms, the man standing there, the children. All this other, only a way of passing time. They talk to one another, they finish each other's sentences. They laugh, they pose with their cigarettes in cigarette holders, but all the time, the little rooms are there. Look in my eyes. You see little rooms? No, I don't have them."

Anders nodded. He put down his manuscript and considered me. "So you are the only one on earth of your kind?" he asked. Of course that was what I was afraid of. "Oh, what a time that is, when you think you are the only one! You think the terror will shake you to pieces! And then you find another one, and that is so good you are drunk all the time, you make no sense to anyone, not even yourself, and the whole world falls away. When it happens to you, you will say to yourself, 'Everything I went through, I went through for this.' But now you don't believe such a time will come because you've never seen it. But it does come, and then comes the real terror. If something should happen to that person! Well, that's jumping ahead. My mother used to say, 'Remember, Anders, all you need is one. Just one.' She was right. Then, of course, I laughed at her."

"Bitterness, bitterness, bitterness," I say. "At the bottom of every-thing a great bitterness." Now he will scold me. He will ask me what I have to feel bitter about.

"Then you must find someone else who understands bitterness," Anders says.

But why such bitterness? Is it Max, the way we are together? We do not sleep together like man and woman. I know he is waiting to see desire in me and as yet he does not see it. But I want to see desire in *him*. I want to be desired by him. If he desired me enough, surely I would learn to feel the same for him. Can I really be as beautiful as he says I am if he does not want to sleep with me as a man sleeps with a woman? I do not understand it. Perhaps it is true and Max is not really interested in women. But even then, even then, I could make him interested—if only he desired me enough! Oh, I am sure of it! Is this why I am so unhappy, because when we sleep in the same bed, I am not treated as a woman and so I doubt myself as a woman and do not feel like one? I do not know why I am unhappy. It is something in the blood, a darkness that thickens with every year that passes.

Yet Max loves women. He is always surrounded by them. And here is Anders. He also loves women. What would annoy Max makes him laugh. The way Anders looks at women, who can describe it? He looks at them with reverence and pity. He loves them all and every one of them loves him. Anders, that great charmer.

In his films he casts the ugliest woman. The thief who died with his wife in the snow, she was an ugly woman, or at least her face was not pretty, so there was never any doubt: he loved his wife. What other explanation could someone sitting in the dark watching the film flash on the screen find for such devotion? A fact of nature, that love, inexplicable, unalterable, without conditions.

"I am lonely," I say aloud.

"Lonely and bitter," says Anders. "Yes."

And now Max raps at the glass door of the compartment, comes in and sits down next to me. They begin to speak of The Studio.

"It is not the same there as it is at home," Anders says. "They watch every penny. And first they must learn to trust you. Spend little, earn a lot, that's their motto. Even worse for you, Max, only the studio heads are allowed to be temperamental. The directors must be calm and stick to their schedules."

"They can trust the pictures I made," said Max.

"Everyone who comes, that person is on trial, no matter what he has done before," Anders says. "They speak of 'breaking us in,' as you speak of a horse."

"You are not broken," Max says.

"I know I can go back," says Anders. "Really, I do not care. They let me do my work, fine. I can't do my work, I am on my way home. In the end, what does it matter?"

"In the end," says Max.

"For me the work is everything," Anders says.

"For me it is not," says Max. He falls silent, thinking. The train is running along a cliff face, the tracks are sending up clouds of dust. Sometimes we can see, sometimes we cannot. "But always," Max says, "everyone gives in to me. Always I get what I want."

Anders says nothing.

"Of course they will let me work with Anna," Max says. Anders doesn't answer. "It was not written into the contract," Max says, "but it was understood." He scratches Gussie under her chin. I think, So many fusses in New York, so many tantrums, so many visits to the local office and yet nothing happened. No one hurried. In their own time, The Studio put us on this train.

"They must let me work with her. She is nothing without me."

I feel Anders' eyes on me. I say nothing. Anders says nothing. I look out the window. The sun is going. I see my face reflected in the window. Who is that girl and why is she wearing that elegant cloche hat? She has no family here. She comes out of nowhere. She forms and re-forms herself like a cloud. The wind blows her across oceans and countries. I cannot believe in these cliffs, this enormous empty country.

TO GET OUT OF THE RAIN, Ivy and I go into the Caribbean Coffee Shop. We've returned my red shoes. The owner comes out from behind the counter, hands us each a menu and says, "How about it, girls? You're splitting the check today? One check or two?"

"One," I say. I don't look at him.

"Where are your manners?" Ivy asks him. "You do that again, we don't come in here anymore."

"All right, all right," he says, standing at the table, waiting for us to order.

"A cup of tea and two cornmeal cakes," I say.

"Why do I ask?" the man says. "And you? Codfish and scrambled eggs with toast and a pot of weak tea."

"You are too smart," Ivy says.

"How old is she, anyway?" he asks me. "And why does she look so happy? Even when she's mad, she looks happy. You ever notice it?"

"Go about your business," Ivy says, but she looks pleased. It is true. Almost always, Ivy looks happy, and suddenly I want to know how she manages.

"You have a special philosophy of life or something?" I ask her.

"I am happy."

"Yes, why?" I ask.

"Maybe because when I was a child, I lived so hard, now I appreciate every little thing."

"If being poor made people happy, there'd be traffic jams, so many happy people dancing in the streets."

"To be honest," Ivy says, "only in the last two years am I really happy. Before, I lived my life for others—first my father, then my husband, then my children, even my husband's sister, that Flora. Someone said that was no life. He was right."

"I don't know what it was, maybe a bad character, maybe something in the genes, I never could live for anyone else," I say. "I could barely live for myself, that was the trouble. Well, since I couldn't do it, I didn't do it. A chicken clucks, it doesn't sing opera."

"In my early days," Ivy says, "the older ones, they used to sit at night and talk, and all the time the talk was about this girl being disbanded and that girl being disbanded, and it frightened me so much I could not do otherwise than listen to them."

"What is it, being disbanded?" I ask.

"You know, when your parents won't know you anymore and the family closes itself against you. And, you know, I am part Indian, and Nanny used to tell me a story about her friend who had this very bad girl, and the mother disbanded her and every morning when the sun came up she would go out in her yard and kneel down facing the sun and she would take her breast from out her blouse and she would pray to the sun and curse her daughter and ask for terrible things to happen to her, and Nanny said people used to see the girl wandering up and down the roads like a hungry dog, her bones sticking out all over, and no one wanted to feed her because they knew: every morning the mother was facing the sun saying her prayers. I was so scared of this disbanded business!"

"Well," I say, "I disbanded mine. Not officially. But after a while, what did I have to say to them? With them, I felt more lonely than with strangers."

"All the time the children were growing," Ivy says, "I looked over my shoulder for death, because I always said I wanted only one thing.

I wanted to live long enough to see them on their own so they would have no stepmothers in their lives. And I did that. Then I should have been happy. But I brought my sisters all over from Green Island. That was where I made my mistake.

"But when I came back from Green Island that last time, when I went out there to bury Tita Lu, I rubbed my hands together and said, 'All right, that's it. No more. Now I am living my life for myself.' And now the shadow is gone completely. Now I am happy. To be honest with you, if I had it to do over, I wouldn't marry. I wouldn't give back my children, but I wouldn't marry. I would be my own person. I wouldn't let my family know where I was if I left the Island."

"To tell you the truth," I say, "I never wanted to marry either. If you marry, then you have children. If you ruin a child, how can you forgive yourself? If your husband ruined a child, how could you forgive him?" *Arms and legs, floating. A soup of bodies. Where did one end? Where did the others begin? Was that one male or was it female? Everything, arms, legs, floating.* "I always thought I was better off alone. Then my will and my mind would be my own. I did what I wanted but I am not happy."

"I live for today," Ivy says. "I'm sitting here enjoying this plate of salted codfish and eggs and that's enough. Whenever I made plans, then I was disappointed. I wanted to go to school, I was so good at it, and I started, but then my stepmother told my father that every night I came home late. I couldn't take the arguing, so I stopped going. Now I'm on my own and I am happy."

"Yes," I say. "But I have been on my own a long time and I am not happy."

"But sometimes you are happy. You are happy when you dust your china dogs. You are happy when you go for long walks and tire out that young man who walks with you. Sometimes you are happy when you sit in your chair looking out at the snow."

"Oh, snow, that always makes me happy," I say. "Maybe I should move to the Arctic Circle."

"Why not?" Ivy says.

I chew on my cornmeal cake and think: this is what it comes to. You become famous. You become rich. Everyone knows you. And what makes you happy? Sitting in your chair watching snow. Dusting your china dogs. Walking with a young man who can't begin to understand you, but you like it, walking with him. It is company. "I should get a cat," I say. "But it will scratch the furniture. It will climb the draperies and cling on there, screaming, out of our reach and we will have to call Louie with his bad heart to come get it down."

"We could keep it in my room," Ivy says.

"All right," I say, jumping up. "Let's get one! Mr. Owner! Where is there a good pet store? We want to buy a cat!"

"You want a purebred or a mutt?" he asks.

"A mutt," I say. "Like me!"

We get in a cab.

"You know," I say, "we are crazy. We look over our lives and decide we are happy when we don't have to look over our shoulder and now when we have no one to worry about, we get in a cab in a rainstorm and go look for a kitten. A cat can live twenty years!"

"Why must we always do what we say?" Ivy asks me.

"That's right!" I say. "Why must we? We have our freedom! We can believe one thing and do another!"

"This cat," says Ivy, "he will be the love of your life."

It is two more hours to San Bernardino.

I am worried about the interviewers, what they will ask me, what I should tell them. Anders says I should tell them the truth.

"Don't tell them the truth!" Max says. "Why should they be entitled to that? No, you must imagine yourself the way you want to be and answer as if you were that person."

"Well," I say, "I am worrying about nothing, I cannot speak the language, I won't understand them and they won't understand me."

"They will have an interpreter," Anders said.

"When they interview you," I ask him, "how do you answer?"

"He asks a great many rhetorical questions and smiles all the time and they think he has a very deep nature," says Max.

"I am a cheerful person and cannot help smiling," Anders said. "I tell the truth. I don't have to tell all of it. Of course not."

At the San Bernardino station we are met by two men from The Studio who take us to a private house where many Scandinavians have gathered to greet us. I nod at everyone but am too jumpy to smile. People say their names but to me they are only moving their mouths. Of course they will think me conceited and stupid.

At last my translator is produced. He is a young man named Tomas Sondquist. "You will be spending a lot of time with me," he says, and I say, "Oh, that is very nice." Then I can think of nothing more to say.

From across the lawn, people nod and smile but they do not come over to me.

Around Max and Anders a crowd has already gathered. A small woman, very tiny, her blond hair finger-waved, is standing next to

Max, holding Gussie, who is squirming in her arms. Either she is a great lover of dogs or she thinks Max is someone very important. She puts Gussie down, turns her back on the little group, and brushes off her pink dress with an intense look of disgust. She doesn't like dogs. It is Max she is after. So that is how it is here.

I pretend to cough and whistle behind my hand. Gussie runs over and I sweep her up against my rumpled navy suit. Max, whose eyes have followed the dog, glares disapprovingly at me.

The house is some kind of whitewashed stone. Red roses climb all over it. It has green shutters and a green-tiled roof. Flowers are thick all over the garden. White lawn furniture is everywhere. People say hello, drift off, and begin playing croquet. Anders and Max, the dog and I, pose together and are photographed. "Now we can go home?" I whisper.

"Can I borrow her for a minute?" says the translator.

Borrow me?

"Two interviewers are waiting for you over there," he says, pointing across the lawn to a table shaded by a great red and white striped umbrella. "Come." He leads me over and sits me down in the middle of them.

"What are your impressions of this country?" the woman asks me.

"Oh, it is very big," I say. "And people run around so fast here. Everyone seems to have a place to go. Always in a hurry. Even when I hurry, I don't seem as if I'm hurrying. I suppose I am slow, really." Tomas translates my answer. It seems to me he is using more words than is necessary to repeat what I said.

"What is the most interesting experience you've had so far?" the man asks me.

I say I haven't had any interesting experiences.

Tomas translates and the two interviewers smile and nod. What is he telling them?

"Do you have plans to marry Max Lilly?" the woman asks.

"How can she ask me that?" I say to Tomas.

"Here they ask anything," he says to me. "What should I tell her?"

"Tell her he is a very great director and a very great teacher and I owe him everything, but naturally one does not marry all one's teachers, and in any case, we have not thought of marriage. I am very young and have a great deal to learn about everything."

"Good," says Tomas, and begins translating. "The gentleman wants to know if it is true you shared a room with Mr. Lilly in New York City."

"No, I did not, and I am too tired to answer any more questions," I say, getting up.

"He wants to know if you will become a great star," Tomas says.

"I didn't come all this way to be an extra," I say, walking away.

In back of me, I hear someone Swedish asking Tomas, "How did she do?" and he says, "I had to change some of her answers, but sometimes she's fine."

"Max," I say, "this translator, he changes what I say to the interviewers. I do not like it."

"This is publicity, this is not real life," Max says. "Let's hope he gives good interviews."

The next morning when the papers come out, I find I have said that I am most impressed with the physical splendors of this wonderful country, the abundance of its natural resources, and the wild beauty of its scenery, so uncramped, so unlike tired old Europe. My most interesting experience came when I was taken to the theater and saw the First Lady of the Theater and of course I was enchanted by all the American films I saw, finer than anything I had expected, and even though I could not read the title cards, still as if by magic I could follow the story and often left weeping. My greatest ambition was to become as good an actress as the wonderful woman I had seen on stage and of course I had no chance at all to become homesick. How could I be homesick when I was so excited and happy?

"How indeed?" said Anders.

"It's not bad, not at all," Max said.

"It is all nonsense," I said. "When can I start to work?"

"That will take a while," Anders said. "It is part of what they call breaking you in. They keep you waiting and waiting until you feel grateful to them when they ask you to come in and do something you don't want to do—like get your hair dyed. You'll see."

"But you are working," I wail. Sitting around doing nothing, in a strange country, left to my thoughts which are not thoughts, but frights, how can I stand it?

"I am now," Anders says. "I am broken in. It's not so bad. You see me. Did you notice a difference?"

"Where will we live, what will we do?"

"Every week you will go in to The Studio, get your check, ask what plans they have for you and go home," Anders says. "Then, when you think they've forgotten you, they'll send for you. That's how it is."

"Not for me," says Max. "Not for me."

• • •

This time it seemed Max was right. Once we were installed in our hotel, the studio called and said they were sending a car for Max. When he asked, they said they would not need me for days. "Then," I told Max, "I will call Tomas and we will look around."

"For what?"

"I don't like this hotel. What can you see when you look out? Shop windows and cars and some palms. A nightmare. They say they have a whole ocean here somewhere, so I will go find it. It is important."

"All right, it is important," Max said, standing before the mirror, fussing, tugging at his suit jacket, adjusting his tie clasp. I came over and reached out to straighten his tie, but he said, "Leave it alone. You make things worse."

What did The Studio want him for? Did they already have a film for him? Well, why not? Except, of course, he usually chose his own stories and wrote his own scripts. Probably that's what they wanted: to know what story he was going to work with.

Tomas had an open car. "Who is paying for the gas?" I asked him, and he said The Studio. "Who is paying for your time?" I asked. Again, The Studio. "Then we will look for the ocean," I said. "It is very far away?"

"Not far and not hard to find," he said.

"And how much time are you to spend with me?"

"All day."

"All day!"

"I keep you out of trouble," he said.

"And how will I get into trouble?"

"Oh, if they decide to do something with you, and the publicity gets going, the termites come out of the wood and start chewing on you. Then you say what The Studio wants you to say."

"No," I said. "Better to say nothing."

"If you say nothing, a poor girl with runs in her stockings who sits at a desk under the roof in the heat types up what you should have said. Believe me, that's how it is. It's all business here."

"So all day you must follow me around like a jailer?"

He didn't answer. *Santa Monica*, a sign said. Thank God this wasn't Russia. Thank God they used the same alphabet.

The land was growing sandier, the greenery thinning out, and the road was climbing. We went around another bend in the road and the car slowed. Tomas pulled into a paved circle on top of the hill and we walked to the edge of the cliff, and there it was, stretching far away, silver in the far distance, blue closer in, and green, green, green, lapping at the shore. A large black dog came flying down the beach, a stick in its mouth. It dropped the stick and plunged into the water, then let out a shriek and flew back onto the sand. "Crabs," Tomas said. "They bite. And there are sharks. Sometimes they come in quite close."

"It is the Pacific?" I asked.

"It is the Pacific," he said.

"And on the other side is China?"

"Yes, China."

"And also Japan and Siam?"

"And also Japan and Siam and Australia."

"Oh, it is the wrong ocean!" I said, beginning to cry.

"I know a nice little hotel near here, not very expensive, not very many studio people, the landlady speaks German, and all day long you can sit on the veranda looking out over the sea," Tomas said.

"Not very expensive?" I asked.

"No."

"Who pays our rent?"

"You do."

So when I heard that, I stopped crying and asked to see the little hotel.

"We can walk to it from here," Tomas said. "Down the beach where the dog came from. Probably he belongs to the hotel.

"You like it?" Tomas asked. We were standing in front of a long, white wooden building, two stories high and very plain, its roof orange tile. Porches ran the length of both stories. Flowering bushes were everywhere, and little trees with oranges on them. "Orange trees?" I asked Tomas.

"All over," he said. "You can pick them anywhere and eat until your stomach hurts. They grow wild here, and grapefruit, and grapes, not like home where the frost shrivels everything and you wait all winter for the ice to break up and the boats to come in from warm countries."

"I will look at rooms," I said.

We stood in the middle of a large bedroom, its plastered walls painted white, its exposed wood beams almost black. The floors were pale wood, unstained, and when we walked across them, sand ground beneath our feet. The curtains were made of a loosely woven cloth I had never seen before and thick cream-colored shades pulled down behind them. I pulled one by its cord and it snapped up into the air and flapped like film that had just unspooled from a finished reel.

"You don't always want the sun," said the landlady. "Sometimes it's blinding. And if you have a tendency to headaches, you'll give thanks for a darkened room."

"Headaches?" I said. "I don't have headaches."

"She is only saying *if*," Tomas said.

I looked at the double bed, its headboard and footboard plain dark wood. It looked Swedish, but the coverlet was a rough, striped material, pink and orange and purple. Who ever saw such colors in Sweden? A little woven rug lay next to the bed. The chest of drawers and the wardrobe were plain pine boards. "Look, from that wood they make poor people's coffins," I said to Tomas. He said here such wood was popular.

"Walk out on the balcony," the woman said and we went out on the porch. The sand was white and shimmered in the heat. The green strip of ocean winked and crashed against the shore. Foam and spray rose into the air.

"How much is this room?" I asked.

"Twenty dollars. With breakfast," the landlady said. "A *big* breakfast."

"What is a big breakfast?" I asked Tomas. A big breakfast was two eggs, bacon, bread and jam, orange juice, coffee and milk, and many rolls, so many you could take them from the table and eat them all day.

"Twenty dollars, two hundred kronor!" I said. "How much is the hotel?" Seventy-five dollars. Seven hundred and fifty kronor! "I will take this room," I said. "Tell her. And she must reserve one for Max."

Tomas said he was under the impression that Max liked the big hotel we were staying in.

"If he likes it, he will stay there. You know Anders Estersen?" I asked him. "He lives near here?"

"Not even a mile away. You can walk," Tomas said.

"Then Max will come here," I said. "You'll see."

The two men who have broken out of prison keep going across the frozen plains where the snow looks like sand. They walk and walk and now they are hungry. They come to a farmhouse where the wife is cooking. "Woman!" they say. "Give us something to eat!" but she refuses. "Work for your food!" she says. But they are crazy with hunger. They take her pot from the stove and ladle the stew into bowls and drink it as if it were water. Then they look around the kitchen until they find the keg of beer and they drink until they fall to the ground like stones. When the husband comes home and finds them, he throws them out into the snow. They wake up and find themselves outside, laugh and slap one another, and begin to walk. They are walking toward the town of Hogeborn. They are walking through snow. Because of the clothes they wear and the way their breath forms little funnel-shaped clouds before their faces, we know they are walking through snow. But if we didn't look carefully, we might think they are walking through sand.

And somewhere in the distance, an old man driving a horse cart tells his dog they are driving to Hogeborn and the dog begins to howl. Even though there is no sound, you know the dog is howling. Yes, he is howling, and the old man cannot make him stop.

That evening, Max and I sat on the porch of the Magnolia Mansions. Of course he was complaining about me. "Any other woman would have been in the stores. Any other woman would have come back with so many shoes and dresses and hats I would have been forced to roar and scold. You go out and find a cheap hotel."

"Cheap and by the sea," I said. "The sound of the waves, it is wonderful, and the sea talks all the time and does not expect you to talk back to it."

"You will be very happy when death comes calling," Max said gloomily. "It doesn't expect you to pay attention or talk back either."

"I want to go to The Studio and see what it is."

"It is very big," Max said. "It would swallow up the Lagerloff, so many sets, they have maps telling you which way to go, and still you can't find anything. Seven directors filming at once! The lunchroom is a surrealism, Pilgrims sitting next to policemen, the kind they call cops, girls in tutus, something called a vamp, something called an *It* (the It, she is very pretty, by the way), a Marie Antoinette, a crazy musician in a filthy coat, girls in swim suits, they're all sitting around the same table, some male doctors in white jackets, hundreds and hundreds of them, and then a whistle blows and they jump up from their chairs and run off, still chewing."

"Where are the famous ones?"

"They have their own room," Max said. "Madness all over. But very nice. What English did you learn today?"

I laugh. *"How much?* I can say that."

"What else?"

"Where, ocean, sand, all those words I can say." Max sighed and stared out over the ocean. "I've learned enough languages," he said. "First Yiddish, then Russian, then German, then Swedish, then Finnish. Now I must learn this one too? Enough!"

I said nothing. He would learn. How could he help it? All day he would hear English. In a few weeks, he would believe he spoke it better than people who were born here.

"So, I went into the offices, I explained my ideas, a story of the country, a myth of the country, like *The Sharp Knives* or *The Mansion of Father Bertil*, something everyone will remember, like a fairy tale everyone tells the children, generation after generation, so no one ever forgets it, and that Pinsky, he said to me, 'Leave America to Americans. What do you know about American myths?' And into my hands he shoves a heap of scripts, oh, one is worse than the next, and I ask him what Anders is doing next, and he turns red like borscht and says, a famous American book, but don't worry, he has plenty of American advisers, and later I asked around, and it's a classic, an American classic, that's why there are so many Pilgrims in the cafeteria! So it's all right for Anders, somehow he's an American, but they don't trust me."

"They are used to Anders," I said. "And the actors, maybe they are also used to him and ask for him. You know how it is. How many times did you tell me? Make friends with the director? Make friends with the stagehands, the cameraman? When the director doesn't know who he wants, the stagehand looks up and says, 'Tora Tellson, she is pretty good.' So probably, yes, that is how it is."

Here I am again, frightened to death, so stiff with fear that if anyone hits me hard I will shatter like glass, and I must give advice to a man twice my age. Once again, I have become the oldest child.

"Probably that's how it is," he agrees. "It's that famous woman and her sister, Maud Marsh, the one you like so much. You come with me tomorrow and I'll leave you there on the set. Bring a book."

A book! I was too nervous to concentrate, too nervous to write a letter, too nervous to do anything but stare out at the sea—what would I do with a book? But Max had his own troubles. Why should he have to hear mine? And then Gussie saw another dog playing in the sand and she began jumping up, her front paws on Max's knees, whining. "I will take her," I said, and Gussie and I played in the sand. I threw sticks for her, she caught them and buried them. I fought her for her sticks and when I got one, I pretended to chew on it until she began barking, and while the dog and I played, I forgot where I was. For a few minutes I forgot, but then I looked back at the hotel, and Max was sitting on the balcony, perfectly still, so still I called to him: would he move? He moved and waved but even from where I stood, I could see what an effort it was for him to raise his arm.

IT WAS EARLY in the morning, and my stepmother was in the house giving birth to Lida. Miss Blue, who usually came to make breakfast, which we called tea, was late, and so Cynthia and Cherry and I decided we would do it ourselves. We had already been down to the river to bathe and were in the skirts and blouses we would wear to school.

I said I would eat the cold ackee and salt fish left over from last night's meal. Cynthia said she did not want the cold food and if Miss Blue were here, she would make cornmeal porridge with red peas, so I began to grate the cornmeal, and Cynthia lit a kerosene bottle lamp.

"Move that lamp," I said to Cynthia. "It almost caught my sleeve."

I believe she moved the lamp before she began making the hot chocolate we always drank in the morning, chocolate we ground from our own beans. I looked down at my skirt and saw its hem glowing red. The fire in the lamp had caught it. With my fingers, I snuffed it out and moved aside.

Jack came in, eating a banana, and put four or five fingers down on the table. "In the towns," he said, "Daddy says they have to share one banana among five people. He said no one expects to have a whole coconut or orange to themselves in the town. That's how fortunate we are."

"I know a girl who moved to Cinnamon Bay," Cynthia said, moving the lamp so she could see better, "and she told me that every morning her grandmother made one scrambled egg and divided it up between the four of them. Four people eating one egg!"

Outside there was a terrible squawking and Jack ran out. A chicken hawk had been after our chickens and had carried off four in the last week. Now a dead chicken was fastened to a stick in the middle of the yard. He was bait for the chicken hawk and Jack hoped to catch the bird when it came for its prey, but my father said it would not work. No chicken hawk was so stupid. Jack came back in and said it wasn't a chicken hawk up there but a vulture.

"Oh, well," I said, and continued stirring the pot of cornmeal. I stirred in the juiced coconut we used in place of milk. I felt a warmth near my knee but paid no attention. Probably it was the sun coming through the window. Then the warmth turned to heat and I looked down. The side of my skirt was on fire. I screamed and ran to the doormouth. The fire climbed me like a dry tree.

When Jack saw the fire eating my skirt, he picked up a large wash basin and threw the water at me and began to shout for Daddy. The water hit my skirt, but it kept on burning. Jack was looking for more water when my father came running out of the house. He took one look at me and grabbed me up and began to tear at my clothes but the fabric would not yield. I stood there, flames leaping from my right side.

Daddy plunged toward me, his mouth open. I thought he was going to take a bite out of my flesh. He thrust his face into my bosom and caught the fabric of the blouse between his teeth and pulled. I heard the material rip. He tore the blouse from me and threw me down in a mud puddle and rolled me over and over. I was crying, not from pain, because I didn't feel any, but because my hair, which I had set in curlers the night before, was drenched in mud and when I got to school, I would be the class laughing-stock.

"Why are you crying?" my father asked me, and I told him.

"You are not going to school," he said. "Oh, no. Cynthia, Cherry, go to the river with her and clean her up and put her to bed."

They helped me wash myself in the river and laughed when the mud streamed out of my hair, down my face, and along my breasts, where it dripped from my nipples onto my stomach.

When Lazarus stopped his truck to pick up my father, Daddy said he was not coming yet, but would be along later in the afternoon. Every ten minutes he would come into my room to ask me how I felt. Everywhere I had been burned I was covered with large, liquid-filled blisters.

"I feel fine," I said. "Go to work."

I did not feel fine, but I did not want to upset my father. When he came home from work that night, he sat on the bed and asked me how I was. I said I was fine and would go to school in the morning. "You're sure?" he asked me and I said I was. I didn't want to interrupt his dinner.

I was having trouble breathing. When I breathed out, my breath was hot, like the steam that rose up from a boiling pot. As the night hours passed, and I watched the sky grow lighter, I became very thirsty, but when I tried to drink the lemonade Cynthia had left for me on the little table at the side of the bed, I could not swallow. The first of the cocks crowed and my body was on fire. I touched my side where the fire had caught my skirt and blouse and felt large blisters. I blew on my hand and my breath was like a blast from an oven.

In the morning, my father came in to see me. "Daughter," he said (*daughter* was what he called me now), "How are you feeling?"

"Not as well as I thought," I said. "I can't swallow and when I breathe out, my breath is hot."

"What do you mean?" he asked me.

"If you will give me your hand," I said, and he stretched his out, and I blew on it.

"My God!" he said. "Why didn't you say something?" He was shouting to Jack, telling him to bring his bicycle. He touched my head. "She is hot as fire!" he shouted to no one in particular. The others came running. Cynthia said he should wait for Lazarus's truck. "I am not waiting for anything," he said. "Help me wrap her in a sheet."

He carried me to the bike and lifted me onto its handlebars. I was dressed only in a sheet and worried that the wind would blow the sheet from me as we drove through the streets of Cinnamon Bay. I remembered how Daddy used to come for us after school, four or five of us riding on the handlebars and back wheel of the bike, all the way back to Mare River. I saw my stepmother's face watching through the window.

"You should have brought her in sooner," said the doctor in Cinnamon Bay. My father did not answer. He was weeping.

They put me in a room on the children's ward and inserted a needle in my arm. Sugar water began dripping into my vein. I said I was thirsty but the nurse said I was not to have any water. Instead she put a drop of something on my tongue, and when it melted, I could swallow it.

"You have no medicine for her?" asked my father.

"It is there, in that bottle," said the doctor.

He asked my father how it happened. My father told him that the woman who usually cooked our breakfasts did not come and we did it ourselves. "If I was a coward before the fire," he said, "she would have burned up."

"My God, man," the doctor said. "You have no beard or eyelashes. Or eyebrows! Every hair on your face has been burned off!"

My father touched his own face. It must have been sore. He withdrew his fingers hastily. He blinked his eyes incessantly.

"Are your eyes dry?" the doctor asked. My father said they were, and the doctor gave him a little bottle of drops. "Use these," he said. "Your eyes will be fine."

"And the child?" Daddy asked.

"Another minute and the fire would have reached her heart," he said. "Another few seconds and it would have been too late. And if the water your son threw had hit her near the heart, she would have contracted pneumonia and died." My father began to weep again. Then he sat down next to my bed and when I fell asleep he was still sitting there. He was there in the morning when I opened my eyes.

He came every morning before work and every evening after work. If my stepmother objected, I knew nothing about it. After six weeks, they let me get up, and I learned to walk by going from bed to bed, holding to the footboard of one bed and taking one step until I had hold of the footboard of the next bed. In the beginning, I could not walk very far, just the distance between three beds, and then the nurses would have to help me back. But after a while, I could walk from one end of the ward to the other, and then the nurses let me sit out on the veranda, wrapped in a robe.

From the veranda, I could see Cinnamon Bay, the clear green water, and the white flowers of foam exploding against the sea wall. Small boats on the horizon sailed into the cove, becoming larger as they approached. I could hear the faint shouts of the men on board ship calling to the men on the dock, who would grab the ropes they threw and tie them onto huge metal links fastened into the concrete. From my veranda, I could see the great palm tree that marked the horizon's edge, the palm tree at the end of the world. In the garden below me, scarlet and yellow flowers burned their colors into the day. In the distance, beyond the village itself, I could see the sun glint bone white on the gravestones of the cemetery of Cinnamon Bay. The sun heated the hospital and heated me under my robe or sheet. The nurses explained that the sun was not to touch me because I was already burned badly enough.

I began to help the nurses with the charts they kept at the foot of other patients' beds. When the doctors made their rounds, I took out the patients' charts and hung them on the rails of the beds, and in the afternoon, I helped the women in the laundry fold pillowcases and children's clothes. The nurses would pay me one or two shillings at the end of the week, and so I was well on my way to earning my keep as a patient. And as a reward I was allowed to walk in the garden outside the hospital. Before I went out, the nurses would give me my big white pill, which I was to take when I was outside. I carried my cup to the fountain, and when I got there, I would drink the water and pretend to take the pill, but because the pill was bitter, I would not take it. I threw it away. One day, I threw the pill and just then the doctor's car was passing and the pill landed in his lap. The doctor caught me and brought me back in and said that from now on I was to remain inside and the nurses must dissolve the pill in water and watch while I drank it.

No one knew why I was not improving. The wound would not heal.

My father had hired a private nurse to take care of me during the day. During the night, the hospital nurses changed my dressing. First, I would sit up at the head of the bed. The nurses would soak the dressing and then they would gently coax it up with tweezers. Sometimes the procedure would take them over an hour. But the private nurse had no patience. She would rip the bandage from the wound, opening it, drenching the pillow, and scold me if I screamed. One weekend, a woman who was visiting her son saw the private nurse at work, and when my father came, she told him what she saw.

At first, my father did not believe her. "If you pick up the pillow, you'll see where the blood gushed out," the woman said. "She turned the pillow over so no one would notice." My father turned the pillow over and there was the blood. He waited in the ward for the private nurse to come back and when she did, he wanted to go after her. "Vidal, don't," said the doctor. "You'll get in trouble."

The nurse was fired. The wound began to heal.

After I had been in the hospital for eight months, my Aunt Lucille came to see me. I didn't recognize her. "I am your aunt," she said. "Tita Lu."

"Tita Lu?" I asked.

"You called me Tita Lu when you were a little bit, you don't remember? Your mother called me Sister Lu, but because you couldn't say Sister, you said Tita. So I became Tita Lu. That is what everyone calls me now. Of course it is a long time since you've seen me, so you don't know who I am."

She talked and made a fuss over me. She brought me chocolate and spice cakes. Finally I asked her why she hadn't come before. Her voice was bitter. "I found out yesterday you were here," she said. "From Mrs. Darlington's daughter, who visits her son here."

"Daddy didn't tell you?" I asked.

"No, he would not," said Tita Lu. "That kidnapper. That criminal."

And so I realized that there was still deadly bitterness between the two families. She asked me if I remembered the kidnapping. I told her

I did. She asked me how I felt after I was taken away. I said I thought her family wanted me to go or they would have come after me, and that she had taught me that I must always do as I was told, and that was what I did.

Tita Lu cried when she heard that. Then she told me the story of how she had ambushed my father with his drinking buddies and gone to Stanny's store and emptied it of half its wares. I liked her. It was as if I remembered her, not from previous visits with her in Cinnamon Bay, but from another, earlier life. I asked her about my mother, Mer, what she remembered of her, but she began to cry.

"What good is remembering," she said, "when she is dead and gone?"

After that, Tita Lu came to visit me every few days until I was released from the hospital. I was released with a scarred arm, a scarred chest and a scarred leg and told that I was not to lift anything for some time because the scar tissue could break open. And it seemed to me that life resumed where it had left off.

Before I went to the hospital, I had never been ill and had known little illness in those around me. When the other children got the chicken pox or the mumps, I was perfectly healthy. I became the nurse, tending everyone.

Lazarus, my father's friend, used to say, "It's a good thing they're not down with poisoning, because they would arrest your daughter," and my father used to look at me and say, "The thing that makes her sick, that thing will kill her." But nothing made me sick.

When I was in the second standard, an entire family, except for one little boy, was found dead one morning, all dead in their beds, their appearance healthy and natural. Yet they were dead. The authorities came and sealed off the house and eventually it was determined that the oldest son had been performing experiments with chemicals and the fumes had killed everyone. Since some of the children were in our class, we were taken to the funeral.

A few days later, one of the older girls, a relative of the dead boy who had been conducting experiments, began to complain that her cousin had been slandered. She insisted that the family had died of food poisoning and nothing in the house was now poisonous. No one paid attention to her.

One night she went thiefing out of her own house, and, through a window, crept into her cousin's house. She left a note for her mother, telling her what she had done. In the morning, her mother found the note and ran down the hill to what the villagers now called the Dead House. She called to her daughter but there was no answer. She broke a window and climbed into the Dead House and there she found her daughter, apparently asleep on her cousin's bed, but the girl was not sleeping. She was dead.

Some people have a thirst for life, some for death.

The doctors said I should not have lived, but I did. I didn't know I wanted to live. I doubt that the girl who slept in her cousin's bed knew that she wanted to die.

Everyone on Green Island believes spirits walk because everyone has seen them. At home in Mare River, we used to sit on the veranda and watch a shadow couple approach our gate. As soon as they approached the fence post, they would turn and go back. When we went inside, they would come as far as the fence post and look at the veranda, and when they didn't see us there, they would go on down the road.

One night, my father was coming back from a domino tournament in Milk River when he saw a woman with a fine figure standing at the crossroads. He asked her if she would like a ride on his bicycle and she said she would. He asked her where she lived and she said she would tell him when he got there. He pedalled and pedalled and finally he came to a place where there was a store on one side of the road and a cemetery on the other.

"This is where I live," the young woman said, and she jumped down from the bicycle. He expected her to go toward the store, but she jumped over the stone cemetery fence and disappeared among the stones. He climbed back up on his bicycle and pedalled home as quickly as he could.

The next day he told Lazarus what happened. "You're lucky," Lazarus said. "Some men take her home and when they wake up, no one is in the bed. They're never the same again. They say they feel as if they've lost their shadows."

In Mare River, there is a small cemetery on one side of the church. One of the graves is covered by chains. Inside the grave, everyone said, was a terrible man. Every night he would get up from his grave and stop people on the road. Occasionally, he would so frighten the horses that he would cause an accident.

One night, the parson met this man's ghost on the road and the parson crossed himself and began to pray. The ghost began to laugh, and said, "You think that can work with me? I can pray better than you can!"

Finally the villagers decided that something had to be done and they tombed the man. They put a heavy blanket of cement over his grave, and over that they fastened heavy chains, chains heavy enough to anchor an enormous ship. The man in that tomb wanted to live.

My mother appeared in Tita Lu's dreams and told her things only a spirit could know. My mother must have wanted to live. In the next life, or wherever she is, she still wants to live.

They say that spirits do not walk as frequently as they used to because these days bodies are put on ice in mortuaries.

And if they are unable to walk as they used to, if they are unable to hang laundry in yards where they used to hang it, they walk now in people's dreams. There are some beings who so want life that nothing can stop them. So I wonder: were my mother and father two such beings? Did they both want life so desperately that they could not live together? Did one of them sense that the other was too hungry? That she might turn on him, or he on her, greedy for what life the other possessed? Can it be that one house cannot contain two such appetites?

But I believe he hungers for her still. Mer is who he remembers. Mer is who he loved best. It was Mer he picked up and drove to the cemetery on his bike that night.

"Well, well," I say to Anna, "that is why I liked helping people, all that time in the hospital." And she says she spent time in the hospital when her father was dying but it did not affect her the same way. Instead she became afraid of everyone. Yes, she says. Yes, she thinks that is where it started.

5

IN THE MORNING, the sun rising behind the house, climbing up over the sea. In the afternoon, the sun overhead. At night, the sun on the rim of the sea, beginning to sink, shadows of palm trees like giant insects on the walls of our hotel. All the time sun and more sun. "Does it ever rain?" I asked Tomas, who said, "Oh, yes, sometimes." And of course there is no snow.

"In the mountains there is snow," he said.

"But as soon as you come down, sun and heat, sand and palms."

"This is California," he said. "You get used to it." He himself felt very lucky to be here. Someone promised him a screen test. He would be the American Erik Grissom!

"But Erik Grissom is already here," I told him. "He has a big part in Anders Estersen's new movie."

"He can't star in everything," Tomas said.

There were times I caught him watching me. *She* was working in a confectioner's shop when Max Lilly came in and saw her so why not me?

I said to Max, "Tomas thinks he will be the American Erik Grissom," and Max said, "If he has so little imagination maybe he will fail even as a translator."

"If they gave him a screen test, perhaps he could do something."

"Not for me," Max said. "There is nothing in the eyes."

"But," I said, "he is young." And Max said if you were young with young eyes, you were useless. When he looked in my eyes, he saw everything from youth to old age. That you had to be born with. He had such eyes but he was hopeless on film. "Well, you know. You've seen it," he said to me. "People said I looked like the most elegant basset hound in the world."

Basset hound! It was true.

"So today," he said, "you will come with me. They want to show me more scripts, tell me more of their ideas. I want something that's right for both of us."

"Then it will be like home."

"Like home," he said, raising his eyebrows.

Always I forgot that Sweden was not home to him, Finland was not, nor Germany. He had no home.

"Anders won't mind you on the set. He says you are so quiet you keep him calm. Today Miss Marsh goes crazy when the storm breaks, so he is worried. She's so anxious to look the part she stays up all night and when she grows tired, she wakes up her sister, and her sister sits up and pokes her awake. Thanks to all this, she looks terrible, her ribs stick out, her clothes hang on her, already she looks crazy and sometimes Anders thinks she is. All he has to do is say, 'Miss Marsh?' and she starts screaming. But worst of all, he wants to know, how will she go crazy? It takes a lot of energy to go crazy and she can barely get herself out of her chair and in front of the camera."

"This is great acting?" I asked him. "You can't tell her a little black paint under the eyes, a little white powder on her face, and she can go to sleep? What happens tomorrow when she's supposed to look strong and healthy?"

He said, "Thank God she dies after the storm and on film you don't see the body. According to her, everything must seem real. If you had to see the body, she'd starve herself and when the camera stopped turning, she wouldn't get up.

"So I said to him, 'You encourage this?' And he said, 'Look, she is a powerful woman. The bosses listen to her. She wants to kill herself, what more can I do about it? I tried. What more can I do?' So I said, 'What you mean is you have lost control.' And he said, 'No, I have complete control. First she does it her way, then she does it my way, then in the cutting room, I pick up a scissor. You think they can remember which take it was they wanted? If it turns out good, it was their way. Bad it was mine. Sometimes the cameraman cranks the camera and there's no film in it. Anders has one camera that never has film. 'That camera,' he said, 'is for the *artistic* shots.' He said that to me in Swedish. Then he said it to her in English. And she was listening to him, looking at him pointing, and she said to him—I know, because he told me—'It has a very fine lens, specially ground in Germany. We're using it all day tomorrow.' '*All day*,' Anders said. She adores him. 'Sometimes a little sugar in the tea, Max,' he said. 'Must it always be salt?' "

"Miss Marsh," I said. "Is she important?"

"Very important. She becomes interested in a story, the studio makes it. If the studio doesn't want to make it, she can pay for it herself. She wanted to make *Dust,* so now they're outside with fans blowing hot sand over everyone. God forbid she decides to make *The Fires of Hell.* Anders is already so sunburned he screams if he thinks you'll touch him."

"So I must make friends with her," I said. "Without knowing the language, that will be hard."

"You'll think of something," Max said. "Make yourself like her. People always know. You like them, they like you back."

"And if I can't like her?"

"Then act."

"Sometimes it is hard to act when any minute you expect lightning to hit you," I said.

"You are complaining about me?" he asked, astonished. "The girl who was a lunatic stork when I found her? You are complaining?"

"I was just saying," I murmured.

"An actor must have good nerves," Max said. "Most don't. Erik Grissom, he has nerve, falling on me that way. And a director, he must have nerves of steel because he has to work with crazy actors, every one of whom is up all night studying, figuring out ways to ruin everything. They sit there with scripts in front of them, you think they're memorizing their lines, but what are they doing? Dreaming up new ways to disgrace the director! And who will get the blame? The actor? No. He was badly directed. Even the stage sets, if they are bad, they blame the director. So a director must have control. Thus, he strikes like lightning. You understand that?"

I was not going to argue with Max.

"Is it safe to leave Gussie with that translator?" he asked me. "He won't sneak off to meet Miss Marsh?"

"He will do as I say," I said. "He wants to meet you. He wants to meet Anders. He wants a screen test."

"Sometimes you are hard for one so young," Max said.

"Well, what can I do about it?" I asked him.

The Studio, when I saw it, was like a city, so big I could not take it in.

"Dust, Dust," I said to everyone. "Anders Estersen?" People began to nod and say, Lot 45.

I peered into sets as I walked along the studio streets.

Two cowboys were fighting one another, one dressed in white, the other in black. On the next set, a woman reclined in an Egyptian bathtub, one leg over the rim, while a man in Roman armor bent over her. Two men passed me, speaking German, one wearing a turban and Turkish pajamas. "I'm not flying through the air," said the man in the turban. "Not until you test it out with sandbags."

"Oh, come on," the other man said.

"Last week Billy flew through the air on that thing and he's in plaster up to his neck," said the man in the turban.

"Oh, come on," the second man said again, this time louder so that I could still hear him. "Your nerve is going."

"You think it's easy, you do it," the first man said. Evidently they had stopped walking. I stopped too, to listen. "Me?" the second man said. "I'm the director."

"Yeah," said the man in the turban, "but they insure the life of the star. Why is that?"

The buildings ran out and the open-air sets began. A huge steamship was marooned in the middle of a field and in front of it people were waving from a pier rising straight up out of the earth. On the deck of the steamship, the passengers waved madly back.

"Dust?" I said to a man walking by. "Anders Estersen?"

He pointed past the steamship. "Thank you," I said in Finnish, but he was gone. I passed beneath a papier-mâché oak tree and saw two lovers twined together under it, and then water began to pour down through the branches, soaking them. When I passed the tree, I saw it had no back. It was propped up by timbers. As I walked toward a house, half of the façade was taken down. I knew they were striking the set, but still I was frightened, and one half of me thought, This is a lunatic asylum, and the other half thought, This is wonderful.

I began to hear the loud roar of airplane engines, and I remembered Anders saying he had two airplanes blowing sand in the desert, and there, where the streets ran out, were two airplanes, and in front of them, a tiny shack surrounded by cameramen. I walked on. There was Anders, a wide straw hat on his head, a thick white cream smeared beneath his eyes, on his nose, and on the point of his chin, shouting through his megaphone, *Cut! Cut!* A small woman in a calico dress walked slowly toward the long, low building to the right and collapsed in a canvas chair. At that moment Anders caught sight of me.

"Oh, Anna, thank God," he said in Swedish. "A normal human being! Look at that skeleton sitting there! She's been going mad all morning and all morning the wind from the propellers pushes her back. She doesn't have the strength, you see. Come, I'm bringing her a cup of coffee, two inches of sugar, *two inches,* for the energy. It's ridiculous. This one, she can't die in more than one movie. Come on, you go up to her chair first."

"Miss Marsh," he said in German. German seemed to be the universal language here. The small woman in the chair looked up at me, her eyes unfocused. She began clawing at her face. I grabbed her hands and pushed them down into her lap.

"What are you doing?" she shrieked at me. "You're in my line of sight! You're taking me out of character! Anders! Get this woman away from me!"

"Come, Anna," Anders said. "Sit in this room out of the sun and watch. Something good can come out of this? You tell me."

I sat inside and watched Anders. He bent over Miss Marsh. He spoke to her softly. She picked up the mug of coffee and began to drink it. Was she pleading with him to begin filming? It seemed so, but he shook his head, no, no, no. Then he nodded as if to say, All right, we'll try it.

Miss Marsh got up and with her arms stretched in front of her, faced Anders, and pushed against his chest. He stood firm. She tried again and he took a step backward. He nodded at her, she smiled, the propellers began to whir, she went into the weathered little cabin, which looked as if it had stood there for all eternity, and she pushed the door open and staggered out into the wind and the dust. When she was clear of the building's shadow, she began to run in circles, tearing at her hair, staring up at the sky, then into the camera, pulling at her clothes, and finally she froze, her hands clapped over her ears. Then she fell and lay motionless. "Cut! Cut!" shouted Anders.

He helped her get up. From his tone, I knew he was praising her. Then he stopped speaking and listened to her. "No, no, no!" he said. "She wants to do it again!" he exclaimed in Swedish. "All right, we use the special camera," he said.

He pointed to one of the cameramen who moved up and Anders peered through its lens. Once more the propellers started up, once more Miss Marsh struggled out through the door, ran in circles, tore at her hair, stared at the sky and fell to the ground.

"Perfect!" Anders cried. He ran up to her. She raised herself up on one arm, said something to him, and collapsed. "She's satisfied," Anders called out to me. He bent over Miss Marsh, spoke to her, helped her up and sat her down in a chair.

"Anna, come over here," he called. "This is Maud Marsh. Say hello."

"Hello," I said shyly. She smiled wanly at me and said something.

"She is sorry she yelled at you before," Anders said.

"I thought she would hurt herself," I said.

Anders said something to her. She clasped my hands and kissed them. "I told her what you said," Anders told me, "and she takes it as a great compliment to her acting ability. Where is Erik? He is about here somewhere. You've seen him? No? And Max? Where is he? Filming already?

"Sit here with Miss Marsh," he said. "I want to check the light for the stampede." So I sat next to Maud Marsh, who said something to me in English that I couldn't understand, and because I couldn't, I smiled and blushed. Eventually, she reached out and took my hand in hers and began to stroke it. She shook her head and turned down the corners of her mouth as if to say, "What a business, eh?" And I liked her. I thought she was completely crazy but I liked her.

"So," Anders said, "you two sphinxes are getting along?"

"It is so exhausting, this not talking," I said.

"Everyone is exhausted. She is exhausted, you are exhausted. Only I am full of energy. Two more days, we finish, we strike the set, and then I will be exhausted, too."

He asked what I would do now. I said I had nothing to do. I would wait here until Max came to take me to lunch. Meanwhile, I thought, I must make Miss Marsh take an interest in me.

"So," said Anders. "They haven't separated you yet. Well, maybe they won't."

6

WHEN I WAS STILL IN SCHOOL in Mare River, a tall, flat-faced woman named Jean Holroyd came there intending to make a living as a dressmaker. But since she was always pregnant, and always carrying a baby with her, and on top of that, usually ill with one thing or another, she did not finish her dresses and suits on time, and so the villagers began to abandon her and either went to Cinnamon Bay or to Mr. Darlington and his daughters in Mare River.

After five years in Mare River, Miss Holroyd had no income and could afford to pay no rent. One day she came to my father, who had a large piece of land, not all of which was cultivated. She asked him if she could rent four of the acres across the river, and in exchange, she would give him a share of the crops. He asked her who was going to help her work the land and she said she would work it alone.

By this time, everyone in Mare River understood that no man who stayed with Miss Holroyd would remain with her for long. She had five children to support and lived in a one-room shack, so there was no privacy, and the men who lived with her tended to earn their living at Gray's Mansions during the harvesting of sugar cane. Many of them were married when they came and went back to their families when the crops came in. Nevertheless, they expected the women they lived with during harvest to prepare their meals and do their laundry.

Miss Holroyd's intentions were good, but she was frequently too ill to finish the laundry on time, and the men, who provided her with bluing and soap and starch, would complain that their shirts were not properly done, or she hadn't used enough bluing or starch, so that now they looked shabby and were too wrinkled to wear. These men also complained that they could not get any sleep at Miss Holroyd's, since a child was always crying, but everyone believed they left because of their rumpled shirts, since what man on Green Island was unaccustomed to being awakened by the cry of newborn infants, as ubiquitous as the crowing cocks who lived even in the back yards of the cities? All these troubles, which she saw as growing out of her faults, made her feel small. No one, I later learned, can endure feeling small for long.

My father told Miss Holroyd that she could make use of the four acres on the other side of the river and she and her children could live in the abandoned chicken coop he had once built there, although he warned her that it had never been cleaned well, and was not yet fit for humans.

The Saturday before she was to move into the chicken coop, my father organized a work party among the villagers, and many couples came to help her. My stepmother and father paid the villagers in the usual way. They cooked goat meat for them, and cornmeal with coconut and peas, and soup with dumplings. They fried plantains and one of the women made bananas dipped in caramelized sugar. It was a festive occasion, as all such occasions are, and afterwards the village took a proprietary interest in Miss Holroyd and watched how she prospered.

She did not have a green thumb, and the villagers soon realized that when it came time to plant, there would be no proper crop unless they helped Miss Holroyd sow her peas and corn and plant her yams. They joked with her and said she reminded them of my aunt, Lucille Clifton in Cinnamon Bay, who, after moving from the city to the country, cooked her grains of corn before she planted them. And the funny part of it was, they said, that some of the cooked grains grew into healthy plants. That was how fruitful Green Island was. Miss Holroyd would prosper, especially with their help.

They helped her willingly since she was so grateful and would send her children on errands for the neighbors and would herself do anything for them she could. Moreover, many of the women looked at Miss Holroyd and saw an image of what misfortune might have befallen them had they been less lucky with their men, a misfortune that might still get them by the throat and shake them if anything happened to their husbands and their sons were not yet old enough to help them. This was not pity. They did not pity her. On Green Island, everyone was accustomed to saying, "If I meet good fortune, I will take it, and if I meet evil, I will take that, too."

Miss Holroyd had met with bad fortune. She was unlucky but she was one of them. And she was helpful. Some people, when struck by misfortune, become bitter and selfish and care about no one but themselves, but Miss Holroyd was not such a one. When a dog was killing sheep in my father's upper meadows, she sat up all night with her two oldest boys, a large stick and a piece of zinc at her side with which to sound the alarm, but while she watched, the dog never came. The villagers insisted that this was not the work of a dog, but of a wolf who came down from the mountains. The Chinese butcher of Mare River was particularly insistent that a wolf was killing the goats in the upper fields.

My father went up to the field one night, smeared himself with mud so that the dog could not smell him, and at three in the morning, Jack-O, the large brindled dog of the Chinese butcher, appeared, scattered the goats, and began running one down. My father, who had taken down his rifle, loaded it and shot him.

The next morning, he brought Jack-O's body down to the Chinese butcher. "Here is your wolf," my father said. Without a word, the butcher took the dog's body. After a few days, we heard that the butcher had dressed him and the family had eaten him.

After that night, we looked at my father with new respect. For years we had heard him threaten, "I'll fill your mouth with lead," but we never believed the rifle was in working order, much less that he knew how to use it. We thought of my father as a strong man, but the kind of man who made empty threats. "A barking dog never bites," Mr. Darlington used to say when my father threatened him. Now we knew better.

After many years, Miss Holroyd began to prosper. At least she did well enough to feed her family of eight. The oldest boys could now help her plant her crops and harvest them and two of the older girls were skilled with an iron and took in laundry from the villagers and from the men who stayed in Mare River during harvest time. Her children now wore shoes to school when previously they had gone barefoot. When she hung their clothes on the line, the sun, shining through them, did not find out the many little holes and tears that incessant wear used to make in them. If the villagers had regarded Miss Holroyd as one who belonged to them and so needed their help, they had come to look upon her as they might view the sickly child of their own family who had now grown strong. The oldest boys and girls worked. The youngest went to school and at night taught their older brothers and sisters. Miss Holroyd was proud of all her children. All of them could read and write. The family was fat and happy.

Then the children began to grow thinner. Miss Holroyd herself grew thin and pale and was often found asleep on her mat in the middle of the day. When my father asked what was the trouble, Miss Holroyd led him out to the field where she had planted forty rows of yams. "See there?" she said. "In the night, someone comes and digs up two rows, sometimes three. If it goes on this way, we will be back where we were."

My father bent over the rows of yams and said, "This is a man's work, a man who wants you to think he is an animal. See how the dirt is scraped back here and heaped up, as if a dog had been digging? But it is not a dog. See the sharp cut a trowel has made in the earth? We will have to help you out of this."

"Oh, no," said Miss Holroyd. "I will do this myself."

"But what can you do?" asked my father. Afterwards he said he had seen something new in Miss Holroyd, a determination to keep what was hers, an unwillingness to depend on others, an unwillingness to always feel small.

"I can do something," she said. "I am not completely worthless." And my father thought to himself, Someone has been taunting this woman, someone has been making her feel small.

She must have decided to wait for him, the man who was plundering her fields. Miss Blue, who was coming home after looking for fever grass, passed her where she squatted in the yard in front of her chicken coop, sharpening her machete.

"That looks well done," Miss Blue said, but Miss Holroyd said it was not well done yet. Miss Holroyd said she had been working on the machete for hours and it would be hours before she finished. Miss Blue stayed for a while and watched her. She noticed how the chicken coop had grown. Rooms had been added to it by the boys and it had been whitewashed inside and out. Curtains, each panel a different pattern, hung from the windows. A tin-roofed structure provided the roof for a large outdoor kitchen. "You've done well," Miss Blue said approvingly.

"It is not sharp enough yet," said Miss Holroyd, looking down at the machete. "Not sharp enough yet." She worked with the concentration of the desperate or the mad. Miss Blue left, and when she looked back, Miss Holroyd was bent over the machete, rhythmically drawing her whetstone along its blade.

This is what must have happened.

Miss Holroyd sharpened her machete and sat up in the field waiting for the thief. She had learned her lesson and smeared herself with mud so that the thief would not see light reflected from her skin, nor would he detect the odor of another human being floating toward him on the wind. She took her eldest son with her and sat in the sugar cane she had planted just above the rows of yams. The moon was not full, but nevertheless she could see clearly. She had taken her son with her, so that if she drifted off to sleep, he could wake her, but she found she had no difficulty staying awake.

At about three a.m. a man appeared. He was carrying a crocus bag and his head was tied in a scarf that covered his face, exposing only his eyes. He looked carefully around him, and, sensing nothing, began digging the yams.

He dug one row and when he was finished, put the yams in his crocus bag. He began on a second row and did the same thing. Occasionally he would bend over the hole he had just dug and paw at the earth as if he were a dog, scattering the earth behind him. When he was half finished digging the third row, Miss Holroyd nodded to her son, made a gesture with her hand that meant he was to stay where he was, took her machete, and began creeping toward the man.

He was bent over the yam row, concentrating on his task. He did not hear her coming because during the day she had swept the field clear of twigs and leaves and in any case she knew how to move silently. When she was behind him, she raised her machete and brought it down on his back. She split him as one would split an animal. Her son said the man did not cry out, but fell flat upon his stomach. Miss Holroyd picked up the crocus bag, took the rest of the yams, put them in the bag, and then started back to the house. "He won't steal from anyone else again," she said. "Now call the police."

Her son ran down to our house and woke my father. No one in Mare River had telephones. My father took his bicycle and he and Miss Holroyd's son bicycled off to the police station in Cinnamon Bay. Within an hour, a police truck carrying my father, Miss Holroyd's son, and several doctors arrived at Miss Holroyd's house. She said she was ready to go with the police, and the policeman took her. The doctors put the split man onto a stretcher and carried him into the truck. No one could identify the split man. We believed he was a worker from Greenstown, who, during harvest, came into the country to find work.

In the morning, the news spread quickly, as it always does. In Mare River, you cannot pass an older person without greeting him, because if you do, when you reach your own yard and gate, your mother will be there waiting for you. "You didn't say good morning to Teacher Banford?" she will ask you, and you will wonder how Teacher Banford, whom you passed not one minute ago, crippled and hobbling down the street, managed to get news of your rude behavior to your mother before you yourself could return home.

At once everyone needed to go to the hospital in Cinnamon Bay.

"I've put off checking the condition of the boy's feet too long," said one mother, whose son had been walking on his heels for two years now. "It's an infection that could go to the brain." Cars and trucks and bicycles began making their way down the narrow red clay road from Mare River to Cinnamon Bay.

The nurses in the hospital soon gave up any pretense of maintaining order. That day their job was to show the people of Mare River past the bed of the split man. He lay on his bed, on his stomach, his body bandaged from the neck to the waist, his head turned to one side. His pupils were tiny and the whites of his eyes reddened with blood. While we stood over him, he blinked rarely.

"She split him like an animal," said my brother Jack. Like Daddy splits a goat, I thought.

"Will he live?" I asked one of the nurses.

"What do you think?" she asked me.

The man died that night, but not before all of Mare River had made a trip to see him, the Split Man. No one ever came to look for him. No one knew who he was. That was the only name we ever knew him by and the name he was called forever after.

The next day we went to visit Miss Holroyd. She was cutting up ackee and preparing to cook it. Her yams were lined up on a wooden shelf. She had peeled some of them and was going to cut them up and put them in a soup. She said she knew the split man had died and soon they would be coming for her, and so she had a considerable amount of cooking to do. The children would be on their own now. She hoped they would manage. She went out into the yard, caught a chicken, broke its neck, and came back in. She appeared to be completely resigned. She looked up at the sky and saw a chicken hawk circling. She shook her head as if to say that was how things were. For every living thing, there was another living thing that waited to take its life away.

On the day she had to appear in court, all of Mare River appeared with her. One person after another testified to how hard she worked to support her family. My father said that if the thief had continued uninterrupted, her family could not have survived. They were beginning to starve when she decided to split the man.

The judge acquitted her and sent her home.

The people of Mare River wanted to celebrate her acquittal, but how was that to be done? To make a party for an act that had ended in a man's death seemed right to no one. Eventually the people began to bring Miss Holroyd cooked dishes. They left them for her and her children, exactly as they would have done if she had just given birth and not taken the life of a fellow creature.

In time, people's curiosity began to die down.

"You see what people will do when they're hungry?" my father said. "You see what people will do to survive?"

A few years later, Miss Holroyd's eldest son got a job as a mechanic at the Greenstown airport and the family moved away. People began to forget Miss Holroyd. But whenever a child stole, whatever it was, a nisberry that had been put up on a high shelf for his father, someone would say, "Be careful or Miss Holroyd will split you."

Green Island is a fruitful place. If a storm devastates a mountain, that mountain slope will be green and productive in six months. A newly planted tree will look gangly for a short time and then will grow proudly into an adult. The weather is the same from day to day, month to month, year to year. It was hard to remember what year something happened, each year is so like the one that preceded it and so like the one that will follow. And the people of Green Island are like everything else that grows there. They grow quickly into adults and then do not seem to change.

A fifty-year-old man who left Green Island returned from another country and went back to his village. He had been gone twenty years. He came to see his mother and some of his uncles and aunts. He remembered them as being very old when he left, but when he saw them, they looked just as he remembered them. Miss Jones, who had been walking with a stick when he left, was walking with a stick now. Old Mr. Morse was old Mr. Morse still. Mr. Vin, who would stop in the middle of the street, point his finger into the air, and deliver a speech to God or whomever he saw in the clouds, was stopping in the middle of the street still.

"What?" he said to his mother. "Doesn't anyone die in this damn country?"

"What do you mean?" said his mother. "Mrs. Bedward died last year!"

"And how old was Mrs. Bedward?" he asked. "Two hundred?"

He said he supposed Mrs. Bedward was the exception who proved the rule. No one ever died on Green Island and he looked forward to retiring, coming back to his own country, and living forever.

They say the young everywhere think they will live forever. Green Island is different only in degree. The earth itself is young and giggly and fruitful and cares about nothing but blooming, and we are like the earth. No, here people's memories are not long. What is there to remember when every day is like the day before? When the girl who drives the goats up the mountain dies and is replaced by her sister, who is so much like her?

Why make an effort to remember the story of our lives and the lives of others when all we need do is wake up in the morning and the world outside the window is unchanged, sufficient to remind us of all that has gone before? When what is outside our window tells us what is to come? The past, the present and the future, all here at the same time. Eternity! Green Island is immortal and so are we. The great, blessed illusion of Green Island. Why complain? Why speak out against it? The happy do not need memory.

But for the unhappy, the unfortunate, it is a different story. When something goes wrong, what do the people of Green Island have to arm themselves with? Without memory, without a story of their lives, they can only suffer like dumb dogs in the sun.

I remember the Split Man. Wherever she is, Miss Holroyd remembers the Split Man. I remember everything I am told about my mother, but people tell me so little of her.

When I ask Tita Lu about my mother, she only cries. My father says, "Oh, she was a nice woman, very nice." My grandmother thinks that when my mother became ill with jaundice and was put in the hospital, she refused to take her medicine. No one knows. No one can tell me what she died of, not even that. No one has a picture of her, not a scrap of paper to show this is what she looked like. Once I wrote my father, asking him for a picture of her. He sent me one of him and said, "You must picture your mother standing next to me."

Someone stole my mother from me, a theft as terrible as the theft of Miss Holroyd's yams. And if I could find the person who stole her from me, I would split them. And I would not care what they did to me. With what little I remember, I have built a little world for myself, a world far away, and very small, as such a world should be, because it is seen from a great distance. And I look back toward that world and say, That is where I came from. This is why I am as I am. I too had a mother. I did not drop from a hollow tree. I had roots. I am as real as you are real. If I did not remember, how could I hold up my head? How could I live?

It seems to me now that I like thinking about the story of Miss Holroyd because this is one of the last times that the yarn of a story unwound neatly and took up the shape of a circle on the floor, a story with a beginning, a middle and an end, and the beginning was like the snake's mouth and the end was the snake's tail, and when we heard

the last of Miss Holroyd, the snake's tail fit neatly into its mouth and
made a perfect circle.

The childhood stories of my elders were such circles, beautiful
things, sometimes frightening, but in the end like bright glass bracelets
I could wear on my wrists. But after Miss Holroyd, the stories become
mine and the skein of thread spills from the spindle and tangles and
assumes fantastic shapes on the floor. To disentangle the thread, I have
to step back, trying to follow the main strand, or stoop over, trying
to pick it out, and it is impossible to do it. I know it is. I have seen a
woman counting grains of salt before.

7

THIS IS ONE of those mornings when I wake up and I don't know
where I am. When I was younger, even ten, fifteen years ago, there
was good reason for it. Hotels in different countries, different countries every week, living some of the time in my own house, some of
the time with someone else, and then whoever it was would say something and out of the house I went, back to my own bed. If I slept on
my back and looked up at the ceiling, and took my time turning on
my side to see what room I was in, was it any wonder?

But now when I wake up and don't know where I am and I'm in
no hurry to open up my eyes, I think, All right, Anna, keep them
closed. One of these days you'll open them and you still won't know
where you are even with your eyes wide open, that's how you'll know
you're in the next world. Of course I don't believe in a next world.
It's just a way of saying something.

Beyond my door the phone is ringing, so I know someone is calling
Ivy. Everyone thinks my phone number is her number. Well, it's better that way. I don't like the surprise of it, a loud noise, and then a
voice at the other end asking questions. "Good morning, how did you
sleep?" Do I know how I slept? Was I sitting up in a chair, watching
myself? And must I always have something to say? The person who
dials the number, that person wants to talk, he's awake, he's had his
breakfast, he's opened up his top drawer and found a freshly ironed

face and put it on, he knows to whom the voice at the end of the phone belongs. But for me it's like getting hit on the head with a stick, and then the person says hello and wants to be friendly.

And who can sound so intelligent at the drop of a shoe? "And what did you do today?" The worst question in the world to ask me. *What did I do today?* Always I try to speak the truth, and this is where the trouble begins. Should I answer, I went to The Studio and watched a woman stand in front of airplane propellers and go mad twice, and then I thought, Yes, even madness can be planned. And then, since the propellers were still going, I thought, Yes, you can walk into most things but you can't walk out, and that thought tired me so thoroughly I didn't do anything for the rest of the day, or at least nothing worth mentioning. It is a great deal of trouble for me to have thoughts, like having a very demanding houseguest, the worst kind of houseguest, the kind who says, Oh, I will keep myself busy, and she does, but then when she comes home, she follows you all over. *If you don't mind, I'll come with you.*

Once I had a houseguest from Finland, a very nice houseguest for the first month. It was during the war; at that time you had houseguests, sometimes for years. After a month, she was at loose ends. We went for a trip into the mountains. By this time, the sound of her voice was like an air raid siren. It was all my fault, really. She was not so bad and I suppose her voice was very nice but I could not stand it. So I said, "Wait in the car or go get a paper, and I will go get some postal stamps," and I went into the post office.

There was a line. I didn't mind. I didn't know anyone on the line. For once no one recognized me or they didn't care. I was by myself. I was at the window, making my negotiations, when I heard the houseguest's voice behind me. My back stiffened. "You see, I bought these stamps by mistake," the voice was saying. "I bought airmail stamps when I need domestic ones. You are buying airmail? To Europe? Why don't you buy mine?" I pretended not to hear. Then the voice was next to my ear so I had to turn around and smile. "Oh, you don't take back stamps?" it said. The other woman who wanted air mail stamps was tired of the whole thing and said she needed a lot of stamps; she would buy hers from the post office. Then the voice said, loud and cheerily, "Oh, Anna, what was I thinking of! *You* can use them!" And she insisted on giving me the stamps.

For this I wanted to kill her. She came in to the post office to save a few cents on each stamp. Fine. I am even worse. But in back of me, on line, where I did not expect her, she began negotiations with a perfect stranger. Well, of course the houseguest was a stranger to the country and you never know where you'll make a friend. If she said that once she said it a thousand times. What a smooth stone that sentence was in her mouth! Why did I want to kill her? Because she was there. Because I wanted silence. Because I am not fit to live with. Really I am not. I am impossible to live with. There are a lot of people who could tell you: it's the truth. *No one can live with her.* You could ask them, but they are all dead, the ones who tried living with me. It sounds funny when I say it. People would laugh. But the sad part is it's true.

A conversation that starts with a loud noise, how well can it go? And the other person has the advantage. I know what I look like at the end of my string: I look terrible. But I think that the person on the other end of the line, he looks magnificent. And I am crazy enough to think he knows exactly how I look. "Oh," said a psychiatrist I met once at a dinner party, "you *want* the other person to see how you look." And why would I want that? I ask, lifting my fork. "So he could come over and rescue you."

Well, maybe it is true I want to be rescued, but who wants to think about it? Really, I want to be rescued from the voice at the other end of the phone. Of course, it is different when *I* call someone. Then I am the invading army banging down doors, occupying bedrooms and kitchens and smiling at the poor victim with the unwashed hair, pushing it back out of her eyes, clutching her towel, backing away from me, bowing and smiling all the time, like a servant in an old film caught using her mistress's perfume.

Beyond the door, Ivy has answered the phone. "Who?" she says. "What?" I love to listen to other people talk. It is a bad habit. "When?" says Ivy. "Where?" she says. Is this a conversation or an exercise in journalism? Next she must ask, How? "How?" Ivy says. Oh, well, something has happened.

Ivy says nothing happens in her life anymore. This thought gives her great comfort. What can happen to her at her age? "I'm a big old woman," she says. Only one thing can happen to me now. But she forgets all the other people she knows. Something is always happening to them.

"So," I say when she comes in, "what happened?"

"This lady on Green Island, she took her own life," Ivy says. "You can tell me why people do things like that?"

How can I answer such a question? Do I know why I am still alive? "She was ill," I suggest. "She was old? Someone she knew died?"

"She was forty-five years old and stronger than a storm," Ivy said, "but she got ideas. She was well off, very fine. The only wrinkle was her line of work."

"Her line of work?"

"A prostitute, but you know, on the Island, it's a little different from here, because unless you're saved, you grow up thinking, Everything has a place, and the loose woman, she has hers too, and the men said she was a very good one and she ran a very clean house and she gave money to the church and she took in children whose mothers ran away from them and sent them to school. Even the women liked her. If it was the husband of someone she knew, she took the money and sent him home. If he was too drunk to walk, her men who worked there, they drove him home."

"A saint," I said. "This woman comes straight out of a movie I've seen fifty times."

"She was a good woman, Miss Anna!"

"All right, all right, she was good. So what happened to her?"

"Guess," says Ivy. But who needs to guess? "It had something to do with love," I say.

"Oh yes, oh yes," Ivy says. "This young man from Portland Parish came to Orange Bay where she was visiting with her sister and he met her on the street and he began courting her and always she would meet him in the cemetery or in the churchyard and soon he had plans to marry her and she began to think, Why not?"

"The woman was an idiot," I say, bored. "Already, I know how it is going to end. Not because you told me but because I know. How many times I played this part! The minute I saw the words, 'a woman of the world,' I knew what would become of me. These people on Green Island don't go to movies? They don't learn anything from them? Listen, I'm so smart, I'll tell you. He meets her in the churchyard and in the cemetery—one stands for the wedding that doesn't happen, the other stands for the funeral that does—and he finds out she is not so perfect, she has this thing called a past. Then he draws himself up and climbs up on a big pedestal and throws his shadow over her, and he says, I cannot marry such a bad woman, and she walks off, proud and straight, and when he's out of sight, she runs into the house and drinks rat poison or a bottle of ammonia or some lye, whatever she has handy.

"Then maybe he feels sorry and comes running back but already she is stiff as a board. He cries at the funeral but this is what he says to himself: Next time ask a few questions before you jump into the water. At the funeral he is already talking to himself with the voice of his own mother. What happened to this woman is a tragedy? The woman is stupid, the man is stupid. Before they went to school, they knew how such a story would end. What does it mean that she killed herself? In stupid people hope springs eternal, that's what it means."

"You must talk like that?" Ivy asks me. "So hard? There are no second chances in this world?"

"For stupid people?" I ask her. "No."

"But I myself had a yard child!" said Ivy. "And still a good man married me—at least at the time he was good. Should the world have turned its back on me as if I were a dirty dog?"

"He knew about the child, didn't he? So, of course he married you. But if you had wanted to become a nun and wear white robes and the story about the yard child got out and everyone started talking about it and then they threw you out in the rain, you would have been surprised?"

"But, Miss Anna! She fell in love with this young man! She took her money and went off and put down two dollars on a bakery in Cinnamon Bay! That was a good distance away from where she used to work! She talked about it to my sister Cherry, the one with fits, how she liked working with her hands, she liked pounding at the dough, she liked the white flour over everything. Even that!"

"Oh, you see!" I said. "A white veil! So how did she do it? Rat poison or what?"

"She killed *him*, Miss Anna! Then, when the police came for her, she ran up onto the roof and she jumped off. She broke her neck and lay there in the hospital for two weeks and maybe she got hold of some stuff from the nurse, maybe the nurse fed it to her, but now she's gone."

"But first," I said, "first she sat in her room and thought of herself in that bakery, giving out nice rolls to the little children and their mothers, wearing a neat black dress and a white apron and a white kerchief on her head, getting fat and respectable, going to church on Sundays, and one Sunday when she knelt down a ray of light would shine on her and all her sins would be washed away and she and the husband would live happily ever after. Oh yes, they would even climb the steps to heaven together. If this is how she thinks, she deserves to swallow rat poison!"

"You are too terrible," Ivy said, but she was sitting on the edge of the bed, thinking.

"She meets him in the churchyard, she meets him in the cemetery!" I said with scorn. "And probably all along he knew all about her and he liked the idea, you know, a woman of the world, and what does he end up with? A matron who wants to open a bakery and he will be coughing and choking on flour dust the rest of his life!"

"It was not like that, Miss Anna," Ivy said sadly.

"Oh yes it was," I said.

"You are getting excited, your pressure will go up," she said to me. I say I am not excited, just disgusted. "And any minute," Ivy said, "any minute you will be crying." Well, that is true, because I am crying now. "Well, she is well and truly dead," Ivy said, "and I feel sorry for her, but that's enough of that lady."

"They buried her in the churchyard?" I asked Ivy. I knew the answer. Why was I so greedy for these stupid details?

"You know they didn't," Ivy said.

"You are a hopeless romantic," I called after her. She came back into the doorway. "Why not, Miss Anna?" she asked me. "You know something better?"

Did I know something better? Did I love Max? Even Anders wanted to know: Did I love Max? Do I know, even today? Some things are so deep down, so secret, you yourself cannot let yourself know what they are. Once I read about sacred objects, so sacred that no one in the tribe could look at them, and if they did, they would be struck blind or they would die on the pathway home. Was he my sacred object? Can I have done that to him, made him into such a thing? It is fifty years later and still I do such a bad job describing him. Always, when I look back, I see him sitting in his carved chair, motionless, the little dog jumping.

But really, Max was always in motion. His eyebrows went up and down, the corners of his mouth turned up or down, he made sweeping gestures, usually with his right arm. When he walked with Gussie, she leaped about his feet and he would bend down and grab her up with his right arm and then point at this or that with his left arm: *Look, Gussie, look!* If a stick was nearby, he would pick it up and throw it for her. And always that look of amusement, as if he were about to burst into laughter, as if he were humoring everyone, as if whatever happened was beyond words ridiculous and he was playing along, out of good humor, with the look either of an overgrown child playing at amusing the grownups, or a grownup playing at amusing the children.

Which was it? Probably both. Whatever it was, it was irresistible.

So even when he scolded and cursed and ridiculed, everyone adored him. When he looked like that, then to see him was to know the whole world was a joke.

The energy, the hilarity, the silliness, it was right beneath the surface, that was what I loved, so much present yet at the same time hidden.

I think this is how it was. I was seventeen, he was thirty-seven, so he was older, he was supposed to know more, and of course he did, he did know more, but both of us knew ourselves very little. Today seventeen-year-olds know everything. In those days we knew nothing. I went from being a young person, someone who sunned herself on the building's lavatory roof and read romantic novels and wondered exactly why people were interested in sex, to being a woman who was recognized on the street, who was seen everywhere with Max, and still I didn't know anything at all.

And Max, well, there was always gossip about him. Did he like boys, or men, or girls, all of them or none of them? To this day, I don't know. I couldn't tell you. We never discussed it. What he talked about, what he thought about, was making movies.

A few days after Anders came to look at the rushes of *The Mansion of Father Bertil,* I was at work very early, around six o'clock. It was still dark outside. The two of them were standing outside the studio door, discussing something in low, tense voices. I stood behind the streetlamp, waiting to say good morning.

One of them would say something, the other would cut in—neither of them finished his sentences. Then Anders said, "Max, sometimes I think that for you the world exists only so you can put it on film!" and Max said, "Yes! Yes! What have I been trying to tell you! Everything in the world exists so we can put it on film, and if life is good, everything in the world will wind up in a film. That's what the world is for!"

I don't approve of people who eavesdrop. It's my opinion that if people want privacy, they should go somewhere they can't be heard. But where is such a place? Even a cemetery isn't private. I used to go to a cemetery and I thought, Here I won't be disturbed. But every melancholy person in Stockholm and every lovesick couple had the same idea. Well, melancholy people and lovesick people, they are the same.

Once Max and I walked into a cemetery and leaned against a shiny gray marble monument and went on and on about something we wanted kept secret from the rest of the cast, and when we finished talking and stood still, looking at one another, a couple came out from behind the stone, sheepishly nodded to us, and walked quickly down the path toward the gate. In cities, if you find a place where you can walk or talk alone, then you are about to be murdered or you are in a padded cell, and in either case, someone is probably watching and listening.

So I had no business standing there. But I was tired of asking myself, Why does Max do this? Why does Max do that? Sometimes he would talk to me seriously, but usually he would tease me or say something ironic and distract me.

Anders said, "For you the world is some kind of quarry?" and Max said, "No, Anders, you weren't paying attention! For *you* the world is some kind of quarry. You dig out of it what you want. Some of it you keep for yourself, some of it you put in your films. For me, the world is something that goes into a film or it doesn't mean anything. A person standing in front of me, he doesn't mean anything. He's missing a dimension. Everything needs a context. The world is no context. It's too big. It contains everything. It's senseless. It's unedited. A film is an edited world. Everything in it makes sense. Behind every film, there's the dreamer. You don't look at a film and say, 'How can God allow this? Is there such a thing as God?' All those questions that drive people crazy. You look at this world, you know there's no such thing as God. You look at a film and you know who God is: he's the one who wrote the script. He's the director. You sit in a theater and watch a film, and the world makes sense. It doesn't have to be simple, but it makes sense. People, what are they? Collections of raw facts waiting to be interpreted. They're pretty or they're not. They don't mean anything."

"Utter indifference to life!" Anders said. "That's what you're preaching! If a person doesn't find his way into a film, he might as well fall off the earth! Once he finds his way into your film and plays his part, you're through with him! You'll even give him a push off the earth!"

"You think I'm indifferent to life?"

"To other living things. What they need, what they feel. You're going to tell me you pay any attention?"

"Without other living things, how could I make a film?" Max asked. "For you, people are ends in themselves. For me they're not. It shows in your films. In my films, people exist as part of a pattern. The pattern is the important thing."

"I don't know who you think you're fooling!" Anders said angrily. "For God's sake, we're not children anymore! We know the world wasn't created for us! So you're disappointed in life! So you want to persuade yourself people only exist for you as raw material! Pigment for the painter! You're fooling yourself! You care about them and they care about you! You're a horse walking around with blinders! You're doing a lot of damage!"

"I don't know what you're talking about," Max said. His voice was cold.

"So now you're pretending to be stupid! Well, my wife warned me. 'If that's what he's doing, that's what he needs to do.' Once again she's right."

I moved from behind the lamppost. "Oh, good morning, Anna," Anders said. Max glanced at me and nodded. At Anders he glared furiously. I went through the studio door.

How guilty Anders looked when he saw me! How furiously Max regarded both of us. I hung my coat from the brass hook behind the flats of the set and thought, They were talking about me.

Before we came to America, while we were still in Sweden, Max took me to see a movie, about a magician and a painter's model. She came into the painter's studio to get something to eat and they induced her to sing, and she sang so badly they begged her to stop. But the magician saw her and to show off his powers, he made her a great singer. Under his influence, she became great. When he weakened, she couldn't sing a note.

I remember sitting in that darkened movie theater, holding a small white box of dark chocolates with cherry liqueur centers, trying to hoard them so they would last through the movie, dutifully offering the box to Max, who shook his head and watched the screen. I remember the screen lighting up and the image I saw there, and how afterwards, I wasn't sure I saw it or if I imagined it—a young girl, standing against a white wall, raising a hand to her cheek, on her face an expression of absolute terror, and a presence making itself felt, felt but not seen, a shadow coming closer. And then the film began and there was the young girl, smiling and happy: was it the same young girl who stood against the white wall?—I didn't know. Her image was there for no more than a second.

The story continued. The magician, big and fat and dirty, his beard matted and grease-stained, saw the girl and he chose to exercise his powers over her. Why her? Did he love her? She began to sing. She forgot that she loved another. She left her own wedding to follow the magician. For years, they toured the great cities of the world. Still under his influence, she married him, not the young man she truly loved. Occasionally, the magician's strength would falter and she would come out of her trance, not knowing who he was or what she was doing. Once she happened to come across the beloved young man and the magician had to exercise all his powers to keep her under his control. The effort exhausted him and he died, and when he died, the scales fell from the girl's eyes, she saw her lover who had come to hear her sing, and married him. Of course, she could no longer sing.

The cinema we sat in was old and dirty. We could hear rats running on top of the boards of the ceiling. It was not the kind of place Max would choose to go. And I remember that when the girl first began to sing on a great stage, Max put his arm around me. For a long time I seemed to sit in my chair without breathing. If I breathed I was afraid he would take his arm away. Finally, I gained courage and turned my head and looked at him.

He was staring straight ahead as if he didn't know what he had done, as if I were nothing but an arm rest. But his fingers had closed around my shoulder; his arm was around me and he was holding on to me. I knew it then: this was what I wanted. I wanted this arm, this person, but I knew also that this was not the time. When we are old, I thought to myself, this is how it will be. When we tire ourselves out, when we finish throwing ourselves at the wrong people, when we run out of punishments to inflict on ourselves, it will be like this. Nothing will separate us then. The trick is to live long enough.

And as I thought these things, I felt very old, very ancient. And at the same time I had my box of chocolates. I was eating them greedily, and when the lights came up, Max would reproach me. He would take out his white linen handkerchief and wipe off my lips and chin, he would say, "Anna, put out your hands. Anna, you are nothing but a child!" So with Max I was very old and very young, all at the same time.

What could I expect? I confused him and I confused myself.

In that theater he bent over and for the first time kissed me. No one has ever kissed me in that way since. The touch of his lips on my cheek flooded everything—my body, my heart, my mind—with pity, pity for Max, pity for me. The walls of the world grew thin and behind them I could hear all the sad voices. There are so many sad voices! And I was in such complete confusion it was an agony. On the one hand Max was so big and so old he disgusted me, the largeness of him, the worn quality of him, his body, his creased hands, his creased face, age all over him like a gray, sad layer of grime. And yet I wanted nothing more than to leave the theater and be with him, but when I thought of it, involuntarily I would cringe and press my eyes closed, and so the two images would alternate, faster and faster, desire and disgust, disgust and desire. *I hate him*, I thought to myself, and I thought it so hard it was as if I had said it aloud, and I was afraid that I would say it aloud, in the silent theater, and no sooner would I tell myself I hated him than I would be overwhelmed with something like love, something like compassion, with desire, I didn't know what it was. And while all this was going on, a large rat walked over my foot, stopped with its paws on my shoe, and with my other foot I gave it a good kick. I was not afraid of rats. We had enough of them in the building at home.

When we came out of the movie theater, it was dark. We were in an old, poor section of the city. The lamplighter was coming toward us, lighting the streetlamps. We crossed one street, then another. We were walking further and further away from Max's car, but such was the nature of the silence between us that I said nothing. Then, when we were about to pass an alley between two small tenements, Max took me by the arm and pulled me into the alleyway.

"What is it you want of me?" he asked me. "Say it simply. What do you want of me?"

I shook my head. My eyes filled. What did I want of him? What did he mean?

"You know what I'm asking you! All right, I know you admire me. You think I make great films, I'm a talented director, all that stuff. I understand that. *We* understand that! You want to be a great actress, I can make you a great actress. That's what you want from me?"

"I want to be very good," I said. "Yes."

"You want to be great!" he said. "That's all you want?"

"I don't know what you mean!"

"You sit in movie theaters with me, you let me put my arm around you, you let me kiss you. You've been with other men before? I don't think so. You come to movie theaters to see the movies? You could go by yourself! Why with me? Why don't you say, 'I'm busy, I have a headache, my mother is sick, I have to stay home and take care of her'? The usual excuses! You're not too young to know them!"

"I go with you," I said, "because I want to go."

"Why? That's what I'm asking you! Don't be stupid with me! How many ways do I have to ask?"

"Why?" I repeated.

"So," he said. "You want to humiliate me? I have to spell it out? People see the two of us on the street, a young girl, beautiful, well dressed, maybe she's sixteen, maybe she's seventeen, and an older man, thirty-seven, maybe forty, and they ask themselves, 'What's that old guy doing with a girl like that? What's in it for her? He must have money. He's got something she wants.' They shrug their shoulders and think, It's the same old story. A man can be rich and ugly and old but if he's powerful, he gets all the young girls."

I didn't know which way to look.

"Are they right?" Max demanded. "That's what you want from me? Because you can have it. From the start, that was our agreement." He was overwrought. There were tears in his eyes. He looked as he had the day he first saw the rushes of *The Mansion of Father Bertil* and decided the film was a disaster, beyond reclamation.

"I go with you because I want to be with you," I said.

"But if someone else came along, you'd just as soon be with him! Someone who was younger, who could make you laugh? You'd rather be with him?"

"What are you talking about?" I cried. "There's nobody else!"

"So while you wait for that person, you go about with Grandpa?"

"Grandpa!"

"I'm talking about sex! I'm talking about. . . . "

Now it was clear. "Love," I said. "You're talking about love."

Now he was tongue-tied.

"But I do love you," I said. "Everyone knows I love you. As much as I can love anyone, I love you."

He smiled; then his face crumpled. He began to cry. "You're too young to know your own mind," he said.

"Then why are you asking me!" I moved away from him. "Is this a game?"

"A game!" He was outraged.

"What is this about?" I asked him. "What? You want me to say I love you? I said it! Now what?"

"Well, maybe you will come home with me for a few hours," he said. I said I'd done that before. "But this time we will lie in my bed," he said. I said we had done *that* before. "We'll see what it's like," he said. "This time."

We walked to his car and drove back to his apartment. In his bedroom, I got undressed. I took off all my clothes and let them fall in a little pool around my feet and then I got into bed. Max was already in bed, lying on his back. In Berlin, in the hotel, when I was frightened, or when Max could not sleep, we would go through the connecting door to the other's suite, go into the bedroom, and crawl into the other's bed.

In the beginning, we would lie still, without touching, until we fell asleep. If I woke up and found my head on Max's arm, I moved away slowly so that I would not wake him. If Max found his legs across my

legs, he would do the same. There were times, in the middle of the
night, when I would wake up and want to put my arms around him,
fall asleep holding on to him, or if it was cold, then I wanted to press
against him for the heat of his body. Sex, whatever it was, was not something I wanted. Now, when I slid into bed, I still didn't want it. What
I wanted was to hold on to Max or to have him hold on to me.

"What a lovely body," he said. "What a young body, no wrinkles,
such white skin, you'll never need powder." His hands passed over my
breasts, my stomach, my thighs. I waited to feel something that would
make me turn to him as I had seen my mother turn toward my father
in the big bed at home. And he too must have been waiting, and must
not have seen it, because he suddenly said, in a cheerful voice, "And
what a young person inside that body! Too young for this grown-up
thing called sex! Let's have a nap!" And he turned on his side. But this
time I turned on my side, my breasts and stomach pressing into him,
and put my arms around him. I was happy, I was warm, I was revolted,
all at the same time.

Gussie jumped onto the bed, tried to push herself between our
bodies, whined and then gave up. She went to the foot of the bed and
slept, her little body across our legs.

It goes without saying that after that day I was not an innocent
young girl, not innocent about anything. I was not initiated, but I knew
what was coming. And we knew: people saw us together and raised
their eyebrows. *We know what she's doing with him, these young actresses
are all the same.* And younger men would look at Max, his arm through
mine, and think, *So, look at the old man! He's not above using his position
to enjoy himself!* It's true we were both calculating, both selfish, but that
was not the whole of it. There were other old men, other young girls.
There were five or six from the Academy in *The Mansion of Father Bertil*
but it was always me that Max wanted.

There were young men all around me but there was no one else I
wanted but Max. And it was not because I found him so attractive;
no, it was nothing like that. All my life, people have looked at me and
thought, She's a hard one, she's cold, her career is all she cares about.
She hasn't got a romantic bone in her body. She could cheat the Turks
in the market out of their rugs. The great romantic heroine doesn't
have an ounce of romance in her. But about Max I was romantic.
Perhaps it was my age. Perhaps all young things are romantic. Kittens
look at you, their eyes full of romance, but the full-grown cat looks
at you out of narrowed eyes, his pupils full of cat food cans. There
are things he wants. He is older; he knows better.

Well, I was young and Max was the one I looked at and thought,

When the storm is all over this is the one I want. This is the one who can give me what I need. This is the person to whom I can bring my soul the way Gussie brings him her bone. When I am old, he can bring his to me. There is something I want to take and something he wants to give. We will be perfectly matched. I will not ask him questions about the others he sees. He will close his eyes when I go home with someone else. We will come to an understanding. The trick is to live long enough.

Well, let me tell you, it is some trick! I lived long enough: here I am. But Max didn't manage it. There is no telling what that was like, to have something in your hand and then to lose it, as if you had dropped it and then bent down to find it, and said to yourself, it can't have gone far, I haven't moved, it's somewhere in the room, and you search and search and it's gone. An instant ago you had it and now it is gone. An instant's carelessness and it can never again be found. Who can tell what that is like? If it's happened to you, you know. If you don't know, good for you.

In any case, we knew better than to hold too tightly to one another. I don't know how we did, but we knew. In Berlin, Max would get tired of me, or perhaps grow restless, and he would say, "Anna, I'm going out." I would shrug my shoulders and sometimes I would go to the window and wave. He always looked back at the window before crossing the street. And later, when I wanted to meet someone else, I would say, "Max, this weekend I won't be home," and he would say he'd see me when I came back. Well, of course, now it all sounds very liberated, very free, very much ahead of our time. It had nothing to do with freedom, no, it had to do with how precious we were to each other. If at any time I had said, "Max, you must choose. You must stay with me and give up the others," what great harm I could have done! I found that out later when I met someone who said, Choose, and I tried to choose, and I did him great harm and myself even more.

Max didn't know what he wanted. I understood it. If Max had turned to me and said, Choose, would I have survived it? Today I think he was everything to me and I was everything to him, and we understood how it was, but we also understood the time had not come for us. It must have seemed, I suppose, that we took each other for granted, used one another, behaved badly, behaved cruelly, were responsible for each other's tragedies.

In the beginning, particularly in the beginning, when I was easiest to hurt and confuse, people never tired of saying Max was the master and I was his speaking statue and without him I would be nothing. But then they would stop, bewildered, and say, Still, what has he done since he met her? What is he known for here but the fact that he discovered her and trained her? And they would begin to stumble on the question that kept me awake at night, stiff with fear: could either of us exist without the other?

8

A COUNTRY WHERE you cannot speak the language, that is the landscape of nightmares. Everywhere people come and go, moving their lips, making sounds, but to you their words mean nothing. It is like being caught in a movie that is not silent, but might as well be, since words that mean nothing are not heard properly by the ear, but are only a kind of noise. It is a movie whose meaning is forever unclear. It is a vast, empty place where the people, although they move about, are so far from you they could just as easily be statues, and all the while your thoughts are inside you, but there is no one you can tell them to and so they grow heavier, until you are so weighed down, so tired, you cannot move. It is a huge country and yet what you feel is claustrophobic.

You must learn the language, Anders said to me. Now, every day, Tomas accompanied me to The Studio, where I followed Anders into the cutting room, watched him as he screened his rushes, listened to him as he talked to himself about which take was best, as he asked himself questions he immediately answered: Isn't that better, less of her running in circles? Isn't that better, the shadow on the wall a few frames longer? Yes, that's better.

And meanwhile, Maud Marsh and I were becoming friends, or at least accustomed to one another. Anna, Anna! she would say when she saw me coming with Tomas. Anna, Anna, come meet this one! Come meet that one!

She was a tiny woman, a face like a cameo, more frail than a slender eight-year-old, but beneath the skin she was pure iron. She knew that if she was in a film, The Studio would make a fortune. She knew what she wanted and she knew how to get it. One day she said to me, "There are other people here who could have plenty of power.

If they knew what they wanted. Most people don't. If you know what you want, you can have everything. But first you must know."

I asked her when she knew what she wanted. From the beginning? And she said no. She watched others, she studied herself. One day she knew. It's like anything else, she said. You have to learn.

She would sit with me while Tomas tried to teach me the language. Once she cried out and scolded him. I asked him what she said. "She said I am not trying very hard," Tomas said. "She says I am afraid if you learn too well, I will be out of a job."

"Is that true?" I asked him.

"A little true," he said.

"But you must teach me and teach me well," I said. "You cannot half teach a thing."

Maud dreamed up little plays in which I had to say the lines. She would run in from behind the flat of the set and say something and whatever I said in response, if that reply was not sensible, I had to pay the penalty. Up I would climb on my metal chair and begin reciting, "By the shining Big Sea Water, lived a maiden called Nokomis, Daughter of the Moon, Nokomis." And when that became too easy for me, she taught me another poem:

> Ghost Lake's a deep lake,
> A dark lake and old,
> Ice black as ebony, frostily scrolled.
> Deep in the darkness, a faint sound whirs.
> Steep stand the sentinelled deep, dark firs.

"I don't know what it means!" I would cry after I recited it, and Maud would laugh and say, "Go on, go on!

"We'll do it again," Maud said, and this time she came through the door and fell at my feet as if dead. "We must help her," is what I wanted to say but now I was stuck. How did I say "we"? How did I say "must help"? I knew how to say "to help." I to help her will! I shouted, and Maud, lying on the floor of the shack, propped herself up on her elbow and shouted with laughter.

"What did you want to say?" Tomas asked me. "Oh," he said. "This is how you say it."

And so it went on. Occasionally, Anders would come out, watch the proceedings, smile at me, shake his head at Maud, and go back into the cutting room. Once he came out with a camera and filmed us at our antics, Maud, who was pretending she was eating and asking for something, and I, who was attempting to tell her there was no salt, no bread, no milk, nothing for which she asked. When I failed to remember the word for bread, I was again up on the chair reciting the lines about Ghost Lake.

"She has been good?" Maud asked Tomas.

"She has been good," he said.

"Translate 'Ghost Lake' for her," she said, and he recited the lines to me in Swedish.

"Oh, it is a wonderful poem!" I said. "It is about our country! It's about the way life is!"

Maud laughed and said something. I pulled at Tomas's sleeve. "She says it's wonderful to be young," he said.

But most of the time it was not wonderful. The Studio did not call me. Perhaps they regretted having brought me here. I knew from the expressions on the faces around me that people looked at me and asked themselves, "What is she doing here? She is not pretty." The small blond girls looked at me and smiled, self-satisfaction disguised as sympathy. Oh, Max was right about sympathy.

Maud was speaking to Tomas and in the middle of the cloud of sounds floating from their mouths, I understood something she said. "Day after day doing nothing?" And then they both looked at me with real sympathy. Maud continued speaking to Tomas, the tone of her voice indignant.

The next day The Studio called and said I was to come for a screen test the following Monday. It was Tuesday when they called.

"Why so long?" I asked Tomas. "Why not tomorrow?"

"They have to build a set for the test," he said.

"A set! They can test me in a room!"

"They're building a set. That's all I know about it."

"What will they ask me to do?" I asked Tomas, who translated what I said to Maud.

"What kind of set is it?" she asked. "You don't know? I'll find out." She spoke to a stagehand, who disappeared. When he came back, she said, "They're building a walled-in Spanish garden. Probably you'll have to climb up a flight of stone steps to reach the top of the wall, speak to your lover, and then collapse in grief. You'll do it."

That night Max came home distraught. Nothing The Studio offered him had the slightest appeal. Nothing he suggested to them caught their interest. "How long can it go on?" he asked me. "Sitting here on the porch looking out over the ocean? There is so much I know how to do and to them, none of it means anything."

"Well, tomorrow you will go in and maybe they will have something better," I said, but he said, No, they said it would take time to look for new things. Not until the end of next week, or even later, would they be calling him. "We can practice English," I said. "I know a few words."

"And I must learn a language to speak to blind people!" Max cried.

Gussie leaped at his knees. He picked her up, settled her in his lap, and rested his heavy hand on her head. She twisted her head sideways and licked the side of his hand. "Gussie here knows more than they do, don't you, Gussie?" he said. So we sat on the porch for hours, staring at the sea. Finally, I grew hungry.

"The young are always hungry," he said. In his tone there was something new. When I looked up, he was staring at me, as if coming to a conclusion.

"Well, we must eat, studio or no studio," I said. I was angry.

"Yes, we must eat," he said. He got up slowly from the chair. "The sea air, it does nothing for my knees or my hips. In this country one gets old quickly."

As we ate dinner, his spirits revived. "So what did this Marsh tell you about the screen test?" he asked. "Oh? Climbing up steps? That's a problem, you are such a stork, tripping over your own feet. So you must practice. And you are to speak to your lover and collapse in grief? Let's try it out."

We went back to my room. He took a small table and set it under the windowsill. "That is the staircase," he said. "The window is the wall. On the other side of the window is the lover. Climb."

I climbed onto the table.

"Get down. Do it again. You're young, the step is small, no one is asking you to climb the Alps." Now he was happy. Again he was directing. "So what are you going to do with your skirt?" he asked me. "Trip over it or what? Pick it up and carry it like a bag from the grocery store? Try to imagine you have nice legs and it won't be such a tragedy if the camera sees them. Climb again. Don't yank up the skirt like that! You were bitten by a flea and you must suddenly scratch? Again. No, it is all wrong. Your lover is coming. Because he is coming you think you are beautiful, you even think your legs are beautiful, so you lift up your skirt to begin climbing and in back of your mind you are thinking, These are the legs he likes so much. Climb again.

"Fine," he said. "Not too bad. You are up on the wall. There is the lover. Speak to him."

"Daughter of the Moon, Nokomis," I said.

"That is how you speak to a lover?" Max said. "What did you say to him? 'Nice weather, isn't it? You know they expect snow?' In the next scene, he rides off and looks for someone who is happy to see

him! You are happy to see him but you are also afraid his feelings
have changed. Why? Because that's what a young girl feels! A young
girl is not a puppy, always confident! Do it again.

"Oh, so now you are insane with joy? He will run away in terror.
Both things, Anna! A lot of happiness, a lot of fear, and then when he
leans toward you, a lot more happiness. You can flicker or not? Like
a candle, Anna, not like a glaring light bulb."

"Oh," I said. *"Flicker!* Oh, I know. I understand that."

"She understands that," Max said. "Go on, then. Flicker. Yes, that's
it. That's very good. Once you have it, you have it forever. All right,
done." He fell back on the bed. "If they would give me *anything* to
do," he said. "Even directing screen tests! But, it is true, I can always
go home. Don't you start crying. I'm staying here until you're on your
way. I promised it and I'll do it.

"What I want, if they would let me do it, it would be such a
wonder, people all over the world would marvel. Not these silly stories, Anna, but stories that twist and turn into myths! Myths, those
are the immortal things. Here they are interested in train robberies
and penny romances. But even them, I could make something of them.
If they would let me alone, if they would turn me loose! Instead they
say, Mr. Lilly, you have done great work, but here we have a different
system altogether. Mr. Pinsky must come on the set and see how
things are going. People must report on the costs. In advance we must
know what you are going to shoot. They are not interested in the
happy accidents. I don't even mention the word revelation!

"Because they don't understand what I understand! You see an
entire film and what do you remember? One image! One image only!
And in advance, you never know what that image will be. So the
whole film is there to let that image come to exist. That one image!
And in advance, you don't know what it is? How can you know until
you have it?

"You know what they praise? My flock of reindeer swimming the
river! And those reindeer, they were an accident! And of course it is
beautiful, one of the most magnificent things on film, but for audiences
here, too strong. In the end the reindeer freeze in the snow. The
audiences here won't stand for that! So I tell them, but that is what
happens to real reindeer in winter! There are blizzards, bad storms,
the temperature drops, the shepherd is unconscious. No one guides
them, they stumble into valleys, the drifts wall them in, they freeze.
The film was about real life, not a visit to happy reindeer in a meadow
or a zoo! Of course they are glad I made the film and my reindeer
froze. It changed their view of life. Now they see what film can do.

It's only that in *their* films, they don't want them to do those things. What are the audiences here, cardiac patients? Everything must have a happy ending? The audience doesn't like to see its heroes and heroines die. Miss Marsh, she is so remarkable she can die and still be box office. Anyone else, if he dies on the screen, he dies also at the box office. People here are so stupid they think the actress lying on the floor is really dead? Such delicate sensibilities they all have, how did they fight the Indians? This is what I have to listen to! Every day the same thing.

"Of course I know what they're doing! They're trying to wear me down. What will they accomplish? They can tell each other: another dream knocked on the head! Another opportunity lost! The people this! The people that! They have too high an opinion of people! People don't know what they want until they see it! Then they know. Then they say they wanted it all along! We proved that! That's why they brought us here, Anders, me! And now they tie our hands and tell us fairy stories!"

"Max, Max," I said. "You upset yourself. You must stop."

"But it *is* upsetting!" Max shouted, thumping the bed table.

"You will hurt your hand."

"Someone cares if I hurt my hand?"

"Let's sit on the porch. Let's go for a walk."

We sat on the porch. We watched the sun balance on the edge of the ocean, the red rays on the water like a path, how easy it looked to walk on water, to walk through that red door. We lay in bed, on our backs. A cool breeze blew in the curtains. Max looked over at me, sat up, pulled up the blanket and covered me. We turned on our sides, away from each other. He thought about meetings in The Studio offices. I thought about the screen test. What if, in the harsh sunlight, my face photographed all caverns and shadows? That everything should depend on five minutes of film! I turned back toward Max and put my hand on his shoulder. He pretended to be asleep, but I knew his eyes were open, staring at the wall. I turned back and stared at my own wall. He had his problems, I had mine. For the first time they were not the same.

Was he tired of sleeping in the same bed like brother and sister? Was I? I didn't know. It wasn't the most important thing.

"This translator?" Max asked me in the morning. He was buttoning his shirt. "You like him?"

"He is very good."

"Very good," Max repeated.

"I can say, 'What must I do?' "

" 'What must I do?' How many times a day you must say that! Well, it is good to know the important sentences."

"On Monday, you will come to the screen test with me? You will look at what the cameraman is doing? You will just stand there on the side so I know you are there?"

"On Monday they will have more discussions. No, I cannot come. But the very good translator, he will come."

"It is not the same," I said.

There are days when time will not pass and then it is best not to struggle. Tomas brought me Swedish novels and German newspapers. I could concentrate only on the papers. I went to The Studio and studied with Maud and Tomas, but my mind was not on learning. I was forever up on a chair reciting my penalty poems. Late in the afternoon, I would come home, send Tomas away and walk on the beach playing my childish game: if I looked hard enough, I would see the coastline of Sweden. I knew it was impossible but now and then it seemed true: there it was.

When the sun began to fade, I would go back to the hotel and wait for Max. Sometimes I did not have to wait. He was already there. If he was sitting on the porch looking out, then things were not so bad. If he was lying on the bed in a darkened room, then, soon after I came in, he would begin raving. *They were not serious, they no longer knew why they had brought him here, why had he not gone home? He was not Anders, he had no patience, he had no understanding of people, wasn't it true? I was right, he should learn the language, but he could not bring himself to twist his mouth around these new words, it was all lowering himself, demeaning himself, but then what was life, you could not forever repeat your old triumphs, forever haunt the old scenes, if you didn't go forward, you went backward, or worse, you mimicked yourself, over and over until everyone was tired of you and one day you realized how long you had been a dead dog performing your old tricks, but still, here it was impossible. How would it work out?*

What could I do but take a washcloth, soak it in cold water, wring it out and place it on Max's forehead? More often he would reach up for my hand on the cloth, and press it there. Often he would pick up the cloth and fling it on the floor, shouting, "Nothing helps! How can anything help!"

Then I would say, "What must I do?" sometimes in Swedish, sometimes in English. Would Monday never come? Would nothing ever be settled? At night, when I got into bed, I would think, another day knocked on the head. Another day dead. Three more days until Monday, two more days, one.

Then it was Monday morning. Max, who was disturbed by a dust mote settling, slept so soundly I could not wake him. "You will not wish me luck?" I whispered, but he breathed in and out, regularly and deeply. He was awake. I knew it. Then I knew: he was more frightened than I was. I went outside to wait for Tomas.

"It is so terrible," I said, getting into the car. "What must I do?"

"You must calm yourself," he said. But I did not. When I got out of the car and stood up, a small snowfall fell from my lap. I had torn Max's linen handkerchief to pieces.

Two days after the train left New York for California, I still slept during the days and read at night. One night Max looked up from his book, threw it across the compartment so that it landed on the seat next to me, and took out a pack of cards.

"What are you doing?" I asked him, completely without interest.

"We're playing poker," he said. "You need to learn."

"Because you're bored I need to learn?"

"Great generals, they are great poker players," Max said. "You can't win if people know what you're thinking."

"No one knows what I'm thinking," I said. "You always complain about it."

"I know," said Max. "When you can fool me, you can fool any-body." I wanted to know what we would play for. "Candy," Max said. "You'd sell your soul for candy."

"How much candy?" I asked suspiciously. Since we'd left Sweden, Max had had me on a diet.

"I want the camera to see the planes of your face, I want it to see the bones," he said. "Fat as you are, I can photograph you, but the Americans need a head start." So for many weeks I had no sweets.

"One bar, before dinner," Max said.

"Before dinner!"

"Then you won't be so hungry at dinner. The way you grab for the basket of rolls, it's frightening. People start hiding food in their pockets! Who knows? You might take to going from table to table, wolfing down rolls!"

"I'm thin enough," I said. "All my clothes flap around me like laundry."

"Five more pounds," Max said. I said I wanted to go back to sleep. Max ignored me and began explaining the rules of the game. As we played, the compartment began to brighten until it seemed the sun was leaning on the window. I reached over and pulled down the shade. "Not bad," Max said, looking at my hand. "Not a bad way of passing the time, is it? But you, as soon as you start to win, that's the end of it, you won't want to play anymore. So I have to pay attention or the game's over."

"I don't know what you're talking about," I said.

The train was slowing. I raised the blind and looked out. We were in the middle of nowhere, the earth absolutely flat and green. The sky above us was blue, but near the horizon, hundreds of miles away, storm clouds were gathering. I watched them. Lightning flashed. I listened for thunder but couldn't hear it. We were too far from the storm. When the train stopped, Max got up and said he was going to talk to Anders. I decided to go out for some fresh air.

We had stopped at a small station, a platform in front of a small gray building, its doors and shutters painted red. There was a signal light at either end of the platform and inside I could see the station-master. His skin was so brown he looked like an African; his bald head was burned red and he wore a green visor. I looked behind me and saw green fields stretching for hundreds of miles. The flatness of the land was astonishing: not a wrinkle, not a bump, not a ripple any-where. To the left it was the same, and to the right the same flatness, the same emptiness. Only the clouds on the far horizon were full of hills and valleys, ravines and colors, clouds purple and lavender, gray and silver, wonderful, a country in the sky, not this terrible flatness where nothing seemed to exist, where the flat land itself waited for something to begin existing.

The train station seemed to cast no shadow, but of course I couldn't see it. It cast its shadow on the side of the building I could not see. I looked out at the fields, the vast flatness. Here, I thought, you could walk away, walk one hundred feet, lie down in the grass and no one would find you. Well, it is a pleasant thought. I took a cigarette from my pocket and lit it. Somewhere inside the train, Max and Anders were talking about something, probably The Studio and what to ex-pect. Or Anders was looking out the window and dreaming up stories that could be filmed here. They knew what they were doing. I was supposed to know what I was doing: I was on my way to Hollywood to become a great star. What was my mother doing now? I looked at my watch. It was already growing dark in Sweden. She would be cooking dinner. In an hour or two, Marianne would be coming home from the department store. Lars would be waiting for a tram to bring him within two blocks of the house. Probably it was already snowing. On the clotheslines, laundry would have frozen. Nightshirts, scrubbed white, would rattle in the wind like boards, their frozen arms out-stretched. When the frigid garments were carried in and placed before the stove and the hot iron, clouds of steam would rise from them.

What a ghostly time it was when women began to iron! It would be a long time before I saw that again.

At night, everyone would get into the one big bed. Marianne and Lars were not too old to argue over who slept nearest the edge. These days mother always slept near the wall. The stove was just on the other side of that wall: her place was the warmest. They would have more room now: I was no longer there. Would Marianne get up in the middle of the night and go to sleep on the bench in front of the table? Would Lars? When they got up in the morning, did they still look for me out of old habit?

At night, I went to Max's compartment or he came to mine and we slept with our arms around each other and even though the berth was small, it seemed very large, as if we took up no space in it. Would I ever want to sleep alone in a bed?

And while I was thinking these things, foolish things, like flies that wake up in the winter when the stove goes on in cold rooms and buzz fatly around the window until they fall to the windowsill, I heard the train whistle and the train creaking and rattling, and the sound of the engine speeding up. I saw smoke coming from the train's chimney and the engine began to move toward me, and then the train began to gather a little speed and it was pulling out of the station, going down the track. I looked at my watch and thought, In five minutes, it will be too far away to walk to. In a half hour it will be out of sight. It was pleasant to sit there in the sun and smoke my cigarette, thinking, it seemed, about nothing. The train was gone from the station. I could see the caboose and its little platform. Often at night I had walked through the cars until I came to the caboose and tried the door. I would have liked to stand on the platform and watch the land recede behind me, but always the door was locked.

Suddenly, I heard a loud screeching and when I looked down the tracks, the train had stopped. It seemed to be growing larger. Then I realized it was backing up. When the train reached the platform, Max jumped out and started shouting, "What is the matter with you? Have you gone crazy? What if Anders hadn't looked out the window?"

"Oh, I'm sorry," I said. "I was smoking a cigarette and thinking and I didn't notice."

Max's fingers dug into the flesh of my upper arm. "Didn't notice! Didn't notice! I pulled the emergency cord! People went flying! Your rolls in the dining car went flying! Who doesn't notice an entire train leaving!"

Anders was in the aisle of the car, his arms crossed against his chest, watching both of us. His eyes were narrowed, like a cat's.

"From now on, no more getting off the train!" Max said. "You're worse than a child! Where are we? In Kansas? In Nebraska? You know what state we're in? You have any money? Suppose we had gone on and left you? Anders! What's wrong with her?"

"She was thinking," Anders said. His eyes were on me.

"I'll teach her to think!" Max bellowed at the top of his lungs.

"They have a saying here," Anders said. " 'Too much school makes Johnny a dull boy.' "

"What does that have to do with anything!" Max demanded.

After that, each time the train stopped, Max opened his eyes and watched me. If I wanted to go out, he came with me. But it wasn't necessary. The train had come back for me. I knew I was going to California. He was right. What was Nebraska? What was Kansas? No matter what I did, the train would always come back, and if it didn't, I would have to find it.

9

IT IS AMAZING how little it takes to build a world, or at least the illusion of it, but perhaps the illusion is all one needs. I used to walk around the studio streets watching the stagehands strike one set—the vaulted chamber of Notre Dame—and in ten minutes, a small, poor dwelling had gone up in its place, absolutely convincing if you didn't look up at the ceiling and find yourself staring at a sky scudding with clouds. Four walls pushed into place by the stagehands, sometimes only two walls necessary. It depended upon the position of the camera and how much of the room was needed, and how much light. Once the walls were in place and propped up, with the pictures already attached, the rugs were laid down, the lamps were hung from their hooks, and the furniture was dragged into place. In five minutes, a world.

Of course you couldn't lean against the walls; there was nothing behind them. The telephone on the table didn't work; it was only a prop, but a few changes, a roof over the room, a few outlets, some heat, you could have lived there. That's how little it takes. And yet it seems so hard. I've always found it hard. Not keeping a roof over my head, no, but wanting to stay under it, understanding why I was under that particular roof.

The last stone blocks of the rose garden walls were set in place the morning of the screen test. I walked over to one of the walls and looked at the stones. From a distance, anyone would have sworn they were real stones, strong enough to build a pyramid, but up close they were made of grayish-white cardboard. I touched them. They had the unpleasant, unhealthy texture of egg cartons.

The rose garden smelled of mothballs. Roses rioted everywhere. I stopped to smell one; the smell of naphtha grew stronger. The roses were fabric, probably silk. No doubt they had just been taken out of storage. Orange blossoms waved from trees behind the walls, sweaty orange blossoms. I climbed up the steps I knew I would have to climb for the screen test to get a better look at them: wax, and in the heat, they were sweating. Below eye level, the trees were only poles thrust into the ground. The third wall of the garden was formed by a painted flat of a white Spanish house, its roof tiled. It was an attractive house. I would have liked to walk into it. Perhaps when they made the actual film, they would build the house, or at least the exterior. The interior rooms would be on another stage.

I walked about aimlessly. Tomas, my interpreter, had receded into the background. An actor, already in make-up, wearing his costume—black tights, an embroidered jacket and a tricorn hat—was strutting about the set. Every few seconds he thrust his tongue against his left cheek so that his cheek looked as if it were stuffed with cotton. Probably he had a toothache and was wondering when he could leave and go to the dentist's. He took great pains not to look at me. By now, of course, I understood English quite well although I still spoke it very badly, if at all.

"That's the one they brought in?" he asked one of the stagehands. "That's the one," the stagehand said. Finally, they called me for makeup. I sat in a canvas chair while they powdered me, outlined my lips in dark red, combed my hair. I went with them and put on my peasant skirt and blouse, and then sat motionless while they began setting up the cameras. "She understands what she is to do?" someone asked Tomas. I understood.

Finally, I was given the signal. I ran over to the wall and climbed the little flight of stone steps, just as I had practiced doing with Max. When I got to the top of the wall, there was the painted face of the actor, and from the shadow I cast across him, I knew the camera would not be on him. Evidently he knew this too, because he said, "Who did you have to sleep with to get here?" and then he grinned, but it was not a grin: he pulled his lips back over his teeth like an animal.

Still, I went on as if hypnotized, I had rehearsed the scene with Max so many times. I *flickered*. Across my face went the required emotions of hope and fear, hope and fear, until, as if from a great distance, I heard the director call, "Cut!"

"Very good, very good," the director said, coming up to me. Tomas asked him when the film would be viewed. "Oh, in a few days," he said.

"What did he say to you?" Tomas said. "That guy in the pajamas?"

"He asked me who I had to sleep with to get here," I said. "He thinks I understand nothing. Let him think that. If I succeed, I will make his life a misery." And then we were back in the car, and I was back at the hotel, waiting for Max.

When he was not there at six o'clock, I ate dinner alone and lay down on the bed. The sound of the door opening and closing awakened me. Max sat down on the edge of the bed and looked down at me. I began to get up, but he pushed me back down.

"The test was a disaster," he said. "A disaster. We have to do something."

I sat up and looked at him.

"The acting, that was fine," Max said. "Very fine, a natural, what emotion, but your face! Black circles under the eyes, a face longer than Italy, don't ask. The photographer didn't know what to do, the lighting man, he must be blind. We must persuade them to do another test. Anders is talking to them, Miss Marsh is talking to them, maybe they will do it. If they don't maybe we can go home together."

"What else happened?" I asked him.

"This dream factory doesn't know about dreams," he said. "They have a silly film they're all excited about, *The Siren*. A good woman, beautiful, naturally, marries a man who sells her to get money. Why she married him, of course we don't know. Why he married her, that's obvious. She is still married but she falls in love with a good man, so you know what's coming next. When he finds out about her past he almost drowns himself. An old lover hangs himself. There's a great scandal. Her husband threatens to drown *himself*.

"They all end up on a plantation in India and four or five more men take a look at her and threaten to drown themselves. So I said, 'I'll do this film. Out of this I can make a great film.'

"Of course they are surprised but also at the same time they are delighted. *You want to make this film?* Yes, I want to make it. Give it to me, let me have my way with it, it will be a great film, you will be praised, your studio will be praised, the history books will print stills from it. So they're impressed with my confidence, they like the idea of the history books, and they say, how much? I said, a big budget or don't bother. A dollar bill doesn't buy greatness. So they want to know what I have in mind, and I begin to talk about Siegfried and Brunhilde and Kriemhilde and I tell them this could be another Niebelung, it's the same story. Of course they don't know what I'm talking about. They think I want to make *The Siren* into some kind of crazy story with Siegfried, Brunhilde and the rest of them running around in saris in India.

"So I said, you know how much money *Siegfried* made? It made millions! And you know why it made millions? Because it was the story of Adam and Eve all over again, except in *Siegfried* there are two Eves and two Adams. If the kings in *Siegfried* didn't want these women so much, they'd still be alive today, never mind the lime leaf. So Pinsky, he is interested now. Adam and Eve, he knows that story. He's nobody's fool. No one has to tell him the Bible sells a lot of copies.

"I tell him the story of Siegfried and how he had to wrestle Brunhilde to the ground in her wedding chamber and how the jealousy of two women killed Siegfried, who bathed himself in dragon's blood and would be alive today, probably running a studio, if his wife had only managed to keep her mouth shut about the lime leaf. What lime leaf? Mr. Pinsky asks. I tell him about the lime leaf that covered Siegfried's skin when he bathed in the dragon's blood so there's a little part of him that's vulnerable.

" 'Like Achilles' heel,' says Pinsky. So now I've got him. He's showing off. He knows his myths. They were so interested in Siegfried, I thought I'd overdone it. They forgot about *The Siren.* Now all they want to know is, Who was Siegfied married to? Not Brunhilde? Then why was he in her bedroom wrestling with her? So I had to explain. I ended up telling the whole story.

"You know, you start to tell these big men a story, they're worrying about whether to spend a million dollars, and now they want to hear the end of the story. And *Siegfried,* that's a story you don't finish with so quickly!

"So it ends up, they ask me, can I make *Siegfried,* but in modern dress, with names normal people can pronounce, and we'll set it somewhere everyone's heard of, like France. And then I said, But why go to all that trouble? Already you have the same story. *The Siren* is that same story. All these men brought to their knees by a woman. Not just any woman, but Woman, with a capital W. We make the woman beautiful enough, we make the men strong enough, we have the story of Siegfried all over again.

" 'So who will be the beautiful woman?' they ask suspiciously. 'There aren't any in Hollywood?' I ask them. So they go on to the next thing. Why must it cost so much? 'Because it is a *myth*,' I say, thumping the table. 'This is the story of Siegfried and Brunhilde, not the story of Gertrude and Sammy down the block.' And Pinsky is starting to smile. But his assistant says, 'How do we know he can do it?' 'Estersen says he can do it,' Pinsky says, thinking.

" 'With enough money and no supervision I can do anything,' I said.

" 'Maybe,' Pinsky says, 'we should look at *Winter Reindeer* one more time,' and he picks up the phone and calls the archive and people run in and set up a screen and in ten minutes we're all sitting there watching *Winter Reindeer*, and no one's talking. You know how amazing that is? No one is ever quiet here. And when the shepherd gets caught in the snowstorm, and the flock of reindeer gets away from him, and five hundred of them swim the river before they freeze to death, then you could hear a pin drop.

"A few minutes later, Pinsky's assistant whispers to him, 'How did he do that? They were real reindeer?' and Pinsky draws himself up and whispers back, 'Of course they were real reindeer!'

"So they say I can do it, but someone must be on the set to keep track of costs, an absolutely free hand, that is impossible here, and they want the script in advance. It costs too much, this European improvisation, and I say, I'm sorry, but that's how I work, and Pinsky says, What can we lose but money? and now no one's talking. If he makes a decision and loses money, fine. They don't want to be in on it.

"Well, then I sat there and waited. This little pulse here leaps in my wrist. I thought, One more minute and I'll jump up and start shouting and pounding on the table, and just then Pinsky leaned forward and asked me, 'How do you see it starting? The first scene, what would it be?'

" 'Well,' I said, 'the woman is Woman with a capital W, so we will see her first at a carnival. All kinds of animals will be there, big ones, wild ones, a lion, maybe even an elephant. And people dancing about wearing giant monster heads so everyone knows this is not a normal carnival but that the forces of nature are loose here. And the woman will be so beautiful, but she will be masked, so everyone knows from the beginning her true nature is always hidden, and she will be confused, so everyone knows that her true nature is unknown, even to herself,' and I went on and on that way, and the smoke in the room got thicker and thicker, long lines of smoke floating in layers above the tables, and Pinsky got up and said, 'All right, we're making a myth about Siegfried and Brunhilde.'

"So," Max said with a sigh, leaning back against me, "that's that."

"That's very nice," I said.

"Yes," Max said. "Together we should do a good job."

We?

"Once they do another screen test, you'll be the siren," he said. "You'll see."

"When?"

"If we can get there by eight o'clock tomorrow, Freddy Feldman will do the lighting, I'll take over the camera, Maud will get the test to Pinsky. What did you do to that woman? You seduced her?"

"Oh, she has an investment in me, all those English lessons. She will say to herself, I wasted my time on a talentless girl? She will say, I don't know whether a face takes the camera? She likes to be right. What must I wear?"

"Wear white," Max said. "And bring this with you. Silverstone Number Two."

I opened the little tin of face make-up. It was almost empty. "Maud swears by it," Max said, "and believe me, you need it."

The next morning the rose garden still smelled of mothballs. A stagehand was dressed in tights, the embroidered jacket and the tricorn hat.

"Now we get to work," Max said happily. Anders leaned against the propped-up wall, smiling. "Mr. Feldman," Max said, "look at that face. You must always shoot her from above. Always if it is possible she should be looking up and most of the time it is possible. Look through the lens. It is a difference?" Mr. Feldman nodded. "And to light her, a lot of light, *a lot* of light. This bleaches out the circles under the eyes, the lines between the eyebrows, the width of the nose. Try it. Almost an overexposure, as if you were photographing a ghost. Now we get to work on the make-up. Miss Rosalie! Where are you, Miss Rosalie!

"She's a hunchback," Max whispered to me, "and almost a dwarf. Don't say anything and don't start laughing!" Anders, against his wall, looked at me, raised his eyebrows and rolled his eyes.

"Now, what we want here, Miss Rosalie," Max said, "is the mouth, perfectly outlined, the lips where they come to a point outlined, the mouth a little bit more full. We want the eyes outlined but thin black lines so on film you don't notice them, plenty of mascara on the lashes, and the face white, very white, no highlighting under the cheekbones, those bones stand out enough, we don't want shadows, plenty of Silverstone Number Two under the eyes. We want a *statue*, Miss Rosalie, a statue that walks and talks. You can do it?"

"I can do it," she said and she bent over me.

"She could make Pinsky look like Cleopatra," Anders said.

"Well, maybe not Pinsky," Miss Rosalie muttered, a paintbrush between her teeth. "There, how is that? White stone, a statue, nothing from this earth!"

"Walk around, loosen up," Max said. "Say when you're ready. You're ready, Mr. Feldman? Two or three takes, a lot of light. Stop!" Max shouted. We turned to look at him. "What's wrong?" he shouted. "What's everyone standing there for?"

"You said stop," Anders said.

"I meant go!" Max said. "It makes sense to call *Stop* when everything is ready?"

I ran to the stairs, I flickered at the stagehand, I came back down. Miss Rosalie dusted my Silverstone Number Two, and I did it again and again. "So," said Max, "now we'll see."

Two days later, the word was handed down. In two weeks I was to report to The Studio and begin filming *The Roses. The Siren* would go into production. Pinsky wanted a shooting script. Max agreed. A script would not materialize in a day and when shooting began, a script was a fine thing to deviate from. With good luck, the script would need so many revisions that we would be finished filming *Roses* before it was completed. What did it matter who directed *Roses*? Max would direct me at night. Freddy Feldman was assigned to the picture. The cameraman agreed with everything Max had to say. What did I have to worry about now?

"Except for the fact that you can't act and that the script is so terrible even I can't believe it, nothing," Max said.

This morning Ivy is very happy and all morning long the telephone has been ringing. She has another grandchild, a granddaughter. Ivy's daughter is fine, she wanted a girl, so now that's over. Ivy is very happy but she is less excited by these things than she used to be.

I have trouble keeping track of the grandchildren, how many there are, which one of Ivy's children has which grandchild. Really I am not interested, although of course I cannot let her know that. A person is always interested in his own life. I learned that when I was making films. No matter how dull the life, how ludicrous the events, if it is your life you are always aglow with interest. Unless of course you have gone mad, because that's how you will look if something happens to you and yet you seem bored.

Ivy comes in with my tea tray and says, "How many more babies does she need? Of course they don't cost much now but when they grow up and need shoes and want to go to school, what will she do then? And still, she promises me: 'Mummy, next year when the baby's walking I'll go back to night school.' For how many years have I heard that?"

I used to love children. Even now if I'm sitting in the park, a child will get loose from its nanny and run over to me and I let it climb all over me. But I never wanted one. I say that to Ivy. "I never wanted a child."

She says, Well, you were too busy, and, as always, I let it go. But the truth is, always I believed if I had a child I would harm it. If it looked like me, already I would have harmed it. People would have followed the child, hounded her. They would have looked at her and asked themselves, Is she as beautiful as her mother? Who could be as beautiful as I was then? I wasn't even human. I was a creation of lights and cameras and camera angles and make-up. Oh, yes, I was the thing casting the shadow, but between me and the screen were the many, many filters of illusion. If people knew how hard Freddy Feldman worked to give me that perfect, white untroubled face! And then, two weeks later, someone would take a snapshot of me, and if I had just seen the rushes, and thought I once looked like the woman in that film, I would think, My God! I have some dreadful disease! In two weeks I have aged twenty years! I never look like that on film!

No, I would have been no good for a child. You act in film, you have one foot in reality, one foot in illusion. It's fine as long as you're confident, as long as you don't notice. But you notice and then you're standing, one foot on the dock, one foot in the little rowboat, and any minute you're going to fall into the water and all of a sudden it occurs to you: do I know how to swim? In the film, you knew how to swim, but in real life do you know?

In front of the camera lens, when you're doing a good job of it, you are absolutely sincere, absolutely genuine. Everyone watching you knows what you are. They fall in love with this confident, genuine thing. But it is only for the camera that you expose this perfectly genuine soul. You create it for the camera. And then the camera stops turning, and you're back to yourself.

And who are you? Not the person you were on the set. The mask is still on tight, so others don't yet understand. And if someone was taken in by me, then I, too, was taken in by someone else. Shadows loving shadows.

Once someone talked to me about children. You had to have them. Otherwise it was like living without seasons, an eternal summer. Well, it was already eternal summer in California. Where were the seasons there? If I wanted seasons, I could take a boat.

Then he said, How do you know a daughter won't be *more* beautiful than you are? Maybe even so beautiful she won't need the make-up and the lights.

Oho, so that was what I was afraid of, little Snow White. I would no longer be the most beautiful of them all. "Now you are talking nonsense," I said. "All around me there are beautiful people, more beautiful than me. I like it when I am not the most beautiful person in the room. Then people pay attention to someone else."

To tell the truth, if I had had a child, a daughter, I would have wanted her to be plain. You can always dress up a plain person, make her more beautiful, more dramatic. At least every night when she goes to sleep, she doesn't ask herself, Why did he come to my door and ring my bell? Did he want to see what I look like without make-up? Did he want to tell his friends he saw the most beautiful woman in the world? At least when she has something to say, she won't spend her life wondering, Are they listening? Or are they staring, memorizing my face?

Well, I had a wonderful face. It made my fortune. But in Sweden, there is a saying: When you take the devil on board, you have to row him ashore. I had enough trouble rowing myself. I didn't want to watch a child struggling in the water. Was I selfish or unselfish?

The lives of people I knew in Hollywood! On screen, people led such wonderful lives, and their families, they led lives out of the most horrible novels. A layer cake, the top layer beautiful, the bottom layer bitter and filled with little devils holding spears.

And nothing could ever keep my attention very long. Oh, perhaps when I was very young, something could, but soon I was completely scatterbrained. People used to notice it. *She's so concentrated in front of the camera, but when it stops turning, nothing. The light goes off. She's a gray mouse. Nothing interests her.* And it was true. I knew how to come alive in front of the camera. The rest of the time I was like a doll. I hate dolls, hate and fear them.

Yesterday I stopped in front of a store window full of dolls and there they all were, staring at me, beautiful, their long curls, their elaborate costumes, their blue glass eyes, almost alive, but they were not. People without souls. Frightening things.

Once, after the screening of *Another Woman,* I went into the ladies' room and caught a glimpse of myself in the round mirror. I looked at myself in the glass and what looked back at me were the blue glass eyes of a doll. I sat down on the little bench and peered into the mirror, looking into those eyes. Were they human? Was there anything human in them? I put my face in my hands, let my head fall forward, and closed my eyes. I pushed back my hair with my hands. I opened my eyes and stared into the mirror. The face of a doll was staring back at me. I was terrified.

I must have been sitting there a long time. Sound had drained from the room. Then I heard voices and looked up. Two women were standing near the door to the room, watching me. Still I could not move.

"Look at her," one woman whispered to the other. "Already so afraid of growing old! Terrible!" Of course I heard every word. I always had ears like a fox.

I was never afraid of growing old. I looked forward to it. I don't mind it now. The loss of beauty, what is that? It's natural. The new face time gives you, there's generosity in it. A new face for a new life. Your face changes, it reminds you it's time to turn the page. If someone gave me a choice, if someone said, You could be a lot uglier than you are but your bones would stop creaking, what would you say to that? Make me ugly! Make me a toad! What are mirrors to me? But if I must see myself in one, let me see human eyes.

"So," I said to Ivy, "you will want to go stay with your daughter."

"Not really," Ivy said. "A baby is a baby."

"Oh, we are getting old and jaded," I said. "But you know, if you want to go, go ahead. I think I'll go the South of France and visit Tinka. How many times can she ask me? She sits in that deck chair and they take her out on the porch in the afternoon and bring her in at sundown."

"On Green Island," Ivy said, "they used to say, 'You'll live so long, they'll sun you.' In the morning, they carry you out. In the evening, they carry you back in."

"I'm not so far from that," I said.

"And the doctor, he says you can go?" Ivy asked.

"A person can be on borrowed time in any country," I said.

"The doctor said so?"

"The doctor said so. Well, of course there are always terrorists to worry about, but then who's going to live in New York and worry about terrorists? If I run into a terrorist, then we can worry about my health. And on the way to France, I think I'll stop in Sweden," I said. "It's not on the way, but it's not out of the way, either. Always I have to touch down there. The strength comes in through the soles of my feet. So I'll go."

"I'll start packing," Ivy said.

"Three pairs of gray slacks, three gray sweaters, three gray silk shirts, the usual thing," I said.

"A red scarf wouldn't hurt," Ivy said.

"No red scarf," I said, but I knew when I unpacked I would find it there. And already I was thinking, Have they taken care of Max's stone? Will it be snowing when I get there? How strange it is that one can go back! Really, I was already gone.

After five days in Sweden, I went to the Jewish cemetery outside of Stockholm. Many years ago, when I first visited, I could not find the stone. I had to find an official who consulted his records and took me down the narrow paths dug out of the snow. It was hard to keep my balance. I kept slipping. Once I fell and grabbed hold of a headstone and the stone went over backwards. I expected the earth to yawn open, a hand to reach up. I had no idea I was so suggestible. "It happens all the time, don't worry," the official said.

We went on. Inside my boots, my feet were cold. The paths were icy and gray water pooled in them. Water leaked through my boots and my stockings grew wet and my toes even colder. This, I thought, is like a dream in which you walk endlessly and are always farther away.

"Here we are," my companion said. *Here we are.* The stone was plain and gray and highly polished. I looked at the name and the dates. MAX LILY. "His last name is spelled wrong," I said aloud. "There are two L's in Lilly."

"God knows who he is all the same," the old man said.

"God did not pay for the headstone," I said.

"Must it be replaced?" he asked. "You are family?"

"Yes," I said.

"Replaced?"

"Yes."

Then I began to complain because there was nowhere to sit. "A little stone bench, can you make room for it?" I asked, and the man said he could. Now when I went to the cemetery I sat on the bench. MAX LILLY read the shining stone. It was kept well polished, I saw to that, no pitting by the rain or snow, always smooth, always well made-up.

This time, too, I sat on the little granite bench. I was wearing Eleanor's fur-lined coat. I was very warm, except for my legs. They were cold.

"I'm back," I said to the stone. No answer. Of course no answer. One day I would come here, hear something, and die of fright.

"Remember?" I said to him. "You said if you were stuffed, you wanted to be dressed like a clown and your hand put on a large globe? What were we talking about, to think of having ourselves stuffed? A few ashes, that will be enough for me. It's not the Middle Ages. I don't want someone walking around bragging that they have my finger bone."

I looked up. Along a path nearby came an old man in a loose black coat and a brown fur hat, and I didn't want to be overheard, so I talked under my breath—my lips moved, but no sound, as if I were praying.

Well, I said, I did everything you wanted me to do, all done, half a century ago. Since then, what? I've been on a long search, it is a very long search, really, trying to find out what normal life is. I thought if I studied long enough, then I would learn. But I am too—that word they always used for you—too *fastidious*. Not about what you called all the dreadful ways of the body. This is my trouble: I can't sink myself in anything long enough. For an instant I can become anyone, yes, that was always my talent, but normal life, that lasts more than an instant.

Poor Ivy, you would laugh if you saw how I study her! No story she tells is too small for me to pore over. *She* has led a normal life, all of it normal, but does she have any idea how remarkable it is? None. She takes it for granted. If she were smarter, if she were richer, she thinks she'd have more to say for herself than this: I led a normal life. A husband, children, grandchildren, up every day happy to see the sun, not forever asking questions: What am I here for? Is it good enough? Not always pounding on doors to earth vaults screaming, *Open up!* Whatever she sees, whatever she does, that is enough. To her, it is all remarkable.

To me, everything she tells me is remarkable: about Miss Iron Front, a lady in her town when she was a girl who lost her son when he left the Island. He was killed in a plane crash, and after that, the mother, who was always smiling and happy, stopped washing, she stopped combing her hair, she put on one layer of clothing after an-other, and walked through the streets thumping her fists against her womb, thump, thump, thump, and the children, when they heard the thumping, began calling her Miss Iron Front, and then they ran away from her. And she complained to Ivy's aunt, Tita Lu, and Tita Lu asked her, What do they call you, and she said, You know what they call me! But Tita Lu said, No, what is it they call you? And she said, They call me Iron Front! And Tita Lu said, They are rude! They are very rude! To call you Iron Front! Not even Miss Iron Front! And later Tita Lu used to laugh and say, The damn fool! She was satisfied! And she, calling herself the very name she complained the children were calling her!

Tita Lu is more real to me than people I knew. I know her better! And the Janga Mumah, the woman who went to the head of the river looking for shrimp, and got lost, and the village had to take torches and find her, oh, you and Anders would have liked that, Janga Mumah. Think what it would have looked like on film!

And you know, that's another trouble. Someone tells me something, something happens, and I say to myself, Think what that would have looked like on film. Today they would say, Oh, it's too symbolic, this trip to the head of the river. But all the same it happened. Today anything that's a little bit less random than a crazy mass murder, that thing seems symbolic. And the ghosts Ivy saw growing up! I am not real to myself, but these things are real to me. If you were here it would have been different. But to be the only one left! Anyway, who knows? I have excuses for everything.

When I was still a child, I was always the one to walk with my father, so when he became so ill at the end, it was natural that they would send me with him to the clinic, to the doctor's office, and I remember that last time at the clinic, when he couldn't breathe, when he told my mother, No, I don't want you to come with me, all you do is get angry, and they put him on the cot in the little room, and the nurse came in with the big needle, and she said, "Don't look, now we're going to take some fluid out of the lung and then there will be room for the air and then he can breathe." I didn't look but I heard this strangled scream, and a few days later he was dead, and I thought, I shouldn't have let them do that to him, I should have said, He's going to die anyway. Leave him alone. But of course I didn't believe he was going to die, how could I believe it?

And then my aunt came, Olga, and she said, If he earned more money, a good doctor could have fixed him up. As if it was his fault! Well, maybe it was. Look at all the money I have. Without it I wouldn't be here.

My mother and Olga. I remember one night years before he died, they sat down and worked it out: if my father worked at night collecting night waste, he could earn enough money so we would all get by. And he did what they wanted. All those bottles of whiskey left for him in the snow, those tips, the drinking to get warm, what did they expect? They sat at the table and worked out a murder.

There was no other way? We couldn't have gone back to my mother's family in Finland? I asked her again and again. *He has his pride.* So many years later and still I go over it. What holds girls so to their fathers? I think about him and start crying. And you know, he was only forty-two when he died and now I'm almost eighty. If he saw me now, he wouldn't recognize me. He'd walk away. He'd say, Who's this old lady? She's not my pretty daughter.

You, too, Max, you'd walk away. All the other actresses we knew, they had face-lifts, they had surgery here and there, all over, so eventually they looked like monsters, young heads on these old bodies, like something out of a fairy tale to frighten children. But me, people say, Oh, now she looks like a bag lady. But this is how people should look at eighty! *This* is normal life! So in one thing I am normal.

Anna, don't marry a poor man. That's the only thing I remember my father telling me. *Anna, don't marry a poor man.* That was my inheritance. Well, I listened. I didn't marry anyone.

A scientist is taken in by a wealthy patron. The patron steals his wife and his theories. He presents them in front of the academy. When the scientist protests, the patron slaps him and everyone laughs. The scientist becomes a clown. He becomes famous. His act is simple: whatever he says, people slap him and the audience roars with laughter. After each act, a huge globe spins in the air and clowns sit on a ring around it. Sometimes they fall off into empty space. There is nothing that people like better than seeing someone else slapped down. But the clown wins in the end. The wealthy patron comes to the circus. He wants to marry the bareback rider. The clown locks him in a room and pushes the lion cage against one of the doors. He is already dying from a sword wound the wealthy patron inflicted on him. When the wealthy patron opens the door, the lion springs out and devours him. This is the last thing the clown sees and he laughs as he watches the great paw of the lion slap the patron down. He has the last laugh.

It's funny to think of that film now. I was on the set during filming. I watched you help Anders edit it. I listened when you two worked out the script. I knew how bitter it was. Life is so terrible our own lives only seem worthwhile when someone else's seems worse.

But just this moment I thought about the lion. I remember how happy The Studio was when they read the script and came across the lion. The lion was their emblem! They *had* a poor tame old lion and now they had a use for him! So that was what Anders intended! The Studio devoured the rich patron! The Studio devoured everything and eventually it would devour itself! Well, Anders must have been happy about that! He got his love scenes past the censors, he got his view of The Studio past Pinsky. Until just now, he got it past me, too. And still he told a story about "real human beings." Remember how he used to come in waving a sheet of paper, shouting, "This is a great story! About real human beings!" And how mad at you he would get when you changed the stories of great novels to suit yourself, and you would say, The writer, she was a real human being! Real human beings aren't perfect! She was writing a book, not a film script! Goats, reindeer, what difference does it make?

And how he used to scold me. "Fight for yourself! Always in the same role! It's like an animal in a cage! Soon that cage is the whole world! Next that world is the only one you know! Finally someone will come along and open the door and you won't know how to walk out! You won't want to walk out!"

We used to wonder: if you had stayed alive, what could you have done? Everything, I think. Once we had a fight. *I don't like sleepwalkers,* you said to me.

Once I tried to explain myself to Anders. He laughed and said, "Oh, you're looking for your body!" I didn't know what he meant. I still don't. Did he mean I was like a vampire? They go out at night but before morning they have to get back to their bodies? But that's not right. It's not their bodies they have to get back to, it's their coffins. What did he mean, I was looking for my body?

I never had much sense of having a body, it was something to hang clothes on, it couldn't get too big or too thin, and I had a nice big head the body held up, that was all the body was for. It kept me alive, it held up my head. And it wasn't even my whole head I noticed. It was my face. So what did he mean?

He used to say, "Anna, it wouldn't hurt you to think a little." So one day, he was hanging from a cliff, starring in his own film (*This way I have one less problem to deal with,* you know he always said that), and when he came back up and we were all sitting next to a little fire on the rocky ground, I said, Anders, tell me. These monster movies, you know, the one about the girl who sings opera because the phantom helps her. The one about the magician who teaches the girl to sing. Why are the helpers so bad? Or even Siegfried. He gets his powers from dwarfs and ugly dragons and before he dies, he stands under a bush and the bush takes the shape of a skull. The phantom looks like a skull. And Faust. The devil helps him, and the devil looks like a skull. These helpers, they all come from the world of the dead. Why is it?

"Anna, that is a good question," he said. "I don't have the answer."

When you are a child, a short little thing, everyone is magic, everyone helps you, but soon enough they are gone, so you look for the old helpers, but they are gone, so really you are looking in the world of the dead. So these helpers, they are bad dreams, really. Anyway, that's what I think. Of course I am not a good thinker and anyway what mind I had is worn pretty thin.

And Anders used to say, "Anna! Fight for better stories! Don't only fight for the money!" But I didn't know what better stories were and you were gone and then he went home, so who was to tell me?

And even that's an excuse. I knew what I was doing. Somehow or other, people around me went under but I kept on floating.

Too many people died. One person dies, it's like living with a secret. And then you look into other people's eyes, and you see in them the same secret. Like a hot coal in the hand. One coal, two coals, still you can hold them. Then your hands get too full, it's too hot, you start to drop everything. You don't make a fist and fight for something if you don't know what you're fighting for. If a few more people had stayed alive, then it would have been another story.

A few years ago, they told me how film decomposes. First it begins to flake. Then it starts to crumble. Then it becomes a solid lump. And it is dangerous. It's nitrate film, like dynamite. It can explode. I was asking about a film of Charlie's. Someone said, It's in the earth vault. So I said, You bury them underground? Because they might explode? And he said yes. But then I asked someone else, Where are these earth vaults? And he said, There are no earth vaults. That's how we say the film is gone, decomposed, it doesn't exist anymore. Dead. But these dead things, they explode. So I thought, It's true. The dead are dangerous. The past doesn't let go so easily.

Someone said the silent film spoke a language after all, but now, because no one watches those films anymore, it speaks a dead language, and sometimes I think, All right, we spoke dead languages but the job we did, I think it was pretty good.

10

ON SUNDAYS DURING the summer months, the men of Green Island played cricket. During the rainy season, or whenever they had a night free, they played dominoes. We preferred it when they played dominoes because my father was captain of the Mare River cricket team, and whenever a game was scheduled, it was our job to see to it that his uniform—white pants, a white shirt—was so clean it would glare in the sun and so well pressed the crease in each pant leg felt solid against the palm of your hand.

I had learned to do this even though my stepmother would not teach me. Instead, when my grandmother, Mother Lize, came to the house, I said, "Granny? How do you get a pleat to stay in the trouser leg?" and she would show me. Later I would hear her shouting to my father in their language, Hindustani, and I would hear the familiar refrain: "But Mother . . . But Mother . . . What can I do? I am not home all day to watch. But Mother . . ." Granny would continue until she had exhausted her supply of insults, and then, as she left, she would look at my stepmother and mutter insults at her.

So on the whole we preferred it when my father played dominoes. There was no laundry to be done for the occasion, and when my father had company, we were free to do as we pleased. If we went down the road and turned on the water in Mr. Darlington's standpipe, we would hear about it in the morning, but for the moment, we were free. When we were all very young, and the men played in the moonlit yard, we would crouch under our windowsills or cry out, trying our father's patience, waiting to see how long it would take him to get up and run into the house and chase us into our beds.

Of course all this meant we were still children, still without responsibility. What we did depended on what the adults did, if their eyes were on us or on something else. And since we never knew what they would do, our lives were either very exciting or insupportably dull. At some point, without our noticing it, this began to change.

• • •

Between our house in Mare River and Swan's Landing, Bevon Berriman, said to be a distant cousin of ours, ran an establishment that was at once a store, restaurant and rum shop. She was an enormously fat woman who had very short and very skinny little legs and she always seemed out of breath, although when someone took something from her store without paying for it, she could run astonishingly fast, and the sight of her running down the road like a large building on two sticks was enough to strike terror into the heart of a thief and hilarity into those who knew her.

We were very fond of her, because when she came to visit, she always brought a bag of sweets, which was, she said, just for us, not one piece for the adults, and if my father and stepmother asked us nicely, even for one piece, we should consider the request, but probably we should refuse it, because they didn't share their things with us. She would laugh and ask when they last shared a bottle of rum with us. This struck her as so funny she would laugh until she was breathless and then she did not seem to be laughing but choking.

I cannot remember her saying a harsh word to anyone, but for some reason my stepmother did not like her. When I grew older, I learned why. In the evenings after the men had finished drinking and playing dominoes some of them would take the women who had come to watch them upstairs, and Bevon herself usually retreated along with them. I know my stepmother complained of this to my father but he paid no attention to her, since, as he said, Bevon was family.

I doubt very much if she was related to us, but once the idea of a blood tie had been established, my father claimed to be helpless and threw up his hands. Yes, it was terrible, but Bevon did what she did and my stepmother could say nothing about it.

We had many such relations, all of whom my stepmother would not have tolerated if my father had not persuaded her they were members of his family. This was not difficult to do since my father would speak to my grandmother in their language, and my grandmother, who did not like my stepmother, would agree to whatever he said. In time, my stepmother came to have a low opinion of my father's family, but by then my father didn't care.

One night the men of Mare River and the men of Swan's Landing were having, as was their custom, a domino tournament at Bevon's, and she asked our father if some of us could come and help her serve. My father sent Cynthia, Cherry and me. We took the bus to Swan's Landing while it was still light and arrived there after dark. Dark falls early on Green Island, or so it seemed to us when we were young. We set up tables while Bevon laughed and talked and offered us bits of cake and candy and I, of course, was always offered chicken, since everyone knew I would not eat it. A small band was hired for these occasions, and that evening, Bevon had retained Buddy Gray and The Swaggerers. I knew Buddy would be there. We were always deep in conversation in the lanes, but whenever my father came along, we would change the topic so that we must have seemed, inexplicably, to have an enduring and obsessive concern with the weather or the proper time for the planting of peas.

Presently the men came and we went outside and sat on the low white-painted benches made of planks stretched between stones, talking about school, about who would continue with private lessons after finishing the sixth standard, and what boys were noticing us. Cherry said the other girls were teasing her because her face was so covered with pimples, but a boy named Marcus had defended her, saying that she was going through puberty and the others hadn't done it yet. "He defended your puberty?" Cynthia asked her, and we burst out laughing. Every few minutes, Bevon would shout for us and we would come in and wait on the men at the tables.

As the tournament continued, the orders for beer and iced drinks came faster and we remained inside. Whenever I looked up, I saw Buddy watching me. He played the saxophone and played so well he no longer needed to look at his sheet music.

When the tournament was over, we began to clean up, working quickly so that we could catch the last bus home, but Bevon had gone upstairs with one of the men and I was afraid to go after her. Cherry said she would go, but when she came back downstairs, she said Bevon was dead drunk, sound asleep, one arm and one leg thrown over a skinny little man in the bed up there, and the other rooms were filled up, too, and not everyone was asleep, and how could we go home now and leave the store wide open? Anyone could come and walk off with what they pleased and Daddy would kill us if he found out it was our fault.

"We can't leave while Bevon is asleep," I said, and we agreed to stay, and while we stayed, we cleaned. Of course the band had finished playing, and Buddy stood next to me, asking if I was going to Duncie's wedding, and I pretended I didn't know, when Stanny, who owned the clothing store across the river from us, came in and went over to Cherry. He talked to her a minute and then left.

"Daddy says we are to come home," Cherry said.

"You know we can't go until Bevon comes down," I said.

"I don't want a beating, so I am going," Cherry said. "Cynthia, what about you?"

"I am tired of beatings, too," said Cynthia. "Ivy, let's go. Stanny is waiting outside with his truck."

I said no, we had agreed to wait for Bevon and I was going to wait for her. If they reached home first, they were to tell Daddy what happened. They left and I began sweeping, talking to Buddy. After a while, I grew tired and stopped for a minute while Buddy brought me a glass of lemonade. I looked up at the top of the steps but saw nothing stirring. No sound came from the upstairs rooms.

"What about Duncie's wedding?" I asked him. Duncie was another girl in Mare River. He knew I thought he had been seeing Duncie and so didn't want to go.

As luck would have it, Daddy walked in just as Bevon appeared at the head of the stairs.

"Didn't I send for you?" he asked me.

"Yes, sir," I said.

"And what was your reply?"

"I said I couldn't come home because Bevon was asleep upstairs and I couldn't leave the store unlocked." I was already backing up, looking for a door out of the room, because my father's hand was behind him, which meant he had a fan belt in his hand and he intended to beat me.

"That's not what Stanny said you told him."

"I didn't talk to Stanny!" I said. "He talked to Cherry!"

"The others came back but you would not," my father said. He looked at Buddy and then at me. I ran through the back door, but my father must have run even more quickly, because no sooner was I through it than he met me there, his fan belt in his hand. He whipped me right outside Bevon's door and didn't stop until he and everyone else could hear me sobbing. Then he drove me off in the direction of the road. I was fifteen. I was fifteen and I wore my best printed dress and a pair of white shoes his mother had bought for me.

Between Swan's Landing and Mare River are many little rivers you have to cross, and many small bridges built over them. I walked in front of my father, and when I came to each little river, I ignored the bridges and walked through the water wearing my shoes. My father made no comment. I sobbed and walked through water until I reached my house.

"What's wrong with *you* now?" my stepmother asked me, and I said, "That damn coolie man you're married to came and beat me in front of everyone." I didn't know my father was right behind me, and when he heard me, he took out the fan belt and beat me again.

"I am not staying here tonight, you know," I said, and went up to my room and packed a nightdress and a few pairs of panties into a paper bag. "I'm going to Uncle Reggie's in Greenstown." Cynthia and Cherry said they were going too. The three of us sat in the bus depot until early morning and took the first bus to Greenstown.

My father sent Uncle Reggie a telegram ordering him to send us back. Cynthia and Cherry went willingly, but I refused. Eventually Uncle Reggie said I could stay with him until I was ready to go home. I got a job working at Mr. Smith's grocery store. Mr. Smith paid me well and called me Sweetie and there was a woman named Rainie who also worked there and occasionally I would spend the night at her house.

My Uncle Reggie was married to a woman much younger than he was and one night he came to me where I was reading and said, "Ivy? You'll have to find someplace else to stay. Before you came, everything was fine, and my wife, she was always content with what she had. But now you come home with a blouse and she wants it, or you come home with a hat and she wants it, and I can't afford these things, you know."

I said all right, I would find another place to live. I moved in with Rainie. Rainie saw that a young man who came to the store liked me and in the evenings I told my Uncle Reggie that I was working late and he was not to meet me. The young man and I began to walk out together. Rainie saw what was what and encouraged me to spend the night with him. I said if my Uncle Reggie found out he would kill me. She asked me if I was crazy. Didn't I know she could cover up for me?

I spent the first night with Marcus sitting up in a chair and eventually I fell asleep there and Marcus fell asleep on the couch. Rainie could hardly wait to hear what happened and Marcus said to her, "Let me tell you about your friend here. She spent the night sitting up in my blue chair!" Then I spent a second night with him and this time I did not sleep in the chair but in his bed. It seemed natural and very pleasant.

Eventually, Rainie and I ran into difficulties and I moved in with my grandmother, Mother Lize, and it was at her house I discovered that I was pregnant and I resolved to have the baby and give it away. Mother Lize sent a telegram to my father and the day he was to come I was back and forth from the window, looking for him. I saw him getting down from the bus and when he came in, he walked past me without saying a word. I could hear them in the kitchen, their voices low.

That night I went to bed early. My father knocked at my door and said, "May I sleep with you, ma'am?" and I said yes. He asked me if I loved the baby's father and I said I didn't know. He asked me if I would take him to the man tomorrow and let him talk to him and I said I would.

The next day I walked with my father to Marcus's place of work, and after I introduced the two of them, I ran and hid behind a coconut tree.

"Come back here," my father called. "I want you to hear what I'm telling him. If you love her," my father said, "marry her. But if you don't love her, leave her alone. If you marry her because she's pregnant, later you'll be sorry and make her pay for it. That's not the way. Let her come home if you don't want her. She is my child and I do love her."

Marcus asked me what I wanted and I said I didn't know but I thought I wanted to have the baby and give it away.

"Give it away to whom?" my father asked.

"It's not your baby, sir," I said.

My father returned to Mare River. I stayed in Greenstown and continued working for Mr. Brown. No one could tell I was pregnant. I met a woman who said she had wanted a baby for years but she could not have one. I told her that when I had mine, I would send a message to her and she could come and take the baby.

When the time came, I went to the hospital and I had the baby. I didn't feel uncomfortable there. The whole wing was full of teenagers about to become mothers. One of the girls had a sister who took a message to the woman who wanted the baby.

The birth was quick and easy. I had a girl. I took her back to my grandmother's and told her I was giving the baby away. "No, you are not!" she said. I said I was, and the woman was at the door, waiting to get her.

The woman came in and I handed the baby to her. My grip was already packed and I had my ticket back to Mare River. Granny began to argue with the woman and the last thing I saw when I turned around was Granny, trying to tug the baby out of the woman's arms. The baby was between the two women. I closed the door, heard the latch click, walked to the corner, and the bus pulled right up and I climbed in.

The bus swayed and tilted its way around the steep curves of the Green Island roads. Many of the passengers were returning from the Greenstown Market and their purchases, packed into huge baskets, were tied to the roof of the bus, and, since rain threatened, were covered with tarps. The bus came to the junction and as it went around it tilted so dramatically everyone began screaming and clutching at the seats in front of them, but then, as it always did, the bus righted itself.

I don't remember who won the domino tournament, the men of Mare River or the men of Swan's Landing. I don't remember if, when I was deciding what to do about the baby, I asked myself what my mother would have done in my place, because if I did ask that, I must have decided to do the opposite. My mother never gave any of her children away. I felt as if I had won a contest with my father. Even then, I knew he was not a bad man. He was very loving but strict, and, at times, unfeeling.

In the days when my father used to play dominoes, there was an old woman who lived alone a short distance beyond Swan's Landing. She was known to be selfish and to traffic in magic and the villagers disliked her.

In Mare River, if you asked a boy to climb your coconut tree and bring down some coconuts for you, it was the custom to allow him one jelly—one unripe coconut—as payment.

One day, a boy named Gabu came down the road and the old woman said, "I beg you to bring down four or five coconuts for me."

Gabu climbed the tree and threw down five coconuts and one jelly, which he picked up, intending to keep it for himself. "Where are you going with my coconut?" demanded the old woman. Gabu said it was his and started off down the road, but the old woman shouted after him, "You're a thief and you'll spend the rest of your life thieving!"

The people who knew the boy said that afterwards he was never the same. When he grew older, he would not work, but lived deep in the bush, and at night came out and stole people's goats. For some time, this dog or that dog was blamed, but gradually the farmers penned up their dogs at night and then everyone realized a man, not an animal, was stealing goats and finally someone saw Gabu. His hair was wild and tangled and he had grown a considerable beard. He no longer wore clothes, only some kind of cloth diaper that covered his nakedness.

Gabu's mother now had no one to help her work her land and was dependent on the generosity of the other villagers. One night, the men were playing dominoes at my father's house and the subject of Gabu came up.

"He should be brought back," my father said. "It is not right for him to live in the bush like an animal. All his mother does is cry out for him."

My Uncle Gusta asked how anyone was to find Gabu. No one knew where he lived and he was an expert at hiding himself in the bush.

"We could form a search party," my father said, and my Uncle Gusta grumbled, reminding my father of how he had built a coffin for Mr. Darlington's wife and how badly that good deed had ended. Mr. Darlington had gone about the village for years telling everyone that my father had built the coffin out of guilt because it was my father who had put a spell on his wife and that spell had killed her. My father said he could not see what the two things had to do with one another. My Uncle Gusta went on to say that we had no business with Gabu because he had never stolen any of our goats.

The houses on Green Island were built on stilts and at night when there was company at our house, we used to go beneath the house and listen to what the adults talked about. It was said that Gabu now did the same thing. At night, when families ate their dinners, Gabu slid beneath the house and listened to what people said as they ate. Apparently, one night he heard my Uncle Gusta talking about him, because the next day Uncle Gusta was missing two goats and there was a visible trail leading from his yard into the bush.

The men decided to search for Gabu. They went into the bush armed with their bottle lamps but they failed to find him. My Uncle Gusta said he had told my father what the result would be, and my father said there was no result. They would have to search again. The second time they searched the bush for Gabu they found him and brought him home to his mother.

I don't know whether he stayed with her or not, but I think I remember my father telling me that he had stopped stealing. I do remember that when the old woman who was said to have cursed Gabu died, no one knew of it until she was dead for five days, that was how much the villagers hated her, and when she was discovered, the officials from Cinnamon Bay had to send the dead wagon for her. There were no mourners at her funeral, not even Miss Coffin Cover, who generally could not be kept away from a grave mouth.

I think it was Gabu's mother who came to our house one Christmas when we were children and gave me a shilling and sixpence because I was the oldest, and gave Jack a shilling, because he was younger. Jack began to quarrel and said he should have the shilling and sixpence because *he* was the oldest child, and when I asked him what he meant (because everyone knew I was the eldest) he said that he was the first of my father's *real* children. Before that we had never quarrelled and now we were fighting over money. We were standing—

I remember that clearly—at the back edge of our garden, near the stone fence, after which the ground dropped off precipitously. I asked to see Jack's shilling, and when he gave it to me I said I would put an end to this quarrelling, and I took his money and mine and threw the coins over the fence, saying that now there would be no more arguments.

The next morning the two of us were up early, scouring the rocky hillside, but we never found any of the coins.

When Jack and I were still very young, my father decided to move our house from one side of the river to the other. He had built the house so that it could be moved easily. One day all the men from the village came to help him move the house which was placed on logs and rolled down to the river, pushed across, and then carried up the opposite bank.

As long as I knew my father, he never went without shoes. If he was in the house in bed, he would not get out of bed and put his feet down on the concrete. He put them into slippers first. The day he was moving the house, my stepmother cooked for the men who were helping. Between one thing and another, the house-moving took a long time, and the men didn't reach the riverbank until after dark. My father took up his place and saw he still had his shoes on. He took them off and threw them through an open house window. "Don't do it, Vidal!" one of the men cried. "Don't come into the water without your shoes! We can do it ourselves!" But my father didn't listen. He waded barefoot into the cold water and the house was moved to its foundation on the opposite bank.

The next day my father collapsed at work. When we saw him, he was in the hospital in a coma. I sat by the head of his bed and said, "Daddy? If you can hear me, show me you can. Blink your eye or something." He blinked his eye and water ran from it.

The doctor said if he had worn his shoes into the river nothing would have happened, but because he had no shoes, his stomach had cramped and inside something had twisted. He was operated upon for eight hours. Eventually he recovered completely.

I think of all these things together, I don't know why: the domino tournament, the beating I got for staying behind, the child I had because of the beating, Gabu, who was cursed for helping an old woman and who became a thief and lived in the bush, my uncle who sent me away because my clothes made my young aunt envious, the coins I threw into the gully so that my brother and I would not quarrel, and my father, who took off his shoes and nearly died.

I think of Gabu, under the floor of the house, listening to snatches of conversation and deciding whose goats he would steal. The smallest things affect us and determine what will happen to us. My father believed I left home and went to Greenstown because of what happened the night of Duncie's wedding, but Duncie's wedding had nothing to do with my leaving. People are always hovering between two points, and it is not the gale that sweeps them away. It is the small breeze that comes at the right time when they tire of their own will and open themselves up to the wind. Then, when they bend down their heads to fate, to chance, to another's will, when they tire of themselves, their own past, whatever comes along can change them forever.

And all these things are pieces of a puzzle, and they fit together to form the picture that is my life. Anna Asta says, What is the past to me? I am what I am. What has the past to do with me? But she broods over it. She goes in circles.

If I could gather together all the pieces, if I could fit them into place, one into another, then I would have the picture of my life, and the blank shape that would be left in the middle of the picture, that shape would be my mother. Finally, I would have found her. So I go back, I go over everything, I sort through things, I place them side by side. To Anna Asta, it is a kind of madness. But her search for forgetfulness which is not forgetfulness, which leads her back even against her will, this strikes me as madder still.

11

IT SHOULD BE no trouble at all to summon up the set of *The Roses*, the director, the other actors, myself, so frightened, so angry, so excited, so hopeful, but no sooner do I think of them than I begin to see something else. It is as if at this instant in my life, the film was double-exposed, and instead of the actors and the director, moving and speaking, this is what I see:

A very young boy comes into his magnificent parlor and stands under the portrait of his grandfather, painted, evidently, while he was playing the violin.

The boy's grandmother comes in and tells him how, long ago, his grandfather went to Lapland, herded reindeer to the south, and made the fortune that bought the family estate. The little boy wants to follow in his grandfather's footsteps, an artist who also made a fortune! As his grandmother tells the boy the story, the grandfather's portrait begins to move: the grandfather is playing his violin. Slowly the boy falls under its spell.

The boy, too, plays the violin. The mother hates this instrument. She does not want her son to become an artist. No, she wants a practical man.

When misfortune falls on the family, the boy, now grown up, goes to Lapland where he intends to duplicate his grandfather's success. But there is little grass along the route and the animals grow suspicious. The lead reindeer will not follow him. To be sure the lead reindeer does not escape, the young man ties its lead rope around his waist, but the animal panics and drags the young man after him through the snow. To the reindeer, it is nothing. He gallops and gallops through the snow. He climbs up and down small cliffs of rock. But the young man has a human body and he is smashed and broken. Finally the reindeer snaps the rope that pulls the young man after him. The young man falls asleep in the snow.

When he awakes the next morning, his fellow herders find him. At first they see only the bruises. They laugh with relief because he is alive. But suddenly the young man sees a black dog and begins to scream. It is a reindeer! A reindeer! Make it go away! When the men look they see only a black dog. When the young man looks, he sees a black animal with antlers and he screams piteously.

This movie, Max said, is about what is necessary for life. The dream of the artist, the practicality and the instinct of an animal, they must be combined or else there is nothing. Madness is a form of nothingness. You see?

No, I said. Madness is seeing the same thing no matter at what you are looking.

The director, Horton Hall, had been ready to begin for weeks. All he needed was a leading lady. I reported early Monday morning and he looked me over. "What language does this one speak?" he asked my interpreter, who said I spoke Finnish, Swedish and German. "Which language is hers?" he asked, his own voice heavily accented. "Finnish," Tomas said. "Finnish?" Mr. Hall asked. "No one speaks Finnish. Even the Finns don't speak Finnish."

He turned his back on us. He went off saying, "It's a Tower of Babel here. Where's Ricardo Bruno? How sunburned did he get?" He disappeared through a door of an exterior wall. I looked at Tomas. He looked at me. It was going to be a long wait.

A few minutes later, Mr. Hall, an exceptionally tall man, reappeared dragging a smaller man by the collar. I knew him at once. The last time I saw him, he had been wearing tights, an embroidered jacket and a tricorn hat. *Who did you have to sleep with to get here?*

Don't worry, I will take care of him later, I had told Tomas.

"Mr. Feldman!" Mr. Hall shouted. "Mr. Feldman! Come look at this! Tell me, what nationality is this?" He thrust the smaller man from him. The stagehands stopped what they were doing. The technical crew came out of the shadows like ants. The small man stood in the center of a growing circle.

Freddy Feldman looked at the small man and took out a light meter. "It can't be done," he said.

"Of course it can't be done! What can be done with you?" he demanded of the small man. "Look what color you are! You read the script? Did it say you were an African slave or something? Did you happen to notice the date filming began?"

"I fell asleep in the sun," the little man said. His voice was high and reedy.

"He fell asleep in the sun," Mr. Hall repeated. *"He fell asleep in the sun.* How long have you been an actor, Mr. Bruno? Have you heard of some of the difficulties we face here?"

Now his tone became confiding, even imploring. He took the small man by the arm. The actor pulled back when he touched him.

"We're making a *film*, Mr. Bruno. The audience has certain expectations. For instance, if, in the first scenes, they see a dark-skinned man making love to a white woman, that blonde standing over there, you see her? Good. If they see that, then how surprised they will be when the movie continues and gradually the dark-skinned man *fades.* This may be a stupid movie, Mr. Bruno. Perhaps it's not worthy of you, but what is it, after all? Is it a fantasy? Is it a sophisticated expressionist work so that the audience can sit back and watch and think, Of course, normally people born with dark skin stay that color, that's the way of the world, but in this parable, the dark actor fades and turns white? Are you, perhaps, trying to make a social comment through this sunburn of yours? Or once again you are envious of the female lead and her Silverstone Number Two? Or do you harbor some idea that Miss Rosalie can perform miracles and paint you white? A face painted white, some red lipstick, I see it. What will you look like then, Mr. Bruno? Something from *The Mummy Walks?* Just what did you have in mind, Mr. Bruno? I'm eager to fathom it. I always want to know what my actors are thinking. You understand that. People say actors don't think, but I know better, Mr. Bruno. Mr. Bruno, tell us, what were you thinking?"

Mr. Hall leaned toward the small man, smiling. Throughout, he had not stopped smiling, his thin lips pulled back, his expression unchanging, only his eyes, suddenly opening wide, then narrowing back to slits: those changed.

"I fell asleep in the sun," Ricardo Bruno said. His voice, his expression, was sullen.

"He says it once more. He fell asleep in the sun," Mr. Hall said. "And I was hoping for an explanation of why he fell asleep in the sun! Well, I am a foolish man, aren't I, Mr. Bruno! Get off my set! Go to Mr. Pinsky's office! Sit there and wait for me! When he shouts about our production schedule, when he explains how much your sunburn is going to cost, I want to hear you tell him, 'I fell asleep in the sun'! I want to see for myself what Mr. Pinsky will do to you!"

"But I can rehearse—" Mr. Bruno began.

"Off my set! Out of my sight! Off! Out! Go!

"And you," Mr. Hall said, turning to Tomas, his lips still drawn back into that imitation of a smile, "what are you mumbling about?"

"I was only translating," Tomas said. He was terrified.

"Oh, excellent," Mr. Hall said. "Than I may take it she knows better than to fall asleep in the sun?" He clasped his hands behind his back, leaned forward from the waist, and inspected me. "Not much shorter than I am," he said at last. "Perhaps Mr. Bruno will grow an inch or two while he fades. So," he said, "you don't look frightened of me. Mr. Feldman, what has gone wrong? The girl is not terrified."

"She worked with Max Lilly," Mr. Feldman said.

"Oh, oh," he said. "I see. Max Lilly. Well, after Max Lilly, nothing can be terrifying, is that it? We don't want you going back to Mr. Lilly and telling him Mr. Hall is a softie. Don't worry," he said, shaking his finger at me, "when you do something wrong, I'll frighten you. Isn't that true, Mr. Feldman? When I'm angry, I lose all control. On my last picture I chased Maud Marsh with an axe."

"Her scars healed quickly," I said.

"What did she say?" he asked Tomas.

"She said, 'Poor Miss Marsh.' "

"I don't think she said 'Poor Miss Marsh.' Well," he said, looking at me, "will we get along? Are you going to do everything I say? Little girl, the director always knows best!"

"Which director?" I asked.

"What did she say?" he asked Tomas.

"She said, 'Of course the director knows best.' "

"I don't think that's what she said. Tell me," he said, leaning toward Tomas, "What did she say? Really?"

"She said, 'Which director?' "

"Which director?" Mr. Hall repeated. "A good question. She doesn't like to be intimidated. She hasn't been to the Hollywood charm school. Anyone can see that. No fluttering her eyes and blushing and sighing, 'Oh, Mr. Hall! You're so clever, Mr. Hall!' I suppose I must learn to get along with *her*?"

Tomas, that continuous buzz in the background, translated everything but his eyes were frightened, almost all white, the pupils shrunken to two dark blue points.

"And you," Mr. Hall said to me, "please tell me how long is this ventriloquist and his dummy business going to continue? Are you going to be like that dumb Czechoslovakian who's been here for six years and still can't say more than yes or no? There are people here who don't think she knows how to say no. Just yes."

"She is studying English," Tomas said.

Mr. Hall took a step back, clutching his heart, raising his eyebrows. "From a book? A book?"

Now I was angry. I glared at Mr. Hall.

"A book," he said again, nodding. This time he smiled a real smile. "Well, go off to costuming," he said. "Take your books. You've got about thirty costume changes. Mr. Pinsky won't spend money to send us on location, but when it comes to clothes, that's another matter. He sits there and watches rushes with Bertha and when he comes out, everyone holds his breath and what does Pinsky say? Bertha says she wants copies of the dresses! And people wonder why he's such a success. Well, it helps to have a simple philosophy: Women want to cry and look at clothes." And then, abruptly, he was through with me.

"He likes you," Mr. Feldman said, going back to his lights.

"Well, how was it?" Max asked when I came in that evening.

"All day long taking off dresses and putting them back on. All day long the fitter saying, 'You must stand up straight or the hem will be uneven.' All day long standing there with my mouth full of pins while she fitted the bodices. All day listening to her say, 'What wide shoulders you have! What a long waist! What long legs! We don't grow them so tall here!' A sheet with a hole cut out for the head, that would be fine with me! Or no clothes at all!"

The setting sun sent its streamers into my little room. The floorboards glowed like fire. I unbuttoned my blouse, took it off, threw it across the room. Then I lay back on the bed. I asked Max what he had done all day.

"Meetings about the script, meetings with Mr. Pinsky about locations. Anders thinks the Painted Desert would do fine for the wilderness where the siren tempts everyone to their doom, but I said, How will they drown themselves in a desert? He said, even a desert can have a lake, or at least an oasis. So that's a good idea."

"A normal day?"

"Normal, yes. Well, one thing was not so normal. Mr. Pinsky has a suite of offices. Here if you're important, you don't have a few rooms, you have a *suite*, and we were in the adjoining room when we heard the most terrible sobbing. The most terrible! I said, 'Who is that crying?' and Anders—he came in to help translating, *to smooth the way*, that's some expression isn't it?—he hardly looked up. 'Oh, that's Pinsky,' he said. But a man should be crying like that? Either his heart was breaking or he was going altogether crazy. So I got up to rush into the room and Anders stood up, got hold of me and said, 'Sit down. Sit down and listen.'

"And on the other side of the door, more and more sobbing, louder and louder, and then suddenly Pinsky begins to shout. *Two weeks! Two weeks behind schedule!* Then the door to our office flies open and a small brown man came running through and ran out the other door and Mr. Pinsky right behind him, chasing him with an American flag!

"So I asked Anders, 'What is that all about?' and he wasn't even interested. 'Pinsky's after some actor,' that's all he said. And then Pinsky walked back in, smiling, beaming at us, saying, 'Go on, gentlemen, go on. What a wonderful feeling, such creativity going on outside my door,' and he disappeared into his office. His cheeks were still wet!

" 'So,' I said to Anders, 'it was all an act?' Let me tell you, Anna, if that Pinsky didn't look like a mushroom with elephant ears, he would be the greatest actor in the world! The greatest! Watch out for Pinsky, Anna! A man who can act like that, he can pull the wool over anyone's eyes!"

"That little man who ran through the office?" I said. "That was Ricardo Bruno, my leading man." And I told him the first part of the story. "So," I said, "Mr. Pinsky was weeping over the man's sunburn."

"And this Hall, what is he like?"

"A difficult man, a sharp tongue, but he is all right. I think he will be no trouble for me."

"Just what you are used to, eh?" Max had turned toward me. The sun was warm on my body. Max put his hand on my breast. "Oh, your hand is rough," I said. "I should rub some lotion on it."

"Some lotion," Max said. His hand rested on my stomach. Over my belly button, it stopped moving. "Sometime we should think this over," he said. "Are you still too young? Am I still too tired?"

"Mr. Pinsky says women like to weep and look at clothes but they don't care if movies are shot on location, so he doesn't want to hear about location shots," I said.

"No?" said Max. His voice was abstracted. I opened my eyes and looked at him. He was staring at my breasts. "You would be still cooler if you took off all your clothes," he said.

"It will be cool now on the beach if we went for a walk." Gussie, asleep in the corner, heard the word "walk" and began yelping happily.

Now every morning at six, Tomas came for me and drove me to The Studio. One morning I came in and found Miss Cotton, the woman in charge of costuming, weeping in her chair. "Oh, what is wrong?" I asked her in my poor English.

"All the final scenes, the ones we're doing first," she said. "Never do they tell me the truth about what is going to happen! First it is that idiot Bruno and his sunburn! Now Mr. Pinsky notices that in this film you are an opera singer and we already have an opera house on the lot because *The Phantom Singer* finished ahead of schedule and so we can use their sets. And nothing is ready! And I am to blame! This dress you are to wear today? The sleeves are only basted in place. Under the arms they aren't sewn at all! But I didn't know! He said he was beginning at the beginning and for the opening scenes you need only two skirts and two blouses and now twenty-nine costumes should have been ready yesterday!"

"Yesterday?"

"It's what he always says: 'Immediately if not sooner. When do I want it done? I want it done yesterday.' "

"So what scenes are we doing?" I asked her. "I come out of the opera house, yes? I wait for my lover but he does not show up? I stand at the top of the steps and the crowd stares at me before I go down the steps and get into my car? We are doing those scenes? Miss Cotton, not once in those scenes do I have to raise my arms. Not once do I have my back to the camera. So if you can fix the front of the dresses so nothing falls down and I am standing there naked, what are you crying about? When we stop filming, then you can fix the sleeves. Who will know?"

Tomas translated and translated. Lately I was barely aware of him, a hum, like a radio turned down low.

"You won't complain?" she asked me. "Some of them do. They say, how can they concentrate if they know they're not sewn up."

She reminded me of my mother, sitting there weeping over her clothes, thick round glasses sitting on the edge of her wide, red nose.

"Why should I complain? Why? If anyone sees the hole under the arm, I'll say I did it. I put the dress on too fast."

Mr. Hall knocked at the dressing room door. "May I inquire," he asked through the doorway, "if we must plan on another week's delay?"

"Why should there be a delay?" I asked. "We are ready."

"Did I hear correctly? We are ready?"

"Yes, we are ready," I said.

"You are ready and that nincompoop Bruno is at home, on salary, fading!"

"Fading and itching," said Mr. Feldman. "Yesterday he decided he should hurry things up so he put a solution of soap and peroxide on his face, maybe some bleach, too. The doctor says the rash will be gone just about the same time he turns white again."

"Rash?" said Mr. Hall. "He used bleach on his face? Get Pinsky on the phone and tell him not to send me any more actors until he gives them some intelligence tests! No, I'm not joking! Think of the money it would save him, if his actors had brains. Get in the cars! We're going to *The Phantom Singer*. Freddy, have you been over there? Have you set up the lights?"

The opera house in *The Phantom Singer* was enormous, the exterior wall seven stories high, the interior set cavernous, stalls receding up toward the ceiling as far as the eye could see, huge crystal chandeliers hanging from the vaulted ceilings. The exterior staircase appeared to be marble. Each step curved. The bottommost step was almost a block long. There was an open-air set representing the roof of the opera house. On it stood twenty-foot-high gargoyles, twenty-foot-high stone angels with unfurled wings.

"Oh, look at that!" I said. "It is a pity not to use them!"

Tomas translated.

"Another country heard from," Mr. Hall said. "I should have listened to my mother and studied to be a surgeon. One anesthetizes one's patients and gets the silence one expects."

He looked at the gargoyles and the angels. In the early morning light, they cast enormous shadows, monstrous angels, graceful gargoyles. "'It *is* a pity not to use them,' he said. "Maybe there's a way."

"Of course if they already used them in *The Phantom Singer*," I said.

"You think the director will tell us?" Mr. Hall said. "He's furious we're using his set."

"A friend of mine's an extra on that picture," Tomas said.

"Can you ask him what they filmed? Don't tell him why. Just ask him. We'll shoot some footage, eh, Freddy? While we have these shadows?"

"Why not?" Mr. Feldman asked.

"You practice going up and down those steps. They're very wide. If you don't get the rhythm right, when you run down, you will trip and fall. Go on, walk up and down."

I climbed up and began coming down. Such wide steps! But then my legs were long. If I took big strides, if I walked the way I normally walked—

"That's fine, that's good," Mr. Hall shouted. "That's enough! Freddy, start the camera setups."

"That's very good," Mr. Hall said. "Miss Asta, as you know, Mr. Bruno is indisposed but we don't need him for filming. He can do his close-ups later. But you would like someone to look at, I think, so you know where to focus your eyes. Mr. Feldman is about the same height as Mr. Bruno. Stand here, Freddy. Put on that ridiculous hat. Now Miss Asta, I know I'm asking the impossible, but look at Mr. Feldman with longing. Your soul is on fire. That's very good, very good. All right, Freddy, today you are yourself and Mr. Bruno as well. Miss Asta, go sit somewhere."

I went into the interior sets of the opera house and wandered through the rooms. Finally I came to what must have been a bedroom. A bed shaped like the prow of a boat occupied one corner. A little flight of gilded steps led up to it. I climbed up the steps, climbed into the bed, lay down on my back, and opened my English grammar. The sheets were satin, the coverlets were satin, the canopy above me was pink satin. The walls were covered in gray silk. The whole place smelled of dust. The mattress was thin, but then the bed was probably meant only as a prop. The dusty smell, the feel of the satin, the carved, curved swan-neck of the bed-prow, oh it was wonderful. I fell asleep. I opened my eyes and looked into the frightened faces of Mr. Feldman and Mr. Hall.

"Please don't do that again, Miss Asta," Mr. Feldman said. "We thought God only knew what happened to you."

On the set, Miss Rosalie applied Silverstone Number Two, put on my lipstick, and settled the brown wig over my hair. Behind a painted flat, I put on my costume, climbed the steps, stood there nodding at a nonexistent crowd, ran down the steps, and gazed at Mr. Feldman with unutterable longing. Then I stepped sadly into the black car filled with flowers and stared straight ahead while a nonexistent woman moved from the nonexistent crowd to say how lucky I was, how I had everything I wanted.

"Very good," Mr. Hall said. "Very good. Miss Asta, go home. If the lab doesn't mess it up, we've saved a week. I'll see you in the morning."

The young man who was dragged by reindeer, who fell asleep in the snow, is now quite mad. He returns home but does not recognize his mother or grandmother. He spends his time filling his pockets with rocks he believes to be coins. With them he intends to pay off the family debts.

A young girl, a violinist with a travelling circus, hears of his plight and comes to help him. But he does not recognize her and so it does no good. Then one day she thinks, I will recreate the events of the day I met him. Perhaps it will take him back in time. So she dresses in her circus costume and stands in the courtyard playing her violin. The acrobat performs his tricks. The fat tight-rope walker crosses the yard on her rope. Gradually the young man becomes aware of the girl playing her violin and as he does, he looks at the rocks he has spread out on his table and once more they are only stones, not coins. He goes into the yard. He recognizes his mother. He recognizes the girl.

The girl has saved him. How? By returning the time, the lost, lost time. Now he remembers the reindeer, the flight through the snow. Now he remembers his dream of an artistic life. Somehow the family mansion is saved and the practical young man spends his days playing upon the piano while the girl, now his wife, plays the violin.

If we could have back the time, knowing what we know now! If it could be done!

This was a film of Max's. How film redeems the time, he says, his eyes full of tears. How it redeems and repairs! If, in real life, we could remember every detail, exactly how we were, how we felt, the exact touch of the air on our skin, if we could do that, we could go back, we could pick up all the dropped stitches, no more walking around in these bodies, these coats full of holes!

But, I say, in real life it cannot be done, because if it could be done, I would do it. He does not ask me to what I would return, what I would undo. Instead, he says: It can be done. By people wiser and stronger than we are. It was done by the girl in the film. And what can I do but sigh? Again he is mixing up the story on film and the life we lead.

In the morning, Miss Cotton had a big box of chocolates, a yellow box decorated with red roses and green ivy leaves.

"Oh, someone gave them to you?" I said.

"Mr. Sondquist said you liked candy," Miss Cotton said shyly. She handed me the box.

"I don't want to eat up your candy," I said. "Such a beautiful box!"

"You think so? It's for you," she said, thrusting it at me.

"You see?" Max said that night. "Make friends with the helpers. You'll be walking around dressed like an empress and that Bruno, he'll be walking around with runs in his tights." He was leafing through the script of *The Roses*, looking for my scenes.

"So, tomorrow you do the scenes with this Bruno. Now you have become the famous opera singer, and this man who has spurned you comes to you and tells you he feels regret. How will you do it? Pretend I am Bruno."

"Max," I said, "let us eat dinner first!"

"After you ate all that candy? Let's rehearse!"

I came up to him. I looked at him with surprise, then with longing, and then I drew back, all as Mr. Hall had told me to do.

"What's this?" Max asked. "Such drama! I can't stand it! He is a dress you're thinking of buying, you go up to it, look at the price tag, and the price is too high, so you turn away and go to another store? We can do better than this, Anna!"

"What's wrong now?" I asked. "Mr. Hall was satisfied."

"Mr. Hall was happy when you didn't break your neck on the opera steps!"

"Then tell me what to do."

"First, what really is going on here? The lover, the great love of your *youth*, comes to see you. Time has not touched you. He tells you that. You are cynical. You say it is the business of a prima donna to be untouched by time. Fine. What do you mean by it? You mean life hasn't worn you out with children, with marriage, with the thousand and one cares of human beings. You're not complimenting yourself. Such bitterness in that remark! Life has passed him by, he says. Fine. You say nothing, but you are thinking, Life has passed *me* by. You can't say it aloud. Who will feel sorry for you, a beautiful prima donna, rich, famous! You must think it. And your love, what does he look like now? A banker, a dentist! What disappointment! In your heart, in spite of all he has done to you, he is still the great romantic hero. But now you look at him and you see he is a banker or a dentist after all. You laugh at yourself for thinking him more. Suddenly he strikes you as ridiculous. And then you see him again as the lover of old. After all, Anna, he is the last bit of your youth! When he goes you will never see him again! When he goes you will be old!"

"All this," I said, tired and lying down on the bed, "is much more interesting than what's in that silly script."

"What did you say? Anna! Sit up!"

"I said, All this is more interesting than anything in that stupid script."

"And that surprises you?" Max asked angrily. "What are they paying you for? Why don't they have Miss Rosalie read the part? What do they need you for? You're the one who makes it interesting! You're the one who keeps the audience's eyes on you! What is this movie about, Anna? It asks, What is happiness? It answers, No one is perfectly happy. Every choice has its consequence. That is not interesting enough for you? To that idea you're going to bring all the depth of a teacup? All right, if you can't do it, you can't do it. Young and stupid, that's one thing, but young, stupid and lazy, that's another. Go eat your dinner!"

"All right," I said. "I'll try it again."

"Not for me! Do it for yourself! Not for me! Someday I won't be here and then who will you do it for? You don't want to do it for yourself, go eat!"

I was tired and hungry. "Oh, you will always be here," I said.

"Start."

"You must promise me. You will always be here."

"Who can promise such things? Start."

"The last bit of my youth. But really, I don't know what that means. They used to say I was born old."

"Then the last bit of happiness. Try that."

I walked up to him. In front of my eyes, he grew older. The lines in his face deepened. The veins stood out on the backs of his hands. His hair turned gray. His voice shook. I looked at him with shock. Then I summoned up the photographs taken before I met him, a handsome young man, laughing, even then with a bulldog like Gussie, strong, an odd face, tall enough to cast a long, long shadow. I felt the muscles in my face soften, my eyes widen. And then he changed again: his back curved. He could look no one in the eye. He had failed terribly. I felt shame to see him as he was. Pity, scorn, ridicule, all went through me like lightning. When I was finished, I sat down on the bed. Unhappiness pressed me into the mattress.

"So," he said. "How silly is it now, what happens to all of us in the end? What are you crying for? You're so hungry? Let's eat dinner. Tomorrow you do it the way you did it tonight, Mr. Hall will be happy, I'll be happy, Mr. Hall will tell himself he's a great director, Pinsky will congratulate himself on picking such a wonderful script, he himself didn't know how wonderful it was. In this business, believe me, you grow old before your time."

• • •

One evening after filming finished, I was very tired and decided to stay on the set and study my English grammar. Max had persuaded Anders to go with him to scout for locations and was not returning until late. Four or five of the sets were constructed on top of a huge turntable so that they could be rotated to take advantage of the sun as it moved through the sky. It was a very warm night and the skies were clear. The gauze diffusers were still in place over the rooms, protecting them from nothing more than mosquitoes.

In the living room of Ricardo Bruno's house, I found a high-backed chair that reminded me of Max's old chair in the Lagerloff Studios. I sat down in that chair and drew my legs up under me. The chair faced a whitewashed wall. It did not occur to me that I would be invisible to anyone coming into that room. I pored once again over the mysteries of the verb *to be*. Mr. Hall and Mr. Feldman were becoming connoisseurs of my abuse of that verb. This annoyed me, because I thought that, under the circumstances, I was doing quite well. *It is raining tomorrow? She is here last week?* They knew perfectly well what I meant. But then I remembered that Mr. Hall's first language was Hungarian and Mr. Feldman's was Russian, and, as far as I knew, they both spoke English perfectly.

Moreover, I was constantly admonishing Max: Learn the language! Please learn the language! They are giving you a film to direct and you are so particular! Particular and with such a temper! If you shout *Stop!* when you mean *Begin!* you will rage up and down because they followed your orders. Nothing will get done. Which hand is this? I said, and held out my left hand. Your left hand, Max said in Swedish. No, no, say it in English, I said. Why? Max asked. You've forgotten how to speak your own language?

So I sat there in the carved chair, the grammar book and my box of vocabulary words in my lap, an impossible language and ugly to the ear, no rhythm in it, and I must have fallen asleep, because when I opened my eyes I heard Mr. Hall's voice, and then Mr. Feldman's answering him.

"Pinsky calls every day," Mr. Hall said. "And every day he asks the same thing. How's the Finn doing? I tell him, fine, she's great, she's wonderful. What do you make of it, Freddy? This morning, she *was* wonderful. In that scene when she sees Bruno for the last time, that was something. I never saw anything like it.

"But this afternoon! All she has to do is sit in a donkey cart and wave goodbye to her mother! Who ever saw a human being wave like that? She lets her hand drop down and wags it like a tail! And was that supposed to be a sad look? She raises her eyebrows and lets her mouth droop? She looked like she had a stroke! And that was the third take! And when Bruno finds out *she's* the famous opera singer and she rolls her eyes and screws up her mouth! Once she gets it wrong, I can't make her get it right. They say this Lilly, he does wonders with her. She's a cooperative girl, sometimes very pretty, but even that! If you shine the light on her the wrong way, she's hard-faced, like a peasant who just counted her cows and realizes one of them is missing. What do you make of it?"

"I see how to light her," Freddy said. "A lot of back-lighting, a hot light on her chin, very hot, some pretty bright light on the rest of her face, all the features outlined, the chin down, almost against the chest, then she looks like a Madonna."

"What are we going to do with her? Is she human scenery? What?"

"How old is she? She's seventeen, eighteen? A child, really. My daughter, she's going to listen to another man who tells her something just because he's as old as I am? No, this Lilly, he is the problem. He's the one she listens to. He's the one she trusts. If she didn't have this Lilly to lean on, she'd lean on someone else and then maybe she'd learn something."

"But sometimes she's very good!"

"Maybe he directs her off the set."

"This is my picture!" Mr. Hall said. "But it could be done. The Studio could separate them. Pinsky hates it when two people get too close. They gang up against him."

"It could be time," Mr. Feldman said. "Time and confidence and experience. Okay, so we get some of them who walk on stage as if they've been on all their lives and they act natural. What are they doing? They're being themselves. Then you want them to be someone else and you're out of luck. Remember Betty? How happy everyone was with her? Until she was twenty-one and got grownup parts and everyone started to notice: she's not a grownup! She can't play anything! But this one, she can be someone else. One flash, it means nothing. Two flashes, three, the storm is coming. And with the right lighting, so beautiful, so beautiful!"

"Can she act or can't she?"

They must have turned back, walked away. I heard their voices fading.

Can I act or can't I? The studio wants to separate us.

I looked at my watch. In a half hour, Tomas would be back for me. Today he had taken my shoes to the shoemaker for heels and soles. He helped me put on my make-up. He went over my lines. He went to the store for the ginger crackers Max likes to eat.

When he's not needed on the set, why should he sit around doing nothing? He should earn his money. When he walks by, carrying my wig stand, Mr. Feldman grins at him behind his back.

I send him out to get the papers and when there's nothing interesting in them, I send the papers back and he exchanges them for magazines. Max says this is terrible. This is how a peasant behaves. But what am I? Not an actress. Something Mr. Feldman paints onto film with his hot lights. What is the proper way to wave? In Finland, people let their hand drop down at the wrist and then they gently flap it. How do people wave here?

Tomas's red car pulled up. He leaned over and pushed open the door. "Congratulations!" he said. "I envy you!"

"What are you talking about now? Someone died and left me a fortune?"

"The rushes! The rushes!"

"The lab ruined them. Good. I have another chance." After what I'd heard, that was reason to congratulate me.

"They just saw the rushes. Everybody's fighting to get in and see them. They say they've never seen anything like it! Pinsky has three people, *three people*, looking for projects for you! *Magic on the screen. Magic on the screen.* They keep saying it."

"I can't act," I said. "Some magic."

"You know how many people can act and when they flash up there on the screen everyone covers their eyes? No, no, after this you don't have to worry!"

"A human decoration!" I said bitterly. "Listen, you found a good shoemaker to put on the heels and soles? I paid one hundred kronor for those shoes. When I wear those shoes, then I feel happy. The shoemakers here, they know how to fix things? Everyone I meet, they see a hole in their shoe, they say, Oh, I have to buy another pair. Here no one keeps anything. When will the shoes be back? This pair pinches my toes."

"You should have more than two pairs of shoes. You have two pairs of plain shoes. You need party shoes."

"Who is inviting me to a party? Why do I need party shoes? When I'm invited to a party, I'll worry about more shoes."

We drove back in silence. The coastline was black. The sea was blue-black except where the full moon lit the water, turning it silver, a wide, wedge-shaped, rippling, fish-scaled path across the sea. A cool breeze blew. The palm fronds swayed gently. Sometimes at four o'clock it's this dark in Finland, I thought. Right now it was possible a snowstorm was blowing up in Stockholm, the snow horizontal against the window panes, slanting down at oblique angles, blotting the buildings from sight, parting its thick white strands of hair so that for an instant the cornice of the house across the street became visible, shaking its head, obliterating the house again, and when you looked up at the sky, there was none, not even a ceiling over the world, just a thick grayness from which the snow fell.

And if the wind was blowing, then people would run along, holding their hats on their heads, pushed from behind by the big white flat hand of the wind, skidding where the wind whipped the snow from the ice on the sidewalks, but scouring everything, the wind scouring and scouring, and people bursting into their warm rooms, exclaiming, laughing, brushing snow from their coats, their cheeks red, their eyes watering, their toes frozen, a puddle forming around them as they hurried to take off their boots, their coats, their hats, to hang them on hooks, little clouds of steam rising from the drying clothes near the stove, someone at the stove pouring a cup of tea, saying, This doesn't look like it will stop so fast, tomorrow the schools will be closed, Poppa's in the shed, he's greasing the runners for the sleighs. Tomorrow it's going to be dark all day. Do we have enough candles? Must I bake some bread? Will the milk wagon get through in the morning?

And all the while, the wind scouring and scouring. For an instant, the round white clock face in the church tower takes the place of the full moon, then it disappears, but the wind is scouring it clean, the buildings are scoured clean, the streets, the people, even they come in from the storm, scoured clean, the preserving snow that people and animals lie down in and fall asleep in and are discovered in later, perfect, rosy, decay hasn't touched them, who can believe that the snow is not an instrument of God, the way it polishes with its hundreds and hundreds of hands, who can be out in the snow and the wind and not come home exhausted, exhausted and exhilarated, exhausted and exhilarated and washed clean.

"Maybe you better borrow some party shoes from Wardrobe," Tomas said. "Pinsky wants you and Max at a party."

"Oh, I don't like parties, all those strange people speaking a strange language. Who can like it? These are the same people looking at rushes? If I look so good in the rushes, when they see me they'll faint with disappointment. Better to stay home."

"Well," Tomas said sullenly, "if you went, of course you would need a translator. I would like to go."

"Everyone always thinking of himself." I sighed. "Always self. I tell you what, Tomas. If you go, I will go also. How is that?"

He nods and smiles. Now he is happy.

In Sweden where it is often dark at one in the afternoon, there is one word for night, another for darkness. They are not the same thing. At home, there are many names for darkness.

12

AFTER THE DOMINO TOURNAMENT at Bevon Berriman's, when my father beat me for not coming home when he summoned me, I went to Greenstown where I worked for Augustus White, a man who owned a grocery store.

Augustus White came from Goose Landing, a town even smaller than Mare River. Because Mr. White's mother was widowed young, and because he had to help support his family, he quit school very early and so he never learned to read and write. As a child, he worked the family land and when crops were harvested, he went with his mother, who did higgling, to Greenstown, where he met the buses that were entering or leaving the city. Even as a small child, he knew whom to approach. He did not, like the others, simply call out *oranges, tangerines, guavas, breadfruit, grapefruit.* No, he looked into the eyes of people who seemed interested in his doings and to them he recited his list of wares. His mother saw his gift for salesmanship and encouraged him to think of opening a general store. When he objected, saying that he could neither read nor write, his mother said that was no obstacle: he need simply hire someone who could do those things for him, or better yet, he could marry a woman who could.

Mr. White was still not married when I moved to Greenstown and began looking for a job. He asked me if I had ever worked in a grocery store before, and I told him that when I lived in Mare River, I worked for Mr. Hajid on Friday afternoons and on Saturdays. Mr. White asked me what I had done there and how I had liked my work. I told him that Mr. Hajid was an Indian and a friend of my grandmother, Mother Lize, and was old enough to be my father. He had daughters who

were seven and eight years older than I was. Until I went to work for
Mr. Hajid, I had no idea there were so many Indians in the district
and thought that the only Indians in our parish were my father and
his relatives. But on Fridays and Saturdays, when the women came to
shop, the store was always crowded.

If Mr. Hajid had not been a friend of my grandmother's, I believe
he would have fired me. The Indian women would ask me for something, and when I would try to explain that I didn't understand their
language, they would curse at me.

"She is not a full Indian!" Mr. Hajid would shout at them. "She
does not know the language!"

Finally, Aza, one of Mr. Hajid's daughters, said, "Do you have a
blank sheet of paper?" and I tore a brown piece from the roll in which
we used to wrap meat. On the paper she wrote the names of everything in Hindustani and across from them, the names of the same thing
in English. Now when someone asked me for something in their language, I could look it up on my sheet of paper. One day when I came
in, I couldn't find the sheet, and was frightened until I realized that I
no longer needed it.

My grandmother, Mother Lize, wanted me to marry Mr. Hajid.
He came to her house one Saturday and asked for me. After that, I
had no peace. "If you are not happy, you can blame me," she said. "If
you are happy, you can thank me."

"But I do not love him!" I said. "He is an old man!"

Still, she kept on, and finally I said, "I don't like an Indian man!"
Then she became angry and cursed at me in her language, but still
she did not give up. I don't know why I did it—the devil must have
taken my tongue—but I finally said, "I don't want him. You take him."
After that, Mother Lize was furious with me and on weekends I didn't
stay at her house for some time.

When I saw Mr. White peering at the bills the bread man left, I
remembered how difficult it was for me when I worked for Mr. Hajid.
I watched Mr. White the first week and was astonished at the multi-
tude of tricks he had worked out to conceal his illiteracy. When the
bread man came, Mr. White handed him one hundred dollars and
asked for change. When he got it, he'd say, "Count it again. Last week
you cheated me." The truck driver would count it again. "Eighty-six
fifty," said the driver. "Thirteen fifty is the right change. You are too
suspicious."

I liked the job. I liked being needed, and soon I was hopping like
a cricket around the store. Mr. White always called me "Sweetie."
Every Friday I would make up an envelope for each bill, for the bread,

for the meat, for the canned goods, and put the proper amount of money in each one. Then I would either wait on customers in the store or go down to meet the buses that brought in fresh fruit and I would buy what Mr. White told me was needed.

After eight months, a woman began stopping in to buy a little sweet cake or a candy, and each time she came, she stayed and chatted with Mr. White. A few weeks later, Mr. White came up to me and said, "Sweetie? I'm leaving a little early tonight. Can you lock up?" I said that was no trouble. Mr. White went into the rear and I heard the sound of splashing water, and when he came out, his hair was plastered to his head. He was newly shaven and wore a fresh shirt. He waited in the doormouth of the store looking down the street, looking for Miss Rose.

Miss Rose came from St. Catherine's and no one in Greenstown knew her or any of her people. I looked at her as she came into the shop, wearing a shiny purple dress to whose lapel she had pinned a giant fuchsia hibiscus, her hair fussily and professionally finger-waved, and on her head a huge white straw hat, and I thought of what my grandmother had told me when I was a child. "Don't go with people unless you know their parents or grandparents," she said. "There are people who aren't really people but spirits who come to take you away. They ask you to follow them down dark alleys or to the edge of cliffs so you can gaze out at the sea. You must look down at their feet and make sure they point forward the way yours do. Mrs. Darlington's daughter June went down to Cinnamon Bay with a little girl who fell out of a hollow tree and they never found her until her body washed up on the shore. Miss Jane's son went up into the hills with a little boy and no one ever saw him again. If you know the parents and the grandparents, you know the child has roots. Someone from a hollow tree, he can fall from a hollow tree and not want to hurt you?" I thought of all these things as I gazed on Miss Rose.

The next day Miss Rose was sharing Mr. White's bed. I was still "Sweetie," but she had become "my Rose." If she had been working before she began living with Mr. White, she was not working now. "When you have a little time," she would call to me from the top of the stairs, "would you bring me up a cold lemonade?"

"Mr. White," I said, "I did not know you hired me as a waitress."

"Certainly I did not hire you as a waitress," he said.

"But that's what I am doing, sir," I said. "Running up and down all day, taking things to Miss Rose."

Mr. White saw the expression on my face and put a stop to Rose's requests. If Rose wanted something, he would carry it up to her himself.

I was fascinated by Miss Rose's appetite. She would come down for a can of baked beans. Whole loaves of bread disappeared upstairs along with jars of grape and guava jelly. Bunches of bananas went up, and armloads of grapefruits and paper bags full of oranges. And then I noticed that nothing came down: no trash from peeled bananas or oranges, no empty cans or paper bags. I began to wonder what was happening to all the food. Miss Rose was not fattening. Her clothes fit her as well as ever.

One afternoon, when Mr. White had taken the bus down to the Greenstown Market, Miss Rose took four empty cartons upstairs to their bedroom. An hour later, she came down with four fully packed cartons, which she stacked near the door. Soon a car pulled up in front of the store, a man got out, picked up the cartons and loaded them into the back seat. The two of them talked together a minute and then the man called out, "See you next week!" and drove off.

Miss Rose was looting the store. I said nothing to Mr. White and he noticed nothing.

One morning Miss Rose came in and I saw she was wearing a beautiful new watch. "That is a lovely watch," I said, and she said, "Oh, yes, I've had it for years."

A few hours later, Mr. White came downstairs, his hair pointing in all directions. He pulled a piece of paper from his pocket. "Sweetie?" he said. "What is this? It is a receipt, isn't it?"

I looked at it. "Yes, it is a receipt," I said.

"When was it given?"

"Oh, a long time ago."

"You're sure?"

"A long time ago," I said.

He left the shop, and when he came back, he stood in the middle of the store and began to shout that he lived among hogs. I asked him what he meant. He said he had gone down to the market and showed the receipt to the man at the breadfruit stand. "It's a receipt for a watch?" he asked him, and the man said it was. "And it's dated when?" he asked the man. "It's dated yesterday," the breadfruit man said.

"Sweetie? Why didn't you tell me?" Mr. White asked.

"Look here, now," I said. "I learned a long time ago that when a man and a woman put their head down on the same pillow, I don't get between them. Miss Rose is your woman."

"But you were here before her!"

"It's not the same," I said. I had not lived with my father and my stepmother all those years for nothing.

Things went from bad to worse. One day the bread man came and when Mr. White took out the envelope to pay him, it was empty. When I came into the store, Mr. White said, "Sweetie? Why didn't you leave money for the bread man?" I went over to the cash register and picked up the envelope beneath the drawer and said, "What are you talking about? Here it is." Mr. White said the envelope was empty and he didn't understand it. But I understood it perfectly. The woman had stolen money from the till and bought a watch and lied about the receipt, saying she'd always had the watch, and she was shipping box after box of groceries to her home in St. Catherine's. Soon Mr. White would cry out for bankruptcy and the police would look around and ask who operated the register and I would be the one carried away.

That Friday when Mr. White had paid me, I said, "Mr. White? I am not coming back." He asked me what I meant, and I said I had to leave because if I didn't, in a little while the police would come to carry me off to Bodmin Town. I said I didn't like what was going on here. Mr. White quarrelled, he pleaded, but I said no, I could not afford to stay.

The next morning, a policeman came to my gate where I was renting a room, but he was my friend Vin, who was also a friend of Mr. White's.

"You're not going back?" he asked me. I said no. "You won't think about it again?"

"No," I said, "because I don't want you to have to come for me and carry me off to Bodmin Town."

"Come and talk to him, then?" asked Vin. I went with him to Mr. White's.

"Sweetie!" he said. "You're coming back!"

"No, Mr. White," I said. "I am not. I'm going to look for a job at the biscuit factory."

A few months later, Vin stopped by my gate. "Ivy!" he called out. "Come out here!"

When I came out, he asked me if I'd seen the morning paper and I said no, I hadn't seen it. He showed it to me. Mr. White had filed for bankruptcy and the door to his store had been nailed shut. "It was because of that Miss Rose," Vin said. "She had a husband and children in St. Catherine's and when she ate out everything he had in his store and he had no more for her to send back to them, she left and went back home."

"You see!" I said.

One afternoon, I was walking down the street past a group of men who sat on the grass eating their lunch. I was on my way to the biscuit factory. "Sweetie!" someone called out. I stopped. It sounded like Mr. White. "Come over here, Sweetie," he called.

"You're working here now, Mr. White?" I asked him, and he said yes, he was working the night shift.

"You see this woman?" he said to the men around him. "It's because of her that I had to cry out for bankruptcy."

"Oh, no," I said. "Tell them the truth. If I had stayed, I'd be in prison right now." The men laughed and I said goodbye and walked on.

Meeting Mr. White made me think of my childhood days.

Not long after I came to live with my father and stepmother, my stepmother became ill with whooping cough, and one day I didn't bring the tea she asked for fast enough. "You better hope I don't get sick and die," she told me as she always did when she was ill, "because if I do, I'm going to come back and gouge out your eyes."

Of course I believed her—in those days I believed everything adults told me—and whenever my stepmother fell ill, I hovered over her like a fly over warm meat. One night when she had a fever, my father heard me sobbing in my room. "Why are you crying?" he asked me. "Why are you always in Bea's room?"

I told him what his wife had told me.

"And you believe it?" he asked. I said I did.

"How can you come back and bother people if you're dead?" he asked. "You believe that stupidness?"

After that, when my stepmother fell ill, I helped in the house but I did not worry.

Almost a year after my mother died, my father agreed to take me to her grave. I didn't tell him why I wanted to go, but still he took me. She was buried in Cinnamon Bay overlooking the water, near the church and near the hospital. People told me that if you went to a person's grave, you could speak to them. My father left me at the gravesite and walked off. I sat down next to the mound and looked at the plain marker: MARIE CATHERINE CLIFTON. There was nothing else written on it, not even the date of my mother's death.

The small stretch of ground beneath the marker was surrounded by an iron railing, so that, from a distance, the grave looked like a small hospital bed. The grass inside the railing was growing wild and was overgrown with weeds. I spoke to the grave but there was no answer.

It was a windless day and it remained a windless day.

After I went back home, I saw the grave everywhere in front of me. For years I had kept a picture of my mother's face locked in my mind: it was my face, only older. Now when I looked in the mirror, I saw only that little plot of ground, weed-filled and silent. At night I touched my face and expected to feel cold earth. These visions went on for weeks and then months. Eventually they stopped but when they did I felt a continual sadness I had never felt before. After a while I stopped feeling that sadness, or thought I stopped feeling it. Probably I still feel it although I am no longer aware of it.

When my father lived in Cinnamon Bay, he owned some land above Mare River, and on weekends, he would go up there and pick breadfruit and jackfruit and tangerines and bring them back into town. As soon as he began to drive down the main street, friends of his would call out, "I beg a jackfruit from you, Mr. Vidal," and he would call back, "There are acres of them up there above Mare River. Get in the truck and we'll pick some," but none of them wanted to go.

Later, he began grafting oranges onto lime trees and produced green oranges that were very popular with the tourists. But when he wanted to sell them in the market, the vendors offered him such a low price he said it wasn't worth picking the fruit and driving it down to Cinnamon Bay for a few pennies. He said he'd rather let it rot on the boughs, and he did.

He used to tell me that story, and I'd think about the trees heavy with fruit, the sun shining on the crop, and the fruit falling to the ground and then rotting under the hot sun.

"Either they pay me what those oranges are worth or they'll do without them," my father said. Whenever he said that, I'd feel a great grief, a mourning, as if the oranges were human beings he had condemned to die, up there in the fields, alone, not knowing what they had done wrong or why this was happening to them.

I walked on to the biscuit factory and thought how great things could make you bitter and how little things could do the same. I thought about Mr. White, who had been ruined by Miss Rose from St. Catherine's, and who never resented her or turned bitter, but laughed with the men outside the biscuit factory and worked the night shift, accepting his fate as if he deserved it.

I am not bitter about my stepmother nor am I bitter about life. I should be bitter but I am not. What I feel is sadness. What I search for is my story. The more I remember, the happier I become. If the memory is happy, if the memory is sad or painful or even tragic: it doesn't matter. What matters is that I remember. I remember my grandmother wanting me to marry Mr. Hajid and I wonder if I had married him, if I had married, not for love, but out of common sense, would I have been happy? I like to remember all this because it reminds me that there were choices open to me, that I myself made my life what it is. This seems important. My father always said my memory was good. It is.

If I spend so much time remembering other people's lives, it is because it is always easier to see the truth in them. In the middle of our own lives, we can see nothing. Everything is so bright and crowded and so we are blinded. To ourselves, we are like sheeted mirrors. But the others: they are the mirrors that truly reflect us.

13

"WE ARE GOING," Max said, "because Pinsky expects it and so we must go, and also I like parties."

"That is a good reason for you to go. Not me."

"Are you not also on his payroll?" Max asked. "Here it is one great big tiny family. You insult him, the relatives will turn against you. It is worth it, not to go to a party?"

And so began the usual, disconsolate rummaging through my drawers, the pulling out of dresses that in Berlin had looked so elegant, but here were too extravagant, too heavy for the heat.

"Throw them out," Max said, "or if you will not throw them out, pack them into cartons and throw some mothballs in after them. Tomorrow we go shopping, we buy you a few dresses, a good cloak, some shoes. If we finish in time we can go to that movie you want to see, the one with that Charles Harrow they're talking about. We'll come home, go to bed, and we'll get up in time to go to the party. In two days at this time, the party will be over, you won't remember why you made such a fuss."

"Oh, I will remember," I said.

"Peasants have long memories," Max said.

"Why does everyone call me a peasant? I was poor. I was not a peasant! I didn't work in the fields!"

"You act like a peasant, naturally people will take you for one.

Why did I have to hear about the rushes from Anders? You have decided I will always be the twenty-third person to know?"

"What was there to tell you? From the beginning, you said the screen made me beautiful but I could not act. Now Mr. Hall says the same thing."

"He says you cannot act? Tell me every word he said." When I finished, Max said, "Oh, so you are still flapping your hand like a seal? Well, we have more work to do. This comes as a surprise? What are you discouraged about? Here, there, everywhere, what counts is what the camera does to you. You *like* the camera, little Anna. You know you like it. You like the great big eye watching you and no one but you. Who can get lost with that great big eye watching her? Don't you like the camera, little Anna?"

"That's enough," I said, turning on him. "Enough!"

"Why be ashamed? Can a human eye look at you so long and so hard without blinking? And all the humming, whirring noises and all the people watching, oh, you become better than you are when that eye opens and watches you. You walk right into the big pupil of that eye. What a wonderful eye that only sees how beautiful you are. Does that eye see a peasant? That eye sees an angel! People, can they be trusted? But the camera, that you can trust, the way it looks at you."

"What are you sounding so bitter about? It was your idea I come to this place!" I slammed shut a drawer. "*If* I had stayed at the Academy, *if* I had stayed in Sweden, I would have gone on the stage! I might never have seen a camera!"

I sat down on the edge of the bed. Max sat in the chair. Eventually, Max got up and sat on the balcony. I stared at my chest of drawers. Finally, I got up and sat down in the chair next to him.

"You can tell me what we're fighting about?" Max asked me. "Because I don't know."

I rocked in my rocking chair. "So," I said, "tomorrow we will go shopping, and then you will take me to see *Wartime*. There is a club somewhere, the Sewanee, where colored people sing spirituals."

Max sighed deeply. "Where is this club?" he asked. "In a terrible part of town from which no traveller returns?"

"Tomas will drive us there and bring us back."

"How do you even hear about these things? You don't talk to anyone. Anders said one night Erik Grissom drove by, he was going to pay us a visit, and he saw the two of us rocking here on the porch and he said to himself, 'I won't disturb the old folks.' Very nice. The old folks."

"So? At the end of the day," I said, "I am tired. And the end of the day is not the end of the day because then you begin teaching me, and then if I cannot sleep I have my English grammar and my big box of words. If I don't dance late at night, why should anyone be surprised?"

"Surprised? I don't think he was surprised. I think he saw us and thought, Those two look depressing. I'll do something else, something pleasant."

I said I was going to write my mother a letter.

"Why not?" Max said. "Why not write her a letter?"

That night, when he got into bed, I was so angry at him I got up, sat in the lounge chair on the porch and in the morning, the heat of the sun woke me.

"Are you ready yet?" Max asked. "What are you doing?"

I was looking for an umbrella. A party on a lawn—if it rained it would be the end of everyone's clothes.

"It is not going to rain," Max said.

"But why must they have a party outside? Weeks in advance they schedule them, but they cannot schedule the weather. They put up big tents but if there is a big rainstorm the tents would not keep out the rain and the food would be wet and spoiled. Such waste!"

"They have the parties outside to show they can afford it," Max said. "A big rainstorm, everyone's mascara running, wigs flying like birds into the pool, dresses sticking to breasts and thighs, tennis sweaters filled with water like sponges, everyone weighed down, the sandwiches wet, rain slanting into the punch, what could make Pinsky happier? Women running around in bare feet, holding their shoes, turning them upside down like cups to throw out the water, what a day it would be for him! Who would forget it? A party in good weather is just a party! A party in a hurricane, people will talk about it for years! They say he has three hundred dressing gowns for such a calamity! A shed full of firewood for his big fireplaces so everyone can sit around and dry out. Who else has three hundred dressing gowns?"

"Of course Anders will not come to this party," I said.

"Of course he *will.* You like to think Anders is such a pure soul? Pinsky pays him, too. And Erik will be there, and anyone else who knows what's good for him. And Miss Marsh, you like her, she will be there, and Mr. Hall, all kinds of people, even Charles Harrow, he will be there if he's back."

"Mr. Feldman?"

"Not important enough," Max said.

"But Charles Harrow will be there?"

"Charles Harrow and his two ex-wives. You've heard of them. They say anyone Charles Harrow marries, that woman becomes famous. If she isn't under contract already, Pinsky comes to the wedding with a contract for her to sign. Now, what are their names? His wife's? His daughters'?"

"Beatrice, Estelle and Vera," I said. "Beatrice and Estelle are the daughters. Vera is the wife."

Outside the hotel, a car horn honked gently. "Oh, that is Tomas already," I said. "Well, let's go. They will all talk about us, they think we don't understand a word, they say the most terrible things and we laugh and smile at them. I tell you, Max, when I am famous, I will make them pay."

"When?" said Max. "Not if? And if you get there, that alone won't be punishment enough for them? They won't look at you and then look at themselves, and ask, Why did it happen to her and not to me? I am just as beautiful. I am smarter. I worked longer and harder. Every time they see you it will be a punishment."

"It will not be enough," I said. "If they suffer, I want to see it in their faces. I want them to know I see it. That will be enough."

We got in the car. Max and Tomas exchanged gossip. I stared out at the sea, flat and blue, no cloud anywhere. In Stockholm, the fishermen were raising their green nets from their boats in the river. "You know," I said suddenly, "I think, even if I can't act, Mr. Hall likes me in spite of it. He does such things to Ricardo Bruno!" I started to laugh. Max's face lit up. Tomas too became a different person. Oh, I should remember this, I thought. When I am gloomy, I feel sorry for myself only. But now I am laughing, look how happy they are. Oh, you have plenty to be guilty about, I told myself.

"Well, you know Bruno, he is very pompous and in the movie, there he is pompous, too. And one night, he comes to my villa soaked by a storm and I am supposed to give him something warm and dry to put on. And Mr. Hall says, 'Let's make this interesting. Why must he have a plain pair of trousers and a shirt? Give him that black and white striped cape.' So I give him the black and white striped cape and he parades around in it, giving speeches about virtue and so preposterous does he look I can hardly keep from laughing and all around the set the stagehands are trying not to laugh and they make barking noises trying to keep quiet. And then Bruno stalks out of the room, still wearing the cape, and when he is offstage he throws it so it comes flying in through the door. And later, when he is older and I see him again? He is so old! Old and fat and gray, they powder him all over.

And short! How do they make him shorter? Short, practically a dwarf! He has the role of a hero but believe me it is hard to look at him and think he is a hero. In the last scene his poor gray wife takes off his shoes and massages his gouty feet and in the last shot, there I am, in my cape, as beautiful as Mr. Feldman can make me, getting into a car, holding all these roses, well, I am trying not to sneeze, but no one knows it. And it doesn't hurt, this trying not to sneeze, it produces the right expression. So what do you think? Isn't it funny?" I began to laugh.

Once again I saw Ricardo Bruno stalking around my room in my black and white fur cape and I burst out laughing and slapped my thigh.

"Well, when she is happy, the weather changes," Max said.

"What does it mean?" I asked.

"It means Mr. Hall does not like his leading man," Max said. "He had to wait two weeks for him to fade? I wouldn't like him either."

"In the last scenes, I must look at him with contempt," I said. "It isn't hard."

"It could be a little harder," Max said.

"What do you mean?" I asked him. He waved his hand and looked out over the flat, shining sea.

At the end of Mr. Pinsky's curving driveway was a huge white arcade covered with pale roses and red carnations, and in front of it stood Mr. Pinsky, his wife and two daughters.

"Smile, smile," said Max as I got out of the car.

Mr. Pinsky was doing the introductions himself.

Bertha was short and fat, her bosom resting comfortably on top of the belt of her navy blue dress. A mother duck! She was not what I expected. Her face was round, jolly, a face from a cookie jar, but her eyes were shrewd. Her finger-waved brown hair was perfectly combed. Both daughters were tall, browned, extremely homely and young, although not younger than I was. They stood, however, like princesses accustomed to receiving the boring tribute of commoners.

When our turn came to be introduced, Bertha nodded and smiled, the girls inclined their heads, a scarcely noticeable motion. Then, just as it was our turn to move off and make room for the people behind us, Bertha unclasped her small, white hands and rested her fingers on my arm. "So you are the beautiful girl I saw last night on the screen," she said. "Tell me, how old are you?"

"I am seventeen," I said.

"And already you speak a little English!" she said. "Good for you! Seventeen," she repeated. "And your mother was willing to sign a contract and let you go? She doesn't miss you?"

"All the time I am writing her," I said.

"But you miss her?" Bertha asked me. Her white, ringed fingers tightened on my arm. She wore a ring on every finger, the bands of the rings sinking into the white dough of her flesh.

"Oh, that is terrible, difficult to speak of," I said.

"But he pays you enough so you could call her," Mrs. Pinsky said. "Saul, you pay her enough?"

"She looks like she is dying of poverty?" Mr. Pinsky asked.

"She is alone in a strange country and she doesn't call her mother!" Bertha said. "How much money can she earn?" In back of us, people waiting to be introduced were murmuring. Who were we? Who were those people the Pinskys were talking to?

"Mrs. Pinsky," I said, "Mr. Pinsky's trouble it not is. My mother does not have telephone. Very poor woman she is."

"No telephone?" Mrs. Pinsky said, "Saul, her mother has no telephone!"

"Everyone must have a telephone?" Mr. Pinsky asked. "So in the middle of the night a terrible fright must throw them from their beds? Good for her mother!" Mr. Pinsky was nodding at someone behind us. I turned to look. Maud Marsh was part of what was now a long, long line waiting to greet the Pinskys. She stood arm in arm with someone who looked very much like Charles Harrow.

"Oh, too much time we are taking up," I said.

Mr. Pinsky nodded and smiled approval. His daughters' eyes skittered over me and away.

"Nonsense," Bertha said. "Saul, her mother must have a telephone."

"Fine, she'll have a telephone," he said.

"But Mrs. Pinsky," I stammered, "there is in Sweden no one my mother can telephone up. No one she knows who has telephone."

"She knows *you*," Mrs. Pinsky said. "The phone, when it rings, means you are calling. Do *you* have a telephone?"

"The small hotel I live in, it has telephone," I said.

"So, Bertha," Mr. Pinsky said, "our guests are restless. It's hot here out in the sun. Let the poor girl go and enjoy herself."

"How does it feel to be seventeen and sign a movie contract?" Bertha asked as if she hadn't heard him.

"Oh, it was very nice," I said. "Very nice."

"And your mother, when she signed it, she was happy?"

"When I told her, yes."

"But she signed it too?"

"Oh, no," I said. "She is not an actress."

"Saul, did you hear that? Her mother didn't sign the contract."

"So?" Mr. Pinsky said.

"She's seventeen," Bertha said.

"So?"

"She's not legal age," Bertha said.

Now Mr. Pinsky's eyes were on me. "You're seventeen?" he asked.

"Almost eighteen."

"A lovely girl like you, you should come into my office and we'll get to know each other. Bertha, you would like that? On Monday, lunch hour, you'll come in? It would be a great favor, a great favor. Bertha, she can go now?"

"Goodbye, dear," Bertha said. The two girls smiled uncertainly. Why had their parents taken so much time over me?

"Oh, thank God we are off the line," I said. "Where is a big tree to hide behind? Where is Anders? Where is Erik? Why is she talking all the time about a telephone?"

"An interesting woman, that Mrs. Pinsky," Max said. "And very smart. She understands a bargain. She gives you a telephone, you stay away from her husband. And the way she puts out her hand and stops the line! Just so she makes it clear. He runs the studio and she runs him. Well, that's the way it is in these families. What fat, fat little hands!"

"What is my mother going to do with a telephone? It will ring, it will scare the whole building to death! Who will pay the bill when it comes?"

"When you sign your new contract," Max said, "ask for twice as much money and stipulate that Pinsky pays the phone bill."

"What new contract?"

"Right now you don't have a contract," Max said. "The one you signed is no good. You're underage."

"He can get rid of me!"

"He doesn't want to get rid of you. He saw the rushes."

"A few feet of film!"

"But enough."

"Anna, Anna!" Maud was calling, pushing her way through the crowd. "Oh, Anna, the rushes! Marvelous! I knew it! I told them! Charlie, you've met Anna? No? Anna, meet the star of *Wartime*. Erik, where are you? Erik, you've met Charlie? Where's Anders? Look, he's over there under that palm tree. Oh, see that! Who's that blonde feeding him pineapple chunks! Oh, he's disgraceful! And the blondes are worse! So, Anna, how does it feel to be queen of the lot?"

"Everyone knows *you* are queen of the lot," Max said to her.

"Flatterer! There's the real queen of the lot! Bertha Pinsky! At night, she takes off her disguise and rises up out of bed a beautiful princess."

"*Someone* rises up out of Pinsky's bed a beautiful princess," Charlie said.

"A regal presence," said Max.

"What we should do," Charlie said, looking at me, "what we should do is get out of here and get drunk."

"I know a place, the Sewanee," I said. "Erik said they have good brown beer and there are Negroes singing spirituals."

"I know the Sewanee," Charlie said. "Maud, how long do we have to stay? I always ask Maud," he said. "She's the one who understands these things."

His hair was curly and black. His huge eyes were brown, almost black, and in the sun his teeth flashed, such white teeth, I'd never seen such teeth.

Maud looked at her watch. "Another hour," she said.

"Then we go to the Sewanee," I said happily.

Max looked at me, astonished. He was holding a glass of gin. I took it from him and sipped it. Over the rim of the glass, I watched Charlie Harrow. He had his arm around Maud's waist and was slipping his fingers beneath her belt. Then, with his index finger, he pulled the back of her brassiere and let it snap against her skin. There is something between them, I thought. Charlie smiled at me, half friendly, half mocking. Oh, I can get him for myself, I thought. I looked over at Max. He was watching me out of narrowed eyes, an expression on his face I had never seen before. At first I could not place it and then I knew what it was. It was rage.

The palm fronds waved. The banners on top of the tents streamed in the air. The grass was green and gold and the palm fronds were gilded. Waiters in white uniforms passed carrying gold trays that caught the light and sent gilt rays through the bubbling champagne glasses. In back of us, a band began playing a song I'd heard before: *I want to be happy, but I can't be happy, unless you're happy too.* And then everything changed. The color was gone from the scene. Everything was in shades of black and white, but worse, everything was a negative of itself. People's faces were black, their teeth black, their hair white. Their white suits were black, their white dresses were black, their skin was black. Their dark eyes shone white. Tomas's blond hair had gone black. His eyebrows were gray in a black face. People in black shoes walked on the gray grass. The sky was dull black, the sun a dark hole.

This was not the world of the living. All around me were shades, what was left of people after they stopped breathing, their images caught on film not yet developed. Max was smiling at me, his teeth black in a grayish-black face.

So this is what it means, I thought. This is what happens when the world exists only to be put onto film. I looked at my black hand and raised it to my black face. My hair was black, my eyes were black. Two brunettes with white hair walked by, arm in arm. Somewhere they were filming us. Somewhere we were caught inside of cameras and in them this is what we looked like. Then the film would be projected and once more our teeth would be white, our blond hair blond, Charlie Harrow's black hair black, not white, and who would notice that we had no dimension, no color?

If the sun shone any brighter, it would shine through us and then we would be skeletons walking beneath the trees.

Did I see that vision then, as I remember seeing it, or now, looking back, do I think that is what I saw?

"Anna! Anna!" said Max. "What's wrong with you?"

"Oh, it's too hot!" Maud said. "These stupid parties, everyone standing in the sun drinking and getting heatstroke! Let's go inside."

"Is there an inside?" Charlie asked. "This isn't a stage set?"

"Quiet!" Maud said to him. "People can hear you. Every word gets back to Pinsky."

"To the Sewanee!" Charlie said, dramatically flinging out his arm. "All in my car!"

"We came in our own car," Max said stiffly, but Maud was laughing and saying it was easier to go along, just go along, Max, and so Max and I, Charlie and Maud and Tomas headed for Charlie's small canary-colored convertible. Erik would follow in Tomas's car.

"Who will be driving this car?" Max asked. "Not someone drunk."

"I alone shall drive," said Maud.

"Maud, driving, Max here in front next to her, me and the big Swede in the back, and Anna on my lap," Charlie said.

Max looked at me.

"The lap is fine," I said.

"The lap is fine," Max mumbled, folding himself into the front of the car.

"Here we go!" Maud shouted and we pulled away in a spray of gravel.

"Good old Maud," Charlie sighed, settling back. "Sit back," he said. I sat back. Charlie's arm was around my shoulders. Carefully I adjusted myself against his knees, his chest.

"I am sorry if I am hurting you," I said.

"No one worries about hurting me," he said. He laughed but his laugh was bitter.

"You must tell me if I hurt you," I said.

He laughed again. His hand moved up from my waist, paused at my breast and then my breast was cupped in his hand. Wherever his hand touched me, there I shone with heat and fire, but when I saw his face, I saw his eyes were closed. I knew he was half asleep, that to him I could be anyone. And so I said, You must not do that.

"No?" he said sleepily, and his hand slid back to my waist.

A few minutes passed. Maud was shouting something to us from the front seat. "You are very beautiful," Charlie whispered in my ear. My ear was touched with fire.

"You don't even know who I am!" I said furiously.

"You are the girl who doesn't want to hurt me," he said.

"Let me out of the car!" I said.

Max turned around. "Is anything wrong?" he asked me.

"I am fine," I said. "Fine absolutely." And then, enraged as I was, I settled back against this deplorable man, this drunken lamentable man, this profligate, this automatic Don Juan, and my body, as if it had a will of its own, sighed with excitement and delight.

The Sewanee was housed in a large square building. The cinder block walls kept out the heat and inside, the walls were painted navy blue. The little bluish smokes rose up from each table, scrim after scrim. From the first time, I loved this place, where Negro singers came and sang of their vanished lives, their lost homes. Always, before when I came here, I grew calm. But tonight I was not calm. The sight of Charlie dancing with Maud, her body pressed into his, kissing her with his eyes closed as if it were too much trouble for him to open them, as if, should he open his eyes, he would be expected to remember her name, this made me incensed. And so, when Charlie left our table to talk to someone else, I leaned over and said, "Maud! Let's flirt with Tomas! Life is too peaceful for him!"

Max heard me and regarded me with disgust.

"Who do you think will get him?" Maud asked me.

"Well, let's see," I answered.

"You are making a fool of yourself over this Harrow person," Max said.

"What has he to do with anything?" I asked Max. "It's all in fun. Let's see what kind of sirens we are!"

"Let's see!" Maud said, laughing.

"She knows him for an hour and already she's lying to herself," Max said in Swedish. I paid no attention.

We lavished ourselves upon Tomas. No matter what he said— "Would you like a drink? Do you want to dance?"—we reacted as if we had heard the most passionate declaration of love. Tomas grew flattered, then confused. Did he dare approach either of us? And if he chose one of us, what retribution might he expect from the other?

Max sat still, one leg crossed over the other, watching us.

I bent forward, I bent further still and sipped some wine from Tomas's glass where it rested on the table. I felt his eyes slide into the space between my breasts. I knew, when I raised my eyes, his face would be flushed, his forehead would be sweaty, he would be in my web. I looked up.

"Dance with me," Tomas said. His voice was thick.

"Satisfied now?" Max asked.

Charlie was returning to the table. He passed me where I danced, pressed disgracefully, seductively, against Tomas. If he noticed, he gave no sign. Later, as we were leaving, I heard him say to Maud, "Your friend goes for the big dumb silent types," and I thought, I hate that man. It is because of him that I am in so much trouble. Because I would have to placate Max, who saw how I had flirted with Tomas, all to attract Charlie's attention, and in the morning, I would have on my hands a love-crazed translator and what would I do with him? I would have to make up a story, I would have to say I was drunk, and in my drunkenness, I mistook him for my long-lost love, the young man who in Sweden committed suicide for love of me, some such nonsense, but a romantic young man, he would believe it. It was embarrassing, it was humiliating, and it was Charlie Harrow's fault. And meanwhile Maud, who was leaning over Tomas's shoulder, whispering in his ear, caught my eye and winked at me. Well, of course, this really is not nice, I thought. Not nice. In the morning, she too would have some explaining to do.

The Negro sang a spiritual about his lost mother, his lost home, and when he was finished, I went up to him, moving through the crowd as if I were very drunk. I pressed a five-dollar bill into his hand, I said something maudlin about how I too was far from home, and the singer, his face wet with sweat, smiled nervously at me, and I thought, Oh, he is not allowed to talk to the customers, perhaps that is why

Max tried to hold my arm when I got up to walk to the platform. I wove back to my seat, and Charlie looked at me as if I were an extra knife or fork on the tablecloth and said, "We better get this one home."

He is bored, I thought. I bore him.

And then I thought, Will I sit on his lap on the way home? I want to sit on his lap on the way home.

And even as I sat on his lap, shot through with a foolish happiness, I thought, In the morning he will not remember me. He will not remember any of this. That is how drunks are. From childhood I have known all about this. And even as I felt it, the disgust and hatred, I nestled closer to him, closer to his starched blue shirt.

"So," Max said later as we got ready for bed, "how did you enjoy the evening?"

"That Charlie Harrow!" I said. "I hate him!"

When we lay side by side, I began to stroke Max's back and shoulders. My hand moved downwards, but his hand stopped mine. "So now you think you want to make love to me?" he asked. "Not tonight, Anna! I don't like being an extra!"

"What are you talking about?" I demanded.

Max sat up and jumped out of bed. "Can she really be so stupid?" he asked the room. "Yes," he answered himself. "The young and the inexperienced can be so stupid."

"It was only harmless flirting with Tomas!" I said. "'Only a little fun!"

"Fun!" Max exclaimed. "Harmless!" He went out onto the balcony. In the morning, I found him there, asleep in the deck chair.

I SAT ON MY BED and watched Ivy pack. In went the slacks, the blouses, the sweaters, the underwear. By now she had it down to a science. She had two lists: one for warm climates, one for cold, and, if both hot and cold weather were possible, she included everything underlined in red.

"Aspirin," said Ivy. "Dental floss, medicine for the fluttery heart, warm socks, toothbrush, toothpaste, shampoo, rubber bands to pull your hair back, what have I left out?" She sat back on her heels and stared into the suitcase.

"It is a civilized country I am going to," I said. "If I forget something, I can buy it there."

"Why should you buy it if you already have it?" she asked me. "A curling iron, or you are not going to bother?"

"I'm not going to bother."

"How many cans of tuna fish in water?"

"One for each day."

"But this time, eat them!" Ivy said. "Every time when you come back, there are the cans and you complain your ankle is swollen!"

"Well, it is not always possible to open a can at a restaurant table."

"Better to have a swollen ankle? Eat the tuna. And some salt-free matzos. I have to buy another box."

"All this is very boring," I said.

"The hospital is more boring."

"Well, go get the matzos then." And while she was gone I sat on the bed and thought about going back to Sweden.

When I first came to America, I said I would go back every year, but of course, in the beginning, that was impossible. I was always working. And then there were personal complications. So all in all, if I was lucky, I went back every two years. My mother was there, my brother, my sister, and it was the landscape I knew, the only place I felt I belonged. But each time I went back, I belonged less. Each time I went back it was more of a duty, more of a disappointment. Was there one of us to whom it did not happen?

We longed for the snow and the long, dark, gloomy days when everyone stayed inside and dreamed, but when we got home, there was more snow than we remembered and it was harder to walk through and the ice, when it appeared, was grayer and more dangerous, with the glint of a shark's fin. We were tired of the way everyone in America rushed about, but at home everything was too slow. How long could it take to make a phone call? Why did it take so long for someone to fix a pair of shoes?

Soon we were discontented and mumbling. The Christmas fruitcake, what was wrong with it? It never had figs in it before! It was never this dark! Before there were more raisins, more walnuts. Whose idea was it to put in bananas? From year to year the fruitcake was the same. What went wrong this year?

The first Christmas I went back, that was a disaster. I expected to settle into the old apartment, to forget about movies, to talk to my mother and sister, to be the same as I was the day I left. And then one morning I heard myself say, "You can never get warm enough here. How do you stand it?" Only two years gone by and already I didn't belong.

And it got into the papers: "Anna Asta Comes Home!" Every time people followed me in America, I would tell Max, This would never happen at home! At home people respect your privacy! And I believed it. I had to believe it. Who can believe the hounds will hunt you forever? But it was no different at home.

Crowds of people outside the apartment building and no one to protect us. So after a few days we all moved into a big hotel with doormen and elevators and gadgets people spoke into from the lobby so we could first speak to them and see if we wanted them to come up. My mother found it very exciting, and my sister too. My brother said if we had to suffer, best to suffer in luxury. He particularly liked room service. We saw quite a lot of the waiters because if we left our rooms we were surrounded.

Our suite had three rooms, but after the first night, we found ourselves rattling about and for the rest of the time we all slept in one of the big beds.

In the middle of the night, I got up and found my mother awake, sitting on the couch. I sat down next to her. "Anna," she said. "Can I unhook that telephone? All the time people are getting the number and all night the phone rings and the telephone company, they are tired of changing the number. You understand?"

I understood. "I will teach you to call me collect," I said.

So snowy, so dark, so cold, such a smell of pine in the air. Did the sun never shine here? What did people do all day? And my father, where was he? Of course I knew he was dead. Still, in the back of my mind I must have thought, Oh, it's been two years, by now he's decided to come back. It was a terrible visit.

And Anders, when he took his wife and children home, the same thing. The children wanted the same toys they had in America. Who were these people kissing them all the time? Why must they be seen and not heard? They didn't like the food, so salty and full of vinegar! When could they go out and play? Why was it always snowing? Always dark? When could they go home? And when his mother heard that, *When can we go home?* she began crying and couldn't stop. *Here is where you belong! This is your home! This is where you did great things! Stay here until the children forget that other place!* Of course it was too late for him also. He went back to America, his face hardened and turned away.

And then, when we were unhappy, what could we say? Now we will go home? Wherever we were, that was home. Wherever we were, that was no good because it was not the other place. Who can understand this? Only another exile. Today, what do I miss that I go back so often? The time of my youth. Now when I walk the streets, they all come back as they were then: Max, Erik, Anders, Marianne, my sister, my brother, my mother, my father. If the place has stayed the same, I can sit on a garden wall and soon I feel as I once did. We come so far only so we can want to go back again.

They say Eleanor is growing senile. She thinks her nurse is her mother or her cousin or a friend from Studio days. Everyone shakes his head and says this is too bad. Does she seem unhappy? I ask them. Oh, no, they say. She seems very happy. But it is terrible to see her! Terrible for them, but not for her! The old warm world has reached out and taken her back.

"Ivy," I say, "you never want to go back to Green Island and live?"

"No, not really," she says. "It was the place I grew up. But now I'm not used to its ways. Everyone in everyone else's business, no, that is not for me anymore." *Not anymore. Not since Tita Lu died.* "The children, they like to go back and say, *This is where I came from. This is the house I grew in. Here I went to school.* When someone recognizes them, they are so happy! *It is Ivy's daughter, isn't it? You still like cinnamon candy, don't it?* It's nice, doing the old things the old ways, for a few days it's nice, and then you want your own ways back. And it is hot, hot, hot! When I first came here, I thought I would die from the cold, but now when the heat beats down on my head, I send one of the boys for a taxi and they carry me to the market. Better just to think about it. For that you don't even need a passport."

Well, that's how it is. Time is so busy with us. Time, that one-way street. Well, I envy Eleanor, going back against the traffic. And Maud, the same thing, all the time talking to her husband who died sixty years ago. And all their relatives after them, trying to push them into the present! *Mother! It's Alice! Your daughter! Mother! Daddy's dead!* Finally they find a heaven of their own and no one will leave them in it. Well, at least someone can go back. But these trips home, they never end well.

I wonder: who does Eleanor think she sees from Studio days? Anyone I know? Oh, I am terrible! I can't grow senile myself, but I must want to borrow her senility! They'll say I died in full possession of my senses, as if I ever had any!

I suppose it means she's going to die soon. Usually that's what it means.

In the end, I miss the old food. When I get home, I'm going to eat pickled herring and meatballs and red cabbage, and brown beans, brown beer and brown bread. To hell with the salt-free tuna! To hell with it all.

14

ONCE, LONG AGO, back home, in the Lagerloff Studios, Anders had finished a film called *Death Train*, in its day a very famous film, a film still famous today in Scandinavia. The studio executives wanted Anders to release the film in time for the Christmas holidays, especially since the hero of the film died on New Year's Eve at the stroke of midnight, and, thanks to the pure love of a dying young woman who had given her life to God, was reborn on New Year's Day.

The film was finished but not edited and Anders asked Max for help. I sat in the little white-walled room and watched Anders and Max pull down the black fabric that was suspended in rolls from each wall, and then Anders began to edit.

"Well, this much of his past life is not necessary. We get the point. He is a drunken brute." And snip, snip went Anders' scissors, and a bit of film fell to the floor and curled up there like a pig's tail. When I grew bored, I picked up a strip of film, took it outside and held it up to a bright light. There were tiny photographs of Anders, who was, as usual, playing the leading role, one after another, each barely different from the next, but of course, when speeded up, there was motion, there was the illusion of life. Each frame was like a little cell, confined by tiny white strips. The actor stood in each cell like a trapped criminal, but when the film ran, there were no small rooms, no one was walled up, everything was continuous. And I thought, in life it is also like that and the problem is always how to jump from one moment to another so that time does not become empty, so that you do not freeze in one position forever.

When I went back into the room, Anders and Max were staring with horror at a reel of film. "It can't be, not the whole reel!" Anders said. "The lab would have told me!"

Max said nothing but took the reel, threaded it through and started up the projector. On the black wall, a white square appeared. The film ran and the white square flickered, changed in intensity, but no image emerged.

"This is a disaster beyond imagination!" said Anders, who seized the hair on both sides of his head and began pulling at it as if he would tear it out at the roots.

"Let's see where the break is," Max said. He picked up the previous reel and looked at the last few frames of film. Then he picked up the next reel and inspected it. "When you are calmer, I have a suggestion," he said. Anders sat at a small pine table, gnawing at his thumb. Finally he looked up. "All right," he said. "What is the suggestion?"

"A caption," said Max. "It will read 'Fifty years later.' "

To Anders, this was nonsense. He shook his head and continued chewing on the flesh of his hand.

"Why not?" Max asked. "The man's been brought back from the dead. He goes home and promises to reform. Do we have to see him reform? Tomorrow we can make you up as an old man and shoot you kneeling in front of an altar and in the back, your wife smiling and nodding, and two middle-aged people on either side of her, also smiling and nodding, both blond, so everyone knows those were the small children from the last reel."

"I don't even want to hear about it," Anders said. "That was always our joke. The lab made a mistake, we didn't match our shots, so we put in a card reading 'Fifty years later.' This is not a joke. This is my life!"

"You can save the picture and no one will know the difference," Max said.

"The author of the story will know," Anders said.

Now Max sat back in his chair, knees crossed, his elbow resting on his knee, a cigarette between his second and third fingers, the smoke rising up in tiny grayish-blue coils, saying nothing, waiting.

"Still," Anders said, "it would work."

"Perhaps even better," Max said. "Not so sentimental."

"An aged man kneeling before a church altar, his decrepit wife and ancient children in the back smiling, that is not sentimental?" Anders asked.

"No one said you had to shine a light on him. You don't have to backlight him so that his hair glows with the glory of God. Just an old man with his family in an ordinary church, maybe with a few broken windows, like the church around the corner from the Lagerloff Studios, a little snow blowing in the windows, the old man on his knees, shivering, the old woman and the children shivering, a little snow blowing across the face of the man on the crucifix, a little snow falling from Christ's face onto the man's old wool jacket, very suggestive, very subtle. How long can it take us to shoot it? We develop it ourselves, we splice the film together, we're done."

"A sentimental ending," Anders said contemptuously.

"A man saved from death by the pure love of a dying young girl, that's the plot. Or do I have it wrong? The whole story is sentimental."

"What I had before was better!"

"Then release this version, get yourself out of trouble with the executive committee and film the sequences again. You can get the actors back."

Anders watched the wall as if a film only he could see was playing there. "It would work. A church with snow blowing through the broken windows, I like that touch. And across the face of Christ, I like that as well. And it's true, after it's released, what's to prevent me from reshooting the lost reel?"

"Even better, shoot the director of the lab," Max said.

"Of course there were shots in that reel I can never duplicate. Light coming down in rays through breaks in the clouds, each ray hitting a tombstone in the churchyard, a miracle of lighting. Well, that's gone."

"Worse can happen," Max said.

"Thank God none of the double exposures were on that reel," Anders said. "Then I would have to kill myself."

He resumed editing. Max sat in his chair. I sat on the windowsill. This frame, yes. This frame, yes. This one, no. Snip, snip. And then he was finished. The film was a great success. Anders shot the last scenes just as Max had described them. Eventually, he reshot the lost reel and later, the new, longer film was shown every year at Christmas, and even later, every New Year's Eve. I myself always preferred the shorter version: when the camera stopped, the title card read "Fifty years later," and life jumped ahead.

Often I have heard people say, I'm sure I've been here before. I know this room, this place, this person. I know what he is going to say because, once before, I was here when he said it. It happens to everyone. Some of us start to believe we have lived many times before because, otherwise, how could we know? I remember the first time I saw Charles Harrow, and I thought, Oh, I know him already. And at that time, I thought, Yes, I have lived before.

And then, after I had been making movies for ten years, I had that sensation all the time. No experience seemed new to me. Everything was slightly worn, a book that someone had read before me, handled carefully so that the book appeared new, but still, when you picked it up, you knew someone else had been there before. And that was when I began to hesitate, that was when my self-confidence began to go. Because if you think, Oh, this is happening again, this has happened before, then you do not react spontaneously. Your instincts no longer tell you what to do. How can they? Instead you hesitate, a slight pause, barely noticeable, as if you had forgotten your lines but quickly remembered them, because what you are doing is comparing what is happening now with what you think happened before. And always: what was it that happened before? Nothing that happened in real life. Something I had acted in a film.

In films, I had loved, betrayed my lover, been betrayed by him, died for love, seen my lover die for love, borne children, had children torn from my arms, married, been faithful or unfaithful, spied for my country, betrayed my country, grown old and saintly, grown old and drunk, taken to prostitution or a nunnery. Did I ever do anything that required brains, that was worthwhile? Once, perhaps. In a comedy. And so, when something first happened in life, it was happening for the second time, or the third, or the fourth. In life, the event was new but the emotions, of course they had happened before, in a film, a strip of celluloid that the director might have held up in his hand, looked at, and said, *Not that one. It will go faster without that one*, and so it was gone, but still, it had happened to me, and emotion becomes memory, takes its place in the attic of your mind. You cannot get rid of it. This emotion, caused by something on a thin celluloid strip— and perhaps it does not exist anymore, perhaps it perished on the floor of the editing room—it is a real emotion, as strong as any other.

And so I was forever remembering things that had not really happened, at least not in the usual sense.

Of course now it is easy to understand, but then? Then, when I was young, I grew mystical and dreamy. I believed I had known Charlie before, in another life. So when I met him, I thought, This is my second chance. There was purpose in our meeting, inevitability, fatedness. Oh, the romance was irresistible, powerful. We spent hours with a Ouija board, with a fortune teller, with a pack of Tarot cards. A strange fat man in a dirty black suit came to our house, mumbled into his beard, and sent us into a trance that would take us back through time. Something went wrong, I don't remember what. Charlie jumped out of his chair, tried to knock the man down, and the two of them rolled over and over on the floor.

Every night for a week we went to a small movie theater and watched a film that began with a wedding, a lovely wedding, but the groom could not use his left arm and so wore it in a sling and became despondent, while his bride had fear in her heart and could not make physical love. When she saw her husband's shadow on the wall, she would tremble with fear. And none of this made the slightest sense until they learned they had lived before, and in their previous lives, he had done something terrible to his wife and so his arm was crippled and in her soul was a shadow which refused her husband forgiveness and trust.

Then came a terrible train crash and the husband and wife were pinned, she against the headlight of one train, he in the wreckage of the other, a few feet from one another, unable to move. And the crash shattered time and space and sent them back to their earlier life, and, when they regained consciousness, they could atone for what had happened before, and so in this life lived happily ever after.

Could it happen? Could it happen? I asked Charlie that. Every night I lay awake, asking myself the same thing. Could it happen? What had I been, what had I done, in my previous life? If I did something wrong, if I was now being punished, how much that would explain! But how to get back?

I tried self-hypnosis. I tried examining my dreams. And I was continually afflicted by the conviction that I had done this before, seen that before, known this person before, and each time, I would stop and think, This is a splinter from a past life. What does it mean?

At The Studio, I often played opposite Walter Drake, not a remarkable actor, but a dignified one. That's what they said about him—an unremarkable man. I've mentioned him before. Again and again I insisted on him. And why? Because from the first I believed I'd known him in a previous life. And now, fifty years later, it is clear. He had Max's face. That face, that lost face.

And now, when I try to go on with my story, I would like to pick the film up in my hand, hold it up to the light, and say, *Not this year, not this one, not this one.* Finally, I would cut out so much, there would be so many celluloid curls on the floor, I would say, All right, now let's put in a title card that reads "Sixty years later." Because it is sixty years later.

But in life things do not happen as they did in Anders' movie. No one dies and is reborn as if new. If we are reborn at all, we are given new strength, but we go on with the same scarred bodies, the same foxed, dog-eared minds.

Oh, yes, in the eighteenth year of my life there were great changes, but did they produce great changes in me? And if they did, what kind of changes were they?

Well, for everything you pay a price. So Anders always said. But

sometimes you do not know what the price will be, or you think you
have paid it, but you paid the wrong creditor, and when the bill comes
due, you look in horror and say, "If I had known!" Like every criminal!

So I am going back now, back in time. We have finished filming
The Roses. Max is beginning work on *The Siren,* in which I am to star.
At last we are working together. What can go wrong now? *Sixty years
later! Sixty years later!* Where are the scissors? Oh, it is unbearable that
life will not let itself be cut up like a film!

Yet while you are living your life, you think it can be done. You
do. This thing that happened today, tomorrow I will fix it. That which
I did not notice today, tomorrow I will notice and take care. Well,
now it is fifty years later, and to go back, to see everything, to speak,
to warn, but not to be heard, now that nothing can be changed, when
people speak of hell, this is what they mean.

I am a tower of sins of omission.

*In the mountains, there is an isolated village. The people who live there are
said to be happy. Few people come to visit this village, and those who do generally
come to bathe in the mineral springs.*

*One day a carriage pulls up in front of the only inn in the town and a
beautiful woman steps out, but this causes little comment. After all, the town is
full of beautiful women. A week after her arrival a grocer begins beating his
wife. An apothecary sends cough syrup laced with arsenic to a small child.
When he is accused, he has no defense. He merely wrings his hands. Terrible
things begin to happen. Wives are seen at all hours, going through the streets,
warm shawls over their shoulders, looking for their husbands. Gradually, it
becomes clear: the woman who came to take the waters is the cause of the trouble.
It is rumored that she has a demon lover.*

*The priest, an expert on demons, says yes, a woman with a demon lover
casts two shadows, her own dark one, and a lighter shadow, in the shape of the
demon she loves. When she stands against the light, the outline of the demon
lover can sometimes be plainly seen.*

*The doctor disagrees. This was not how one knows a woman has a demon
lover. No matter what such a woman does, he said, men fall in love with her.
This is one way we know she has a demon lover. And what is a demon lover?
He is not the man she is with, no, never. He is a man the woman has seen, seen
once, and forgotten she has seen, but with every breath, she thinks of him. She
thinks only of him. He is what hovers at the edge of eyesight. He is the man
she kisses with such passion, the man she regards with such longing. We know
she has a demon lover when we see how ordinary are the men she kisses, yet
how radiant is her look, how her eyes light up and burn as she looks at them.*

We know she has a demon lover because of the shine on her skin, by the way she is lit from inside, as if there were always a full moon casting its ray only upon her.

People say that if you photograph a woman who has a demon lover, his outline can be seen just behind hers, but, said the doctor, this is nonsense; this is what the vulgar believe. She is lethal because she is a woman in love with her own creation. Nothing is more beautiful than a young woman in love with a man she cannot see but whom she senses every moment of the day. Every move she makes she makes in relation to him. When she sits, she inclines slightly, bending herself toward him. Every word she says she says to him. The slight pause before she answers, this is the time she listens to him.

This is what makes her so deadly. She kisses with great passion, she touches the body of the man she lies with as if there were nothing more precious. She weeps at the very idea of harm coming to him. She insists he is the pivot on which the universe spins, that the universe is inconceivable without him. And yet the man she is with knows: he knows he is not the beloved. He knows, in her terrible hunger, she has taken him for someone else. But who can resist the concentration of her, the splendor, the magnificent intensity? No one human can resist it. Everything she touches shines with romance, romance which wraps passion at its core. She transfigures the world. Who could turn from her?

Does she know she has a demon lover? asked the doctor. No. She does not. This is the secret of her power, her absolute power, her easy, almost thoughtless subjugation.

What happened to the woman? What could happen? She died by her own hand. Wherever she went, the same thing: church bells tolling, women grabbing her hem and pleading, men she spurned throwing themselves into rivers. And for what? She could not understand it.

I am truly innocent, she told the priest, who turned from her in revulsion. I am truly innocent, she told the doctor, who believed her. Then what must I do? she asked him. The doctor left a bottle of white powder on his table and left the room. When he came in, she was sitting very still in his chair.

And probably, said the doctor, the demon lover was nothing much: an ordinary man. Isn't that always how it is?

Maud Marsh has arranged a private screening of *The Roses*, for Max and for me, for Anders and Erik, all of us who worked in Sweden together. Tomas is coming too.

The small room darkens, the screen lights up, the title flashes by and there, right beneath the name of Ricardo Bruno, is my own name, almost as large. Max is holding tightly to my hand. Scene after scene flows onto the white screen. I watch each scene and remember what happened the day of the filming. I remember sitting in the donkey

cart and flapping my hand and the outraged screams of Mr. Hall:
Wave! Wave! But I was waving! Why was he still shouting at me?

Or the scene in the garden when I sit down and play the piano
and how I began to laugh when I was supposed to sing. "What's the
matter now?" Mr. Hall asked and I told Tomas, "Now I must do two
things I cannot do: sing and play the piano." At the time, this struck
me as unbearably funny. And Mr. Bruno stalked around the garden
muttering, "Amateur! Foreigner!" and that only made it worse. Everyone in America thought he was a Spaniard when really, so Mr. Feldman told me, he was born in the Bronx.

I sat in the dark and watched myself change from a poor girl who
fed chickens and carried pails of slop out to pigs to a famous opera
singer who wore beautiful clothes and learned the bitterness of success. I was awkward. Sometimes I was terrible. But the story was worse.

It was not a story at all, only a silly dream. No European would
dream it: only an American in a country where everyone likes to say
that any child born here can hope to grow up and someday become
President.

When it was over and the lights went on, I looked around from
beneath my eyelids. No one was in a hurry to look at me. Finally Erik
said, "Well, Anna, it's a beginning."

"She was very good when she sees that fat old lover," Anders said.
"That was very good. Impressive. Wouldn't you call that impressive?"
He looked at Max, who, stricken, looked at me.

"Well," I said, "a disaster is a disaster. There is no point in wasting time thinking about it. Stupid from beginning to end, and what's
worse, next week they release it and the whole country will be laughing at me."

"No, no," Anders said. "They will put the blame where it belongs."

"And in any case," Erik said, "the whole country has better things
to do than laugh at you. You think it will happen, but you walk down
the street, they don't know who you are, and their minds are on the
price of gasoline."

"Gasoline?" I said. "Why not? Why spend time talking? Let's go
to the Sewanee and get drunk."

"But Anna," Erik said, "you cannot get drunk! You drink and drink
until you fall asleep."

"I can try," I said.

And so I had no hopes. The Studio had photographed me wrapped in
Ricardo Bruno's arms, and that photograph was printed on all the
posters advertising the film. Mr. Feldman did a series of portraits and

those were sent to magazines and newspapers. Publicity flacks hinted that the passions of the screen reflected the ardors of real life. Ricardo Bruno smiled mysteriously whenever he was asked about me. "A gentleman from my country does not speak of the women in his life." That was what he said and no thunderbolt struck him dead. Interviewers who must have been bribed, arrived and asked predictable questions to which I had no answers: What was my life like before I came here? How was California different from Sweden? Had Max Lilly really discovered me sitting in a geography class when he came to film scenes at our school? I would try to answer, but if Tomas was dissatisfied with my reply, he would give his own.

Eventually, The Studio decided to portray me as a poor girl from a poor but noble family, a deep creature whose passions were so strong and so secret they left her speechless.

"Oh, I am really a very ordinary girl," I said during the third interview. "The people who call me a peasant are not so wrong." This was changed. In the papers, I said, "I would like to be an ordinary girl, a peasant working in the fields. Instead I am born with a talent that throws me out of bed in the morning and does not let me rest at night. I pray to have it lifted from my shoulders, to be, as others around me are, normal. But since that is not to happen, I must resign myself and become what I was born to be. People believe talent is a wonderful thing, but it is a master you must serve with all your heart and soul. Often I feel unworthy. But there are times when I know I am not. It is for those times that I live."

I went to Mr. Pinsky's office in great agitation. "This must stop," I said.

"What must stop?" he asked me. I showed him the interview.

"Not one word of this did I say. Not one word. I will not have people putting words into my mouth. It is all silliness. It is undignified. You must stop it." He was astonished.

"What am I hearing?" he cried in amazement. "All day long, a parade of actresses in here, and everyone with the same complaint! No publicity! If there was some publicity, the world would know them, they would make a fortune! Instead I let them spoil like potatoes in a cellar! And you come in and complain that all over the papers there are stories about you! It is making you unhappy? This attention is making you miserable? This being a movie star, you don't like it? Tell me now. I'll find someone else. You're telling me I should find someone else?" I said, No, no, that was not it. He misunderstood me.

"What am I misunderstanding?" he asked me. "It is part of the job or it isn't part of the job? You don't know your own life? So they take a plain handkerchief and they embroider a little. It hurts you? Later, you become a big, big star, then you can give an interview. Then tell the truth. Then insist you're a peasant. The Studio doesn't hire peasants! I don't have peasants working for me! Even Bettina, she can't speak one word of English, not one word can she speak, she worked in an iron factory, a welder, I'm going to let her say she's a peasant? She has an imagination! She's a countess! With an accent, you can be anything here! When you're a big, big star, then you say what you want. In the meantime, where's the harm in it? It's undignified? It's dignified to stand all day in front of a camera and make faces? Go home and pray *Roses* doesn't lose a fortune. You know how much this undignified business is costing us? I'm going to spend a fortune on *The Siren* and in it I'm going to put a peasant? You want to be in *The Siren?* You want to work with Mr. Lilly? This is ingratitude! You know you are being ungrateful?"

And so he went on, working himself up until he had tears of self-pity in his eyes, but he had made it clear: I cooperated with The Studio or Max worked with someone else in *The Siren.*

And even Maud had no sympathy when I complained about the interviews, the campaign of rumors. "Pinsky knows what he's doing," she said. "He's the best there is. Let me give you a piece of advice. He's a powerful man. You don't fight someone powerful until you have more power than they do. You remember that, you won't have any trouble here."

And so I was sitting on the porch, studying my grammar the night the picture opened. There was no opening night party. Mr. Pinsky sent a note saying that, given my state of nerves, he was sure I would be happier without one.

"You see?" Maud said. "He's punishing you."

But, I told her, I didn't want a party. To pretend pride in a movie I thought was so bad!

"You *should* want one," she said. "When people start coming up to you and saying, 'Don't worry, next time you'll have a party,' then you'll feel it."

"I won't," I said. Of course I was wrong.

Roses was an enormous success. I became "A Fiery Star from the Frozen North." Columnists announced that "beneath that black wig lay the golden hair of Nordic beauty." "Her eyes are so blue that she has to look up from under lidded eyes or her blue eyes photograph as white!" "A hundred photographs, a hundred different women!" "Are we seeing the birth of a goddess?" And on and on. It was inexplicable, shaming, exciting, all at the same time. Whatever it was, I didn't trust it. It could not last.

"Is it Pinsky?" I asked Max. "This publicity?"

"People are seeing what I saw," he said.

I said, "You were the first."

He said, "How long will that matter?" And then we began work on *The Siren*.

PART THREE

THE TEMPTRESS

I LOVE THE WAY Ivy tells the story of her life, such a straightforward account, and such a sense of inevitability. But she says the clarity and inevitability are just an illusion. Nothing was clear. Nothing was inevitable. If her stepmother hadn't lied and said she came home late from her private lessons, then she might have become a schoolteacher and a writer like her sister Cherry. If the spirits who came to her had warned her about Neville, the man she married, as they had warned her about the man she saw before meeting him, of course she would have had nothing to do with him and the life she lives today would be entirely different.

She says it is all in her way of telling the story. She does not immediately get lost in the trees the way I do. She says that is because I am a more complicated person but I know that is not so. I am more confused. That is not the same as being more complicated.

Still, I tell her, I think I will try your way. How can it hurt?

I was born in Ekeborn, Finland. Well, we already know that. At night we all slept in one bed. I still have nightmares about that bed, arms and legs floating, breasts and buttocks floating. But enough of that.

From the time I was a small child, I wanted to be an actress—even before I knew the word for such a profession. I was never comfortable inside myself. I was always happier when I was someone else. Often I dressed up as other people: kings, queens, tragic women, hunted men who had stolen to feed their families. I was sure that if I became what I wanted to be, then I would be happy.

Then how, when I got what I wanted, did I become so miserable?

Why, when I became famous, did everyone call me selfish or cruel?

One man who wrote for the papers called me the most evil woman in Hollywood. Yet I was, for many years, a simple creature, blank as the blackboard in my school classroom after I had washed it. And I loved washing it, erasing all the grammar lessons from it with the wet cloth, so that it shone and no one could write on it. But when it was wet, the blackboard was like a mirror, reflecting everything. Perhaps that is the fate of blank things: they reflect everyone else and in the end no one can see them.

In school, I went along in a dream world. When I walked with my father, he told me stories about the people he met during the day. Those stories, too, were like dreams. Then he fell sick and died and without warning I found myself in a confectioner's shop. I was still no more than a child.

Mrs. Berger, who ran the shop, saw that and taught me how to behave toward the customers, particularly the men. The men, she said, were the backbone of her business. Few women would come in. But men came in day and night to buy candy for women who were furious at them. They left the shop holding boxes full of anticipated forgiveness. So, she said, I must learn to be nice to the men. It wasn't difficult. A monkey could have been taught to do it.

And one afternoon, Max Lilly came into the shop. (You see! says Ivy. It is your life that had inevitability! Yours that had clarity! Not mine!) He said I had the face he wanted and he put me in a movie. The movie was a great success. People pursued Max. Max refused to go anywhere without me. He brought me with him to Hollywood. I was still a child.

It is just here that my understanding of my own life begins to part company with everyone else's. No one succeeds so easily! She must have done something for such success! No one has such luck! She must have been clever, selfish, shrewd! She must have used Max Lilly! She was ambitious! Ambitious people do terrible things!

Well, probably it is true ambitious people do terrible things. Later I did them. But at that time, if I had a will of my own, I didn't know it. Max Lilly was one of the strongest men in the world and he knew what he wanted of me. I loved him and wanted to please him. He was twenty years older than I was, almost the age my father would have been. When I stood in front of him, I was like a child, not the child of seventeen that I was, but a very small child.

It was my job to please Max. I thought he would raise me all over again and, this time, I would be perfect. Through him, I would learn to understand others, to get along with others. I would learn how to dress, how to move, what to say and what not to say. I tried very hard. But I never pleased Max. Always I said the wrong thing. I did not move gracefully enough. I did not learn fast enough. So I began to feel that I had failed terribly. At seventeen I was already a failure! I did not understand that Max was always hopelessly displeased with himself, that he saw me as part of him, and so he would always be displeased with me. I was much older before I understood that, and of course by then he was gone.

He was, in every way, my second chance. In Hollywood, when he fell ill with rheumatism, I came home from The Studio and nursed him. I coddled him. I talked to him. I fed him the ginger crackers he liked. I helped him up from chairs. I insisted he walk on the beach because walking would be good for his health.

I had done all this with my father, but my father had died. Max would not die. I would not allow it.

When we came to New York, I waited in the hotel room while Max argued with officials from the Studio office. Only once did I go with him. He would shout in Swedish. They didn't understand a word he said. If someone came in who could translate, the officials would listen to the translation, smile and shrug their shoulders, raise their eyebrows, and grimace in annoyance. Max understood that his words sounded childish and silly when they were translated. This made him even more furious, even irrational. Often I felt desperate, even disillusioned. But what was I to do? He had brought me here. I was entirely dependent on him. His days became a chase after "useful" people. I grew unhappy and stayed in the hotel. Occasionally we went to movies or to Broadway shows. Then we went out with other Europeans with whom we could talk and for a while life seemed normal, not the nightmare it had become.

And in the city the heat was so terrible, and the boredom so terrible, that I would turn on Max, or he on me. Why did he bring me here? I would ask him and then I would cry. It was a mistake! Let's go home!

He came back to the hotel one day and I had my trunk entirely packed. When he saw that, he sat on the couch and cried. Of course, I unpacked immediately. I didn't want to see him cry. Max must have no weakness, I thought. He is the only solid thing.

We came to Hollywood. Again we waited. My screen test was disastrous. Max had it done over. Accidentally Mr. Hall saw the new test and decided I was what he wanted for his movie, and so I had a starring role in The Roses. The movie was a tremendous success.

That was when the talk began. What did she do to get the role? Who did she sleep with?

And the next movie I was in, The Siren, that was even more successful, and the third, well, that one made movie history.

So I led a charmed life all right. But when the snake charmer casts a spell on the snake, who is to say the snake is happy?

I was only eighteen. I still looked to Max for everything. And Max was dissatisfied with everything I did.

After the screening of *The Roses*, everyone tried to be polite. For an hour or two, even Max said nothing: he was too depressed. Then he began shouting about my hair, the way I waved, the way I rolled my eyes to show surprise. I spent the night of the screening weeping and apologizing. *Next time I will do better.* Max asked me: How could you help but do better? A cartoon! I was a cartoon! The movie was ridiculous! I was ridiculous! Why had he wasted his time? So when the movie was a great success, naturally I did not enjoy it.

What you are seeing, said Max, is the stupidity of the American people.

At this time The Studio discovered how very badly I gave interviews. I was forever apologizing for my acting, for the script, even for the film's painted sets. And if I knew an interviewer was coming, shooting was held up for the day while I shook in my dressing room, broke out in rashes, and vomited. So they decided on a policy: Anna Asta would give no interviews. Of course it turned out to be a wonderful policy, a masterstroke. Everyone became fascinated by me.

But they also made up their own Anna Asta. I was too haughty to give interviews. Like Max, I was arrogant. I was too sure of myself. I must know important people. Who were they? These things don't happen out of the blue. So they said. But they *do* happen like that: like lightning. Still, even when lightning strikes, there are always people who try to explain it.

How did I become so reclusive, so shy? I did not become that way. I had always been so.

If you have little to do with people, you are not up at night wondering why they haven't stopped by to see you, why they haven't written or called. You don't ask yourself, Was it that letter I wrote? Was it what I said on the telephone?

You save yourself agonies.

A night with other people is a night of risks. Later, what will they say about your dress? Was it cheap? Too long? The wrong color? The wrong style? Will they think you drank too much? If you make a joke and they don't know you are joking, will they go home and say you are insensitive, with skin like leather? They will. If your opinions are not the same as theirs, will they despise you and ridicule you? Many of them will.

It is easier to stay home.

Who can endure such cross-examinings, such dissections under the dining room lights? I cannot. Max always said so: it is a weakness of mine. Other people take their chances. Why not you?

I could not.

So this is the truth of it: a shy girl, uneducated, sensitive, cowardly, came to Hollywood with Max Lilly. In the great tradition, she was discovered. She was put on the screen where she was made to seem worldly and sophisticated.

At night, when she went home, she became herself, skinny, shy and frightened. Max Lilly, the great director, told her she was hopeless. She believed him. As a result, when people interviewed her, she was terrified and confused and said idiotic things.

The Studio put an end to this. *Anna Asta will not be interviewed.* On the screen, Anna Asta grew mysterious and famous, apparently irresistible. In daily life, Anna Asta remained the girl she had always been. Thus, when strangers came up to her, she fled in terror.

From this a legend was born.

Of course later Anna Asta became quite a monster, but that is a different story.

2

WHEN I LEFT my father's house for the last time, I left because my stepmother began calling me my father's woman and threatened to leave the house to me and to him. At first I stayed with my grandmother, Mother Lize. Then I asked about and found a woman who had a spare room to rent in her house.

I began to see various young men, all of whom told me I was pretty. One of them, a handsome young man named Robbie, worked for the airport. He was particularly persistent. Occasionally we went to movies, and one night, we were to go to a domino tournament in Gordon Park. "You could come home with me, you know," he said, and I said I wasn't going home with anyone.

He said he could come live in my house. I said I liked it where I was, the rent was right, and I didn't want any trouble with my landlady, so he must stay where he was.

"Come see me is one thing," I said. "Come live with me is another."

"He's handsome," my friend Kitty said. "But what else does he have?"

"A good job," I said. Kitty said that wasn't what she meant, but when I asked her what she did mean, she wouldn't explain.

The night before the domino tournament, my grandmother dreamed me. She took me by the hand and we floated over Gordon Park and settled in the middle of an empty field.

"See that woman over there?" she asked me. "That tall woman on the bicycle? That is the mother of Robbie's children."

The next night, a bus took us from Greenstown to Gordon Park. Neville Anderson, a friend of Robbie's, was on the same bus, and so was Stanny, whom I had grown up with in Mare River, and who was Robbie's cousin. We brought our picnic baskets and sat on the grass while the tournament went on and then a band began to play and couples walked over to the dance floor set up the night before. Robbie went off to get me some peanuts and a soda. I watched him go and when I turned to the road, I saw a tall woman on a bicycle, a very pretty woman with two long black braids.

"Look," I said, pointing at her. "The woman with the bicycle! That's the mother of Robbie's children, isn't it?"

"Oh, my God," Stanny said. "She knows." He looked at me and he looked at Neville. "Neville?" he said. "Did you tell her?"

"We haven't said two words," Neville answered. He smiled at me. His lips were soft and fine and in his smile there was something sad, sympathetic and sad.

"Two words exactly," I said.

Robbie came back, but when he asked, I refused to dance with him. "What's the matter with you now?" he said. He became angry and walked off. Neville and I sat on our blanket, talking.

Neville came from a small town on the south coast of Green Island, Vulture's Beak, a town said to have earned its name because the inhabitants would wait for ships to become wrecked in rough weather and then would row out in boats to pillage the cargo.

"Is any of that true?" I asked him. Neville smiled and said he didn't know, but more than one house had the wall of its dining room decorated by the figurehead of a ship.

"Is that true?" I asked again, and he said that his parents' house had one of these figureheads. Little worm holes were eaten in it, and every week his mother polished it with palm oil.

"What does it look like?" I asked, and he said, "Oh, it is a mermaid, half woman, half fish, unclothed from the waist up, and the funny part is that when we were young, my mother hung a napkin around its neck."

I looked up and saw Robbie on the wooden dance platform, dancing with the tall woman who had come on the bicycle, his arms tight around her, and, as they danced, she leaned back in his arms, her head back, her eyes closed, her braids swaying as her body swayed.

"She is a beautiful woman," I said aloud, and Neville looked at me, looked away, and said, "So are you."

For no reason, I began singing, "Every morning the red sun rises, rises hot and bright," and when he asked me what I was singing, I told him. He looked at me a long time before he looked away. I felt a strange tingling in my scalp and toes.

Eventually, Robbie came back. The tournament ended. We took the bus back to Greenstown. When the bus stopped at my gate, Robbie started to get off. "Don't get off here on my account," I said. "Don't do it." But he got off the bus and followed me to my gate.

"I'll see you in," he said, and I said, "No. You won't. You go back to that woman and her children. What more do you want?" I opened my gate, closed it, and went in. Robbie stood stunned, staring after me.

The next day, at lunch hour, Stanny came to the biscuit factory where I worked. "Why did you tell Robbie I told you about his woman and children?" he asked me.

"Is it true?"

"Yes, it is true. But if you tell Robbie I said so, he will kill me."

"Why didn't you tell me?" I asked Stanny. "We've known each other since childhood days."

"I was afraid of Robbie," he said.

"You didn't tell me," I said. "My grandmother told me."

"He's threatening to kill me and he's threatening to kill Neville," Stanny said.

I told him not to worry. Robbie wasn't killing anybody.

I left work early and went to see Robbie. "I want to see you, sir," I said to him. "Why are you telling lies about me? Why are you accusing people who haven't done anything? Stanny didn't tell me about your woman. Neville didn't tell me about your woman. My grandmother came and told me." He glared at me.

"Look here," I said. "I didn't fall from a hollow tree. I have a father and brothers. You ask Stanny about my father and my brother Jack. My brother Jack is in charge of the baggage at the airport where you work, you know. My brother Bobby works there too. I don't want all this trouble. Stop telling stories about me and stop telling stories about people who don't even know what you're talking about."

After that, I didn't see Robbie again.

One day, Stanny stopped by the house to help me move a china wagon I had bought and he brought Neville with him.

"This man has been saved," Stanny said, nodding at Neville.

"True?" I said. "You're saved?"

"It is true."

I laughed at him. "You don't drink and you don't go to parties? Not even on your birthday? I heard you do drink, you know."

"I don't drink anymore."

"True?"

"True."

"Can you go to movies?"

"Yes, I can go to movies. It's a church, not a prison."

"I like movies," I said.

"There's a movie coming this weekend. Would you like to see it?"

"With you?"

"All you want to do is laugh at me," Neville said.

And so we began to see one another.

He wanted to know everything about me. He asked me questions about my life before I came to Greenstown. He asked why my step-mother had so disliked me. He listened when I told him how I had to go to Inspection Day at school dressed in a long frock my father bought me from the Hang Upon Nail man when everyone else wore their best navy blue skirts, white blouses and brown shoes and white socks.

I told him how I had sneaked off and paid a woman sixpence to cut my hair because I couldn't stand the half hour of pulling and tugging with my stepmother on the veranda. Eventually I told him about the baby and how I had given it away.

In turn, he told me of life in Vulture's Beak, where almost no child went to school beyond the second standard. This was because the weather was so rough and windy and the soil so poor that everyone worked or families would starve and in drought years it wasn't uncommon to see mothers carrying babies with swollen bellies because the children had so little to eat.

The people of Vulture's Beak were not affectionate. Certainly his mother was not. His father died shortly after he was born and he had no memory of him. What he wanted now, he said, was to live peacefully and happily. He said he would take me to meet his mother, but

I would be frightened of her, she was so cold and showed so little liking for him. Naturally I would think he had done something to deserve such treatment. I said I would think no such thing, but we made no plans to go to Vulture's Beak.

One day when he came for me, I was not yet back from work, and my landlady asked him to come in for some tea and crackers.

"You shouldn't be seeing her, you know," my landlady said. "You should be going out with a virtuous girl."

"I would have to take a blowtorch and search the streets of Greenstown before I found one of those," he said.

"What about my daughter?" she asked him.

When I came home, he told me what had happened and we agreed that I should remove. Kitty knew of a woman who was renting a two-room apartment. I went to look at it. It was in the back of the house and had its own doorway. It was private and clean and I took it. Neville began to spend nights there and soon the two of us were living together. He gave up his apartment and we began to share the rent.

Tita Lu came one Sunday to visit, and when Neville left, she asked me why I didn't marry him.

"Because I don't want to get married," I said.

"But whenever he moves, your eyes follow him," she said, "and he is the same about you."

I wanted to tell her how I loved the feel of his cheekbone beneath my hand, how I loved the way he waved his hand when something displeased him, but I was accustomed to keeping my thoughts to myself.

"He is good to you?" she asked. I said he was. "He doesn't beat you?" I said he didn't. "And you love him?" I didn't answer. "You do love him," she said. "Your mother was stubborn too. She was stubborn and look what happened," Tita Lu said and began to cry.

Time passed and finally we had lived together for two years. On weekends we went to the local gardens or we rented a car and drove out into the country. We drove down to Pecan Bay and dove off the cliffs and swam in the green water. Once we even drove to the Sunken City, so close to Cinnamon Bay, but I didn't mention my father's house or how near to it we were, and so we drove back to Greenstown.

It seemed that Neville was really and truly saved. He no longer drank and the friends he had before were his friends no longer. Now we went to parties given by the people in our courtyard or we made parties of our own. Kitty and her husband, Neville and I often went to the movies on Thursday nights.

Eventually Neville decided against going to movies. The members of his church had concluded that sitting in the dark watching people do things we would not approve of in broad daylight was no activity for Christian people. But since I was not a member of the church, I continued to go. I went alone, for the late afternoon show on Sundays, and Neville attended church services.

One December night I came out of the movie theater, alone as usual. I was wearing a low-cut green dress and the night was very chilly. I walked to the corner of the block where Neville was attending his Pentecostal Church and leaned against the streetlight. The light inside shone through the stained-glass windows and their colored shadows lit up the sidewalk, so that where I stood looked warm, but it was cold and I was shivering.

Every now and then a car passed, and occasionally one of the drivers called out to me. I grew tired of shivering in the cold and opened the heavy wooden door of the church and sat down in the back row. It was my bad luck to walk in just as the pastor was calling people up to the altar to testify.

"Lady," he said, motioning to me. "Lady, come up here." I ignored him. "Come up here now, lady," he said. "Don't be afraid." I stared into space. The whole congregation had swivelled in their seats to watch me. "Lady in the green dress," he said. "Come up here."

I lost my temper. "You are all right," I said. "Nice and warm up there in your wool suit, but I am cold."

I got up and walked out. Neville came after me and caught up with me on the next block. He was furious. "Did you have to answer back? You couldn't just keep quiet?"

"I was cold and he wouldn't leave me in peace," I said. "What kind of Christian charity is that?" He was still angry. "All right," I said. "From now on, you go to your church and I'll go to the movies." And for some months, that was how it went. He went to church and I went to the movies.

Stanny began to talk to me. It wasn't right that I went one place and Neville went another. He spoke of the uneven yoke. He quoted from various passages in the Bible.

"Since when do you know the Bible so well?" I asked him. "Who's telling you what to say to me?"

He said he was concerned for Neville's immortal soul. Suppose something happened to Neville while we were still living together without benefit of marriage? Neville would go straight to hell, and every day of my life, I would reproach myself for what I had done to him.

I said I hadn't asked Neville to live with me.

The next day Neville asked me to marry him.

"No," I said. "I don't want to do it. I want to be free to do as I please. If we come to a place where we can't get along, I want to be able to walk out that door a free woman."

He nodded and I thought that was the end of it.

But that Friday I came home and Patsy who lived next door came running out to meet me at the gate. "There are strange men in your apartment!" she said. She came to the door with me. From inside I heard unfamiliar voices. I turned the key, opened the door and looked inside. Neville was there, Stanny, and the pastor of Neville's church along with another man I didn't know.

"It's all right," I said to Patsy. "I won't go to church so the church has to come to me."

I went inside and the pastor began speaking of the uneven yoke, and Neville's immortal soul, and how, when he looked at Neville, he could see the flames licking at him. Last month they had been licking at his shoelaces. Now they reached up to his knees. Did I want this on my conscience? Did I want to damn a soul to hell?

I said I didn't believe in souls or in hell and I didn't believe in churches and I wished they would all go home. I thought if I was rude enough, they would be hurt and not come back.

The next Friday night they were back again.

On Saturday, Tita Lu visited. I told her about the pastor and how he came to my own house and hounded me.

"But what is wrong with marrying?" she asked me. "You have lived together in friendship for two years now. You know one another so well. Do you want him to go off with another woman? Do you want to go off with another man? Try it. What can you lose?"

I said I wanted to be free to walk through that door if anything went wrong, and Tita Lu asked me if I thought it was such a great thing to walk through a door and have no one care enough to follow and bring me back.

"Come now," she said. "If you decide to marry, I'll make you a beautiful dress and you can wear your mother's red felt hat."

"That is your hat," I said.

"It was your mother's first," she said. "She gave it to me when I told her how badly it fit her. Once when we were moving house, I pretended I was sick and lay on the bed, and when everything was moved except for a little suitcase, I got up and said I thought I felt well enough to carry that suitcase out to the van and your mother never suspected. That was how she was. The hat's her hat. You can have it if you get married."

The churchmen kept appearing.

Finally, the pastor said that if I refused to marry Neville and Neville intended to remain in the church, he and I could not see one another anymore.

In the end, it was my own guilt that persuaded me.

When I was a child, my stepmother used to say that if she died, she would come back and gouge out my eyes, because it would be my disobedience that had killed her.

My grandmother believed that my father and mother would have remained together had I not been born and had my mother not decided to take me to Albion Bay to visit her relatives.

Now a pastor and his committee were coming round every week to tell me that I would be responsible for the damnation of Neville's immortal soul.

I loved Neville. He knew about the baby I had given away. He knew about the burn that scarred my side, two inches from my heart. He knew about my stepmother, about Miss Blue and her stories—but I married him out of guilt.

Tita Lu and Brother Beckwith came to the small civil ceremony. I wore the beautiful white lace suit she made me, the suit trimmed with red satin buttons, and of course the red felt hat.

My brother Jack came, but no one else from the family, because I had not told them. After we were married, life went on just as it had before.

In Mare River, when I was growing up a woman named Esther lived with a man who beat her. I asked my father why no one helped Esther and he asked me what he could do. Half of Mare River had tried to interfere, but a few hours after Esther and her husband finished fighting, they were back together again. "If she wants to get beaten," he said, "let her take her beating."

One night Jack and I were sitting out on the back step and the men were playing dominoes in the front yard. "If ever a man beat me," I said to Jack, "you know what I would do? I would friend him up, and then when he was asleep, I would take a little can of condensed milk and throw out the milk, and fill it up with palm oil and heat up the palm oil on the fire, and I would lean over him and pour it into his ear."

"Oh, my God!" said my father, who had come into the house and heard me. "Where did you get ideas like that? Who talks to you like that? My God! My God! The things she thinks of!" He said he would speak to me later. He went back and joined his friends.

"And," I told Jack, "if my husband ran around with other women, I wouldn't stand still for it. I'd sleep with a machete under my side of the bed and a scissor under a pillow."

"To do what?" asked Jack. But I could hear my father's steps coming toward us and I put a finger to my lips.

We think we know what we will do, but of course we don't. Neville and I lived happily together for fifteen years and when those years ended there was nothing but trouble.

The spirits in my family warned me against Robbie, who had a tall, beautiful woman and many children, but they did not warn me against Neville. When I married Neville, he was a wonderful man. He was handsome, he had a good job, and he loved me. We could talk together for hours. There must have been signs—there always are—but I did not see them.

I believe now that spirits are like the rest of us. They can see what is, but not what will be. They can see from one end of the past and the present to the other, but the future is closed to them just as it is closed to us.

3

DAY AND NIGHT now there was constant raving about shoes and elephants and from this lunacy I knew Max and I were once more working together. Sets for *The Siren* were under construction. Every day I reported to Wardrobe and was fitted for dresses, dresses no human being would wear, but only a creature out of a fairy tale, and every day I stood still for hours, my back straight, my mouth full of pins, while Miss Cotton fitted satin sheaths to my body, adjusted the drape of lace collars, lowered the décolletage until it could go no lower, and then, while Miss Rosalie made up my face, while Mr. Feldman watched her make up my face, the shoemaker was busy with my foot.

The feet of women! Max said. In this film the feet of women are important! There are women in bare feet who walk through the dust and the mud and there are women like Helen here whose feet must never touch the ground. The shoe must be a sign of her divinity! Work on the shoe!

And the shoe was never right. The gold satin did not glisten enough under the eye of the camera. The shoe was taken away and encrusted with gold braid and rhinestones. Ah, said Max. That is the shoe I want. *But I can't walk in it.* You don't walk in it. You step out of a carriage and the camera is on your feet. You walk two steps and the camera is on your feet. Then we throw the shoes away.

Throw away such shoes! I would keep them and use them as containers: for hairpins, for rings. How could such shoes be thrown away?

You know, your feet are not good, Max said. They are big, big feet. You have the feet of a platypus. Your leading man has tiny feet. He will have to wear very big shoes. Otherwise, when you stand together, it will look like the giantess and her child.

The sets for *The Siren* were no less elaborate than the shoes. The initial set, where I was first to appear, was an enormous ballroom with one balcony. Next was a formal garden, built to resemble Versailles, wide lawns, stylized white marble statues, a wall for a lute player to sit upon, and beyond, a thick glade, a Garden of Eden. These sets were intended for the opening scenes.

For subsequent scenes, Max had found The Studio's Grand House and pronounced it acceptable. Its enormous curving stairway winding down to a marble tiled door, its immense French doors, its windows from ceiling to floor, this was the house of his imagination.

But, he said, he would not tell that to Pinsky. He would tell him that out of consideration and to show his good faith, he was making all possible economies. Only after the movie was made did we realize how frequently this house appeared in The Studio's productions. It appeared so often it was almost a character. Actors who appeared on the set would sigh with relief. Here they were again. They felt right at home. At the time we did not know.

Was this what led me to understand that Max viewed *The Siren* as his only chance to accomplish what he wanted to do in this country? Because, under ordinary circumstances, he would have insisted on building his own set. He would say, I don't want used visions! Up on the screen everything is mine!

There were the endless meetings he would not talk about afterwards, although in the evenings when we sat on the porch, there would be outbursts. "Now they want a cut-rate Siegfried and a bargain-basement Brunhilde! And I must explain why I want an elephant! They said there would be no interference! And I am in the hall, and I hear

Pinsky's toad doing his croaking. 'Insolent! Insolent! Insolent!' Well, better men than he have said that of me!"

"Max," I said, "why must we have an elephant? Everyone will be frightened."

"You too?" he said. "Even you don't understand why we must have an elephant?" And he looked so stricken I didn't mention the animal again.

And there was the question of where we would live. One day Max came into the fitting room and sent everyone out. "Look, Anna," he said, sitting down on Miss Cotton's folding chair, "I'm going to take a room in the Golden Palms. You know how I like big hotels." I said I didn't know. I thought he was happy where he was. "I am happy," he said. "That's not the point." He was uncomfortable. He hated explaining. "They think it's bad for the picture, particularly bad for you, the two of us living in the same house, always sitting on the same balcony. How will it look to *the people?*"

"Well, I am sick of these people, whoever they are," I said.

"It's a question of appearances," Max said. "You can live in my hotel room. I can live in yours. But we must have separate addresses, separate places to entertain people from the press, people from The Studio, people like Bertha Pinsky!"

"Bertha Pinsky?"

"You saw how it was at the party," he said. "Anna, it will make no difference! We can do what we want! Only now we have two places! Don't argue!"

Several days later, Max was working with the dancers who would frolic like wood nymphs as I walked with my lover into the thick wood. A messenger arrived on the set and walked up to Max. Once more he was wanted in the office. When he came back, he was shaking with rage. "It came to Mr. Pinsky's attention," he said, "that when I made *Masquerade*, I commissioned an entire original opera! He looked at the movie last night and what did he see? A lot of people moving their mouths and no sound coming out! No original ballet for his movie! Let them leap about the way they usually leap!"

"Max," I said, "do as *you* usually do. Instruct the dancers. Don't argue with Pinsky!"

"I can listen to such nonsense and keep quiet?" he shouted at me. "You have been speaking to him?"

"I haven't seen him since the party. I am sensible and stay out of his way!" That was the first thing my mother and sister taught me: stay out of the boss's way.

Of course, when Max began a production, life was always a tense affair, but how can one say when things cross a line and become not merely tense but killing? When he began directing me, at night, after everyone else had gone home, in my hotel room or in his, this is what I knew to be happening.

One night, we were sitting on my porch looking out over the sea. Gussie had been for her walk and slept on Max's lap. The sun had dropped below the horizon, but still it lit the sky. Max now officially lived in the Golden Palms. Unofficially he still lived in our small hotel. In the morning, we were to begin filming the festival, the opening scenes of *The Siren*.

"Now, before we do anything else," he said, "I want you to understand what goes behind all this. Every tiny detail, I want you to understand it. You just look out to sea and I will describe two things to you: what things the camera sees and what those things mean. You are paying attention? You are not hungry? You don't want a glass of water? Anything you want, get it now.

"In Paris, where this is set, on the other side of the river, in the Bois de Boulogne, is a great castle set in a park. In the castle and in the park is a wonderful festival. No one knows what it's for, but that becomes clear as you watch. A title will come on: 'O woman! Thou are not the creation of God, but of man!' Then a hand is seen strumming on a lute. So it is clear we are in this world, but at the same time we are not in it. This is the shadow place between what is real and what we want to be real.

"So when you act, you do not act like a real woman, although of course you are real. Instead you act like a creature in someone else's dream. And how do you do that? You must act as if you yourself were dreaming someone else's dream. Of course if that were to happen, if you were to fall asleep and believe you were dreaming someone else's dream, you would be frightened and confused. So you must act frightened and confused. But most of all, you must act as if you were beautiful. Not beautiful as you are in life, but beautiful as these others dream you to be. You must become the ideal thing. This part is not easy. How do you become an ideal?

"By never waking up. On the screen you must seem like someone whose eyes are open but who is still asleep, someone who is in this world but who does not belong to it. You understand?"

Although I did not understand, I nodded. When Max finished with me, I would understand. This was an old story.

"Well, of course you understand," Max said. "You and your demon lover. For these scenes, summon him up. What are you getting mad about now?"

"Demon lover!" I said. "I don't want to hear it again. Always when there is a silence you talk about the demon lover. It is all nonsense!"

"The camera agrees with me, not you," Max said. "The rushes will prove who is right."

"If I didn't know better," I said, "I would say you are losing your mind, but of course, you have already lost it, long ago. This demon lover, who is he? You, all over again. You have so much to do, there is so much pressure, you dream up another Max, you give him another name, but he is you all the same. I know."

"Anna," he said impatiently, "you don't know anything and I hate listening to such stupidity. Back to work. Pay attention. So. In love with an ideal. A demon lover can do only so much. I have to do the rest. It's always that way, what else can I expect?

"The dance floor is crowded. There are people wearing heads of monsters. You come onto the balcony dressed in white, the same color as the moon. You look at the dancers and something disturbs you. A man dressed in a black cape wearing a black mask comes up behind you.

"He has the appearance of a devil and he frightens you. It is evident he has power over you because he tells you to sit down and you obey him. On the dance floor, everyone is rioting, everyone is happy. Again and again he asks you if you love him. You tell him you don't.

"Now you run into the throng. He tries to follow you. You are running away but the people are thick. Clowns, devils, soldiers catch you up. Everything frightens you. Finally you fight your way out through the streamers, the balloons, the confetti, all the hands grabbing at you. This is a nightmare world you are caught in.

"Then a man in black grabs you. You think he is another devil and you fight loose. You run out onto the lawn and yet another circle of dancing devils and clowns closes in on you. All this sickens and frightens you. Why? Because you do not belong here. You are not part of this world. The man in black, the second one, the one who let you go, now comes to your rescue. He takes you away. You walk with him down a path lined with white marble statues, nude women, perfect, beautiful, carved from stone.

"But what does the man in black want? Has he come to rescue you or is he like the other men: a devil? Until you know, you are confused and exhausted and above all, frightened. You will be frightened anyway, on the first day the cameras roll, so concentrate not on how frightened you are but how beautiful you are, how unsure you are of what that means.

"Your first reaction to this man must be disgust and anger. Then he will ask to see your face, but first he will slowly remove his mask. When his mask, the mask of a devil, is removed, you see the face, not just of any man, but the perfect man for whom you have been waiting. You must look at him as if you are overcome by love, as if you have just seen the face of God although you do not believe in God. It is like being drunk and sleepy. Everything you do is slow and exaggerated and at the same time muted. Do you understand? *He*, on the other hand, although equally enchanted, is not in the same dream, is not drunk, is not asleep. He too will seem to have found the perfect woman, a dream creature, but what he is is practical. He is not a dreamer. What he sees is a beautiful woman, and that is what he says to you: *You are beautiful.*

"The two of you walk across a brilliantly lit meadow and into the trees. Devils and clowns laugh but do not follow you. Now you are in your own Garden of Eden. You begin to cry. You tell him they are tears of your first happiness. And then, what does he want to know? He wants to know if you are free to love him.

"This is the danger signal: he is a man bound by codes and rules. You have made a mistake. He is not a dreamer. The audience knows this but as yet you do not know it. The lute player is asleep on his wall; the full moon comes out from behind a cloud.

"And then the night is over. The camera shows the Paris skyline. It is on the other side of the river. It stands for real life. Now you must change. You are going back across the river, back to real life. You are still dreaming, dreaming, but once more afraid and angry.

"In this story, men are either good or bad. They have their honor, they have their work. They are honorable or dishonorable, good workers or bad workers, but not you. You are neither good nor bad. You are all emotion, all dream, an ideal creature in search of an ideal. Yet your husband has sold you! For money!

"If you play these scenes properly, the audience will understand everything. What is honor, what are codes when one has found the ideal world? Such things are not needed in such a special realm! But not everyone who stumbles into such a place knows where he is. This is your tragedy. You know but your lover does not. He will see adultery where he should see innocence. He is misled by proprieties, by appearances. Every time you appeal to him he will fail you. In this way he will be worse than the husband who sold you, a devil who knows himself a devil.

"And so things will continue, woman, the eternal dreamer, man who cannot dream but who deifies the worker ant! This is the fundamental opposition of the movie: men's work and the dream. And the movie is full of irony! Throughout the movie, your lover insists you are destroying everything around you when really he is destroying you! He is destroying the delicate vision! So you see why this will be a great movie! Every little detail will establish the theme!

"The way your husband flirts with other women and sits at the table and builds little people out of fruit and swallows the fruit people down whole. The long banquet table, so long it seems to hold the whole world. The behavior of the people at this table, shown only by shots of their legs under the table, the women removing their shoes, their stockinged feet dancing on the carpeted floor, unseen. The way the women rub the men's legs with their stockinged feet. The difference between what goes on above and below the table. The woman whose antics produce a run in her stockings. The villains who always look first at women's legs or feet. These are men without dreams. The villains, always seen first as shadows on the wall, and in the end, even your lover's shadow enters the room before he does.

"All these little touches, what a movie it will make! I don't even need to look through the lens to see it! The last scenes which bring everything full circle. You go into a café, drunk, fallen, and you look at another drunk and what do you see? You see Christ, his head surrounded by a golden nimbus, looking at you. And now you play the scene as you played the opening scene: half drunk, half asleep, slow motion. You see why? Tell me why."

"Because," I said, "finally I have found him, the man who died for love. He is the ideal."

"And when you walk away from him, what are you going to do?"

"I am going to die."

"By your own hand?"

"No, not by my own hand."

"Very good, very good," Max said. There were tears in his eyes.

"You are exhausted," I said. "You see I understand. We can go to bed now." But he said, No, there was too much to do. We should work on the opening scene at once; he would be the man on the balcony. Tomorrow he would have so many problems. Armando Torres, the leading man, he would be a terrible problem. He was so beautiful he thought he was the leading lady! He had to wear bigger shoes but he didn't like it. He was proud of his dainty feet. And of his moustache. That had to go. The Brazilian villain who dynamites the village has a moustache. The villainous husband has a moustache. How is the audience going to keep track of them?

"And Torres has such a beautiful face, that's why we picked him and now he shows up with this, this—aberration!"

Had he told me he wanted this Torres to play both the husband and the Brazilian villain? What a touch that would be! When the Brazilian villain shoots the evil husband, he is only shooting a version of himself and so he goes on living and this too helps explain my despair. But will he want to play a villain? He will say he is not being paid to play two roles and his fans want to see him as a hero. He says this and throughout the entire movie he is the very opposite of a hero! Well, he understands nothing, but he doesn't have to understand. In fact it is better if he doesn't. Then he will play the thick-necked practical man even more convincingly. What did I think of all this?

"Oh, Max," I said. "You know me. I like to avoid trouble."

"That is all right for a girl in a confectioner's shop," Max said. "Not for me or you." He was so tired he began to cry again.

"All right," I said. "Let's try the scene. Here I am on the balcony. Come up behind me."

And so we played the scene.

"Now you will go to sleep?" I asked him. Yes, now he would go to sleep. But a few hours later, when I awoke, there he was, standing on the balcony.

"All right, now what is it?" I said. He looked helpless, almost abject. "This has something to do with me," I said. He didn't deny it.

"Long ago," I said, "you asked me what I wanted of you. Now I am asking you the same thing. What do you want of me?"

He sat down and motioned me over. I sat on his lap. "If I thought I could keep you, I would want that," he said.

"If you thought you could keep me," I repeated.

"Yes."

"Why can't you keep me?"

"Someone else will come along," he said. "What is inevitable is inevitable. Oh, I have my passions, but they don't last long, they're not so strong, I don't take them so seriously. *You* still look first at the feet."

"At the feet?"

"The legs, the feet."

"You can try and keep me," I said. "Why not?"

"Why not? Already you are acting your role."

"Then," I said, "let's see how well I do."

"Things will change," Max said.

"Yes?" I said. "I will no longer be your ideal woman?"

"I will become jealous."

"And I won't?"

We were in the room and I stood still and took off my clothes. "So," I said. "Are my hips too big? If I get in bed, you will come in after me?"

"All right," Max said.

"Oh, such enthusiasm," I said.

"Get in bed," Max said.

And afterwards I was happy, I was warm. "So this is what it is," I thought to myself. "So this is all it is." And I looked at Max, asleep in the bed, and felt the familiar mixture of love, pity and revulsion. "This is nothing to be afraid of, this is normal, this is nothing to worry about," I told myself, "and besides, now Max will be happy." It surprised me, that the idea of his happiness made me happier. Lately, what did I feel? Afraid, worried, listening to Max explaining ways of conveying emotions I had not yet felt.

Oh, he was good at making me do that, with his fishing rod and his chocolates swinging in front of me! Such longing, such sexual ecstasy in one so young! People marvelled so at these things, at my ability. They guessed at what experiences I drew upon when in fact I had none, when in fact it was Max's life I was drawing upon. And it seemed to me then, turned on my side, watching Max's back, smooth in the moonlight, that I had no life of my own. I saw that it was possible to go on as I was for years and years, to grow old as I was, and one day I would wake up and think, If I die today, I still will not know anything. Still I will have no experience of my own.

Then I thought about my mother in her bed in the little room in Sweden and I thought, I have had contempt for her but she has had experience. There are things she knows. You can see it in her face, the way she smiles when she thinks no one is watching her: she has memories. The room can be empty and quiet but there is something she is smiling at. She has a life inside her. When nothing happens around me, I go dark, like a lamp unplugged from the wall. What was missing in me? Had I had not enough time? Or was it Max, who made it unnecessary for me to live on my own? Oh, I thought, turning on my back, it is always best to blame someone else.

A little later I was still awake. To tell the truth, I thought, everything is a little disappointing. Why not sex?

I was not a passionate lover, but I learned quickly. From childhood I knew the sights and sounds of passion, and in disgust, I had turned away from them. And from childhood I knew, too, that Max was not a passionate man. After all, hadn't he explained *The Siren* to me? There were men who looked at women's legs and there were men who looked at women and saw something ideal, something not of this earth. But near the end of the film, when the lover decides to give everything up and follow the woman, when he tells her she is too strong for him and nothing else matters, doesn't he look at her and see both the body and the ideal? Doesn't he want both? So it seemed to me. So it must also seem to Max, who had gone over the script line by line, word by word. But there was no question: the later scenes did not obsess him as the earlier ones did.

Well, Max was a romantic, a visionary, while I was not. There was nothing I had that I did not already know could be taken away. No matter what was given to me, that knowledge—that it could be taken away, that it *would* be taken away—spoiled it. No, I was not a romantic, but still, there was something that drove me on. If it was only animal energy? Then what was I? Was I any better than Gussie, who lay at the foot of the bed across Max's legs?

It is easy to look down on a dog, not so easy for one human being to love another as a dog loves. There were times I thought, Well, I am not human. I am only a doll. But my eyes were closing; soon I would sleep.

Did I feel closer to Max now? To be honest, I did not. And yet there were times, frightening, unleashed times, not many, almost few enough to forget, and always the next day, I did want to forget, and usually, as people do, I succeeded, times when Max would turn to me and I would become as a creature possessed, and afterwards, I would lie on his chest and sob out of sheer happiness. And once I pushed myself up on my elbow to look at his face, and his face too was wet, and when he saw me watching him, he turned on his side and pretended to sleep, and so I knew there was something in these sudden onslaughts of passion that hurt him and because I did not know what it was, I would hold him, hold him until my arms first ached and then grew numb. But these times were the exceptions. Now it was as if we had tied ourselves to one another with rope, loose ropes, loose knots, so that escape would still be possible. But now the ropes were there, while before it was not necessary to think of escape. Knots, rope: I fell asleep thinking of such things.

And then the next day the trouble began. The shoes, the moustache, the elephant, three small things: well, one of them not so small.

4

THE ELEPHANT WOULD not move. He slept in the center of the festival like an enormous prehistoric rock. Because everyone had been so frightened of him, he had been thoroughly drugged, and now no one could rouse him. Extras who had threatened to walk off the set if an elephant walked on began to approach the sleeping beast and, bending from the waist, peered at him with concern. *Is he dead? Is he dead?* He had been painted white and in the hot lights, the white paint was drying and soon it would be flaking.

"Get up! Get up! Get up!" Max was shouting at the elephant, who, of course, remained oblivious. Max was holding a riding whip and with it he began slapping the palm of his other hand. When I saw his hand beginning to bleed, I went over to him.

"Max," I said. "It is a sleeping animal. You are not even near his ears and besides, he doesn't even know you. What can you do? You must wait for him to wake up."

Max stared at me without seeing me. He went on shouting at the elephant. A camera went by on its dolly. In exasperation I climbed on and rode around the set.

In every corner, people were blowing up balloons for the festival scene. Now the extras were growing bolder. Some of them had taken their balloons over to the elephant and were bouncing the balloons against his side.

Well, I thought, the fun will be over the minute he stirs. And then I heard a commotion in one corner of the set. Armando Torres was shouting. "First I am upstaged by that flatfoot, and now by an elephant! Who decided on the billing? Was it him? Why should her name go above mine?"

People crowded around him trying to calm him. Not, however, Max. He was bellowing at a man I had never before seen.

"Off my set! Off my set!" he shouted. I jumped down from the dolly and walked over to him.

"Who is that man?" I asked Tomas, who was standing behind Max.

"A studio supervisor," Tomas said.

"Oh," I said. "What does he do?"

"He spies for the front office!" Max roared. "Off my set!" He picked up his whip and menaced the man with it. The man fled.

"This is normal?" I asked Tomas. "A supervisor?"

"Here it's normal," Tomas said. "He stands around and keeps an eye on costs. If he sees a way to save money, he makes suggestions."

"A stranger has no business on my set!" Max shouted. "No interference! That was our agreement!"

"Mr. Lilly!" someone called. "Telephone!"

I followed Max to the telephone. "Yes, I threw the man off the set!" Max said. "Why? Because I am the director here. He has no business being here! Don't send him back! I can't be responsible! When the elephant wakes up, then we'll film him! You want footage of a sleeping elephant?" He slammed the phone down.

"Max," I said, "the man could stay. What really is the harm in it?"

"Don't talk to me!" Max shouted. "I am having enough trouble! No one understands a word I am saying! When I open my mouth they pretend not to know! *You* understand!"

"I speak Swedish, I speak German," I reminded him.

"Go away! Sit down somewhere! Elephant, get up!"

I sat down on the sidelines and watched the balloons blown up, the confetti taken up to the rafters where, during the dance, it would be loosed on the crowd of extras. The elephant, unperturbed, slept on.

The supervisor was back. "We are falling behind schedule," he said, and then Max pursued him and he ran from the set.

"Oh, boy," I said to Tomas.

"I don't think they'll get to your scenes today," he said.

"Maybe not even this week."

"If he would tell me what he wanted, if he would let me translate," Tomas said.

"Please," I said. "He is not a reasonable man."

Through a gap in the painted flats the supervisor was watching. Thank God Max did not see him.

And I thought, Why must it be an elephant? From the beginning, everyone explained the problems of having an elephant on the set. An elephant was heavy. The floor of the set would have to be reinforced. An elephant was unpredictable. At any moment, it might decide to spray the cast with water from its trunk. And everyone knew The Studio had its own very tame, very old lion. They were always happy to put the lion to work. For the festival, the lion could be suspended in his cage from the ceiling. Wouldn't that be exotic? The dancers could feed him by hand. Wouldn't that be dramatic? Wouldn't that make the point? Who could look at a lion fed by revellers and not understand this was no ordinary revel?

"I am sorry," Max said. "It has to be an elephant."

"Why an elephant?" Mr. Pinsky asked.

"Because an elephant is what it must be!"

"You think an elephant has a long memory!" Pinsky shouted. "A head of a studio, his memory is even longer!"

I was sitting in a corner, studying the script, when a cry went up on the floor of the set. The elephant was waking up! The extras began cheering him on. The elephant's ears fanned out and he began struggling to get up. He got to his knees and then struggled erect. The extras were cheering wildly.

Max walked over to the elephant, smiling calmly: *What was all the fuss? I expected the elephant to wake up.* But before Max reached the elephant, he sank back to his knees and refused to stand up again. The trainer took Max aside for a conference. When it was over, Max picked up his megaphone and said, "Everyone go home. No more for today." Then he handed the megaphone to Tomas who repeated the same words in English.

Max came over to me. "It is a sick elephant," he said. "So naturally it will not stand up."

I asked him what the trainer said, and he told me that the trainer said it was very hard to judge the proper dose for an elephant, and the elephant would be fine after he slept it off. And how long would that take? The trainer didn't know. One day, two, by the end of the week the elephant would be ready to work. In the meantime, Armando Torres and I would begin rehearsing our scenes together.

He called Mr. Torres over and told him we would be wanted on the set at eight in the morning. Immediately, Mr. Torres began to complain. Why should he clomp around in huge shoes just because my feet were too big? What was this about shaving off his moustache? He was hired because he was beautiful? He was a great actor! He was supposed to be Spanish, a Brazilian. He wanted it understood: he was not shaving off his moustache. Max began shouting in Swedish. Tomas translated, but not so loudly.

"Oh, so this is *her* picture," Mr. Torres said. "Well, anyone can see that! She's the only woman in the picture, except for that virtuous mouse who shows up for twenty feet and the mouse is going to end up on the cutting room floor! Anyone want to take bets on it? And I, I who am the great love of her life, I who am on-screen through the entire movie, I must clump around in ridiculous huge shoes and break my neck? I must shave off my moustache? All right, I said I'd take second billing and now look what happens! I'm going to the head office."

"Where you can pick up your check!" Max shouted.

Mr. Torres turned and looked at him. "*I* am not going anywhere," he said. His voice was so full of venom, pure poison, it took my breath away. And it occurred to me: Did he know something? Was he spying for the front office? Always I heard rumors that some people on the set were paid to report to Mr. Pinsky. But not one of the stars! Surely that was not possible.

That night Max directed my scenes again. In the morning, I rehearsed with Mr. Torres.

"You know," I said to Max, "we could film these scenes now. Everything is ready."

"You know I don't like to film out of order," Max said. "You lose the most important thing, how it is like life, one thing leading to another. Suppose we do the end scenes now? Then we are trapped by them. Then everything that goes before has to aim toward them. That is not like life. In life you don't begin knowing the end. All the little balances, they shift when we film. So then when we get to the end, we accommodate. No, first scenes first, last scenes last."

"But Max," I said, "that's not how they do things here. Tomas told me."

"For a translator, Tomas is a great theorist of film," Max said. "We will wait for the elephant. How long can an elephant sleep?"

By the end of the second day, the elephant was awake but the trainer called to say that the animal could not stand up straight. When he stood up, he staggered. The veterinarian thought the drug had affected his inner ear. "I think," the trainer said, "you better forget the elephant."

"This is a trick of The Studio," Max said to me. "After work, I am going to the zoo to see this tilting elephant."

We went to the zoo. A miserable elephant, one ear up, one ear down, was leaning heavily against a chain link fence.

"Oh, the poor elephant!" I said.

"Poor elephant!" Max said. "The Studio did this!"

"Please," I said. "Please."

In the car, Max said, "Obviously the elephant is not well."

"No."

"It is not right to torment a sick animal."

"No."

"So tomorrow we begin filming."

We drove along the shoreline. Clouds blocked the sun. The sea was the color of pewter.

"You remember everything I told you? The man you see, he is your ideal, he is an incarnation, an ideal made flesh and blood." I said I remembered. "Then we can do no wrong," he said.

Once upon a time, a great sinner, a great drunkard, found himself freezing to death in the cold, and so he took refuge in a mission house. A young woman worked in this house, and when she saw the man, half dead from cold, she helped put him to bed, and when he slept, she took his coat, which was torn and full of holes. The night was very cold, but all night she sat at the side of his bed and mended the coat. Before daybreak, she placed the coat on the foot of the bed and went out of the room.

The other sisters scolded her. "You have stayed up all night in the cold mending this coat," they said, "and you are not very strong." But she said she was glad to do it; it was her first chance to serve one of God's creatures.

Just then, the great sinner, the drunkard, the wife beater, the tormentor of his children, awakened and came into the room where the sisters sat together. "Who fixed my coat?" he asked them. "I did," said the sister. The man looked at her, took off his coat, ripped apart the seams, tore the pockets so that they once more dangled. "This is how I like my coat," he said to the sister, and he left.

The sister was shocked, but she began to pray for the man's soul. Of course she fell sick from her exertions, and soon she was on her deathbed. The sinner, too, was soon on his deathbed, but that was of no consequence to him. Did he regret tearing his mended coat? No. His will had been done.

Time and time again, when I was working on *The Siren*, Max would explain his vision of the film to me. Each time the explanation was more desperate, more feverish. Then one day he thought to ask me how I saw what happened between the man and the woman. And I said I saw all stories in the same way. It didn't matter what the story was or who the people were: always one person was trying to impose his will on another. The greatest thing was to impose your own will. If you failed at this, then you subjected yourself to someone else's will. This, I said, was what the world was about.

"Everyone is a masochist or a sadist?" Max asked me. "That is what you are saying?"

"Everyone wants his own way," I said.

"And will do anything to get it?"

"Anything."

"And when he doesn't get his way, then he enslaves himself to someone else? He lives vicariously through him?"

"Yes," I said. "That's it."

"Anna," he said, "there are people who are not like that." I said I didn't know any. "I am not like that," he said. I said there was no one else who wanted his own way more than he did. "Yes," he said, "but what I want I pay for myself."

"It is yourself you punish," I said. "You are like a horse that learns to whip itself. But always it is your will. Not for nothing are you a director."

He said my view of life was appalling. If it were true, then life was a dreadful business. "But still . . . ," he said, thinking.

"Yes, but still," I said, laughing at him. "Still, it would make a good film."

"SOME PEOPLE ARE ADDICTED to drugs, some people to food, I am addicted to travelling," I said.

Ivy was closing my suitcase. "You have nothing to say today?" I asked her.

"I have a sore throat," she said.

"And?"

"And the man in the hat with the pink ribbon, I saw him again," she said. "If he only came to tell me about Neville, what is he doing in front of the building? He already told me about Neville."

"You're sure it's the same one?"

"Miss Anna, go to the window and look."

Across the street, under the apartment building's maroon awning, a man stood, wearing an ancient fedora trimmed with a pink satin ribbon. "I'm calling the police," I said, but just as I picked up the phone, Ivy said, "Miss Anna, he's gone." And when I looked again, he was not there.

"You know," I said, "sometimes it is easy to see signs everywhere, to suspect everyone. I have such tendencies."

"Well, I don't," Ivy said. "We didn't dream him up. If you're going out later, be careful."

But when was I not careful? When did I walk out of my door and go up and down the sidewalk as if I were a normal person, invisible? Sometimes, when I walked, I knew—it becomes a sixth sense—that no one was aware I was there, no one's eyes were on me, and then I would follow someone, track him, drop back when he stopped in front

of the fruit displayed in front of the grocery, listen when he talked to
the man at the newsstand. If I was very lucky, I would follow two
women or a man and a woman and listen to what they had to say.
Oh, this was an uncontrollable passion! Some day, Ivy said, I would
be arrested for it.

It is a wonderful day when I can follow two people and listen. I
come home and sit on my bed and think, That is real life. That is
what people do in real life. They talk about their sons who cannot
manage in school. They go for walks and look in windows of jewelry
stores. Then they go home and sit in their rooms and drink coffee
and write whatever it is they write. When they talk about their sons,
their sons are the important thing. When they are in their rooms,
what they do there is important. Real life is full of many things, not
just one thing at a time.

And then I ask myself, Did I once know this and then forget it? I
tell myself, I must remember it now. I tell myself, You are like a person
who has had a stroke. Everything in life you must relearn. These are
the little things they forget to put in scripts.

5

BALLOONS FLEW AND DRIFTED. The confetti snowed down so that
the light the revellers moved in was pearly, almost frosted. The monsters, nearly sixteen feet high, danced gracefully, their deformed heads
nodding, their huge white hands floating and swaying before them.
When I took my place on the balcony and looked down, I was frightened by the carnival I saw below me. Tall men in black held the ballet
dancers in their white dresses aloft. Why should there be such gaiety
if death had already announced his presence? This was celebration.
This was defiance.

And that morning, all the shadows fell perfectly. The monsters
cast their monstrous shadows. The ballet dancers whirled through
them, into the dark, back out into the light. When I stood on the
balcony and a dark shadow fell over me, my body went rigid.

Afterwards, I took off my make-up and went to look for Max. I said, It is perfect! This is the best you have done! No one who sees these scenes will ever forget them! And he looked at me as if I were a speck of dust, as if he were trying to remember who I was.

"Tomorrow we do it again," he said. "What is a crowd scene without faces? The eye looks at it, the mind gets used to it and hears a hum, a buzzing like a bee. When we do it tomorrow, there must be many close-ups, many details, the open mouth of a dancer, the painted eye of a clown, many such shots intercut. Now you see why I needed the elephant? What a focal point he would have been! But I tell you what," he whispered, "tomorrow the elephant will be here! I spoke to his keeper!"

Exhausted, I went to my dressing room and lay down on the little camp bed. The elephant! Again!

The next day the festival was reshot. The elephant stood on his four feet, his eyes open, and did not sway. The extras kept a safe distance. Mr. Feldman shot his scenes with a special lens. When the film was developed, it would appear that the extras were pressed against the elephant.

That night Max and Mr. Feldman developed the reels themselves. "I am not trusting the lab with this!" Max said.

"He is a little suspicious, isn't he?" Tomas asked me, and for an instant, something crossed my mind, not a thought, but its shadow.

While they were developing the film, I slept on my dressing room bed. At six thirty, Mr. Feldman shook me and said, "It's perfect, every frame perfect, not one frame you couldn't blow up and hang on your wall!"

Where was Max? Max was asleep on the floor of the cutting room. I went back to sleep. Rain on the roof of my trailer, *ping, ping, ping.* The roof must be made of iron. Why hadn't I noticed it before? That was why it was always so hot in here.

I liked the heat. It was like sleeping on the bench in front of my mother's wood stove.

I awoke and thought, Rain! How will we shoot the scenes in the gardens now?

"You could shoot the scenes in the husband's house," Tomas said, and Max said, "I do not shoot scenes out of order."

"Now you want to be a director?" I asked Tomas.

I had my eye on Mr. Torres. Always when he was not in front of the camera, he was sulking and whispering. His moustache had been shaved off. When I walked toward my dressing room, I deliberately passed in front of him. "No moustache?" he was saying. "By the time my scenes are shot it will grow back!"

We waited three days for the rain to stop. "Thank God," said Mr. Feldman, "two wasted days were Saturday and Sunday."

The next week we shot the scenes in the garden. We rehearsed the scenes in the husband's house. The following Monday, we shot the recognition scene in the house: the lover comes to visit his old friend, the husband, and recognizes his wife as the woman he met at the festival. The woman searches his face for signs of understanding. Does he see in her the woman who longs for her ideal love or does he see only an adulterous wife? He sees the adulterous wife. Again, Max and Mr. Feldman carried off the reels and developed them themselves.

That night, Max and I lay in my bed in the small hotel.

"Well, how is it going?" he asked. "What do you think? All the extra effort, it is worth it?"

"It is beautiful," I said. I yawned. I was so tired I was only a stain on the bed. I had no dimensions at all.

"Lazy beast!" he said. "That's the most you can say? But it is beautiful," he said. "Still, when people see it, will they see what I saw?"

"I hope so," I said. I wanted to sleep.

"She hopes so," he muttered. He sat up. I wanted to put out my hand and touch him, but I couldn't move.

In the morning, he was full of enthusiasm. From the porch, he could see the light was just right. We would film the first of the Brazilian scenes.

"It is all downhill from here," he said. "Except, of course, you. There is a lot of work to do with you."

Either I was too stiff or I hopped about like a stork, nothing in between. "Every bit of grace, every bit of sex, that we have to rehearse," he complained.

When Tomas came for us, I sat in the back, my chin on my chest, half asleep.

When we came on the set, it was very quiet. Of course it is very early, I thought. I waved to Mr. Feldman, who only nodded and looked away. Film makers were moody people. I went to my dressing room, put on my kimono, and waited for Miss Rosalie. She was never late but today she was.

Then, outside, I heard a terrible roar and the sound of crashing. A disaster, an earthquake, something terrible! I ran back to the set. Max was roaring like a mad thing, waving something white. People were all around him. A stagehand who got too close was hurled through the air. An ashen Mr. Feldman looked at me and shook his head.

"What happened?" I asked him. "The film was ruined?"

He shook his head. "Lost?" No. "Then what!" He couldn't speak.

I stood stone still. Max was raving in a language I didn't understand. He tore about the set waving what I now saw was a piece of paper. His eyes were everywhere but what did he see? Probably nothing. Then they settled on me. "Fired!" he shouted. "I am fired."

"Fired?" I repeated.

"Fired! They're replacing me with Luria! That idiot Luria!"

"Fired?" I said once more.

"Don't say it again!" he shouted at me.

I grabbed the sides of my head, pressed my hands into my skull, pressed my teeth together.

"Very good," Max said. "Very good. Remember that gesture, that expression. Use it when Torres tells you he's sending you away. Maybe if you pulled your hair a little." A smile erased the rage and was erased in turn.

"Come to my dressing room, come on," I said. If he was going mad, he didn't need all these witnesses. What did these people have to do with him?

Now he turned on me. "You want me to hide in your dressing room? They have fired *Max Lilly!* And not even in person! No, they send this courageous piece of paper!" He shook it under my nose. "Give me a piece of cheese!" he shouted.

Cheese? In pure panic, Mr. Feldman and I looked at each other.

"To lure that rat Pinsky out into the open! I'm going to his office! I am no writer of black notes on white paper!"

"What does it mean?" I asked Mr. Feldman.

"They fired him," he said. His hands were shaking.

"But why! What did he do?"

"Production delays, cost overruns, that damn elephant, Torres and his shoes, the moustache, all those things."

"For that they would fire Max Lilly?"

"You didn't know Torres was a stockholder? His wife is, anyway. We all know it. And Max, he threw the supervisor off the set. They won't stand for it. That crazy Rumanian, he's spoiled things for the rest of us. Ten thousand dollars filming women's hands! In gloves. In soapy water. Lying on tablecloths, on backs of chairs!"

"What crazy Rumanian?"

"Also, probably," Mr. Feldman said, "we have a spy on the set."

"Mr. Feldman!" I said, shocked. "Everyone cannot go crazy at once!"

"A spy," Mr. Feldman said. "What else? The rushes are perfect, but who's seen them? You, me, Mr. Lilly. The spy hasn't seen them. The extra costs aren't so bad either. If you've seen the rushes, you know where the money went. It's in the film. But someone carrying tales about a drugged elephant, telling Pinsky what it's like here, Mr. Lilly shouts one thing and means another, everyone confused and resentful, the supervisor thrown off, and still Mr. Lilly cannot speak the language! And a spy, he could repeat what people say about Pinsky, particularly what Mr. Lilly says—who knows what he means half the time, but he's very funny. 'If Pinsky were a cabbage, he'd spoil the soup.' "

"I know who the spy is," I said suddenly. "It's obvious! Tomas! Of course Tomas!" Because who else knew the language? Who else knew what Max was saying? Helpless, Mr. Feldman and I looked at each other. "It is too late now?" I asked. "They will give him another chance?"

"Will he walk in, hat in hand?" Mr. Feldman asked me. No, he would not do that.

"So," I said, "soon I will be going home."

"You!" Mr. Feldman said. "You're not going anywhere! This is your picture!"

"This is Max's picture!"

"Please, Miss Asta," he said. "We mustn't argue. They want you. They don't want him. That's how it is."

Perhaps if I spoke to them? If I went to Pinsky? But if Max knew, he would never forgive me. If I asked Pinsky not to tell Max I'd come? But Pinsky would see to it that Max knew. If Pinsky saw the rushes?

But if he liked them, he would keep those scenes in and the new director would pick up where Max left off. What could I do? Nothing.

"I'm going home," I said. "If you see Max, tell him I went home."

I paced up and down in my room. I paced up and down on the porch. No Max. There was a chill in the evening air, a smooth, cool dampness against the skin, on the inside of the arm where no hairs grow, a prediction of rain. Oh, I thought, this will be bad weather for filming, and then I thought, It is bad weather now and the weather will never change.

I walked out to the jetty. I climbed on the black, slippery rocks. Ten feet in front of me, blue-black waves crashed and sent up a white, violent, feathery spray. Drops of water floated through the air. Before I knew it, my clothes were wet. How was it possible to feel such fear and live? I should take my pulse, I thought. Of course, I didn't know how.

MY FATHER AND I are walking along the edge of an ancient pine forest. The pale white sun is behind the wood. The wood casts a sharp, thick, cool shadow on which we walk. We are both carrying homemade fishing rods, twigs, string, and a hook made from one of my mother's hairpins. My father carries a wicker basket filled with herring sandwiches and biscuits and bottles of lemonade. By the crumpled and now slightly wet and twisted neck, I hold a brown paper bag inside of which are two misshapen apples out of which something or other has taken small round bites. When I take one out to eat, my father will say, Be sure to rub it first on your skirt.

Ahead of us lies the Ebba River, always cold, even in the summer. Only when the sun is overhead, at the very edge of the river, can one see through the water to the smooth brown and black pebbles on the bottom. Only there is the water warm enough or shallow enough to walk into. A few feet further and the narrow shelf drops away and the river becomes bottomless. Pine needles carpet the slope that leads down to the river. The wind carries them from the trees and into the water. In summer, the brownish-orange needles are shot through with green. They bob on the water like wreckage from tiny boats.

I like to think of the tiny, wrecked boats and their miniature sailors. When I sit in the sun holding my fishing rod, I look for them among the pine needles. Surely one of them is going to call out to me and then I will scoop him up in my hand and take him home where I will keep him in a box with holes punched in the top and he will tell me stories. Of course I will save the best bits of my dinner for him and when no one is home I will take him to the kitchen window and let him walk up and down on the windowsill. I will teach him to keep quiet if anyone else is in the room. He will belong only to me.

We have almost reached the old jetty. Once there was a summer house in the woods up on the hill, but the owner died or lost his money, no one knows. Now the house is in ruins and we are forbidden to go there. All the same, I have been there many times with Marianne and Lars. Parts of the roof have collapsed. Swallows nest in the angle between the ceilings and the walls. They have built their nests on rafters. They swoop down like bats. Everywhere there is a thick carpet of pine needles. In the dining room a crystal chandelier is still suspended from a rafter but the sunlight streams through what used to be the roof.

Clouds scud by and cast shadows on what is left of the dining room floor. The floorboards are weathered and rotten, in some places soft as fur. Some windows have been shattered. Others are in fine shape, painted by the rain with little gray circles.

Whenever we come to the house, there is the sound of something scurrying, something slithering. I think there are snakes, said Marianne.

I suppose my brother and sister told themselves their own stories about the ruined house. To me it was a ruined castle. Once a prince had lived in it, but he fell in love with a beautiful princess who was lost in the wood, and so of course he took her home to her own kingdom and there he lived with her and they ruled together. But one day they would come back and then they would fix up the ruined castle.

Whenever we visited the ruined house, I stood at the window peering beyond the shadow into the dark pines, looking for a sign of their presence. I was the one who knew their story. Surely it was right that I would be the one to see them.

At home, at night, I would cry, thinking how terrible it would be if my brother or sister were to see them before me.

The old jetty is grayish-brown and spidery. It leans this way and that, every board askew. It has a demented look and smells of mold dried out in the sun. Occasionally, a rowboat is moored to one of its stilts and that means someone else is fishing or hunting in the woods. Today there is no rowboat. My father and I sit on the jetty and begin fishing. I look for the shipwrecked men.

I am always happy when I am with my father but annoyed when he speaks to me and interrupts my search for the little, drowned people, the plans I am making for what I will do with them. I watch him surreptitiously, wondering if he will fall asleep and I can sneak away to the ruined house.

Look! he says. *A swan!*

Far out on the water, a beautiful white bird goes sailing by. I know it is not a swan. It is a goose. I tell my father, Oh, you don't know anything! It is a goose.

"A goose!" he says. "I am disappointed."

We sit on the edge of the jetty, our lines in the water. Where they disappear beneath the surface, you cannot see them. "You are like me," he says. "Such a dreamer."

I don't think he is a dreamer. Does he look into the water and see small people clinging to pine needles? What does he know about the true owners of the ruined house? He is my father who loves me. In the morning, he gets up and asks himself, What must I do now? Will

I cough this morning or will today be a good day? Will I bring home enough money, or will they shout at me because I come home drunk? This, I believe, is all he thinks about. In our family, I am the only dreamer.

The sun is very hot. How old am I? Seven? Eight? My chest is still flat as a tombstone. I take off my shirt and slacks and lie on the soft boards of the jetty. I am wearing my underwear only. My father lies down on his stomach and falls asleep. I pick up my shirt, steal away, and find the narrow, overgrown trail to the ruined house. Animals rustle. The pine trees sigh in the dry, hot breeze. My skin is hot and smells of iron. In the dining room, under the chandelier, I stand looking up at the sky through the crystal pendants. A shadow falls across me. On the other side of the room, someone is watching me. His back is to the light. He is only a thick, dark shadow. I turn and run back down the path toward the jetty.

My father is sitting up. From the look on his face, I know he has been shouting my name. I tell him, There is someone in the ruined house! and he grabs me by the wrist and with his other hand slaps my face. He has never hit me before.

When I stop crying, I will not go near him. We sit in silence watching the water. What was I to think? he asks me. You could have drowned. The undertow here is terrible. Gradually, I give in. I inch toward him. As for the house, he says, someone's come to look at it. Of course if someone buys it, they'll tear it down. It's beyond repair. What they're buying is the land and the location.

Tear it down! And he says it so calmly, as if it were permissible, as if it's all right to tear down the ruined houses of absent people. I move away from him again, my back to the water, facing the pine forest. Its shadow is longer and falls over us. Cold, even on the hottest day of summer.

MAX IS BACK. He walked out to the rocks and found me. When I saw him coming, I waved but he did not wave back. He climbed up on the rock and sat down behind me, Max, in his elegant suit, sitting on a rock, sprayed by the salt sea. For a long time, I waited for him to begin, but he said nothing. A crescent moon lay on its back and drifted through the silvery blue sky.

"What did Pinsky say?" I asked him.

"Not much," he said.

"You know it was Tomas? Tomas was the spy."

"Even a spy has to have something to report."

"But what *did* he report? About the elephant? Was that it? Mr. Torres' shoes? What?"

"They want me to do things their way. Well, I cannot do things their way." Again, silence. "You're the one I'm worried about now," he said. "They'll go on with the picture. Don't worry, I'll direct you at night. All this talk about compromise! You compromise a little bit here, you trick them a little bit there, and soon whatever it is you set out to do, that thing is gone. And something else. Pinsky wants me to like him. Well, I cannot like him and I cannot pretend. No one is that great an actor. So," he said. "I am getting wet."

We went back to my room.

"Get undressed," I said. "Get under the covers. You'll catch your death."

"For a young person, always to be so worried about health."

"When I was a child, my knees swelled. For weeks my father had to carry me everywhere. They took me to doctors. People stood around and worried and looked at me as if I were already dead, so now I am careful."

"While you worry about a chill, the roof will fall on you," Max said. "Of course you are worrying. In the morning, I will call Anders. Of course he already knows everything. When I got to Pinsky's office, Maud was outside. You know they call her the Virgin Queen of the Lot? Anders always has a plan for catastrophe, and not only for himself. He has plans for everyone. Of course I have a contract for three pictures but it's no good. They'll let me start, then they'll fire me. No one's nerves can hold up under it. If I don't find another place, then I'll go home. But you, you will be fine."

After that, we lay on our bed, on our backs. At one point, Max laughed. "A camera up above would see a dead king and a dead queen," he said.

"But not a translator," I said. "Tomas is gone."

"Gone?" Max asked.

"Suddenly I have discovered how very well I speak English," I said. "Who will employ him now? A company spy?"

"It is not necessary to take revenge," Max said.

"Not necessary," I said, "but very pleasant."

"You are a good girl, Anna," Max said.

"If we could only talk about the time before this all began," I said. "When you were a child. When you lived in Russia."

"First of all, I was never a child," Max said, irritated. "Second of all, what is there to tell? I was not poor. My father made very good hats. Everyone bought them. I went to a good school. I did my work. I watched the men and women who made the hats and never did anyone see anything so boring or frightening, these brown and gray people hunched all day over pieces of leather and fur, occasionally a needle glinting when the sun got in. Then the soldiers came, my father was killed, my mother hid in a stove and afterwards suffered from chest pains and one morning I went to wake her and she didn't get up. So that was the end of Russia and relatives sent me to Germany and from there I went to Sweden. A short and uninteresting story."

"More," I said.

"More?"

"You liked your mother?"

"Of course I liked my mother. She was my mother. Not very interesting, but a good cook, a calm person, not very strong. I was not supposed to excite her, so you can imagine, with my temper and my tantrums, I spent a lot of time in the fields shouting and screaming to the birds and the bees, and all the time dreaming up stories, all the time drifting in and out of stories in nice clothes at the most interesting parts. It wasn't a bad life."

"You looked like her?"

"Like my mother? She wasn't a monster. A woman with a face like mine! No, I looked like my uncle. He was in the army the year I was born, so there was no gossip. I got into fights, I had such a temper, and I was big and furious, so I usually won. Yes, I always won. But this Pinsky! What was he? A glove manufacturer! We come from the same house! We talk the same way! I know a man like that. You make a glove, you make a hat, there's only one way. Now he makes movies, there's still only one way. So I wind up back in my little village with a glove manufacturer, not a hat manufacturer, and this time I lose."

"But, you know," I said, "there must be more than movies. There must."

"Why?"

"Sometimes one wants something human to love."

"Humans," he said, "can be very disappointing."

He meant: messy, without glamour, confusing, unpredictable, un-shaped, unaesthetic, raw material, all potential, frustration and despair.

"Well, what else?" I asked. "It's not such a short life, yours."

"Can't you see?" he demanded. "It's all a desert." And he began to weep. I got up and drenched his linen handkerchief in water, wrung it out, and pressed it to his forehead. Eventually he lifted his arm and his hand closed over mine.

• • •

The maid came to the door. "I've come to see Mrs. Pinsky," I said, and the woman showed me into the hall and disappeared.

From behind the curtained glass doors, I heard voices, conferring. Then the doors swung open and Mrs. Pinsky burst into the room.

"Anushka! Anushka! What a surprise!" She rushed up and threw her arms around me. Her head fit neatly beneath my chin and I looked down into her immaculate, soft brown hair. When she did not release me, I managed to raise one arm and pat her on the shoulder. At my touch, she drew back and searched my face.

"What is it?" she asked. "Something is wrong? I can see it. Don't try to fool *Mrs.* Pinsky. Someone at home is sick? Your mother is not well? She did not get her telephone? Tell me what happened."

I gestured with my hands, a foolish gesture, as if I were holding a crystal bowl.

"Oh, how can you talk, standing up, and you're so pale, come in, come in! Now," she said, settling me on a chintz settee in a room that was part parlor, part greenhouse, "tell me."

And so I told her that Max was fired, I had come here to work with him, if it weren't for him I wouldn't be here, and no matter what the complaints, he was making a great movie.

"So," said Bertha, "you want to know what I can do about it?" She clasped her fat white little hands together and settled her plump chin on them. "Well," she said, "this is a hard one. Of course I can do something, but what should I do? He is happy working for my Saul? Of course not. No one who works for him is happy. He has weapons with which to fight my Saul? Of course he doesn't have them or he would still be working. They see eye to eye? They don't. So let's say I interfere. Your Mr. Lilly, he goes on working. My Saul, he finds little ways to interfere. The film is finished, The Studio ships out the film missing one reel, maybe two. It can happen. And all the time everyone looks at the paper boy with more respect. How long will your Mr. Lilly stand it? You will like to see this happen to him?"

I clenched my hands into fists.

"You upset yourself, and what for? What's done is done. Now what must we do? We must think of how to help Mr. Lilly. You are a smart girl. A stupid girl, she would have gone to my Saul. You came to me. So you come from a little town in Sweden and I come from a little town in Poland, but we know. Everywhere families are the same."

She picked up her long strand of pearls and began to finger them. When her fingers reached the diamond clasp, they stopped. She dropped her hand and hit her thigh.

"I have it!" she said. "I have it! See how this sounds to you. You've heard of Ben Levine the producer? A good friend of mine. Probably you've heard rumors? No? Well, a fat little thing like me and a short little thing like him, it's hard to imagine. Anyway, the rumors about us, they were true. Tomorrow they could be true again. A great producer! So everyone asks themselves, How does she hold on to Saul? But he knows, he looks at me the wrong way and I'm out the door. And he does so well because if he doesn't, Ben will do better! Oh, Anna, life is funny! So what I think, Anna, is we should send your Mr. Lilly to see my Ben Levine. A different kettle of fish altogether. He doesn't interfere, always he encourages, he doesn't pinch pennies. Of course he doesn't make the money my Saul makes, but what is money? And if he likes you, he likes you forever."

"Mrs. Pinsky," I said, "no one can *send* Mr. Lilly."

"He can be sent for, no?"

"But it would—well, you know, it would have to be done just right."

"Just right, *of course* just right."

Then I became nervous. Tomas had spied for The Studio. Here I was, in the mouth of the lion.

"Mrs. Pinsky," I said, "why do you want to help me?"

"Look, my dear," she said impatiently, "sooner or later these problems come to me but by then they are dead mice on a silver tray. Who knows enough to come talk to me first? All over the lot, beautiful women. They look at me and think, a mouse, but I'll be nice to her. She sleeps with the cat. So how did you know to come to me? So yes, you're smart. But you like me, don't you? Come on, Anna! You like me!"

"You look like my mother," I said shyly.

"Your mother!" she said. "Oh, I feel proud! Stay for lunch! You know, my own daughters, they bother with me because they know without me they accomplish nothing, but they don't like me. They look in the mirror and they see my face looking back, so they don't forgive me so fast. You don't look like your mother?"

"I look like my father," I said.

"He was a good man," Bertha said. "I can tell."

And so I stayed to lunch. Max would be gone all day, meeting with Anders, making phone calls. We ate shrimp salad served in cantaloupe halves.

"You like sweets?" she whispered, leaning toward me. "Oh, I know we can't have them, but you like them?" I said I loved them.

"Come look at my jewelry," she said, and I followed her into her bedroom. From beneath her blouse she pulled a gold chain with a little key and with it she opened a small carved chest. "Look, look!" she whispered. She opened the bottom drawer.

"Chocolate-covered pecans!" she said, taking out a box. "Chocolate-covered cherries! Old-fashioned Swiss biscuits! Dark chocolate! Which do you like? Here, take two of each, you're up all night worrying off the pounds. Sit on the bed and eat."

I ate until I couldn't breathe.

"A good healthy appetite, I like to see it. So. Let me look at you. Chocolate all over your mouth." She leaned over and dabbed at my lips with her handkerchief. "Anything on my face? Yes? Here, take the handkerchief." She sat back and studied me.

"You're a nice girl," she said. "And smart. Very smart to decide you like me. Anything goes wrong, you come to me. Look, Miss Asta. Anything I say to you, you can repeat to Mr. Lilly. But if we are friends, you keep my secret about this little chest here. Tomorrow morning, he'll put me on the scale and all day long I will wring my hands and ask God how can I eat one crumb a day and not turn into skin and bones. Well, this is married life. So, we have an understanding? I talk to Mr. Levine?"

"Is it the right thing?"

"It is the right thing," she said. She looked happily at her thumb. It was smeared with chocolate. She licked it blissfully. "And you," she said. "You should like your next movie. Even if you don't, remember I said it would make you. After that, you won't need to come to me. You'll be like everyone else."

She patted her hair, stood up and straightened her dress. My eyes drifted to the carved chest. "Well, maybe not like everyone else," she said.

6

ON FRIDAYS when I came home from work, it was my habit to cook liver and green bananas. One day, I came home early and because I was still wearing my white uniform (I worked then at the National Biscuit factory), and because the uniform already needed washing and

I did not want to soil my other dresses, I went out into the yard kitchen and began to prepare the liver. As I spiced and salted the meat, I thought how far away my father's house in Mare River seemed, how small, as if it shrank a little every week and every month I was away from it. I thought about my brothers and sisters who still lived there, and about my stepmother, and I wondered who she found to sweep the yard now that I was gone, but as was my custom, I put them out of my mind.

Neville was still at work but he would soon be home. On Fridays, he always had extra work, because women wanted their jewelry repaired for the parties they would go to over the weekends, and men who wanted to give presents were anxious to pick up whatever they had ordered.

At that time, we lived in a rented apartment in a house built around a courtyard. In one corner of the courtyard, opposite our apartment, was the kitchen, which was roofed in but stood apart from the house.

I turned and saw Mrs. Brown's son, Jimmie, who liked to joke with me, standing in the doorway.

"We don't need any nurses here," he said to me.

"Don't worry," I said. "I may have to nurse *you*," and then I went back to my work. I was distracted, and instead of cutting the onion, I cut my finger. It was as if our small conversation had taken place in a disturbing dream, yet there was nothing out of the ordinary about it.

Later, Neville and I were sound asleep when we heard terrible screams from the next apartment. I threw on a dressing gown and when I rushed out onto the veranda, there was a man on a bicycle in front of Mrs. Brown's door. Mrs. Brown was running up and down the yard in her white nightdress.

"What happened?" Neville called, coming out behind me, still buckling his pants belt.

Mrs. Brown flew like a demented moth, back and forth, up and down the yard. Neville ran into the yard, caught her and held her. Then she told us that Jimmie had met with an accident on his way back from Gordon Park and now he was in the hospital.

"Don't worry," I said. "We'll go with you." This happened before my husband bought his car, which brought him so many police friends and so much trouble. We waited while Mrs. Brown dressed and the three of us walked out to the road and waited for the bus. The swamp turtles croaked, and the crickets chirped, and from across the empty fields we could hear the church choir, now faint, now strong, as if they were coming closer, then moving away. They were practicing.

When we reached the hospital, Jimmie was unconscious. His

mother begged and pleaded but he could not speak to her. Her son's friend, who was also there, told her that Jimmie had been sitting in the front seat on the way back from Gordon Park, but when they decided to give a young woman a ride home, he insisted on sitting in the back so that the girl could ride more comfortably in the front seat. Apparently, when another car hit them, he was thrown forward and hit his head on the front seat. His friend kept apologizing. He said he should have known. He shouldn't have let Jimmie change his seat; if he had stayed where he was, he would be fine now. Both the driver and the girl were bruised, but neither was badly injured. Mrs. Brown and I listened to this and she began to cry. Neville took her to a bench and sat with her. I told Jimmie's friend none of it was his fault. How could he have guessed his car would be hit, and as far as I knew, it was usually safer to ride in the back than in the front.

The next day a messenger came from the hospital. Mrs. Brown wept at the sight of him and could not be persuaded to dress herself and go to the hospital. Finally I asked her if she wanted me to go for her. By the time I reached the hospital, Jimmie had died. A doctor asked me to identify the body. We went down to the morgue, and they pulled out the first drawer.

"No, that is not him," I said. They pulled out the second. I lifted his left hand and saw the familiar gold bracelet Neville had made for him. I knew his face, although it was so changed, so smoothed out, his nose so much larger, that I might have hesitated had I not seen the bracelet he always wore. "It is him," I said, and they closed the drawer.

Afterwards, I thought about it often, how strange it was that he came to the door of the kitchen, saw me in my uniform and said, "We don't need any nurses here," and I said, "Don't worry. I may have to nurse *you*." I never wore my uniform once I left work. Jimmie was never home that time of day. Even though my uniform was white, I don't believe I looked like a nurse in it. This was one of those small events, so small that if it were a stone you would be unable to find it on the ground where it lay, but even as it happened, it shimmered with strangeness, was swollen with meaning, as a fruit ready to burst, and it did burst later that evening.

Jimmie and I were talking about one thing, but we were really talking about something else, something that had not yet happened.

Perhaps spirits can see into the future after all, but can only tell us what we are willing to hear.

Neville and I had been married fifteen years and for fifteen years we had lived happily. I joined the church and on Sundays I no longer went to the movies while he attended services. I gave up dances and large parties. When the church gave dances or had a youth meeting, I baked and cooked. I read the Bible and studied it. We had two children, one boy and one girl, and on Saturdays we took them into the country and on holidays we took them to see the dancers in their animal costumes as they made their way through the crowded Greenstown streets.

Then a man knocked at my gate, and when I told him to come along, he asked me if my husband Neville was no longer a Christian. I said, "I don't know. You'd have to ask him." I had a trusting nature. People in our yard always commented on it. But this time I asked, "What is this all about?" and he looked at his shoes and said he didn't want to cause trouble.

"I am his wife," I said, "and I have a right to know."

"He owes me money," the man said.

"For what?" I asked. And he said my husband had sent a woman abroad and every week Neville was to pay him for getting the woman a visa, but months had gone by, and he had not been paid.

"I would like to try that plan myself," I said. "Who is this woman?" I asked.

"I don't want to cause trouble between you," he said.

"Who is this woman?" I asked again.

"Her name is Merle Janesmith," he said. As soon as I heard the name, she became real, and I knew that this life, this good life I lived with my husband and children, was over.

When Neville came home that night, I said, "A man was here to see you."

"What did he want?" he asked me.

"He said you owe him money," I said.

"For what?"

"For Merle Janesmith's visa," I said.

"I don't know any Merle Janesmith," he told me. But when he sat down at the table, he was restless and he could barely eat the liver and green bananas I set before him. Before I had a chance to get the teapot, he jumped up and said there was a bracelet he had to deliver to a man on the outskirts of town. When he came back I asked him if it was all taken care of and he said it was.

A few weeks later a letter for Neville arrived at the house, and when I turned the letter over, I saw it was from a Merle Janesmith in Maryland. Merle Janesmith! I took the letter and held it over the steaming teakettle and while I held it there I heated up a sharp knife and slid it under the glued envelope flap. I opened the letter and read it. "I am so lonely here and you promised you would come and join me and if you don't I don't know if I can wait for you," said Merle Janesmith, who had many other things to say as well. I took some glue and sealed up the letter and put it on Neville's pillow.

"There's a letter for you, sir," I said. He put it in his pocket and said he'd read it later. He asked me if I wanted to wake up the children and put them in the back seat of the car and take them for a ride, but I said no, I didn't. He said he would go for a short ride himself and he left.

Every week when I came home from work with my pay envelope, I handed it to Neville, and on the way to work he passed the bank and deposited the money in our account. We had planned to buy a house in the Lavender Hill section of Greenstown and we went to the building society. They were very helpful and we put some money down. When an architect inspected the building site, he said it was too swampy and warned against building there. The building society made no objection to refunding our money and suggested that we build a house in a development under construction near Queen's Lane, but I said, No, I don't want to live there. There's too much traffic and the neighborhood is not good. The officer of the building society promised to contact us when he heard of something promising.

I had not looked at the bank book in years. Every week I handed Neville my salary and every week he deposited it. I assumed we had a great deal of money. Now I went to his dresser and found the bank-book under his folded white handkerchiefs. I opened it up. Six hundred dollars withdrawn! Two hundred dollars withdrawn! For what? We had less than a thousand dollars left.

When Neville came home, I said, "Neville, look at this bankbook. What happened to all our money?" He said the car he bought was expensive and so were the repairs. "This money sent Merle Janesmith out of the country," I said, and he didn't answer me. "You might as well tell me," I said, "because I already know. This is why the man came to the house and said you owed him money."

"She doesn't make any difference to me," Neville said.

"Then why are you paying all this money to send her away?" I asked him. "Aren't you going to join her?" I asked him. He said he wasn't. "You're a liar!" I shouted at him, and when he tried to push me backwards, into the bedroom and onto the bed, I hit him as hard as I could. He picked up a bottle of perfume to hit me with but I already had my sewing scissors in my hand. He put the bottle down but I held on to the scissors.

After that, I took the rest of the money out of the account and opened an account of my own in a different bank. I waited for more letters from Merle Janesmith, but none came. I thought perhaps her letters were going to his place of work, and I spoke to a woman I knew in the office. One day she called me at the biscuit factory and said a letter had come. "Fine," I said. "I'll be there lunchtime."

"You have a teakettle?" I asked the woman, and when she said she did, we steamed the letter open and I read it. Merle Janesmith had grown tired of waiting for Neville and was writing to tell him that she was getting married. It was too hard and too lonely, living on her own in such a big country. I kissed the woman and thanked her and we glued the letter's flap. I went back to work.

That night when Neville came home from work, everything about him was drooping. His cheeks drooped, his clothes drooped on his thin frame, and even his hair drooped across his eyebrows. He went into the bedroom and lay down on the bed. "What's wrong with you?" I asked him. He didn't answer me. "Oh," I said, "maybe Merle Janesmith is getting married. Maybe your girlfriend got tired of waiting for you." He still didn't answer. "I'm putting your food on the table," I said. "If you want it, come and get it." He didn't sit down at the table. He left the house.

I didn't see him go. He must have climbed out the bedroom window. Climbing out of bedroom windows! I hadn't done that since I'd been a child in Mare River. That was when I knew the marriage was over. I didn't trust him and he climbed out of windows to avoid me.

How had it happened? I never asked him. I was too proud. He'd met Merle Janesmith and stolen my money to send her out of the country. It all began when he decided to buy a car. Before that, we never had a minute's trouble, but after he bought the car, everyone in the world was his best friend, particularly a group of policemen who lived nearby. They would stop by the house and soon they would all roar off for a drive. Neville began to drink one beer, then two beers, and finally he began to come home drunk.

"Neville," I said, "I always said I wouldn't marry a man who drank."

"It's too late now," he said.

Stanny, my friend from Mare River, came and talked to him. My brother Jack came and talked to him but he continued to drink. "She will leave you, you know," my brother Jack told him, "and she'll take the children with her." I refused to set foot in the car with the children. I pleaded with him to stop drinking because one day he would kill someone else or himself. He didn't listen. And all the time I thought that the novelty of the car would wear off, the drinking would stop, and everything would go back as it was. I never believed that anything could separate us or undo the many-knotted rope that tied us together.

When Neville and I first came to live in that apartment, there was a couple who lived next door to us. Doreen was a harder person than Nash, and we always said if she decided she wanted to marry him, he didn't have a chance against her. Doreen met Nash's mother and his mother told Doreen that Nash would marry her if she were pregnant. From that instant, it was Doreen's ambition to become pregnant, but months went by and nothing happened.

Meanwhile, I bought a little hen and kept her in the yard. I liked her because she had such beautiful red and bronze feathers and so I did not have her killed but decided to keep her for her eggs. We would hear her clucking and clucking, but we never saw an egg. Then I noticed that the little hen was always disappearing and one day I saw her go beneath the house. There was an old man named Crony who lived with his daughter in an apartment across from ours, and he came up to us and said he thought we had a good little hen there and when she vanished from the yard, she must be sitting on her eggs, hoping to hatch them.

"Neville," I said, "Crony thinks the chicken is laying her eggs under the house, so when you come home tomorrow, I want you to go look under there." I went to work and I didn't think about the chicken or Doreen or Nash.

The next day I worked late, and Neville and Crony crawled beneath the house, looking for the little chicken, and they began to find eggs. They found one dozen eggs, then another dozen, and they were crawling further and further under the house when Crony called to Neville and said, "Look what I found here! It's made of wax."

Neville said, "Bring it out so we can look at it."

When he crawled out and stood up in the sun, they found two long waxen things tied together.

"Are they candles?" asked Neville. "What are they?"

"You don't know what they are?" Crony asked him.

"I don't know. How should I know?" Neville asked.

"Whosoever put it there, she knows," said Crony. "This is magic. These are two figures. See where the heads go? And the arms? And the feet? And the string that binds them? Someone is casting a spell to tie two people together. The ladies, they set traps like this."

"Well," Neville said, "I don't know what it is, but it belongs to someone, so let's put it up here on the clothesline and whoever it belongs to, he or she will come and get it."

"And where did we find it?" Crony asked. "It was right beneath Nash's bedroom, that's where it was."

"We're going to have three dozen eggs when we get through," said Neville, who was very impressed with my chicken, and had already forgotten about the wax things.

That evening, I came home to find Neville and Crony and many of the tenants standing about in the yard staring up at my clothesline where it was fastened to a bough of the plum tree in the corner of the yard.

"What is that?" I asked, coming over. "What have you been making?" I asked Crony.

"I didn't make it," Crony said. "I found it under the house where we went to look for your eggs. She's laying her eggs under there and setting."

"Two things tied together," I said, looking up at it. Other neighbors saw us gazing up into the plum tree and came over to look. I went into the house to cook dinner and to look at the eggs and I heard Doreen's voice, high and shrill.

"Who put this there? Who put this there?" she cried out.

"Doreen, I did," Neville said.

"And how did you find them?" Doreen asked. "What are you doing with them?"

"I found them when I was under the house looking for eggs," Neville said.

"Whosoever found them, it was him they were set for," Doreen shouted at Neville.

I put down the knife I had used to slice the bread and went out. "What is this now, miss?" I asked Doreen.

"You see those things there?" Doreen asked me. "He put them up there to shame me, but whosoever found them, it was him they were set for."

"Why don't you ask me who set them, Doreen?" Nash asked her. "My mother knew you went to that magic man in Christine Street."

"It was he who set them!" Doreen shrieked, pointing at Neville.

"Oh, no," I said. "Neville and Crony were under the house looking for the *chicken* and they found those things. You found them there, Neville?" I asked, and he nodded. "And you put them up on the line to keep them out of harm's way?" He nodded again. "So don't you go lying after us and say *I* set them there for Neville. Where were they?"

"Under Nash's bedroom," Crony said.

"Am I going to set magic spells for Nash?" I asked Doreen. "You think I am so stupid? You think I will set magic traps for anybody?

All I want of life is to come and go as I please. A man doesn't please me, I go. I don't please the man, he goes. I am a free woman, Miss Doreen, and I don't want any man I have to set magic traps for."

And then, because I could feel Neville's eyes on me, I looked at him. He looked at me as if he were seeing me for the first time. I saw him look at Doreen, a woman he hated, with a kind of longing, and then look back at me, puzzled and disappointed. So I would not set magic for him! I wanted to be a free woman! Neville disapproved of magic and looked down on people who practiced it, but in that moment, it seemed to me, Neville decided that I did not love him as he wanted to be loved.

But I had no time to think about it because Doreen threw herself at Neville, intending to gouge out his eyes, and I threw myself upon Doreen in order to prevent her, and I heard Nash shouting at Neville, "Don't get involved in this!" and Neville said, "I have no intention of getting involved," but when I had Doreen down and was taking off my shoe to beat her, Crony got someone to hold me and he held Doreen.

After that Nash would have nothing to do with Doreen. Crony said that Nash was ashamed of her because she had disgraced him in front of the neighbors and one afternoon his mother and two brothers came with a cart and removed all his things. Doreen, her belly swollen, watched from the doormouth as they drove away.

When I was ten years old and living with my father and stepmother in Mare River, my father decided to work out of the country as a farm laborer. He wanted to buy more land, and salaries out of the country were far better. As he was about to leave for his examination, I sneezed.

"Oh, that is bad luck," said my father. "When your firstborn sneezes as you're about to take a trip, it is very bad luck." His mother, my grandmother Lize, was there and she said, "No, Vidal, if your firstborn is a girl who sneezes as you're leaving, that is good luck." My father turned to me and said if he had good luck and passed the examination, he would bring me something special when he came back from foreign work.

He passed the examination and when he came back to Mare River, he took me down to Cinnamon Bay and bought me an enormous doll with hair I could comb. On Saturdays thereafter, the other girls of Mare River would come to my house and we would marry our dolls. We would make clothes for our dolls and buy or bake little cakes for them. The wedding of my doll was always the day's main event. I had the doll when I married, and for years afterwards, it sat in the middle of our bed. Then when I left the country, I gave it to Tita Lu to hold for me.

My father always said he was not superstitious, but he was. He was very superstitious. Everyone, I think, is superstitious, because everyone wants to know why his life goes on as it does, and people want to believe that they themselves can affect the course of that life, as I want to know why, one afternoon, after fifteen years of a happy marriage, a thin man knocked at my gate and when I told him to come in, he asked me if my husband Neville was still a Christian. When I think back to that afternoon, I still believe there was something I could have done to change the way things were happening. Even now, I think I could go back in time and change the way things happened if only I knew how to do it.

In those days, I wanted to know why lives ran on as they did, although I would not ask for an explanation. I still want to know. Perhaps once I am dead and buried, I will be seen walking the earth because I will still want my questions answered. The more time passes, the more I want to know: what is this life all about? We feel our stories within ourselves, growing, trying to hatch, pushing at us, wanting to live themselves out through us. Perhaps our stories possess us and are, in the end, more real than we are. But where do they come from? Are they like ghosts, possessing us? Or are we ghosts, existing to harbor these stories and give them a home?

We think ghosts live as we do, but we believe ghosts are weaker than the living. They flicker on and off. They have less power than the living and can only make themselves seen some of the time. So we think. But are we all brides and grooms of ghosts who fill us with their stories so their stories can have a second life? A second chance? Are we leading our own lives at all? Can we do anything to change the stories we feel growing within us?

I like to think there is a thin red thread of meaning connecting my life to other lives, as a red clay path in the mountains always leads from one house to another, Jimmie, Doreen, Merle Janesmith, Neville, the chicken, the woman who told me about the letter and helped me steam it open, my father, my sneeze, all of us and everything, tied together, part of one another's stories, bound together like the two wax figures suspended from my clothesline in Greenstown.

Anna says I am mad and crazy and romantic and there is no such red thread and life is such a rag bag anyway who would want to try making something of such trash, but when I see her sitting up at night I know she is sifting through those rags looking for the same red thread and if she doesn't find it, one day she will take some red thread from a drawer and stitch the pieces of cloth all together whether they belong together or not.

7

THERE ARE TIMES when something happens, it is like a flood, and you are on one side, the water is in the middle, and everyone else is on the other shore. Then the trouble is: how to get across to the other side? Everyone else is over there, waving, walking off, going about their business. It's not that they don't care: they see you across the water, but to them it is perfectly evident how to get across. Perhaps there is even a bridge and perhaps they already crossed it to get to their side and so they don't understand why you haven't done the same. If you are not with them yet, you soon will be. Any minute, you will be with them.

I don't know, really, if this is a dream or if it is a memory, or even a scene from a movie, but it is very clear, very vivid. Everyone is on the other side. I am on this side. The water is black, the tips of the waves are white: except for that the whole thing is shades of black and dark, dark blues. If I could paint it, I would do it. It is a waste of time, seeing these things, and off they go, you can't hold on to them.

Nothing like this ever happened, so it must be a dream. And what happens next is this: I am on the other side with everyone else, walking around, and everyone takes this for granted. Well, here she is at last. But I am still there, on the other side. So now I want to know: when are they going to notice me, over there, alone?

That is what it was like when Max was fired from *The Siren*.

Now every morning I went to the set and Max went off who knows where. I knew he spoke with Anders. I knew he talked with Maud. There were businessmen he met at hotels and some weekend afternoons I accompanied him. They talked about the weather. They talked about Sweden and Germany. They never talked about movies. But something was going on.

At night, Max took my script and we went through the scenes step by step. In the morning, I came to the set and said, "Mr. Luria, I am ready to begin," and after a few days, Mr. Luria said, "What an angel she is, already she knows everything, already she has everything worked out, what an angel," and we would get busy.

Then it was time to film the scene where Armando Torres is challenged to a duel fought with whips. I was to stand on the balcony and watch. In bed the night before, I said, "Max? When I stand on the balcony, of course I am afraid."

"Of course," Max mumbled. His back was to me.

"So what else must I be? I cannot stand there afraid the whole time. It will be boring."

"You can be happy," he said, again without moving. But what was I to be happy about?

"Happy?"

"Because two men are fighting over you."

"Oh, that is ridiculous," I said. "This woman would not be happy because her lover is fighting for her."

"She is a woman, isn't she?" He shrugged his bare shoulders.

"Well, anyway, it is only one scene, it is not so important," I said mutinously. I knew what he thought: every scene is important. He lay still, his back to me.

"Look, Anna," he said, sitting up, "if I spent more time in the Golden Palms it will be better. I am not always in such a good mood."

"I begged you to stay here?" Of course I knew he had troubles, but I had my own. Tomorrow I had to film a scene I didn't know how to play. For a few minutes he could stop being troubled!

"You've heard of Ben Levine?" he asked me. "The producer?"

"No."

"He wants to see me. Probably it will come to nothing."

"Probably."

"Well, you are angry, but frankly I don't have the energy. If you could leave me alone."

"Should I sleep on the floor?" He didn't answer. "Next to the bed? Like a dog?"

"You are trying to make me fight with you, but it won't work."

So the next day, when filming began, I didn't know what to do. I remembered how Max had directed me in the past: different emotions should flicker on and off. But which?

Mr. Luria was not happy with the scene. "It's a simple film, right, Miss Asta?" he said. "The men do their work, the women come along and distract them. The Garden of Eden all over again. The men are busy, the women cause trouble. That's your idea: the more trouble you cause, the happier you are.

"So you watch and look very pleased with yourself, and a little excited, in a naughty way, you know what I mean? Because he's whipping this other man instead of making love to you. But *you* know better. You know he's really making love to you. It's clear. Let's do it."

I was terrible. I knew I was terrible. For as long as I lived, never would I hear the end of that scene. Of course Mr. Luria was very pleased.

Almost every night, Max would direct me in the scenes for the next day. Every night, when I came home, he would ask me what Mr. Luria had done with this scene or that scene, and when I would tell him, he would say, "Good, good, he's killing it. Maybe they won't even release it. You'll be the only good thing in it." I said, believe me, I was not so good.

He said I was dragging the picture after me the way a dog drags a sled across the ice. I said I was being dragged like everyone else. We were competing: which of us was more miserable? It was a question.

The film previewed in Santa Monica and the usual group went to see it: Erik Grissom, Anders Estersen, Maud Marsh, Max and me. I came in wearing a pair of Max's slacks, tied around my waist with a rope, and his shoes. They were too small for me and they pinched. I wore his hat and hid my hair under it.

"So," said Erik when he saw me. "You make a very convincing man. But tell me why." I said I wanted to stand around in the lobby afterwards and listen to what the people had to say. How could I do that if they knew who I was? He said I was a glutton for punishment.

"Pinsky should see this," Maud sighed. "He spends ten, fifteen thousand dollars on portraits of this one and she shows up looking like a tubercular poet."

We sat in the back so we would be first into the lobby. "You will see," I said. "They will be laughing. In their place I would laugh. It's not a comedy but by God it is funny."

Women came out, crying, pressing white handkerchiefs to their eyes. Astonished, I looked at Max. He raised his eyebrows. Two men passed us. "How about when she raises her arm?" one of the men said. "Did you ever see anything like it? Pure sex!"

"Do you think she drinks?" a woman asked. "I think she drinks."

"She's very convincing," said her companion.

People drifted by. Some women cried, some women glared at their husbands as if to say, See? You are no better than the men in the picture.

"I wonder if she dyes her hair?"

"She's engaged to that Torres."

Outside, two men, sent from The Studio, stood on either side of the door, handing out questionnaires and little pencils. They looked very happy.

"Another hit," Maud said. Anders shook his head.

"How does he do it?" Max asked. "How does he know?"

"Who?" Anders asked.

"Pinsky. How did he know? If I ran The Studio, I wouldn't have touched that story, and then, after I fired myself, I would shut it down."

"That's why he's head of The Studio," Anders said.

"Not in Sweden," Max muttered. "Not in Germany."

"He wants prestige," Anders said. "But not if it costs too much."

"At home, the movies I made had prestige and also they made a fortune," Max said.

"Here they screen a new picture every week," Maud said. "Every single week. They need something in the theaters all the time. Every one of them has to make money or he has trouble with the distributors."

"*Dust* made a fortune?"

"He has two categories: his 'backbones' and his 'prestiges.' He doesn't make 'prestiges' for the money. People see him and say what an artist he is, how his heart's in the right place, look what he would do if his hands weren't tied. That's what he likes Anders for, right, Anders?"

Anders smiled and nodded.

"And you," I asked her. "What category are you in?"

"I make fortunes so he can afford to indulge me. I asked to make *Dust*. I asked to make *Madame Butterfly*. He said they won't make money, and he was right."

"But we are happy we made them, eh, Maudie?" Anders asked.

"A hundred years from now people will still see them," she said. "I keep my eye on that."

"But to have to wade through so much garbage first!" Max exclaimed. "Who can do it?"

"You have to do it," Maud said.

"Ben Levine's office called me," he said.

"Oh," Maud said. "Ben Levine!"

"He is the same as Pinsky?"

"The same but different," Anders said. "Smarter, but not such a businessman. Keep him warm."

"Let's see what Pinsky does with *her* when the reviews come out," Maud said.

"He already knows," Anders said. "He doesn't wait for anybody." And it was true. The next morning, Pinsky called me to his office.

"No, no," he said. "Not the chair in front of the desk. Everyone hates that chair. To my face they don't say it, but I know. It's so low, it's how I make them feel bad. That's what they say. I like that low chair. Why should I sit in a tall chair, my feet up off the ground, when I want to sit in a comfortable chair and look out the window? Who spends more time in here, me or them? Anyhow, sit at this table. We'll have some *kuchen*, a little jelly, maybe a cup of tea. Good? Good.

"So," he said as we sat down, "you're looking at me as if I bite. Who do I bite? This Studio, it is a big family, you can see how big it is. Remember, you said to the newspapers, if someone didn't bring you, you'd never find the set? A little country, everyone related, and I am the poppa. Something is troubling you, you come in here and I'll explain. You tell me what you want, I talk you out of it. You go out happy. Are you ready to make another picture?"

I said I was very tired.

"Who is not tired? I myself am exhausted. They are still arguing over *Wartime*. What country must show it first? All the time it goes on and all the time I am sneezing. We went to *The Siren* and such a terrible cold I had, I was on the edge of pneumonia, and Bertha, she said to me, 'Be quiet! This is a picture you paid for!' And I said to her, 'Be quiet? I *made* this picture. What can't they hear? You can hear people's voices?' So she got mad at me and said I didn't understand a thing, how could she feel a mood with all this sneezing? All these things happening and she wants to feel a mood? Well, German Jews, that's what they're like, very superior people. Of course you don't want to know all my troubles. Why should you want to know them? Even I don't want to know them. You were saying? You are tired?"

"Very tired."

"Too tired to star in a *film* opposite Mr. Charles Harrow, the star of *Wartime?*"

"Is it a good movie?" I asked.

"Not a movie, a *film!*"

"Is it good?"

"The best that money can buy."

He took a bite of his *kuchen*, looked up at me and saw I was not yet persuaded. "And," he said, "you will have people you know. In it,

Erik Grissom is your best friend, you can talk Swedish all day long. And my wife, she is so excited. Let me see, can I get this right? She said, 'Mr. Hall, he must direct her.' She said, 'This will make her. After this, nothing can touch her.' She is never wrong, Bertha. Will you do it?"

"If I could go home first," I said.

"You have a telephone. Your mother has a telephone? She should have one, I pay the bill for it. Why go home now? Finish this film and then go home. I'll pay for the tickets. Why not? How famous you'll be when you get off the ship! Your mother will die from joy!"

I stirred my tea with a tiny teaspoon. A rose leaf formed the crest of the spoon. Its stem resembled a rose stalk. Its basin was shaped like a rose blossom. "What a lovely spoon," I said at last.

"Take the spoon," Mr. Pinsky said.

"Oh, no, no," I said. "I can't take the spoon. You won't have a set!"

"Take the spoon!" he said. I was about to put it in my handbag. He said no, when I was finished, he'd wash it for me and wrap it in a napkin.

"Now, about the film," he said. "Let me tell you what it's like."

I sighed and sat back in my chair. I said I wanted to go home for Christmas. After that I would come back and do anything.

"So," said Mr. Pinsky, as if I hadn't spoken, "this film, we call it *Sin and Salvation.*"

"The title is long," I said.

"Never mind the title, listen to the story. From boyhood, two men are friends. In the army, they become heroes. Wonderful costumes, wonderful adventures, and such a script, what a script, a gilt-edged writer does this script! They go home on leave, and one man falls in love with a beautiful woman who is you. What love scenes! The women in the audience falling in love with both of you! In the dark, the wives don't even poke their husbands in the side so they should wake up after their big meal and stare at you! So wonderful, who can tell you?

"Anyway, this woman, she is married but of course she does not tell the young man. The husband comes home, surprises them, there is a duel, such excitement, the husband is killed, never a dull moment! The young man, he is exiled: of course, duelling is forbidden. Meanwhile, the young woman—that is you—marries the best friend. She loves money. The exiled young man comes home and the trouble begins. He tries to stay away from you but you want him.

"The two friends come to blows, there is another duel, a last-minute repentance, you rush across the ice, the ice breaks under you,

you drown. You are wearing a fur coat, it's heavy like an anchor, it pulls you under. You can see it? Wonderful! And so full of mysteriousism! A minister who gives thundering sermons! A European *Scarlet Letter!* Maud Marsh, she wanted to do it, but I said, No, Miss Marsh, the country wants to keep its pure, perfect girl! There is a good, pure little sister, but the role is too small for you. She was so disappointed, she cried! So, what do you think? Look what Mr. Pinsky finds for you!"

I said, "It is the same thing all over again, a married woman in the middle of two good friends! And in the end the two friends live happily ever after! That is a happy ending? The men walk off holding hands? Only men can love with a pure love? So what will I do in this picture? How many dresses I must be fitted for? Twenty? Thirty? I will spend more time with pins in my mouth than on the set in front of a camera. No, Mr. Pinsky! This is not for me! A good picture, please! A real human being! Not a beautiful dress with a head!"

Mr. Pinsky turned a deep tomato red. A flush spread from the top of his tight white collar, up his neck, his cheeks, to the top of his bald, shining head. He jumped up from the table. The little teacups and saucers slid and flew. The porcelain teapot slid to the edge of the table. I watched in fascination: it teetered and fell to the carpet. Where it fell, the colors of the carpet darkened.

"I tell you what is good and you say no!" Mr. Pinsky shouted. "I bring you the best film The Studio has for years and you say it is no good! An idiot is what you are! A flathead! What they say on the set! All that and worse! Tell me the truth. That Lilly! He told you, Come in here and whatever he says, to that you say no. Isn't that what happened? But your Mr. Lilly, he's taken care of himself! He's making *The Left Bank* for Ben Levine! He didn't tell you that! Instead he tells you, Don't listen to that Pinsky!

"Well, let me tell you. You have a contract. You break it, you never work again. Not here, nowhere. And your Mr. Lilly, he doesn't work either! You think Ben Levine will go ahead if I talk to the distributors? Don't count your feathers!

"Idiot! *Salvation*, it's a great film, a great film! And with Charles Harrow, no less. That bastard! Old women come in on crutches to see him! At his openings, we have a doctor. Already the theaters fight for bookings and we don't have a cast and you stand there and tell me you want a good film! You will do this film!"

"I am tired," I said.

"You are tired, then go to sleep!" he shouted. "Go to the casting office! Look at the hundreds of girls sitting there! Every one as beau-

tiful and talented as you! Tomorrow morning, fittings! Don't argue!
Here! Take your spoon! Take this envelope. Your reviews. You're a
big hit, Miss Asta. See what it says here? *'Men die like flies for the sake
of her. I would too.' 'If you don't fall in love with that raised right arm, go see
your doctor.' 'The Siren packs them in for the sixth straight week.' 'The Siren
breaking records across the country.' 'Who is Miss Asta and where has she
been? Mr. Torres is good but we wonder what she sees in him: he is, after all,
a mere mortal. In The Siren we see the birth of a goddess.'* This I did with
my bad choices? Tomorrow at eight on the set, Miss Asta!"

I SIT ON MY BED, my legs crossed, drawing on the back of some
letters: Would I consent to be interviewed for this magazine or that
magazine? Would I consider reading a book about my life? Would I
sign the framed photograph someone had mailed to me complete with
return packing and postage?

Probably I would keep the picture. I like it. Strangers should know
better than to bother an old woman.

"What are you drawing now?" Ivy asks me, coming in with the tea
tray.

"Oh, the usual nonsense," I say. I like to draw, I do it so badly, it
doesn't occur to me to try to do better. Ivy looks over my shoulder.

"That house again," she says. "Always the same house. Holes in
the roof, no glass in the windows. They lived on Green Island?"

"Oh, just a house somewhere in the forest," I say. She sits down
next to me.

"It doesn't stand on the ground," she says. "Why not?"

I look at the house: it floats in the air. And the tree next to it, all
gnarled, there were its roots, an inch away, but not connected to the
tree.

"If you drew a line here," Ivy says, pointing, "then it wouldn't
float."

"No, no," I say, pushing her hand away. If it was floating, it was
supposed to float.

"You know," I say, "a long time ago, we made a film on Green
Island. Remember? I told you, I think. Oh, so many years ago, maybe
fifty years ago, I was an old man's young wife, and my husband wanted
to start a coffee plantation and go boar hunting, and Green Island,
well, it was supposed to be India, you see. I forgot all about it until I
got a letter from an extra on the picture. What was it called? *Bitter*

Almonds? *Fools of Fortune*? Orange Bay, that was where we stayed, everyone in a different little house."

"Orange Bay!" Ivy says. "Right next to Cinnamon Bay! My mother used to walk there with my father."

"The women were so beautiful," I say. "So beautiful."

"Oh yes, oh yes," she says. "Orange Bay. Hope Bay." She bends over my drawing and looks at it. "Here is something new," she says. "A road to the house. And paving stones in the road."

"No, they are not stones."

"They aren't stones? No, they are not. All these round things here, are they faces? What does it mean, these faces stuck in the road?"

"Just faces looking up at the sun."

"And if a car comes and goes over the road, then it must run over these faces?"

"It is only a picture and a very bad picture!"

"Go on with your picture, Lady Clare," says Ivy. "That man in the hat, when I walked out this morning I saw him again."

"There is something he wants," I say. "Everyone wants something."

"From you, maybe," Ivy says. "Not from me."

After she goes out, I ask myself, What are these faces? Who knows what they are? But of course I drew them so I should know.

AFTER WE FINISHED *Salvation,* a reporter asked me what I was thinking in the last scenes when the young girl came to see me and fell to her knees next to my bed and began to pray. All I did was sit up in bed and watch her, but what a powerful scene it was.

"Well, really, to tell the truth," I said, "I don't know."

"Who would know if you don't?" he asked me. And when I stood up abruptly and made a gesture Mr. Pinsky already knew too well, one hand up, palm out, he answered for me. "Do great artists need to know what they're doing?" he asked, and then he declared the interview over.

I am looking at my picture of the house and the road. Hundreds and hundreds of faces in the road. The road does not stop at the edges of the paper. It is only cut off by them. Presumably it goes on forever, into the distance behind the house—that is the future, don't ask me how I know—and the distance in front of the house—that is the past, and everywhere, the road is filled with these faces.

• • •

"Of course you must attend the screening of *The Siren*," Bertha Pinsky said. "Without you there is nothing. All these men want to stand around and interview another phony Spaniard?"

"Then I want Mr. Lilly to escort me," I said.

"That would be very foolish."

"Why?"

"He should sit there and be humiliated? *'Personally directed by Mr. Igor Luria.'* That's how the credits read now. He must sit there and look at that?"

"But he will know what he directed! He will know he directed me!"

"Look, Anna," she said, "on this earth there is nothing more brazen than a director unless it is a producer, and Mr. Lilly is both. But that is only how they are on the outside. On the inside it's a different matter."

"If he wants to go, I want to bring him."

"My Saul will throw himself in the goldfish pond."

"Can he swim?" I asked. We both started to laugh.

"Come look at my new necklace," she said. "I don't know how it is, I live on air, I don't lose an ounce," she said loudly. She was very pleased with herself. I worked for her husband but I had no interest in what he said. I listened to her. "So, at a time like this we should separate a young girl from her oldest friend?" She held out a tray of pralines. "I'll say that to him."

For the screening of *The Siren*, Mr. Pinsky had the festival sets resurrected. The guests were driven from the front gate to the set, a band played, balloons were everywhere, confetti floated down like snow and tangled in everyone's hair. In the middle of the guests were the male dancers, in black tuxedos, holding their female partners aloft. It was inexpressibly lovely. "Look, Max," I said, "it's your set. Even the monsters!"

"Without an elephant it's no set of mine," Max said.

Yet somehow it was known, Bertha let it be known, that Max directed the festival, Max ordered the balloons, Max was sorry the elephant was otherwise engaged, and all night people came up to him and shook his hand. And at midnight, everyone was driven back to the studio gates and limousines drove everyone to Mr. Pinsky's private theater and the movie was screened.

Of course I had sat in the dark and watched myself on the screen before. Now, I watched my face on the screen, and thought, That face is not my face. That face is like a balloon that has floated away from me. All those faces up there, they should belong to me, but now they are lost. How perfect were those faces! How hard Mr. Feldman worked to be sure the nose shadow was very short! How long he adjusted the lights until I could feel the heat of the small spotlight on my chin. How he fussed with a strange celluloid shape suspended above my head so no harsh light fell on my forehead.

So really, I told myself, the huge faces on the screen, they are not my faces at all.

But I felt as if they had been stolen from me.

When I was a child, my father used to tell me a story about someone who lost his shadow. Until he found his shadow, he could not be happy. Ivy tells stories about ghosts. On Green Island, you know you are in the presence of a ghost when that person casts no shadow. There were my shadows, up on the screen.

When I was a child, I gave people a piece of my mind. My mother told me a story about a child who gave people a piece of her mind and then one day she gave someone a piece of her mind and found she had none left. That, she said, will happen to you. How many shadows could I afford to lose?

"What's the matter with you?" Max whispered. "You're shaking."

"Shhhh!" said Mr. Pinsky.

I sat there and watched the rest of the film, but really, I was completely crazy. Every time I saw my face, I saw it floating off. Max knew how to catch it, but Max was going away.

"You're overtired, what?" Max whispered.

My teeth were clamped together. If I opened my mouth, who knew what I might say? When the lights went on, the entire audience turned toward me and clapped: my first standing ovation.

"Stand up, Anna!" Max said. I stood up. He held me up. All those hands clapping, the loud noise woke me. With my loosely stitched-on face, I smiled at everyone. I turned to Max and bowed to him. Finally, he bowed to the crowd. The applause grew even louder. So they knew. They knew it was him.

People moved down the aisles to the reception room.

"Tonight you will stay with me?" I asked Max. He seemed surprised.

"Whatever you want," he said.

That night, on the way home, Max said, "Fine, now you are on your way. I am also on my way, but it's not such a good road I'm travelling. Still, now you can go on by yourself. You think so too?" I said nothing.

"So, in one thing anyway I've succeeded. We see a little less of one another now, I understand. You go outside, people will stare and talk. You have your own business to attend to. Is it good?"

The car drove on. There was no moon. The car followed the white line down the middle of the road.

"Anna, it is good," he said. We made a turn. A lone palm stood on the edge of a cliff as if it were floating in air. "So, anyway, when you were standing on that balcony watching the men fight, what were you doing? You thought you were watching a bullfight? Your lover is nearly blinded, he's bleeding all over the place, and you're grinning like a mad person. That was Luria's idea? You didn't know any better?"

In the dark, I smiled to myself. He couldn't help it. I was on my own but all the same he had to say something, and because he did, I knew nothing had changed. We might see one another less or more. Nothing could separate us.

ALL THOSE FACES in the road. A person without a shadow, that was a dreadful thing. But why did it happen? Somehow you didn't live properly in the world? And when there's a shadow but no person?

Why does no one ask how the shadow feels?

Ivy's son says, "Mommy, you cast a long shadow." She does.

Of course her shadow is attached to her body. It may flow from her heels, but it is part of her.

In my drawing, the road is still cobbled with faces. I take the pencil and erase them one by one, but when I look at the sheet of paper, still I see them there, blindly looking up at the sun.

8

SO I SAT THERE on a chair, fully dressed, wearing my best dress, a blue dress with a white belt, white shoes, and a white hat with a red flower on it: in Brooklyn, all night. My brown suitcase sat next to my chair. My sister-in-law sat in a chair across from me, watching me.

Eventually she fell asleep. My husband Neville lounged on the couch, watching me and watching his sister Flora, and saying he had something to do on Nostrand Avenue, but no one answered him, and eventually he fell asleep.

I must have fallen asleep in the chair, because the next thing I knew a milky light filled the room, and when I looked at the windows, they were filled with a gray light, the color of light on the ocean when the fog rolled in. Neville got up from his sofa and said he had to go to Nostrand Avenue. His sister Flora, who was sitting up straight, picked up the little ashtray next to her and flung it at him.

"She comes here after five years and she expects my life to stop?" Neville asked. "Doesn't she think I have a job and business of my own to do here? She can do whatever she wants. She did whatever she wanted on Green Island. If she wants to look a job, let her look one. If she wants to stay in the apartment, let her stay. She can sleep on the couch there."

"What's wrong with your bed?" asked Flora.

"It's my bed, not her bed," Neville said.

"Let the man keep his own bed," I said.

"I'm going out," Neville said.

"You're going out and she's going out, and how is she supposed to get back in?" Flora asked him. "You have a key for her?"

Neville took a key out of his pocket and threw the key into Flora's lap. She picked up the key and threw it back. "I'm your older sister!" she shouted. "You can travel across a room and hand me something!" He picked up the key, walked across the room, and handed it to her.

I took my first good look at Neville. He was still a fine-looking man. From a distance, you would say he was handsome. He was tall and thin and had fine, sharp features, but as I looked, I saw he was too thin and when his hand reached for the doorknob, it shook. The sun lit up his belt buckle and I saw that the belt was drawn tight to hold up his pants, which were loose. He had punched an extra hole in the belt. I could see that clearly. The texture of his skin had roughened and become leathery and there were deep wrinkles around his eyes and at the corners of his mouth. His cheeks were hollow. The man drinks too much, I thought. He drinks too much and probably he does not eat well or sleep well and he looks old. It was true. He now looked years older than I did. He went out the door, and when he did, he didn't look back.

I walked to the window and looked down at the sidewalk. There was Neville, making his way along the thick gray ribbon of concrete. On the other side of the street were apartment buildings, five stories high, built of gray stone. The gray and black trees cast short morning shadows. What is this dead world? I asked myself. What is this dead world and where in it is he going?

I looked at Flora, wanting to ask her, Did he ever ask after me? Did he ever ask after the children? He left Green Island five years ago. In all that time, did he remember me? But Flora had fallen asleep in her chair.

I looked around. The apartment was small and dark. There was a living room and a bedroom, a small kitchen and a bathroom. The walls, which had once been painted white, were now streaked by dust and had turned a dull gray, dirt-gray, not real gray. This was the color of poverty, of stuck time, of hopelessness. Here and there, where the walls met the ceiling, the original paint had escaped the drifting dust and a white streak glowed brilliant and pure, like the sun when it burst through fog.

I went into the bedroom. The window looked out onto the back courtyard, gray and stony. Nothing would grow there. Plants would not grow. There was not enough light.

In the bedroom was an old double bed with a cast iron headboard that reminded me of hospital beds in Cinnamon Bay. The white paint was flaking from it and left behind irregular black shapes. The mattress sagged. I sat on the bed and the springs creaked. A dead man's bed, I thought to myself. Someone owned this bed before Neville.

A tall, narrow chest of drawers was next to the bed. It looked like wood, but it wasn't wood. The veneer was peeling at the edges. I opened them. In the top drawer were a few pairs of blue and brown socks. In the second drawer were five white shirts. Otherwise the drawers were empty. In the small closet hung another pair of Neville's pants. There were no shoes on the closet floor. Apparently he owned only one pair.

There were no pictures on the wall, no photographs on the dresser top. Thin, dirty curtains hung from the unwashed windows. This was not the home of a man who cared much for life. Everything in the apartment—the brown tweed couch with its armrests worn through, the cheap black chairs, the straw matting that served for a living room rug—everything had been used and used up in another life and when the owners were through with the things, when they looked at them and pronounced them worn out and dead, Neville had come for them and brought them here.

Then I thought, Perhaps Neville does not live here at all. Perhaps he lives somewhere else, with a woman in her apartment, and there the windows are curtained with flowered chintz and a nice rug lies on the floor and the furniture is new or shines like new because the woman oils it every week. I went back into the living room and sat down in my chair. Flora was still sleeping. The first thing I had to do was find a job. Never let something hurt you twice. I could hear my father saying it. *Don't let them beat you,* he said. *If they beat you, you must fight them.* I thought of my children, Priscilla and Junior, living with Tita Lu in Cinnamon Bay. I will fight whoever I have to fight, I thought.

Flora was awake and was looking at me. "He doesn't mean it," she said.

"Don't tell me nonsense," I said to her. "Don't tell me he's glad to see me but he doesn't know how to show it. It was your idea that I come, not his. You took care of the papers. You gave them to him to sign. He isn't happy I'm here. He has another woman somewhere and that's why he had to go to Nostrand Avenue."

"He will be happy to see you," Flora said. "When he has time to think."

"He's had five years to think," I said.

"But he doesn't think," Flora said. "Look at this place. A thinking man would live like this? You'll see. He'll wake up to the error of his ways now that you're here."

I had to laugh at her. The error of his ways! When we were children, my father was always telling me I'd see the error of my ways, and my teachers said the same. In those days, we saw the error of our ways. But when I was older and left home, and someone pointed out a man or woman and said they would see the error of their ways, it always meant the same thing: whoever that person was, he was beyond hope.

"Don't be bitter," Flora said. "He loved you once, he'll love you again."

"No," I said. "He won't."

"But you will try?" she asked me anxiously. "You are still man and wife, you know."

I got up and went to the refrigerator. In the freezer there was some ice. In the door rack were two bottles of beer. An orange covered with blue mold rested on the bottom shelf. Otherwise there was nothing. "What I must worry about first," I said to Flora, "is a job. Look at this."

We put on our coats and went outside. The wind blew hard and cold and I shivered in my coat. Flora saw me wrapping the coat around me and said that tomorrow she would get me a real winter coat and a wool hat. We walked for blocks. Every block was the same: gray concrete houses pressed up against one another, no space between them. People walked by, bending into the wind, their heads down. No one looked into our faces. No one said *Good morning.* There was no color anywhere. The clothes the people wore were dark. There were no flowers.

"What happened here?" I asked Flora. "All these trees died?"

Flora laughed and said, "Oh, I forgot you don't know winter. In the spring all the leaves come back." Of course I didn't believe it.

"Here is where I live," Flora said, stopping in front of a three-story brick house. She turned the key in the door to the basement apartment and I went in behind her.

She had painted the walls of the hall and the living room aqua and the woodwork bright pink. A flowered couch and chairs splashed themselves against the bright rose of the carpet. Curtains covered with pink and aqua hibiscus hung from the windows. The windows shone, not a speck of dust on them anywhere. In the corner, a huge rubber tree bent over just beneath the ceiling. I began to cry.

"Don't cry," said Flora, whose own face was crumpling. "I have salt fish and rice and peas and breadfruit pudding and even some sugar cane. You can get everything here."

She steered me to a chair and sat me down. I was shivering uncontrollably. She brought me an afghan and covered me with it. I looked down at the woolen blanket crocheted of aqua and pink wool and began to cry harder.

"We are all unhappy in the beginning," Flora said, "but then we get used to it. You'd be surprised how fast you get used to it. And when you get a job, you can buy a ticket and take a plane and go back."

On the wall opposite me was a painting of a house on Green Island, a small pink house nestled among palm trees and banana trees and coconut trees. In the yard in front of the house were pigs and chickens and one rooster which the light picked out. A woman was at the kitchen window, about to throw a pail of dishwater into the yard. I cried harder.

I heard a key turn in the lock, and Flora's daughter, Jeannette, came in. "This is your Aunt Ivy," Flora said. "She just came in last night."

"Where's Uncle Neville?" Jeannette asked.

"On Nostrand Avenue," I said. "Doing something very important." *Don't let them beat you,* my father said.

"Not on her first day here!" exclaimed Jeannette.

"It doesn't matter," I said. "Let the man do what he wants. I need to find a job."

"I can take her down to Mr. Martin at the factory," Jeannette said.

"Let her rest a little," Flora said.

"When?" I asked Jeannette.

"Today, if you want," Jeannette said.

"Let's go," I said, getting up. "How much money do I need? I have ten dollars to my name."

"We'll lend you some money," Jeannette said.

"He'll *give* you some money," Flora said.

"Eat something first," Flora said, but I said no, I'd take a piece of bread with me and I'd eat when I came back.

Jeannette and I walked several blocks but I saw no train. Suddenly Jeannette stopped. "Here we are," she said. "No, here, Aunt," she said, laughing. "We go down these stairs. The train runs under the streets."

When the train came roaring into the station, I thought, This is a frightening sound. I looked around me to see if anyone looked frightened by the noise of the arriving train, but no one did. Women sitting on benches with books in their laps got up and moved toward the opening train door. People began crowding to get on. In an instant, we were pressed between the people who packed the car.

When we got out of the train and climbed the steps into the gray day, the buildings around us were enormous and shut out the sky. I thought of the dominoes I played with on Green Island. These buildings were like giant dominoes, sharpened at the top, cutting the sky into pieces like bits of broken glass. *Yet people live here,* I thought. I was here, the buildings were tall, the ground underfoot was hard, concrete covered the earth. This was how it was.

We came to a large building. Its windows were enormous.

"This is the factory," Jeannette said. "Everyone starts out here." We went inside and took an elevator down to the basement. A small bald man in a small ugly office looked at my papers and asked if I had worked before. He had a swollen round stomach, and red suspenders cut into the shoulders of his blue and white striped shirt. I said yes, I had, for fifteen years in the biscuit factory on Green Island. I had letters of reference. "That won't be necessary," he said, and asked me when I could start work.

"I can start today," I said.

"Go home and get some sleep and come back at eight thirty tomorrow morning," he said. "The salary is seventy-five dollars a week."

"That's not much," Jeannette said. "Does she get a raise if she works good?"

"Of course, if she's a good worker, she gets a raise," he said. He was bored and impatient, already picking up the papers on his desk.

"Let's celebrate," Jeannette said, and she took me into Chock Full o'Nuts and bought me a cream cheese and nut bread sandwich. I drank three cups of coffee, not because I liked coffee, but because it was hot and I was cold. Then we went under the streets and back to Brooklyn.

Jeannette walked me back to Neville's apartment and came in with me. She looked in the refrigerator. "Oh, there's nothing here," she said. "Stretch out and go to sleep, Aunt, and I'll run out to the store." I remembered what Neville told me about not sleeping on his bed, and lay down on the couch still in my coat. I was cold.

When I opened my eyes, Jeannette was gone. I went to the refrigerator and saw that she had bought a dozen eggs, two loaves of bread, some ground meat and ketchup. On the counter were cans of soup and baked beans, a large jar of peanut butter and a jar of grape jelly. A box of tea bags was on top of the refrigerator. A bunch of bananas sat in the middle of the table.

I made myself a cup of tea and ate one banana and then another. From where I sat, I could see my brown suitcase in the living room. I had a nightgown, two skirts and four or five blouses, two pairs of stockings and two pairs of shoes, two sheets, two towels and my sewing scissors. In Cinnamon Bay, Tita Lu had my china wagon, packed with dishes and curios. She had my cartons of books and a closetful of clothes. She had my two children, Priscilla and Junior. If I were on Green Island and wanted to list everything I had, I would be busy for days.

I got up and looked out the window but there was no sign of Neville. It was four o'clock. I hung my skirts and blouses in the closet next to his pants and placed my two pairs of shoes on the floor. I did not want to put my nightgown or stockings in Neville's drawers. I left them in my suitcase and put the suitcase on the floor of the closet, and then put my shoes on top of it. I opened my purse and looked at the pieces of paper in it. I had the address of the factory and directions telling me how to get there. I had Flora's address and phone number. I was tired and lay back down on the couch.

The phone rang and I answered it. It was Flora. "Is Neville there yet?" she asked, and I said he wasn't. It was almost eight o'clock. Four hours had passed since I last looked at my watch but it seemed no time had passed. "I'm coming over with a coat," Flora said. "Jeannette got it from the woman she works for. If it's long, you can take up the hem."

She came in with a purple quilted coat. "Is that a coat?" I asked her. It looked like a blanket.

"Put it on and tell me it isn't warm." In it I felt warm for the first time. "And this green hat, put it on too." I put on the hat. "Now all you need is a good pair of boots and you're ready for winter," she said.

We heard the key turn in the lock. Neville walked in. "She's still here?" he said to Flora.

"This is her home!" Flora shouted at him. "Going out and leaving her on her first day here!"

"She better get used to it," Neville said.

"What did she do to you?" Flora shouted at him. "Tell me that? You thought you could steal her money and she'd stay there and like it? She's here now and you make the most of it! And that food in the kitchen? Don't eat it out unless she says you can eat it. Jeannette paid for it, and it belongs to her. You hear me, Mr. Anderson?"

"What do I want with her food?" Neville asked. He went into the bedroom and came out wearing another shirt.

"Where are you going?" demanded his sister.

"Out."

After he left, the phone rang again. I picked it up and a woman's voice asked for Neville. "He's not here," I said. "Where is he?" asked the voice. I said I didn't know. "You goddamn bitch," the woman said, "get the hell out of there before I come and scratch out your eyes." I stared at the phone and placed it back on the hook.

"Who was that?" Flora asked me.

"A woman cursing me out," I said.

She and I drank some tea and Flora made a peanut butter and jelly sandwich and divided it with me and watched me eat it. "Not bad, is it?" she asked, and I said no, it wasn't. "He will come around," she said. When she left, I went to sleep on the couch, the purple coat over me like a blanket. In the middle of the night, someone shook me awake.

"Ladies call here and you curse them out?" Neville asked me.

"What are you talking about?"

"A woman called here and she said you cursed her out!"

"What woman?"

"Never mind what woman!" he shouted.

"Am I so stupid," I said, "that I would answer the phone and curse a woman and not know who it was? You think I am so stupid that I would do that?"

"If you do it again I will beat you," he said.

I sat up on the couch and looked at him. "You will beat me?" I asked him.

"I'll beat you," he said, but now his eyes raced around their sockets like mad, trapped animals.

"I told you and told you, Neville, in my life three people have hit me: my father, Mistress Banford and Teacher Williams, and the fourth one, he won't like it."

"Maybe he will like it," said Neville.

"No," I said. "He will not." I took the sewing scissors from beneath my pillow. "You see this?" I said. "It is *sharp* and if you don't want the ambulance to come for you and the police to come for me, you won't hit me."

"You sleep with a pair of scissors under your pillow?"

"You said I am not to sleep on your bed, and I am sleeping here on the couch, and if you come near me when I don't want you near me, I will do for you with these scissors."

"Give me those scissors," he said.

"No."

He picked up his hand as if he intended to strike me. I slid the scissors deep under my pillow, jumped up and jumped on him. He lost his balance and fell against the brown chair. When he righted himself, he lunged at me, but it was too late. I had him by the shoulders and pushed him back until I had him pinned to the wall.

All the years he had been in Brooklyn drinking and not eating or sleeping I had been on Green Island where I worked in the garden every day and after coming home from the biscuit factory, I scrubbed the house and painted and planted and lifted and did all the things a man would have done for me had he been there. I was always very strong and now I was stronger than Neville. I watched his eyes and when I saw he was too frightened to move I let go of one shoulder and grabbed him by the hair and knocked his head into the wall, once, twice, three times. Each time I hit his head against the wall hours seemed to pass until it seemed as if I had been standing in that dark apartment hitting his head against the wall for years.

"I will brain you, I will kill you," I said, "if you touch me or any of my things." I let go of him and he sat down on the chair.

"You are so angry," he said to me. "I am not even as angry at you."

But I wasn't angry. "What should you be angry about? What did I do to you?"

"You don't know what you did to me?" he asked.

"I asked you to take up with Merle Janesmith?" I said. "I asked you to steal our money so you could send her here to work? That's what I did to you?"

"You did do it to me! I bought myself a big white car. That was a crime?"

"You bought a car and you started to drink and all of a sudden every policeman in the world was your friend and every woman in the city was their friend, and that's how it started. I saw how it started!"

"A man can have a car!" Neville shouted at me. "He can have friends! But not you! You don't have friends! You don't want friends! It was your brother Jack this, your brother Jack that, and then Robert and his wife moving in with us! You didn't have time for me! And my mother! Who asked you to go up to see her and clean house for her? I didn't marry you to get a maid for my mother!"

"Your family was my family," I said. "When we married, we were flesh of one flesh."

"Your brothers, your father, my mother, the children, you could have all that but I couldn't have a car? You had to hate the car? You didn't care where I went! You didn't care what I did! You joined the church and I was disgracing you in front of all your saved friends! That's what it was."

I sat down on the couch, my hand under the pillow, touching my scissors, and watched him. There he sat, motionless on the chair, as if inside a cube of ice, a tear frozen midway down his cheek. Everything stopped. I thought back to one late afternoon in Greenstown, the day before Christmas.

I was baking a fruitcake in the yard kitchen and was sitting on top of our veranda when Neville came over and sat on the step above me. "Look what I have," he said, and took out a rifle. A cool breeze blew. The evening was cool and I thought, I should get up and get a sweater. The sky was bright blue but its color was deepening and the palm trees and bananas were glistening. In a few minutes, the sun would drop a little lower and then it would seem to sit on top of the coconut trees like an enormous, hot blossom.

"Is it real?" I asked Neville, taking the gun from him, and he laughed and said, "Of course not," and he showed me the little cork bullets that fit into it. He began pinching me and poking me and I began to feel it, so I said, "Neville, stop! Neville, stop! Will you stop?" But he wouldn't stop, so I picked up the rifle, placed the muzzle against his ear and fired it. Immediately he crumpled down. "Neville, get up," I said. "Get up, Neville."

Mrs. Brown came running across the yard. "What happened, Ivy?"

she asked me, and I said, "He was pinching me and he wouldn't stop, so I picked up this toy gun here and I fired it at him."

"Uh-oh," said Mrs. Brown. She went into my kitchen, took a pot, and filled it at the standpipe with cold water. She threw it over Neville. He still didn't stir.

"Maybe he's playing dead," I said.

"I don't think so," Mrs. Brown said and she ran to her apartment and came back with a small bottle, which she held under Neville's nose. He began to stir and then pushed away the bottle as if he were swatting at flies. His eyes opened. He looked around in surprise and sat up. "Neville, now will you listen?" she said. "When she tells you to stop, will you stop?"

"What happened?" Neville asked her.

"I shot you," I said.

He stood up, took the gun, and broke it over his knee. "That's the end of that thing," he said. He sat back down on the step behind me and put his arms around my shoulders. "The first slice of that fruitcake is for me, right?" he asked, and I said, "You touch that fruitcake before company comes and I'll kill you," and he laughed and said, "Again?"

We were so happy then. I already had Junior and was pregnant with Priscilla. My brother Jack was head of the engineers at the airport and Robert was almost finished with technical college and living in Greenstown. My father had gone to England and was sending money home and in a few months was to come back himself. Everyone was safe and on his way.

I looked at Neville. The tear I had seen before, frozen on his cheek, had fallen. Time must have passed. "You can't blame it on me," I said. "I never turned to another man."

"Have it your own way," he said. "You don't change."

Around me everything was strange. But Neville looked strangest of all, as if I'd never seen him before or heard his voice before. "I'm going to sleep," I said. "On this couch."

"I'm going out," he said.

"When will you be back?"

"When you see me."

"You want me to cook something?" I asked him.

"I have someone who cooks something," he said. He looked at me, hard, as if trying to place me, and then walked out. I sat on the couch and thought. What did he mean, I did it to him? After I found out about Merle Janesmith, I didn't sleep with him. I couldn't. The minister from our church came and talked to me of Christian forgiveness and I said once I might have been able to forgive, but now it had gone on too long. He was always out late and came home drunk and I didn't need anyone to tell me what he was doing. After that we were two strangers living together.

When I lost all patience, I took the two children and left them with Tita Lu and moved out. I rented a room in Greenstown and spent weekends with Tita Lu and the children in Cinnamon Bay. There was nothing I wanted from Neville and he made no effort to find me or to offer me anything. He had been living in the United States for eight months before I heard about it.

The next morning I got up early. Neville was not in his bed. I washed and tidied up, dressed myself and found my way to the subway and went to work.

In the factory, no one came from the United States and some women were there illegally, as I was not, since Neville had filed for me.

The foreman led me to my station and showed me where I was to go to pick up the boxes of children's clothes. I was to fold the clothes and pack them into smaller cartons.

A tall, thin woman wearing a turban worked down the table from me and looked once at me when I came and then looked away. The Chinese woman on the other side of me tapped the table and when I looked up, she said, "She fights with everyone, that one." I nodded and watched the Chinese woman until I saw how the clothes were to be folded and so I began.

Green Island disappeared as if it never existed. All I thought about now was the concrete city, where to go to find the cheapest pair of shoes, the cheapest cuts of meat, and how much money I could save and how much I had to send to Tita Lu for my children.

Some evenings after work, I would stop at Flora's house and we would sit there and have tea, but since Flora could not persuade me to eat anything at her house, I would come back early to the apartment. Neville was rarely there, and when he was, he came in late.

But one night when I came home, he was there, and when the phone rang, he jumped up to answer it, and as he spoke into the phone, he looked at me and smiled and talked on. "Cook me some liver, now," he said. "And some potatoes and buy a few grapefruits. I like that, you know. Yes, I'll be over soon. No, there's nothing here I have to do. You think so?" he asked, laughing. "I am? You are? Yes, there's someone here, but she's nothing. I used to know her in Green Island, that's all. Oh, she sleeps on the couch. I don't know why she won't go away." He laughed again.

"You wouldn't do this at home," I said to him. "At home I have a father and brothers. You wouldn't dare do it."

"Shut up," he said to me, and I was flooded with anger. I grabbed the phone out of his hand and yanked the cord from the wall.

"Now talk to your woman!" I shouted at him. He looked down at the table and picked up an ashtray and threw it at me, but I ducked, and the ashtray, a heavy glass square, hit the wall behind me. I picked it up and threw it back at him and I didn't miss. I hit his forehead and the blood streamed from the gash I made there and poured into his eye and I watched with satisfaction.

Then there was a pounding at the door.

"Neville! Neville! What's going on in there?" someone shouted and I recognized the voice of the landlady. I opened the door. Neville was standing still, his hand to his forehead, then looking at his hand and the blood that covered it.

"What happened here?" the landlady demanded.

"Look what she did to me," Neville said.

"Tell her what you did to *me*," I said. "Tell her how you threw the ashtray at me and I threw it back at you. Tell her how you were talking to your woman, telling her what you wanted for dinner, and how I was here like a pest around you and how I slept on the couch and wouldn't go away. Tell her all that."

"I don't like this, Neville," the landlady said. "This is a quiet house. I don't want trouble here."

"It's up to him," I said.

The landlady walked up to Neville and looked at his forehead. "Put some ice in a towel and press it against that cut there," she said. "No more of this, you hear me?" She looked at Neville and then at me. "Can't you remember you are man and wife?" she asked us.

"Get me some ice," Neville said to me.

"Get it yourself," I said.

Neville glared at me and went over to the phone and then plugged it back into the wall.

"Don't worry," he said. "You didn't break the phone. You pulled the jack out of the wall." He called Flora and proceeded to tell her what happened. Finally, he handed the phone to me.

"He says you sleep with a scissor under your pillow," Flora said. "True?"

"It is true," I said. "If he gives me any trouble, I will do for him."

Flora went on about how we were married so many years and had two lovely children and how much better it would be if we would make it up. "Tell it to him," I said and handed the phone back to Neville.

"Don't worry," he said to Flora. "I'm getting out of here. I have a place to go."

9

HOW DID THIS CREATURE, this evil woman, this seducer of best friends, this disdainer of morality, this cold beast who slithered over bodies toward sparkling bracelets, this creature who sinned even as she sipped from the communion cup: how did this creature move? She couldn't walk like any other woman; she wasn't any other woman. On the other hand, she was not a snake, not without a soul, not entirely cold-blooded. In the end, the sound of a pure girl praying wakes her from her dream of selfishness and sex and sin, her face softens, once again she becomes a creature of God. But before she wakes, how must she walk?

The first week on the set of *Sin and Salvation*, whenever I was not standing about with pins in my mouth, sighing into Miss Rosalie's hair, I was outside the set, pacing up and down the sidewalk. Was this walk the right one? Was this? Finally I had it: a kind of stalking walk, a gliding along the walls until the last instant and then advancing into the center of the room. A walk half big cat, half rat. The cat always creeps along the wall. His prey does the same.

Time and again I've noticed it, how the habits of the hunter mimic the manners of the hunted. So now I had my walk and once I had that, I had my character.

I was wandering around the set, watching the cameramen and the propmen, wondering when Max would begin filming *The Left Bank*. Just then Charles Harrow came on the set. He saw me and waved. I remembered the night in the car coming back from the Sewanee. I continued to wander.

"Look," he said coming up to me, "I forgot my lipstick. Can I borrow yours?" There was something in his tone, I didn't like it, something familiar, as if, although he barely remembered me, he remembered that I had sat on his lap. So, I thought, now he thinks we are familiar.

"Next you will be wanting to slap my bottom," I said and turned away.

These Americans, they come up to women they don't even know and slap their bottoms. When we first came to New York, Max said that.

"Miss Asta," Mr. Harrow said, "if you don't mind, I'd like to write that down."

"Write what down?"

" 'Next you will be wanting to slap my bottom.' "

"So if you already remember it, why are you asking me? It's a free country."

"Do they teach you that on the boat? *It's a free country.*"

"I have a fitting," I said.

"Get the hat a few sizes too large. Your head is swelling."

"My head is swelling?"

"Ask Miss Rosalie. She'll tell you. Your head is swelling. Sometimes they can do something about it, sometimes it's fatal."

"Miss Rosalie," I said, "my head, it looks swollen to you?"

"Who said so?"

"Mr. Harrow."

"Don't listen to him. The girls are crazy about him. *His* head is swollen." I made a face. "You know what it means? A swollen head?" She proceeded to tell me.

"Oh, he thinks I insulted him," I said. "He is a big puppy, isn't he?"

"He's no puppy, Miss Asta," she said. "He's left two wives and two kids in the dust. Everyone falls in love with him, men, women, everyone but Mr. Pinsky. They hate each other. Don't ask me why. You haven't met him before? I thought you'd met him before."

"We weren't introduced," I said. "Not really. Not properly. Probably he doesn't remember my name. A lot of us packed into the same car, that's all it was."

"And he was drunk and the next day he didn't know where he'd been the night before," Miss Rosalie said. "Always the same thing. His ex-wife said he never could remember the night he conceived their little girl. How was he supposed to know it was his? Still, Miss Anna, he is adorable. Who can resist him?"

"I can," I said.

Later that day, Mr. Hall called us on the set to rehearse the scene when we first meet. "You see her," he said to Charlie, "and you fall in love with her. She sees you and she is first bored, it's so predictable, and then amused. See what you can do with it."

I sat on a chair and pretended it was my carriage. Charlie came and asked me for an invisible flower. I hesitated, then handed it to him. I smiled slightly.

"Excuse me, Miss Asta," Charlie said, "but that's not quite right. That's how my mother would smile at me. You should smile at me as if we're spies for the same side, as if we know a code and no one else knows it. I'm frightened of you, you're so beautiful, and so it takes me a while to catch on. Can you try it that way?"

"Why not?" I said.

"That's *very* good," Mr. Hall said. "Very good. We'll keep it that way. Spies. Whatever you ask her to do," he said to Charlie, "she can do it."

"And if you don't ask her?" Charlie said.

Mr. Hall ignored him. "He used to direct, you know," he said. "He writes, too. Did you see *Underground*? Good, wasn't it? That was his story."

"Not just another pretty face," Charlie said.

"You two, can you try to get along?" Mr. Hall asked. "This whole picture is love scenes and more love scenes. Miss Asta, *The Roses* was nothing compared to this. Every day, all day, you're going to be kissing. Every day you will look at each other as if you wanted to eat each other alive. You don't know what it's like when two actors start to fight in a picture like this. It's hell! The leading man munches on garlic before he comes on the set. The leading lady tucks mothballs in her cleavage. I know. He sneezes, he chokes, he coughs, his eyes water, the cameras stop turning and it takes two days, two days, to film one kiss. I've seen it before. If either one of you, *either one* starts that on my set, I won't forgive you. How hard is it for a director to make you look bad?" he asked Charlie.

"Usually you don't do it on purpose," Charlie said.

"No mothballs, no garlic, no biting his ear until it bleeds, no nonsense. I hope we understand one another," Mr. Hall said.

"I am a professional," I said.

"She is a professional," Charlie repeated solemnly.

"Charlie? Do we understand each other?"

"Of course, Horton," Charlie said. "This picture could take six months. You mean I am to eat no garlic for six months?"

"Unless Miss Asta develops a passion for garlic, no garlic. It's very simple. No garlic. Everyone on the set promptly. No drinking on the set. No expensive jokes. No destruction of the sets. A few simple little rules, that's all."

"Am I not always good?" Charlie demanded. He seemed genuinely offended. "When haven't I given it my best shot?"

"That's not what we're talking about," Mr. Hall said. "Anna, you can go back to Miss Rosalie."

I turned and began walking away, when *thwack*, someone slapped my rear end as hard as he could. Furious, I whirled around.

Charlie was laughing, his head thrown back, his white teeth flashing. "Well, I did it!" he said. "Your worst fears confirmed! I slapped your bottom! And let me tell you, there's nothing very wonderful about it!"

"You slap my bottom, I slap your face," I said. I advanced on him, but he danced two steps to the right, then two to the left.

"All right," I said. "I am not chasing you across this set. I will wait my turn."

As I walked away, I could hear Mr. Hall: "What did I say? What did I just say? I won't put up with it, Charlie! I'll go straight to Pinsky! Stop laughing! It's not funny!"

But Charlie kept on laughing and by the time I got to my dressing room and Miss Rosalie, I could hear Mr. Hall laughing too.

"Miss Asta!" someone shouted. "You're wanted on the set!"

In my evening dress, half sewn, half pinned, I went back. Charlie and Erik were already there. "Stand together for Mr. Feldman," he said. "In the middle," he said, when I tried to stand next to Erik. "Look at that, they're taller than she is," Mr. Hall said. "That's going to save time."

"Are you finished with me? I can go back?" I asked. He nodded: *go back.* "Erik," I said, "come with me and talk to me." Charlie watched us. Then Mr. Feldman said something to him and he turned away, and as he did, I moved slightly. When he turned to face us, I slapped his cheek, hard and fast. "Now we are quits," I said, and turned my back. He began wailing, a lament fit for the death of a king.

"What did he do to you?" Erik asked.

"Never mind what he did."

He sat down on a metal folding chair and slid down so that his head rested on the curved chair back. "So," he said, "I'm getting a little tired of this sunshine and these oranges. After this, I think I'll go back to Sweden. You know, before this place goes to my head. I miss Mitzi."

"Mitzi?"

"The little dancer from *Death Train*. You don't remember her. No one does."

"I never saw you with a woman," I said. "Only with Max."

"Well, so many leading ladies, they're too much trouble, everyone lifting her skirt *just so*, turning her head *just a little* to the right. Well, Anna, I'm not a casting director! Anyway, never let anyone know your business, that's my rule."

I asked him, "How is Max?"

"You spend the nights with him and you don't know?"

I said I didn't spend so many nights with him and he was working very hard.

"Yes, yes," Erik said. He took out his cigarette case and when I shook my head, he lit one for himself. "Yes, he's trying to make something of it. It's not much to work with, is it? A wounded soldier stranded in occupied territory plots with a chambermaid to take information to his own side. Some romance, some danger, two reels of romance, two reels of danger, two reels of local color: already he's bored. So how to make the man into the spirit of war and the woman into the self-sacrifice of the little people during wartime, that's what he's figuring out."

"His leading lady is good?"

"The same woman who crossed the country to come to see the actor buried. You remember the funeral in New York?"

"But she is good?"

"Very emotional. A *very emotional* actress."

"And pretty?"

"They're not holding the femme fatale roles for her."

"No?"

"No." He puffed, leaned back and closed his eyes. "So," he said, "you had a reason to slap the leading man?" I didn't answer. Miss Rosalie took the last pin from my mouth. "You looked at the script for this movie. What do you think?" he asked.

"Oh, it's the usual nonsense, isn't it? A married woman, no better than she should be, kills one husband, exiles a lover, remarries, is still no better than she should be, again takes a lover and this time two men are almost killed. Duels, drowning, one pure girl, one evil woman, two pure, weak men, well, it's not real life, is it?"

" 'No better than she should be,' " Erik said. "What an expression! People still use that expression in real life?"

"In the poor section of Stockholm, they use it."

"It's based on a book, this film. You should read it."

"Why? Would my opinion be higher?"

"Very possibly. Here." He fumbled in his pocket, extracted a small, blue paper-covered volume and threw it over to me. *The Devil in the World.*

"This is the same story?"

"Max didn't teach you to first read the book? Of course he taught you. So, because he is making a film without you, you're sulking. A drowning man is not so particular about the passengers already in lifeboats."

Miss Asta! Mr. Grissom! Mr. Harrow! Wanted on the set!

"Yes, yes, extreme pallor," Mr. Hall was saying. "Mr. Feldman, you can do it without making them look like corpses? Miss Asta, here on my right, Mr. Grissom, behind her. Where's Harrow?"

From behind a painted flat, Charlie came dancing onto the set, and, as he approached us, he whipped off his white scarf and used it as a toreador's cape. He pranced this way and that before us, inviting me to charge.

"All right, stop the nonsense," Mr. Hall said.

Charlie grimaced and pointed to his left eye. It was swollen and red. Tomorrow it would be black and blue.

"This girl doesn't come from a rich family," he said. "This girl was a tough kid."

"His eye, it will hold up shooting?" I asked, ignoring him.

"The first seduction scenes are all profile," Mr. Hall said.

Charlie bowed to me and smiled. He radiated self-satisfaction.

"Charlie, we're through with you. Go back to Wardrobe. You too, Grissom. So, Miss Asta, I see you're worried."

"You are angry at me?"

From behind the flats Charlie shouted, "How much mist can there be in one picture? It's not a murder mystery!"

"Angry at you?" Mr. Hall asked. "For what?"

"IF THE MAN WITH THE HAT is still around, then we have to do something about it," I said.

"What?" asked Ivy. "If you won't let me call the police?"

"How long must I live? In a few years, I'll be eighty. I must live the next few years worrying about a man in a hat? At least let's find out who he is."

"I must know who he is?" Ivy asked me. "Why? What do I have to do with him?"

"I am going out for a walk," I said. "Yesterday when I went to the

doctor, he said my joints would freeze up if I sat still all day long. I
don't want to live on a porch in a steamer chair like a fancy plant."

She said she would come with me. She looked at the soft white
rag in her hand, smeared pink with silver polish, black with tarnish,
and turned to go to her room, but I said, no, finish polishing the silver.
Tonight that young man was coming to visit, and why had we bought
so much pickled herring and salami if we weren't going to feed him?
What looked worse than badly tarnished silver?

Well, silver when it began to tarnish, then it was beautiful, the
soft gold it turned, but when it blackened the resembled cast iron,
that was another story. The people who lived in the house didn't have
the money to polish it or their lives were too busy or they were too
feeble, something was wrong. Blackened silver trumpeted everything
to the world. Still, I filled the house with silver: the way it tarnished,
it was almost human, first turning gold, then blackening, like flesh
itself.

"You're going alone?" she asked suspiciously. "You're going to buy
chocolate and come home dizzy and fall asleep?"

"I am going for a *walk*," I said. "Look, there is my handbag. If I
leave it home, I have no money."

"Don't be so foolish," she said. "Take the handbag. I don't know
your tricks? There is some storekeeper in the neighborhood who won't
advance you a thousand dollars' worth of chocolate? The chocolate
man, he'll give you the store for an autograph!"

"I never give autographs," I said.

The end of autumn was in the air. What leaves were left on the trees
rattled and clacked. The wind puffed up the awnings in front of the
buildings and dropped them down. The doormen wore their topcoats.
Taxis drew up to the buildings, women stepped out and paid them,
hurried inside, their hands holding their hair in place.

Once I used to be concerned about my hair like that. In August I
would sit in taxis with the windows closed so that the wind would not
blow the curls loose.

The chocolatier was three blocks away. I waved to the doorman
and started off.

Well, how long would it be before I could no longer make this
walk? Every year I walked more slowly. Now when people recognized
me they caught up with me easily. Just a few years ago if someone
followed me, I would walk faster, and faster yet, and just as the light
was changing from red to green, I would stride across and there they
would be, still on the other side. If it was someone who often followed

me, and I recognized him, sometimes I would turn and wave before disappearing into the crowd. Fifty years later, to still have such power. And for what? Max said it: What the gods give they don't take back. But even the gods can get a little confused. When you are young and beautiful, then people are wonderful mirrors, so you think, When I am old and ugly, they will be mirrors still. They will see an ugly old woman and turn away from me. But after all this time, they still see the beautiful young girl. Only someone who loves me sees the ugly old woman. Yes, yes, everything is backwards!

Backwards, upside down! Always Charlie said that. "You mistook this for normal life?" he asked me. "That's funny! Before I came West, I carried pails of beer from the saloons to the tenements! You worked in a shop! The Queens of the Lot, what were they? Waitresses! Horton Hall, the great director? An electrician! What's the difference between you and a waitress? The bones of your face take the light better. And as for acting! To get through one day of real life, *one day*, any housewife does a better job than we do! Without make-up! Without rehearsals! Without special lights!"

He grabbed my arm; he yanked me toward him. Sometimes, when he was drunk, he hit me.

Was it any wonder I fell in love with him? *Salvation* was my third American movie. At any moment I expected to be sent home. And still: I noticed the change around me, the way the crew moved aside when I passed, Miss Rosalie's anxiety: did I really like my make-up? It wasn't too white? The eyebrows weren't too arched? Was I comfortable with such a low-cut dress?

Or the way Mr. Hall would say, "Miss Asta! It might be better if we didn't see so much of the whites of your eyes." On the set of *The Roses*, he shouted, "Miss Asta! Don't roll your eyes like that! You look like a dog with epilepsy!" Suddenly my opinion mattered. And why? Because they respected my judgment? Because my face on the screen made money! Even before you know you have it, you can become drunk with power, drunk and a little sick.

"All right, you're beautiful," Charlie said. "What next?"

What next?

A few days after filming began, Max picked me up in his new black limousine and we drove to the Sewanee.

"You know, Max," I said, "I am pleased to be here, but outside they are stealing your car. All this time plotting and scheming to make money, and then you are so reckless."

"Plotting and scheming to make money," he said.

"You say it yourself. Without money you are a beggar, not a producer."

"Plotting and scheming," he said again.

"We are going to have a fight? I am exhausted. After five o'clock, I am good for nothing."

"Sit," he said. We had a good table, near the stage. "There's not enough sorrow in the world for you?" he asked me. "All these sad songs, Anna, I could do without them. So, Anna, sometimes I am tired too."

"I must feel guilty because you are tired? I know you are tired. I can see it in your face. You should sleep. There is nothing like food when you're hungry. There is nothing like sleep when you're tired."

"Now we hear from the peasant," Max said wearily.

"Look, Max," I said. "I want to know. What is going on here?"

"You slapped someone's face today?"

"Yes. So what?"

"All the time my shoulder and my knees hurt," Max said. "So I am getting old, we know that. And even as I get old, I get busy. For you the door to my room is always open."

"I know that," I said.

"But if you don't open it, that is all right, too."

The singer on the platform wore a checked suit. He was down on one knee, holding out his hat, singing. Thick smoke blued the room.

"I see," I said.

"*The Left Bank*, well, it is not so easy for me. The leading man, someone carved him out of wood. The leading lady, a nice girl but hysterical. Not even a squirrel jumps around so much. Yesterday I took her out and said, 'Look around. What are these people doing?' She said, 'They are doing nothing.' I said, 'Yes, but they are awake. They are not under anaesthesia. It's a big room. Someone in it is talking about divorce. Someone suspects her husband of adultery. Another woman, her child is dying. But they are doing nothing. They are not jumping all over the place. So, Gemma, how can that be?'

"You know what she said to me? '*Maybe today nothing is happening.*' So I said, 'Listen, Gemma, if you don't start to think, you won't get anywhere with me. These things are happening. You have to look at their faces. Normal people don't run around flinging their arms and screaming. Look at the little things! That woman with her head on her hand? She doesn't have the strength to hold up her head. Why? *Maybe she is tired.*' So Gemma is stupid, Gemma has no imagination. Everything I have to first act out for her. You, at least, were like a sled. We pushed you up to the top of the hill, you came down by yourself."

Were. Were like.

"I have heard all these complaints a hundred times before. So really, what is on your mind?"

"Of course you feel your little wings starting to sprout. It's natural. I expected it."

"I don't know what you're talking about," I said.

"You know."

"I don't know!"

"We will have this conversation again in a month and then if you still don't know, I'll apologize."

"For what!"

"How is your movie?" he asked me. "You notice you're going from bad to worse? In the first, a good woman who falls once too often. In the second, a mad Eve. In the third, Eve again, but evil. In the first, no man dies for you. In the second, a crowd expires. In the third, everyone dies but the pastor. What comes next?"

"If you won't talk to me," I said in a fury, "let's go home."

"To my house or yours?"

"Oh, so now they are different!"

"Anna, in a month we'll talk again."

"This movie is so important to you?"

"Now you are deliberately stupid," he said. "I don't like it."

The chocolatier is across the street. No one is following me. After all these years, I can tell. It is absolutely an instinct. Have I ever made a mistake? I don't think so. I stop in front of the plate glass window and look at the display. The window reflects my face, so many wrinkles, my eyes red-rimmed and watery, my nose red and chapped, my skin made blotchy by the cold wind. From under my blue knit hat some iron gray strands escape and float in the wind. My face floats over the fancy chocolates like a decaying lily leaf.

Well, what do I want? If Bertha Pinsky were here! What a time we would have!

These days, Ivy says, her business is to stay alive. No cholesterol, no sweets, no salt, no sugar. She lives on steamed vegetables and fish heads. Unless we go out, she never weakens.

The chocolatier looks up and smiles. I smile back and walk on. I want to go into his shop with Bertha Pinsky on my arm but I have not yet summoned her up. A leaf blows from a tree. The wind takes it.

"WHO IS IT? Who is it?" I asked, and Jenny, my housekeeper, said a Mrs. Pinsky was there to see me. I grabbed a kimono and put it on and was still tying it when Bertha came in carrying a small, shiny white cardboard box tied with gold ribbon. She looked around her, set it on a table, and stood there looking at me.

"So tell me the truth," she said. "What really do you want?"

Because I had signed my first contract when I was underage, it was invalid, and for months, I had been negotiating a new one. My lawyers had told me, Speak to no one. If you have anything to say, speak to us. But Bertha was my friend. In those days I still believed in friends.

"You want more money?" I nodded. "You know he won't give it to you." I nodded again. "And you won't give up?" I shook my head. "Well, we are where I thought we were," she said.

She picked up the white box, sat down on the sofa, and opened it. "Here," she said, handing it to me. Dark chocolates! "We can eat and talk at the same time," she said. I took a chocolate, but my throat clenched.

"You can't swallow?" she said, looking at me. "That's too bad, they're good." She ate one with great relish. "So, what are you accomplishing?" she asked me. "Everywhere people talk about how greedy you are, you come here a poor girl with holes in her stockings and now you want a million dollars a year. Do you fight for better stories? No, you don't. You fight about money. That's what people say. So they resent you a little, but they resented you before. Everyone resents someone who makes a fortune, we know that.

"And what is my Saul accomplishing? He brings a poor, friendless girl to this country and he pays her sweatshop wages. So no one likes him much either. Every day he plays the poor poppa with the bad daughter. Well, he is used to that. He has plenty of practice. But if you win, you make him look foolish. And still you are working for him. A studio head cannot afford to look foolish. Give it up. Next year you sign a new contract. Then ask for your money."

I shook my head. *I cannot do it.*

"Why not? You are starving to death?"

Still, I didn't answer.

Bertha lowered her eyes and when she raised them, she was crying. "For my sake, change your mind! He is sick! He can keep nothing down! It tears my heart out. If I get down on my hands and knees, that will make a difference?" And without warning, she threw the box aside, flung herself from the couch and crouched in front of me.

"Bertha, get up! For God's sake, get up! You make me angry! This is all acting, don't think I don't know!"

"Oh, all right, it is acting," she said, getting up, straightening her skirt. "But don't think you don't upset him."

"If Max goes back to Sweden, that will not upset me?"

"I thought you had someone else on your hands," she said.

"On my hands!" I said contemptuously.

"Well," she said, "I tried. Look, nothing spilled out of the box."

I said I wasn't hungry. Bertha said women mustn't fight. When everything was over, when the fires burned down, what was left? Two women sitting in chairs, talking.

I took a chocolate and ate it. It was good. To the end of her life we were friends.

A MOUNTED POLICEMAN rides by, his horse the color of polished cherry wood. He raises his whip and smiles. Whenever I walk, I see him. I do not think he knows who I am. Everyone I meet, I ask myself that question: do they know who I am? What little energy I have I waste on this foolishness.

Now I am back at the chocolatier's and this time I am certain someone is following me. I stand in front of the window, waiting. Sure enough, the man in the hat is reflected in the window.

"You!" I say. "Come inside!" This time I plainly see his face. He is white, not black, a thin man in a shiny dark-blue suit. He wears wing-tipped shoes, well shined. "I know you," I say as we go through the door. "I've seen you before."

Inside, it is warm and the air is thick and smells of vanilla, cinnamon, chocolate. An odd mist drifts through the air, brilliant, white. I move my hand through the white haze: sugar dust? I ask the chocolatier. Sugar dust, he says.

"This man is following me," I say. "Also he follows Ivy. I know his face from somewhere. You know it?"

"The face of a man who buys candy bars at newsstands," he says.

"What's wrong with candy bars?" the man asks.

The chocolatier throws up his hands. The man in the hat looks at me, half afraid, half wondering. Why am I not more afraid of him?

Because I know that under the counter, the chocolatier has his famous panic button. If he touches it, a siren goes off, a strange machine dials the police station as well as two neighbors. "For me such a thing would be useless," I said years ago. "Who knows so many people?" All the same, Ivy persuaded me. I had one installed.

"It will come to me, who you are," I say to the man in the hat. "So why not tell me?"

"I live here, I walk around, so what's the big deal?"

"Miss Asta," says the chocolatier, "don't waste time. Call the police."

"I know this man," I say.

"Then who is he?"

Who is he? "You! You are the photographer! Mr. Kodak! This is the man who followed me for fifty years! Do you have any idea how miserable you made me? Why did you do it?"

"They paid me for the pictures," he said.

"Fifty years stalking the same woman? What kind of man are you?"

He mumbles something.

"Explain it to me! I have a right!"

"I saw you in *Sin and Salvation.*"

"So?"

"It's a living."

"It's a living! What kind of living is it? Every time I got out of a cab, a flashbulb. Every time I came out of the hospital, a flashbulb. After *Salvation,* I came out of the hospital with a broken nose—that was you, too?" He nods. "You followed me across the country?" He nods again. "The man is crazy," I say. "All right, that I understand. All my life I've been followed by crazy people. But you follow my house-keeper. What do you have to do with her?"

"Her husband was following her first," he says. "Then he saw me following you, so he said, Why must two of us stand out in the rain? He gave me a couple of dollars and his phone number."

"You are not following her anymore?"

"He doesn't answer his telephone and he doesn't pay me."

"So what will it take to make you stop? When you follow me, you frighten her."

"You were so beautiful when you put on that black veil," he says.

"Will you stop?" I ask him. "Here, take as many pictures as you want! Only stop!"

Then I think of what his picture collection will look like. Hundreds of pictures of a beautiful woman staring him down, then pictures of a not-so-beautiful woman hiding her face, shading it with hats or her own hands, and finally pictures of an ancient crone. I start to laugh. Now he is frightened.

"Impossible," he says. "It's my life's work."

"His life's work!" I exclaim.

"So beautiful, staring into that mirror, putting on that black veil."

"Really, he is insane," I say.

"Miss Asta," the confectioner says, "get his name and phone number."

"Give the man your wallet," I tell him. Mr. Peterson takes it. "Archibald Ellington, Thirty-two St. Mark's Place. Archibald," Mr. Peterson mutters, writing it down. "And his Social Security number, I'll write that one down, too."

"Mr. Ellington, you go home," I say.

He left the store.

"His skin, it is the color of wet newspaper," I say. The chocolatier says he will keep a copy of the man's name and address.

"The homicide squad should be very pleased. So now you see the power of nostalgia," I say. "Well, no one has to tell me. Anyway, let's pick out some chocolates. What time is it? Four o'clock? Soon everyone will stop in on their way home."

"Two pieces? Three?" he asks me.

"A pound," I say. "What I don't finish I can feed to the squirrels. In this city, only the squirrels flourish."

I walked to the East River and sat on a bench. Charlie understood nostalgia. Who could look at him, his entranced eyes, his wondering face, his stunned, hurt look and not remember their first love, their first sorrow? Who does not want back those first things? Charlie had that gift: he gave them back, that and more. And so he was a great star. Even when he turned bitter, you could see it in him, the longing for first things. Whereas Max: even before I met him, he had given up on personal happiness. The myths, people who were not people, those were his creatures. And one day I looked at him and thought, No, I must get away. A person who is not a person, I cannot become that. Charlie could save me. I believed it. He believed it. It was a wonderful dream.

AFTER NEVILLE AND I FOUGHT, after I threatened him with my scissors, I went to The Junction and to the street market and I was standing in front of a produce stand looking at the sugar cane thinking, *Ribbon cane, striped cane, white cane,* when a man touched my arm and said, "Ivy Cook?" I looked up and there was Stanny, Stanny from Mare River. I asked him what he was doing there.

"What am *I* doing here?" he said. "What are *you* doing here?"

I said it was a long story. He asked me if I still didn't eat at other people's houses and I said I didn't. He asked me if I would eat at restaurants and I said I would eat at a clean one. And so we went out for dinner and after that Stanny began calling me and then coming for me.

One snowy night, we were eating roast beef sandwiches in a diner and I looked up at Stanny and said, "You're the reason I had to leave Mare River, you know." He put down his fork and stared at me.

"That night we went to help Bevon Berriman at her bar with the dominoes tournament, you came and told Cherry that Daddy wanted us to come home and then you went back to Daddy and told him I said I wasn't ready to come and for that he beat me there in front of everybody. And when I walked in the door, my stepmother said, 'What's wrong with you now?' and I said, 'That damn coolie man you've got there beat me in front of everyone.' And Master Vidal was right behind me and heard me and beat me again. And I decided, That's it. I'm going to my uncle's in Greenstown. That was where it all started. You never liked me back in Mare River," I said.

"I did," said Stanny.

"Then why did you tell lies about me?"

"I was jealous. You were standing up there with Buddy Gray like the whole world belonged to him."

"You were jealous of Buddy?"

"Any fool could see it," Stanny said.

I buttered a piece of bread. "I didn't see it," I said.

"That's what I said. Any fool could see it."

We sat there in silence, chewing and saying nothing. Outside the window, I could see a bus drawing up to the bus stop and a crowd of people shoving one another in their hurry. Drops of moisture collected on the inner side of the window pane and snaked down the glass like rain. I remembered the sound of rain on the zinc roof of our house in Mare River before our father put the rafters up, the *ping, ping, ping* of it. It seemed to me now the most wonderful sound in the world and I tried to put it out of my mind because I thought I would never hear it again.

"So why you don't divorce this man?" Stanny asked me.

"When I married," I said, "it was until death do us part."

"That's not Mare River talking," Stanny said. "You're doing for him, Ivy."

"No," I said. "I am not."

"You don't want to remarry? You're afraid to take the chance?"

"You don't understand," I said. "I turned very religious in Greenstown," but even as I spoke, I flushed, and Stanny was laughing at me.

"You turned Catholic?"

"Pentecostal."

"Then you can divorce," he said.

While we ate, I watched Stanny. He was of medium height, not as tall as Daddy or Neville. His hair curled around his head like a wreath. The top of his head was bald. He was powerfully made.

Here he rebuilt and restored houses and now he had gone out on his own and was doing well. He owned two houses. He lived in one and fixed up the second and then sold it for a profit.

The snow had turned to rain.

"Listen to that rain," he said. "When I was a child in Mare River, Miss Blue used to stay with us when my mother was sick, and she would send us in to the bath house for showers, and when I came out, Miss Blue would say she knew I didn't take a shower. How did she know? Because the sound of the water coming out of the drain pipe was different when it didn't run over a human body first. And I believed her!"

I laughed. That was Miss Blue all over.

"So after that," he said, "I used to put an arm or a leg in the water and I thought I fooled her, but one day she put her hand against my back and said the water running out of the drain looked different when it ran over a whole human body, and she knew I wasn't all the way under the water, and I had to go back in. I thought she was a magician, you know, but she was feeling my back to see if it was damp or dry."

"We all know that," I said. "That Miss Blue had magic powers."

You can change your story, said Miss Blue. A nip here, a tuck there, and it fits you better, like a dress that was too long but now the hem's taken up, it fits you fine and you feel comfortable in it. It's the same dress but now you're happy wearing it.

"So why not leave him?" Stanny said. "He doesn't come home sometimes for weeks. He comes home drunk as a bat and he taunts you with his women. Why do you stay there?"

"You chat too much," I said. "You talk to Flora?"

"I talk to Flora. People from Green Island must stick together."

"He won't let me sleep on his bed. I sleep on the couch."

"With a scissors under your pillow," he said. He was grinning at me. "You want to live like that?"

"Until I have enough money to move out, that's how I'll live."

He didn't answer and we got up and walked back to the apartment near Nostrand Avenue. Most of the windows were lit yellow squares the color of flypaper. Some people hadn't pulled down their blinds and inside those cubes of light we could see them moving from table to refrigerator, from bathroom to bedroom. They looked, not like people, but animals in cages.

"I don't like coming in there," Stanny said. "Not to another man's home."

When we walked, he walked with his arm around my waist or around my shoulders. I was happy when Stanny had his arm around me.

"I want a wife, you know," he said. He was married on Green Island but his wife died of a stroke. His two children were both in high school. "Why should you make the same mistake twice?" he asked, pulling me closer. We walked in silence. Finally I said, "I won't be at the factory much longer. I'm tired of it. When I get my next job, I'll take a place of my own."

"And Mr. Neville?" he asked me sharply.

I shrugged and didn't answer. Stanny sighed.

"I'll help you move," he said. "I have a truck."

When we got to the door of the apartment building, he kissed me good night and I went upstairs and sat down on the couch. I thought about the factory. The girl who worked down the table from me was from one of the Islands and pretended she couldn't speak English. In the morning, one of the men would bring me the boxes of clothing I was to fold and pack, and, if the girl got there first, she would take the boxes the man put down for me. One day I got angry and grabbed the boxes from her and slid them down to my station at the table.

"Look," I said. "He puts the clothes here for *me*, not *you*. If you want my things, you must ask me. You can't take them."

She began to curse me and I heard her say quite distinctly that she was going to cut me.

Don't let them beat you, said my father.

I walked up to her and banged my hand on the table. "Look, you," I said. "You need a turban to hold your head on?"

Behind me, I could hear the other women beginning to laugh. She was long and thin and always wore a turban and she must have been shortsighted because she swayed snakelike, back and forth above the clothes she was packing.

"You come from a country where people cut up chickens to do magic," I said, "but I come from a country where we cut off people's heads and the heads roll around on the ground and bark like dogs. You want to fight me, you wait for me after work and we will fight. You understand me," I said. "You pretend not to understand the language, but you understand it. You must have manners in this world, and if you won't have them, I will teach them to you." I went back to my station at the table and began working.

That night after work, I went downstairs and looked for her, but she was not there. I sat on one of the cartons and talked to the foreman, waiting for her, but still she did not come. Finally, I put on my coat and went home.

In the morning the foreman came up to me and said she was in his office, afraid to come into the big room. She was crying and said I was going to beat her.

"She said she would cut me because I took my boxes back from her and I told her I would beat her," I told him.

A little later she came back to her place at the table.

"You take your things and I'll take mine," I said to her. "That way we can be friends." She nodded. "Friends?" She nodded again.

After that, when one of the men brought me my boxes, I shared what I had with her, and when she went for her boxes, she gave me one of hers.

There was nowhere you didn't have to fight. My father had taught me well.

Letters arrived weekly from Tita Lu. The children were doing nicely. Priscilla ordered Junior about. When she went into the bathroom, she would shout for him and ask him to bring her a pair of panties, but when he went into the bathroom and asked her to bring his slippers, she would argue and ask him if he didn't know he would need them before he went in and why hadn't he taken them with him?

Then Tita Lu would lose her temper and shout at Priscilla, "Bring the boy his slippers, come!"

They were so far away. When I thought of them, it was like watching a film where they moved jerkily: tiny, tiny figures, so tiny I could barely make them out. So small they could have danced on the back of my hand.

I got up from the couch and unfolded the sheet and spread it out over the cushions. I took down my pillow from the closet and placed it at one end of the couch. I went into the bathroom and undressed and put on my nightgown. I spread the blankets out on the couch and thought it was time to leave.

But how could I leave Neville without turning Flora against me? Oh, I was sick and tired of it. All my life it had been the same thing. In Mare River, when I wanted to run away, people would say, "You can't run away. Your people will disband you," and I would be frightened. And now here I was in a great cement city and the only person in the world I had was Flora, my husband's sister. She had persuaded Neville to send for me. She and Jeannette called every day after work and convinced me that I was not dead, because there were times, in the apartment, listening to the silence, that I thought I was. I sat alone until I heard the sound of my heart, *thump-bump*, *thump-bump*, stupidly going on as if no one had thought to tell it to stop, and I thought if it did stop, things would be better. But then I would think of my children with Tita Lu in Cinnamon Bay. I knew what it was to be a motherless child.

"Something will work out," Stanny said one night as we sat in the diner. "An opportunity will present itself."

Only in the diner did I allow memories of Green Island to come back. Memory Gems, I thought irrelevantly. I asked Stanny if he remembered the Memory Gems they had taught us in Mare River. " 'If you throw minutes away, you can't pick them up in the course of the day. You may hurry and scurry and worry and flurry but you have lost them forever away.' Remember that?" He smiled. " 'If you smile, smiles come back to greet you, but if you frown, frowns shall ever meet you.' "

"I remember that one," he said. "And this, too: 'You can't curse the cow and ride the cow's back.' " He looked at me hard.

"You think that is what I am doing? Staying with Neville and complaining?"

"You don't complain. Flora complains."

"To myself I complain," I said.

"Then you will stay with him until chicks grow teeth and cats lay eggs?" he asked me.

"Do you remember that man who hanged himself from a plum tree?" I asked him. "The one I found when I was bringing the goats down from the fields?"

"We all came and looked at him."

"Hanging there like a stopped pendulum, his head on his chest."

"He was the brother of the Split Man, the one Miss Holroyd cut with her machete."

"I never knew that."

"I remember how two men held his feet and a third one cut the rope," Stanny said. "Wasn't your father the one who cut the rope?"

"I don't remember that," I said. "Why did he hang himself?"

"Something about a woman. Who remembers now? If they ever knew." *If they ever knew.* I had travelled so far from my early days in Green Island I could not remember them, not unless I sat here, in this diner: but when I was elsewhere, not then.

I asked him if he remembered the slapping girl who slapped herself until her face was swollen. He remembered her. "She was possessed by spirits," he said. "You can't tell anyone those things here. Green Island," he said.

"Green Island," I said. "The Sunken City. The palm tree at the end of the world."

"The palm tree at the end of the world?" he asked me.

"Next time," I said. I shifted uncomfortably in my seat. I was beginning to have pains in my stomach.

||

ONE MORNING the phone rang early. "Max," I said when I hung up, "it's snowing in the mountains."

"So you're going," he said. "How long?"

"Two days, three days."

"Snow," he said. "I wish I were coming."

"You could come," I said.

"Not today. Today Gemma shoots the general. She doesn't understand how it comes to look like suicide. He's in a tub, in a locked room, a gun in his hand, and she doesn't understand why they think it's suicide. Stupid but adorable," he said.

"Our lives are ruled by these stupid stories," I said.

"But one thing I want to settle. About this standing up straight all the time. You shouldn't do it. Don't listen to them. From all this stooping over you do, your spine curves naturally. On you it looks right, stooping over to see the world so far down below you. On Gemma, preposterous. For her I'd make up a back brace."

"These stupid stories!" I said again.

"As if even gravity were too heavy for you," Max went on, following his train of thought. "Stupid stories?" he said with surprise, as if he'd just heard me. "Life is stupid? Everyone's life is a story, happy or sad, long or short, many people, few people, but still, always a story."

"What I mean is, what I mean to say is, we could walk off, we could stay together, for just one day!"

"You think we could?" Max said. "You are so young!"

"Young! This is about will!"

"Then I don't have the will," Max said.

"For whom would you have it?"

"When my elbow and knee stop hurting, then we can fight."

"Elbow and knee!" I said furiously, throwing some clothes into a suitcase.

"Take something warm," Max said.

"So?" I said. "To you I am still a child?"

Outside, the studio van honked and honked again. "Wish me luck," Max said. But I was angry and left without a word.

"Things are going well enough," Mr. Hall said over the telephone to the studio supervisor. "No, why come up? The roads are impossible, snowdrifts everywhere, trees falling down, you can hardly walk, the heating system's primitive, no one can get warm. There's no love lost between them but they're professionals. No, I don't think Miss Asta would like it. Yes, I'll ask her." He turned to me. "Anna," he said, "do you have any objections to The Studio manufacturing a romance between you and Charlie?"

"Of course I do," I said.

"Of course she does," he said into the telephone.

Charlie bounded onto the set. "Horton," he said. "I see what you're trying to do. It's not that I don't understand. Every room lit through stained glass, every room a church. Everything turns on that one line:

'Sometimes when the devil cannot reach us through the spirit, he creates a woman beautiful enough to reach us through the flesh.' She's a devil, she's an angel, fine. But do I have to cower every time she comes near me? What am I supposed to be? The world's most sinful weakling?"

"Actually," said Mr. Hall, "that's Erik's part."

"I'm this dashing officer, but when I'm with her, I'm a child with its mother!"

"That's it," Mr. Hall said smoothly. "Play it that way. It's perfect."

"Why me? Why not a little boy in short pants? He'd be cheaper."

"Maybe, but the Legion of Decency wouldn't permit it."

"She's the smooth seducer and *I'm* the cowering virgin? You damn fool! It's ridiculous!"

"It's in the script," Mr. Hall said. "Read the script."

"Then it's a stupid script," Charlie said.

"It's in the book the script's based on. Read the book."

"I have read the book! It's a stupid book!"

"Yesterday you said it was a wonderful book."

"Yesterday I hadn't seen the rushes!"

I put on my fur coat. Charlie put on his. We were to walk through the snow toward a little cabin on his property. It was supposed to be abandoned, and for no reason whatever had a fire in the fireplace. Just before we reached it, I was to point to my shoes and show him how wet they were. Then I would catch a sight of the blazing fire and run inside. He would follow me. Once inside, I would take off my fur coat and stretch out my naked arms to the fire. As usual, I was wearing one of the thirty thin dresses stitched up by Miss Cotton. It was the dead of winter in the German forest, but none of my dresses had sleeves. Well, the wealthy did not need to dress warmly. It was other people's business to keep them warm.

"I don't know what to do with this scene," I told Max.

"Make love to the fire," he said. "It's not a fire, it's your beloved. You understand."

"Oh, I understand," I said.

The cameras rolled. We began. Charlie kept his raccoon coat on. As we had planned it, he stared at me. I took off my coat, and I stretched out my arms to the fire as if I were coaxing it toward me. I raised my eyebrows as I looked into it. I parted my lips as if I were about to speak and then closed them again. I leaned in to the fire as Mr. Hall had told me to do and suddenly, in the cold room I felt its heat and without thinking, I wriggled my legs and stretched them straight out before me and held out my arms like a child playing. I threw back my head and laughed and turned to smile at Charlie. I was so happy to be warm!

He stared at me as if he'd never seen me before. "You are so beautiful," he said.

"Thank you," I said, still laughing. The fear in his gaze, the rehearsed fear, was fading. Suddenly, adoration replaced it. He threw himself at my feet. Oh, I thought. This is what Max means when he says the scene grabs up the actors and inspires them. And then I leaned over Charlie and looked worshipfully at him, all as we had rehearsed it, and suddenly, there he was, that beautiful face, those sad eyes, why had I never seen how sad they were?

She caresses his face. She kisses him, read the script. My head was next to his.

"Are you cold?" he whispered, and I nodded, nodded and put my arm beneath his shoulder and drew him up to me and when he was half reclining, I seized him with both arms and began kissing him, eyebrows, forehead, cheeks, eyes, throat, until he lay back in my arms as if unconscious, and then he sat up and took me by the shoulders and hugged me to him.

Somewhere I heard Mr. Hall calling, "Cut! Cut!" but we didn't stop. We went on. I didn't dare look at him nor he at me. Automatically we looked for the cameras and the crew but they were gone. I passed my hand over my lips. They were sore and chapped.

"I'm sorry," Charlie said. He touched his moustache. "It's like sandpaper."

"I like it," I said.

"You do?"

"Yes."

"We better find the others."

"Yes."

"So," said Mr. Hall when we came back into the main building, "the scene needed more rehearsing?"

And so it began.

THE YOUNG MAN CAME to visit at four o'clock. I took the chocolates from their box and put them on a plate and handed them to Ivy. She looked disapproving, but what could she say? Guests must be fed more than air. He was a shy boy, very nice, someone I met at Tinka's last winter, a nephew of a friend of hers.

"What would you like to talk about?" I asked him.

"If you wouldn't mind," he said, "what it was like back then, when you first came here."

"Oh, but I would like to talk about what it is like now!" I said. "That was sixty years ago! How do young people live now?"

"I don't know," he said. "The same as always. They date, they break up, they don't break up, they get married or they don't get married. The difference is in the appliances."

The appliances!

"Then you had horse-drawn carriages, ice boxes, no computers, no televisions. Everyone sat around and listened to someone play the ukulele."

"No, no," I said. "I am antique but not that antique. When I grew up, already there were automobiles. I remember an automobile trip to the country in an open car and my white straw hat kept blowing off and my father stopped the car for it three times, four times, and at last he said, 'Anna, get up,' and when I got up he put it on the seat and made me sit on it and I cried because I knew it would be crushed."

"And was it crushed?" the young man asked.

"Oh yes, the stick-up part, what do you call it, that was crushed, but it worked very well all the same."

"Did you mind?"

"I minded! I was old enough to be vain about my hats and, before I sat on it, it was so pretty! And what a trip! My father was a great lover of mushrooms. He saw one on the side of the road, he stopped the car. Of course in those days there was not much traffic, but he saw one special mushroom, he stopped the car and he backed up right on the big road. My mother screamed, we all screamed, we thought we would be killed, and out he jumped and got his mushroom and jumped back in. It wasn't our car, you know. We didn't have a car. Well, poor people don't have those things. My mother's family, they must have lent it to us."

"All those hats in *Sin and Salvation*, they were so beautiful, remember them?"

"Hats?" I said vaguely. Just then Ivy came in with the tea tray and the dish of candies. "You're talking about *Salvation*?" she said. "Miss Asta saw that just last week."

"Today people see that movie and ask themselves, Who is more beautiful, the woman or the man?" he said.

"Young people?" I asked. He said yes, young people.

"Oh, well, that is a question, isn't it? And to think that today nobody remembers Charlie Harrow! He *was* beautiful, wasn't he? That high forehead, that curling black hair, those huge black eyes, that perfect nose, I thought it was a better nose than John Barrymore's! You look at some pictures of him, you mistake him for John Barrymore. He taught me a lot."

"Not Max Lilly?"

"You know, I don't talk about these people," I said. "It's a rule."

You're very pleased with yourself, Max said, but be careful a little. Who doesn't fall in love with her leading man? And how long does it last? A movie set's like nothing else on earth. The director broods over every little move you make. The lighting man can't take his eyes from you, he worries about every shadow that falls on you, he arranges the shadows that do fall on you, people adjust your clothes, they pat your hair, always you are bathed in this endless, endless intense attention that is just like love. What is more wonderful? What can compare with it? You must be perfect to deserve all this! And the leading man, he is bathed in the same attention and this beloved person, he turns his precious gaze on you! The same drug as before, but now twice as powerful. The two of you kiss, the whole crew swoons in ecstasy. The world exists to approve of you! You grow certain you love him because they are certain. Their passion fuels your passion; yours grows greater, theirs grows greater, so erotic it is almost unbearable. Soon it is the greatest love on earth. Then the cameras stop, your hair is a mess, his eyes are bloodshot, he comes home late, you lose your temper, and where is the crew? Where are the perfect people? Disillusionment, bitterness, anger, it ends badly. Believe me, I know. It is the oldest story in the world. Don't walk into this story.

"I have my own copy of *Salvation*," the young man said. "*They could be twins.* That's what I thought when I saw it. They could be twins."

"What do you mean?" I said, sitting forward. "What do you mean, twins?"

Who coached you? Max asked. This was Hall's work? The two of you look like twins! All the gestures the same, all the facial mannerisms the same! You part your lips and close them, he parts his lips and closes them. You raise your eyebrows, he raises his eyebrows. You open your eyes wide and stare at him and swoon. He does the same thing. This is some new style of acting? Falling in love means imitation? At least his eyes don't roll up in his head! When you're guilty, your eyeballs have to disappear? Also he doesn't cover his face with his hands. Never have I seen an actress cover her face! No, you shouldn't stop! That bit is very good. You can tell him I said so.

When you try the hats on in front of the mirror, who told you to make love to the face you see there? You didn't think it up yourself! It was Mr. Hall? No? It was him. So. They said when he directed you he was good.

You see where he's taking you? Where I was taking you. No common gestures, no raising the eyebrows up like windowshades, no screwing up the mouth, no shop girl shrugging of the shoulders, no shaking the head like a wet dog, everything slowed down, that's the right way for you. Not all this flapping and fluttering. Now I can go back to Sweden. You don't need me anymore.

You know, Anna, when you try on the hat in the mirror, you can see it happen, the instant you fall in love with yourself. You didn't fall in love with yourself? Then that was great acting!

"I don't know," the young man said. "It crossed my mind. Twins. One blond, one dark, both tall, one male, one female, but both the same. Silly, really."

"Well, of course he was older, but then you know that. The Firebrand and the Ice Princess. That's how they used to talk. And there were other differences: strength of character. All that drinking. Well, today they call it an illness, don't they? But still they don't have any medicine for it! Once I lived on carrots and boiled onions for two weeks. He couldn't have done it. Of course, why should he have wanted to do it: carrots and boiled onions! But if he wanted to, still he couldn't. That was a problem. And we both turned black, like potatoes in a cupboard, absolutely black. In the moods, you know what I mean?"

"Miss Anna," Ivy said. In the morning I would regret it; I'd said too much.

"So, young people today," I said. "They are very free? All the papers say so. You sleep with anyone you want to sleep with? Men sleep with women and also with other men and no one notices, and the other way around too. But when they part, they still swallow sleeping pills, they still write threatening notes? Or do they walk quietly away? Of course they do both. Why do I ask? But they feel free to do as they please, that is the wonderful thing."

"In your day, it must have been the same," he said.

"In my day it was not the same. What do you think all those movies were about? There was the good woman who stayed at home and had babies and cooked at the stove and darned socks on her darning egg and there was the bad woman. Oh, she was so bad she wasn't even human. A devil, a spy, a murderess, believe me, it wasn't the same. You took a step outside the circle, you didn't come back in."

"Did it matter?" the young man asked. "Out there? In Hollywood?"

"You think it didn't matter?"

"I thought it was like the sixties, only forty years earlier."

I shook my head and picked up my coffee cup. So much gets lost! Where do you even begin?

"Look," I said, "somewhere in this house are wonderful albums. I am photographed with everyone but Hitler and *he* wanted to be photographed with me. You think of a famous person, I'm standing next to him in a picture, or a letter came through my mailbox asking if he could meet me. If I cut my hair, women everywhere cut their hair. If I wore short skirts, everyone cut up their dresses. But was I acceptable? I was never acceptable, no, not even in Hollywood. Only with the movie people, and sometimes not even with them. For everyone else, what was I? A whore! If I had married, if I'd had children, maybe then, but I didn't do it. The great producer of our studio, he wanted to know why Charlie Harrow thought he had to marry me. We were living together, what more did he want? That was all I was good for.

"And I had friends, Vera Polovna, we were very good friends, and then she got married, and all of a sudden I wasn't respectable enough for her anymore. *Why don't you get married, Anna? Why don't you get married?* Like a parrot! Do you think they forgot what she was because she got married? So, she had a rude awakening. Sooner or later, we all did.

"Well, today maybe it isn't such a sin to be beautiful. Then it was a sin. The beautiful one caused the trouble. Great beauty, great temptation. A normal person, a little homely, who is she going to tempt? What ideas will she get into her head? Oh, it's all nonsense, but then they believed it. One film after another! And let me tell you! The *worst* woman I knew, the *worst*, the most unscrupulous, she had everybody's husband, she was five foot one, absolutely round, gray-haired, prematurely gray, she looked like a wrinkled apple! Completely respectable! No one expected anything of her. Who could believe it?

"We were very good friends, the two of us. She told me stories about her exciting life, I told her what I read in bed when I came home from work. Well, it was ridiculous! Is that still the same? I don't think that is still the same."

"No," he said, smiling. "Today everyone's cynical. Everyone's the same as everyone else. Everyone's bad."

"But that's a mistake! There are good people!"

"It's not the fashion to think so."

"Did you believe it? Did you believe you were—?" He hesitated.

"What? A whore?"

He flushed. "No," he said. "A force for destruction."

"Listen, young man, it crossed my mind. Year after year playing these terrible women, I began to think, There are things you do that are not so different from what these dreadful women do. Always you are not so particular about whom you hurt. When is there just one man in your life? Always there are two and then you have the triangle the films love so much. And all the time you are acting, it's not so innocent. You live these other lives. Someone used to say, Think what you do, Anna. You practice sinning. With practice, everyone gets better. I can't deny it. I got better. I blame myself for a lot, a lot. I should have been honest. I should have said, All I trust is the woman in front of the camera. The camera stops turning, who knows what I'll do?

"I should have said, Look, I cannot trust myself so you cannot trust me either. You can be so many people, someone meets you, he doesn't know he's meeting a crowd! Well, it is all very complicated and I was too stupid or in this I was like Charlie: not enough will. Never enough will. Not in those days."

"It's interesting," he said. "Like Dr. Jekyll and Mr. Hyde."

"First you decide to become someone else, then you don't decide, but still you become that other person. Yes, like Dr. Jekyll and Mr. Hyde. I suppose you'll go home and write this down for a magazine and then I must say I never met you, I never talked to you, I don't know who you are, and everyone will believe me, because all my life I refuse to talk about these things."

"Don't you remember?" he asked me. "I don't write for magazines. I'm a biochemist."

"A biochemist! You must stay longer! Have another candy! Ivy, what do we have to eat?"

"Sardines and boiled potatoes," Ivy said wearily. "What else is on my list to buy?"

"You will eat sardines and boiled potatoes?" I asked anxiously. He said he would be happy to eat them. "And you will tell me what it is to be young today?"

"Miss Asta," he said, "that's not what you want to know. You want to know what it is to be ordinary."

"DO YOU WANT to meet him?" I asked Max. The set of *Sin and Salvation* was closed down. We were waiting for more snow.

"Why should I want to meet him?" Max asked. "He is your business."

"Well," I said, flustered, "he is important to me."

"Now you want me to approve your lovers?"

"What is this about?" I asked angrily.

"I suppose it is natural," he said. "I pick your clothes, your roles, I show you how to behave, so of course I should meet him."

Now I was furious. "*You* were the one who said our lives must be separate! You were the one who said your door was always open but I should come less often!"

"Come here as often as you want, but without him."

"And if it gets as far as marriage, what then? What then, Max?"

"That's another story," Max said. "We understand one another?"

There was the famous incident of the blue teeth. In those days, if something was to be pure white, a dress or a shirt, then our dress or shirt was blue. Of course, on the set we looked ridiculous, a morning coat worn over a blue shirt, or a blue silk wedding gown in the middle of fifteen other lovely colors, but when the film was developed, there was the shirt, the color of sun-struck snow, the gown, bridal.

After Charlie made *Wartime*, he was invited to a party and came straight from the set wearing his blue shirt. All over the country, people began wearing blue shirts. He was amazed. How far would it go? People were ridiculous, like sheep: he talked that way all the time.

Then, one morning before we left for The Studio, we were drinking little, bitter cups of coffee, the kind of coffee I made, where you put the grounds in the bottom of a teapot, poured the hot water in over them, and then put a little sweater on the teapot.

Charlie looked up from the paper and said, "Miss Rosalie says not to drink so much coffee. We'll get yellow teeth, but look here! Here it says we have the whitest teeth in the world."

"Think how much whiter they would be if we painted them blue," I said.

I should have kept quiet. Charlie put down his newspaper.

"Painted them blue," he said. "Let's do it!" I said it was nonsense, we couldn't put oil paint in our mouths, and he said, No, no, the same black stuff he painted on his teeth when he was supposed to be missing a tooth, it came in blue.

Now I was curious. "How does it dry in there? You have to keep your mouth open?"

He said no, we painted it on, we stuck our faces into the mouth of a hair dryer or we pressed a curling iron to our teeth. I wanted to know if it hurt. He asked if seeing Horton's face wouldn't be worth it. So we found a friend of Charlie's, a make-up man, who painted our teeth blue and told us to keep our mouths open and breathe through them. Then we went to the set.

"Here come the happy children," said Mr. Hall. "What's wrong with the two of you? You went to the dentist? Why are your faces all pulled down?" Charlie mumbled something and we went to our dressing rooms.

During the first scene, I was to come in out of the cold into a warm inn where a fire was blazing. Charlie was to look up, see me and smile. After an instant, I was to smile back. The cameras began turning. Charlie smiled. I smiled back.

Pandemonium! Mr. Feldman, who never laughed, was making whooping, choking noises. Mr. Hall stared. He was, for once, speechless.

"It may not be the greatest picture," Charlie said, "but you're going to get a lot of mail asking where your stars get their dentists."

"Go brush your teeth!" Mr. Hall said.

"Horton, let them leave it," Mr. Feldman said. "Look through the lens here! In their mouths they have jewels!"

Mr. Hall did look. "I hope you've got a lot of that blue stuff," he said, "because you're going to paint those teeth blue in *all* the love scenes."

So, for the remainder of the shooting, we painted each other's teeth. I sat still while Charlie painted mine and rhapsodized about my lovely rose-colored tonsils, streaked with coral-colored blood vessels. He sat still while I painted his and announced that his two back teeth looked chipped and one of them had a black hole on one side.

Mr. Hall would pass by and always, he would say the same thing: Look at the happy children.

And for the first time I knew, I was really happy, and even more astonishing, I was really a child.

Because I liked the sea, Charlie bought a yacht. I couldn't understand it: why buy a yacht when you could rent one? So much money when you could sail on someone else's boat! He wanted to name it *Sin and Salvation*, but I said that was asking for trouble. People would believe the first part but not the second. Still, once we had the yacht, I liked it. Whenever we were not shooting, we were out on the yacht, not standing at the rails like normal people, looking out from under visors, but wrapped in terry cloth robes wearing wide-brimmed straw hats because otherwise we would burn and ruin the picture.

"This picture," Charlie said to me one day. "I was looking at the rushes. Horton's a great editor. No scene goes on too long. That scene where the husband comes home and finds us in bed, that's perfect. The whole thing filmed through his clenched hand, it's wonderful. We challenge each other to a duel: then *Cut*. The next scene: a few inky trees, something out of an expressionist film, my face, his face, some smoke, then *Cut*. Then your face in front of the mirror, trying on a hat and mourning veils. Or the parson warning me to stay away from you, then *Cut*. Then you and I walk into church together and *Cut*. Does anyone wonder what people say to one another in the middle? Think about what's left out. The husband comes home, finds his wife in bed with an army officer, she cowers on the bed, the officer accepts the challenge to a duel, and leaves her there with her husband. What do they say to one another? They don't sit there like a tableau, frozen all night. What do they talk about? Isn't that the interesting part? Does he ask her why she does it? Is he angry at her or at the officer? Does he care? Does he hit her? What goes on in that room all night? Everything's left out. If these were real people, you'd want to know."

"Max should have made this movie," I said. "He never makes movies about real people."

"If these people aren't real, what are they?"

"Myths," I said.

"Myths," Charlie said contemptuously. "I want to make movies about real people, human beings. They have faults, they have stomachaches, they scratch themselves, they break out in rashes, they drink too much and fall down the stairs, they worry about losing their jobs, they beat their children, people like that."

"Sometimes real people are happy," I said. "It happens."

He kissed me. I kissed him. Soon our clothes were off and we had to go below: we couldn't afford the sunburn.

"Could we speed the tempo up a little?" Mr. Hall asked us. "It's a love scene, not an underwater ballet."

"It's right the way it is," Charlie said.

"Anna, every now and then you could drop your eyes," Mr. Hall said. "You don't have to stare that adoring stare the entire time."

"It's fine the way it is," Charlie said.

"I tell her something and she looks at you before she does it!" Mr. Hall said angrily.

"In that scene where the three of us toast friendship?" Charlie asked. "What if Erik breaks his glass and cuts his finger and while he sucks at it, the two of us toast one another? *Our* oath of friendship, not his. I think it's better."

"Don't think so much!" said Mr. Hall.

"Think about it," Charlie said.

"Ready everyone?" Mr. Hall asked. "Erik, Charlie, don't open your eyes so wide. It's not a contest."

"It has a dramatic effect," Charlie said.

"It's overdone," Mr. Hall said. "Not so wide. It's a love scene. You're both smitten with her. Smitten. Instead you look like you wandered in here from a horror film."

"Put in more love scenes," said Mr. Pinsky. "That son of a bitch, Harrow, this is the best work he's done yet."

"The scenes are a little slow," Mr. Hall said.

"They could be even slower," Mr. Pinsky said. "So the movie will run a little longer. We're making history here."

"HE WAS A NICE YOUNG MAN, Lady Clare," Ivy said. "You liked talking to him?"

"Well, I did talk to him," I said grumpily. "Who knows what got into me? Now I will be up all night."

"You want something to think about? Think how you will feel in the morning if you stay up all night."

"Always I walk around half asleep, that's how I like it, and these people come along and wake me up. The least little thing preys on me. This morning, Tinka calls up to say this is the Year of the Sheep, last year was the Year of the Horse, and for days I am washing my hair of this information. What a nervous system!"

"What really are you complaining about?" she asked me.

"Oh, who knows! *We were like twins!* What a foolish thing to say. Why did he say it?"

"If a person can't sometimes say what's on his mind," she began.

"Never mind, I am taking your advice and going to bed," I said.

They say women are more interested in the past, that, for them, the beauties of the past are guarded carefully, like lights that shine through into the present, because, should they go out, the present would become darker. Someone said it has something to do with children, because women bear them, so that when they look at the adult, always they see the golden little child.

I don't know, really. I was never very interested in the past, and after I left home, I didn't like to remember it. Of course I remember the country of my childhood, dark cliffs with big black and gray stone faces, dark rivers running far below, the two places we lived, in the country, in the city, no one forgets those things.

What you remember, how much, it is not entirely involuntary. For a long time, I said to myself, one foot in front of the other, this is what you are doing, everything else: Out. Well, during that time, everyone said, Oh, she is selfish and superficial, just as we thought she was, hardly even a person. I agreed with them so I didn't mind. I spent my time dreaming up practical jokes and laughing a lot. I swam, I was always brown, and really, I was very happy.

Then this plague of tiredness came over me. And one day sleep turned against me. Someone would say something, anything: I would be awake. Awake and watching. But for what?

So then I made a new rule: always home by seven o'clock. No phone calls after seven unless I made them. If no one said anything to me, then I could sleep. And then even that no longer worked.

A ceiling, when you stare at it, has as many wrinkles as a face. Time would pass. Faces would begin to form there. Then I would get up, look at my clock—two o'clock, three o'clock—and call someone. Naturally no one was awake. I was waking someone up. But I knew what I could get away with.

"Oh, she's a strange one, that one," they would say later, but even as they complained, they would be advertising: We know her! See how close we are! She calls us in the middle of the night!

Well, in their dealings with one another, all human beings are shopkeepers. No one gives away anything, everyone keeps an account.

Then Ivy came to work here, and when her children married, she moved in, so during the week, when she is here, I sleep better. Of course I talk more. I remember more. Who can help it? Always Ivy is trying to remember: did she see her mother after she was kidnapped? Someone said they had a picture of her mother: who was it? Not her aunt. Her aunt said she lent it to someone. Who did she lend it to? Someone in Mare River or was it Orange Bay? How could anyone vanish like that, not even a picture of her? Every little detail she polishes, she sets it shining on her windowsill. Every bit of earth to be turned, she turns it.

At first I thought, This is dog behavior, this digging things up, this is foolish. Her mother will not come back, no one comes back, why bother? And then I saw: there was a way to make her mother come back. She could become her mother. Anything she knew about her mother, she drew it into herself. If she knew something she didn't like, she made herself the opposite, but everything, it must be done in relation to the mother.

And I thought, This is just like acting! First there is Ivy. Then she learns of her mother. She brings the mother alive by taking her in. With her own gestures, she moves for her mother. Who can tell them apart any longer? Every moment is a conversation with the mother. *You died young but I am still alive. My children are not stepchildren. No one beats them with an Indian broom.*

I know I too am interwoven with someone or other. But who wants to be interwoven with a dead thing? *Don't be so stupid, Anna,* Max would say. *If you remember them, they're not dead. What is there to remember about a dead person? There's no such thing as a dead person, only a body.* I can remember Max and still sleep.

But the other one: I can hardly say his name. Sometimes, when I'm talking to someone, I say, Someone once gave me a pool cue and said, This is what you do with it. Of course then I am remembering. But I keep him hidden. So many terrible things happened to him, now he is nobody's business.

Other people, all day and all night they think about their first loves, they go on about it: What can compare to them? Of course their husband is nice, but he's not the same. Their eyes grow misty. They say things like, It only happens once and after that you go on. It couldn't have lasted. Time would have ruined it anyway. How many people do you know who married their first loves? Did they stay married? It's not the same this time but it's better.

What, really, are they saying? *Once I was young. Then I grew up. What a disappointment, to be an adult!*

I should be able to speak of Charlie without staring from an armchair down at the graying concrete city, watching the streetlamps, pale yellowish-white, the color of summer suns in Sweden. It embarrasses me. What do I have to say about him? I loved him.

When he was there, I saw nothing else. The rest of the world, if it was on fire, I didn't care. I looked at that face, that long, straight, fine nose and wanted to touch it. I watched the forehead and learned the language of its folds and wrinkles. A furrow between the eyes meant worry or a headache. A raising of the eyebrows, the wrinkles of the forehead closer together: worry. The mouth slightly open, the eyes narrowed: disappointment and hurt. In the beginning, I saw little of that. Later, I saw it often.

If I could not touch him, I felt alone in my own body. To touch his hand properly: that could take half an hour. I felt each fingertip, rubbed it until it was warm between my fingers, then each finger, joint by joint, then the palm of the hand, massaging it in a circular motion with the tips of my fingers, listening to the dry sound my fingers made, like the sound of dry leaves in autumn, the sound of taffeta, rustling. His face! I rubbed my cheek into his cheek. He lay on his back. I pressed my cheekbone into his until I couldn't bear the pain. I bit. I pulled the hair on his chest, I traced the outline of his ribs, I sank my head in the hollow of his rib cage. One day I chewed on his knees and shin bones. I was cannibalistic. He stroked my hair, stroked it and stroked it. When I got up all the curl was out of it. He used to say: like the Miracle of the Loaves and Fishes. Such devourings! And when we got up, still there was more.

I never looked in mirrors. I never liked to. Now I stood with him in front of mirrors, marvelling. Look at those two together! Is it possible? Do the gods say, This one and this one, they must go together? Her blond hair, his black? Her blue eyes, his black? In those early days, there was no bitterness in me: no unhappiness. In the pictures that survive, you can see it.

We are in his garden, behind the tennis courts. I am leaning against his legs in their white, pressed trousers, those sharp creases, they looked so expensive and elegant, who would believe he pressed them himself, because, when I lived with him, he was forever sending the servants away.

"I do a better job than you do," he said. The light is falling badly. He is a blur of black hair, black eyes, eyebrows and moustache. I am tall and skinny and the shadows give me a long, misshapen nose, but my body is like rubber, nothing could look more content. We have the exhausted look of the very happy, the look of people who climb a mountain and collapse at the top in amazement and surprise: Look! We have made it!

When I moved into his house, we had parties. At first I hid. I wouldn't come down. Then one afternoon he dragged me downstairs and pushed me through the front door. He handed me a tray of champagne and strawberries and said, "Horton looks thirsty." I marched through the garden like a waitress. After a while I was laughing and talking. Later, of course, I scolded and said how shy I was, how hard it was for me, but he slapped my bottom and laughed at me.

We began to have friends, to go places. He never asked me if I wanted to go. "Get dressed," he said and threw something onto my bed. Whatever it was, I put it on. We went out.

One Sunday, Anders and his wife Esther came to one of our tennis parties. Of course Charlie knew that Max and Anders were close friends, so at first he avoided him, but then they began to talk about films with "real human beings," and soon we were planning on a trip to the Sewanee. I like this, I thought. This is not so bad.

"So how is Max?" I asked Anders.

"I never mix business and disaster," Anders said.

"How is Max?" I asked Anders' wife.

"He hobbles and he complains: he's on his second movie and they're talking about a third. How should he be? But, you know, who ever heard of ice-cold swims to cure rheumatism? My mother, she heated old towels in a big pot and when they steamed, she wrapped them around what hurt. Heat! Heat! I tell him, but he doesn't listen."

"You think he will begin now?" I asked her.

"Who here had a happy childhood?" Charlie asks me. We are lying in bed, in that severe black bed, in that stark white room, but the far wall is all glass and looks out over the sea. "Maud's mother washed clothes for a living. She hired Maud out back in New Jersey to make a few dollars. People here don't know what childhood means. Even Pinsky, you can begin to feel sorry for him. They say he walked across Poland with a pushcart when he was eight years old."

"Who believes these stories?"

"The trouble is, they're true."

"And you, I read about you before I even met you. In *Photoplay.*"

"In *Photoplay!* No one tells the truth to *Photoplay!* Oh, sure, my mother was an actress. One day she noticed her dress was tight and the next thing she knew she was back home in Minnesota waiting to get thin again. I was the unsightly bulge. She left me with her parents until they got tired of it and then she took me on the road. I slept in drawers. For a few years I slept under her bed. She needed the sleep because she was working. If I couldn't fall asleep, she gave me a drink. Once we stopped in Chicago for three weeks and I tried to play ball with some of the boys on the block but I couldn't catch anything. They thought I was a bad player, but I wasn't. I was drunk. At ten years old.

"At night, the leading man came in, peeled off his moustache, wiped off his make-up and got in bed with her, and the springs almost touched the floor so I had to roll out from under. Sometimes I watched them. Sometimes I didn't. She said my father was off with another company. He used to laugh at me, that man. I was going to grow up hating women! Mr. Johnny One Note. That was all he had to say to me.

"Well, so I used to think, I'll find my father. He'll take care of me. I found him two years ago. He was an extra on the set of *Wartime*. Two weeks before we shut down, he came up to me and introduced himself. Then he asked for twenty bucks. I threw him out, it got in the papers, heartless son turns his back on penniless father.

"So there was my mother. She spent her time getting rid of me. There was my father. I never knew who he was but when he found out who I was, he wanted twenty dollars. It's some town here. We drift in and out of these terrific stories in dandy clothes living dandy lives and where do we come from? The bigger the star the worse it was for him before. *That's* the truth!"

"Once," I say, "I was walking with my father. A woman ran out of an apartment house and pressed some money into his hand. She was crying hysterically. It was snowing, well, it was always snowing. She didn't have on a coat, just a white flannel nightgown and bare feet. She grabbed me by the cheeks and kissed me on the top of the head and ran back in."

" 'Daddy,' I said, 'why did that lady give you the money?' and he said, 'Oh, no reason.' But I was a child so I didn't give up. 'Does she run out and give everyone money?' I asked, and he said, 'Of course not.'

" 'Then why does she give you money?'

" 'Because she's grateful,' he said.

" 'For what?'

" 'You know at night I drive the hearse and come for the bodies?' he said. 'I came for her husband's body.'

" 'But she paid you then,' I said. 'Didn't she pay you then? Everyone pays you when you come.'

" 'This was different,' he said, but I wouldn't stop, so finally he told me. Her husband had fits and one night he died in the middle of one of them and by the time the doctor got there one arm was out stiff, going one way, and one leg out stiff, going the other, so how were they going to get him down the stairs? My father said he figured it out, so she was grateful and now when she saw him, she ran out and gave him money. And he had to take it, because if he didn't, she started crying and screaming and throwing her nightgown over her head."

"What did he do? How did he get him out?"

"He never said. He must have broken the bones."

"Broken the bones! My God!"

"What else could he have done?" I ask.

I know what he is thinking: How can people like us make anything good?

"Anna?" he says. "Let's have a child."

It is impossible, you see, to tell how it was. We fell in love like everyone else, yet we were not like everyone else and so, in some important way, it was different.

Once more, I will try.

One day during a break in the shooting, I started walking through the deserted back lots, past the remains of the great horses, once five stories high, now missing their heads and tails, large white looming torsos of horses, through the Roman amphitheater where the chariot race was filmed, and onto the set of a little western town, all storefronts and saloons. For no particular reason, I climbed up the steps onto the dry wood porch of the saloon.

The sets had been weathered by the California sun. Now they looked ancient and authentic, and I stood in the small town and looked back, through the amphitheater to the ruined horses, and just then Charlie came into view, also walking aimlessly. So that he would not see me, I moved back behind a post and stood in its shadow, and my foot went through a rotted floorboard. I didn't notice. To steady myself I wrapped my arm around the post, and the shadows fell right, the light was right, the air was cool and washed and the smell of rain and wet wood was everywhere, and I watched Charlie walk. I watched him turn around to look behind him, I saw him tilt back his head to look at the sun, and he was so beautiful, of course they built an amphitheater for his backdrop, an amphitheater and the great ruined horses, everything from the beginning of time spread out only for him.

But what does this tell you? Another lovesick female! If he was near me, I had to touch him. We held hands and even when his fingers squeezed my ring and hurt me, I thought, it is good to suffer for this! Oh, yes, during this time, I was like any other woman, absolutely obsessed, absolutely boring.

This may give you an idea: two weeks after we finished shooting, Mr. Hall had a rough cut of *Salvation*, and, as a courtesy to an ex-fellow director, he asked Charlie if he would like to watch it with me.

"On one condition," he said. "No complaints, no criticism." So we sat alone in the screening room and the white path of light cut through the dusty air, Charlie and I lit cigarettes, the smoke rose up to the

light, mixed with it, we sat up straight like children in school, the
credits came on and there he was. I began to smile. I sighed and
relaxed. He stiffened, watching himself clown around with Erik.

Then the scene changed and he saw me for the first time in the
railway station. I dropped my flowers. He picked them up. In the
screening room, his hand tightened on mine. We sat in our chairs
watching our best, our most beautiful selves falling in love, making
love, and everything else in the picture dropped away—the jealous
husband, he didn't exist, the best friend I later married and betrayed,
he didn't exist—there were only two of us, giant, beautiful shadows
like beautiful souls whose only business was with one another, whose
only scenery was one another, just as it was in life! Just as in life. Two
people fall in love, a common thing, and they look at one another and
ask, What is the rest of the world for? They don't know. We didn't
know.

Why should we know what the husband and wife said to each
other before the duel in the morning? If the world burned up, if it
shrivelled to an ash and floated away on a breeze, what difference did
it make to us? The world was not part of our story.

We sat in the dark and marvelled at one another. I marvelled at
myself: Was it true I was so beautiful? Was it true I was so human? I
must be if I could look at someone like that. Everything he had told
me, that no one before me mattered, that before me he had never
seen anyone's face, all that was true when I saw how he looked at me
on the screen. We sat in our seats and looked at ourselves in another,
more perfect, more intense, more purified world, and as we watched,
we fell doubly in love, hopelessly in love.

And even in the middle of this, as we sat there, I was frightened.
I said to myself, Those are hellish creatures. When they face the
camera, there are no backs to them. When they turn away, they have
no faces. They are not real. But it did no good. I was enchanted, by
Charlie, by myself. We were seducing ourselves, we who were already
seduced. This is how we differed from the others and what a sorrow
it is to think of it now.

"So?" Mr. Hall asked us. His indifference was studied and desperate. "How was it?"

We looked at one another and smiled.

"Say something!" he said.

"One scene is not good," Charlie said. "The scene in the park.
When I lean toward her and say, 'I love you,' it's too sudden. I jump.
I look like someone stuck me with a pin."

"That's it?" Mr. Hall said.

"That's it."

"No one is going to notice."

"I noticed."

"Charlie," he said. "Don't complain."

"Well," Charlie said later, "that's it. Our afterlife. Other people have to wait and wonder, but we've already seen ours. It's up there on the screen."

"Who wants an afterlife in the middle of this life?" I asked.

What did he mean, our afterlife? As if it was already over, as if we were caught, as if we were already dead!

"Forget about afterlives," he said. "Madame, the screen's greatest lover is going to ravish you!"

"Again?" I said.

We were very happy.

12

BUT HE HAD SAID, *Anna, let's have a child.* He had said, *All my life I wanted a family. That's all I ever wanted.*

Months passed. We began new films. One morning I found myself pregnant. I knew it the morning after it happened. I came back from location, and the next morning I threw up. So I knew. But I didn't tell him. Instead, I waited a week and went to see Max.

It took him a long time to come to the door and when he opened it, I saw why. He was leaning heavily on a heavy black wooden cane and with every step he grimaced in pain.

"Come in, come in," he said. "As you can see, the cold swims in the Pacific aren't doing the trick. But, filming is almost finished. So? You're getting married?"

I leaned my head on my hand; I shook my head. "Come on, come on," Max said. "I'm prepared. So what is it?" he asked.

"He wants children," I said.

"Yes," Max said. "That is expected."

"I don't want them. Not yet."

He didn't ask why. He didn't say, women in love want the child of that man. "What are you going to do? You didn't come here to ask me to fix it for you. You know better."

"I know better."

"So what do you want to know?" he asked.

"What will he do? It will end if I put a stop to the child?"

"Must he know about it?" Max asked me.

"He knows. I threw up and he said, 'Anna, you're pregnant. We'll have a child!' Believe me, he knows and he's happy about it."

"If he didn't know, you wouldn't have told him?"

"No," I said. "No. It is such a serious thing, I have to think about it. Look what happened to my mother!"

"Your mother? Your mother is a fine woman, happy with her lot."

"She is not happy!" I said.

Max closed his eyes and imperceptibly shook his head. He looked down at his fingers, drumming on his knee. "You are asking me what to do?" he said sadly. "Never, never have I been in this position." He absentmindedly massaged his right elbow. "But you want to know what I think? I think if you 'put a stop to the child' he won't like it. How can he like it? You hear the way men say 'the mother of my children'? 'How can I leave the mother of my children?' So we know it is something special. Anyway, one thing we know absolutely. If we are sitting here working it out like a math problem, we are over our heads."

Time passed. A little wooden clock ticked. I looked around the room for it.

"Over there," Max said, pointing at the tall cupboard. "The only hotel guest who appoints his own room."

"Well," I said, "how are you?"

"That's my Anna," he said. "On to the next subject."

"I want to know."

"When have I ever been able to answer that? If I could answer that, I would be a different person. I am busy, my mind is occupied, I limp, I take aspirins and go for cold swims, I am visited by you. At my age, what will change?"

"Oh," I said, "that is your delusion, that you are beyond change."

"No, that is not my delusion," he said. "Not at all." He stirred; he shifted his weight from the afflicted hip. "So, something else is important. I saw *Salvation*. I wept! It should have been my movie! Perfect! That one will last. And you, you are better than good. You know when to slow down, you know when to become what you are, so silly, so playful. Who is this Mr. Hall, who has stolen everything I know?"

"A great admirer of yours," I said. It was true.

"So, a great admirer with some talent can now do everything I can do. So quickly we become pointless in the world! They keep coming, don't they? Just like waves. Have the child."

He passed his hand in front of his face, once, twice. I shook my head no. I was ashamed to look at him. An instant before I had been thinking, Who can I ask? Who will tell me where to go, how it is done?

Charlie would be unhappy and bitter but a morning would come when he would get over it. But now it was as if Max was the child's father, Max who wanted the child, Max who would be broken the day I came to him and said, The child is gone. "If it were your child . . ." I said.

"Yes?" He looked up, tense, eager, almost greedy.

"I don't know if I could say no to you."

"But you don't love me."

"I do love you!"

"You don't know what you're saying. Don't say any more."

"You are suffering!"

"The hip is painful."

"I am not talking about the hip!"

"Anna, I am asking you. Don't say any more."

"How many chances do we get in life?"

"You come here lovesick and pregnant," he shouted at me, "lovesick and pregnant and talk to me about—I don't know what we're talking about! And now you start to cry! Really, what is it you want to say?"

"You know!" I said. "You know!"

"Go home. Go home and calm down. Tomorrow I'll still be in the world. Tomorrow, you know what you want to say to me, come back."

"Tomorrow?"

"If not tomorrow, the next day or the day after that, it doesn't matter, but today you don't know what you're saying. Go home."

I got up and went to the door. The brass knob was cold against my palm. "Here," said Max, hobbling to me, "here." He took his big white handkerchief from his pocket and wiped my face. "All right?"

I looked around the whitewashed room, at the black wooden beams in the ceiling, at the painted pine furniture. Sunlight streamed in thick paths through the window and formed brilliant rectangles against the polished wood floor. Max followed my eyes. "A good light for filming," he said. He smiled a terrible smile. I said, I will be back. "Of course you will," he said.

But I didn't go home. I stopped in the lobby and called Bertha

Pinsky who told me to come straight over. She babied me, she fed me candies, she coaxed me, she held my head against her breast, and eventually I told her.

"You're sure?" she asked me. I said I was sure. "Then I know someone you should talk to," she said. "Also he does cosmetic surgery. Well, in a studio town, what can you expect? They still want your nose thinner? Maybe he can do both at once. It's not funny? I know it's not funny. That's why I'm making such stupid jokes. You see why it's a good idea? You come out of his office, everyone thinks you're improving on nature. Look, you have time. Think it over. Sometimes it doesn't turn out so well and later when you want them you can't have them." I said I would take that chance.

"The young girl thinks she can speak for the older one, but the older one doesn't always like what the younger one had to say," Bertha said. "To have such regrets later, that's a bitter thing. You love this man? Of course you love him. Anyone can see it."

"But," I said hesitantly, "everyone falls in love like this. I hear people talk. It's like—"

"Like what?"

"Teething!"

"Teething!"

"You do it and you're finished!"

"This is a schoolgirl crush? Is it?" I said of course it wasn't. "Anna," Mrs. Pinsky said. "Go home and get some sleep. Here is the name and number. Two hundred dollars. Don't do anything so fast. The child doesn't start walking tomorrow."

"You won't tell Mr. Pinsky?"

"This is his business? He has to know everything? You think his own daughters tell him everything? Go home, get some sleep."

I have taken off all my clothes. He faces me. He puts his hands on my hips. He leans forward and takes a nipple in his mouth. My body has a will of its own. It presses itself against him.

He takes little bites, little chewings, from my breasts, my belly, from my upper arms. My arms are tight around his neck. His head is beneath mine. I rub my chin into his hair, hard against his skull. With my toes I trace the shape of his leg, up and down his leg, from the shin bone to the knee.

I hold his head with both hands. I push my nose into his cheeks. He has a taste: it is like eating. I make low noises. I am a hot, golden animal. I love this. No matter what happens, I cannot get enough of this. He says I love him for his body. I do love his body. After this is over, after he falls asleep, I will lie in bed and watch the sun move like a hand over his body. I will go to the window and turn and watch my shadow move over his body. He says, One would think you've never done this before. I haven't.

He picks me up and carries me to the bed. He crouches over me. I sit halfway up, put my arms around his neck and pull him down. Now we are on the floating bed, breasts, arms, buttocks, floating. Oh, I have been here before.

We spend hours like this. Later, I think, I do not feel more of a woman. I feel part woman and part man. I feel complete.

I used to ask him, Why do you love me? Is it because I am so beautiful? and he would say no. Then I would ask, How do I know that? and he would say, Because you are not so beautiful. Then I was insulted. You're trying to tell me I'm ugly? I said. No, you're all right, he said. Just all right? I asked. If you're fishing for compliments, he said, give an interview.

Every room in his house was copied from one of his movie sets: the living room, high and vaulted, like a church, came from *The Magic Forest.* This is normal? I asked him. They strike the set but you're still living in it? Souvenirs, that's all, he said. The best movies, the best sets, there's something odd about that? So, yes, there is something odd, I said. You, he said, your idea of a nice place is a little kitchen and a bed big enough to eat on. There is something more I need? I asked him. Ambition, he said, and I said, I am very ambitious! He said, You need the ambition to get dressed!

Then I would put on one of his shirts and put on a pair of his slacks and tighten my belt around my waist and we would go shopping. These were the good times.

It was a big house, the house on Cathedral Road, and Charlie had many friends while I, I was a lone wolf, and his friends, they had a tendency to move in when their wives threw them out or they couldn't pay the rent or they had a deadline and their children made too much noise. I was surprised. I liked having them around. When Charlie was on location, we sat up and talked. They bought me books to read. I picked up the books they dropped.

One of them, Walter Arnett, became famous later for his screenplays. We would sit and talk about Charlie.

"Look," I said, "I know you're a drunk, so tell me, how does anyone live with a drunk? You go to a party, he says terrible things, he throws something in a punchbowl, and what does he remember? He remembers *you* insulted him. Then I should apologize!"

"No one ever called me a drunk to my face," Walter Arnett said, and I said, "Oh, I'm sorry. Is that bad manners? How should I say it?"

"Look here," he said. "You really want to know about drunks?"

"If I am living with one, I must."

"You're never living with a drunk," he said. "You think you're living with a drunk but he's not living with you. He's living with this glass and this gin. That's the whole of it. Nothing and nobody is more important to him than that bottle. Just remember that, you'll have a good time, you'll know where you are."

"He thinks he loves me anyway."

"You rate high on the list," he said. "After the bottle."

He was one of Charlie's friends, very nice men. All of them, very intelligent.

Once I came back from location and found four of them playing cards around the kitchen table. The house was unrecognizable, furniture in the wrong rooms, mattresses on the floor, open Chinese food cartons everywhere. When they saw me, they did their Pinsky imitations. Oh, they were very funny. They would sit up late thinking up Pinsky plots and Pinsky dialogue and then they would act everything out. I played all the roles: the mother, the old woman, what Walter Arnett called the antivamp, and of course, I parodied myself. I parted my lips and closed them like a goldfish in a bowl. I raised my eyebrows and narrowed my eyes and lifted one arm and put my hand behind my head. At night the muscles of my stomach hurt, I laughed so much.

One man, a famous writer, came in the middle of the night and said his wife was chasing him, he was afraid for his life, so of course Charlie let him in. Later this same man drowned himself. They found his body floating in a canal, but that's another story.

So we sat around until late. They talked, I listened. "You're not the usual thing," the writer said to me. "No?" I asked. "What is the usual thing?" and he said the usual thing was a pretty little lady, her ankles crossed neatly, one over the other, leaning forward, saying, "Yes, Charlie, no, Charlie."

"Charlie," I said, "I'm going for a drive." And I got in the car and drove to the Golden Palms and let myself into Max's room.

Sometimes he was asleep. Often he was awake. "Come whenever you want," he had said. "But come alone." I would sit in one chair, he in another. Sometimes we sat that way for hours, saying nothing. If, when I came, he was in bed, I would crawl in next to him and sometimes I would fall asleep. Later, I would leave and go back to Cathedral Road.

I came in one night and found Max crying. "Gussie is not well and I am not well," he said. "Time to go home, eh?"

"When?" I asked.

"Next month. Well, it has to be done."

13

NO ONE WAKES UP in the morning and says, Today I will become less human, but one day you wake up and realize you are less human than you were. Some of the reasons are almost too obvious to talk about. Overindulgence: that is one reason. When every whim is gratified, when every idle fancy is taken as a command, when people scurry about, scouring a city because you said, out of boredom, in a state of nostalgia, I wish I had an apricot macaroon, then sooner or later you will want to see how far this can go. You want to know the extent of your power. So in the beginning, there is something innocent, almost childlike, about it. A child lying in his crib wiggles two fingers and it occurs to him, Can I wiggle them all? And so he tries.

This is how it begins. You think to yourself, I must have this book. I would be a better, more intelligent person, if only I had this book. You mention the book: someone gets it for you. Then you need another book. Your shoes need mending. Someone brings the book, mends your shoes. If only someone would comb the tangles from your hair. Your arm is so tired. Someone combs it. If only you had a peaceful, quiet place to stay. Someone lends you his house. But it is so hard to clean the borrowed house! The owner lends you his maid. If only you had something to wear; if only you had thought to pack some clothes! The owner of the house lends you his wife's clothes. It is sad, not to see the pines of the Swedish forest. The owner plants pine trees in a corner of his property. Yes, but now the trees remind you of Ekeborn where once there was a waterfall. The owner builds a waterfall and the sound of falling water soothes you to sleep at night. But on some nights you cannot sleep. If only you had a companion when you walked through the quiet, empty rooms. The owner stays awake and walks with you.

Slowly, this is what happens. The owner of the house who was your friend becomes your familiar. You grow impatient when he does not do your bidding. After all, he has always done it before.

Now you are no longer two human beings living together. Now

one of you is the wizard and the other the servant. But the servant does not want to be pressed into service; he does not want to be less than he was. Eventually he will tire of it. Probably when that occurs he will want his revenge. But it is hard to foresee what will happen later. And even when you foresee the result, you are powerless to stop yourself. Your own power intoxicates you.

The things you do become less innocent, the games you play more complex. Oh, I do not want a child, you say, and the owner of the unborn child weeps and says, Then we will get rid of this one. But next time, we will have one. And you say, Yes, I want a child that looks like you. Next time we will have it. And next time, you say, Oh, I want a child, but not right now. It is so inconvenient. You can understand. And the owner of the unborn child whitens and ages before your eyes. But he says, Will it make you so unhappy? And you say, Yes, it would make me very unhappy. I do not want you to be unhappy, he says, and so the second child is gone. Afterwards he asks, Are you in very much pain? and you say, Oh, yes, the pain is terrible. And you say, You must not feel guilty. These things happen between men and women and this happens to a woman's body. Of course he feels guilty. And you say, But next time we will have it.

And the third time, you say, The third time is the charm, and you see how happy you have made him, but then you cannot sleep, you are sick to your stomach, you find a doctor who says it is dangerous, you are too nervous, too thin, too tired, and so the third child is gone.

And you begin to ask yourself, How many times will he let himself be tortured? Five times! Now he begins to complain. A man feels less of a man when he knows a woman does not want his child. How sympathetic you become as you explain that he is no less manly in your eyes because you have not borne his child. Now he begins to drink more and when he is drunk he shouts about the unborn children. You are very rational and gently remind him that he drank long before this trouble came upon him. He threatens to throw you out of the house. One night he does throw your clothes over the balcony and onto the lawn. In the morning he is remorseful and brings them back in. He washes the mud-stained blouse himself, with his own hands.

And now you find yourself strangely excited. Is this the limit of your power? Does your power have a limit? And you determine to find out. You do not move out of the house but you spend a night with someone else. In the morning, he is frantic and pleads with you to come back. So you have not yet reached the limit. Perhaps there is no limit.

And then one day when you are off somewhere, you read in the newspaper that he is engaged to marry someone else. Now you rush back to the house, now you plead, now you are ready to have children, twins, triplets! But it is too late. He wants no more of you. He has, after all, such a thing as pride. Even love, humble, suffering, generous, forgiving love, can be broken.

Have you learned your lesson? No. You are like a cat who has just discovered the joys of hunting mice. You tell yourself, I will not do that again. But you return to your home and you begin again. How can you help yourself? The game was so exciting. Now it is a form of drunkenness, a splendid addiction. Not *Will I do it?* but *How much will I do?* And now you have a reason, while before you had none. After all, he abandoned you. He left you for someone else. He broke your heart. See? Here are the pieces. Now you have an excuse. People are not trustworthy. Perhaps they are not even people. And it begins to creep in everywhere, in everything you say, in things so small you no longer notice them, in the way you enter someone's house and fail to say hello, but announce that you do not like rooms on the east side of the house because the early sun wakes you and your eyes are so sensitive to light. In short, you are becoming a monster and where are the monster-tamers? It is astonishing to discover how people adore monsters!

These are some of the ways one becomes a monster. People mistreat you, call you names, order you about as if you were less than a cow. You decide that when your time comes, you will make them sorry. This is natural. This is good. Without hope of revenge, how could one endure the humiliation? But then your opportunity comes and you have a choice: will you or won't you take it?

Ricardo Bruno asked me who I slept with to get my part.

In those days, musicians were called onto the set to play music that would put us in the mood for our scenes. Whatever music I asked for, he would object to. *Who can stand this heavy foreign stuff?*

When we were next in a picture, his star had faded. He was nervous in our scenes together. He asked the band to play Negro spirituals. I loved Negro spirituals. He had hired a singer from the Sewanee. I loved that singer. But I would wait until the music began to play, and as soon as the singer began, I would say, I can't stand that music! No matter what Mr. Bruno asked for, it was always the same thing: I can't stand that music! It destroys my concentration!

By the third interruption, Mr. Bruno was stumbling through his lines. His hatred of me hung in the air and glittered like a knife. I could see it but no one else could. And he didn't dare say a word, not one word. The reviews of his performance were my revenge.

Later, when we were making *Another Woman*, the actress who had made fun of my big feet and my odd way of walking had worked herself up for an emotional scene. I began to hiccup. Oh, how innocent it seemed, that hiccupping! But as a school child, my friends and I would sit outside practicing hiccupping.

The director, the other actors, and Mr. Feldman all brought me water. By the time I stopped, the other actress was beside herself. She ran up to me, burst into tears, and ran off the set.

"Well, if she cannot handle emotional scenes," I said, "we must get someone else." Of course she heard me. I wanted her to hear me. When she came back to the set, she was nervous and unsure of herself. When Mr. Pinsky saw the final version, he said, "We'll reshoot Miss Linder's scenes. Get someone else, maybe that Veronica person."

I was an actress. They said I had genius. No one ever suspected what I was up to. And yet it was obvious. Max would have seen through me. Probably he would have stopped it. He would have said, That is like kicking someone under the table and letting them take the punishment when they hit you back in full view. But he was not there to stop it.

And at times I did extraordinary things, things utterly out of character, all to attract attention, I, who was always so anxious to avoid it.

At a party, a young woman was to sing a song for Mr. Pinsky's birthday, but when he walked in, I stepped away from Charlie and began to sing, "I'll Never Be Happy Unless You're Happy Too." Naturally I brought down the house. Naturally the next day's papers were stuffed full of my photograph. Of course Mr. Pinsky was delighted. Normally I would not look at him.

Why had I done it? Was I jealous of the spotlight swinging to this young woman who saw a boring party as her chance to be noticed? I was jealous of her appetite for public display. I was envious of her tolerance of the spotlight. So I dared myself to do what she was going to do: I stepped forward and sang her song.

There are times when you are so horrified by your own limitations, so frustrated by them, you dare yourself to overcome them, and when I did dare myself in this way, I did not care who I hurt.

I went to that party with Charlie. Afterwards he was speechless with rage and didn't speak to me for days. Max, who was more tolerant, only shook his head. "At it again?" he said to me.

Once, in Sweden, when I was making *The Mansion of Father Bertil,*
a German producer came onto the set. The reviews of his last film
had just come out and all were terrible. That night I called him at his
hotel and told him I hoped he was not too upset. I had seen his film
and it was wonderful.

"Who are you?" he asked me.

"Oh, no one important," I said.

"Yes, but what is your name?" he asked me.

"Anna Asta," I said.

He went to Max and asked Max about me. After I finished work
on *The Mansion of Father Bertil,* perhaps I could make a film for him.
Max accused me of double-dealing. I said I had only tried to cheer the
poor man up. "You wanted attention!" Max said. "You want to be sure
everyone knows who you are! You want two eggs in your basket! So
the little dunce can be shrewd! Once more and I don't know you!"

I never played such a trick on Max again. It was hopeless anyway.
He was master of the game.

Taken one at a time, none of these deeds was so very reprehen-
sible, but then came a time when one followed close upon the other,
and after that a time when I could not stop, when I grew hungry for
the look of humiliation, of defeat, of misery, on someone else's face.
Because I did not have to see these things on my own. How superior
I felt to the others then, those who suffered, when I was not suffering!
There were times when, by making others unhappy, I could even
persuade myself I was happy. And so one grows a little more monstrous every day.

But not everyone is taken in. One afternoon, I came into a house
and failed to say hello and later the hostess introduced me to a very
old lady, a very famous European actress, Elena Grushenskaya, a wonderful actress, someone I worshipped ten years before. I barely nodded
my head. She put down her wine glass so that it clattered against the
glass surface of the lawn table.

"Life will knock some stuffing into her," she said.

Her voice was very loud. It carried. Everyone in the garden heard
her.

The hostess laughed nervously. "You mean, 'Life will knock the
stuffing *out* of her,'" she said.

"No," the old woman said. "I mean what I said. With luck, life will
knock some stuffing into her. She is empty as an Easter egg they suck
the insides from. You are empty, Miss Asta," she said to me. Then she
picked up her glass and began to sip it. She never took her eyes from
my face. She finished her wine, put the glass down, struggled out of

her chair, leaned on her stick, and walked slowly away. No one had anything to say. People could not look me in the eye. I could not look at myself. I lasted it out for five minutes. Then I retreated to my room, my room with the western exposure. Finally I began to think.

I followed her. I tried to speak to her. She had no interest in me, and I no longer knew how to speak to such a person. On the day she was leaving, I drew up behind her and she turned to me and said, "I knew Max Lilly." Then she turned her back on me and went out the door. She knew Max Lilly! Oh, how clear she made it. I had failed him. I had betrayed him. It was as if Max had stood before me in her body. If he were to come in now, he would not forgive me. I wanted to follow her, to implore her forgiveness. But she wanted no part of me. So I began to realize I had taken a path into a deep wood and it was time to find a way back. One day you wake up and find yourself less human. How do you wake up the next day and find yourself more human? Can it ever be done?

EVERY DAY HE WOULD SAY, "Anna, will you marry me?" and I would say, "Not yet." Then he would ask, When? And I would say, Why must we marry? We are happy. We can go on as we are. This was almost a game. He would ask me in front of friends, and I would say, Not yet, and he would ask, When?

In those days, I was always tired. Without make-up, I was the most exhausted thing anyone ever saw. My "noble, alabaster forehead," well, that was furrowed and pale. My "remarkable eyes, twin drowning pools," they were bloodshot. "That elegant, marble pallor"—I was anemic. I would finish work at five or six and then report to the Studio dentist where they filed down my teeth and gave me a wire brace to wear at night, so at night I was not so ravishing.

And there was another reason for the exhaustion. In two years, I had put a stop to five babies. I could not bother to be careful. Each time, I thought, this will never happen again. And it is amazing what can come to seem routine. The third time it happened, I recognized the symptoms before Charlie did, and I remembered Bertha Pinsky's advice and, to hide it from him, I had cosmetic work done on my nose. Afterwards it was narrower, more aristocratic. When I recovered, I made a film about a narrow, aristocratic woman, a mother tragically separated from her child.

"No more," Charlie said. "Leave your face alone! Look how sick you are! It isn't worth it!"

But the fourth time it happened, he knew, and the fifth time, we quarrelled terribly. Would I marry him or wouldn't I? I said I wasn't ready to get married. He knew I wasn't ready to get married. I was afraid to get married. I wasn't ready to be pregnant, but still I became pregnant and when it was inconvenient, I went somewhere filthy and they scraped it out. Well, he said, what are you? A whore! A common whore!

I said I was leaving but he said no, I was not leaving the house. I said, I *am* leaving this house, and started walking to the door. Something flew past my head and exploded against the wall: a vodka bottle. Now I was frightened.

"Either you marry me or you move out," he said. I said I would move out. "Not when it's convenient for you!" he shouted. "Right now!"

"All right," I said. "I'm going.'

"You're not going anywhere!"

"You said I must go!" He had hold of my wrist. I begged him to let go, and when he would not, I kicked him in the shins. He began to hop up and down and in a fury he hit me and knocked me to the floor. My head hit the leg of a carved table and when he saw that he was sorry. "I hurt you," he said. "I'm sorry I hurt you!"

Well, if you've seen his films, you know. When he suffered, you forgave everything. They say the perfect woman is both mistress and child. That was not true of me. But he was the perfect man, the lover, the son. Who could not love him?

He was stroking my hair, saying how sorry, how very sorry he was, when it came to him: for the fifth time, I had put a stop to his child. "This can't go on," he said. He pushed me away and looked at me. "Your eye's not swollen," he said. Time passed. "What are you thinking?" he asked me. "You have no regrets at all?"

Did I have regrets? At night, I had bad dreams, but I always had bad dreams. Lately, I dreamed that I had a doll, and when I finished playing with it, combing its hair, straightening its dress, I put it on a high shelf in a cupboard and closed the door and then I went to sleep, and just as I got in bed, I heard the doll begin to cry, *a-beh, a-beh, a-beh!* the annoying staccato cry of a small baby. Always the same dream: sometimes there was only one doll in the cupboard, sometimes the shelf was full. Only one would cry, but I knew that at any moment, the others could start.

"Well," I said, "I must not have any regrets or I would not do it."

He stared at me until I grew uncomfortable. "So," he said coldly. "You're not human."

"All right, I'm not human." He could look at you as if you were lower than a worm.

"May your baby be born with teeth, to bite the nipple it sucks on," he said. He picked up another bottle of vodka sitting next to him on the floor and began drinking from it. I didn't like his abrupt changes of subject. His moods changed with them.

"What?"

"You heard me," he said. He picked up the bottle. It was two-thirds empty. "But you know, maybe I shouldn't be upset. Maybe I'm upsetting myself over nothing. Five babies. To some people that would be a lot of babies. But are they my babies? How do I know that? It's what you want me to believe, but how do I know? You're on location. You have plenty of opportunity. And this Max. What about him? He keeps threatening to go home but he doesn't go and you tell me these fairy tales about sleeping in the same bed like brother and sister and I'm not supposed to mind. No, you stay here. I think I'll go talk to Max."

"Leave Max out of it!"

"Oh!" he said. "Leave Max out of it! If I went over there and broke this bottle over Max's head, you'd regret that! Not the baby, but Max!"

"Leave me alone!" I shouted. I tried to get up but he pulled me back down. He put his hand through my hair, then tightened it. If I moved my head, he tightened his grip. "Infidelity, I could understand that. Everyone here's unfaithful. People go away together. In five minutes they think they're in love. But a woman, *a woman*, to kill off five babies! And then she turns around and tells the man she loves him!" He got up and went to his gun cabinet, unlocked it, and unlocked a drawer. "Look, I'm loading the gun. Take it. Wouldn't it be simpler to shoot me? Go ahead. Shoot me!"

"I'm not shooting anyone. I'm leaving."

"You're not walking out that door."

"I am walking out." I turned and moved toward the door but before my hand touched the knob I heard the crack of a pistol. I smelled the acrid smoke. He had killed himself! But when I whirled around he was laughing. "You think this is funny?" I demanded. "This is your idea of funny?"

"Go, go on," he said. "Don't worry about me. Go make baby number six! Whore! Bitch!" The words followed me out the open door. "She looks like a woman! She acts like a woman!" he shouted from the doorway. "But guess what, folks? *Something's missing!* Is she selfish? You bet your goddamned life she's selfish! She eats her kittens! You know what she eats for breakfast? Little, little babies! One after another! Little, little babies, some with ketchup, some with cheese! Little, little babies, some boiled, some broiled! What a bloody mouth she has, all those little, little babies!"

I was crying, trying to start the car, but I couldn't see the ignition. Below us, the famous drunken actor came to his window and started to shout: "Shut up, up there! Shut up, Harrow!"

"Edmund! You want to know how to stay young!" Charlie yelled back at him. "Forget sheep's testicles! Eat little, little babies! Anna Asta eats little, little babies! That's her secret! Little, little babies! Plates and plates of little, little babies!"

The key turned. The motor started. I floored the accelerator. I skidded around curves, but still I could hear him shouting. *Slow down,* I told myself. *Slow down.* Then I heard the siren. "What are you doing?" the policeman said. "You're trying to kill yourself?" I was sobbing, my forehead against the steering wheel.

"Lady, give me your wallet," he said. I couldn't look at him. "Lady, I'm taking your wallet out of your bag," he said. "Would you look at me, please, miss?" he said. He said I was to come with him; he would take me where I was going. Where was I going? The Golden Palms? All right, he would take me. My car? Leave the car. "You do this again," he said when I got out, "I'll have to take you in. I know The Studio pays the fine but it's not just yourself I'm worrying about. You could kill someone." I stuffed my fist in my mouth. I was making terrible animal noises, grunts, choking.

"What happened to you?" Max asked. "What happened?"

"Little, little babies," I said. I began laughing hysterically. "Little, little babies."

"What about little, little babies?" Max asked, steering me to the edge of the bed. He put his hands on my shoulders and gently pushed me down. "What about them?"

"Some with ketchup, some with cheese! Some boiled, some broiled!"

"Of course you are talking about something," Max said. "Tell me what you are talking about."

"Charlie is angry about the little, little babies," I said. Now I was giggling.

"So," said Max. "So. That was expected. It was expected, wasn't it?"

"I eat the little, little babies," I said. I clawed at my mouth. Max gripped my wrist with one hand. With the other he reached out for a bottle of scotch. "Drink this," he said. "Don't sip it. A *big* drink!

That's good. Isn't it good? Now another drink. That's good. Now lie down."

"I don't want to lie down!" I shouted.

"Then you must sit up," he said. "Of course you must sit up." He sat next to me, his hand over my hand. "Here," he said, handing me the bottle. "Drink." I began to cry quietly.

"Five little, little babies," I said in despair.

"And now you want them?"

"No! I don't want them! What's wrong with me?"

"You are as you are," Max said. "He doesn't understand."

"*How* am I? *I* don't understand!"

"You are your own baby, aren't you, Anna? Is it so bad? A cow in the field can have babies, is it so wonderful? But everyone cannot make such films."

"A cow in the field is better than I am," I said, starting to cry. "A duck, a chicken, a snake can do what I won't do. I like babies! Wherever I am, they come to me! Even if I make nasty faces, they come to *me!* And then he says such things!"

"He shouldn't say such things, of course not, but Anna, they were his babies."

"He said maybe they were yours!"

"Mine," said Max.

"You could have babies!" I said. "You could have them! Dogs, babies, it's all the same thing!"

"Must we talk about me?" he said. "What's that noise? You hear that noise?" I said I didn't hear a noise. The liquor was making me sleepy. Maybe I would lie down after all. "Gussie?" Max said. The little dog was at the French doors, growling, her ears down, her lips rolled back over her teeth. "Now we have a prowler," Max said. "This is all we need." He picked up his black cane and advanced on the windows. The French doors flew open, Max raised his cane and brought it down on someone's shoulders.

"Where is she?" asked Charlie's voice.

"Make him go away!"

"How did you get in here?" Max was asking him.

"Where is she?"

"How did you get in here?" Max repeated.

"Up the trellis," Charlie said. His tongue was thick. He was drunk.

"You see too many movies," Max said. "So, now you will go home."

"You," Charlie said to me. "Come with me!"

"Look, Mr. Harrow, you can go out the door or you can go back the way you came. I will open the door for you." He walked over to the door and opened it. Gussie lay on the floor, growling. "That dog is waiting for an opportunity to sink its teeth," Max said. "The door is open."

"Not without her," Charlie said.

"Anna?" Max asked me. "You want to go?" I shook my head.

"The door, Mr. Harrow," Max said, but Charlie moved toward the bed instead.

Max was a very strong man. I knew that. When we made *The Mansion of Father Bertil*, he lost his temper with an electrician and picked him up, threw him across the room into a painted flat where he became a hole in a frescoed bedroom wall. When a sleigh ran into a drift, Max lifted it by its rear end and set it down on the road.

"Must I lose my temper?" he asked Charlie. "I am afraid you must," Charlie said, for all the world as if he were in a movie. Max advanced on him. Gussie, following Max, advanced as well. "Sit down, Gussie!" Max ordered. Charlie tried to hit him. Max grabbed him by the arm and pinned his arm behind him. "All right, onto the balcony," Max said, and he propelled him out of the room. From where I sat on the bed, they were two shadows struggling in the air beyond the room. Then I saw Max, who was taller, lift Charlie bodily and drop him off the balcony.

He had killed him! What had I done now? And then we heard a great bellow of outrage and on the lawn Charlie was dancing up and down, shaking his fist at Max, threatening police, threatening disgrace, threatening lawsuits. "I don't think he is too badly damaged," Max said calmly, closing the French doors.

"He will call the police!" I said, walking frantically up and down. Still growling, the dog followed me.

"Good, let him call them," Max said. "They will pay attention to him when he is stinking drunk? It is legal in this country to break into someone's room? Let's not worry about nonsense."

"He thinks you don't go home because of me," I said.

"I have my tickets," Max said. "Of course, he is not wrong either."

"What must I do?" I asked, but Max said, "How can I answer that? You think you are well suited? How can this go on? Unless it is so convenient for you, then you don't change anything. In this world there is such a thing as selfishness."

"I should go home. We came together. We should go together."

"More nonsense," Max said. "We came to succeed. You succeeded. I failed. Still, part of your success is mine."

"All of it," I said. "Yet you are not envious."

"Oh, inside I am maybe a little hollow but not selfish. You remember the funeral in New York? I would like a funeral like that. Well, I won't have it. But you, you were horrified. So as you always said, you are a different kind of bird. Someday you'll find it, a different kind of nest."

"A nest," I said, lying down on the bed. "No nests for me."

"Don't talk silliness," Max said. He took a blanket from the foot of the bed and covered me.

"Little, little babies," I said.

"No more silliness, go to sleep," he said. I felt Gussie jump up on the bed and snuggle into my side. I raised my head and looked up. Max was sitting in a chair, smoking, legs crossed, elegant in his silk bathrobe, watching over me.

The day Max left to return home, I was on the set of *Another Woman*, so I did not see him go. We were filming the most intense scenes: the heroine, having been rejected by her true love many times, has just suffered a miscarriage and nearly dies of it. The ins and outs of the plot do not matter. The tragedy arises because the hero and his father value honor more than love, although they do not really understand the honor they claim to advocate and moreover, do not understand that I, the heroine, am capable of the finest, strongest kind of love. What kind of love is that? Who knows? I didn't understand it then and I don't understand it now. In plots such as this, it is best not to look too deeply.

In any case, spiritually I am superior to them. In this film, I prove the strength of my love by letting my beloved jilt me or misunderstand me at least four times. About this the film leaves the audience in no doubt because, in the final scenes, realizing this world is not good enough for me, I sacrifice myself by leaving it.

So: Max is on a train headed for New York, where he will meet the steamship *Ingeborg Holm*, and then he will sail to Sweden. I am on a film set, lying like a corpse on my hospital bed in a Catholic nursing home, a huge bouquet of lilies clutched in my arm. Am I alive or am I dead? Charlie, my beloved, disappointing lover, whose child I have just lost, has been called to France to see me, having been told his presence is the only thing that can save me.

He comes in to speak to me but I am still unconscious and do not respond. I tell you it was a pleasure lying in that bed like a speechless corpse, listening to Charlie's pleading. When he gets up and leaves, the doctor tells the nurse to take the flowers from me, I don't know why, but probably he believes the old tale that flowers eat up the oxygen around the patient. Many times I've been in hospital surrounded by flowers and never have I found myself gasping for breath. How much air can a flower eat up and how hard is it to open a window or a door? But people will believe foolish things, and writers of scripts will believe them longest. In any case, they must get the flowers from my room into the hall, because when I wake up and find the flowers are gone, I am to go after them as if I am going after my lost child. In my state of mind, I think they are my lost child. And in the hall, as I go to the flowers, Charlie watches me and begins to understand what he has done.

Probably no one will be surprised to learn that Charlie and I were barely speaking as we made this film and that the new young star carried messages back and forth between the two of us. When was I going to come for my clothes? I didn't know. If they were so much trouble, throw them out. Or: Charlie thinks the scene would work better if, when I came to look for the roses, I played it as if I were blind. Then I would send back an answer: Tell Mr. Harrow I am completely blind and I have been for a long time. Another message: Tell Miss Asta that, as she goes through the scene, her blindness should gradually clear up. My response: That's fine. Please tell Mr. Harrow to open his eyes so I do not fall over him.

We went through the scene, once, twice, and Mr. Hall, who, when things were going well, was the calmest of souls, shouted, "I can't stand this! Tell her! Tell him! What am I, the child of divorced parents?"

"Believe me," Charlie said, "it's better if we don't speak." Did I, Mr. Hall wanted to know, agree?

"Absolutely it is for the best," I said.

"You will speak to one another on the set!" Mr. Hall shouted. "You will behave normally on the set! Mr. Feldman! Are you ready? Once more. Anna, even more tortured, even more twisting of the upper body. Let's go!"

With the crazed look I'd so carefully rehearsed, I wove from my hospital room through the hall, looking for the roses. I spoke my lines. I heard my voice tremble with agony. I picked up the flowers and cradled them as if they were a small, infinitely precious baby. Then Charlie came up to me and gently gripped me by the shoulders. He pressed his face into my hair, his mouth against my ear.

"Amazing!" he whispered. "Someone would think you were human!" I moved away from him as I was supposed to. The camera stayed tight on my confused, tormented face.

"Good! That's it!" Mr. Hall said. I dropped the flowers, walked up to Charlie, and slapped him as hard as I could. For an instant, he stood still, staring at me, and then he slapped me back.

"Go to your rooms!" Mr. Hall shouted.

• • •

"Miss Asta," Mr. Hall said afterwards, "do you know what I'm doing in your dressing room? Is it too much to inquire what's going on? We all know what privacy means to you. Believe me, I'm a great respecter of privacy. But now we have a slapping match on film, the crew is out there talking, and some of them are upset, and of course by morning this will be all over the lot. That's your difficulty. Mine is how long it takes to shoot a simple scene. I tell you to drop a ring to the floor. You think the ring should drop later in the scene than I do. Fine. We discuss it, in a few minutes we have a decision.

"Then Charlie thinks you should twist the ring and what do we have? A half-hour delay while someone tells you what he says, and then someone tells him what you say, and then I tell both of you what I say, and we start all over again. How many times have we worked together?"

"Four."

"Four. Were the movies good?" I said they were very good. "Do you trust me?" I frowned and shook my head. "You don't. All right. Then tell me: how are we going to get through the next two weeks of filming?" I said he should talk to Charlie. "Miss Asta," he said, "you're being childish."

"We have," I said, "a very big difference of opinion."

"And can it be resolved?"

"I don't think so."

"He said something to you while you were playing that scene," Mr. Hall said. "Didn't he?" I said, Yes, he did. "All right," Mr. Hall said. "No more talking. Send your messages. If this is how it has to be, what else can I do?"

"Are you going to talk to Charlie?" I asked him. He said he was. "Do you think it will do any good?" I asked.

"No," he said. He advised me to go home and get a good night's sleep. But lately I hadn't slept. I sat up in an armchair and stared out the window. When there was no moon, there was nothing to see, blackness, an even blacker almost imperceptible outline of black palms. When there was a moon, the palms were edged in silver; there was a path of light across the water. *Someone would think I was human.*

"Oh yes," Anders said, "I think I will be going home soon. Esther is homesick, always the same thing, where is the snow, where is the darkness? And the children, if I wait much longer, it will be too late for them. Maybe it is too late already and already they are little Americans. And what is there left for me to do here? *Dust,* I made it, it's done, I don't know what they fuss about. If I go home, then I make more *Ghost Trains*, and the head of the studio doesn't ask me, Why should women like this picture? Put some romance in, not a lot, just a little."

His wife brought us a pitcher and set it down on the glass-topped table. "Kvass!" I said. "You made it yourself?" She smiled and nodded, made an excuse and went back into the house, and I thought, Well, she knows. My interest in her is only polite. Her husband is my friend.

"So," Anders said. "Not that I am unhappy to see you, but what brings you here? You're busy, you're filming, every night you study the script and drop into bed. You are homesick? You miss speaking Swedish?"

"I don't want to be melodramatic," I said.

"Good."

"But it is the end of the world."

"Yes," said Anders, "it is always good to avoid melodrama."

"He is somewhere in the middle of the ocean and the other one, well, the other one, he slapped me on the set."

"Man trouble," said Anders. "You know, Anna, the triangle is not such a pretty shape. It makes for nice plots, but not in real life, no, not in real life."

"And perhaps I don't want either one of them!" I said, standing up abruptly. Anders watched me, poured himself a second glass of kvass and drank it. "What have I done wrong? What?"

"You are asking me?" he said.

"Always I am unhappy!"

"You come from Finland," he said imperturbably. "And anyway, no one is always unhappy. It's impossible. Your mind wanders, you forget your troubles, the sun is shining, and what happens? You're happy."

"No! No! I come home at night, I'm tired, I get into bed with my script, I study, I turn out the light, my eyes fly open and then I sit in an armchair and look out the window. Sometimes I go to the beach and go into the water, it's so black I can't even see my own hand, I can't see the shore, nothing, maybe a light from the hotel if I look the right way, I don't know how far out I am, there could be a shark, I couldn't see it, I float on my back, I stick my leg up in the air, nothing. Nothing! How far out I am I wouldn't know but the water's not over my head so it's not far. So black! After that I go to sleep."

"Swimming alone at night, it's not safe."

"You will see Max when you go back?"

"Of course. You know that."

"You must tell him I will come home soon."

"Must I? Even if it's not true?"

"It is true!"

"You know, you don't strike me as a woman who knows her own mind. This is a change."

"You have a wife, you have children," I said abruptly. "You're happy you have a family?"

"I'm happy, but my brother's wife, every day she says she's sorry she didn't raise cabbages, and she's not joking. She means it."

"And when I die, who will remember me?"

"What is this, really? You want to marry Max? You want to marry Charlie? You want to have children?"

"Who will remember me!"

"No one gets married to be remembered."

"Yes, they do! Max said his father wanted a son so someone could light a Yahrzeit candle!"

"There was more to it. You can be sure of it."

"Then what is it! What is it for!"

"Oh, you are very like Max," Anders said, shaking his head sadly. "He would ask a tree why it wanted to put down roots. Wives, children, it's a way of loving the world."

"I don't understand!"

"No."

"But if I had a child, I would learn!" I was speaking wildly, running my hands through my hair.

"Maybe," said Anders. "And maybe not. Some animals devour their young."

"It is important to leave something behind!"

"Who have you been speaking to?" Anders asked impatiently. "The wardrobe lady? Everyone is not the same. And anyway, you are leaving something behind. Other people will be long dead, and their children after them, dead, and their grandchildren, dead, and still they will remember you. You are already immortal."

"I don't know these people! Who are they to me? Why should I care if they remember me?"

"You picked a strange career if you don't care."

"I thought I did. Once."

"If you don't care, then you are in a good position. Maybe you'll find it, that thing called happiness." He said *happiness* in an inexpressible tone, part derision, part longing.

"So," I said, getting up. "I'm going home. You have work to do."

"Anna, enjoy it. Enjoy what you have."

"I cannot!" I cried. He shook his head sadly and walked me to my car. "And Max? What of him?"

"Max will be all right. No matter what happens, Max cannot give up."

"You think so?" I asked him, and he said, "Anna, don't look for trouble."

14

THE DOCTOR Flora took me to see was a woman. When she finished examining me, she said, "You're pregnant."

"No, I am not," I said.

"You are pregnant," she said.

"I am not pregnant," I said. The doctor looked exasperated. "Look, miss," I said, "do you think I am the last ass to walk into this city? I *know* how a person gets pregnant and I am not pregnant."

"No, she is not," Flora said. The doctor looked at the two of us and sighed.

"All right," she said. "I'm sending you to a specialist." We were sent to another clinic in the hospital.

"I am not pregnant," I said to the doctor who was examining me.

"No, you are not," she said. "You have cancer."

I sat up straight. "Cancer?" I said.

"What kind of doctor are you?" Flora shouted at her. "To come out with something like that! How do you know? You can't tell by looking!"

"I'm referring you to a specialist," the doctor said.

"Another specialist?" Flora asked.

"He'll do a biopsy," said the doctor.

"When?" I asked.

"Today," said the doctor.

We went to another clinic. When the doctor finished examining me, he said he didn't think I had cancer, but he wanted to know if I had any children. I said I had two. He pulled up a chair and asked me if I wanted more. No, I said. I didn't. Then, he said, he would advise me to have a hysterectomy. I had a tumor and it was causing the pain in my stomach. Of course I would want to consult my husband.

"Why would I want to consult him?" I asked the doctor.

"Women usually do," he said.

"I don't," I said. "It is my life and my body and my husband has nothing to do with either one."

"He doesn't," Flora said.

"Who are you?" the doctor asked her.

"The husband's sister," Flora said.

"My sister-in-law. When could you do the surgery?"

"Next week."

"Fine," I said. "I'll have time to give notice at work."

"Now you'll see," Flora said. "Neville will be right there by your side."

"You think so? You are too stupidly hopeful," I said. I shook my head. "When trouble comes, it comes on a fast horse, but when it leaves, it leaves on an old donkey."

"That is nonsense," Flora said smugly. There was a smear of triumph in her eyes.

The next week, on Tuesday, Neville drove me to the hospital. He sat in the front and Flora and I sat in the back. When Flora protested and said, "Let your wife sit in the front, man!" he said we would be more comfortable in the back, and Flora snorted, saying all he needed now was a chauffeur's cap. We drove through gray streets until we saw the hospital, a huge gray building that stretched out for blocks.

People go in here and never come out, I thought to myself.

"Here's Admitting," Neville announced. "I've got to go to work."

"You're not coming in?" Flora asked.

"Why should I come in?" he asked. "All she has to do is fill out a few forms."

"Go to work!" Flora shouted, so loudly that I jumped in my seat. We climbed out of the car and Flora took my suitcase from me. We stood watching the car drive off. "You'll see," Flora said to me. "He'll come around." She was his oldest sister. She had raised him. He was more child than brother. She couldn't see him for what he was.

We filled out forms in a small office packed with people. I followed the painted yellow footsteps along corridors to rooms where I was X-rayed and blood-tested, and then I was sent to a room on the fifth floor.

It was a small room and the woman near the window was talking to someone else. I sat on my bed and Flora sat on the chair. Gradually we began listening to the other women.

"The radiant energy," the woman on the chair said to the woman in the bed, "comes from your stomach and pours from your eyes, your ears and your nose. Put your hand up to your mouth. You feel the heat? You are a furnace of light. You feel it?" The woman in bed nodded. We stared. "Let us pray," said the woman on the chair.

Flora leaned closer. "A faith healer," she said. "They come in during visiting hours."

"What do they want?" I asked her.

"Money," said Flora.

"Do they do any good?"

"I have seen them on the slab like everyone else," Flora said.

Flora stayed with me until visiting hours were over. She called the switchboard and arranged to have the television near my bed turned on. She kissed me good night before I left. "They'll be coming for you early in the morning," she said, "but Neville and I will be here when you come back up."

"Back up?"

"From the recovery room," she said.

After she left, I lay on my bed and cried. I cried for Tita Lu and my children, who did not know what was happening to me. I cried for my father who would not have let me come to a hospital alone. I cried because never again would I see oranges with green skin. I cried for Neville, who had been such a fine man when I married him and was now less to me than a snake, and when I looked at my watch, it was five in the morning, and the nurses were coming for me with needles and encouraging words.

In the operating room, they told me to count backwards, and as I did, I saw my own body, dead and cold on a slab, and from the sky, I could see a vulture diving, and I could hear Miss Blue's voice saying, "And the little boy said, 'Sister, sister come look. Your husband is in the gully eating stinking meat,'" and that meat was me, and I saw my own body as if from above, and it was small and shapely and looked like the body of a young girl, and I thought, It is a pity she has to die so young and no one will ever touch her again. My eyes filled and I would have begun crying but I was sound asleep.

The next thing I knew I was in a stainless steel cradle in a room where everything was quiet. Gradually I could make out the shape of the nurses and I wondered when the doctors would operate on me, but as I tried to turn on my side to look for a button to press, I felt a sharp pain, and when I reached down, I felt a large bandage on my abdomen. It had been done.

You never miss your mother 'til she's gone. Where did that refrain come from? From an old song I used to sing while I swept the yard of my father's house in Mare River.

Now, I thought, I can move out of Neville's house and Flora will not blame me. But what if Neville comes every day and sits there for an hour and asks how I feel? It was not Neville I was worried about losing, but Flora. She and her daughter were all I had.

I needn't have worried.

When I was brought up from the recovery room, there was Neville, slumped on a chair, half asleep, and when I was settled in bed by the nurses, sipping at some ice water, he opened his eyes and said, "Oh. You're back." His voice was slurred.

"Oh," I said. "You're drunk."

"Well," he said to Flora. "I've seen her. Can I go now?"

"What kind of a man are you, to come drunk to see your wife and then leave before she's even out of the anaesthetic?" Flora demanded.

"And the world will end in fire and brimstone and the wicked shall be punished," said the woman from her bed near the window. She sat up straight and pointed at Neville.

"You hear that?" Flora asked. "Even strangers sit up in their beds and accuse you."

"We are all family in the eyes of God," said the woman in the bed.

"Amen," said Flora. "And what is your name, miss?"

"Miss White," the woman said. "God sees what you do," she said, addressing herself directly to Neville.

"Then He sees I'm getting up and going home," Neville said. He came over to my bed. "Good afternoon," he said to me and he bent over me.

"Don't try to kiss me," I said, "or sick as I am, I'll do for you."

"You see what she is?" Neville asked the room. "You see?"

"A lake of fire and brimstone and you swimming in it," Miss White said, pointing at him.

"When are you coming back?" Flora asked. "Visiting hours are every night from seven to nine."

"Maybe this weekend," Neville said.

"This weekend!" Flora exclaimed. "Don't talk to me, you hear! I brought you to this country so you could disgrace me in the eyes of man and God? You come tomorrow or you forget you know where to find my house."

"I see his soul and it is shrivelled like a pea left to dry in the sun and I hear the wings of birds with talons for feet and they are coming to eat him up," said Miss White. "Their talons will tear at his flesh and he will be shreds upon bone."

"You see!" shrieked Flora. "You see!"

A nurse poked her head in. "This is a hospital!" she said. "There are sick people here! Quiet please!"

"Who is causing trouble?" Neville asked his sister. "You are."

"A pea eaten by birds, flesh ripped to shreds," said Miss White.

"You women have a good time without me," Neville said, and he walked out of the room. Flora sat back down, banged her fist against her knee and began to cry.

"Don't cry over him," I said. "I cried enough over him for both of us."

"Why did you leave him?" she asked me. "In Greenstown, what did he do?"

"Merle Janesmith," I said.

"Who is Merle Janesmith?"

"You don't know?" I was getting tired. "The woman he sent to this country with all my money?"

"And God came down in a cloud and He tore the faithless limb from limb and He flung them to all eight quarters of the globe," said Miss White.

"Thank you, Miss White," said Flora. She was still crying. My eyes were closing and soon I was asleep.

On Wednesday Neville didn't come, nor on Thursday, nor Friday, nor Saturday. In her bed, Miss White waited for the faith healer's visit and afterwards she would look from me to the clock and when visiting hours passed and Neville was nowhere to be seen, she would begin preaching against him and against men in general. On Saturday when the nurse was making her bed, she said, "Miss White, hush up. We all know it. 'And God created woman so He could torture her.' That's the long and short of it. Here," she said, handing me an Italian ice. "I brought you an extra one." Everyone in the hospital who came near me felt sorry for me.

"Don't worry," I told the nurse. "This won't go on forever."

"No?" the nurse said.

"When I go out of here, I go out of his life," I said.

On Sunday, visiting hours were from one to three o'clock and Flora was there at one. "Neville is coming today," she said wearily. "But he says he can't stay long because he has a company party."

"Let the man enjoy his party," I said.

"And the devil sought out sinners and filled their souls with pins as if they were pincushions," said Miss White.

"Miss White," I said, "tell my sister-in-law about your eyes."

"Oh," said Miss White, "sometimes I can see things quite clearly and other times I can see nothing at all. It is God's will, you see."

"She has diabetes?" Flora asked me. She had worked in a hospital for years.

"Diabetes and high blood pressure and kidney trouble," Miss White announced proudly. "*And* a broken toe."

"That is a lot of affliction to bear," Flora said.

Soon the three of us were discussing how we came to this country and Flora was telling Miss White how afraid she was that her daughter, Jeannette, would marry a good-for-nothing Puerto Rican whom she met when he was painting her apartment, and how slowly he painted when he heard he was being paid by the hour, when Neville walked in and fell into a chair. As if we had agreed in advance, we ignored him and kept on talking.

"So how are you?" he asked me. No one answered him.

"And I have no one left in the world," said Miss White, "but sometimes it is better that way."

"I brought you some daisies," Neville said. He got up and banged into my mail tray. "Ring for the nurse, now," he said. "She'll get some water." Everyone ignored him. He poured some water in my glass and drank it down. Flora and Miss White stared at him. "I can drink water!" he said, his voice rising. "I come to visit and no one talks to me! People look through me like I'm a ghost! I have a party to go to!"

"You are damned foolish and out of order!" said Flora, rising from her chair. "Damned foolish and out of order and not too old for a beating!"

"Let the man enjoy his party," I said.

"You're coming for her on Monday when they release her," Flora said to him.

"No, I am not," he said. "I have to work."

"You're not coming for her?" Flora asked. "Say it again so I can hear it!" She was shouting.

"I am not coming," said Neville. "You may come, but I am not coming."

"And God saw him in his crib as an infant and foresaw what was to happen and yet did not strangle him," put in Miss White.

"Forget you have a sister!" cried Flora. "You have no sister!"

"Flora," I said, "when I get out of here, I am setting up on my own."

"Of course she is setting up on her own!" Flora shouted. "You presume too much! She will not live with something like you!"

"Leave the man alone," I said. "Let him do as he pleases."

"What pleases him does not please God," said Miss White.

Neville, who was by now infuriated with her, weaved his way toward her bed. "How does what I do concern you?" he demanded. "Who are you to me? You chat too much, old lady!" he shouted.

"Help! Murder!" screamed Miss White.

"You will talk to an old woman that way?" Flora asked. "You are rude and out of order! Go from my sight!"

The floor nurse flew into the room. "What is going on here?" she asked. "We can hear you down at the nurses' station. You, sir! You are the cause of this trouble?"

"He threatened me," said Miss White.

"He didn't threaten her," I said. "He is rude and drunk and out of order."

"He is not my brother!" Flora said. "Coming in here and mashing up lives! He is not the boy I knew!"

"I think you should leave," the nurse said to Neville.

"*You* think I should leave?" he said. "*I* think I should leave!"

"There are sick people here," the nurse said. "Show some consideration."

"I'm leaving," Neville said. "You want more consideration than that?"

He left the room. Flora was crying. Miss White was sitting bolt upright, clutching her blanket under her chin. "He was going to do for me!" she said. I was disgusted and turned on my side and pretended to sleep. Eventually, I heard Flora getting up, preparing to leave. She said goodbye to Miss White. "Did you ever see such a thing?" Flora asked her. "In your life did you ever see such a thing?"

"Worse," said Miss White.

"I can't believe it," Flora said. She was crying again.

"They drink and they drive right over people," said Miss White. "That is what they do."

That night, Flora called to tell me she could not pick me up on Monday because she had to work and had already taken too much time. "Don't worry," I told her. "I will get there."

I called Stanny and said I was coming home on Monday and all I wanted to do then was pack up and leave, but I had no place to go. Did he know of any apartments to rent? "Don't worry," he said. "I'll find you one." And then he asked, "Who is coming for you Monday?"

"An old friend," I said.

"Oh," he said. "I'll come by the house Monday night."

When I hung up, I called Mrs. Drummond, Neville's landlady. "I'm coming home tomorrow," I said. "But I need some help. Could you bring me my blue dress from the closet? And a pair of boots? Take a taxi and I'll pay for it." She asked me what time she should come, and I told her to come at one o'clock.

And she came and I went home with her. Neville was not in the apartment and for the next five days I did not see him. The windows brightened and darkened and brightened again and the television talked to me and I began to feel stronger. Every day, Mr. or Mrs. Drummond came in and brought me something to eat or asked me what I wanted at the store and went out and got it for me.

Then one day I heard one of the women using the hall telephone. "I have to go back home," she said, "and I just got this job from the agency. I paid fifty dollars for it and if I even knew someone who would pay me even ten dollars, I would sell them the job." She was crying. Lately, everyone I knew spent their days weeping.

"Mrs. Drummond," I said when next she came, "I heard a lady on the hall phone out there and she said she paid an agency for a job but now she has to go home and if someone would pay her even ten dollars, she would sell that job. Do you know what it is all about? I want that job."

"You want that job, you can have it," she said. "It is my sister-in-law who was out there. Her husband died back home so she is going. You have ten dollars?" I took the money out from under my pillow, where it lay, folded, beneath the scissors.

"Okay," she said, smiling. "Now you have the job."

Then it occurred to me: I didn't know what kind of job it was.

"What kind of job is it, Mrs. Drummond?" I asked her, and she said I would be taking care of a sick old lady who had cancer and couldn't eat, and it wouldn't be a bad job, because I could live at the old lady's and save my rent money and her sister-in-law said the old lady hardly weighed anything, so she thought I could manage it if I was careful. I asked her when I started. "As soon as you can," she said.

"Next week," I said.

I called Stanny and told him. "Where is the old lady's place?" he asked me.

"In the Bronx," I said.

"And you get time off?"

"On Sundays."

And how much do they pay you?"

"One hundred and fifty dollars."

"I'll come for you tomorrow," he said, "and you look at the apartment I found you. If you like it, they'll have another one when you're ready."

And he did come for me, and I liked the apartment, one big room with a little kitchen and a bed that pulled down from the wall, but I said I didn't know how long it would be before I was finished working with the old lady, and he said, "Don't worry. By the time they hire someone from Green Island, the patient isn't long upon this earth."

Then we went to Stanny's apartment and he asked me if I was tired, and I said I was, and he told me to lie down on his bed, and when I did, he lay down next to me, and after we lay down on our backs, looking up at the ceiling, he turned toward me and began unbuttoning my sweater, and then the blouse beneath it, and I did not stop him, and when we were finished, I lay upon his bed, looking up at the ceiling, and I was pleased with my body, which was small and slender and full-breasted and young and I was even pleased with the scar on my abdomen, still livid and swollen, because now I was finished with having children. That part of my life was done. And in two years or three I would have enough money to bring my children here from Green Island and they would prosper.

"I don't want to come between a man and his wife," Stanny said.

"There's nothing to come between," I said. And then I said, "To think I never noticed you in Mare River!" And he said sometimes you have to travel a long way to find the thing you had all along, and when he said that, I turned to him and kissed him and the light flooded in and we were happy.

And I worked with the old lady until she died, and then I came to work for Miss Asta and I have been here ever since. I don't know where Stanny is now. In the end, I was afraid to marry him. What if he couldn't accept my children? One thing I had determined upon: my children would have no step-parents.

15

AFTER MAX THREW CHARLIE off the balcony, I thought, My life is a drunken crow flying in crazy circles. I moved back into my little hotel and began to look for a small house. It was difficult because everywhere I went, newspapers followed. Was it true that Max Lilly had thrown Charlie from his second floor balcony? Had Max Lilly really tried to murder him, as Charlie claimed when he went to the police? Because that is what happened: Charlie went to the police. He wanted to press charges of attempted homicide against Max, but apparently he was so out of order that the police arrested him instead. He spent the night in jail, giving speeches to the other inmates about the inadequacies of the judicial system and the sinful, iniquitous, corrupt, depraved, evil, ungodly nature of women. Evidently he made quite an impression. In the morning, two inmates swore that when they got home, they were beginning divorce proceedings against their wives. They reported themselves very surprised to hear that the eloquent Mr. Harrow was himself unmarried.

A detective came around to speak to Max, who explained that Mr. Harrow had climbed up the vines onto his balcony, broken into his room, and tried to kidnap the woman he found there. That was the end of that. Apparently the detective liked sherry. He enjoyed the glass Max offered him.

The closer it came to Max's departure, the more time we spent together, although now I returned to my own room at night. Often Charlie would stand outside the hotel window, calling my name. I would lie on the bed, rigid, listening, waiting for him to stop. Several nights, other guests called the police, who came and warned him that he could be arrested once more.

"You actors lead very exciting lives," I heard the policeman say to him. "Drunk again?" asked the other policeman.

"If you are through with me, leave me alone," I said to him the first day of filming. "If you're not through with me, leave me alone also."

"Pregnant again?" he said. "Moody?" After that we didn't speak at all.

One night there was a terrible storm. The sky turned an evil purple, then changed until it was lavender and muddy yellow, the colors of a black eye, and soon after, the moon disappeared from view and the wind came up. From my balcony, I could see the palms lashing, left, right, left, right, a row of mad women. The sound of the breakers was louder, a frightening roar. The coming storm would be huge and violent and for a moment I thought, I should go inland, and then I thought, No, the hotel manager says we are too far back to be flooded, unless of course there's a tidal wave, but there are no tidal waves here, and I settled myself in my armchair next to the closed window to watch the storm.

From behind closed windows, I watched the lightning flash, the sheets of water, the chains of rain driving horizontally into the windowpane, then breaking against the glass, spreading out and snaking down. I sat in the chair, my arms on the armrests and thought, in a few minutes I will be asleep but everyone else in the hotel will be up, staring at the ocean to see if it advances, shivering when they see the lightning.

Once, when our family still lived in Finland, we were at my grandmother's farm. She had five Alsatians and one of them I adopted. They were all terrified of thunder, but he was the most terrified. One night there was a violent thunderstorm and the dog jumped down from my bed and tried to go beneath it, but the bed was too low. The dog was so strong that he lifted the bed with his back, lifted it and dropped it, *thunk, thunk, thunk.* I laughed at him and coaxed him back out but he would not come. In the morning, he was lying in a corner, his nose wedged between the wall and a cupboard. The cupboard was solid oak but he had cracked its side trying to squeeze himself between the cabinet and the wall. To be so strong and so terrified, for no reason at all!

After I came to this country, after I had already made two films here, I needed a hat. Everywhere Max took me, the prices were too high. One hundred dollars! That was one thousand kronor! So I found this very nice store called Woolworth's. They sold plain felt hats you could pull down over your ears. I bought the hat and got on a little line and watched the salesgirl. Everyone who came up to her, she had something to say. So I thought, Imagine knowing all these people! She must have been born in this store! Naturally I got off the line to watch her.

Little old men, little old ladies, young girls with rubber bands in their hair, she talked to all of them. Finally, when there was no line, I took my hat up to her.

"How much is this hat?" I asked in German. She answered in the same language. "Two dollars, fifteen cents. There's a sale today. You're lucky."

"All these people?" I asked her. "You know them?"

"Know them?" she asked. She looked at me oddly.

"You talk to all of them," I said. "They don't frighten you?"

"Why should they frighten me?" she said. "If they don't come in, if the store doesn't make money, I lose my job."

"Oh," I said, remembering the confectionery shop, "you are pleasant so your customers will come back again."

"Oh, no," she said, putting down the hat and looking around. There was no one else on line. "I like people. They tell me all kinds of things. This morning a woman bought the same hat as yours. You know what she said? 'I'm buying this hat for my daughter-in-law so maybe, God willing, she'll let me in my son's house.' I asked her, 'Do you think she will like this hat?' and you know what she told me? She said, 'This is my ticket in the door. Every time I go I have to pay my way in. She doesn't like the hat, she'll tell my son, "I don't want that woman in the house." That woman! Me! His mother! God forbid you should have such a son and he treats you this way!' So I said to her, I said, 'Your son shouldn't allow it. Isn't he master in his own house?' And she said, 'God will curse him, he has no backbone. He is frightened of her, the *meshuganah!* She gets angry, she throws perfume bottles into the tub! She could kill a person! One day she threw a hot potato from the oven. What did he do? He got up and took a towel and wiped his face!' All day long I hear stories like that. You know, this job would be pretty boring if people didn't talk. My husband, he says people come in here like they're going to confession, but he loves to hear the stories too. You married?"

"No," I said, "I'm not."

"That's too bad," she said.

"Well," I said, "first I want to see what the world holds for me."

"More men," the salesgirl said. "Pick one you like, get it over with. Who wants to spend her whole life shopping?"

So I went home and thought, This terrible shyness, what am I to do about it? Why can that salesgirl talk to everyone and have a good time, but someone comes up to me and opens his mouth and I jump off the curb into traffic and am nearly killed? And then I thought, It is easy for the salesgirl. She doesn't know the people who come in but neither do they know her, so everything is equal, everything is normal. But people I've never seen, they come up to me as if they know me, there's nothing normal about it, no wonder I'm frightened.

I worked in a confectioner's shop and Max Lilly happened to come in.

If anything had happened differently, I would still be home, rubbing my hands at night in front of the coal stove, toasting my wool scarf on the poker protruding from the stove, and wrapping it around my face to heat up my frozen nose. My mother would be saying, 'Take off your shoes, your toes will warm up faster,' steam would be rising up from the pot of boiling potatoes and from the windowsill she would bring in the meat for dinner.

What you do not deserve, that should be taken away from you. No, I did not like strangers, probably all of them thinking, What did she do to deserve this? Nothing. Let her give what she has to me! Everywhere I walked among thieves, I who was the biggest thief of all.

Because the dentist is going to drill on her teeth and has given her gas, she sits in the dentist's chair unconscious. Asleep, incapable of movement, how beautiful she looks, how trusting! Even though she might as well be dead, he falls in love with her. Of course he is falling in love with a body the soul has gone from, a corpse. He kisses her lips; there is no tension in them. His lips press against her teeth, then his teeth against her teeth. He is careful of her: a person asleep like that could choke on her tongue. Her hair is soft. He strokes it as if she were a little animal. If she is so wonderful asleep, how wonderful will she be when she wakes! But when she wakes, her eyes are hard, her gestures are brittle. He tells himself she is afraid of the drill, of the office's strange smells. He tells himself, she will think I kissed her in a dream. She will want to dream that dream again. Those soft lips, almost slack! She will come back to me.

Outside, the rain is hurling itself at the window, but now it has turned to hail. Hail? How can that be possible in California where there is no hail? I get up and look out the window. Outside in the furious wind and rain, Charlie is standing, his clothes plastered to his body. As I watch, he picks up some stones and throws them at my window. I open the window and shout, "All right! Come in!" In that second, I am soaked to the skin. Then I hear him on the stairs and open the door. I give him a blanket to wrap himself in. I wrap myself in a white bathrobe.

I sit on the edge of the bed, he sits in the chair. I stare at my toes.

I raise my eyes to his face. He is staring at his wrist. Every so often he looks at me.

"Let's get married," he says. I am still staring at my toes.

"All right," I say, without looking up.

"When?"

"Before filming starts next month."

"Can I tell anyone?"

"Really, I would rather keep it quiet."

"All right," he says. "Let's have a drink to celebrate."

"I don't need to celebrate and I don't need a drink," I say.

"I need a drink. I always need a drink."

"I know."

"But you'll marry me?"

"What can I do about this drinking? Nothing."

"No more abortions," he says.

"I cannot promise that."

"But someday, you might want a child?"

"Someday. Yes." He has two daughters he never sees. Why is this so important to him?

"I can't stay away from you," he says.

"You talk like someone in our films," I say.

"Can you stay away from me?"

"Yes, but I don't want to."

It is the coldest winter anyone remembers on the Finnish coast. The outlaws, looking for a ship to take them away, take up residence in an inn. A young girl meets one of them and falls deeply in love. Of course he is the man who murdered her mother and father, her sister, all of her servants. When she finds out, the dead come back to her and beg for vengeance and so she betrays her lover.

The wind howls, the snow swirls and falls, the ice on the coast thickens, the ship cannot move. The outlaw, whom she loves, seizes her and uses her body as his shield. She does not struggle. She lets herself be killed. When the townspeople come for her on the frozen-in boat, she is already dead.

Then the women of the town dress in their black clothes and black scarves and come out for her, carrying a bier. They form a procession and march back into town, carrying the body of the young girl who loved an outlaw, betrayed him, and died to save him. Slowly they make their way across the wastes of ice back to the little stone town, a small, black trail, a black, curving line on the snow, patiently returning with the young girl. As they go, they sing a dirge. From a distance, they look like a low, moving black wall. As they walk, as they sing, the ice breaks up behind them, the gates of the sea open, the ship unfurls its sails and grows smaller and smaller until it vanishes altogether.

• • •

Once, I thought, I loved this story but did not understand its meaning. Now I understand it and no longer love it.

"Probably we are not so good for one another," I say to Charlie, but he says all we need is time.

"Oh, you are an optimist, such a romantic and when I am hard and practical," I say, "it hurts you."

"If you were so practical, you'd board up that window," he said. He sat down on the edge of the bed. He began combing my hair with his fingers. His left hand massaged small circles all over my body, around and around until the skin beneath was warm. Time passed and passed. We lay back in bed, we made love. The passion was almost greater than the sadness.

Then the wind blew enormously, the window shattered, the lovers found themselves making love in a snowstorm of glass, but because they were very careful when they moved, when they got up each had only a small cut, he on his left wrist, she on her right. Or so they thought. Years later, she had persistent pains near her heart and when the doctor probed, he found a splinter of glass. When he, too, had pains near his heart, he too went to the doctor, but the doctor could find nothing. What is that swelling? the doctor asked him, and on his neck, near a large vein, the splinter had lodged itself. We will have to leave it there, the doctor said. Be careful. Don't let anything touch you.

"A very nice day for a wedding," Elska said. Elska was a screenwriter who had worked on the script of *The Roses*. Like me, she came from Finland. We understood one another. "Very nice."

"Last night I had the most terrible dreams, the worst."

"What does that mean?" she asked me. "Nothing. Less than nothing."

"Shipwrecks, storms, drownings, trying to talk through water, God knows what."

She suggested I go for a walk. I said I would go for a drive and come straight back. I drove to the Golden Palms, sat in the parking lot, and looked up at the balcony of Max's old room. So, I said to him, wherever he was, in Sweden you have good doctors, your rheumatism is better, and already you are forgetting the humiliation of this place. Anders told me Gussie is gone but soon you will have another dog. What film are you making now? I know you think about me and of course I think about you. So it will be no surprise to you when you hear I am getting married but maybe you will be a little surprised to hear that the next day I am going to the cosmetic surgeon for the usual thing, but again I won't tell him.

I started the car and was halfway back to Elska's when I put my foot on the brake and stopped the car in the middle of the lane. No, I said, and turned the car around. When I stopped again, I was in front of a gas station filling the tank, and when I next stopped, I was in Nevada. I found a motel, signed in as Lisa Miller, and paid in cash. Later that night, I called Elska.

"What a thing to do!" she said. "He was mad with pain! Everyone standing around saying how sorry! For four hours he stuck it out and then everyone went home. Don't talk to him, don't go near him. He will try to kill you and who can blame him? He went away with three bottles under each arm. Anna, what a thing to do! Tell me why!"

"If I knew," I said, "I would tell you. Look, I'm tired. I'm going to bed."

I stayed in Las Vegas for almost two weeks. This is what I remember: it was very hot. The buildings were low and many were painted pink or aqua. There was sand everywhere. For two weeks I lay on my narrow white bed and looked at the ceiling or slept. I thought, This is what dying is like. This is what it's like to be an invalid. Then one day I dressed, got in my car, and drove home.

NOW WHEN I TRAVEL, I am very impatient. I want to take nothing with me. One suitcase seems a terrible encumbrance. A book to tuck under an arm, a few bottles of distilled water in a plastic bag, that seems more than enough. When I drink the water, I throw away the plastic bag. When I finish the book, I leave it on the seat of the plane. Then I have nothing to carry, only my handbag, and often I don't take that, only the little black folder with three credit cards.

Ivy also complains when she packs to return to Green Island. "What more do I need than what I have on me and a change of clothes?" she asks. "What I wear during the day I can rinse out at night and in the morning it will be dry, it is so hot there. Why must I carry all these things? They know I am coming and they sit down to write out their lists." She complains and complains but always she leaves with two suitcases full of rice, flour, toothpaste and shoes of all sizes and when she gets on the plane, she struggles with her shopping bags and the carry-on suitcase I lend her. But what we both want is to travel as if we were dust, so light we could be borne along on the currents of air. We are, I tell her, getting ready for death.

"You are," she tells me, "not me. I still have children."

"The children are middle-aged!" I say. "Well," she says, "once Tita

Lu had two cats, a mother cat and a son. The mother cat was twenty and the son was nineteen. Every day she would see the son sleeping with his head on top of the mother, so she said, 'The mother, she is dying and the son, he won't leave her.' But she got up one day and when she went to throw out the dishpan water, the mother cat was sitting up and the son was dead. 'Oh,' Tita Lu said to the mother cat, 'you waited for death to carry your son. Now you can come eat out the house.' But until she buried the little cat, the mother cat wouldn't leave him, not even to eat. That's how these things are."

"Well," I say, "for sure I don't know about these things. All my life I took trouble to stay alive, and now when I don't care, my heart decides it wants to keep on beating so the rest of me has to keep on going too. If each part of the body had its own mind—the heart, the lungs, the brain—one of them could decide to live and the rest of us, we would have to go along. Just like Russia! What do you think? It could be like that."

"Anything can be like anything," Ivy says.

"Yes, well, if I had my way, I would walk around with nothing on, nothing at all. Every day in the house I wear the same thing, you know why? That way I never have to think about clothes. If I don't think about them, I don't have them on. Really, I'm naked."

"At home alone I walk around naked," Ivy says. "In girlhood days, we went down to the river to bathe, all of us naked, boys and girls. What did death have to do with that?"

"To travel like a beam of light, that's it," I said.

"And to have no clean underpants when you get there."

"Have we lived before?" I ask her. "What do you think?"

"If I had to live my life again, I wouldn't have the strength," Ivy said.

"Oh, you, you will come back as an angel."

"And you, Lady Clare?"

"A toad under the wheel of an emperor, maybe a vulture over the ice fields of Ekeborn, all the time feeling sorry for the chicken I'm circling."

"You're mixing up the hawk and the vulture," Ivy said.

"So?" I say. "I will come back first as one, then as the other."

That morning, it was very mild, no wind at all, so I went out to get the paper and I stopped at my favorite antique store. In the front window was a huge bouquet of tiny white flowers, ice flowers, the way the trees looked at home when the snowfall came early, settled on the trees still heavy with their leaves, and then the weather warmed, so the snow melted a little, the temperature dropped again, and everything was covered with a thin sheet of ice and in the right light, the whole world was a garden of ice.

I stood there a long time, looking at those flowers, and then I said, Yes, I want to have them. It is a bad habit, this talking to myself, but on these long walks, who is there to talk to?

"These flowers," I said to the owner. "I would like to see them." Of course he rushed to get them. A word from me is still a command! He set the huge bouquet in front of me. "They're magnificent, aren't they?" he said. "And you know what they are? Beaded flowers, that's all. A few of them, they look like nothing, but so many of them, arranged like this, stunning."

"Who made them?" I asked him.

"Oh," he said, "some old lady in one of the rent-controlled apartments. Probably you used to see her going by in a wheelchair? Her son bought her a little kit to make a few flowers and she liked it so much he bought her another kit and another. Finally he went to the wholesaler and came home with cartons and she made her own designs. He said it gave her something to do, it kept her alive. I said in all my life I'd never seen such a huge bunch, such a gorgeous display, and he said he asked her why she was making it so big, and she said she couldn't stand the view from her window and when this was finished, she'd look at the window and all she'd see were these flowers and the light coming in behind them. He didn't want to sell them, Miss Asta. He said they were the story of her last years."

"But of course he did sell them," I said. "Once you're gone people can't wait to get rid of your things."

"He was leaving the country," the owner said. "He only stayed to see her out."

The courtesan has died and all of Paris comes to poke through her apartment. They pick up her bracelets, her necklaces, lying on her tables. They look at the bed and think, this is where she slept, this is where she died. Some of the women and some of the men, when they think no one is watching, touch the coverlet gently as they turn away. They paw through her things. Later that day they will auction everything off. People will go home with a piece of her. Relics, bits of bone. This is what it is to die, to be scattered to the four winds. We should go back to the Egyptian ways: when a person dies, everything she has should be buried with her. Unless she has children who say, I want this, I want that, this will remind me of her, let me keep it. Otherwise bury it all, the things that kept the soul alive, bury it all together. The courtesan: what did she die of? Of course she died for love. She was consumptive; she would have died anyway, but she died for love. It is impossible to kill a legend.

• • •

"Are they for sale?" I asked him.

"For sale, but very expensive," he said. "Because, really, Miss Asta, I would like to keep them. But for you, that's another matter."

"Yes, why?"

"You are everyone's first love," he said, his eyes shiny. "You walk in and I am back in the days of my youth."

"And who wants to be everyone's first love?" I asked. "What good did that love do me? People see me and right away they're nostalgic for their happy days. Who can do that for me?"

"If we could, we would."

I waved my hand angrily. "Are the flowers for sale?"

"One thousand dollars," he said. "Half of what I was offered this morning."

"I'll take them," I said. "My housekeeper will come in with the money."

"I trust you."

"You shouldn't trust people so fast."

"Miss Asta, may I ask you a question?" When I didn't stop him, he went on. "It must have meant something, making so many people happy. So many people watching you, learning to dream! What a destiny that is!"

"If it makes you happy to think so," I said. "Dreams!"

"These are dream flowers," he said, touching the white blossoms. "While she made these, the old lady dreamed and dreamed. You see it in the blossoms."

"That's silly, all the time this sentimentalizing. How do you know, really, what she was thinking? Old and dying, in a wheelchair, knotting these little wires with the white beads, maybe she was counting the people she hated, maybe she dreamed up tortures for her son, he didn't come to visit enough. Maybe it was an old Medea up there making these flowers! They are any less pretty? Men are the worst! They are the most sentimental!"

"Well," he said.

"Well," I said. "I am sorry for this outburst."

"You say what you mean," he said.

"But each time I walk into a room, to provoke an attack of nostalgia! The past was such an idyll? Tell me that!"

"For you, yes."

"Do me a favor, if they auction my things, don't come."

"Miss Asta," he said, "you're going to live forever."

"Don't threaten me!" I said.

• • •

I was still filming *Another Woman* when the telegram came from Anders. MAX SERIOUSLY ILL. CANNOT SAY HOW LONG HE WILL LAST. I went to see the director, Mr. Hall. "Principal photography is over," I said. "I must go home."

"We may need to reshoot," he said.

"I must go home," I said again.

"What happened?" he asked me. I handed him the telegram.

"Yes," he said. "You have to go."

"But for now we can get back to work," I said. Charlie came over to me. "What happened?" he asked me. I showed him the telegram. "A trick of Lilly's," he said. "There's nothing wrong with him."

"Anders doesn't lie," I said. "He sent the telegram."

"Well, if you're going, go, but when you come back, don't come to my house."

After the wedding that didn't come off, Charlie was enraged. For weeks he refused to speak to me. When I called, his gardener answered the phone and said he wasn't home although in the background I could hear him drunkenly roaring. Production on *Another Woman* was delayed because he was incapable of getting to work and when he did appear, he swayed. Bertha Pinsky warned me he was in danger of being suspended, or worse, fired. When I heard that, I came down with a sore throat, and when Charlie still failed to appear, I called my doctor, coughed a few times, and he wrote a note saying I had pneumonia. For however long it was necessary, I was prepared to remain in the house, feigning ailments.

When filming started, and Charlie and I were once again barely speaking, Mr. Hall tried to improve matters by reminding him that my "illnesses" had saved his professional neck. "That bitch!" Charlie shouted. "I don't want anything from her!"

But as filming went along, he softened. I was the proper wife of an army officer who fell in love with him, the dapper card shark, and I threw everything over to follow him. In the end, of course, I died as I always did. There were times, especially when the cameras were turning, that he would look at me with such compassion, such pity, such regret, tears came to my own eyes.

"What is it?" I said one day. "You believe the role you are playing?"

"It's what I can't believe," he said.

"It's my fault, I told you," I said.

"If I drank less, if I were less jealous," he said.

"No," I said. "Nothing would make a difference. It is my fault."

"So," he said. "It's over."

"Yes."

"No regrets?"

"I don't want to get married," I said. "If we could go on the way we were before—"

"But we can't."

"No. So you always say."

Now we agreed to be friends. We swore that if one of us needed anything, the other would come. This, however, did not stop him from becoming angry when the telegram came and I said I was going home. He crossed his arms over his chest, leaned back against a painted flat, and the four walls of the room we stood in came tumbling down. For an instant, everyone stood stunned and then we burst out laughing.

Behind the painted walls, one of the electricians was kissing one of the make-up girls. Someone else was scratching his head. One of the extras hitched up her skirt, examining her stockings for runs. Someone was sorting out cans of film. The whole, hidden world behind the flats, suddenly exposed: it struck us as hilarious, who knows why? We knew it was there. It was always there.

Four hours later, disguised by a black wig and a dress padded to make me look heavier, I was on a train headed for New York.

Like weather reports, telegrams from Anders followed me across country: MAX WORSE. MAX BETTER. Like weather reports, I thought they would go on forever. In the same ridiculous outfit, I boarded the ship. Everyone thought I was still filming in Hollywood. For once, no one was looking for me. Still, I spent the voyage in my cabin, reading, or writing letters, and when it was foggy, walking on the deck and staring into the thick, impenetrable mist. I thought about nothing. I felt nothing. I suppose that when I got there, when I walked into Max's hospital room and handed him a box of glazed pineapple slices from the old confectionery shop, I intended to ask him what I should do with my life.

16

WHEN MAX RETURNED HOME, to Stockholm, the first thing he did was rent a suite of rooms in the most expensive hotel, the Continental. Then he made a journey to England, where he had several suits made in Savile Row. While the tailor was doing his work, he paid visits to financiers and producers, and then, dressed in one of his suits and carrying the others, complaining about how in the United States it had been impossible to find anything worth wearing, he departed once again for Stockholm, which he claimed he was only visiting.

Upon his second return to Sweden, he was satisfied with the greeting he received. News of his presence had spread from England. Everyone knew where he had stayed while in London and everyone spoke of his extravagant habits, which they assumed flowed from his great triumph in America. It did not hurt that Gemma Rambova, whom he had directed in three movies in the United States, was a great favorite in Europe, and that her movies had been very successful there, so it was naturally assumed that Max had been successful as well.

He took the ailing Gussie, whom he now carried everywhere, with him on a tour of the Lagerloff Studios, commenting aloud on everything he saw, as if he could not believe how backward and quaint the place was, as if he were astonished to remember that there he had made such films as *The Sharp Knives of Hogeborn* and *The Mansion of Father Bertil.* "Swedish amateurism!" he was heard to exclaim. "It is the most wonderful thing! What confidence it gives, to try anything, even the most impossible thing, and then of course, since we try, we succeed! In the United States, they are too smart to try, so nothing gets done." Then he carried Gussie to his car and drove home to his hotel.

The same day the board of directors of the Lagerloff sent for him and asked him to come back. Would he consent to make two films? Did he have any ideas? If he had none now, and why should he, since he had just returned for a visit, surely he would have them in a week or so after he had given the matter some thought. When he left the offices, one of the board members shook his hand and said golden days were back for Swedish film. Hadn't Anders Estersen returned last month? And now Max was back, and soon he would be at work! It was like old times.

On his second day in Stockholm, he paid a visit to the Dramatic Academy and watched the students put on two plays. He took down the names of two girls and three boys, put the paper in his pocket and disappeared. The Academy began to hum with gossip. The gossip spread through the theatrical world. Lighting men and cameramen stopped at his hotel and left their phone numbers and addresses. Rumors grew up about the stories he intended to film, the most popular of which was that he intended to make a film about the American Civil War, or was it the laying of the tracks of the transcontinental railroad? Soon newspaper reporters converged on his hotel. "Why should I make movies about America, that young country?" Max was quoted as saying. "I will make films about what it is to be Swedish and I will call the first one *The Many Names of Darkness.*"

Professors of linguistics wrote letters to the editor on this subject. The Sunday papers ran a long article on the effect of the short Swedish day on the national character. There were many photographs of Stockholm in the winter, of twilight sheep in the fields, all with Max's face in the corner, floating over the landscape.

Soon young girls took to sitting in stuffed chairs beneath potted plants, hoping to ambush Mr. Lilly in the hotel lobby. He spoke to all of them and looked them over. As he had done five years ago, he dismissed them, saying "There is so much talent in Sweden!" For a while, he took care not to mention my name. Then, when asked if it was true he had his eye on a certain young woman at the Academy, he said, "Why should I search the country when I need only wait here for Miss Asta. She is filming now, but even that film will finish some day and then she is coming home." When he was asked if he would like to work with me again, he said, "We have never stopped working together."

He took his furniture out of storage and examined it. After five years, he announced, it smelled musty and all of it was to be reupholstered, especially the seat cushion of his carved chair.

"Max Lilly Home to Stay," announced the papers. A photograph of Max, a portrait, really, of Max, the chair and Gussie, was promptly published.

Now that he had created sufficient commotion, now that he could not walk through the lobby without being greeted, stopped, interrupted, bowed to, offered screenplays rolled up and tied with ribbon, Max went to visit Anders.

"Come on, Anders," he said. "You always have ideas. Give me one you don't want." Anders asked him, "What about *Kristin Lavransdatter?*"

"That woman and her boring books," Max said. "You know, what about a fairy tale? For years, there's one I can't get off my mind. A young girl looks out the window and the ice queen puts a sliver of ice in her eye, ice or glass, something like that, and after that there's something wrong with her, her feelings are frozen or gone, she doesn't see properly. Tragedies, magic, a happy ending, she gets rid of the splinter in the end, by Andersen, I think the story is, a real story about the Scandinavian character, perfect for Anna."

Anders asked, "Why bother coming to me for ideas? I should come to you. Why that story for Anna?" Apparently Max said, "You know Anna, she has such dreams. She dreams that story." When Anders questioned him further, he said, "Well, anyway, she dreams of sleeping in a bed with broken glass. That's close enough."

"So you're on your way," Anders said. "Now all you have to worry about is health." Max agreed. He said, "These swollen joints are terrible. All this hobbling around, it looks bad to the producers. I swallow so many aspirin I click like a child's rattle. See something odd? These red flecks under my nails? I don't like them but what can I do? Red nail polish doesn't suit me."

Anders said he should see a doctor. "What will the doctor do?" Max asked him. "Put the nail polish on for me? A manicurist does a better job."

Producers began to arrive in Stockholm, "only sweeping through," on a tour of many countries to see what was available. The Germans, in particular, came to see Max. In a few weeks he had several investors eager to back him.

Then one morning he got up and Gussie, who was at the foot of the bed, didn't creep up on her stomach to lick his cheek. When he picked up the dog, he realized she was dead. He took her to a veterinarian and made arrangements to have her buried in a private animal cemetery. He spent several days working on the monument's design but he was satisfied with none of them and finally he called on his old set designer, and they came up with a fantastic castle whose turrets and towers looked as if they were alive and growing, a gnarled tree growing in the shape of a small castle. For two days after the dog was buried, Max vanished from sight. Then he was seen, walking through the hotel lobby, carrying another miniature bulldog, the image of Gussie. "This dog is my trademark," he told Anders and added that no one was to talk to him about Gussie. Her growls woke him at night.

"Well," said Anders, "she is only a puppy." But Max said that wasn't what he meant. Disembodied growls woke him at night.

Meanwhile, the rheumatism, or what Max called the joint pains, worsened. During the day, Max took aspirin, pulled himself from chairs and stood up, smiling, and strongly implied that the California sunshine was the cause of his troubles. "Now in Sweden, where we have to provide our own sun, where we know it has to come from inside, we take care, we are on our guard, and so we are always healthy. Besides that, the cold climate kills all germs." Crazy as they were, Max's health views were duly published.

Plans began to materialize for *The Ice Queen*. The directors of the Lagerloff Studios were horrified to hear that a German company might finance and take credit for the film. They began serious negotiations with Max, who described the story, something about a modern version of the ice queen who slept in a bed of broken glass, and—probably because there was nothing on paper—everyone assumed he knew what he was talking about, that he was only days away from finishing a shooting script.

"It will be wonderful, you'll see," Max told them, "but why should I say that when you can already see it yourselves?" In whispers, they asked if it was really possible that I would come home to star in it.

"Of course I admire Miss Rambova," he said, "but Miss Asta and I, we are the team." And so excitement was running high when Max went to a manicurist who took one look at his nails and said, "Mr. Lilly, you are a very sick man. Look at those red marks."

"Are you a manicurist or a doctor?" Max asked her.

"I've seen nails like that before, you must go to a doctor," the manicurist said.

"Please!" Max shouted. "File!" The woman, shaking her head, filed his nails in silence, then began to buff them. "All right," Max said at last, "you're almost finished. Tell me what you see in those nails."

"Those little red marks, sometimes they mean an infection," she said.

"A bad infection?" Max asked.

"Is there such a thing as a good infection?" the woman asked.

"A bad infection or not?" Max asked.

"Yes. Bad."

"And you know about it?"

"Well," she said evasively, "I hear things."

"You could be more direct," Max told her.

"Sometimes it involves the heart," the manicurist said.

"The heart! Spots under the nails! What nonsense!" Max said. "Maybe I caught my fingers in a drawer!"

The woman shrugged as if to say if he wanted to have things his own way, so be it.

"What other symptoms?" Max asked uneasily. "Joint pains?"

"Yes," the woman said.

"Oh, you want to frighten me," Max said. "Let me tell you, young lady, that's no way to get a good tip." Nevertheless the tip he gave her was very good.

Now it was a question: Was Max going to take the advice of a manicurist and go to a doctor, hold out his hands, and say, "A manicurist looks at my hands and tells me to see a doctor! Are there no uneducated people left in the world?"

Several weeks passed while Max consulted with the directors of the Lagerloff, began to write an outline of *The Ice Queen*, and apparently wrote letters to me, none of which he mailed. After a while, he must have looked at his nails and said to himself, I don't like the look of that, and, forgetting the manicurist, believing it was his own decision, he went to see a doctor Anders recommended. "Don't tell anyone," he said. "No one gives money to a sick man."

The doctor, whose office was in the hospital, took one look at Max's hands and said, "That is almost surely an infection of the heart. How long have you had those joint pains?" but instead of answering, Max jumped out of his chair, tumbled his new dog, Jenny, onto the carpeted floor, and demanded to know how the doctor could talk so bluntly and with such confidence to a man he had never met before in his life, much less examined. Had the doctor taken his pulse? Had he examined his chest? No, he had done nothing and yet he was talking about an infection of the heart! Max slammed the office door and stood in the hall. A few seconds later, he went back in. The doctor was waiting for him. "So," said the doctor, "I am glad to see you are not completely crazy."

He began to take a history while Max sat in front of the desk and wept. "All right," he said finally, "let's get you on the examining table. Any swelling of the extremities?" Max said that sometimes his ankles were a little swollen. "They are both a lot swollen," said the doctor. "Your face, it is a little puffier than usual?" Max said he always looked puffy when he was tired. "You are unusually tired?" the doctor asked. "Short of breath?" Only because of the pain in the joints, Max said. It wore you out.

Of course it took the doctor some time to get the whole story.

First there had been pain in the back. Where? The right flank was always tender. The ankles began to swell although some days they were normal. After that the joint pains began and Max initiated his program of cold morning swims in the sea. When this caused no improvement, he stopped plunging into an icy ocean and instead soaked in baths so hot that mists rose from his skin when he left the tub. All these expedients made him feel stronger in himself, but the pain in his knee and ankle joints grew worse, not better. Occasionally, he noticed a yellowish cast to his skin but thought nothing of it. Probably he had eaten some bad seafood and after a few days, his skin returned to its usual olive color. Of course, during this time, his hair also began to gray, so it was depressing, if natural, to attribute these developments to advancing age. When his heart began skipping beats, he chided himself for being an old woman who would soon be afflicted by fainting fits, but of course that was brought on by the extreme stress he suffered when he was fired from *The Siren*. To this day he could not smell the odor of mothballs without his heart stopping, skipping a beat, and then thumping as if it wanted to escape through his rib cage.

What did mothballs have to do with it? Oh, the set of *The Siren* was covered with silk flowers reeking of camphor. All the sets in The Studio were.

"Is that all?" the doctor asked. That was all, Max said, except for the sudden attacks of exhaustion. He would be in the middle of a meeting or a scene and suddenly he could not move a muscle, his eyes would start closing, he would have to make up an excuse, go to his dressing room, lie down and sleep for an hour, even two. Yes, he thought that was all.

"Well, I have to run some tests, but I have a pretty good idea already," the doctor said. "Those red marks under your nails, we call them petechiae, and when we see them, we think, Infection of the heart. Now where it started, I don't know, but your symptoms indicate it began with a kidney infection that ran rampant. Probably the cold swims didn't hurt, but they didn't help either. The hot baths, they may have been of some use. And for four or five years, this has been going on? Someone else would have said goodbye to this earth years ago. The questions for us are: Do you have this infection now, and if so, can we treat it? Next, how much is your heart damaged? Next, why the swelling? Are the kidneys functioning properly? If there's a heart infection, we can account for the joint pains. The sleepiness, who knows what that is? We can check your blood sugar. You must come in to the hospital right away."

Max said he needed another week.

"You don't have another week," the doctor said bluntly.

"I could hire nurses. I could be cared for in my hotel room," Max said. "A pinched nerve, a slipped disc, I could let it be known that is what keeps me in bed."

"No," said the doctor. "Day by day this gets worse. Isn't it true? In a few weeks, you won't be able to get up. If you won't admit yourself, I can't take responsibility."

And so, after a night's delay, Max was admitted to the hospital, an IV was attached to his arm and he was given huge doses of sulphur. Anders, who came to visit him daily, brought various bitter drinks, herb concoctions prescribed by his mother-in-law. Max drank these eagerly. His diet was limited to gelatin, plain biscuits and an occasional banana. Meat, fish, nuts and cheese were forbidden to him. He began to complain that the doctors were trying to starve him to death, although at the same time he seemed to improve. The swelling in his ankles lessened. The pains in his joints grew bearable. "I will be out of here soon," he told Anders. "Bring me a herring sandwich next time. Put it in your overcoat pocket. What they don't know won't hurt them."

"He thinks he is getting better, but really, it is only an illusion," the doctor told Anders. "Because he lies in bed, no pressure is on the joints, so they feel better. The heart gets a rest so there are fewer palpitations. We control his food, so his kidneys are not overworked, and the swelling goes down. But the heart is infected and has been for a long time and it's enlarged. You can see it on the X-rays. He should have been dead two, three, four years ago. Does he have any family? If he does, you should call them. Yes, the sulphur is doing something, but how much we don't know. The blood is full of microbes. At any moment, things could get worse."

"Or better," Anders said.

"Not likely," said the doctor. "Look, you are his friend. You will want to know."

Every day Anders came to visit. They talked about Anders' new film, a silly effort, Anders said, about a French assassin in the time of Richelieu who is reformed by his love of a good woman. "But I think I can make something of it," he said. "Two people in love, one good, one not entirely bad, and how they affect one another. It won't disgrace me." They discussed holding meetings in the hospital room, but Anders protested and the doctor said he wouldn't allow it. Max said, "But surely it will be better to have the meeting here than to have me climb out the window and walk through the streets in these blue pajamas?" A meeting was held. There was more talk of *The Ice Queen*.

Meanwhile, oblivious to all this, the real ice queen was filming *Bitter Almonds.* "Leave her alone," Max told Anders. "You know what she's like when she's filming. It takes all her energy. Everything she has is on that film." Nevertheless, Anders sent me his wire.

Three weeks in the hospital, then four. Max seemed stronger. Oddly, the doctor seemed more nervous. Then one night Anders came and the nurse said, "I'm sorry, Mr. Estersen. No visitors." But Max put up such a fuss they let him in. Anders was shocked to see him. His face was swollen, his eyes squeezed almost shut. He moved constantly in the bed. His joints were so sore he winced if a sheet touched them. "Let's talk about Anna," he said. "All her life, triangles. In her movies, triangles. In life, triangles. And what do these movies teach her? That beauty is power. That power destroys. When she comes home, you must put her in movies that are good for her."

Anders said, "The plots are crazy but there is truth in them. All this is as old as the Garden of Eden."

"She needs other, better truths!" Max said with tears in his eyes. "Better truths! I should never have allowed it!"

"Allowed what? She is her own woman now."

"No, she is owned by that story! A beautiful woman is powerful, a destroyer, and if she isn't careful, she destroys herself. That is no story to live by!"

"Who takes these stories seriously?" Anders asked.

"These are not stories, they are myths," Max said. "People live by their myths."

"This old argument again."

The nurse came in and told Anders he would have to leave. Max became overwrought. "Come back tomorrow night!" he pleaded. "You must come back tomorrow night! Nurse! Let him stay for a minute! I have something to tell him! Anders, I must tell you this!" Tears rolled down his cheeks. Anders pulled away from the nurse and went over to the bed. Max grabbed his hand and held it so tightly Anders' own hand hurt. "Come back tomorrow! I have a story to tell you! It's about human beings! A real story!"

The nurse had gone to fetch the doctor. Behind him, Anders heard their disapproving voices. "Can't I stay a minute?" he asked the doctor, but the doctor said no. "Tomorrow night, Max, tomorrow night without fail," Anders promised.

"I must tell you this story," Max sobbed. "About two human beings, real human beings. You won't forget?"

"I won't forget." He left the room, looking back. The nurse was

easing Max back onto his mounded pillows while Max sobbed, hopelessly, as only the utterly exhausted can.

When Anders came back the next morning, the doctor was waiting
for him. "I'm sorry, Mr. Estersen, but Mr. Lilly died last night."

"Last night?" Anders said.

"A little while after you left."

"But what happened?"

"His heart gave out, that's all. Everyone expected it."

"I didn't," Anders said. "I didn't expect it."

All this I found out from newspapers, from reporters, from the doctor,
from Anders.

"So you see, it's a mess," Anders said. "Of course he didn't leave a
will. He didn't think he was going to die. I have the things he kept in
the hospital room: a book of fairy tales, a picture of you, a description
of the new movie. You want to see it?" I wanted to see it.

A young woman and her lover are running away through the forests in Finland. They come to a cave protected by a forest of icicles
thicker than a man's leg and they take refuge inside it. As they sleep,
a large bear comes to the entrance to the cave and sees them. The
audience thinks the bear will attack the sleeping couple but the bear
moves surprisingly lightly and goes further back in the cave and also
goes to sleep. The moon is full but covered by clouds. The wind
comes up, the clouds blow down the sky, the full moon bathes the
landscape in blue light. The icicles glitter and flash so, they hurt the
eyes. The wind blows harder and the icicles are blown into the cave
where they shatter with a terrible noise, covering the lovers and the
floor of the cave, even the bear, with a carpet of ice that looks like
glass.

The young woman sits upright, clutching her chest. She shivers
slightly. It is apparent an icicle has penetrated her body. Her lover
shakes his head and with his first two fingers rubs the space between
his eyebrows. It is evident that an icicle has lodged itself between his
eyes. The young woman and the young man look at one another, first
with love, then with fear, then with little recognition, then none. The
bear sits up and looks at the girl, who stands and walks over to him.
She sits down at the bear's feet. The bear lifts the girl and walks out
into the snow. The young man stands at the entrance to the cave,
rubbing his forehead, watching the bear walk off, carrying the girl.

The wind rises again and the shards of ice are blown this way and
that, chiming like glass bells. The young man inclines his head to

indicate how lovely he finds the sound. He rubs his forehead, deciding whether he should pursue the bear.

"There is no more?" I asked Anders.

"It ends there."

"And his things? What will become of them?"

"There will be an auction in a few days," Anders said. "Everything is on view in the Lagerloff Studios."

"And the burial? When was that?"

"Three days ago. For that he left instructions. He wanted a Jewish burial. He wanted to be buried in the Jewish cemetery, so according to Jewish law, he was buried forty-eight hours after his death. We couldn't wait for you."

"No," I said. "Of course not. There's a stone?"

"A wooden marker."

"There must be a stone," I said. "Send the bill to me."

"And you?" he asked me. "How are you?"

"This is not what I wanted," I said. After a while I said, "Really, it is unbelievable."

"If he had gone to a doctor earlier," Anders said. I made an impatient gesture. What was done was done. An infection of the heart, how curable was it?

"I can go see his things? Perhaps I can buy something? You can arrange for me to go alone?"

All of Max's possessions, the furniture from his old offices, the antique armoire, the bed whose headboard curved, carved with a border of thick pears, many small tables, silver cigarette holders, sheets of thick cream-colored vellum paper with an unintelligible crest, even pairs of unworn kid gloves, were laid out neatly in the middle of a set at the Lagerloff. To me, this seemed entirely appropriate although I could have wished that Max's possessions were displayed in the middle of something other than a medieval chapel. Still, he himself would have appreciated it, the way the stained-glass windows let in the colored rays of light, the way the rays picked out various objects making them smolder and glow.

The studio guard appeared genuinely stricken. He said, "Hello, Miss Asta, this way, Miss Asta, this is a sorry business, Miss Asta," but I was suffering from the cold politeness that put any thought of conversation at a distance, and he retreated, his face hurt. The door shut behind me and I was left alone with the props of Max's life.

For a while I wandered through the huge room, touching this and that. Here was the carved chair in which Max always sat. This small hooked rug, green, with its center of roses, was the little rug Gussie lay on next to Max's chair. Here was the armoire where he kept his best suits, and here was the bow-shaped chest of drawers where he kept his shirts and socks. I opened the drawer. The little bag of cedar shavings was gone. Well, why would anyone think to preserve that? His inlaid collar box—I looked for it but could not find it.

Across the room, I saw a very bad portrait of a woman, her hair piled on top of her head, and wondered when Max had gotten it, and what he wanted with it, but when I went over to it, I understood: she looked like me. Perhaps it was me. There was a photograph album with a celluloid cover, and a design of a horse, rearing. The cover shone with the colors of a summer sunset, all green and gold. I picked it up and opened it: photograph after photograph of me on the set of *The Mansion of Father Bertil.* I was about to set it down when some loose photographs slid out and fell to the floor. I picked them up. Old photos, carefully labelled by hand: *Max, five years old. Max, Mother, Father, Vavara. Max, ten years old,* standing next to a huge mastiff. *Max, thirteen years old,* wearing a white kind of shawl, being blessed by someone: it must be a rabbi. *Max, eighteen. Max, twenty.* As the scenes behind him grow grander and more splendid, his expression grows happier. In the last photographs, he stands alone, his eyes blazing with joy. *I have done what I set out to do.*

No stranger must get this and gut it for their own pictures, I say out loud, and then I go up to Max's carved chair, stand in front of it, and finally sit down. It is really not a comfortable chair. The carving pushes uncomfortably into your spine, unless, of course, you sit very, very straight. Max always sat very straight. When he lounged in a chair, he leaned on its arm, and tilted his body elegantly to one side.

Outside the snow was falling heavily and as a result it was very quiet inside. In the distance, on one of the other sets, I could hear something heavy being dragged across a bare wooden floor. An old cuckoo clock sat on top of an oak chest. I got up and wound it and when I heard it ticking, I sat down again. Now the room had a heartbeat.

"So, you know this was not supposed to happen," I said. "We were supposed to wait for each other. Now it will be a very long wait." The little clock ticked. The cuckoo sprang through its small brown painted doors and cried three times. "You know," I said, "I don't think there will be anyone else. Charlie, he is fed up with me, and who can blame him? Some day I'll ring his doorbell and the gardener will come to the door and say, 'Miss Asta, your clothes are in the greenhouse.' So I should move out before that happens.

"No one followed me here, no one knows I'm in the country. You should see me in my black wig and my dress with the fat padding. Even in the middle of tragedy, I have to dress like a clown. Of course you don't feel sorry for me. It proves you succeeded.

"Look, Max, I read the notes for *The Ice Queen* and I don't understand them. Don't worry, I'll get the original story. I'll read it. But before I came I had a dream, or it happened, I don't remember. It's strange because it wasn't so long ago. I was in a bed, lying there with someone, there was a storm, and the wind shattered the window and blew splinters of glass all over us. It must have been a dream. If a window sprayed us with glass, I'd have a cut somewhere, a bandage at least, but there's nothing, not even a scratch.

"I would get them to make this movie, you know, if I knew what it was about, but I don't know anything. Who is the bear, who is the boy, who is the girl? What are they doing in that cave? What is the cave? All the questions you would ask me. I don't know the answer to any of them.

"So I suppose you died mad at me? Why not? Did anyone tell you I was coming? Did Anders? He sent me telegrams. He was certain I would come, but who knows? Maybe he was not so sure, so maybe he didn't tell you so you wouldn't be disappointed. Anyway, here I am.

"I won my fight with the studio. They raised my salary. I'm the highest paid actress in Hollywood, I choose my own directors, my cast members, everything. It's a little late. Everything is always a little too late. And they say in a few years, maybe a lot sooner, we'll all be talking: no more silent movies. No more directors megaphoning it. No more love scenes with the director shouting, *Tighter! Hold her tighter! Miss Asta! Grab him! Grab him!* So maybe that will be the end of me with my accent.

"What is it you want me to take from here? You know I don't like possessions. I will take the chair and this album, but the rest, other people will have to have it. You would like me to take the armoire but it is so big! If I buy a house, it will have little, little rooms. If I buy the armoire and give it to my mother, first, it will take up almost the whole room, and second, she will only sell it when the money runs low and then who knows what will happen to it?

"When we were children, in the country, she used to say, if you give away a horse, they treat it badly. Therefore you must always sell it. Well, this is still good advice."

Then I sat like a stone and listened intently. It seemed to me the wind had picked up and was howling and behind the stained-glass windows the light was fading. *Wolf-hour.* But wolf-hour was in the middle of the night. Still, my mother called the time of day when the light began to fade and it was neither day nor night wolf-hour. As long as I could remember, I thought of it in that way.

Was I listening for a voice, some words to tell me what to do? Of course I heard nothing. And then I tried to picture Max's face but nothing would come to mind. I looked at the opposite wall and let my mind float: nothing. In panic, I opened the photograph album: *Max, twenty*. That was not the Max I knew! I should cry, I thought, but I was not crying.

I stood up and began to walk around, circling the pieces of furniture. Finally I stopped in front of the armoire and touched it, and as I did, I saw quite clearly, as if I were looking at a screen that had just lit up, a little boy in a black felt coat running across a snowy field, and in back of him, its head down and charging, an enormous ram. The little boy tripped and fell flat in the snow. Puzzled, the ram stopped, looked around, came over to the little boy, nudged him once, twice, with his horns, and turned and trotted back in the opposite direction. In the background, a woman's voice shouted, "How many times have I told you to leave that animal alone? How many times?" I looked for her but I could not see her. Well, this is odd, I thought. A new kind of hallucination. Probably they are showing rushes on the other side of the wall and somehow I see them in here.

So I began to walk around again. On the bow-front bureau was Max's silver brush set. I thought, It would be nice to have that. Really, the brushes are not so heavy. I picked up the brush and looked at its back: cupids riding dolphins in billowing silver waves and at the top of the handle, the entwined initials *ML*. I set the first brush down and as I was about to pick up the second, I saw a woman sitting, naked from the waist up, in front of a dressing table, brushing her long hair. She raised an arm as if she were about to rest her hand behind her head and then she moved the brush through her hair. Again and again. How had I never noticed how beautiful it was to lift a naked arm, how erotic!

Suddenly, the arm stopped, the woman's naked, marble-white back stiffened. "If you are behind that door again, I'll take this brush to you!" she said. Outside I could hear the sough of the wind in the pine boughs. "All right!" she said. "Come out!" A small boy, his thumb in his mouth, emerged from a wooden wardrobe. "Give me my robe," the woman said. The little boy picked it up, covered his eyes, and walked slowly across the room. "To spy on your own mother!" she said. "Shame on you!"

Well, I thought, so I am going crazy or this is some new kind of magic, but of course, whatever it was, I was curious. I went back to the carved chair and rested my hand on its back, and sure enough, there was Max, about fifteen, as he had looked in the album, standing in a cemetery filled with wooden headstones, the trees light with chartreuse buds, a damp wind blowing, and in the distance, a young girl with the full cotton skirt of a peasant, her hair hidden beneath a red kerchief, coming toward him. The gusts of wind blew her skirt against her body, outlining her legs, her thighs. She began to run.

She came up to Max. She stood facing him. She cupped his face in her hands. She pushed his hair straight back from his forehead, she smoothed it back over his ears. His face was wet. She wiped his face with her dry, chapped hands. The little winds blew. On the wooden headstones, the pieces of parchment with their inked-on names tore loose from their nails and flapped in the wind. She pulled his head down so his chin rested on top of her skull. "How long will you even remember my name?" she asked him.

"No one will know about you," he said. "You will always be only mine."

When I placed my hand on the box of vellum paper, the leaders of the herd of reindeer stepped from the riverbank into the strong current and started to swim to the other side. "One cameraman in the boat!" Max shouted. "It's not safe? Give me the camera!" and he climbed into the boat and the rowboat bobbed up and down at the edge of the swimming herd while he filmed the reindeer's heads and faces, their popping, brown eyes, those liquid eyes.

A little silver bell whose knob you hit to summon a servant: when I touched it, there was Max, naked in a hotel bed, the covers pulled up to his waist. A young man stood in front of a mirror, drawing up his pants, buttoning them, buckling his belt. Max nodded and smiled slightly. When the young man was finished dressing, when he had taken his collar and buttoned it to his shirt, when he had put on his coat, he smiled, waved, and went out the door.

Well, I said, this is no surprise. This we talked about, how it made no difference. *All the untidiness of the human body.* It is that other one, the one whom no one must know about, she is the one for whom I feel jealousy. Of course, it is all nonsense. This is all dreaming. But what if it is true, what if, after a death, the spirit clings on and what I see here is real? Those bits of film curled up on the cutting room floor, outtakes from the official version of the life? For a practical person, I am becoming crazy.

I touched a picture of some sheep grazing: nothing. A chair with a triangular seat, carved all over with animals: nothing. So you are through with me, I sighed. I sat down in the chair. "Well, look," I said to the room, "I must see about the stone for the cemetery."

On the sideboard was a silver dish. From my handbag, I took an apricot macaroon. Max's people had a superstition about wine. At one of their religious holidays, they set out a cup of wine for the angel, Elijah, and then they opened the door and waited for the liquid to sink in the glass, and when it did they knew the angel had passed. If spirits came back, if they haunted the things they loved when they lived, then he would come back here, and if he came, he would want this macaroon. And if you don't want it, I said aloud, then let the little mice have it. Even in the Golden Palms, Max would leave crumbs for the mice if he thought he had found a mouse hole.

"Mice lead very hard lives," he said. "They work very hard for their food and half the time it is poisoned or it is set in the middle of traps. They are so big that I must be afraid of them? Let them come in here and eat."

"All right, then," I said. I left the set and walked to the soundstage where Anders was working. "So," I said, "that's that. I will buy this album and Max's carved chair. How do I get it? I don't want anyone else to have it."

I looked around the set. Clouds painted on the flats, some clouds cut out, lights shining through them. "So what is all this?" I asked him.

"The afterlife," he said, smiling. "The hero wants to get married but he doesn't know if it's the right thing to do so he starts climbing toward heaven and finally he makes it. Through the next door is the kingdom of heaven and you don't even have to climb."

"All these clouds, heaven must be very damp."

"The hero decides to go back down."

"Well, who really has a choice?"

"I would give anything, anything, to know what he wanted to tell me, that story about real human beings. Anything! It was so important to him! As if he'd found out the secret behind everything!"

"Every time he got excited, he found out the secret to everything."

"This time was different, believe me," Anders said. "I thought, I'll come back in the morning, he'll tell me the story, we'll have a discussion like old times, but there was no morning. And, you know, I slept well, very well."

"It's nothing to be ashamed of, a good night's sleep."

"Well, now he is out of all this," Anders said sadly.

"Except he was in no hurry to go."

"He was a good friend but a hard man to know. I didn't really know him."

I thought of the crumbs he left for the mice. "He didn't want anyone to know him. 'Let them think I'm arrogant. Let them think I'm crazy! They're going to pay a normal person what they pay me?' He used to say things like that."

"A colossal temper, yes. A colossal ego."

"A colossal idiot, those cold swims in the sea! Cold swims to cure rheumatism!"

"So you're going back?"

"What's left for me here? My mother, my sister, my brother? Famous people can't come home. No, I'm going back. On a very slow boat and every hour I will curse him! Every single hour!"

Anders looked shocked. "For what, Anna? For what?"

"For leaving me here," I said.

17

A NIGHT JOURNEY is a romantic thing: there is no landscape, only your imagination. I like them. I like trains taken late in the afternoon, the little towns wet and dark and black in the snow, all the funny things abandoned in the yard where the owners think no one can see them, the laundry flapping from the lines, nothing a bright color in that light: you think, how can those things ever grow clean? The trees are a strange alphabet against the sky, and then it grows darker, and your face is reflected back at you, and soon you are looking at the landscape through your own features. Then it grows entirely dark, and every so often, one house with its lights blazing. Something is going on there. What? You can think anything and it will be true. No facts come to contradict you.

An ocean voyage is the same thing, but emptier, better for the unhappy person. Here there are no little towns soaking and steeping in the rain, no people glimpsed walking by with their heads down, no black dogs rising lazily when the train passes, then lying down again on their muddy bellies, no men dressed in work clothes lounging elegantly against the back railing of their houses, holding a steaming mug of coffee as if it were a cigarette in a holder, as if they had all the time in the world, no housewives opening their doors and shouting with their round, deep well-mouths into the emptiness. There is nothing in front of you or behind you unless you set it there. Of course this is a time for nightmares, bad dreams, but even they are good for you.

When I was a child, my grandmother would come twice a year, her suitcase, made from an old carpet, filled with purgatives and emetics and we would have to drink them. *To get rid of the poisons,* she said in her authoritative way. *Drink them down. Now you are vomiting. In the morning, even the angels will not be so pure.* Nightmares are like these purgatives. You wake shaking and sweaty and the world around you, how terrible it seemed the night before, but now it is wonderful, solid, something you know. Even its horrors, familiar.

On the third day, the *Majestic* steamed straight into a fog bank. Of course the few other passengers were unhappy. I heard them when I walked through the wet mists, the talking ghost-bundles of clothes. Where were the whales? Where were the porpoises? The flying fish, the sea changing its colors, the waves rearing up like horses, all the things they had read about? Really, it was horrible, like walking in the rain. You couldn't see your hand in front of your face. On a trip like this, you could die of boredom.

Whereas I said, Good. Now I must close my book and do some thinking. What things will come back to me!

Once more I was sitting in the little kitchen in Stockholm. The wooden kitchen table had been polished so often the white paint had been worn from it and the pale pine beneath gleamed with the oil my mother rubbed into it every Sunday after she took out her pail of sand, scoured the floor, and wiped down the table top. Here and there, a thin layer of white paint clung on, like the thin little clouds that resist the wind when it clears the sky. My father sat across the table from me, a bottle of vodka in front of him. Every so often, he would sip at his glass, inspect it, and if it was not full, he would pour a few drops from the bottle into the glass. The more often he did this, the slower and more deliberate became his movements.

"Do your homework!" said my mother, passing behind me, pushing my head down. "Do your homework," echoed my father, leaning forward, peering across the table as if he were trying to find me. Then he would pick up the glass, drink a little, inspect it, and pick up the bottle.

"A bottle like this costs something!" my mother complained. "They couldn't leave you some money instead?"

"This," he said slowly, taking care to form the words, "this keeps me warm."

"You know that is nonsense," my mother said. "The doctor himself told you. You will freeze to death all the faster."

"But nicely, nicely." He picked up the glass and sipped at it. My mother nodded at my brother, who crept up behind my father, waited until he lowered his head onto his hands, and then took the bottle from the table. "Don't think I don't see what you're doing," my father said. "Even if God is drunk, still He sees everything. Nothing falls to the earth that He doesn't see."

"Drunk and blaspheming," said my mother, disgusted. "You," she said to me. "Stop that. Show some respect." Sitting across from him, still wearing the skirt and blouse I kept clean for school, I began imitating him, his movements, his manner, the way he let his eyes droop, the way he strained to keep them open, how his eyelids fluttered, the way his eyeballs rolled back in his head so that the pupils disappeared, the difficulty he had in keeping his head up, the way it rolled, at first imperceptibly, from side to side, then fell back in little jerks, hastily righted, and then began sinking, until his head rested against his breastbone as if he were bending his neck to an executioner, the rest of the body limp, without tone or expression.

"I don't like to see that," said my mother, shaking me by the shoulder. "Like father, like daughter. Heaven forbid you should follow in his footsteps."

"She looks like a drunk," my brother said. "Why do you want to look like a drunk?"

Those days across the kitchen table, imitating my father before he put down his head and passed out, those were my first acting lessons. Later I played a drunken woman three times and each time the rumor went around: *Anna Asta drinks! What does Anna Asta do alone? Anna Asta drinks!* Then would come the studio-planted interviews. "In all the time I have known Miss Asta, I have sometimes seen her sip at a cocktail or a glass of wine. She accepts a cocktail to be sociable, but really I do not think she likes the taste of alcohol." Or the famous quote from Charlie: "Anna Asta drinks? If Anna drank, do you think we'd be living in different houses?" Of course then they asked him if I approved of his drinking. "You don't speak of rope in the house of a hanged man," he said. No one quite understood what this meant, but they took it to mean I did not approve.

Of course I did not. Still, we never argued over his drinking. If he proposed to me and I accepted, if he then celebrated by getting drunk and shouting from his garden to the actor who lived beneath us on Cathedral Road, if he took beer bottles and threw them onto that actor's roof, all the time shouting the good news, I would get in my car and drive off. What is the use of arguing with a drunk? People in the graveyard have more to say and they're less likely to hit you.

Even my father who loved me would sometimes hit me when I passed behind his chair, and when I asked him why, he would say, You'll do something to deserve it. In the morning, he would wake up and see everyone's angry faces, dress quickly and go to work. If I walked with him, he would ask me, "What did I do last night? I said something I shouldn't?" I would lie and say, "I was asleep. Ask Lars."

Now, with the ship steaming through fog, the foghorns opening their wide throats in the mist, I asked myself, Do I really mind the drinking? And I said, No, I don't mind it. It is what I'm used to. Of course, those who drink die young, they make noise, they attract attention. I don't like any of that. People who drink are romantics. But I like them, they are so unlike me. And then I began to remember how I had loved Charlie before I even met him, sitting there like a schoolgirl in the darkened theater, next to Max, watching *Wartime.*

He was the finest actor I'd ever seen, no popping out his eyes like Erik to suggest passion, the way he moved his body, so graceful. He stood still and his face expressed every emotion. He took you out of your own body. Before the titles came on the screen, you knew what they would say. You looked at his face, you read his mind.

And he was unselfish. Once he let you in, you were in forever. If you wanted a book, he bought it for you. He bought you books you wanted that you'd never heard of. At night, when he came home exhausted, he would stay up coaching me, teaching me English. "No, say it this way. This way. This way!" If you loved him, he was stunned and grateful as if no one had ever before looked benevolently upon him.

He was not faithful. Probably he was not capable of it. "Oh, sex," he said once. "It's a nice thing to do." He was a generous lover, very funny in bed. No woman he spent time with ever forgot him. His first wife used to have her chauffeur drive past the house hoping to get a glimpse of him. When I lived with him, a limousine would go by, he would fall silent, drum his long white fingers on the arm of his chair, and stare at his shoes, and I would think, That is Vera.

I loved his face. The way some people go to museums and look at a favorite painting I would look at his face. Even when I was angry at him—especially when I was angry at him—I would go to a theater showing one of his pictures and sit there all day with a white paper bag of chocolate-covered almonds and when I came out, stunned, into the sunlight, I was happy.

Then there were the other times. He would get out of the car to adjust the carburetor. I sat in the front seat, completely happy. And I would look up and there was a stranger, the face of a stranger, a person for whom I felt nothing. I would ask myself, Who is this man to me? He would finish what he was doing and get back in the car, turn to me and smile. I smiled back, but only the muscles of my face formed the smile. Inside I was asking myself, Who is this man? What do I care for him? What is he to me? Then I would tell myself, Wait, say nothing. This will pass. Always it passes. Sometimes it took days, other times, weeks. But always it did pass until the night he drove me out of the house. *Little, little babies, some with ketchup, some with cheese.* I could have a baby. Was that so much to ask? How could The Studio complain? I had my contract. I approved my own movies, my own schedule.

Outside, the foghorn sounded. The ship steamed on to its next stop, finding its way.

But the bed, the floating bed, the arm here, the breast there.

I would go back, I would find Charlie, I would say, You are right. We should have a child. We will get married. We will make up for all those times we were separated on the screen. When we come home tired at the end of the day, we can be tired together. We can wander around the house at night, you with your glass of gin, me with my buttermilk. Two insomniacs, we will be perfect parents for a baby. We will hire nursemaids. We will take it on location. If I am a bad mother, we will hire a good nurse, and I will learn to act like her. Of course it could be done! I should have seen it sooner. Max was gone. No more triangles.

Of course you will not like having a baby. Of course you will still want to do just as you please. Of course there will be nights when you don't come home, when he doesn't come home. Of course you will look at him across the cradle and think, Who is that man and what does he mean to me? All the same, I told myself, this is what you want. No more nonsense. If another woman is in the house, throw her out. This is love, this is innocence. Take it back.

Three weeks later, the *Majestic* steamed into her last port of call. Elska, whom I had cabled, drove up to meet me in San Bernardino. We threw my suitcase in the car and I got in, laughing. "What is that shadow on your face?" I asked her. "One of the boys has the chicken pox?"

"Oh, they are always sick," she said, "always something. Anyway, you had a good trip on your freighter? You look happy."

"He is dead and buried," I said. "Now the job is to believe it."

"Even when you stand over them and watch, you don't believe it," Elska said. "Not even then."

"You will stop the car at a gas station?" I asked her. "I'm thirsty, I want to find the bathroom, I could use a candy bar."

"Why not wait until we get home?" she said. "I was up all night cooking."

"Not guests!" I said. "Not so soon!"

"Noodle pudding, stuffed cabbage, everything indigestible, sweet potatoes with sour onions, my latest invention, and," she said, "no guests."

"Oh, there's a gas station! Let's stop!"

"What do you want? I'll go," she said.

"No, no, I want to use the bathroom."

"It's so important?" she asked me.

"What's wrong with you?" I asked, laughing. "I'll be right back!"

I went inside, found the lavatory, came back out and inspected the candy bars. Probably they were old. Not many cars stopped here. The windows were dusty and fly-specked and a deep amber roll of twisted flypaper was well populated. "You have some newspapers?" I asked the man. He rubbed his wrinkled bald head. "They're right under your nose," he said. I pushed a dollar bill across the dusty counter, folded the papers, and put them under my arm. "Lady, your change," he said. I reached out to take it and the newspapers slid from beneath my arm. They fell, open, to the floor. The man sighed. I bent down to pick them up, and saw the headline: *Charles Harrow, Louise Castle Wed Tomorrow.*

"These are today's papers?" I asked the man.

"Lady, look at the date on them."

In back of me, the screen door slammed, loosing a small cloud of dust. I smelled it as it stirred through the air. Elska had come in to find me. Now she looked from my face to the papers and back again.

"I guess he got tired of waiting," I said. She took my arm but I shook it off. "Who is Louise Castle? The Broadway actress? How did he even meet her?"

We got in the car. *Slam, slam,* went the car doors. More dust. Here everything was dusty, dry and sandy. "What am I going to do?" I asked Elska. She started the car and began driving. "I have to do something." Elska drove on. "Tomorrow! If I came back even a day later, it would be over with!"

We went around a curve. The road straightened out. To our left, the blue sea stretched seamless, to the horizon. Now Elska turned slightly, looked at me out of the corner of her eye. "What can you do?" she asked me.

"It's been in the papers before? And no one told me?"

"We thought you had enough troubles," she said.

"No one told me!"

"What can you do?" she asked again. "If he wants it."

"He doesn't want it! He's spiting me!"

"But even if that's so," she began.

"I will stop the wedding!" I cried.

I walked into Elska's house. The children ran up to me, but I barely looked at them. Instead, I headed straight for her husband's study, seized the phone and dialled Charlie's number, but someone else answered. "Walter?" I said. "Is that you?" At the other end, silence. "Walter, I know it is you!"

"Anna," Walter said. "I thought you were in Europe."

"Let me speak to Charlie."

"He's not here."

"Where is he?"

"I really don't know."

"Look, Walter, I'm coming over there. I'm going to sit there and wait for him."

I heard him take a deep breath. "I wouldn't do that," he said. "It's not a very good idea."

"Why, if he's not there? He told you not to let me in?"

"That's not it. Listen, don't come. Stay where you are."

"Why? Why? Oh, I see! *She's* there! That's it, isn't it?"

"None of this is my business," Walter said.

"It's your business now because I am borrowing someone's car and driving over."

"Please! Don't do it! There are photographers all over the place. Think a little bit. What are you going to do?"

"Tell him he can't marry her! He's supposed to marry me!"

"She may not be impressed by that. She doesn't know you. She'll think you're a jealous, hysterical woman, or worse, that it's only sour grapes."

"Sour grapes? What are you talking about?"

"You're going to walk into a nest of reporters and tell them what?"

"Never mind what I'm going to tell them!"

"Look, don't come. He's not here. Stay there."

"I have to talk to someone!"

"You can talk to me. He's got to come home sometime. When he gets here, I'll talk to him."

"You will talk to me?"

"Cookie, of course I'll talk to you! All those late nights playing gin in the vault! Who can forget them? Pick a place. I'll meet you."

"In front of Edmund Ashley's house, you know, right below Charlie's house, the house he throws beer bottles at. I'll pick you up."

Walter started to say something. It sounded like "Be careful," but I had already hung up the phone. "Elska," I said, "I have to borrow your car."

"You can't go like that. Everyone will recognize you. Put on that black wig and that padded dress. Anna, you can't just stop a wedding!"

"I have to stop it!" I said. By now I was crying.

When I pulled up in front of Edmund Ashley's house, Walter was walking up and down, pacing in front of a large palm tree. I leaned over and opened the front door. "Get in," I said and we drove off. "He's still not there?" I asked as we turned the first corner. No, he said, he wasn't. "She's there?" Yes, he said, she was. For God's sake! he said. Slow down!

"Kidnapped by Anna Asta," he said. "Look, I know you're not a great talker, but where are we going?"

"To the beach."

"Oh, the beach."

"We can talk there." The convertible top was down; I was shouting over the noise of the wind.

When we got to the beach, I climbed down a little path cut in the stones and then sat on a ledge big enough for two people. Walter sat next to me. "Listen, you don't have to say anything," I said. "He can't marry her! I love him, he loves me, we belong together. He belongs to me. He's only marrying her to spite me. Can't you see it? You must see it."

"I heard some pretty serious fights," he said.

"Yes, yes, we had fights."

"About babies," he said.

"We had fights but we won't have them anymore! Now it's all different! I know what I want! I want a baby! It's not because I came home and saw the papers! It's not, what do you call it, green grapes! You don't know what it's like for me! How can you know? I come here, I don't know anyone, everyone laughs at me, they call me Flatfoot, they call me Dumb Finn, and then everything changes, suddenly

I am a goddess, they measure the height of my forehead, how high I can raise an eyebrow, my lower lip is full and seductive, my upper lip is thin and severe, from the front my face is voluptuous and angelic, from the side severe like a nun's, they want my opinions on everything, but I don't have opinions, they follow me onto the set where I'm not myself, I'm someone else, and I have to stay someone else all day or I ruin the picture, they wave at me, they ask me to sign things, they stare at my legs, are they really so bad? They stare at my upper arms, are they really heavy? Look at these arms, like two sticks! They look at my teeth, can they see where the caps are? They pull my hair to find out if the hair snaps back, if the curls are real. They make me talk so they can hear the stupid things I say, my bad accent!

"Because in front of them I won't cry they think nothing hurts me but I go home at five o'clock, I'm so tired all I can do is fall into bed, and to whom can I talk about it? To whom can I say, my skin is thin, everything hurts me, everything! Every little thing, it bruises me! All these things inside me, I can't talk about them, it's like pulling out something live and bleeding! Who wants to be so reserved? Who wants to be so secretive? You think I like it? I was born this way, this is how I'm made, what can I do about it? Only in front of the camera, then everything can come out, that's how it is, I don't have a choice. People should be warm, people should be loving, I want to be those things, but I can't! Only Charlie can I talk to! You think I can talk to anyone like that? To whom can I say, I'm a plain farm girl, not even a peasant, a plain farm girl, with this ability so I become other people in front of the camera, and it's not hard, but it takes so much energy to do it. The ability makes it easy but the energy, the energy! And I don't have much energy! I would give anything to be rid of this ability I have!

"Who is there who would listen to this? Oh, she feels sorry for herself! Listen to her, the sacrifice of the artist, poor thing, she should try working in Woolworth's.

"All those dresses, these beautiful women, these sirens, I can't stand it! This is not real! This is not life! What happened to my body? I want to walk up to people and say, 'Look, I have a stomach! I'm nervous, it hurts!' Who hears a word I say? Who? They get this silly look, they're thinking, 'What would she do to me if I touched her face? Just a little touch. Who would it hurt?'

"He knows I have a stomach! To him I am not an angel dropped down on the earth to make these silly stories! We walk around together in our bathrobes! We come from poor families. We're the same! You have to help me! Please help me!"

"You have to stop crying," he said. "Stop. Your eyes are swelling shut."

"I'll claw out my eyes!"

"I don't drive."

"You don't drive?"

"No. Stop crying. If you don't stop, we can't get back."

"I will go to the wedding. I will stop it. When they ask if anyone objects, I will object."

"You have to have a reason."

"I will say he's marrying the wrong woman."

"That's not a reason."

"It is a reason!"

"It's been in the papers every day, for weeks. What took you so long?"

"I told you! I was in Sweden, I was busy, and then I was on a boat. I didn't see a paper the whole time, not once, not until we stopped at a gas station."

"Naturally everyone thought you didn't care."

"He said that? He said, 'She doesn't care'?"

"He never said anything."

"Where did he meet this Castle person? He never knew her before! A Broadway actress! What is she doing in California?"

"What everyone else is doing. She came to make a screen test."

"She passed?"

"Well, the day he met her, she was renting an apartment."

"What is she like, this woman? I come to the wedding, I make a scene, she will be frightened off?"

"You're going to do that? You're going to show up tomorrow and hide behind a tree until the bride and groom walk to the altar and then you're going to jump out and yell, 'Stop!' And every man, woman and child in California—in the world—is going to see pictures of you in the paper waving your arms? And then if he doesn't want the wedding to stop? All over the world, people will read about how he looked when he told you he was through with you. That's the kind of attention you want? Even if he says, All right, I'll forget about her, I'll go with you, will the two of you be able to look one another in the eye in the morning? It's a folly!

"And let me tell you what will happen. Pinsky will get the publicity machine going. 'Anna Asta Has Nervous Breakdown.' He'll have it in all the papers. He'll tear up your contract. If you can't work, then he doesn't have to honor it. Or he'll show how big-hearted he is and put you in a private asylum and pay the bills. He'll let you out in time for the premiere of *Another Woman*. Think what a show *that* will be! And when you come out, then how will you like it when people come up to you and ask you questions? Tell me, Miss Asta, does insanity run in your family? Miss Asta, do you have a history of nervous disorders? You feel quite confident now, do you, Miss Asta? Anything in the script that might set you off? Of course this is the end of playing jilted women, eh, Miss Asta? When did you realize you loved Charles Harrow? Before or after your mentor Max Lilly died? I'd rather be on trial for homicide. You'd never stand it. Never."

"No."

"Of course not."

"So what must I do? I must do something! When is the wedding?"

"Noon."

"Noon tomorrow!"

"I'll talk to him. He'll come home late, he'll come home drunk, but not so drunk he won't listen. If he wants to talk to you, where can he find you? Anna, stop crying!"

"At home, at the little hotel, or I could go to Elska's, she has a private phone. Which is best?"

"Where will you be least miserable?"

"Alone, where no one can watch me!"

"Then go to the hotel. I'll talk to him. He can call you at the hotel? Good. He has the number?"

"And if he doesn't call?"

"If he doesn't call, then by one o'clock tomorrow you'll know it's over."

"She is a nice woman? A good person?"

"She's a nice person, a little high-hat, but otherwise."

I looked out over the ocean and cried on. "Listen, last it out," he said. "Worse things can happen. With his record, he'll be single in six months. Can you drive? Can you stop crying? You'll be all right alone?"

Alone! It was as if I'd never heard the word before. I began to sob. "What a mess," he said. "What a mess."

I dug my fists into my eyes. He was right. If he was going to talk to Charlie, I had to drive him home. "At least you don't say, Everything happens for the best," I said. "At least you don't say that."

"I don't say that," he said, "because I don't believe it."

"OH," SAYS IVY, "the nice young man is coming again?" Now he is the nice young man, but when anyone first comes into the house, he is suspected: Who is this stranger? What does he want here? Let him go about his business! Then, if he passes some kind of test, Ivy will turn the house upside down for him, so if I don't want to live in a storm of wagging dust cloths and the pine smell of some yellow liquid she pours into a pail to scrub the floors, all that mixing in with the dust she stirs up cleaning, the smell of furniture polish, everything gleaming, but I am under orders not to touch anything until the polish dries, if I want to escape that, I don't say, until the last minute, The nice young man is coming.

Then we have a short squall of tidying up, muttered reproaches while the clean house is made even cleaner, the opening and shutting of cabinets, finally the slamming of cabinet doors when in them is found nothing good enough to put on the table, and at the end of all this, Ivy appears in my room with her coat on and a scarf tied around her head. So here she is now, saying, "Miss Asta, if you will not shop for this nice young man, then I will take some of my money and go out on the street and find a thing or two."

Well, it is so predictable I say, "All right, buy something. Buy some of your salted codfish, and if you feel you can afford it, buy me a few cornmeal cakes." She is almost at the door, her back stiff, when I call out, "Of course I will pay for it. He is my guest."

The slam of a door, the sound of rain driving at the windows. The loud *ping, ping* of rain on the air conditioners in their winter coats. It is damp in the house, not very cold, but still you feel you are never warm. When it stops raining, the light will be flat and gray. These things one knows in advance, at least at my age, when there are no more surprises but instead a delight at finding one had predicted correctly. Well, one should, after all that experience.

There were times I walked around drafty movie sets in satin dresses that barely covered me and I never felt the cold. And once I went dancing at the Sewanee and the straps that held up my dress snapped and there I was, dancing away, the only white woman there, naked from the waist up, and when the music stopped, everyone clapped and I laughed and smiled and my escort was furious. He said, Anna, pull up your dress, and he took off his jacket and put it over my shoulders, and I laughed and laughed at him, and then we went home.

"So," I ask the young man when he comes, "what brings you back here to talk to an old woman?" I wait to hear what answer he's going to pull out of the old trunk, but he says, "I like you, Miss Asta."

"You like me?" I ask him. "Not so many people like me. What is there to like about me? I am old and cranky." He smiles and says he likes old and cranky people. "All of them?" I ask him. He smiles and says he doesn't know very many of them.

"Well, really, I shouldn't see you," I say. "After you were here last time, I was up all night."

"Oh," he says unhappily, "if I upset you, I should go." And he gets up out of his chair. This brings tears to my eyes. Other people, once they get in here, I cannot get them out again, not even with a shotgun.

Now Ivy comes in carrying a tray full of cookies. "She never sleeps at night," she tells the young man. "Why she is blaming you I can't imagine."

We are like dogs, Ivy and I. People come in, we sniff at them. We don't like them, we nip their heels. They come in looking like robbers, we like them, we sit them in chairs, put hot-water bottles on their heads and wrap them in blankets. We are not normal people, the two of us.

"So," I say, "what should we talk about? What is interesting in the world out there? You have a girl you care about?"

"Oh, that doesn't interest you," he says. "Really," I tell him, "I am interested." Yes, he says, he has a girl. "You love her?" I ask him.

"How do you know if you love anyone?" he asks me. He likes two girls. One is exciting and unreliable. The other is very sweet and innocent. Which one should he marry? "Well," I say, "if you have to ask that, maybe neither." He says the sweet and innocent one has her moments. "Really?" I ask him. "What kind of moments?"

He took her to a dinner party, everyone there was very sophisticated, the kind of people you meet at Tinka's, and one of the women was talking about someone else, a famous woman, and what a nice affair they had until a husband came home and spoiled it, and another woman said that France was the perfect place to live, because the French understood adultery; it was part of married life. Even the priests understood it and encouraged it. In fact, the priest was part of the affair. No French woman would have an attack of guilt and confess all to her husband. She would go to confession and that would be that, and all of a sudden this particular woman stopped talking, and looked at his girlfriend, the young and innocent one, and said to her, "Well, you lead a quiet life. A few years in France, you'd be a different person," and she fainted, fainted right into her soup.

"Into her soup?" I asked. "Hair and everything?"

"Hair and everything," the young man said. "Pieces of mushroom in her blond hair. I had to carry her out. Probably I'll marry her."

"Don't marry her because she fell into her soup," I said. "I know how it is. There she is, white and pale, soup in her hair, what could look more vulnerable? What could look more pure? So now there is no one else like her, your emotions are at high tide, and for this one minute, for this little picture, you marry her and then you have the rest of your life to regret it. How often can a person fall into her soup? Maybe the exciting one would be better. Or a third person you haven't met yet who is innocent *and* exciting, if such a thing is possible. Of course you should not listen to me. What do I know about romance?"

"If you don't, who does?" he asks me.

"Change the subject," I tell him. "You have been reading? Of course you scientists don't read."

"Now I will bore you to death," said the nice young man. "I read biographies."

"Oh, biographies," I said. "I don't like them at all. How can they be true? Who knows what we think? The real life goes on behind here," and I tapped my forehead. "It would do a biographer some good to know you visited me and two times we had a nice talk? What did we talk about? What did we think about it? Who can know the truth of a life?"

"Oh, well, Miss Asta," he said, "you're exaggerating. You can know *something*, probably more than something. The police prove that every time they investigate a homicide. You sit there in the courtroom and ask yourself, 'How the hell did they find that out?' 'How the hell does he remember so much about a specific day?' You put enough little details together and soon you can make a big inference. It's the same in science. You don't want to think it can be done. One little piece after another. You travel down a road in the dark and every so often there's a flash of light, a lit window, and you look in."

"But most of the time the road is dark and those are the important times," I said. "The soul cannot even know itself, how can anyone else know it? No, there should be no such thing as a biographer."

Well, he said, he had to disagree. Today he was reading a biography of a great writer, a terrible man, but a great writer. He died in a mental hospital and they buried him on the grounds and after he died, everyone wanted to know the story of his life, especially the doctor who attended him, and one day, he was walking in the cemetery and some workers were digging, and they disturbed this man's grave and they unearthed the body and there was the skull, and as luck would have it, the doctor was a phrenologist, so he picked up the skull and examined it.

"And the skull told him that everything he already thought was true!" I said.

"Oh no," he said. "Just the opposite. He found good development in the front of the cranium, the area controlling interest in theosophy, no exaggeration in the temporal region, the area of ferocity, no exaggeration in the area behind the ears, the site of combativeness, no exaggeration near the mastoids, which would have meant a tendency to excess in physical love. In a word, if he hadn't known better, he would have thought he was examining the skull of an elder of the church."

"At least," I said, "this man was not dissected while he was still alive. Why must people try to explain what cannot be explained? A few different bumps on the skull and the doctor would have gone home satisfied. 'So now,' he would say, 'I know why my poor patient was thus and so.'"

"Of course now you are talking about yourself," the young man said.

"Well, of course, what they did to me, that was dissection, dissection without an anaesthetic. And for what? *We* are supposed to be the narcissistic ones, but who sees a woman looking into a mirror with a caliper in her hands? You know how many centimeters it is from the arch of my eyebrow to my hairline? I know. The exact measurements from my chin to the base of my nose? From the base of my nose to my upper eyelid? I know. I read it in the papers. The length of my body from pelvis to kneecap? From waist to the hip? All these measurements they got from the make-up lady, the wardrobe lady. So, yes, it's a crazy kind of narcissism, but it isn't mine! *I* want to know how far it is from pelvis to knee so I'll know why I walk as I do? And do I always walk the same way? I look in a mirror and think, Yes, the forehead is high, the mouth is wide. That's enough for me. Who doesn't look in a mirror and get a surprise no matter how many times you do it?

"*The secret is in the proportions.* What nonsense that is! I was an ugly teenager, I had the same proportions! So the narcissism was not mine. It was theirs! They were the ones who wrote the articles! They were the ones who pored over my face! Was it the Rosetta Stone? But how to explain it? They are being narcissistic about me! And still it goes on. A film of mine shows up on television and they get busy dissecting again. Is it the remarkable eyes, so wide-spaced? The perfect nose? The big, generous features? The wide shoulders, the narrow hips? What does it mean, that they are so narcissistic about *my* face? After all, it is not theirs. So maybe all the time they are playing with a doll. All the time they are imagining they are being me. And what am I doing? I am imagining I am one of them! It is funny!

"What is on my mind in some of the scenes they talk about and talk about? I stare into space. What profundities pass through my mind when all the time I am wondering, The chicken I left out on the kitchen table, will the cat get it? Is it starting to spoil? My stomach hurts, when will it be five o'clock?

"Such a great mystery that was, how I always knew it was five o'clock and yet I had no watch. *Her pulse and the speed of the film*, there were guesses about that. Back then I had an assistant—Bessie Brown— and she sat there on the set and at five o'clock, she took out her handkerchief and blew her nose or put on lipstick, whatever came into her head. So then I knew it was five o'clock because we arranged it. What mysteries were made of it! The artist is narcissistic all right, but the audience, it is worse."

"All these things still bother you?" he asked me.

"Oh, when you get old, sometimes your mind drifts back," I said. "But to talk about these things, never! Why am I talking to you? Who knows? Of course now I will be wide awake watching clouds drift by the moon."

"Is it really that bad?" he asked me, smiling.

"Now you are laughing at me, you fresh young puppy!" I said, reaching over and swatting his knee with my fork. "You've probably heard most old people don't sleep so well, so you are off the hook."

"If I don't go home now, you can blame me with good reason," he said. "I brought you something, though."

When Ivy brought his coat, he took a flat package from his pocket.

"Oh, give it to me!" I said. "I love presents!"

"You may not love this one," he said. "Open it."

I tore off the paper. A book. "Fairy tales?" I said.

"Something to do instead of staring all night at the moon."

"Andersen's fairy tales?"

"One of them reminded me of you."

"Oh, yes? Which one? Read it to me!"

"Miss Asta," Ivy said, "the nice young man has to go home to his bed."

"Oh, please! Read it to me!" Now I was flirting with him. At my age, with my looks, but still, it worked. He flushed, sat down, and opened the book. He said he would read me the first bit, that was the part that reminded him of me.

"All right?" he asked. "Ready?" I said I was ready. I shut my eyes in bliss. Once Max used to read me stories. Once Charlie blackened my eye and in penance read me an entire book all about a woman who always said she would think about things when she had to and not before. I suppose he thought there was a lesson in it.

"Now," he said, "this story starts when a demon invents a special kind of mirror."

"A mirror!" I said. "No more mirrors!"

"Not an ordinary mirror. Miss Asta, you have to be quiet if I'm going to read this story."

"That's right, tell her," said Ivy.

"I will be quiet," I said.

"I love these simple stories," Ivy said.

"Be quiet!" I told Ivy. "Now," I said, "begin."

" 'One day this demon was in a high state of delight because he had invented a mirror with this peculiarity: that every good and pretty thing reflected in it shrank away to almost nothing. On the other hand, every bad and good-for-nothing thing stood out and looked its worst. The most beautiful landscapes reflected in it looked like boiled spinach, and the best people became hideous, or else they were upside down and had no bodies. Their faces were distorted beyond recognition, and if they had even one freckle it appeared to spread all over the nose and mouth. The demon thought this immensely amusing. If a good thought passed through anyone's mind, it turned to a grin in the mirror, and this caused real delight to the demon.

" 'The demon even wanted to fly up to heaven with it to mock the angels, but at last it slipped out of his hands and fell to the earth, shivered into hundreds of millions and billions of bits. Even then it did more harm than ever. Some of these bits were not as big as a grain of sand, and these flew about all over the world, getting into people's eyes. Once in, they stuck there and distorted everything they looked at, or made them see everything that was amiss. Each tiniest grain of glass kept the same power as that possessed by the whole mirror. Some people even got a bit of the glass into their hearts, and that was terrible, for the heart became like a lump of ice. Some of the fragments were so big that they were used for window panes, but it was not advisable to look at one's friends through these panes. Other bits were made into spectacles, and it was a bad business when people meaning to be just put on these spectacles.'

"Miss Asta!" the young man said. "What's wrong with you?"

"Lady Clare?" said Ivy.

"What is that story?" I whispered. "What story is that?"

" 'The Snow Queen,' " he said. "A famous story of Hans Christian Andersen. Surely you know it?"

"No, it's not 'The Snow Queen,' it's 'The Ice Queen'! You know how many years I have been looking for that story?"

" 'The Snow Queen,' " he insisted. "Look, its title is right here!"

"Give me the book!" I said, grabbing it from him. "What happens? Someone gets covered by some of this bad glass? That is what happens?"

"So you remember," he said.

"A young woman, she is covered by some of this bad glass?"

"No, a young man," he said.

"No! A young woman!" I said.

"This is upsetting you," he said. "Maybe I should take back the book."

"Don't touch the book!" I said.

"Lady Clare!" Ivy said. "You were raised in a yard? Where are your manners. Sit in that chair and breathe like a person!"

I sat down. The nice young man sat down and watched me uneasily.

"So," I said finally, "a long time ago, long before you were born, a man told me a story about a man and a woman who went into a cave, and the cave was curtained with ice, and a big wind came up, and the ice blew in and covered them. And even before that, I had a dream, or it happened, I don't know anymore, I was sleeping with someone in a bed and the wind blew in the window and covered the bed with splinters of glass. The man who told me the story, he was going to make a movie about it and call it *The Ice Queen*, so for all these years I've been looking for this story, but really, I thought he made it up. He made up so many stories."

"Maybe he did make it up. Maybe he didn't know this story," the young man said. "How many stories are there in the world? Sooner or later, you tell the same one someone told before."

"*This* is the story," I said. "This is the one he meant."

"Good, so now you have it, you can go to bed," Ivy said.

"You are perhaps a distant relative of his?" I said. "It's possible. Why else bring me this story? Why should you even think of it?"

"I thought they'd remind you of home."

"Home!"

"Miss Anna!" Ivy said.

"There are no Lillys in your family? You're sure of it?"

"None that I know of."

"Well," I said, getting up, "thank you for bringing me this book."

He asked me if he could come again. He said the book belonged first to his mother and she'd given it to him. I said of course he could come again. But really, I didn't want to see any more of him. You go along complaining that no one understands you, and then someone comes along who does, and really, it's too much of a shock. You complain about the empty rooms and how lonely it is and how the sounds echo and someone else walks in and on the shelves all the delicate things vibrate and rattle and suddenly you notice the floor is made of stone and you see how easily things smash, and you tell yourself, and probably it's the truth, I like empty rooms. I like them.

18

I WAITED ALL NIGHT for a call that did not come. How can I say what that was like? It happens to everyone and I am sorry for every one to whom it happens.

At ten o'clock at night I thought, Well, Charlie is not home yet. Walter has not talked to him. At eleven, I thought, Well, Charlie is drunk, but he will be home by midnight. At midnight, I thought, Now Paul is talking to him. By one o'clock the phone will ring. Outside a wind came up singing all the old familiar songs. See? I told myself. The world is still going on. At two o'clock, when there was still no phone call, I thought, They are having a very long talk. If it is a long talk, certainly that's a good sign. At three I began to think, He is home, he does not want to talk to me. At four, I thought, He is home, he is with her, he does not want to talk to me but still, miracles can happen. At five I began to cry and thought if I leave the room, if I go for a walk on the beach, when I come back there will be a message saying Charlie has called me. At six I came back and the clerk said, Sorry, no messages.

Clerks all over the world say, "Sorry, no messages," and every-where in the world people go to their rooms walking more slowly and heavily than before. Around the world, hundreds and thousands of miles of hotel corridors, sad men and women walking, holding their hotel keys, their heads bent down. At seven, I lay down on my bed and thought, How could this happen? I will never get up again. Around eight, I thought, Whose hair will I tousle now? Then I felt sorry for myself and began to cry until I cried myself to sleep.

Later in the morning, I woke up and found Elska sitting at the foot of my bed. She said it was eleven o'clock; she wanted to see how I was. I said I was fine: Go home. It was nice of her to drive such a long way. "Well," she said, "I couldn't call, you would only think . . ."

"I would only think it was someone else," I said. "Elska, thank you, I said, but go home. In another hour he marries this woman from Broadway."

"You know," she said, "Mr. Pinsky himself is sitting outside in a car."

"Outside where?"

"Outside your hotel."

"So," I said wearily, "he wants to stop me if I rush out of here ready to make a cake of myself. Well, I am not going anywhere. Not anymore."

"You know, it is terrible to say, but you will get over this."

"Well, no," I said. "Some things you don't get over. Of course you are still alive, still you are walking around, even a little different or better, but you don't get over it." And then I said, "Everyone I love dies."

"Everyone *everyone* loves dies," Elska said a little impatiently.

"Well, good, so everyone is stronger than I am."

"And if they put you in a film together?"

"Then I will go to work."

"So," she asked after a few minutes, "what are you thinking about?"

"That, in close-ups, I must no longer tilt my head way back. See how one nostril is smaller than the other? The result of surgery and a deviated septum. That was what I was thinking. Also that I must consider films in which I look anguished or pout. Everyone says I look most beautiful when I pout."

"No, this is not what you were thinking."

"These things are important."

"All right, I am going home," she said.

I lay on my bed until three o'clock, watching the ceiling, then looking at the clock on my chest of drawers, from clock face to ceiling and back again, until, lying still, I gave myself car sickness. Then, when I was sure it was finally over, I fell asleep.

A nobleman is going away from home, to a war. He leaves his wife and child behind him, but he has his suspicions. As soon as he is gone, his wife calls her lover to her. Her husband, who has hidden himself, sees everything. He comes in a secret doorway, climbs up a secret stair. His wife hears him coming and hides her lover behind an unfinished wall covered by a thick velvet curtain. The husband, who pretends to know nothing, kisses his wife. I see that what I value most I have left unguarded, he says. His wife says nothing. Oh, he says, looking at the wall. In the haste of departure, I left the wall unfinished. He calls his servants, who lift great blocks of stone and slide them into place. Inside, the lover who is hiding, sees the light growing dimmer and more narrow. Finally there is only one block of light. There is nothing you want behind that wall? asks the husband and the wife, to save herself, says, No, nothing. The last block slides into place. The lover is walled up forever.

I first saw that film with Max. The actor who starred in it was the man who lived in the house below Charlie's. I remember telling Max, This movie is silly! No one would let someone be walled up like that! Max shrugged his shoulders.

Now I thought otherwise. To save yourself you will let yourself be walled up. A little air, a crumb of bread, more than enough. Behind different walls go the others. You don't think of them. Some of us are better at this than others.

Months passed, then a year. Bertha Pinsky sent a car for me. I will say for Bertha that she never wasted time on polite conversation.

"So, sit down, eat," she said. "You've heard the talk about Charlie?"

"Yes," I said. "He's married."

"He's drinking," Bertha said. "This is of course not news to you. Really, the marriage is over. This is probably not news to you, either. After the big honeymoon, they moved into different houses. You didn't know? So this is what I got you out of the house for. My Saul doesn't want him anymore. Every day, new stories about how he falls down drunk and throws up blood, every day stories that Louise Castle gets called off the set to take him home. He can't finish a picture, she can't finish a picture, an impossible situation. Last month, he got drunk, he called my Saul—well, some of the names he deserves to be called, but I don't want to repeat them either. Anyway, my Saul doesn't forget an insult. Sometimes I think he writes them down in a notebook. He's still mad at me because twenty years ago when we were married I said, one pant leg is longer than the other. A bride should notice such things on her wedding day? So he was furious. The short and long of it is, he wants Charlie out.

"So the question is, can he get him out? Next month, everyone comes in for voice tests for talking pictures. Maybe he can get him out then.

"So of course—have a cookie—you want to know why I'm telling you this. You're out for revenge or what?"

"I don't want to see anything bad happen to him, if that's what you mean," I said. "I owe him a lot. A lot."

"But do you want to help him? That's another matter."

"If I could help him, I would do it. Why not?"

"Because, to tell you the truth, I'm very fond of him, and the girls, they are too, and you know they don't like anybody, but in this house you can't say a word for Charlie Harrow. My Saul, he brushes dog hairs from his coat, and he says, 'There goes Mr. Harrow.' Dust, dirt, that's what he thinks of him." She bit into a candy, clamped it between her teeth, and sat still, thinking.

"But I can do something, you know I can," I said. "My contract—"

" 'Highway robbery, she held me up at the bank,' " Bertha said, mimicking her husband. "Your contract. I thought of it. You have a clause. You can choose the others."

"Not necessarily the leading men."

"But if he said no and you got sick again—"

"Yes," I said. "It works every time."

"How can it not work? You're so skinny, so pale, who won't believe you? They have something in the works for you?"

"The End of the Road."

"It's any good?"

"It's good. A story about a woman who thinks society's rules don't apply to her, so she falls in love with a gangster, and then he won't let her go. There's a good man who loves her and shoots the gangster, a big trial scene. The Studio loves trial scenes."

"One of the parts is a big part?"

"The gangster. He's the picture."

"Charlie as a gangster? What would he think?"

"He hates the romantic hero roles, he doesn't like wearing velvet, he doesn't like wearing tights, he doesn't like make-up: he'd be very happy."

"It's too bad they're not considering him," Bertha said.

"It is."

"Anna, have a cookie. You know, some day my Saul, he'll find the key to my jewelry chest, and the game goes up in smoke. This morning, he says to me, 'Always I see you in there fussing with jewelry and you come out wearing the same pin. What do you do with it? You pawn it? Another Jewish woman whose mother told her, Always have money for yourself? That's it? You have an account I don't know about?' So tomorrow I'm gardening in a diamond choker."

"Won't he know I pulled a string?" I asked her. "He may say no. He's proud."

"Why should he think you'd lift a finger? He married someone else. The first few days give him the cold shoulder. Men are pretty stupid really. My Saul still thinks all those places I turned up when I first met him, what a coincidence it was all the time. Well, if they weren't so stupid, bees would be ruling the world, not people."

"He wasn't so stupid," I said. "He didn't marry me."

"How could he, Anna? All the times you turned him down. They're stupid, but they're not crazy."

"Throwing up blood?"

"He'll behave with you on the set. That's enough business. Let's eat. You like candied apricots?"

"Are they locked up?"

"Locked up? They're *fruit.* God forbid every day we don't eat enough fruit."

Three days later, a huge bouquet of white roses arrived at my door. There was no note, only Charlie's initials.

"He knows," I said. I let the flowers lie in their box. I went for a walk and came back and saw them. When I picked them up, and smelled them, I thought I smelled mothballs. I asked myself, Who can let flowers die? How did these flowers hurt anyone?

I went to look for a vase, came back, and stuffed them in the water. A little later, I came back in, saw them out of the corner of my eye, and thought, Those flowers look dreadful. Why can't I arrange flowers? I picked them up. They dripped all over. I loosened one from the other. How easily the stems tangled! One at a time I put them back in the vase. They were glorious. A porcelain vase, white roses, spots of water on my table. As if it were a rag, I used my hand to wipe up the water.

CHARLES HARROW, LOUISE CASTLE SEPARATE read the newspaper headlines.

This interviewer asked Mr. Harrow if he would marry again. "No," said Mr. Harrow. "After a while it gets to be a little ridiculous. Who could take me seriously? No, I think I'll do women a favor and retire from the race."

"People say professional jealousy caused trouble between you," said this reporter. "Miss Castle who is so famous on Broadway is a fish out of water here. In your judgment, it is impossible for two people, both so successful, to marry?"

"No," said Mr. Harrow. "Miss Castle is in no way to blame. She is a generous woman, not an envious bone in her body. I

am simply impossible to live with and so we are living separately."

"Is there any chance of a reunion?" asked this reporter.

"Unless Miss Castle suffers from amnesia, that's not in the
cards," Mr. Harrow replied.

The third day after we were called to the set of *The End of the
Road*, I was, as usual, pacing up and down on the streets of the back
lots. I walked up to the old saloon. It was dustier and more weathered
than ever. An impulse sent me through the swinging doors, and there,
sitting on a stool at the dusty bar, in front of the dusty, fly-specked
bottles, was Charlie.

"Good morning, Miss Asta," he said. He smiled at me. His face
was dead white. At first I thought he was already made up but then I
saw he had no color.

"Miss Asta?" I asked, climbing onto a stool next to him.

"The bottles are empty so you can throw them without spilling a
drop," he said.

"Why should I throw things?"

"A woman scorned, that sort of thing." I sighed and stirred the
dust on the counter in front of me. "How have you been?"

"I go to work, I come home. What can change?"

"You speak as if you're a very old woman."

"I am a very old woman."

"No one's taken my place?"

"Who could take your place?"

"You're very gallant, Miss Asta. More than I was."

"Let's not speak of it," I said. "It's not necessary."

"I should have sent a message," he said.

"Oh? Yes? What were you going to say? Thank you, but I have a
better offer?"

"I was angry."

"I knew you were angry."

"You think we made a mistake?" he asked.

"We?"

"Then me?"

"No."

"I like it in here," he said. "This is where I always come when my
hands start shaking. Look at them shaking now. I promised Horton,
no drinking. I love bars, the bottles, all the different colors, the way
the light shines through them, the labels, what a beautiful thing."

"You're not talking about a church," I said impatiently.

"We all worship in our own way," he said.

"Well, I must walk," I said.

"You have to slink," he said. "For this role."

"Who can slink? You know what I do. I bend the knees and droop against the man. How can a stork slink?"

"Stand up," he said. "Now put one hand on your hip. No, not like that: open your hand. As if you were pushing your stomach in. That's good. Stand up straight. Thrust your pelvis out. Come on, you know where your pelvis is! Like this! Like this!"

I started to laugh. "What are you laughing at?" he asked me.

"You make a very sexy woman," I said.

"Shoulders back, head back, just a little, keep that hand on your hip, now move one shoulder forward. As if you wanted to rub your ear with it. Well, that's it," he said, and sat back down on his stool.

"How can I remember all this?"

"Do it again," he said, staring down at his hands. "Tell me when you're finished."

"I'm finished," I said.

"Oh, my God," he said, looking up. "You're going in five directions. You have a stomachache and a bad back, maybe even a crick in your neck. All right, once more. Like this. I put my hand this way. You do the same thing. Pelvis out. Shoulders back. Come on, you want to look like you have breasts. Head back, shoulder up toward the ear. That's good."

"It's impossible."

"Do it again," he said.

"You want to walk?" I asked when we finished.

"I spend my time between takes resting. That's how it is these days."

"This trouble with your health, it's serious?"

"The doctor's very nervous."

"And you?"

"If I don't drink I can live forever, but as you say, who wants to live forever?"

"Why turn out the lights so early? It gets dark soon enough."

"Not soon enough for me."

"So," I said. "You're starting to get black again. Tomorrow people will talk to you and no answer. I know these moods, never any reason for them, terrible, like death."

"You know your lines?" he asked me.

"You know me. I know my lines, I know everybody's lines."

"I can't remember! One minute I know them, the next, nothing. They'll get rid of me. They're only waiting for a chance."

"We will go over your lines," I said. "When you look at me, you'll remember them." He shook his head and began banging his forehead against his folded hands. "Stop that!" I said. "Is that a new way to learn your lines? Stop it! Now you'll have a headache!" He straightened up and looked at me. His face was wet. "When you look at me, you'll remember," I said.

"And if I don't?"

"You will, so why bother yourself? You will remember." He nodded. "So you're a gangster and I'm a sexy woman. This will be a disaster," I said.

"You'll be fine," he said.

"Not if you're not fine. All those movies, everyone going on about how passionate, how beautiful I am, well, if I hadn't been looking at you, what would it have been? You can tell me? A silly girl putting on faces! So, no drinking, no hysterics, no black moods, you learn your lines, we come early, we rehearse, everything fine. Fine, fine, fine!"

And it was fine. But when we came to the passionate scenes, I said, "Mr. Hall, I think perhaps a little bit less hot. Mr. Harrow is still a married man."

"Not in this picture," Mr. Hall said.

"Still, the scene goes on too long, I think," I said.

"Charlie," he said. "When I say Cut, let her go. Anna, you're the next best thing to a nymphomaniac. A nympho doesn't turn off when she finds out the man is married. This is a movie, it's not real life. Just do your job."

"So," Charlie said at the cast party, "I did it. No drinking during filming."

"And what now?"

"Now no one cares."

"Oh, so now the excuses start?"

"Come with me to the Sewanee."

"All the reporters," I said wearily.

"Then come to my house."

"All right," I said. "For an hour. No funny business."

At Charlie's house, we sat in the living room. He disappeared into the kitchen and returned with some damp crackers and some moldy cheese. "This is all I have. Probably you don't want the cheese. It looks pretty bad."

"Give me a knife," I said. "We can scrape that off." I handed him a cracker. He took a bite and said it wasn't bad. "So, what do you want to talk about?" I asked.

"I'm talked out," he said. "Louise was a great talker. She talked and talked and talked. Every little thing that happened to me, she knows about it. What it means to take a drink: she's told me. How I'm afraid of happiness: she went over that. How I'm really an overgrown child: we agreed on *that*. How I spoil everything I touch, and what a shame it is because otherwise I'm such a wonderful man, such a lovely person, a terrific lover. She's good at it, the way she mixes the compliments and the insults. It gets so you're afraid of the sound of a human voice."

"So," I said, "you still have your own projector? Let's watch a movie."

"I'll fall asleep."

"Put something on." He got up and threaded a movie into the projector. "Can I sit next to you or will you scream?" he asked me.

"I'll scream, but sit down," I said. The screen lit up, the title came on in Swedish: *Witches' Brew.* "You knew I was coming?" I said. "You're very confident."

"No, I'm addicted to these Swedish movies. They fit my mood. They start out badly and they end worse, just like life."

"So," I said, "keep quiet."

Witches were stirring their cauldrons in the basement of an old house in the country. Old women, fat women, a woman whose skin had disappeared under a network of wrinkles, they looked like the women my mother bought vegetables from when we lived in Ekeborn. Someone dragged in a long package like a rolled-up rug. One of the women began to unwrap it: a human corpse. She pulled the hand from the wrist, pulled a finger from the hand, complained the hand was shrivelled and because of that the brew would not be strong enough, put the finger into a barrel, and hammered the stopper back in. "My God," I said.

Next to me Charlie's breathing was deep and regular. As he slept, his body settled against mine. A fat peasant woman came to the witches for a love potion and went home and fed it to the friar she wanted to woo her. He began chasing her around the table.

Some men unwrapped the corpse of a woman and before they began to dissect her, they prayed to God to forgive them. *Felotame,* said the student, who bent over the body and with the knife, made an incision between her breasts. "This is a terrible thing," I said. "Where did you get it?" Charlie was sound asleep. I sat in the dark and watched the picture.

In the village a man died and his wife blamed his death on witchcraft. She denounced an old woman who came to her house to beg for food. At first it appeared the old woman was innocent, and the tortures the friars administered horrible and unjust, but the old woman began to confess. This one was a witch, that one was a witch. Soon she had named almost everyone in the town. One of the friars thought he was possessed by the devil. One of the nuns felt herself tempted. They went to others for help, but the others were already under the devil's spell. The whole town was damned. In the dark, Charlie groaned, a low, frightened sound. I put my arm around his shoulders. Still, he moaned to himself. I held him tighter.

Then the scene changed. Now it was modern times. A young woman, a shoplifter, was caught by the shopkeeper. "Since my husband died in the war," she said, "I feel I've been going mad. Mysterious forces make me do this. They will put me away!" The shopkeeper felt compassion and let her go. That was the end of the movie. *Snap, snap, snap*, went the film. Charlie slept on. My arm was tight around his shoulders.

That movie is a true thing, I thought. Who knows why we do what we do? When something goes wrong, it is good to believe in witches and devils, always an explanation for everything. The poor woman in the shop, they think they can fix her, they can send her to a doctor, they can put her away, when really, who knows what causes anything?

Always there are forces loose in the world, they move us here and there, why should we think we can fight them? Why should we think we have anything to do with it? So he drinks. Why blame him? I sit here in the dark, I put my arm around him, I'm happy. He's so white: nothing living is so white, lilies are that color. Why should I go away from him? Nothing is perfect. If I could accept people! If I had some tolerance! I am not perfect, only lucky.

Charlie stirred, I patted his shoulder. *It's all right*, I whispered. *Snap, snap, snap*, went the projector. What a comforting sound!

Hours passed. The night was clear. The moon shone. Outside, the pine trees Charlie planted when I first came to live with him sighed in the wind, the wind telling its old old stories. When he planted them, they were small. Now they must be above the roof of the house. My foot fell asleep. I shifted my weight from one hip to the other and wiggled my toes. The weight of Charlie's head on my arm numbed it.

I made slight movements with my wrist. Outside I heard an owl calling in the trees, another owl answering. The breeze was cool, my dress was thin. Charlie's head rested on my shoulder. I let my head rest on his.

What is it I said in the movie? *Love is just a beast you feed all through the night and in the morning it dies.* Did I believe it? Probably I did believe it.

A weak gray light was streaming in the windows when my eyes opened. I knew that light. In a few minutes, the sun would slide higher up the horizon, a gold tinge would enrich everything, saying, In the morning, everything begins again. What a threat! Everything beginning again! Who has the strength for it?

Charlie's head lay like a stone on my shoulder; my eyes closed again. When I shook my head and looked toward the window, I moved carefully. I didn't want to wake him. Then I moved my shoulder. He wasn't there. I looked up and saw Charlie standing in front of me. "It appears we fell asleep," he said.

"Yes," I said, yawning. "Sound asleep."

"Was the movie good?"

"Very good." I patted the cushion next to me: sit down.

"It was nice of you," he said. "I don't sleep through the night anymore."

I said I would make some coffee, but Charlie said he couldn't drink coffee. These days he drank a lot of milk. "Well," he said, smiling sadly, "things change."

"I don't like coffee," I said.

"You always drank coffee!"

"I drank it for you."

"Listen, you know I'm no bargain. You know what I'm like. But if you'd come back, I'd give anything. Anything."

"If you want me back, it means you give up hope," I said.

"What do you mean? Give up hope?"

"A family, children, you give up hope for that. Always you say if you love a woman you want to possess her."

"I do. I think it's normal."

"But you know I don't want to be possessed. I'm afraid of being possessed. I don't even know what it means to be possessed."

"It means you belong to me, no one can have you but me."

"That's too frightening," I said. "I'm sorry. You can give up hoping for it?"

"Use the past tense," he said. "I gave up hope. You'll stay?"

"To tell you the truth, I would like to stay. But I cannot live here and watch you die. That I cannot do. You begin to drink, the vomiting begins, the bleeding, I have to go. I am not good, I am not strong. Oh, I have the strength of a lobster, I crawl along, I take care of myself, something comes near me, I bite it. Someone takes care of me, I am even stronger. So you must understand what I'm telling you. I cannot watch you die under my nose."

"You mean you will not."

"I will not."

"Stay," he said. And I said, All right, I will.

PART FOUR

THE PHANTOM CARRIAGE

"ALL THE TIME you are saying you want to go back to Green Island," Ivy said. "How about this week?"

"What happened?"

"Headless chickens are hanging in trees all over Cinnamon Bay, so you know what that is? It is voodoo."

"And what does that have to do with you?"

"When Tita Lu took sick, Brother Beckwith, he went to the hospital with her, and then they found he had pressure, so they put him in a bed, too. You remember?"

I did. Ivy is upset. It was too much to hope she would say, I want to go home this week and here is the reason. Each time it is back to the beginning. Once again I think, if we could edit lives like movies. *Snip, snip* go the scissors. Oh, but I am ungenerous and impatient.

"So there they were, both sick all together, and so the people, they started to talk. Two together, it must be spells. The people, they came to Brother Beckwith, they said, Bevon, her cow runs away from her, maybe she is the one who did it. The next day, hanging from her tree, some stinking meat and sticks and feathers stuck in the meat.

"Old Mr. Griffin, he walks his donkey past Brother Beckwith's house every morning, and the donkey stops and screams and won't walk further, so in his tree a dead chicken and some sticks. And Brother Beckwith, he is going all about the town saying, This is not Christian! This is not right! And the people, them, they ask him, What about the donkey? Why he will not walk past the house? He will not walk past the house because there some years ago Brother Beckwith beat him when he ate out his garden.

"So it is very out of order, very much out of order and soon there will be so much bad feeling, something will happen. So I am to come and tell them the truth. She had diabetes, I used to send her the medicine, I used to come out to care for her, and every time I turned around, she poured sugar into her coffee. If they will believe me, he thinks I must go."

"They will believe you?" I asked her. "They will decide you cast the spell!"

"All the way from the United States?" Ivy asked me.

"When I was in England, there was a man there who cured sheep over the telephone, long distance. He called a man in India and his sheep were cured."

"No one on Green Island heard of such a thing," Ivy said.

"You know, in my room I am watching the movie we made on Green Island. Come look at it. Forget this nonsense."

"What I know is nonsense and what they know is nonsense are two different things," she said.

"You want to go?" I said.

"It is where I come from," she said. "Brother Beckwith, he and Tita Lu took my children in when I came to this country. He cannot live there with his pressure, every morning getting up and chickens hanging in the trees. If I can do something, I have to."

"In the morning," I said, "I'll call the travel agent."

"You will go?" she asked me.

"What else do I have to do?"

I went back into my bedroom. In the movie, two women were walking down a dusty road, their arms around each other. I remember them, I thought. I remember their faces. I remember that day. There was a storm warning. Everyone was worried about a hurricane, but Mr. Hall said we must not worry. I was sitting on a rock when those two women walked by, really just girls. The one on the right, she wore a nice red hat. I remember that hat. I always liked red hats. They looked so happy! I remember I thought, Probably they are sisters. One of them had nice, shiny shoes, the other one was barefoot.

One was plump, the other very thin. They stopped and looked at something in the field and the woman in the red hat picked up a stone and threw it. Then they started to laugh and walked off down the road.

I switched off the television. On Green Island they still believe in magic. On Green Island they are still innocent. Ivy doesn't like magic. She says it leads to trouble, even killings. Still, they know why things happen. It's not a bad place to be. I say this to her.

"Oh, yes?" Ivy said. "And if you got up in the morning and found yourself looking at a headless chicken, you would be happy? You would want to leave the house?"

"I don't want to leave the house anyway," I said. "Is a headless chicken worse than a photographer?"

"This movie you made on Green Island," Ivy said. "You are still watching it?"

"Oh, it just finished," I said. "I will play it again."

"You will do no such thing, you will go to bed," Ivy said.

"WE'RE HAPPY?" Charlie asked me.

"Very happy," I said. He was nervous. His forehead was wet. "The doctor said something?" I asked.

"I'd be better off with more blood, that's all."

"But better than before?"

"Every week a little better," he said.

"All right, so that's good enough."

Then we sat beneath the pine trees and talked about the films we were making and when I would go on location and how happy we were we had passed our voice tests. "So from now on, they have to find stories with foreign ladies. Otherwise, why do I have an accent?" He said now they would scour all the great European novels for me. "You know what I want to do?" I said. "I want to buy a farm in Montana and raise wheat."

"Why wheat?"

"It can't run anywhere, like cattle or sheep. Always you know where it is."

"And the movies?"

"Oh, enough of movies! How many have I made? Nine, ten? The public wants so many from me? I make sixty movies, I won't be one step farther than right this minute."

"You mean quit?"

"Yes, quit. We go live on a farm and look at our wheat."

"I would die of boredom looking at wheat."

"And you are so healthy here?"

"Out of sight, out of mind. That's the credo of this place."

"It's so bad to be out of mind? I'd like to be out of mind."

"You're not serious?"

"I am serious," I said. "Maybe this is our last chance."

"When you come back, then we'll talk about it. Green Island. It sounds like paradise."

"Mosquitoes as big as pumpkins," I said.

I was on Green Island when Mr. Hall came onto the set and called me over to the side. "I have some bad news," he said. My skin went cold. Oh, I have heard this before, I thought. We went outside and walked away from the others.

"Charlie's dead," he said.

"Oh," I said. "Don't be silly."

"Look at the telegram," said Mr. Hall.

"I won't look at it!" I pulled away from him and walked rapidly down the road.

He caught up with me and walked alongside me. Finally, I stopped walking. "All right," I said. "What happened?"

"He may have started drinking," he began.

"That's what happened? He bled to death?"

"Something like that, I imagine," Mr. Hall said.

"Tell me!"

"He wasn't well, they hired a nurse, she gave him a shot so he'd sleep, he didn't wake up."

"He died in his sleep?"

"Yes."

"What are you not telling me?" I cried. "There is something!"

"Why do you want to know? Dead is dead."

"Tell me! The drug killed him? It was the wrong dose?"

"He choked on his own tongue," Mr. Hall said. "It's a tragedy."

"Who was there with him?" I asked. I seized his arm. "Who was there?"

"No one was there," Mr. Hall said.

"He died alone? No! He didn't die alone!"

"Anna, stop," he said.

But I couldn't stop, and that night, the company doctor gave me a shot to make me sleep but all night I sat up in bed crying and staring. Mr. Hall sat on a chair and slept. Next to him, Miss Rosalie sat on a chair and worked on her embroidery. In the morning, Mr. Hall asked if I wanted to stop and go home or go on.

"What difference does it make now?" I asked him. "Montana! Wheat!"

"Then we go on?"

"What else is there to do?" I rested the remainder of that day and night. The next day, I went back to work.

Now I find ways to keep myself amused.

IT IS FUNNY the way life moves. One day after I left the lot forever, I went into a movie theater. I wanted to see someone enjoying herself on the screen, and who was up there going through her paces? Gemma Rambova playing a Hungarian spy. Her accent was so thick you could hardly understand her, and I thought, Well, she will not be here long.

Then came the serial, and a lovely young woman, blond, naturally, because in the movies no one ever menaces a brunette, and of course she was tied to the railway tracks, and in the distance, a black locomotive bearing down upon her, black smoke and sparks flying from its funnel. In front of me, a woman whispered to the little girl with her, "Not again! Not another train!"

But I was on the edge of my seat. Look at that! I thought. That is my life! My life exactly! First you are bored and nothing happens and you tell yourself, Nothing will ever happen, and you take your book outside and read on the lavatory roof and think melancholy thoughts. Then your mother sticks her head out the window and calls you in for dinner and you sit on the kitchen bench giving her a martyred look: how can this familiar stone of a person understand such sadness, such sorrow for the empty days you know are coming? You sigh deeply and lean on your hand. Your mother looks at you and says you should drink more milk. Probably you are coming down with something. Coming down with something! So that is what the Great Stone thinks!

Oh, such sad times, when looking down at your ankles brings tears to your eyes, because as you look, you see them thicken and wrinkle, and you say to yourself, I will grow old and die and nothing will happen. You get up and look out the window so the Great Stone stirring her pot will not see you and take out her bottle of tonic.

Oh, this is a wonderful time! The sadness is sweet and piercing, quite splendid really, because really, you are completely safe. There is the Great Stone at her pot. There is your father, at work somewhere, doing whatever he does. Soon your sister and brother will be home, you will go to bed, and in the morning you will get up and go to school. How marvelous, this sorrow in such comfort, surrounded by such thick walls. Opera stars must feel like this, plunging plastic daggers with retractable blades into their whale-boned bosoms, while all around them the townspeople sing their hearts out, four thousand people sit in their seats dabbing at their eyes, and the entire crew works the lights, moves the scenery, cranks the curtains up and down. Such pure, such exquisite sorrow, it can take place only when the singer of sad songs knows she is completely safe.

So there I was, dreaming on my lavatory roof, an outhouse, you call it here, pouting when someone came in to use it: imagine, a world where such common things interrupt such resplendent dreams! Oh, really, it is too much to bear. Then, just as you are looking at the back of your hands, weeping as time passes and they become wrinkled and gnarled, a big bear paw picks you up and throws you into the middle of the life you thought was passing you by, and before you know it, you are tied to the tracks, and the locomotive is bearing down, shaking the earth. Well, then it is a little late to look up and say, Really, what I think I want is a peaceful life.

After the serial came a newsreel. Someone in London was giving a speech in front of a rubble-filled lot, and in front of me, a young boy said, "I want to be a general, but the trouble is I'm afraid of noise."

I had to laugh. There it was, the truth. We would like to be a doctor, but we don't like blood. We would like to be an actress, but we don't like it when people look at us. We don't like it when people ask for our autographs or our opinions. We would prefer it if people ignored us. We want to be a great star, an enormous success, but when we come into a room, we want to be like everyone else. Really, we want to be two people: the great star, the gray mouse. We want to be a great beauty, but we complain when men follow us for no good reason. Well, this is how we are.

When I was a child, I walked with my father. I saw the actors in the snow. I stood still and said, I want to be them! That's what I want to be! But of course I made the usual mistake. I put myself in *their* place. I was enjoying the idea of being someone else. How could I know what I would feel when I myself put on their shoes? Well, when I put on their shoes, they pinched. *Don't put on someone else's shoes unless you're prepared to walk his road.* My grandmother used to say this. Who knew what she meant?

They say even as a child I was sensitive to everything. A change in the light, the light moving across the floor, a shadow on the wall,

all these things made me laugh or cry out. There is no virtue in this, any more than there is in genius. It is something you are born with, like the color of your eyes, and to be frank, all this sensitivity and talent, whatever it is, leads to trouble when it shows up in the wrong person. Sometimes the sword is put in the hands of a baby; he cannot manage it and so he causes himself and others untold misery.

"She overreacts to everything, always." This was my mother's perpetual complaint. And it was true. What was nothing for someone else was a calamity to me, and whatever it was, the memory of it stayed on, like a burn on my skin. So very early I learned to avoid everything I could not take in, and soon I tried to avoid everything, because always there was too much. By the time I knew what I was doing, by the time I saw the harm in it, of course it was too late.

I tried to fight off Max. I tried to fight off Charlie. Always I tried to fight off anything new. And I fought by finding fault with every new thing: The Studio was too big, Charlie drank too much. Who could live in a place of perpetual sunshine? It was unnatural. I fought against Hollywood when I was there, and then, when I began to live in New York, I slowly grew used to the idea of Hollywood as I sat in my apartment three thousand miles away. Then I missed the climate, the people I knew there, the routine of going daily to The Studio. Of course by then it was too late. I could not go back, not really.

I fought against the idea of marriage and when I grew used to the idea, well, the prospective groom was dead.

When I worked, the role I played took everything I had. While I played a part, there was nothing else. Every nerve in my body strained toward becoming the character I became when the camera began to roll. And when the day was over, I was absolutely exhausted. I could not lift an arm or a leg. Once Max carried me off the set and into the car.

Of course everyone thought this was affectation. I wish it were. I would come home so tired, worn so thin, the voice of another human grated against my skin like a rough cat's tongue. I felt persecuted by the world. Another sunset, another rainstorm, raindrops on the roof, more things to become aware of! The sound of another voice, the sight of another face: I could not bear it. I had no energy for it. I needed to sleep, to become blank.

And then one day I came home from The Studio and I realized that this need for sleep, this need for blankness, for quiet, for privacy—I could no longer control it. I made an attempt. But by then it was too late. This is one of the prices of precocity. You are so far down the road, so far ahead of everyone else, you don't realize there are other roads, less twisty, less hilly, but for you, impossible. You have had no practice. They say that as an actress I was a genius. Perhaps I was. But as one person carrying on a conversation with another, I was an idiot. Ineducable. And yet you do not say to yourself, Well, when I am up there on the screen I am a genius. No. You torment yourself. If I am such a genius on the screen, why can I not do the simple things everyone else can do with no trouble? And you tell yourself, if I am such a dunce at small talk, at feeling affection, at receiving it, then I am a dunce at everything.

I do not praise myself for my virtues. Lately I do not castigate myself for my faults. This was the nature I was born with. I could not help it.

You realize, of course, you are listening to the tale of a misfit.

Yet even misfits learn to get their way. When I disagreed with the director, I explained why there was disagreement. If I knew I was right, and still he would not agree, I argued no further.

My maid, Bessie, had a little monkey named Evelyn. One day Mr. Hall and I disagreed. "Bessie," I said, "the animal is hungry. Give her to me." I walked off the set and up and down the studio street, the monkey sitting on my shoulder. In my pocket, I had sesame seeds. I fed them to Evelyn one at a time.

"We are ready now, Miss Asta," Mr. Hall called.

"Oh, yes," I said. "But Evelyn has not eaten."

Again and again, this went on. "But Evelyn is still hungry!" I exclaimed. "But she is still chewing!"

Finally Mr. Hall gave in. "All right," he said. "We'll try it your way."

"Oh," I said, looking at the monkey. "Who can overfeed a monkey like this? Why didn't someone say something?"

I walked back in, handed Bessie the monkey, the make-up woman adjusted my make-up and my hair and I did the scene as I wanted to do it. It is a very good scene, too.

Max used to say, What is genius but the overdevelopment of one capacity at the expense of the others? He knew. He knew from experience. Why should other people know? Instead they have opinions. When you have no experience, then it is very easy to have opinions. Everyone had an opinion about me but no one had the slightest idea. And I would not explain. When you need to explain, you realize how far from the shore you really are. The more you explain, the smaller and farther away grow the people to whom you are making your explanations. Soon you are so far from shore that if you had to swim back you would certainly drown. Well, this is what it was like. This is what it is still like. And now time and my own nature have closed the doors of The Studio to me. Because, after enough time passed, I grew used to the idea of being a film star. All the things I had complained of, they seemed small and unimportant.

But no one forgot how often I had called The Studio a factory. No one forgot how I got on a boat and left for Sweden before they finished the final editing of *The Spy*. No one forgave me for turning down so many of the projects chosen for me with such great care. The times I had refused to return calls, the many times I told Bessie to say I was not home when someone rang my doorbell: of course people remembered these things and so, when they had a chance, they slapped me down. They took pleasure in humiliating me. And I cannot even say I did not deserve it. The bitterness, the humiliation, it was unspeakable. I have spoken to no one of it. *Don't apologize*, Max used to say. To this I have added another rule: *Don't explain.*

Of course I have had my revenge, if that is what it is. I've outlived those who said, Oh, we have another Swedish star, and that Asta, she is so expensive and temperamental. Even now every mail brings the most extravagant offers to come back, but it is too late. I don't believe in the resurrection of the dead.

Max used to say, She has tremendous energy but no stamina. Who understood what he meant? But it was true. I used what energy I had and then there was none left. Then it took time and quiet and privacy to recover.

Really, I have travelled through life as an invalid.

There was no other way. If there had been another way, I would have taken it. People think you live as you do out of choice when there is no choice in it.

After Charlie died, after I finished filming *The Spy*, the sets on my films were like crypts. No one was allowed onto the set unless he had a purpose there, and what was that purpose? He was in the scene, he was directing the scene, he was lighting it, and if he wasn't, everything came to a stop until he was thrown off.

"Oh, she's like an animal," Mr. Hall said. "A stranger can't get in here. The hair on the back of her neck rises, her eyes look past the camera, and she says, 'Who is that man?' Believe me, it's not worth sneaking you on."

And then, as if that weren't enough, I decided it was too distracting to have *anyone* watch me, so for the close-ups and the medium shots, I had myself surrounded by blank flats.

"I don't know about this," Mr. Hall said uneasily. "This may interfere with the lighting."

"I'll take care of it," Mr. Feldman said.

The next day Mr. Pinsky appeared on the set. He looked around. "What is this, a crypt?" he demanded, astonished. "You're dressed in black, the set's dressed in black! Take these things down!"

"No, Mr. Pinsky," I said. "When they come down, then I cannot concentrate."

"All over the lot actresses are concentrating in the middle of Grand Central Station!" he shouted. "A great actress can concentrate anywhere."

I said I was tired and it was time to go home. "You know, Miss Asta, I am fed up with this," he said. "No one can talk to you anymore. One harsh word, one word, you threaten to walk off! This is not good for morale! Look what is going on here! Your leading man is back there playing poker. He knows how you are playing this scene? In a few minutes he has to walk on and he doesn't know what you've done here. I want these flats down!"

"Well," I said, "they are not coming down because if they come down I cannot do a good job."

"You refuse? You refuse to take the flats down?"

"They are too heavy for me anyway," I said.

He turned away from me angrily. "Horton! What's this nonsense about rehearsals? She won't rehearse?" Mr. Hall said, "Well, not exactly. She rehearses at home. I rehearse the actors here with someone standing in for her, and then she comes in and does her scenes. Saul, this is nothing new. She never comes on the set until she knows exactly what she's doing."

"This is good?" Mr. Pinsky asked him. "The other actors cannot have the benefit of her presence? What about reaction shots? The actors don't know to what they are reacting. She is not the moon so that we have to wait until she is full! You," he said, turning to me, "you will rehearse with the other actors! You don't want to see the rushes, fine, but I have to see them, and let me tell you, they are nothing to brag about! There are five stars on the lot bringing in more money than you! You want to wind up back in Stockholm selling needles? Believe me, it is possible!"

The silence on the set was deep. At the least thing, I developed a headache, a stomachache, the cameras stopped turning, the budget soared into the sky, Mr. Hall sighed and put down his clipboard, and Mr. Pinsky tore his hair. Bessie, my maid, folded her hands in her lap and stared at the little emerald ring I'd given her for her birthday.

"All right," I said. "I will rehearse with the cast."

"And the flats come down."

"No, the flats stay up. This is not something we discuss."

"All right," he said. "They stay up. Miss Asta, you are out of hand completely! For your own sake, stop it! It's your interest I have at heart!" He looked genuinely stricken.

"All right, Mr. Pinsky, that's enough," I said.

"You come to my office, you talk to me," he said. "What am I there for? Thirteen years you've been working here, you can't come talk to me, who can you talk to?"

"Oh, certainly I will come," I said. He smiled, grabbed my hand and pressed it. His hands were like his wife's, plump and white. The backs of his hands were thick with black hair. When he walked off the set, I said, "Good, he is gone."

"About rehearsing," Mr. Hall asked me. "You'll work with the others?"

"I keep my promises," I said.

I went home and sat cross-legged in the middle of the bed and thought. The eternal sun was shining down. The sea was green and aqua. It was true: I was getting out of hand. Strangers on the set frightened me: I had them barred. Someone moved and caught my eye and my concentration went: I was out of character. If I had a fear, I gave in to it. If I had a weakness, I humored it. My exhaustion was becoming legendary. After two hours on the set, I wanted to go home and sleep. Between takes, I sat in my dressing room and thought about my bed, how appealing it was, how my body would feel when I sat down on its edge, then drew my legs up onto the mattress, then slid my bottom downward, and finally, finally, lay down. I imagined my head sinking into the pillow. I imagined stretching out my left arm, extending it to its full length, my fingers curling up toward the ceiling.

I could spend hours thinking about this bed.

Soon I would not be able to get out of it. I would wake up in the morning, feel the quilted surface beneath my hand, pat it as if it were a dog or a cat, and pull the blankets up over me. This is a breakdown, I said to myself. Under ordinary circumstances, you are bad enough. Now you must pull yourself together.

I could feel Bessie standing in the doorway, a Mexican widow whose five children depended on her. Every week, she sent money back to her grandmother. "So," I said, "you're afraid you'll lose your job? Well, don't worry. I'm not going anywhere." And I thought, even leading my kind of life, no husband, no children, still there are people who depend on me.

"You are depressed," Elska said later. "It takes some time to get over a death."

"Which death?" I asked her.

Bertha Pinsky came to see me. "I am glad you listened to my Saul," she said. "You know he is not always wrong."

"No one is always wrong," I said.

She regarded me narrowly. "You are bored with this movie business?" she asked me.

"You are here as a spy?" I asked her.

"He has more spies than the Emperor of Austria. He doesn't need me."

"And still, he doesn't find your cookies?"

"He can't find everything." For the first time I noticed: she was adorable when she smiled. People say eyes twinkle. Hers really did. A happy, chubby child in its carriage. There should be room on the screen for a woman like that.

"You see what's happening?" I asked her. "The more I get bored, the more I get restless, the more money the pictures make. They are worthless, every one, and still, people line up outside the theaters."

"Well, that is a tribute to you."

"But what am I doing? Making idiot movies for idiot people?"

"The people are not idiots," Bertha said. "They don't pay money to see nothing. There is something you are doing, even you don't see it, but still, it's there. Maybe they go in, sit down, and see a soul."

"A soul!"

"You don't have one?"

"What is my soul to them?" I asked, outraged.

"Oh, Anna, you are impossible," she said. "When the lights go out, when the lines don't form, then you'll cry to the high heavens. How many times have I seen it happen?"

"Not me, not to me."

"Irene is in an institution. Eleanor is in a rest home. Gemma has run back to Hungary. She can't face what happened here. Betty is married and pretending she likes to cook. Isabel is having children and believe me, she can't stand them, so later they'll be lying in wait for her. They found Madelaine floating in the ocean. The papers said she went for a swim at night and went out too far. A lot of people are swimming out too far. Don't be in such a hurry. Here you are. Make something of it."

"I make something of it," I said. "I make myself unhappy."

"That's something to be proud of?" she asked me.

"You know, at night, I drive my car to the Chinese restaurant, I go in the back door, right into the kitchen, always the back door, and I pick out something that fills up two little cartons. Then I drive back here. I sit here and eat, and I think, all over the world there are people, rich people, handsome people, all of them thinking how they would like to eat with me, thinking up what they would feed me, even the Prime Minister in England wants to meet me, and I sit here in the middle of my bed eating out of cartons with chopsticks."

"Accept an invitation every once in a while," she said. "Why not?"

"It's my nature," I said. "What a terrible thing, to have such a nature. Really I am quite crazy." She didn't contradict me.

So the years went by. Every year, I made a movie, sometimes two. Once someone crossed the set and I ran up to him, seized his shoulder, and turned him around to face me.

"Oh," I said, starting to cry, "I thought you were someone else."

When we were about to film *The Red Dress*, the leading man, who was wooing a new starlet, jumped a fence, fell from his horse, and broke a leg. Mr. Hall came to me and said, You have approval over your leading men. Who do you want? And I said, I want Mr. Drake.

"Mr. Drake!" Mr. Hall said. "Mr. Drake is five hundred years old! He's a contract player! He's going to be the first actor to live long enough to draw his pension!"

"I want Mr. Drake," I said stubbornly.

"Look, in his day he was fine, but he was never *very* good. If we use him, we have to change a lot of things. Someone else has to supply the romance."

"Then change them," I said. "I want Mr. Drake."

"When he hears this, he's going to drop dead," Mr. Hall said. "From the shock."

"I certainly hope not," I said.

Mr. Drake was two inches shorter than I was, a very dignified man, and that was what people called him: Mr. Drake, the dignified actor. His hair was snow white, his short, thick moustache still black. His face was long, his features rough, a deep furrow bisected each cheek.

When he came onto the set, Mr. Hall sat down in his chair and refused to talk to anyone, but I was happy.

"Come talk to me in my dressing room," I said to Mr. Drake, who said I must call him Walter, or better yet, Wally. While Mr. Hall sulked, and we sat in my dressing room, I sent Bessie for sweet rolls and coffee, and we talked. Had he always been an actor? No, no, he began as a soldier during the Spanish-American War, but he came down with the flu, and so he was sent back. His intention was to become a newspaper man, but he was in Chicago visiting a friend, and one of the actors was out with food poisoning, so as a joke, he went on. "Well, in those days, an actor was the next best thing to a thief," he said. "My parents weren't happy but I thought, it's not such a bad life. You work late but life in a coal mine is worse."

"I saw you," I said, "in *The Prisoner of Zenda*. You were very good."

"Oh," he laughed, "I was all wrong for the role. You need one of these swashbuckler types, a real glamour guy, not a compact, solemn man like me. I never knew what I was doing on the stage either. Way back then they called me a matinee idol, but the minute the play closed, I packed up my wife and kids and we climbed up into the mountains and went fishing. I shot a few things, too. A couple of years ago, we moved the moose heads into the garage. My wife said she couldn't sew with those big eyes reproaching her."

"I would like to meet your wife," I said.

"You would frighten her," he said. "She's a very private person."

"Maybe you could sneak me in."

"Miss Asta! Sneak you in!"

"She could come here."

"No, no, you come to our house."

"Good," I said. "When should I come?"

"Friday night? Just knock on the door. She won't know you're coming. It will be a nice surprise. Otherwise, she'll worry herself into a stomachache."

"Okay! We have a deal!"

"Your Mr. Hall isn't so happy to have me," Mr. Drake said. "Well, he knows what he's up against. He'll have to order shoes with soles two inches thick, you know that takes two weeks, either that or *you'll* have to sit down through the whole movie. He won't have to worry about lighting me. You can't light me. Why did you want me?"

"We need something human," I said.

"Well," he said, smiling. "That's very nice. You're a very nice young lady."

Seven years passed. I made seven more movies.

When I came to Hollywood, I was seventeen. Now I was twenty-seven. Mr. Drake appeared in almost all my movies. Between takes, we sat in my dressing room and played cards or he told me stories about his early life. On weekends, when I wasn't tired, I drove to his house and sat on the porch with Emily, his wife, and we waited for him to come home from fishing. Occasionally one of their children would visit.

"You know," Emily said, "when we moved out here, it was completely wild. There were wild geese, wild ducks, coyotes, all sorts of small animals I never knew the name of. Now it's rows and rows of houses and paved streets."

"You should move further out," I said.

"If we move further out, he won't be able to come home at night, so that's no good."

"Oh, no, don't get separated," I said.

"After lunch, we'll do some weeding," she said. "But don't attack everything so hard! The flowers throw themselves out of the ground at the sight of you!"

"You adopted him so he would adopt you," Mr. Hall said, but of course that wasn't it at all. "He reminds me of someone," Mr. Hall said. "Doesn't he remind you of someone?" Who should he remind me of, I asked him. "He wasn't a bad idea after all," Mr. Horton said. "He gives the pictures some much needed gravity."

"Now you sound like a reviewer," I said.

"But, Anna, there is no role for him in *Double Trouble*, absolutely no role at all, and Mr. Pinsky wants him for a series that could go on forever."

"A bit part, something," I said.

"Let him have the series or you'll stand in his way. Let Emily buy some new curtains."

"He is my good luck," I said uneasily.

"And what am I?" he asked. "Something the cat dragged in?"

IVY HAS DECIDED to paint her room, which means she intends to paint the apartment. She knows I will never hire strangers and let them come in here. When she first mentioned it to me, I said, Oh, no, I cannot stand the upheaval. I am happy here sitting on my bed. How many people come in here? And, you know, the color of the rooms is nicer now than when I first decided on it. Now it is the color of burnt peaches. She will wait until I go out walking and then she will open a can of paint and begin on her room. She will spread newspapers everywhere so that she makes a path from her room through the living room and to the kitchen. When I want something, I will have to call her.

After a while, I will become curious and begin to stand in her doorway and peer in. By the time she finishes putting on the first coat, I will fall in love with the sight of the pure, clean walls.

Well, I will say, really sometimes it is worth the trouble. She will tell me to sit on her bed and watch her. I will ask her if her neck doesn't hurt from painting the high ceiling and she will say it hurts today, but tomorrow when she lies on her bed, the ceiling will look like new-fallen snow.

I will begin to feel lonely and start bringing my meals into her room and eat sitting on her bed. She knows that to me there is nothing so wonderful as watching old stains, old cracks, disappear under a new coat of paint. Sitting there is like sitting in the middle of an egg yolk. It is like being reborn.

So she will win. When I go back to my room, I will notice every smudge, every bit of soot that has settled on the walls. I will take down the small painting over my bed and see the square of apricot paint so bright it looks like a postage stamp pasted on my graying wall. Well, really, I will say to myself, why shouldn't I wake up in the morning in a bright, new room? All right, I will say to Ivy, we can paint my room.

It's not such a good idea, Ivy will say. If we paint your room, then when you come out to sit in the living room, you will see how dirty it is.

All right! I will say. We will paint the living room! And then I will ask her, Can't we paint around the pictures on the walls? Who wants to take everything down? And she will say, Lady Clare, go hide in your room. You don't have to do a thing.

And so the apartment will be painted. What do I need with such a big place? If I had a smaller place, I might go out more, but with all these rooms, I can go from one to the other and think I've actually gone somewhere. I tell this to Ivy who says, Miss Anna, you would go crazy in a small place. Look at that path you wore in the carpet!

So once again I am outsmarted. I will be sitting on the sofa, on top of newspapers, watching Ivy paint while I complain about the smoke pouring out of the chimneys across the street. What a place to live! It is so dingy! When it is all done, you will like it here, she will say, and of course she is right.

So now I am propped up on a settee and the kitten she persuaded me to buy is skidding through the newspapers, tunnelling beneath them and then exploding into the air, and I am laughing in delight. "Don't fight with him, Miss Anna," Ivy says. "He is cute now but he will get bigger."

"What must I do?" I ask her, annoyed. "You know, I have had cats before."

"When he attacks your hands, put a toy in the middle of his paws," she says. "Then he will grow up to be a good cat."

"That man in the hat," I ask her, "no one has seen him? No one has seen your husband? He is dead?"

"He's been gone a long time," she said. "He must be dead."

"You are getting his pension and Social Security?"

"My son took care of it. 'Well,' he said, 'Daddy was useless when he was alive but now he's doing all right.'"

"That's pretty hard," I said.

"That son of mine there, he talked me into taking that man back and I was so fool, I did do it. When that man brought his women home, it was my son who had to throw him out. He threw that bag of bones out into the yard and threw his bottles out after him. When my son got married, he called him up. He said, 'Daddy? I am getting married. You are going to come?' Of course he was going to come. Then that man called up and said how could he come when he had no suit? My son said he would pay to rent a suit, but he never showed his face. My daughter, when she got married, she drove over there and knocked on the door, and he said, 'Who are you?' She said, 'Daddy, I am your daughter!' So he opened the door and let her in and he went to get her something to drink. He didn't even have a glass! He gave her a bottle of beer! 'Daddy,' she said, 'you know I am a member of the church! I don't drink these things!' When she looked in his refrigerator, what was there? Bottles of beer, bottles of rum. Well, it is hard to believe for fifteen years I was married to that man."

"And if you had to do it over again?"

"I don't regret those fifteen years," she said. "I have my son, I have my daughter. For fifteen years I was happy. So," she said, standing back, "how do you like this wall?"

"This wall," I said, "makes me happier than twenty years in the movies."

"Well, that is ridiculous," Ivy said.

I say, "You weren't there."

"SO, MR. PINSKY, here I am," I said. I stood in front of the desk. "*Double Trouble* is no good for me. I will be a laughingstock."

"You didn't want to do *Secret Agent* either. You didn't want to do

Salvation. You didn't want to do *Roses.* You didn't want to do *Bitter Almonds.* You have something against success?"

"This is not a role I can play," I said.

"You can play anything."

"That's very flattering, Mr. Pinsky, but I cannot play this role. All this silly fluttering around, all this coyness, I will look ridiculous. This is a role for Norma or Edna or Mary, someone who is cute. I am not cute. Look at me! I am built like a scaffold!"

"I tell you what," he said. "You play the role, and if it is no good, never listen to me again."

"Not this one," I said, all the time thinking, it is useless to bargain with this man. He is a master at it. Where is someone to fight for me? Before there was always someone.

"Miss Asta, sit down," he said. "I want to show you something. I know you actors, you live in a dream world, you in particular. Outside this room, there is a war raging. This means every day people are dying, very sad. If this Hitler wins, my family goes to get cooked in the ovens, so believe me, I know what's going on. You, I know, don't like to think about these things so you don't do it.

"But this you have to think about. Look at this. See this big number? This is how much it cost to make your last picture. See this number? This is The Studio's profit. You can subtract, Miss Asta? We lost a million and a half dollars on that movie! This is not good business! You can see that?"

"This is true?"

"I don't lie about money," he said.

"But everyone tells me these movies make a fortune," I said.

"Let me explain the reality to you. You and Elska get together, you decide to make a historical romance. Fine. It's a good picture. We like them here, the kind of thing we're proud of. The research takes months, the sets are out of this world, the costs are too. But we don't mind. We know the movie will make a lot of money. We go on location, the costs are terrible. Still we don't mind. What's your salary per picture? A quarter of a million dollars? So right there, we start out with a big gamble, but always, we've made it. Even if not one single person in this country goes to see your movie, we know we're going to make a big profit.

"Why? Because in Europe everyone who knows what a movie is goes to see you. But now there's a thing called a war, the market there is gone. Now if people don't come, from Brooklyn, from the Midwest, then we lose our shirts. And let me tell you, Miss Asta, in this country people are not rushing to see you. And why? Believe me, I have racked my brain. When people are miserable, they want to come into a movie theater and see you suffer? Norma and Mary, they make people laugh, so people come to see them. So if you can't make people laugh, maybe for a while you should stop making pictures. We can't afford more of these bills."

"But *The Secret Agent* was funny and it was good for me," I said. "*Double Trouble* is no good for me. Believe me, it will ruin me."

"One picture can ruin you? Please! Miss Asta, right now a factory is turning out plaster casts of you and they can't make them fast enough! Show some confidence in yourself!"

"It is the picture I have no confidence in," I said. "Or the director. Only Mr. Hall could make this picture and he is retired."

"Look, you make this picture or you don't make any picture. Believe me, I know what is best for you. You don't trust me? This studio didn't make you the most famous woman in the world? More people know you than the Queen of England! The Queen of England wants to meet you! Of course you don't want to meet her. You don't want the world to bother you. You can afford not to be bothered. But we can't afford your pictures anymore. When the war is over, maybe. Not now. So you will go home and think it over?"

I went home, sat on my bed, and read the script again. A man goes to Aix and meets a simple, healthy girl whom he marries on impulse. After a few days, he becomes bored and lives to regret it. He goes back to Paris and again takes up with his mistress. His wife, the simple, healthy girl, comes to Paris and sees the true state of affairs. She decides to pretend to be her own twin sister and overnight turns herself into a sexy seductress. Naturally, the man falls for her and wants to marry her, but she won't hear of it; after all he is married to her sister. Some of the scenes were very funny and, as I imagined Norma or Mary playing the double role, I laughed. But then I tried to imagine myself both as the healthy, health-conscious simpleton and the beautiful, seductive siren and I began to tremble. This was the story of my life!

The simple girl was the peasant everyone said I was. What chance did she have for happiness? She was only ridiculous. The siren, what was she? Something to watch the way you watch a spider as it walks across the table, something fascinating, but in a little while you pick up a book and drop it on the bug. So, I thought, they wrote this script especially for me.

The simple girl, she was me as I was off screen. The siren, she was me as I existed on film. In the end the good, simple girl wins. Well, that is very nice, but to win she has to kill off her other half.

I cannot, I said to myself, make a movie about my own suicide.

• • •

The husband takes his good, plain wife out in a boat. In the middle of the lake, he gets up, intending to strangle her. In her eyes, he sees the woman he married. He cannot do it. By the time he reaches the mainland, he is in love with her again. He takes her to a beauty shop where they do her nails and then a man comes over to her to unpin her coiled, braided hair and cut it into a new more flattering style. In her eyes, there is pure animal panic. She knows if she cuts her hair she will become someone else, when her husband looks at her he will no longer see the woman he fell in love with. She says, No, no. She gets up out of the chair. Her husband's beard has been shaved and his face has been powdered. When he sees her he takes her face in his hands. Never has he seen anything more beautiful. She is beautiful precisely because her face is the face of the woman he has always loved. A beloved image never dies.

"I cannot do this picture," I told Walter. His wife Emily rocked on the porch.

"Do the picture," he said. "It's a long career. Believe me, I know. People remember the good things and the war will end, wars always end, and then Pinsky will owe you. And if it doesn't work out, well, then you can say, I told you so. Otherwise he'll put you on the bench and if no one sees you, you don't exist. Anyway, that's my advice. How big a mistake can it be?"

"We want to give you a whole new look," the director said. "We'll cut your hair, we'll curl it, less Silverstone Number Two—these days people use less make-up, too much looks like a mask. Believe me, you're going to like it."

"Don't cut my hair," I said.

"Mr. Stone," I told the director, "I don't want to cut my hair."

"Everyone's cutting their hair," the director said. "Women are going to work. They don't have time to fuss with their hair. We want them to identify with you. You'll look great."

"Mr. Feldman!"

"Look, why make such a fuss?" Mr. Stone asked. "Hair grows back."

They cut my hair, they curled my hair. When I looked into the mirror, I cried.

"Oh, Miss Asta," Mr. Stone said, "can't you see how gorgeous you look?" I looked at Mr. Feldman, who avoided my eyes.

The filming began. At night I went home and wept. A nice simple girl who becomes a glamorous woman. And neither one of them is real! Neither one! This woman was two people and neither of the people was real! My nightmare! Exactly my nightmare! And every day I had to go to the set and show people what I was, a thing split down the middle, a thing made of plaster. And to everyone else, this was a comedy. To me it was an agony.

You know what they always tell us? Charlie once asked. *Someday we'll beg for these romantic hero roles. Not me. I've done more swashbuckling than Attila the Hun. I've kissed more women than Don Juan. Get this glamour away from me!*

"Charlie," I said, "they were right. When we made those movies, we did something. The passions, how beautiful they are! After all, they are beautiful and true. But *this* woman, *this* man, this is not passion. This is sex, like a cat or a dog. This is an animal in heat, and not so very hot! They are making fun of me! If you were here, they would make fun of you, too. Well, Mr. Pinsky is right, I live in a dream world. You were right. I am selfish. I sit here crying because a war interferes with me! So, really, I should go to work and keep quiet."

"I don't know," Mr. Stone said to Mr. Pinsky. "She seems very unhappy."

"If the preview audience is happy, she'll cheer up."

"Not just a little unhappy. She's late to the set, she doesn't remember her lines. Mr. Feldman worries about her."

"She's had an easy life," Mr. Pinsky said. "Let her suffer a little." I knocked at the door and walked in.

ONE SUMMER, ANDERS STAYED in my guest room. Occasionally we watched the old films.

"Sometimes I was not so bad," I said.

"You had great genius," he said.

"For what?"

He thought for a long time and then he said, slowly, "Your great genius was for self-pity."

Self-pity!

"Yes," he said, "I think it was self-pity. You felt so sorry for yourself playing those unfortunate women, and so sorry for those poor women you played, who could watch you and not also feel pity for you? And since they all identified with you, what were they doing? They were pitying themselves. Yes, I think that was it. You justified their self-pity. While they sat there and watched you, the world stood up straight. Everyone saw what they had to put up with and how they suffered and everyone pitied them."

"Self-pity!" I said again.

"Self-pity is a greatly underrated thing," Anders said.

"Self-pity!"

"When you have no mother, you mother yourself. When you have no father, you become your own father. When you have no one to pity you, you pity yourself. Yes, I think that was your genius."

"It is ridiculous," I said.

"Think about it and you will see I am right," Anders said.

3

PEOPLE WHO COME to see Miss Asta always want to know how I came to work for her. Like all important things, it was an accident.

After Mrs. Bell, the old lady I cared for in the Bronx, died, I didn't want any more sleep-in jobs. I went to work for a company who sent out five or six women at a time to clean houses. I was walking around in Manhattan after finishing one job, thinking about going to a Manhattan agency rather than a Brooklyn one, because I heard they paid better.

I was on a very wide street, and when I looked down it, there was a pretty house way at the end. I stopped and stared at that house. It had a gold-domed roof. I saw my shoe was untied, so I bent down and tied it. When I straightened up, I happened to look at the wall near me. On it was a sign saying *Woman Wanted. Inquire Within.*

Flora had told me that I must always get my jobs through agencies. New York City was a dangerous place and people here wanted to get hold of you for all the wrong reasons. "Remember the catch-a-man they used to warn us about in school?" she asked me. "They all live in New York."

But there was something about the sign, its childish scrawl. And there was the gold-domed building at the end of the street, and here when you looked up, you could see a generous portion of sky. And across from the apartment house were green trees and a kind of park across the street. I went into the building and the elevator man stopped me.

"Who do you want?" he asked me.

"I saw the sign outside," I said. "Woman wanted."

"That's apartment Eleven-B," he said. "I'll call and see if she's in." He rang a telephone built into the coffee-colored marble wall and watched me. I stared at him. I made him uncomfortable. "Look, lady," he said, "see that sign there? We have to announce everyone who comes in here." ALL VISITORS MUST BE ANNOUNCED said the sign.

"She's not in," I said, but he said, No, it takes her forever to answer. Where are you from? he asked me.

"Green Island," I said. He said he was from Antigua. "This woman," I asked him. "Is she all right? It's safe to go in there?"

"She won't hurt you, if that's what you mean," he said. He began to listen to the phone and then spoke into it. "Yes, yes, she's down here," he said. "Yes, she looks respectable. Should I send her up?" He looked at me. "Eleven-B," he said again. "The elevator to the right."

I found her door, a great slab of wood, a tiny eye set in the middle of it. I rang the bell. No one answered. I must have stood there for three or four minutes and I turned to leave. Just then I heard bolts drawn back and the door opened. Inside was a woman of about sixty, her fine skin criss-crossed with tiny wrinkles, her limp blond and gray hair falling straight to her shoulders. She tossed her head so that her hair no longer covered one eye. When her hair fell back across her eye, she lost patience, and lifted both hands and pushed her hair back behind her ears.

"So," she said. "Come in. You know who I am?"

"Who are you?" I asked.

"Please," she said. "Let's not begin with foolish games."

Perhaps she was senile, as Mrs. Bell had been, so I asked, "Do you know who you are?" I asked.

"Who sent you?" she asked me.

"Look," I said. "I saw your sign. I need a job. I sent myself. I don't want to work for a crazy woman, so please open up the door." *Your mouth will get you in trouble*, said my father's voice.

"I insulted you," she said. "I'm sorry. You don't know who I am?"

"Did you put your name on the sign outside?" I asked. "Am I supposed to know everyone in this city?"

"If you worked for me," she said, "there would be certain conditions. You would have to swear not to talk about me. You can't give anyone this telephone number. You would have to leave through the service entrance and if anyone stops you and asks you questions, you can't answer them. Is that agreeable?"

The woman was mad. "Please open up the door," I said. I looked around me. A heavy green ashtray rested on a table near my hand. I could hit her with that ashtray if she refused to open the door.

She began to laugh. She laughed until she had to hold on to the back of the couch and then she let herself collapse upon it. She shrieked with laughter. She was mad. I picked up the ashtray. I thought, No madwoman will take my life when I have two children back on Green Island staying with Tita Lu.

Tears streamed down her face. She saw the ashtray in my hand and laughed even harder. Her laughter was low and deep and filled the room. I looked at her and began to smile. *Follow-fashion-monkey cuts his own throat watching the machete,* whispered my father. She pointed at the ashtray and bent over, hugging her ribs. I fought against my own rising laughter.

"You think," she said, "you think I'm going to hurt you!"

"Look, miss," I said, "I come from Green Island. I don't know this city. All I know is what people tell me. They say that the city is full of crazy people who will do all kinds of things to you if they get you alone. You lock me up here and ask me crazy questions and you don't let me out. You don't tell me what kind of job you're advertising for. What should I think?"

"There's a fruit knife on the table there," she said. "You can use that to fight me off." And she began to laugh all over again. She slapped her thigh, threw back her head and howled. Now she reminded me of Eugenie, a girl I went to school with in Mare River. When Eugenie laughed, the whole class laughed. I was often sent to the principal because of Eugenie.

"Will you let me out of here?" I asked her.

"Oh, don't you want to work for me?" she said, going kittenish. "Look at all this dust. I had to shut off two rooms with all my best dresses in them." She was pouting through her laughter. There was something girlish and pleasing about this woman. I would be sorry not to see her again.

"If you will open the door," I said.

She stopped laughing and looked me up and down. "You really don't know who I am?" she asked.

"Mistress Eleven-B," I said, "I am out of patience."

"Watch me," she said. And she got up and stalked across the room until she reached a carved chair and slumped against it. I was afraid she would faint. What would I do then? "I am so very tired," she said, her voice throaty and low. She had a pronounced accent. "*Now* you know who I am," she said triumphantly.

I went to the door and rattled the doorknob. I turned the knob, but the door would not open. I tried to undo the bolts but they would not yield. "I am a mother with two children," I said, "and I will let no one hurt me. I will fight you."

"I've frightened you," the woman said. Her face changed. She looked so sad, tragic, as if she'd seen the end of the world.

"Isn't that what you wanted?"

"No," she said. "No. But I have to be careful too. I'm very famous, you see." I stared at her. "You don't believe me?" she said. She watched my face. "She doesn't believe me!" she said, her face blazing with delight. She clapped her hands and then clutched both fists to her chest. "She doesn't know who I am!" she said.

"I told you," I said wearily.

"Oh, sit down," she said. "I will make us some tea. I have some good English biscuits. Sit down. I won't hurt you. I never hurt anybody. I'm not even real. Sit down. I'll make you some tea and show you something interesting."

In that instant, I don't know why, I trusted her. I sat down gingerly on her brocaded couch, running my fingers over its raised flowers. From the kitchen, I heard the sound of running water. What kind of nonsense is this? I asked myself. I come in here for a job, into an apartment like a palace, and the woman is mad as a mongoose and now she is in the kitchen making me tea. She laughs hysterically, she asks me senseless questions, she collapses on her sofa, and now she is cooking for me. Everything is upside down.

"Here," she said, coming out of the kitchen. She was carrying a heavy silver tray. A beautiful flowered china teapot sat in the center and around the teapot were four or five little dishes of biscuits and chocolates. Small lace napkins were folded into triangles and placed beneath two of the plates. She poured a cup of tea for me and then poured one for herself. "Now," she said, getting up, "let me get the book." She disappeared into one of the rooms.

I looked down at the tray. I had never seen such beautiful cookies or such chocolates. There were chocolates that looked like roses and irises, carved so beautifully they seemed alive.

I reached out with care and touched a chocolate iris with my finger. All my life I loved flowers. I looked at the cookies, some of them in the shape of tiny English houses and I felt hunger. But I never ate at other people's houses.

Even as a child I would not do it. When people offered me food, I would say I had just eaten, or I was on a diet, or that my stomach hurt. I could not bring myself to eat something someone else offered me. Once when I went to my Uncle Gusta's, he insisted that I eat something because it was dinner time, and when I refused, he gave me a covered plate to take home so that I could eat when I was hungry. When I got to the river I had to cross to reach my own home, I looked about me, saw no one there, and emptied out the plate in the reeds. Of course, it was my bad luck that someone saw me and the next morning my father asked me if I liked my dinner at Uncle Gusta's.

"I didn't eat it, sir," I said.

"Where is the plate?" he asked me. I said I didn't know. "The plate is down by the river, isn't it?" he asked me, and I said yes, it was. "That is very wrong," he said, "to take food and not eat it. Next time tell the person flatly that you do not want the food."

I was eleven then. I was forty-four now and still I did not eat at other people's houses, not even my sister-in-law's.

The woman came back with a large black scrapbook and sat down beside me. She picked up a dish of chocolates and offered them to me. "The roses have a cherry center," she said. "Have one of those."

I hesitated.

"What now?" she said. "You still think I'm trying to hurt you? They're not poisoned. Look, I'm eating one." She popped one into her mouth and chewed it greedily. She was very thin. I looked at the dish as she held it before me. The china was so thin the light shone through it. I could see her fingers through the glass, holding the plate. I took a chocolate rose and bit into it.

"You should see your face," she said, and she looked at me and mimicked me, and as I looked at her, I felt I was looking into a mirror. What an odd ability, to make yourself look like someone else.

"I don't eat from other people," I said.

"Why not?" she asked, leaning forward, her elbow on her thigh. She concentrated on me as if I were the only creature in the world.

"I don't know," I said. "My mother and aunt wouldn't do it either."

"A religious thing?" she suggested.

"No, no," I said. "Maybe when I was young, we heard stories. When we went to school, two women used to sell sweets from a cart and they competed with each other and they told stories about each other. The first woman said a snake licked the second one's candies, and the second one said a man came up to the first lady and asked her if her cakes were clean, and her little daughter who was sitting there said, 'Oh, yes, they are. Mommy always makes me wash out my mouth before I chew up the coconut.' Maybe that is it." But I didn't know, really, why I wouldn't eat other people's food, or why I wouldn't eat chicken. I picked up a chocolate iris, ate it, and thought it over.

"So," she said. "You come from Green Island."

"Yes. Green Island."

"Where did you go to school?"

"First Mare River and then Cinnamon Bay."

"Cinnamon Bay," she said. "What a wonderful name."

"It is a very interesting little country," I said, "but hard to make money there." By now I felt quite relaxed.

"I come from Sweden," she said, "where it is cold and dark and snowy."

"It is always hot and bright on Green Island," I said.

She picked up her black scrapbook and laid it across our laps. It was an old-fashioned scrapbook, its covers made to resemble pebbled black leather, and inside, pages of black construction paper held endless photographs, their corners affixed to the pages by little black triangles.

"See, here I am," she said. "And here. And here, and again here."

I looked at the pictures. The woman was very young in all of them, and in all of them she wore wonderful clothing, heavy furs, antique dresses, enormous straw hats, bits of shiny cloth that covered her breasts, the rest of her barely concealed by transparent veils. I stopped at that last picture. "You must get very cold dressed that way in Sweden," I said.

"Oh, no," she said. "That is not Sweden. That is Hollywood. I am making a movie in those pictures."

I stared at her open-mouthed. A movie!

"You see, I am very famous," she said. "One of the most famous women in the world."

"The most famous woman in the world," I said.

"One of them," she corrected me. "I don't go out in public, I will not be photographed, people don't know what I do or what I look like now. I've had enough of that. If you worked for me, you'd have to swear to keep it that way. You know there are people who can't go out in the sun? They sit inside wrapped in layers of white cotton? And if they have to go out, they swell up horribly and become violently ill? That is how I am if I think people know me and watch me. Do you want the job?"

"I still don't know what the job is," I said.

"Oh, cooking and cleaning and running errands and answering the phone."

"I don't like to sleep in," I said. "I don't want any more sleep-in jobs."

"You can leave by seven," she said.

"You want a housekeeper?" I asked her. She said yes, she wanted a housekeeper, and someone who would talk to her and tell her stories. She loved to hear stories of other people's lives.

"My life isn't very interesting," I said. "I was raised on Green Island in a big family and then I married and the marriage, it didn't work out, and I came here to find a job and bring my children over. That's the story of my life."

"We'll see," she said.

"I don't know movies," I said. "I went to a few when I lived on Green Island, but then I was saved."

"I don't talk about movies and you don't ask me about them," she said. "Especially why I stopped making them."

"I never knew you made them in the first place."

"But now you do."

"I still don't go to movies."

"Never?"

"Never."

"But you watch them on television?"

"On television, yes, but not so often, you know. I come home late, I bathe myself, I lie down and watch the news and the next thing I know, I'm asleep."

"Good," she said. "That's very good."

And so I began to work for her. After my children were grown, I lived in her apartment during the week and on weekends I stayed with one of my children. And then, after fifteen years, when Miss Asta became older and more frail, and I myself was older, I began to stay in her apartment even on weekends. In fact, I lived there, and we got along well. We still do.

Well, I love her and I believe she loves me.

PART FIVE

Happiness

"YOU REALLY REMEMBER Green Island?" Ivy asked me. "After all this time?"

"Oh, yes," I said, "it was very green, very pretty."

"I remember it so well from childhood days, you would think it was yesterday," Ivy said.

"If you remember so well, tell me something about it, I have such a headache, I can't open the blinds, I can't turn on the lamp, I can't read a book. Probably I ate bad shrimp."

"Probably you sat up all night in your chair brooding," Ivy said. "Since the day the nice young man gave you that book, headaches, headaches, headaches, that's all it is."

"There is some story you can tell me?" I ask her. She is picking up the pillows I've thrown from the bed, and, when I sit up, she settles them behind my back.

"What story do you want to hear?" she asks me.

"Anything."

"Anything. Well, I can tell you a walk I took one day with Miss Blue, not really a story, but it's what I see when I close my eyes."

"So," I said, "tell me that."

"Well, one morning, Miss Blue, the story tailor, got up early and found her daughter's bed empty, so she went to look for her," Ivy began, and she described every step of the journey from Mare River to Cinnamon Bay.

"You really remember all those things? You don't think it up as you go? All your family, they are good story tellers?"

"I close my eyes and there it all is," Ivy said. "The people, the talk, all of it is there."

"What do I remember?" I said. "Almost nothing."

"Lady Clare, you don't want to remember," she said.

"What happened to Elaine? She drowned?"

"They never found her. Probably she drowned."

I lay back on my pillow. "The travel agent says Green Island is not such a good place for white people," I said.

"What does the travel agent know about it?" Ivy asked indignantly. "He has been there?"

"It has changed very much?"

"Nothing ever changes on Green Island. In the city, maybe, but in the country, nothing. Where the roads are so bad, change cannot rush in. Every new car breaks an axle, spends two, three weeks in the shop, and the garage man, he says, Yes, mon, any day now. What is the hurry? Any day now the part is coming. My brother Robert, when he goes to Cinnamon Bay, his whole trunk is full of spare parts."

"Still, I would like to go. I listen to the story and I want to see these things for myself."

"Every story you hear, you want to step into it. They are like ponds you walk by on a hot, hot day. That's the trouble with stories," Ivy said.

"So we will go and put an end to these naked chickens in trees. Probably they will hang naked chickens outside our windows."

"Oh, no," Ivy said. "I have a plan."

DOUBLE TROUBLE was released. I went to the screening and after twenty minutes, I got up and walked out. My skin looked like clay, my gaiety was hysterical. I looked fifty years old, a woman making a fool of herself. Who could believe I could seduce anyone? My leading man was overweight and snide. Who would believe women were fighting over him? The movie wasn't funny. Its view of life was small and mean.

"Well," I said to Elska, who had come with me, "they've done it. They've ruined me."

She tried to talk to me: Anna, be reasonable, no one can ruin you. So it's not a great picture. Pray it does badly! Next time they'll listen to you. No, no, I said. They made me film my worst nightmare! How can I ever forgive them?

Your worst nightmare, she said. What does that mean? Everyone has a failure. Listen to me! You are going off the deep end!

A beautiful woman is lying on her bed fast asleep. Is it a noise that disturbs her? Does she feel pain? She moves her hand to her heart. She floats free of her body. She hovers above herself. She looks down on her body with distaste. She floats to the window, opens it as she hovers in the air, looks back at the body on the bed and floats away.

In the morning the beautiful woman gets up, goes to the mirror and brushes her hair. Something is wrong, she doesn't know what it is. She begins to walk around the room; she is uneasy and frightened. She stops in front of a doll on a shelf; she takes it down. She sits in front of the mirror holding the doll. This is what she sees when she looks in the mirror: she sees her face, she sees the doll's face. It is one face, doubled. She jumps up, picks up the doll, holds it over her head. She intends to smash it. At the last instant, something stops her. How can she kill herself? She is no more real than the doll. Both of them have eyes made of glass. Neither of them is human.

What is the beginning to this story? I didn't remember how it began. "Max," I said aloud, "first you failed. Now it is my turn."

It seemed to me that one morning I got up and said, All right, the story of my life is over. From now on, it is one foot in front of the other. I remember sitting in various chairs in various rooms of various houses, looking out the windows at the scenery, sometimes the Alps, sometimes the beach, even at the dunes of the desert, my hand on my chest, listening to my heart beating, and it seemed to me that the heart was a small animal that had its own reasons for continuing to live while the rest of the zoo, the head, the arms and legs, all said, Enough, we are ready to stop now.

For a long time, I thought that everything important came to a stop when Charlie died, but now I see it began earlier.

I remember the day my father was buried. Everyone was already outside, waiting for the horse-drawn carriage. I said I was looking for my gloves and stayed behind. I opened my mother's bottom drawer and took out her tin box. Once it held candy. On its lid, a pretty girl in golden curls wearing a light blue dress sat in the middle of a swing whose ropes were made of roses. I suppose it was the prettiest thing she had. I opened the box and picked up an old photo and before I turned it over I read what my mother had written on the back. *Our wedding day.* There on the other side were my parents, my father, of whom I was the living image, in his badly fitting suit, the tops of his socks, the cuffs of his shirt, sticking out from the trousers and the jacket.

I thought I remembered my mother saying, in one of her fits of bitterness, that on his wedding day, my father had to borrow a suit from his uncle.

My mother wore a white dress, well starched, very brilliant in the photographer's light. Her cheeks were fat and round and red. Even in a black and white photograph you could see that. When she smiled, her fat cheeks squeezed her eyes so that her pupils disappeared.

In the picture, they looked very happy.

I held the picture, I sat on the edge of the bed, and thought, This is how things begin. Then I got up and looked out the window. There was my mother, dressed in her good black church dress, my brother and sister also in black standing there with her. And this, I thought, is how things end. Really, it hardly seems worth the trouble. Twenty-five years together and in a second it is over, and in a few weeks it will seem like a dream, even to her. Then she will look around and ask herself, What should I do now?

People will tell her it is time to find someone else. *He wouldn't want you to live alone like the old loon on the lake.* How would they know? I never thought my father was selfish, but maybe he was. About some things we are all selfish. Maybe he would want my mother to be the old loon on the lake, flying across the water, looking for him. That's what people do in fairy tales: someone gets lost, they spend the rest of their lives looking for him. They don't stop in the middle of the story and say, All right, that's enough, I've had enough adventures. I'll marry someone else. So about this one thing maybe I was romantic.

I was a great believer in fairy tales, perhaps because they were the only stories I knew and usually they ended happily. Of course we knew the Bible stories. Every family had a Bible, every child went to church, and when we still lived in Finland, my mother took us every week to a Bible study class. I thought she was very religious. Later she said she took us for the cookies and candy and the hot chocolate.

Who can like the Bible? God torments an innocent man because He likes to gamble and so He bets with the devil. He has someone else swallowed up by a whale so he can take a message to a city saying He is going to destroy it, and then He changes his mind and leaves the poor man sitting under a gourd in the desert.

And then there were the parables. If a man plants two rows of radishes, and something happens to them, and it goes on and on, and who knows what it means, and who cares about radishes? After a while, who cares about God? You read and read, and you get to the end, and He is busy destroying the world. Last trumpets, graves gaping open: oh, my mother's voice used to tremble when she read that.

So I would get exasperated. "That is more frightening than real life?" I would ask her. "Last night a fire in the tenement down the street burned up twenty-six people! In the hospital there is a woman so swollen up the doctors are afraid her skin will burst open! Look at all the stones in the graveyard. You think they had a good time getting in there?"

"How do you know these things?" she asked me. "How do you know about the swollen woman? Your father is talking again?"

"Everyone knows," I said. "You don't know anything. You stay in the house ironing."

"You are impudent," my mother said. "No dinner for you."

"Don't talk to your mother that way," my father said.

So now we were burying my father. A little time looking into the camera on your wedding day, thinking, Now life begins, and then a short ride to the cemetery, for once going in style, and that's the end of that. And in the middle, so much trouble, such a struggle! Who could take anything seriously? Who could take the trouble? So many stories, all different, all so fascinating to their owners, but all ending the same way. What did it mean?

If there was a God, He got bored writing His story of the world, just like a child who tells the story of a boy going out into the world, and the boy has many adventures, he meets talking birds, he slays dragons, and then the child gets tired, and at the bottom of the page, he writes, "And then I ran home."

God is any better? He starts all these stories, and then at the bottom of the page, He writes: "And then he died. And then she died. And then the sparrow died. The End." His favorite words: The End. Maybe He didn't have much imagination. Most people don't have it. Why assume God is some kind of artist? Maybe He is a statistician.

I was fifteen when my father died and already I was disillusioned. My mother complained: he didn't bring home enough money.

In the middle of the night, when they thought we were sleeping, he would climb on top of her. I hated the noise. I didn't say, as others did, When I grow up, when I get older and leave this house, it will be different for me. I will find a man and we will live happily. I didn't believe in that kind of happiness. Instead, I said, When I get older, I will have a lot of money and live in a nice house and never have to ask a man to take crumpled bills from his pocket and lay them on my kitchen table. I will have my own money. It will be neat and clean. If I iron anything, I will iron dollar bills or better yet, I will have only gold coins. You could do something about money. About the way people's lives went you could do nothing. I saw that early.

So Max died, and Charlie died, and I said, All right, I am worn out. That's enough for me. But I was still alive. I made more movies. Everywhere I went people followed me. I became very rich, I had the nice house and even a maid who thought I was crazy but who ironed the bills I left every night on the counter.

Then the war started, I made one bad movie, and Mr. Pinsky said, It's nothing, even wars come to an end, and then we send them your pictures and you are back on top. But now I had my excuse. "No, Mr. Pinsky," I said. "I think I will stop for a while."

"You're going to go home?" he asked. "You can't go home. At home it is all bombs and people dying. Every day I get bushels of letters, bushels, asking me to bring someone over here. Probably you get the same thing."

"I will just stop and look around," I said. "All the time in front of a camera, you don't see anything."

"Look around?" Mr. Pinsky asked me. "Listen, Miss Asta, I looked around. Everywhere the same thing goes on. In every room, an alarm clock, if you could hear them all together, you'd be a deaf woman. They get up, they stumble into things, on their faces they dash cold water. The men cut themselves with razors and curse. The women stir pots in the kitchen and try to smile when the man walks in on them. The children eat fast, they don't want to draw attention. They're tired, who thinks to look out the window to see if it's raining? They care if the sun is shining? So they're outside without an umbrella and they get wet and already they're mad and the day hasn't started. Then it's sweat, sweat, sweat and come home and yell at everybody. This is what you want to look around at? You didn't see this before you came here? That's what you see when you look around!

"When they look around, what do they look at? You! They save up their money and go to a movie theater. After ten minutes, believe me, you know all there is to know. Look around!

"But maybe there's something you want to do? You want to direct something? You want to write your own stories? Nothing we have here makes you smile, so maybe you should write your own. A family, some children, maybe, I could understand. You're not too old."

"Mr. Pinsky, please. I have absolutely no talents. What child would be happy with me? I can lie in bed for days. For weeks I wear the same thing, every night I wash it, hang it out, in the morning it's dry. Write a script! It takes me all day to write a letter! No, I want to look around. This is not life, this making faces for the camera."

"Learn the hard way!" he said, raising his voice. "Life is not such a wonderful thing!"

"I want to know what it is."

"I can tell you! It is family and money!"

"So," I said, "if you are right, you save me a lot of time."

• • •

"I want," I told Bertha Pinsky, "to be a human being. So I have to go out and learn how to do it."

"Look, darling," she said, "Charlie would have died no matter how human you were. From the first minute I knew him, he drank like a fish. Other people get away with it. That man who lived near him, he gets away with it. Charlie was a bad drinker. He said terrible things. And a man who goes on drinking when he's throwing up blood, when he's getting transfusions from other people, when the doctor tells him he's drinking rat poison, you're going to blame yourself?"

"I don't know, really," I said. "But somewhere there is more."

"When you find it, you let me know."

"If I don't find it, at least I will have looked."

"Yes, well, looking is a good thing."

"And along the way I will see interesting things."

"You will see other people looking, that's what you will see."

I sighed and picked at a thread in my skirt.

"Maybe you could look in some nicer clothes," Bertha suggested. "Maybe you could finish looking before the war's over and then you could come back and make some pictures. We're not put on this earth for a hundred reasons. For most people one is enough and most people don't find even one. It's true. You'll see."

"Yes, well, I will go home now," I said.

"And do what?"

"Put on a black wig and look at train schedules."

"A very exciting life," Bertha said. The corners of her mouth pulled down.

"And really, I am not so pretty anymore. Yesterday I saw some new portraits and I looked at them and said to myself, A cold-hearted bitch, and her face is drooping."

"Were you ever the prettiest?" Bertha asked me.

"Oh, yes, in the beginning, for four or five films, then I was beautiful. After that, people said how beautiful I was, but I knew what I was before so I didn't listen. For a short time, really, I was. I used to complain, you know. To be so beautiful, it's like being a freak. When it happens, you think you can keep it forever. To me it seemed important. 'Don't waste it,' Charlie said. You can save something like that up? It's not money you put in a bank. So that's over, that won't come back."

"You were put on this earth to act, don't tell me differently."

"Charlie used to say the ordinary housewife acts more and better than we do every day."

"She is not in front of a camera," Bertha said. "She knows her little audience." Her small fat hands were clamped together; her rings bit into her fingers.

"I will always come back and see you," I said.

"You will come back for the camera," she said. "They always do."

"SO," I SAID, "this is Tita Lu's house."

It was a small, square house built of cinder blocks, painted pink, its door aqua, its roof bright sheets of tin. Its small, square garden was surrounded by a white, wrought iron fence, and there was the gate, a gate like any other gate, the gate at which people always knocked. Inside the metal fence, flowers crowded one another, thick, fleshy-leafed flowers, their leaves as bright as their blossoms, purple and red striped, poinsettias everywhere.

"Oh, they are weeds, they grow wild here," Ivy said. "Lady Clare, if you don't want to stay in this house, Robert will come later and take you to a nice hotel."

"I want to stay right here. Here is fine," I said, and Ivy told me the mason had been in last week, fixing up the bathroom.

"Not for me, I hope," I said, but of course it was for me.

"Well," Ivy said, "things should be nice. You go look around. I'll make some tea."

Inside the house it was surprisingly cool, the rooms small and square, the ceilings low. The walls were thin panels nailed into place, dividing up the rooms.

"The rooms were larger," Ivy said, "but Tita Lu, she took in so many children, half the village grew up in here, and the more children, the more rooms. Come, I'll show you your room."

My room was in back of the living room, so small that when I sat on the bed my knees pressed against the chest of drawers. It was an old-fashioned chest of drawers, the veneer peeling from the corners, well-oiled, a lace doily on top of it. On the doily stood little plaster figures, shepherdesses, Chinese dolls whose heads, attached to their bodies by springs, nodded back and forth. Brilliant red and yellow plastic flowers in plastic vases meant to resemble crystal shadowed them. The room was painted a bright pink, and the shade at the window had been mended several times. The mattress was thin and sagged in the middle. I knew, before I lay down on the bed, that the pillows would be hard as rocks.

"These pillows will kill your neck," Ivy said, coming in. She took the pillow out of the case and stuffed the case with clean rags. "I should have brought a pillow," she said.

"No," I said. "Don't be silly." It was hot. I began to drift off. When my eyes opened again, I heard voices in the living room.

"Brother Beckwith, this is Miss Asta," Ivy said.

"Oh, very nice to meet you," he said. "This house is your house. You must take whatever you want." Then he and Ivy continued talking. "Bevon will be here shortly, and Mr. Griffith too. Here I am, sixty years a minister of the church, and because of me there are dead chickens hanging in the trees." He looked at me and started to laugh. "Oh, to you this is all nonsense," he said.

"In my country, too, they believe in witches," I said. "Of course they don't talk about it, but they believe."

"You have a plan?" he asked Ivy.

"We must fight magic with magic," Ivy said. "This is what we do. We use the old ways. We take a coffin, in it we put some earth from Tita Lu's grave, then we use Mr. Griffith's donkey cart, and we drive the carriage from the church to the cemetery."

"Oh, no, that will never work!" Brother Beckwith said. "Griffith's donkey, he will stop and bray at Granison's house and then *his* trees will be full of chickens!"

"It's true we cannot use Mr. Griffith's donkey. We must hire a good, obedient horse."

"Your father, he has a good one," Brother Beckwith said.

"It will work, don't it?" Ivy asked.

"God forbid the horse should stop," said Brother Beckwith.

"If my father drives it, it won't stop," Ivy said.

"Miss Asta, you understand any of this? On Green Island, the old ways still flourish. If a person dies because someone cast a spell, then when his funeral procession is on its way to the cemetery, the casket will refuse to pass the door of the evildoer. If men are carrying it, suddenly they cannot move. Oh, you should see them straining and sweating and they cannot move even one inch! Somehow if the dead person died and someone still owed him money, the casket will not pass that house and there it stays until that person comes out with the money. Then the coffin moves! Mischief, and more mischief!"

"So," said Ivy, "if the coffin goes without stopping from the cemetery to the church, then the chickens will come out of the trees."

"Because it means no one cast a spell," said Brother Beckwith.

"And if the horse stops?"

"If it stops, then you will come back to New York with me!" Ivy said, and they both laughed. "I'll go to my father's tomorrow, but Lady Clare, the road is very bumpy. You should stay here."

Oh, no, I said. I wanted to go.

On the way, we saw a cow dead on the side of the road, a vulture tearing at its side. We saw a newly slaughtered cow and the man who owned it sitting on top of it, waiting for someone to come and pick them both up. A sudden flock of white birds flew out of the forest and settled on the backs of the cows grazing in a field. A man carrying a machete, walking with his small son, suddenly plunged into the wall of greenery and disappeared.

I could live here, I thought. There is no history here.

We sat on Ivy's father's porch. The woman he lived with, young and fat, brought me a green coconut, cut the top from it, and told me to drink. A small boy brought me oranges from the trees in the yard and peeled them. Their skin was green.

"He likes engrafting things," Ivy said of her father. "Look over there. Plums grow on the apple trees."

"Oh, yes, oh, yes," said her father. "I am a lazy man. I want everything on one tree."

"Who is the little boy?" I asked. "A relation?"

"My son!" her father said, slapping his thigh and laughing. "Oh yes, oh, yes, he is mine, and the girl, there, she is too."

"I am a sixty-year-old woman and I have half-brothers and sisters young enough to be grandchildren," Ivy said, exasperated.

"Oh, she is still angry because I didn't live with her mother," he said. "I wanted to. I asked her to come back, but she refused. She doesn't believe it."

"That's not what Tita Lu said," Ivy said angrily. "She said it was your women!"

"Tita Lu was there?" he asked.

"There were no other women?" Ivy demanded.

"If you know so much, must I bother answering?"

"Last year I wrote him," Ivy said to me. "I asked him for a picture of my mother. You know what he did? He sent me a picture of him! 'You must imagine her standing next to me.' Very funny!"

Her father laughed. His left foot was propped up on a stool. "It swells up," he said to me. "But if I keep on the shoe, it comes down. So why must you have my horse? Oh, they think someone could kill off that teg reg, Tita Lu?"

"Don't talk against Tita Lu," Ivy said.

"Oh, she was one," her father said. "She came here to buy the child clothes and she bought so much, I worked two years paying for it!"

"And the time you flung an iron at me because your wife said I came home late?" Ivy said suddenly.

"The teacher always beats the best pupil," her father said, unperturbed.

"In his young days, anyone who bothered him, that person he threatened with his gun. 'I will fill your mouth full of lead,' he said. Oh yes, he had a gun. We didn't think he knew how to fire it, but he did fire it. He shot a dog killing our sheep."

"The old Chinaman's dog, Spike," said her father. "And after I brought him the body, they ate it."

"Ate it?" I said.

"Oh, yes, oh, yes," said her father.

"Well, we have to go," Ivy said. "Where's Robert? Looking at the chickens and the pigs?"

"Here I am," Robert called out. "A lot of ackee on these trees. You ready?"

"Only these two of all my children talk to me," her father said. "Since I took up with this young woman here, they don't want to know me. Well, a young woman makes you feel young, eh, Miss Asta?"

"You will drive the horse?" Ivy asked him.

"Oh, yes, oh, yes," he said.

"He will not stop?"

"He will obey me."

"You will come with the procession or you will stay in the house and rest?" Ivy asked me.

"Oh, yes, oh, yes," I said, imitating her father. "I wouldn't miss it."

All night long people knocked at the gate. "Everyone on Green Island knows everything before it happens," Ivy said.

The next day the procession began at six o'clock in the morning. It was still cool. The grass was still wet. Mist clung to the valleys and, as we travelled toward the village, it began climbing and thinning out. When we went through the town, no one was on the streets, but through the windows, we saw faces peering, eyes wide. Ivy was dressed in black, every so often dabbing at her eyes. Brother Beckwith, Ivy and I sat on a bench behind her father.

"If this horse stops, I will kill him and eat him," Ivy said to her father, who snorted and ignored her. When the horse passed a house, people came out and began following us. The horse reached the cemetery without stopping.

"So now what do you have to say?" Ivy asked them. No one said anything. They looked at their feet. "Now everyone can go home and eat their chickens," she said. "Chickens don't grow on trees."

I sat in the wagon and watched her. Here, on Green Island, she had the dignity and power of a queen. What was she doing in New York, taking care of me?

"Now Tita Lu is well buried," Ivy said as we began the drive back to her house. "Now I will make you ackee and codfish. Here," she said, pouring something from a milk bottle. "What is it? It is juiced soursop. You like it?" I said it tasted like buttermilk.

"My favorite drink," Ivy said, pouring herself a huge glass. In New York, she never ate, only a fish head, steamed vegetables. "This ackee, you have to be careful with it. You pick it at the wrong time, it's poisonous. I won't eat ackee from anyone. Every year someone goes up the eleven steps to the courthouse charged with poisoning. And the vendors at the side of the road, they pick it early and force it, and then you're in the hospital. When the pods open up, then the poisonous gas comes out."

"I like it here," I said. "The peace."

"Oh, there is trouble enough here."

"To stand at that door and look out over these fields to the mountains, the beauty is almost killing."

"It is beautiful, but hard to earn a living," Ivy said. "Tomorrow if you are not too tired, I will take you to see Miss Blue. You know about her, the town story teller. She looks at your hand, asks you questions, and tells you the story of your life."

"I know the story of my life."

"No, no. Remember what Anders said. All of us live out a story that came before us? That's the story she tells you."

"I would like to think there was a story, a pattern, anything, some kind of plan," I said. "You believe it, that idea?"

"Who knows?" Ivy said. "Who knows? Still, we can listen."

BECAUSE I WAS on Green Island, Charlie's funeral went on without me, but when I came back, Bertha described it to me. Apparently every woman in Hollywood was taking care of him before his death.

"It's a miracle he had time to die," she said. "That Gemma Rambova, she came to the funeral crying like a waterfall, a veil down to her heels, so naturally she tripped and fell across the casket. Horrible, who could believe it? And I, I was crying so hard, my Saul said, Stop, you were one of his women, too? That Rambova, first she crosses a country to go to the funeral of a dead actor, then she comes to this one with a broken heart, at night she turns into a vulture and circles the cemetery. I said to Saul, The woman is demented, don't hire her anymore! He said, These deaths are good for business.

"And all his ex-wives were there, that woman from Broadway, the one who coached him for talking movies, she came, his first wife and the two children, I don't think they knew who he was, she never let them come near him, she was there weeping, oh, I felt so sorry, for him, for everyone, I missed the Lower East Side."

"The Lower East Side?"

"A slum, that place we all came from," Bertha said. "And you, how are you?"

"The Ice Queen is frozen."

"Well, at least eat something," Bertha said.

"That cabinet, he still doesn't know about it?"

"The day he finds out, I move out of this house," Bertha said, drawing herself up, thrusting out her bosom. "A person must have some satisfaction."

2

I HAVE NOT LED such a wonderful life, I said to Miss Blue. Believe me, it is not something to boast about.

You will tell me everything, she said. Then I can tell you the story of your life, but when I do, I make changes in it. This is why they call me story tailor. I am a different kind of story teller than the usual kind.

Miss Blue was ancient, a mass of wrinkles, tiny black eyes like the eyes of a turtle. Her body was plump, bloated like a spider's, but her hands were large and flat, her fingers thin, like claws. *Don't be afraid of her*, Ivy said. *All it is is great old age.*

She was very old. Next to her I felt like a girl again. You know, I thought, she will not understand anything I say. Therefore I can tell her anything.

So I told her: first I was a girl, then there was Max, then I came to America, then there was Charlie, then I made more movies, then I stopped, then came all the wandering, then I was old, now I am older. So that is what it all came to. Her little apple-seed eyes narrowed until they disappeared, until I thought she was asleep. Anyway, I said, it was a nice dream: a lot of the time it was a nice dream.

"You're tired," said Miss Blue. "Lie down on this cot."

The cot was soft and comfortable; the air was soft and hot. "Go to sleep," she said. "Sister Ivy will come back for you."

"Why does everyone call her that?" I asked sleepily.

"The eldest daughter, she is called Sister, the eldest boy, he is called Brother."

"I thought it was something religious," I said. Fat bees buzzed at the windows. A big black fly flew over me, buzzing. In the corner of the room, a homemade bird cage covered with chicken mesh was filled with orange butterflies.

When I came to America and The Studio cast me again and again as the vampish woman, Max protested every time. "She does best playing the innocent young girl," he said, but no one was convinced, not even me, really. I was young, but how innocent was I? When I first met Max, before I met him, I was determined to like him, *to like him as much as was necessary.* And I did. And I was lucky. After a little time, I did like him as much as was necessary. In fact I loved him. But I was not good at loving. Perhaps no one is at that age.

And at that time what did I know of the world? When I lived at home I read silly romances that made me laugh, while my sister, who read the same books, wept and shivered as she turned the pages. The story I believed was the story that I saw going on every day in the one bedroom we slept in, in the kitchen all of us ate in. We read Bible stories, but what did whales and mountains and stone tablets have to do with me? In church, the pastor banged on his pulpit, waved his arms, and said crime was always followed by punishment. I never went home without feeling guilty. So when I came to this country, I was empty of stories.

Well, not entirely empty. In Europe, I had already made two films. In the first, I was a beautiful young girl married to an evil man, but my beauty redeemed a defrocked priest and we lived happily ever after. In my second, I was again a beautiful young girl who was going to sell her virtue for the price of meat to feed her starving father and sister, but at the last minute a virtuous young man rescued me and I

lived happily ever after. And off the screen, Mr. Pinsky had come to
Max and asked us to sign a contract and come to America and I was
so ambitious, I was so happy, I had no fears about life. Still, I believed
in happy endings, and why not? What had gone wrong in my life?
My father had died, but other people's fathers die.

Then came my first film here. In it, a girl with an ordinary heart
but great talent is plucked from her family and thrown into a world
she never knew existed. In my second film, a girl with great beauty
ruins the men around her, although, still, her heart is good. In my
third film, a great beauty ruins one man after another. In my fourth
film, the same thing. And I would study those scripts, over and over,
for months on end.

Other children had fairy tales, family stories. I had these scripts.
They were my stories. I believed them and this is what they taught
me: beauty tempts the soul and distracts it. The beautiful woman lives
in a dream of her own beauty. Her beauty is the poison in the poison
ring. Without intending to, she destroys the men around her, but still
she dreams on. Finally a man comes who wakes her from her dream
and then she regrets her past life and tries to undo it. But the past
cannot be undone, and the harder you struggle, the more you are like
the fly in a web. I could be great, I could be ambitious, I could even
be a queen, but if I loved, I would be undone.

This is what I learned: beware great love, that makes demands you
cannot meet, that destroys everything. If you stand out, the ordinary
world closes against you. What do the great dream of? Of ordinary
happiness that goes on and on because it asks so little, like a humble
cactus that lives almost on air, while the beautiful rose lets its petals
fall after two or three days. How curious, how wonderful, how busy
are the lives of the ordinary! Great unhappiness comes, but still the
ironing needs to be done, still the children need to be fed. What
romance there is in the rhythms of ordinary life, how beautiful is the
sound of the word *daily!* *Quotidian.* It took me two days to learn that
word. It was worth it.

I remember how bitter my mother was, how angry my father came
home, his nose red, his eyes bloodshot, no money in his pocket, how
bitter she was sitting there, looking out a window, seeing her life
suspended in the air before her. And those views from the windows
of trains, the back yards speeding by, the child in his snowsuit banging
on the back door with his mittened hand, the woman dragging the
bags of groceries up the wooden steps, one at a time. The romance of
shopping for groceries, thinking, If I buy this meat, this is what I will
make of it! How much everyone will like it! Instead of the usual

potatoes, I will buy yams and mash them. How pretty they will look on the table, so bright orange! Days going by, one just like another, people coming in and out, always the same people, what could be more perfect?

Either you should live that life, or you should die very, very young. When you die young, you miss the cancer scares, the disappointments, the deaths of others. Of course it is a selfish thing to want to die very young, but that was what I wanted, and then, when I saw I was not to have it, I envied everyone who envied me.

You may want anything, you *must* want things, but you must not get them. To get them is to go too far down the road and become lost.

You see, said Miss Blue, you are telling the story all wrong. Talent, greatness, these things confuse you. No story is about these things. All our stories are about animals who act like humans, and since they act like humans, they are human. During our festivals, people dress up in heads of beasts, the ram, the goat, big fangs, big claws. They run at the crowd! And the children, they jump back, screaming. You know there are children who are afraid of this festival all year, and when it comes, nothing can make them come out from under their beds? And then when it is night, the dancers lift off the animal heads and they are once again people.

So that is the only story there is, beasts who are human, humans who are beasts, sometimes one, sometimes the other, but no one knows that story, even on Green Island, where it is the only story there is.

I don't understand you, I said. There is more than one story.

No, no, there is only one. Think about it. Human selves turning animal, animal selves turning human.

No, there are other stories, I said sleepily.

Talent, it is seeing the animal self. Greatness, it is acting with the animal self. For the animals, passions are as real as bones. They sniff after them, they bury them, they dig them up again. For animals, all the rest of the world is decoration.

Max used to describe his movies in that way, I said. He called them myths.

Myths, passions, what is the difference? she asked me. You did ask Sister Ivy what is her favorite story? A story about a woman who marries a vulture, but she doesn't know it, she thinks she's married a man in a nice black suit. This is a story about marrying death. When the animal is not well, when he mistakes one thing for another, there can be such a passion.

I remember, I said, a café Max took me to in Berlin, very elegant, very decadent. In the middle of the dance floor was a boxing ring and boxers hitting one another. In one corner of the ring was a referee. In another corner, a violinist played a concerto. And all around the ring, the dancers turned and dipped and swirled. Max was such a good dancer. Well, he did everything well. He danced me around and around the boxers. One of them was taking quite a beating. His eye was black and swollen. He had a cut over his eye. They were both dripping with sweat, and there we were, the dancers, in our beautiful dresses, the men in their perfect tuxedos, and Max tilted me back, way back, and he said, "Isn't this perfect? The Germans *know.*"

What did Max mistake me for? What did Charlie? Or did they see in me what I am, a strong thing that lasts forever?

"The nice young man," I said, "he brought me the story of my life. It is called 'The Snow Queen.' A piece of glass lodges in my eye and after that I can only see things in their worst aspect."

"The piece of glass," she said, "that is seeing the animal inside the human. Once you see it, you cannot unsee it again. After that you are not innocent. Well, everyone should be able to see it but everyone cannot."

"He used to say, 'If you love a woman, you want to possess her.' "

"Who did?"

"Charlie. And I said, 'I will not be possessed. You can possess a lamp or a chair. No one has title to me!' "

"Some animals, when their mates die, they die too. Other animals kill their mates and then get hungry for another one. And then there are other animals who go from one den to another. And all these animals are the same as people. How long can Brother Beckwith live without Tita Lu?"

"He's lasted a long time," I said.

"He doesn't know she's dead. No, he doesn't know. On the day he knows, then he will die too."

I waited for her to say something more, but when she said nothing, I spoke again about my life.

After Charlie died, after my last movie, I began my wanderings. I thought: somewhere between this business of being a great star and the troubles of monotony there is another country. In that country you can say, my feet hurt. I have a toothache but I am afraid of the dentist. Someone's fist is knocking at my door and I am afraid of him. Will you see who it is? See how terrible I look, my hair is limp, it's too much trouble to pull myself together, let's stay home.

And all this would go on while everyone was there around me. There would be plenty of time. While I lay on my bed, I could think over what happened. I could learn to understand what it meant. Ordinary life could be studied. Why not? But of course it turned out I had no talent for that. What you must have above all is patience. People grow angry and cool off on their own schedules. They refuse to skip steps: you cannot say to them, All right, now we know we love each other, we throw everyone else out. No, they must think it over, they must decide how to do it nicely.

And I would say, "All right, then, I am going."

Or a baby. After a few months, I would have walked up to it and said, "All right, you have been a baby long enough. This is not interesting any longer! Now you will grow up!" Well, in a fairy tale you could do it, in a film you could do it. Snip, snip! One second the child is a newborn. In the next frame he is going off to school carrying his cricket bat.

So slowly I went back to my old ways. People I knew from my Studio days would invite me: Would I like to go to Switzerland in the summer? It was so cool there. The Bahamas in the winter? In February, one appreciated the sun as if for the first time. Of course we were all rich.

I decided to move to New York. Why? Because there I was closest to the ships that left for Europe. When my friends came from abroad, I would see them right away. And there I could forget everything. If there was a palm tree in New York, I had never seen it. There was an ocean nearby, an amusement park I'd seen in films, a parachute jump, a roller coaster, a ride called a Whip. If I wore my black wig and went there, who would recognize me? In the winter, there were blizzards, great drifts of snow blowing up against the parked cars, stopping everything. I would start again. I would forget Max, I would forget Charlie, I would forget my days in Hollywood, that place of eternal sun.

And for a while I was happy. Then I began to grow irritated. I walked the streets and no one noticed me. Weeks went by and no letters came describing absurd plots, absurd salaries, plans to bring me back to the screen. What? Had they forgotten who I once was?

"You see?" Bertha said on a visit to New York. "It is not so easy to grow a new skin. A habit becomes a habit exactly because you don't know you're getting it. Everyone looking at you, you have that habit. The excitement about the next movie, that's a habit. You're afraid it won't turn out, a habit too. You're disgusted with it? Another habit. You finish, you turn gloomy, another habit. Who can live without habits? Let me tell you, no one can do it. All those love triangles, you don't miss them?"

Love triangles?

"You and Max and Charlie, you and all those men in your movies," she said. "Triangles and more triangles. So what do you do all the time?"

What did I do? I visited people's houses. I read books. I walked, miles every day. Sometimes I went to parties, but always I came home early. "This is no life," Bertha said.

"I am waiting for something to happen," I said. "Something will come along. Usually it does."

Bertha snorted.

Then I was invited to a benefit dance. The war was still going on and the Red Cross needed money. I called a woman I knew and asked her where I could go to buy a dress without anyone seeing me. She made some phone calls and took me to a French designer's salon. I came home with a gray silk dress, its epaulets covered with spangles.

Now I had a dress, but my hair was hopeless. Long bangs hanging in my eyes like a horse's forelock, my hair uneven because I cut it at home. I would hold out a strand and cut off an inch or two inches, then another strand, and so on until it was short enough so that it didn't tickle my neck. I called another woman and asked her where could I go so a professional could get at my hair. She said she would make some calls and send someone to my house. So that night I went to the benefit dance looking like The Siren.

To tell the truth, I had grown bored with my life, bored with my stomach, bored with my tired feet. All right, so I lived like a lizard among other lizards, but how interesting was it? It was not interesting. And I was beginning to think it was a mistake altogether. They say if you amputate an arm or a leg, still you think it is there, and in the phantom limb the pains are even more intense than in the real one.

But to go back to the screen, to look with love on the face of a man I'd never before seen, to touch his skin as if the spirit it enclosed meant something to me, that I didn't want to do. It was there I always stopped. Perhaps it was my way of being faithful. Well, if it was, I was a strange sort of nun.

The dance was in the grand ballroom of a hotel. A lovely woman came up to me, touched me on the arm, and spoke to me in German. Just last month she had been in Sweden. They were showing some of my old films there, but she supposed I had seen them often enough. She stood on line in the snow to see *The Roses*, *The Siren*, even *Bitter Almonds*. Well, she said, it was so nice to meet me, but she was going home early, she was always so tired.

"I like tired people," I said. I saw myself, in Charlie's pajamas, padding through his house, barefooted on his tile floors. He was still asleep. In those days, I was up before the sun. "You must come visit me."

She looked surprised but I gave her my address.

"Who is that woman?" I asked a friend who was standing near me. "Janine LaCoste," she said.

"And does she do something or just stand around looking elegant?"

"She's a famous painter, the daughter of a famous painter, the one you like, the one who paints people sleeping in forests under full moons."

"Janine LaCoste," I said. "Is she married?"

"To Henri LaCoste, the financier. Before the war, he bought an old town in the South of France and he's going to fix it up."

"He bought a whole town?"

"A whole town, so when his friends come to stay, or when they retire, they can move in and live together. Well, why not? With his money, he can do what he wants. But, you know, it's nice he needs a whole town. A man that rich, often he doesn't have any friends."

"Who knows if they are real friends?" I asked her.

"They say he has the gift for friendship," she said.

"The gift for friendship," I repeated.

Janine and I became good friends. She took me with her when she shopped. Once again I had clothes. One day she called and I said, "Janine, I need shoes," and she said, "I'll come by in an hour." We went to store after store, and finally I found a pair of shoes I liked. "I will wear them," I said to the salesman. But late in the afternoon, the shoes began to pinch. "I will take them back," I said. "They hurt my feet."

"Anna," she said, "you can't do that."

"They hurt my feet," I said. "I must take them back."

Her car took us back to the shoe store. The clerk called the manager and the manager was very nice about it. "Really, that is not right," Janine said. "These people must eat."

"If my shoes are standing between them and bankruptcy, they are not in very good shape," I said.

"Well, come home and meet my husband," Janine said. "He's in town for a few days." And so I went.

Henri LaCoste was tall, slender and elegant. His face was long, his forehead high, his lower lip full, his upper lip narrow. He wore a thick, neatly trimmed moustache and his eyebrows were heavy. Above all, he was European. Immediately I felt at home with him. I remember thinking, It is not wise to flirt with him. How many friends do you have?

Nevertheless, by the end of the evening, he seemed enchanted.

"Janine," he said, "let me show Miss Asta the paintings in the drawing room," and he took me off to look at them.

"Oh, they are beautiful," I said, "all these people asleep in a forest. If I had dreams, this is what they would look like."

He asked if I didn't dream, and I said no, I slept so badly I had no time to dream. "No time to dream!" he exclaimed, laughing. "For that everyone makes time!"

"I will have time enough one of these days," I said, and he looked at me, surprised, and said, "A woman of your type lives to be a hundred."

"And what is a woman of my type?" I asked, insulted.

"A woman who knows the world but takes offense when it is pointed out to her," he said.

"And why should such a woman live to be a hundred?"

"Because she is thin and eats well," he said.

"Mr. LaCoste," I said, "you are not interested in my health."

"Certainly I am interested. It is so much harder carrying on a friendship with an invalid."

"Suddenly we are friends?" I asked him. I understood I was flirting. The old gestures were coming back, the parted lips, the intense stare, what Max called the *flickering*, anger, then interest, then anger. "Then perhaps you can help me with something."

"With what?"

"Income tax."

"Income tax!"

"Oh, I keep such terrible records, and my lawyer on the West Coast, he is senile, so next week I must go into their offices and probably they will take everything I own."

"I doubt that," he said.

"But you will have a look?"

"It sounds as if it will take a great deal of time."

"Possibly it will."

"Then I should start soon. Tomorrow morning? And we will meet Janine for lunch?"

"She will not mind?" He raised his eyebrows and smiled at me.

When we returned to the dining room, Janine was pouring espresso into small cups. It did not seem to me her smile was strained.

I began to see Henri. He helped me with my taxes, he gave me advice on what to do with my money. He would bring bank balances showing how my money had grown in two months, three months, six months and, like a child, I would squeal with delight. Sometimes we would spend a few hours at my apartment. Other times we would walk about the city. When he was out of town, Janine and I went shopping or we went for walks. In the winter, she and I walked to Rockefeller Center where we watched the ice skaters in the rink. Occasionally we went to Central Park and rented a rowboat and I always rowed. I was the one with the strong back and arms.

One day we were walking and I stopped in front of an antique store window to look at a pair of Chinese dogs. "Do you think they are mahogany?" I asked her. "They're very nice."

"Of course," she said, "there are only two of them, but there are three of us."

"I wonder if they are very expensive," I said. "He might come down. They say the market is very bad."

Janine said, "Do you have any particular plans or what?"

"They have ivory teeth. I like it better when they have carved wooden teeth."

"Because, naturally, I intend to keep my husband," she said.

"I wonder if they come from Thailand."

"Once you appreciate that, perhaps we can come to a better arrangement. After all, there are only so many hours in the day."

"I will just ring the man's bell," I said. The shopkeeper unlocked the door. "How much for the dogs?" I asked him. He named a price. "Oh, that is a lot," I said. "One of them has a crack."

"A crack?" the shopkeeper asked. "What crack?"

"Oh, they always have a crack," I said.

"I know you," he said.

"Yes," I said. "Well."

"Make an offer," he said.

"Oh, I don't like to make offers," I said. "I offer too much, you cheat me. I offer too little, you are insulted."

"Two thousand dollars," he said, coming down a little.

"Well, you know, I think I'll carry one home," I said. "Janine, I will make you a present of the other one."

"That's very nice of you," she said. Her voice was chilly.

And so we became a threesome. At first I liked it. Always there was someone there, and a man, no matter how wonderful, well, you cannot talk to him the same way you can talk to a woman. And in bed I liked it too, three bodies, although in the beginning, when the playing began, either Janine or I would leave. But then we stayed together, all three of us. It was sinful. I was once again becoming a child.

So time went by, five years, six years, and one day I opened my eyes and thought, What is she doing here? Really, I don't like it.

"Remember what I told you," Janine said. "I intend to keep my husband."

"Yes, fine," I said.

Two weeks later Henri and I left together for Spain. "And Janine? She doesn't mind?" I asked him.

"I didn't tell her," he said.

But of course she knew, possibly not immediately, but pretty soon. Then she and I began to avoid each other. "I don't know what he sees in you," she said one day. "You are empty-headed and selfish. You feed on people."

"Oh, yes, but I eat very little."

Another time she said, "He admires you because you were a poor girl who made up your mind to escape and you did it. But still, when you think of it, you have nothing of your own."

"I like to rent," I said. "Let the owner have the headaches." She said I was vulgar and vile.

Another time she said, "Once you were pretty but now you are not. And those ridiculous arched eyebrows drawn on with pencil!"

"Really, I was never so pretty," I said, "but what can I do about it? He follows me like a duck."

Of course, soon we were not speaking. Great efforts were made to keep us apart. "I have no interest in fighting," I told Henri. "I dislike violence."

Then he and I went everywhere together. People said it was like a marriage, and it was. He looked after my affairs. My cook looked after his meals. If we went to a party in the winter, and my shoes were thin, his driver carried me to the car. We went to Switzerland and visited Elska. We played tennis in the mountains. When he skied, I stayed home and read.

"You are satisfied?" Elska asked me, and I said really, it took very little to satisfy me, but to tell the truth, sometimes I missed Janine, watching her paint her strange canvases, walking with her, asking her advice on dresses, all sorts of things. I even watched old movies of mine with her and she said the most interesting things. She combed that long black hair of hers in such fascinating ways and she could wear a towel and look elegant. I could have learned a lot from her, I said.

"I think you are satisfied," Elska said. "You know, last week I heard the most ridiculous rumor."

"Oh, tell it to me!" I said.

"Someone told me that you married Max Lilly in Berlin before you came to America, to protect him, so no one would know he was interested in men, and that's why you never married Charlie. Well," she said when she saw my face, "I told you it was ridiculous."

"What is ridiculous is the things people dream up," I said.

"Well, naturally I said it was pure silliness."

"You should not deny anything," I said. "Then people will think you know something and you won't have any peace."

"You are not angry?" she asked me anxiously. When friends gossiped about me, that was the end of it. I never spoke to them again.

"Of course I am not angry," I said. "But be careful. Who wants to spend her time talking about me?" After a while, I said, "This thing with Henri, it is fine. It is not like it was with Max, or even with Charlie, but it is not bad either. We have the same interests, the same sense of humor, which is to say we neither one of us has any. And there are times I look at him and I think, I know every inch of that body. Every inch of that body is familiar, there is no other body I know as well, and I think, at my age, that is love. Maybe there are other kinds, but for me this is love. If he's late, I don't suffer. If he's with someone else I'm not jealous. Really, it is very nice."

"Is he a man or a candle in the dark?" Elska asked me.

"Is there a difference?" I asked her.

So now I lived with a married man I had taken from a very good friend and my conscience was untroubled. I thought, Well, it is all right, tomorrow he will go back to her, and meanwhile I am happy. Finally I am happy.

I had learned an important trick: do something slowly enough, whatever it is, and you can get used to anything. You can forget you disapprove of yourself. You can learn to hold your head just so, so that the face of the victim never comes into view. Of course this is selfishness and selfishness is close to evil, but now you are used to what you are accustomed to.

And so, when I heard the terrible thing, at first I was unmoved. One morning, Janine awakened, got up, ate her breakfast, and when she sat down in front of a mirror to brush her hair, her face was entirely black and her eyes red and gorged with blood, just as if, in the middle of the night, she had hanged herself. Her maid said she looked at herself and asked, "How did I let this happen? This woman has taken my husband!" Then she lay back down on her bed. In a few hours her face had returned to normal, but from that day forward she told everyone she spoke to that I was an evil woman, a witch. She took to wearing a heavy cross. In the morning, before she got out of bed, she would scream for her maid. "Look at my face! What color is it?" and until the maid could assure her that she was her usual color, she would not get up.

I heard the story. It frightened me. For nights I did not sleep. Then I began to sleep longer, then a little longer, and finally through the night. Eventually I slept very well.

So five years passed, then ten, then fifteen. From friends I learned that Janine crossed herself whenever my name was mentioned. One night, Henri called from Antwerp and said he would be back in the morning, probably by ten o'clock. Fine, I said, I would buy an extra roll. But ten o'clock came, then eleven, then twelve, and still he was not there. I called the airport. His plane had been on time. It was a cold autumn day. At any moment the season would slide into winter. At that instant people were digging through their closets, dusting off their winter coats. Who could I call? Not Janine. So I wrapped up the rolls and went for a walk through the park.

The last of the yellow leaves were rustling on the branches. Dry brown leaves crinkled underfoot. The usual lovers sat on the usual boulders, huddled together against the cold. Every species of dog was out, their owners taking them for a walk. The dogs were excited and leapy, feeling the winter.

When I got home, the phone was ringing. "Oh, hello, Elska," I said. "Your son is in the city?"

"You haven't seen the papers?"

"No, I never touch the papers until dinner. Why spoil the whole day? What is in them?"

"There's something about Henri."

"Henri is dead?"

"He died on the plane."

"Of what?"

"Of a heart attack."

"So," I said. "Janine will not let me into the funeral."

"You must come here," Elska said.

AFTER THAT, I told Miss Blue, I began to wander again, and then I grew too old to wander, although people always drifted in to see me, and then I put a sign in the basement apartment of my building, saying *Woman Wanted*, and Ivy came to work for me, and now here I was. So that is my story.

"I wish I'd seen these movies you speak of," said Miss Blue. "I've never seen a movie in my life. Ivy's mother, she was crazy about movies, and Tita Lu, she was, too. Mer—that was her mother—she said she was once an extra in a movie, but did they ever make a movie on Green Island? I don't think they did."

"Oh, yes, once they did. *Bitter Almonds.*"

"The almonds here are sweet," Miss Blue said.

"Lady Clare!" Ivy called from outside. "You are ready to go home?"

3

DID I WANT to go home? Home was freshly painted. Signs of the last fifteen years of life were obliterated, the black marks on the wall above the settee where I pressed my slippers when I was so ill five years ago, the round mark on the wall, like a dark halo, where I used to lean my head when I made phone calls, all gone. Paint purifies. It also keeps secrets and for so many years I've kept my secrets. This is something you should do for your friends: keep their secrets. In the end, perhaps this is all you can do for them.

But here I was on Green Island, a place almost no one had ever heard of, talking to a woman who lived in the forest above Cinnamon Bay, a town almost no one on the island knew, and I thought, whatever I say here will stop here. When I was young, and then not so young, how I envied the Catholics who had their priests to whom they could confess! But then I thought, After all, the priests are born like everyone else. They have families. When they go home, they may talk about what they hear. Certainly they talk to other priests. So nothing can be kept secret after all.

But here, who would Miss Blue talk to? Ivy herself told me that talking to Miss Blue was like talking to the river. What you told her, all that was carried out to the sea, and there the fish ate one word, then another. *Go talk to the fishes,* my mother used to say when she was tired of our chattering.

"No," I told Ivy, "I don't want to go home so fast."

"Oh," she said. "You want to talk more to Miss Blue."

I said she was a very interesting woman. How old was she? Ivy said no one knew how old she was, so that meant she was very, very old because people on Green Island lived to great old age. She was well, well past one hundred.

"My brother will take you back tomorrow," Ivy said.

"So," Miss Blue said, "now you are ready to tell me your secrets."

"Well," I said, "they are not so remarkable, but they are terrible to me."

"If a secret is not terrible, who would keep it?" Miss Blue asked me.

EVEN BEFORE I MET Max Lilly, I knew his reputation. It was said he liked men and was as happy, if not happier, in their company than he was in women's. At the Academy, the students sat around café tables and talked about Max Lilly and Erik Grissom. "Really, they are a couple," someone said, and someone else said, "Really, he is part of a great many couples."

So when I met Max, I thought, What must I do so that he will like me? For a time it seemed that I must obey him, I must become what he wanted. And he used to say, She is like clay! I can make anything of her!

Then things changed. I began to care for him. Of course he expected me to care for him. Men who are spoiled by their mothers always do. But I wanted to do it, and then I began to know what he had grown to mean to me.

When we sailed for New York, Erik Grissom sailed with us. He had gone ahead, made a film, and returned to Sweden to make the crossing with us, but he stayed out of sight, and when the ship came in, he was far from the photographers. No one knew he was there. Already there was friction between the two of us. A week before we boarded the train for California, Erik left. When we saw him off at the station, Max went to get a cup of coffee, and Erik said to me, "After a year here, I'm going home. Then you'll have him to yourself. Then you'll see how you like it!" His voice was poisonous. "Anyway," he said, "I thought you were interested in girls." I didn't answer him.

Everything about sex embarrassed me. When I was in Germany, a great actress I worked with helped me to meet the famous German directors. Of course she and I were very close and of course other people heard about it or guessed. So from the beginning, I felt I had secrets to keep, my secrets, Max's secrets.

And then I made *The Roses* and became so famous, I was frightened: why should the public know the truth of my life, of Max's life? And then I fell crazily in love with Charlie, and there was so much trouble, so many babies I put an end to, and I thought, What will happen if people know? From the beginning, I was so secretive, so afraid of other people's eyes. Even now, I lock my journals in a safe. People might think, Oh, she has a lot of money, a lot of jewelry, that's what's in her safe, but what's in there are the ten notebooks.

The jewelry, that lies all over the tops of the tables or I stuff it in my drawers. When Janine still spoke to me, she said, "You know, Anna, this is very smart. No one will ever steal it. Everyone will think it is costume jewelry. Look at the size of these stones! Who gave you this? The King of England?"

"His prime minister," I said. "During the war."

"Of course during the war," Janine said. "Of course the prime minister."

"So these," I said, "are my secrets."

"They are not such terrible secrets," Miss Blue said.

"Yes, but for me they were terrible. I was in love with Max, he was in love with me, but he was also in love with Erik, and who knew who I was in love with? And he was so much older, almost twenty years older, but always, always I thought we would end up together! Then there I was, not sure how I felt about men *or* women and suddenly I was this great goddess. Then the glass splinter blew into my eye and then I saw the worst in everything, and you know, I don't think I see differently yet. So," I said, "now you know everything. What do you think of me?"

"Just another person," Miss Blue said, her voice bored. "Just one more person on the face of the earth."

A great stone rolled from my shoulders. *Just another person on the face of the earth!* So I had succeeded!

"Now you are happy?" Miss Blue asked me. "Good. I like to see people happy. Of course if they aren't happy, I like them too."

"This life," I said. "It is so funny. Walter Drake, an old friend from the movies, he died when some young kids stole some porch furniture and he chased them. He had a heart attack. Pierre Lapidou, the famous director, he retired to France and he spent almost fifteen years translating mysteries from English into French. They found him dead, his head on some trashy novel, right on the paragraph about how a dead man was found slumped over his book and everyone thought it was a heart attack, but really he was poisoned, so they did an autopsy. The police read the page, and poor Mr. Lapidou, they cut him up.

"Eleanor Ralston, she was so famous, she got so drunk all the time they put her in a home but she got out and went up and down the highway calling, 'Murray! Murray!' And for all those years her husband lived, they took so much trouble to hide his Jewishness, so she never called him anything but Mark. Well, time passes. It turns everything to comedy. Tragedy is for the young."

"Is that so?" asked Miss Blue.

"Lady Clare!" Ivy called. "Are you ready to go home?"

I was ready.

THE DOORBELL RANG, and I thought, That's the trouble. Once someone finds his way here, he can always find his way back. But maybe it was only a Jehovah's Witness. Then Ivy would stand in the doorway discussing theology with him. I used to stand behind the door and listen, asking myself, What are they talking about? Everyone knows what we see is everything there is.

All morning I have been sitting in my room looking at the bare apricot walls, wondering at the creaminess of the color, admiring the places where the apricot meets the white border of the ceiling or the woodwork. I can pass hours in this way. Really, these days I am so ambitious I am like a talking radish. Now I hear voices in the living room. Soon Ivy will come in and tell me someone is here to read the electric meter and I will say, "I don't like strangers in here. Let them send an estimated bill."

Instead, Ivy comes in and says, "The nice young man is here." She knows I don't want to see him anymore but she gives me a look which means, If you don't want to see him, I will have tea and cookies with him in the kitchen, so I get up and go into the living room with her, still wearing my robe. Resisting her is not worth the effort. If she stands here a few seconds longer, she'll pay too much attention to the paintings stacked against the wall and decide it's time to hang them up again.

The nice young man smiles shakily at me. His mouth trembles a little. He says, "I brought you another book," and I say, "Really, I don't want any more books. They're too upsetting. Who knows what will be in them? I like those afternoon TV shows, what do you call them?—the ones that go on for thirty, forty years, where everyone marries everyone else because they can't keep hiring new actors, so they try every possible, what do you call it, permutation? A nice mathematician taught me that word. You don't watch these shows? You should. They're very soothing. How can anything surprise you on such a show? For months and months they discuss what's going to happen, and then for months and months, it happens, and then for months and months, they talk about what did happen: it's wonderful. That's what I should have done, you know, not those movies. After five minutes in a film, everyone had to know all about you. At least one big thing had to happen. If real life were like that it would be a train wreck! Now, young man, you see I live even more slowly than those shows and anything that speeds things up, well, that thing I must get rid of."

The kitten, as if to mock me, runs by, runs back, leaps on my lap, streaks across the carpet, and hangs from the curtain.

"Well, of course that animal, he is safe from me," I say. "He is really Ivy's cat. Occasionally it is nice to see something move so fast, especially when it can't talk. So," I say, smiling, "tell me why you come to visit me. Really, you want to ask me why I left the movies."

"No, I don't," the young man says.

"Oh, you do," I say. "Everyone does. Do you know something? The year I left the movies, Mary left the movies, Eleanor left the movies, and at the time, they were more popular, but it's me they make the fuss over. The dust dies down, they show something on television and it starts. So that's what you want to know."

"Of course," he says, "I'm curious. It's only natural."

"But what happened wasn't natural," I say. "All right, I made one bad picture. The reviews were terrible. Everyone knows about them."

"Look," says the young man, "there's no reason to talk about it. Really, everyone knows why you quit."

"Oh," I say. "Why?"

"You were getting older. You looked into your mirror and you saw a wrinkle or something. Your vanity was hurt and when the reviews came out, you thought, 'If I stop now, people will remember me the way I was. I don't want to end up playing grandmothers.' "

"You don't know anything," I say. "Only a year before, I made *Double Trouble* and I was not old! How can you get old in less than a year? No, no one knows what happened. It was a shattering. You've seen a mirror hit the floor and shatter? That's what happened to me."

"A breakdown?" he asks me.

"Maybe it was a breakdown," I say. "I don't know what it was, really. I never think about it. I went around telling everyone I knew I wanted to start again, on my own, find people who knew I had a stomach. No one knew what I was talking about. I didn't either. You know those nice little toys they make for children? Little animals with a key in their sides? You wind them up and the animals twirl around, they wag their tails, they walk across the tables, and then they wind down and they stand there until someone winds them up again. So, after that movie, something happened, I lost my key. Well, you know I was never very good at moving around. Always I wanted to sleep, to sit in a quiet room. But before, there were people who would come over and see this little animal sitting on the table top and they would set me going. Well, you can't live on top of a music box forever so I got down. That's all it was."

"And you are happy you got down?"

"Well really," I say, "who is happy in this world?"

"But happier than you were before?"

"It takes so much energy to be anything," I say, "and really I never had much energy. Always I was tired."

"My mother says you walked her off her feet," he says.

"Sometimes I am not tired in my body, but always I am tired."

"You don't get tired?" he asks me. "Of being tired?"

"Oh, it is too late to change," I say. "Really, I don't mind. I am quite used to myself really. So I accomplished what I wanted. Yes, that makes me happy."

"You don't get bored?"

"Young man," I say, "at my age, waking up in the morning is enough excitement for me. And who said acting was so interesting? You sit there for hours waiting for the light to be right. A whole day preparing, and then three minutes in front of the camera. This is an interesting way to spend time?

"When I came to look at this apartment, that was interesting. Would they rent it to me or wouldn't they? You think, Well, certainly they'd want to have her, but landlords don't think like ordinary human beings. They think, an actress, noise, commotion, drinking, scandal, complaints from the tenants, well, they're just like people were fifty years ago. An actress! My God, raise the drawbridge! Anyway, now I am tired. And I have something important to do. You know what it is? I'm going into my room and look at my walls. See how bright and clean it is in here, like a sunset! It doesn't last, not with the pollution here! So while it lasts, I'm going to look at it. Really, I am quite crazy."

• • •

"You were quite nice to that young man," Ivy says.

"Someday," I say, "I will do a perfectly unselfish thing. Then I will die in peace."

"Oh, no one thinks you are as bad as you think you are!" Ivy says.

"Well," I say, "they are wrong."

The woman gets up from her bed. She goes to the window. Someone has stolen my body, she says. She touches her wrist, but she doesn't feel her own fingers. If I am not real, she asks herself, what am I? She looks out the window. There on the lawn she sees herself walking up and down. What am I going to do now? she asks herself. How can I get her to come back? Why should she want to come back? Into this terrible, boring story that is my life? How can I tempt her back? She sits on the edge of her bed. I will let her go, she says. She lies down on the bed, and her heart slows. In the morning, when the doctor comes, he says, she died in her sleep. It was a good death. She died happy.

4

SO MUCH TIME PASSED and then still more time passed. If Max could have been here to see the machines people have now! You can send a letter across the world in a few seconds and someone can send one back a few seconds later. They could be around the corner. Think how Max could have ordered people around with machines like this! No one adds or subtracts anymore. They have computers. Before we had Mr. Pinsky. Well, things change.

For example, lately Ivy is not well. I threaten her. If you die before me, I say, I will have you bronzed and they will use you as a garden ornament. Her family wants her to come home and live with them, but she says she is used to it here. After so many years of living with me, she is also part radish.

Yesterday I hired a woman to take care of both of us, but I said to her, You are here to teach me painting. You understand? Only when Ivy is asleep can you clean anything. Really, this is a hard job. If she sleeps at night, you must clean at night, never in front of her.

You must keep an eye on her but you cannot notice anything is wrong with her. When she talks about Green Island, when she thinks she lives in Cinnamon Bay, you must not correct her. If she is unhappy, you must come and get me and if I grumble, you must ignore me. You really want a job working for two difficult old women? She said she wanted the job. Jobs are not so easy to come by. The papers say times are bad.

Once Ivy told me this story her father told her.

A young boy has murdered someone, but the judge tells his mother, If you can tell me a riddle, and I can guess the answer, then your son will swing from a tree, but if I cannot guess, then your son will go free.

This is the riddle the mother told:

> Love, I hold fast in my hand,
> Love I stand upon,
> Love I sit upon,
> Love I see
> But Love cannot see me.

The judge could not find the answer. The boy went free. Here is the answer to the riddle: The mother said, "I had a dog named Love. I killed that dog and skinned him and from the skin I made a pair of gloves that I held fast in my hand. I made a pair of shoes that I stood upon and I made a cushion that I sat upon. I see Love, but Love cannot see me because Love has died."

At first I thought, No one could guess the answer to this preposterous riddle, but now I think, There is only one answer to all riddles and it is always the same answer. The mother was a wise woman, the judge a foolish man. True, true, all of it. Love is a dog. Love is the thing we stand upon. Love is the thing we see when it can see us no longer. If Love is anything, it is always the mother.

What is wrong with Ivy? She is almost sixty, not very old, really a spring chicken. Is it her kidneys, her bone marrow? Whatever it is, the doctors can't do anything about it. Still, they can keep me going, a useless old woman who doesn't have anybody.

One day I'm not going to wake up, Ivy said to me, and you'll be so frightened, you'll run away. I'm not going anywhere, I said. Well, one morning it will happen, she says again.

Today is the nurse's—the painting instructor's—day off. I go into Ivy's room and she doesn't wake up right away. This is not usual. Then she opens her eyes and looks at me, leaning on my stick, leaning over her. So what is wrong with you? I ask her.

Oh, she says, I don't think I'll get up again.

Of course you will get up again! I say. Don't be so silly! You have that wonderful house on Green Island.

No, she says, I will not get up again.

Here, drink some water, I say. I hold up her head while she drinks.

Where is Tita Lu? she asks me. She went to help that woman up the hill? You know how selfish that woman is? For Christmas, she gave Tita Lu a dress, it was so old you could see through it, so I took the dress and I said, Here, put it in front of the door for the dog to lie on, and the woman came and she said, "You like the dress?" and Tita Lu said in her high voice, "Yes, I like the dress." And then the woman saw the mat and how her eyes popped and we started in laughing, and Tita Lu, she said later, That was not nice. You know how that woman stays. So Tita Lu is up the hill with her again?

Of course she is there.

Well, she will be back soon.

I get up to call the doctor, but Ivy says, Don't go out there. Don't go away. So I sit back down on the bed. Well, what will I do without you? I ask her. You're not going anywhere.

Granny, she says, I will brush your hair. She strokes the back of my head with her hand. I did a good job? she asks. Oh, I say, a very good job. These plaits, I cannot manage them, she says. Well, it is very hard, plaiting hair, I say.

Probably we both fall asleep because when I next open my eyes the afternoon sun is streaming in the window, a real summer sun. It is hot in the room. Neither of us likes air conditioning. I go over to the window and look out. The people on the street are hardly dressed, little shorts, little halters. A long time ago I dressed like that and everyone shouted, Put on some clothes!

Mer! Ivy says. I turn around. The light is behind me so of course to her I am just an outline, a black figure against the light.

Oh, yes, here I am, I say.

You know how long I have been looking for you? she asks.

A very long time, I say.

My whole life.

Well, now you have found me. Here I am.

Miss Blue said I would find you, she says.

Miss Blue was right.

Miss Blue said this is the oldest story. Always at the end, I find you.

Of course you find me, I say. I'm your mother. My name is Mer.

Mer? she says. You will sit here and say a prayer?

A prayer?

I know the Lord's Prayer. Once I learned an Egyptian prayer. I sit down on the bed and put my hand on Ivy's head. She is not hot. Probably she is just slowing down. How can she slow down? Never in her life has she been tired. Never in her life has she been discouraged. Never did she feel sorry for herself, not for more than a few seconds. Everything good about me I learned from her. There should be dispensations. Someone like this should live forever.

Mer? she says. You are still here?

Where else would I be? I begin to recite the Lord's Prayer.

That is a nice prayer, Ivy says. I recite it again and again. Then I think she is not breathing, and I begin to say the prayer I hope I will have time to say:

"Grant that I may enter into the land of everlastingness. Let not my body become worms but deliver me. I pray thee, let me not fall into rottenness even as thou dost permit every god and every goddess and every animal, and every reptile to see corruption when the soul hath gone forth from them after their death. And when the soul departs, a man sees corruption and the bones of his body rot and become wholly stinkingness, the members decay piecemeal, the bones crumble into a helpless mass, and the flesh becomes fetid liquid, and he becomes a brother unto the decay which cometh upon him, and he turns into multitudes of worms, and he becomes altogether worms and an end is made of him and he perishes in the sight of god even as doth every god and every goddess and every feathered fowl and every fish and every thing whatsoever. Let life come from its death and let not decay caused by any reptile make an end of me and let them not come against me in their forms. Do not thou give me over to those slaughterers.

"I shall not decay, and I shall not rot, and I shall not putrefy, I shall not turn into worms, and I shall not see corruption. I shall have my being, I shall germinate, I shall wake up in peace. My intestines shall not perish. I shall not suffer injury, mine eyes shall not decay, the form of my visage shall not disappear; mine ear shall not become deaf, my head shall not be separated from my neck, my tongue shall not be carried away, my hair shall not be cut off, mine eyebrows shall not be shaved off, no baleful injury shall come upon me. My body shall be stablished, and it shall neither fall into ruin nor be destroyed on this earth."

When I feel her hand, it is still warm. So I pick up her telephone and call her son. I say, Your mother is dying. She said she did not want me to bother you, but I think it is your decision. He says he will be right over.

I detach her hand from mine and creep out of the room and unlock the front door so that when her children come they can walk in. Then I go back to her bed and sit down. Once again I pick up the phone and call the doctor. I will be right over, he says.

When he comes, he says she may wake up a few times, but he thinks she is ready to go to sleep for a long while. He tells me to go to my own room and go to bed, but I say, No, I will stay here. She may wake up and look for me. I want to be here when the breath goes. So we sit and keep the vigil.

Her children arrive. Of course they are crying. I move away from the bed and sit in a chair near the window, but her son says, No, come back. If she wakes up, she will look for you. Her daughter kisses me.

So this is the end of the story, I think. All her life she has looked for her mother and now she has found her. This is a story with a happy ending. Her children will grow old and die and no one will remember her, but everyone comes to this. She has mattered in the world. Who knows where the effects of her life will come to an end? This is a better death than Max's. This is a better death than Charlie's. I would like to think we get the death we deserve, but of course in this world there is no justice. What will my own death be like? *My visage will live on. Part of me will not decay. No, there is no justice. I do not deserve to be preserved.

I sit in my chair, thinking these thoughts, in the enormous quiet, and I think, Finally, the world stops. And when I listen carefully, I think I can hear the sound of the earth spinning through space and another sound I cannot quite place, like a giant scissors, snapping. But the sound the world makes, it is the sound of a woman's taffeta slip, stirring. And I try to summon them up, all the missing ones, and I see how little of them I remember, and I think, This is what it comes to, a few ashes, a few bright pieces. And then I remember what Max taught me. Anna! One image is all you need! The rest is dross! Garbage! The setting for the jewel in the ring! Who keeps everything? Not even a mad pack rat! You think a pack rat is happy? One day he runs out of the crowded house and looks for an empty nest! Who can live in the middle of all that rubble! But I cannot yet believe this, not even now, so I suppose I will never believe it. So much life and for what? Well, who knows the answers to these questions? And then I think, I have sent my image spinning out into the world and it has pleased people. Is that something to be proud of? And Max says—oh, now I can hear his voice—You know you should be proud of it! I was proud and I am not even you! You should be proud of it if only because I found you! And then, suddenly, as I sit still, I hear Anders (where is Anders?) saying, *Just here we'll change the story,* and a great peace settles upon me, and I grow sleepy, as if I were falling asleep in snow, except I am warm, very warm. And then I hear the sound again, the sound of a taffeta slip rustling, and when I look up, I see a woman bent to the ground and I know she is counting grains of salt, and I say to her, I know the number! And she looks up at me and smiles, and right then and there I tell her: two million four hundred thousand and six! And she looks at me, she smiles, she steps over the line of salt and she goes into the house and she bends over Ivy and when she turns to the window to look out at me, she is still smiling, and I see I know her face, I've always known it. And right now I know: she will give me whatever I want, whatever it is, that I can have. And in front of me is a wrecked truck, coconuts and nisberries all over the road, and on the side of the road, a sheeted body, and as I come closer, I lift up the sheet, and there is Charlie, not a day older than when I first met him, every wrinkle erased, every sign of age and trouble gone, and he sits up and says to me, *Strike the set, let's go home,* and of course I am ready, so I say yes. And just then I hear someone coming up behind me, and it is Miss Blue, and she says, Just here we change the story, and I think, that is what Anders just said. And I think, Of course! How could I have been so stupid! She is Anders! She was Anders all the time! The things that are right under your chin and you don't see them!

And when I look out the window, it is snowing, but a funny snow, all gold, as if the heat were falling down in fat flakes. So, I think, even here we are on Green Island. And then I think, but on Green Island everyone kills goats! And I don't want to kill any goats! I have to tell that to Miss Blue. She will do whatever it is she does—*snip! snip!*—and on all of Green Island there will not be one single goat! And I think, I have to tell this to Ivy! No more killing of goats. And then I think I wake up. But I am not sure I was asleep before. No, I am not sure of that.

And then I think, I have done this one unselfish thing. I have seen her off. I remember, after Tita Lu died, when she came back from Green Island, she said, *Go on your way, Tita Lu.* Go on your way, Ivy. I don't say, Take me with you. For once I don't ask for anything. I hope I will die soon but I don't ask for it. I don't ask for anything. Who would have thought I could do one unselfish thing? All my life, this is what I wanted to do. I have done it and it was not hard. It was what I wanted to do. So perhaps I have done other things that were not so bad as well. Just another person. Just another person on the face of the earth. So yes, I have done it. I sit on my chair and think, I outlast everyone. This is my punishment. But if I am being punished, why am I happy? In the twinkling of an eye, I am happy. I have seen things! Just now I have seen them! In the twinkling of an eye, I look back over my life and see things I am proud of. Yes, for the first time in my life I am happy.

A Note About the Author

Susan Fromberg Schaeffer was born in Brooklyn and educated at the University of Chicago, where she received her Ph.D. in 1966. In addition to First Nights, *she has written five books of poetry, one collection of short stories, and eight other novels, including* Buffalo Afternoon, Anya, *and* The Madness of a Seduced Woman. *She is Professor of English at Brooklyn College and a founding member of its Master of Fine Arts Program in Poetry. She lives in Brooklyn and Vermont with her husband and two children.*

A Note on the Type

The text of this book was set in Weiss, a typeface designed in Germany by Emil Rudolf Weiss (1875–1942). The design of the roman was completed in 1928 and that of the italic in 1931. Both are well balanced and even in color, and both reflect the subtle skill of a fine calligrapher.

Composed by Creative Graphics, Allentown, Pennsylvania
Printed and bound by R. R. Donnelley & Sons, Harrisonburg, Virginia
Designed by Iris Weinstein